SPINE OF THE DRAGON

SPINE
OF THE
DRAGON

KEVIN J. ANDERSON

A Tom Doherty Associates Book · New York

SPINE OF THE DRAGON

Copyright © 2019 by WordFire, Inc.

Maps by Bryan G. McWhirter

A Tor Book
Published by Tom Doherty Associates
175 Fifth Avenue
New York, NY 10010

www.tor-forge.com

Tor® is a registered trademark of Macmillan Publishing Group, LLC.

The Library of Congress Cataloging-in-Publication Data is available upon request.

ISBN 978-1-250-30210-6 (hardcover)
ISBN 978-1-250-30211-3 (ebook)

Our books may be purchased in bulk for promotional, educational, or business use.
Please contact your local bookseller or the Macmillan Corporate and Premium
Sales Department at 1-800-221-7945, extension 5442, or by email at
MacmillanSpecialMarkets@macmillan.com.

First Edition: June 2019

Printed in the United States of America

0 9 8 7 6 5 4 3 2 1

With special warmth to my entire supportive and ambitious Tribe from the Superstars Writing Seminars. Learning and creativity go both directions, and working with you over more than ten years has helped make my life as rich as any fictional universe I could create.

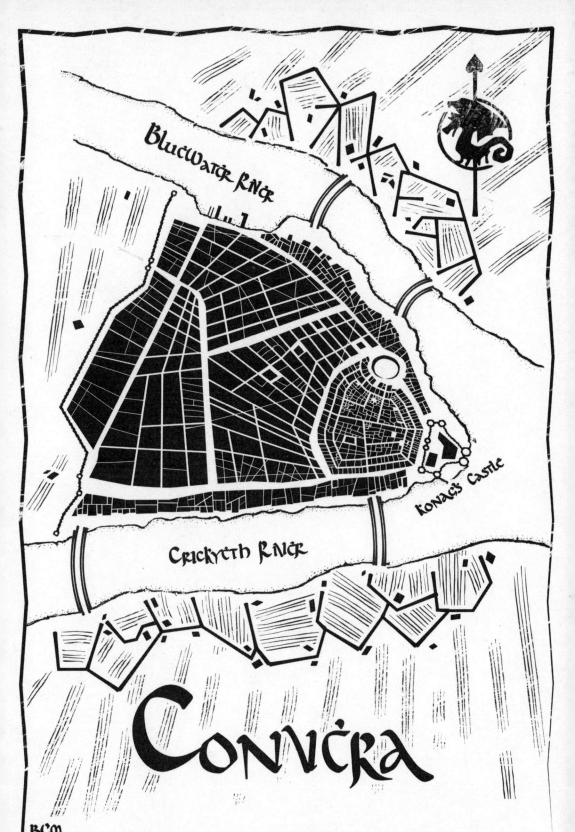

Bluewater River

Konacs Castle

Crickyeth River

CONVERA

BGM

Fulcor

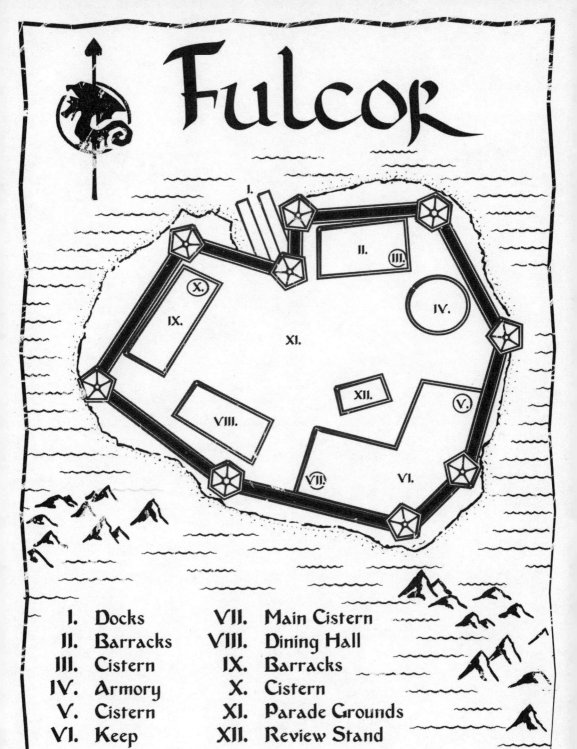

I.	Docks	VII.	Main Cistern
II.	Barracks	VIII.	Dining Hall
III.	Cistern	IX.	Barracks
IV.	Armory	X.	Cistern
V.	Cistern	XI.	Parade Grounds
VI.	Keep	XII.	Review Stand

BGM

SPINE OF THE DRAGON

1

᪥

THE great dust storm prowled over the boundary mountains like a living thing. Brown and angry, the murk loomed in the sky as it approached the capital city of Bannriya from the west. On the high sandstone towers of the central castle, red flags whipped and twisted in the rising wind; they served as warning signals to alert the people to prepare for rough weather.

Protected within the city's walls, men and women scurried through the streets. Spice merchants covered baskets of cinnamon bark, lumpy turmeric roots, and dried peppers before dragging them inside their shops. Innkeepers rolled up canvas awnings and lashed them in place. Food vendors pulled tables into sheds. Mothers called in their children, and the bang of closing shutters echoed through the lower alleys.

Adan Starfall, the young king of Suderra, stood alone on Bannriya Castle's highest tower, watching as his great city prepared for the storm. "This will be a bad one," he murmured. "Very bad." More warning flags were raised on towers across the city, and rumors spread just as quickly. The ministry buildings closed for the day, with the business of the kingdom pausing to weather the storm. Councilors, commanders, and trade representatives returned to their homes in the outer districts.

The fortified main castle had been built on the high point inside the great walled city. On clear nights, Adan loved to stare at the stars from this gazing deck, but today it only offered him a view of the thickening curtain of dust. The oncoming clouds roiled like smoke, stirred up by some titanic disturbance in the desert far to the west. In the face of such a storm, his power as a king meant little.

The stiffening breeze whipped strands of reddish-brown hair across his face and high forehead, and into his eyes. He brushed the hair aside, securing it with the plain circlet crown he wore, and ran his hand down along the goatee that punctuated his rounded chin. His blue eyes looked young for a king's, compassionate and curious. The weight of rule had not yet made him feel older than his years.

He guessed the full force of the storm would strike within two hours. Adan had reigned here for only three years, but Bannriya had stood for nearly two thousand years and had endured many a storm. The citizens of the capital knew how to find shelter and wait until the weather passed. Afterward the people would emerge with brooms and brushes to scour their walkways and outdoor stairs, then shake out the banners of celebration for which the ancient city was known.

He would not abandon his people to their own problems, though. His father had taught him better than that, instilling in him compassion and a desire to work on behalf of the people he ruled. Adan had promised to be a different sort of king when he accepted the throne of Suderra, one of three kingdoms in the Commonwealth. As he stared at the labyrinth of streets below, he tried to think of how to help. Adan wanted to show his people he was not like the aloof kings or corrupt regents the Suderrans had endured before he arrived.

Behind him, a door into the castle tower opened unexpectedly, and Penda emerged onto the gazing deck. He felt the familiar rush of pride that came to him each time he saw his clever, beautiful wife. Penda was slender, with large brown eyes even darker than her rich brunette hair, which hung long and loose. Her quick wit, heart-shaped face, and confident movements were typical of the wild Utauk tribes, the nomadic trader clans that ranged across the Commonwealth.

"I can feel this storm coming even inside the castle, my handsome Starfall." She stepped past him to look at the approaching dust cloud. Out of habit, she traced a circle around her heart. "*Cra,* that's a powerful one!" The green reptile bird on her shoulder ruffled his wings and hopped from one clawed foot to the other.

At twenty-one, Penda was two years younger than Adan, yet in her travels with the Utauk caravans, she had seen more of the world. He liked to think that he had tamed his exotic wife, though it was more likely she had tamed him. He accepted that. She was no fawning princess and never would be—and he would not want her that way. They had been married for two years, and he still felt caught up in new love for her. Penda adored him back, he had no doubt of that.

He wasn't sure he could say the same of Xar, his wife's mischievous pet ska. He was the size of a falcon, with emerald-green scales on his body, pale green plumage, and faceted eyes like a moth's. A thin collar around his scaly neck was inset with a central diamond. On her shoulder, Penda wore a protective leather pad to provide a perch for Xar. Only Utauks could keep and tend the flying creatures, and some owners, like Penda, had a clear heart link with their pets, sharing sensations. The ska haughtily tilted his head from side to side, as if expecting Adan to do something about the coming storm that troubled his Penda.

"Easy, Xar." She stroked the side of the creature's narrow face and turned to Adan. "I've weathered many dust storms as they tore at our tents out in the hills, but I sense that this isn't just a storm. It doesn't feel natural." She seemed to be fighting off an unconscious shiver.

Above them, a yellow banner snapped and strained against its pole. The air smelled of bitter dust and woodsmoke when Adan inhaled. "It's a storm. What more can it be?"

Penda closed her eyes, as if she could visualize the storm better by not looking at it. Xar stirred on her shoulder, sensing the world for her. "It was created deep in the Furnace. It could be a . . . harbinger." Her eyes snapped open, and she looked toward the hills again. With a buzzing sound not quite like a growl, the reptile bird buried his face in her thick hair and peeked out at Adan. Penda sighed. "Skas are sensitive to these things."

"So are you." Adan put an arm around her and drew her closer, and Penda leaned against him. He trusted his wife's senses, knew that Utauks had a special affinity for the scant threads of magic that remained in the land. "The city is already preparing, but let's see what we can do in the time we have left. I'll call out the Banner guards, and we'll ride from neighborhood to neighborhood, offering assistance."

As they turned to leave, a squarish older man with a neatly trimmed dark beard burst through the door onto the platform. "What are you still doing here, dear heart? *Cra*, get inside!" Hale Orr, Penda's father, gestured with the long-healed stump of his left hand. He wore crimson and black silks, a loose jerkin sashed over his belly, and baggy pantaloons. One of his front teeth was gold; the others were bright white. "When we lived in caravan tents, a cloud of dust like that would have struck fear into our hearts."

"Then be glad you gave up the nomadic life and moved into the castle with us, Father Orr," Adan said. "We'll be safe enough behind the walls, but

I will do a quick patrol of the city before the storm hits. I know we have several ministers and visiting vassal lords in the castle, but most of the advisors, businessmen, and clerks have gone home to shore up their own doors and windows. Nevertheless, I'll see the streets for myself—and be seen to show the people that I care about them." His father, konag of the entire Commonwealth, king of the kings, had prepared him for this all his life. "They still consider me new here."

"Nothing you can do about the storm," Hale snorted. "Better to stay inside and protect my daughter."

Penda took the king's arm. "Actually, I'm riding with my Starfall. Let's go."

The older man huffed, and Adan said in a commiserating voice, "You won't convince her otherwise, you know."

Grumbling, Hale traced a quick circle around his heart. "The beginning is the end is the beginning." He followed them back inside and barred the wooden door behind them and trudged after them down the stone steps. "I'd best get to work in here. The castle won't blow away like a tent, but there'll be plenty of cracks and crannies the storm can find. City dwellers may not know the best way to make a structure secure."

With Xar balancing on Penda's shoulder, they entered the main keep, where the staff busied themselves securing outer shutters and covering the interior latticed glass windows. They stuffed rags into cracks, then cocked their ears to listen for any whistle of stray wind.

Adan's eleven-year-old squire, an overeager boy named Hom, hurried up, his curly hair tousled, his tunic askew. "Sire, how can I help? Can I bring your slippers? Some tea for the storm? Or—"

Adan held up a hand. "The storm isn't here yet, Hom, and we still have work to do outside. I'll keep you busy, no doubt of that." As the younger son of one of the recently ousted regents, Hom Santis worked overtime to prove his reliability. Every day, the squire followed Adan around, trying to anticipate his needs, though he seemed oblivious to the king's need for privacy. He took constant notes about Adan's favorite foods, favorite color, favorite clothes. Given the boy's diligence, Adan thought he might someday be appropriate for a position in the trade or tax ministry.

Hale Orr put a big arm around Hom's shoulders. "Come, boy, you can help me make sure these people know how to ready the castle for the storm."

Not wanting to disturb Xar further by taking him outside, Penda left the ska on his stand in the main dining hall and accompanied Adan to the stables, where their horses had been saddled. A group of Banner guards were ready to ride as escort, while numerous other patrols had also spread out through the streets to help.

A skinny young soldier of fifteen led two chestnut mares forward for the king and queen, their favorite mounts. The young guard, Hom's brother Seenan, had similarly unruly dark hair beneath his leather-and-steel helmet. "Got them ready for you, Sire. Word came down, and we didn't want to waste any time."

The guard helped him into the saddle, while Penda swung up onto her mare with the grace of a dancer. Once everyone was mounted, the king and queen led the procession of twelve Banner guards. Riding out of the stables, Seenan glanced uneasily at the sky. "Are you sure you want to do this, Sire? The streets are half empty already, and we need to be behind closed doors well before that storm hits."

Using her knees, Penda nudged her mare into a trot, and the party sped up. Horse hooves clattered on the cobblestoned streets that spiraled out from the high castle. Passing under the main arch, Adan looked down at the statue of an ancient wreth king, symbolically toppled and left lying on the ground outside the castle. The creator race looked similar to humans, but haughtier, with large almond eyes, pointed chins, high foreheads, broad chests. This statue was a trophy brought here from one of the ruined wreth cities that still dotted the landscape, despite the many centuries that had passed.

Though relatively new in his role as king, Adan could feel the weight of history all around him. Bannriya was the first city built by human survivors after the devastating wreth wars two thousand years ago. The people had raised defiant banners to declare independence from their creator race. The wreths were long gone now, barely more than legends. After the disastrous magical conflict, humans had tirelessly worked to restore the damaged land, building homes and cities, not as slaves to the ancient race, but as free people.

On upper floors of the city's brick-and-timber buildings, residents latched shutters. A woman in an apron hammered a lid onto a half-full rain barrel to keep the dust out of the water. Two boys hauled a cart against the wall of their home and turned it upside down to keep it from blowing away.

Adan and the escort party offered assistance to those who needed it. They dismounted to help shop owners move barrels, sacks of grain, or rolled-up rugs. Optimistic potters called out reduced prices, even though the streets were rapidly emptying; one seller even tried to haggle with King Adan.

As she rode along, Penda flicked her attention from one building to the next, as if trying to sense which ones would be most vulnerable. She pointed out an Utauk family, travelers from a small caravan, who had struck their pavilions and sought shelter in a narrow alley. Adan pulled his horse to a halt and addressed the Utauks. "You shouldn't stay out in the open. Don't you have a better place to ride out the storm?"

The caravan leader, a man with tangled white hair and a fluffy gray beard, crouched close to his horse. "This is better than out in the hills. The walls will shield us enough." He glanced up at Penda and acknowledged the crimson and black colors of her tribe. "We just rode in yesterday."

Penda called to one of the guards. "Take them to the stables in the next block, where they can stay with their animals. It'll be safer than out on the street."

Before the caravan leader could demur, Adan added, "We will pay the stable owner if he protests."

With her finger, Penda drew a circle in the air, and the caravan leader responded in kind. The grateful Utauks gathered their packs and possessions and hurried off.

After another hour of rapid riding through the streets, an anxious Seenan pointed at the ominous bruised sky. "Sire, we really need to get back." Dust was already pelting through the air.

Adan looked down the street, saw the last few people rushing inside, the final shutters being drawn closed. Knowing he had done what he could, he nodded. "That's enough. I'm satisfied."

Penda wheeled her chestnut mare, glanced back at her husband. "I'll race you, Starfall! The Banner guards can find their own way back." She galloped off, and Adan chased her through the streets toward the gate of the castle.

The young king and queen entered the dining hall, brushing dust from their clothes. Pennants showing the open-hand symbol of the Commonwealth and the flag-within-flag banner of Suderra hung on the inner walls. Xar rested on a stand behind her seat, bobbing his head in agitation, as if wondering why Penda had left him alone for so long.

She ran her fingers through her long dark hair, straightening the wind-blown strands into some semblance of order; Adan knew he must look just as windblown. Seeing the rags stuffed in cracks and around windows, he said, "Looks like your father took his duties seriously."

"We Utauks place a high value on sturdy shelter," she said with a smile.

Hale chose a seat at the long banquet table. "Indeed I do, dear heart." The squire at his side looked exhausted. "And young Hom was a great help."

The boy was apologetic. "There won't be a formal dinner, Sire, but we have bread and cold roast fowl. Unless you would rather—"

"A small meal will be fine, Hom," Adan said. "Send word to the visiting ministers in the guest quarters, and any staff who haven't gone to be with their families. We can hunker down in the storm and make the best of it." He quirked a smile. "And you can join us. Get a plate of your own. No need for formalities during a storm." The flustered squire dithered before running off to get the food.

More guests tentatively arrived, taking seats, trying to make conversation against the howling wind outside. As the meal was delivered on platters, Hale looked at Penda and Adan with a glint in his eye. "On a night like this, young couples should hold each other close, perhaps even make a storm baby."

Penda placed a palm over her stomach. "We already have a son or daughter on the way." She didn't show yet, but she was three months along. "One at a time, Father."

"It never hurts to practice, dear heart."

During the meal, more servants came into the great hall to tend to the king and queen, joining the awkward clerks, trade ministers, and noble merchants who had been caught in the bad weather. Adan tried to make them feel more comfortable as they took reassurance in one another's company. Hom was too shy to join the conversation, even with the staff. Busying himself, the squire picked up an armload of wood for the fireplace and began adding logs in among the flames.

The winds outside took a sudden raging turn, like some angry force trying to batter its way in. With a moan, air rushed up through the chimney, and Hom yelped in surprise as the fire flared. He dropped a log onto the coals, which made sparks swirl like falling stars.

Before Hom could get to his feet, another blast of dust-clogged wind slammed against the shutters that covered the glass side window, splintering the latch. The left shutter tore open and banged against the outer stone wall with a sound like a cracking whip. One of the diamond-shaped panes of glass in the window popped loose and fell to the floor.

Hale Orr and Adan both ran to the window as the noise of the storm doubled in volume. "Get rags to plug the hole!" Adan shouted. "Anything will do." One woman quickly offered the linen runner from a side table. Hale fumbled to hold the cloth while Adan stuffed it in the hole in the window.

Outside, the loose shutter slammed and crashed against the wall, tormented by the winds like a rat shaken by a terrier. Several more small panes in the now-vulnerable window rattled loose.

Adan looked at his father-in-law. "If we don't secure that shutter, the whole window will fall apart."

Hale nodded. "We'll have to be fast, Starfall."

"I will be." He released the latch on the glass window, which opened in a burst of breezes, and he barely caught it before all the panes could smash into fragments. Hale fought to take it from him.

From the windowsill, Adan leaned out into the storm wind, stretching his arm to snatch the flapping shutter. His fingers slipped and he grabbed again. It was like catching a wild horse. Finally, he seized the edge, pulled the shutter back toward the window.

As he did, Adan had a moment to look at the brown and smoky storm lashing through the streets of Bannriya, scouring the ancient walls. Other shuttered windows groaned under the barrage of sand and wind. Roof tiles flew about like dandelion fluff and clattered against walls. The sandstorm roared along, and for a moment he thought he saw what Penda had sensed: something dark, rumbling, ominous.

He pulled the shutter back into place, blocking out the storm. "Quick, lash it!" Hale and the squire wrapped twine around the latch. The wooden shutter creaked as scouring wind pressed against it.

With a sigh, Adan gently closed the leaded-glass inner window, too. Xar flapped his wings on his stand, as if acknowledging the king for taking care of a bothersome problem. Penda brushed her husband's ruffled hair back into place and kissed him on the forehead. The dining hall finally returned to normal.

The squire looked flushed and disconcerted. Hale Orr used his good hand to sweep dust from his fine silks. "There, now let us see what we can scrounge for dessert."

⁊⁊

Adan and Penda held each other through the night, although the howling winds kept them awake. The storm died down by dawn, and as day broke, the last vestiges of dust wandered through the streets like camp followers after a great battle.

Adan got up early, anxious to see how the city had fared. He donned linen trousers and a silk shirt. With her ska riding precariously on the pad on her shoulder, Penda joined him. Hom hurried in, disappointed to find the king already dressed. He looked as if he hadn't slept a wink. "Breakfast, Sire?"

"Not yet, Hom." Adan moved at a swift pace with Penda at his side.

In the main hall, servants removed coverings from the windows and opened shutters to let bright sunshine through the streaked glass. Attendants tugged open the great castle doors to a cascade of fine dust.

Outside, Adan saw no torn-off roofs or collapsed buildings, although drifts of dust blocked many of the doorways. "Now we clean up."

Shopkeepers emerged to assess the damage and used straw brooms to sweep away the accumulated sand. Children ran about stomping in the powdery mounds, sending up clouds of dust and leaving footprints.

Joining Penda and Adan, Hale Orr used his arm stump to wipe grit from his forehead. "*Cra*, I'm glad we weren't out in tents. It could have been much worse."

Suddenly, shouts came from the watchtowers on the city's western wall that looked out upon the distant mountains. Signal flags went up on the high towers, and a bell rang out. Before long, Seenan and a second Banner guard ran up the hill toward the castle, wading through pools of dust. Their faces were caked with dirt. Seenan called out, "Sire—strangers! Visitors unlike any I've ever seen before!"

"The storm brought them," said the second guard.

"Then let's go greet them," Adan said. "We always welcome visitors."

After saddling their favorite horses in the castle stables, Adan and his companions rode off down the drifted streets. Xar flew above the party and circled back to settle on Penda's shoulder.

When they reached the outer city wall, armed Banner guards were staring nervously down from the wall above the gate, which was still closed and barred. Riding up, Adan signaled for them to open the barrier. "Is this any way to greet visitors? If they rode through the storm, they may need help."

"As you command, Sire," called one of the tower guards, but he sounded uncertain.

Penda pulled her horse to a stop beside him, curious. Seenan looked worried, but he kept his horse back and held his tongue. Hale Orr sat in the saddle, quiet but curious.

Sentries worked the two-man cranks, winding ropes around giant wheels to the sound of ratcheting gears. The huge gates swung open on groaning, dusty hinges. King Adan's horse shied and snorted.

Outside the city, a hundred or so figures waited, dressed in scales and tan leather. At first glance, they looked like humans, but they were not human. Tall and angular, they had warm brown skin and topaz eyes that tapered to elongated points. Their long, wild hair glittered a pale yellow, as if spun from gold and bone, and was adorned with twisted metal that gleamed in the harsh morning light. Though they had arrived with the dust storm, they appeared spotless.

The strangers rode on stout, two-legged lizard creatures with large heads and yellow eyes. Remembering his history and the drawings he had seen in ancient records, Adan knew that these creatures, called augas, were beasts of burden shaped from desert reptiles. Three of the scaly mounts plodded forward, their riders looking imperiously at Adan, who could hardly believe what the storm had brought.

A harbinger, Penda had said.

Wreths, the ancient race that had created humanity as their slaves, had not been seen for more than two thousand years. Their statues and ruins littered the landscape, and Adan looked at the toppled stone figure each day as he passed outside the castle. Everyone thought the warring wreth factions had obliterated each other long ago.

Now a hundred of them had emerged from the wasteland to stand before his city. To see King Adan.

2

⚇

THE striped sails of the Isharan warship strained against the magic-induced breezes pushing them toward the coast of Osterra, easternmost of the three kingdoms in the Commonwealth.

At the bow, Priestlord Klovus clenched his hands on the salt-weathered wood of the deck rail and watched as the ship cleaved the water. Glancing at the iron fist of the battering ram that thrust forward at the prow, he felt ready to smash the hated Osterrans.

The lookout called down from the mainmast, "Coast ahead! We'll reach Mirrabay within the hour."

"If we're on course," the captain muttered from the middeck, pacing back and forth and ready for battle.

"We are on course," Klovus affirmed, making sure all the sailors could hear him. "The godling guides us to our destination."

As key priestlord of Ishara, he focused the energies of the sailors and soldiers. Their faith was strong because the godling down in the hold was strong, and they would witness its power soon when Klovus unleashed it against the weak fishing village. Enemy blood would flow, and flames and smoke would rise to the sky like celebratory cheers.

The anxious crew consisted of a hundred toughened men and women who were eager for the raid. To build excitement and certainty, Klovus called out, "Bring out your swords and shields. Don't expect the godling to do all the fighting for you!"

The sailors rushed to the ship's armory closets. The first mate unlocked the doors and handed out curved swords, daggers, and ironwood cudgels. They had set sail in secret from Serepol Harbor under cover of darkness, determined to reach the shore of the Commonwealth across the sea. Klovus had prayed with them, rallied them. Every member of the crew was primed and hungry for war.

The godling was hungry as well.

The summoned wind swept the warship along, bringing the foreign coast noticeably closer. Ahead lay the tired old world, the continent the Isharans had abandoned long ago after the devastating wreth wars. His brave people had claimed a new land for themselves, virgin soil that sparkled with magic, unlike the weary and damaged Commonwealth.

"The godless are vulnerable," Klovus called out, though the crew needed no further inspiration. "Our war never actually ended decades ago, and while they may have forgotten what they did to us as they scrabble for their pathetic existence, we have not forgotten." He smiled. "And today, we will give them a painful reminder."

Eager sailors, dressed in light hemp pants and rough-spun shirts, strapped on swords, buckled leather armor over their chests, tucked daggers into their belts, tried on and exchanged helmets for a better fit. Klovus, wearing his dark blue caftan with his golden rank symbol around his neck, nodded encouragement, glad to see the crew's eagerness, their jaws clenched in hatred.

Even though the two continents had established an uneasy peace with a treaty signed by Empra Iluris and Konag Cronin thirty years ago, there was no peace in their hearts. Klovus and the twelve district priestlords never let their followers forget, even if their own empra didn't understand. This raid would reawaken their fervor, heat up their blood.

The robust warship approached a sheltered bay, where local fishing boats trolled their nets in the calm waters. The smaller boats tacked against capricious breezes, but the Isharan warship rushed along on an arrow-straight course, driven by magic.

Turning his back to the doomed harbor village, the priestlord raised his voice. "We strike quickly! Set fire to their town, kill as many as possible, and take some hostages. We will sail home, borne on the sounds of their grief."

"Hear us, save us," the crew chanted. It sounded more like a cheer than a prayer.

The godling heard them. Even through the deck boards, Klovus could feel the simmering power of the restless deity that huddled within the cargo hold, waiting to be set loose.

Cinching the caftan's sash around his stocky waist, Klovus scratched his cheek. In preparation for their victory, he had shaved his head and round face with a razor-edged dagger and applied oils to his skin. He wanted to look imposing, not unkempt . . . though he suspected that Mirrabay would remember little more than the godling once it attacked.

Driven headlong and churning a white wake, the warship sailed past frantic fishing boats that scattered to escape the invaders. Klovus wanted those poor wretches to witness the devastation of their homes, the slaughter of their families. None of them would be able to reach shore in time to help in the fight.

Some villagers had already identified the Isharan ship by its distinctive red-and-white sails and battering-ram prow. They would know this ship was not part of the Commonwealth navy, but a raiding vessel from the new world.

Neither continent wanted all-out war, according to Empra Iluris, but the provocative raids continued, with or without her knowledge. Skirmishes like this one kept the wounds open and the pain fresh. The godling that Klovus had brought—a secondary entity from the harbor temple in Serepol—would show the three kingdoms that they could never hope to win.

During the voyage from Ishara, the sailors had slashed their forearms, collectively spilling fresh blood into a glazed clay urn. When the offering urn was full, Klovus had sealed the cap with wax, using a hint of magic to preserve the blood and keep it fresh for the sacrifice just before battle. Now that the ship approached Mirrabay, it was time.

"I offer the sacrifice as you offer your warrior hearts," Klovus called. "Say your prayers, and I shall deliver the blood."

The armed sailors raised their voices in a loud summons. "Hear us, save us!" The chant so often spoken in the temples used the power of faith to strengthen the godlings that they themselves had created. The magic inherent in the new land was made manifest through their own beliefs, and now the priestlord could control it.

Two sailors carried the blood-filled urn to the middle of the deck, where Klovus waited at a small access hatch. The gold-plated hatch had an upraised lip to capture any stray droplets of blood meant for the sacrifice. "Our godling drinks deeply and draws strength from your belief."

"Hear us, save us!"

As they chanted, Klovus tilted the urn and poured the collected blood through the chute into the hold. The restless godling stirred, consuming all the anger instilled in the blood by Isharan believers. Klovus felt the entity's presence increase.

The magical wind picked up, and the Isharan warship surged toward the coast. Ahead, signal fires blazed on towers as watchers called Mirrabay to arms. Loud bells rang out. Villagers ran about, some gathering weapons, others fleeing inland.

As the warship passed fishing boats and coast-hugging cargo ships, Isharan archers launched fire arrows. Klovus enjoyed watching their sails catch fire and their crews dive overboard to escape the conflagration. Many would drown before they made it back to shore.

Simply causing pain to the godless Commonwealth was sufficient reason to conduct this raid, but the key priestlord had more at stake. He was eager to make his point to Empra Iluris, to demonstrate the power and effectiveness of their godlings. The stubborn woman frustrated Klovus, but he would find a way to convince her.

After the blood sacrifice, the hull boards swelled and groaned as power grew in the hold below. The priestlord would have to unleash the godling soon, or it might destroy their ship.

He hurried along the deck, looking over the side and down the hull. The wooden hatch covers remained in place, sealing the hold shut, but they could be opened quickly. He shouted for the sailors. "Grab the ropes! Be ready to release the latches."

The impatient godling battered against the coverings, trying to break free. A crack shivered along one of the hull planks.

"Hurry! Turn the godling loose. Let it do its work."

"Hear us, save us." The sailors grunted as they tugged on the ropes, jerking pegs free so they could lift the hatch covers.

With a wash of steam and spray, the imprisoned godling burst forth, only partially corporeal. It poured out of the openings like some gelatinous, unstoppable force, sparkling, thrashing as it tried to pull itself into a physical form: a fearsome monster made of liquid and beliefs. Klovus let out a gasp.

The warship rocked with the disturbance, as if heaving a sigh of relief, and the freed godling surged into the harbor and swept like a boiling storm toward the defenseless people of Mirrabay.

"Go," Klovus whispered, not as a prayer, but as one speaking encouragement to a friend. "Wreak your divine havoc."

3

MIRRABAY held dark and haunting memories for Utho. He had traveled here to face his personal demons, but now that the detested Isharans had arrived, the blood, death, and pain would begin all over again. He still wanted to kill that entire race for what they had done to his wife and daughters so many years ago. At least this time he was here to fight back.

Utho of the Reef, an elite Brava guard, was tall, lean, and muscular, with close-cropped steel-gray hair. He was a grim and incomparable fighter, right-hand man to Konag Conndur. Utho's wide, clean-shaven face had prominent cheekbones, his eyes narrow and slightly almond shaped, indicating his half-wreth blood. As a Brava, he wore black leather chest armor and breeches, black boots, a shirt of protective finemail, and a black cloak, also lined with finemail. He was an imposing figure.

When he saw the enemy warship approach Mirrabay, his face hardened into a mask of challenge. The sight of the red-and-white sails spurred him to action. "Stand and fight!" He ran out onto the piers, his boots thundering on the wooden slats. "You know what these animals will do."

The village responded. Nimble boys with torches clambered up towers on either side of the bay to ignite greenwood signal fires, sending curls of smoke into the sky. The gray plumes could be seen for miles up and down the coast, but Utho knew the raiders would strike, burn, kill, and retreat before any other town could send reinforcements.

The threat of an Isharan raid was a constant concern, and the coastal villages could never be truly ready—not for this. In their hearts they were just fishermen and townspeople, not ruthless warriors. Not Bravas, like him.

Utho thought of his wife, Mareka, and their two girls butchered by Isharans while he was away at the war thirty years ago. Today, though, he was here. He and his companion, a young Brava man named Onder, were the only hope for these people.

The town's defenders rushed into their homes to retrieve spears and pikes mounted on walls, bows and arrows used for hunting, swords that had been in families for generations. Mothers kissed their husbands goodbye and swept their children into the hills, while other women stayed behind to fight for their town.

Onder, the other Brava, who served as a new paladin on this part of the coast, joined Utho at the end of the dock. He had sandy-blond hair and a pink complexion that made his face look freshly scrubbed; he also had the distinctive features of a wreth half-breed. Though only in his early twenties, Onder was a good fighter and enforcer, familiar with various weapons. Utho had sparred with him several times, but he doubted his younger companion had ever faced a real Isharan enemy before.

As they watched the ominous oncoming ship, Utho saw an unexpected flicker of fear cross the other Brava's face, but he quelled it. "Will we be able to fight them?"

"We are Bravas. It is in our blood and our destiny to defend the Commonwealth."

Villagers scrambled to build makeshift barriers in the streets. These people remembered when parts of Mirrabay had burned to the ground decades ago. Some older fighters still bore scars from that defeat, and everyone knew the horrific stories. Utho was proud to watch them pull together and face their fears.

"They are brave," he said to Onder in a low voice, "but they don't hate the Isharans as much as I do. Are you ready?"

Onder clenched his teeth and nodded.

The Isharan vessel plowed into the harbor like a wild bull. Side hatches lifted up, and something monstrous sparkled and stirred in the warship's hold. Utho caught his breath even before the ravening thing exploded out of the hull and surged into the bay. He gasped, unable to believe what he saw. "The bastards brought a godling! To *our* shores!"

Set loose, the entity swelled and swirled, a storm of water, shadows, and anger incarnate. Its features shifted, then resolved into the suggestion of a snarling human face with an unkempt beard, wild hair, and blazing eyes, attached to a complex body that charged through the water.

The villagers screamed in dismay, and Utho heard a clatter of dropped weapons. Though many defenders steeled themselves and remained in formation, he doubted they could stand against this. He motioned to Onder. "We will need our ramers."

The young Brava gave a grim nod. "I guessed as much."

Each man removed the hinged golden cuff clipped to his belt, a band adorned with ancient wreth symbols. In the unnaturally warm metal, Utho could feel the power in the weapon that only a Brava could use. With his left hand, he folded the golden band around his right wrist and squeezed, clicking it tightly into place. Sharp metal prongs at the edges of the ramer bit into his flesh. The barbs pierced his veins and drank deeply, activating the power of the ancient weapon, which was triggered by the wreth magic in his Brava bloodline. Crimson trickles ran down his forearm as he raised his hand high, then used magic to ignite a corona of flame on the band of the ramer.

With a roar, Utho *pushed,* and the flame brightened. His magic fed the fire, expanding it into a blazing ball that engulfed his hand. Straightening his fingers, he extended the flame into a bladelike whip as long as his arm. He held the fire high, shining against the oncoming enemy. From the end of the pier, he defied the warship and the unleashed godling.

Onder also clamped his gold wristband in place, drawing blood and igniting his own torch. The Bravas stood with fiery hands raised, ready to defend Mirrabay with their incandescent fury.

Undeterred, the godling boiled toward them, sending up geysers of water. Rough waves capsized fishing boats and rolled toward the docks, smashing the larger ships tied to the piers. The unleashed deity rose from the water and lunged toward the dock and the two burning ramers.

Utho realized how vulnerable they were. "We can't fight it here!" He and Onder raced back to shore as the godling crashed into the pier, scattering planks and pilings in all directions. The vicious entity plowed ahead, sank every boat, and smashed supply sheds and boathouses into splinters.

Reaching solid ground, Utho held up his ignited ramer and faced the oncoming creature. He drove back a twist of atavistic fear. Beside him, Onder looked terrified, but his hand blazed bright, curling the flames into a burning lash.

This thing was not natural. The godling was a being beyond their comprehension, a force that didn't bleed. Utho wasn't even sure if it could die. Nevertheless, he was a Brava, and he drew upon his magic, intensifying the fiery lash. Calling to Onder, he ran directly toward the half-corporeal entity as it struck smokehouses and dock shacks, sending fragments of wood high into the air, setting the village ablaze.

Out on the water, the Isharan warship was close enough that the invading soldiers disembarked in landing boats and rowed toward shore. They raised their curved swords, shouting insults and threats as they attacked the harbor village, but the monstrous godling did most of their work for them.

The shifting creature drew upon wild emotions and ripped the air with howling winds. A rowboat spun into the air and smashed down as Utho leaped out of the way. He regained his feet and stood his ground, lashing with his ramer. "Stop!"

He flung a crack of magical fire at the roiling entity. It extended arms that writhed with tentacles of liquid steam, but the blazing ramer sizzled into them. The godling flinched. Utho yelled, "I don't believe in you, abomination."

Isharans possessed a corrupted form of power in their new world, an ability to create their own godlings as constructs of blind faith manifested by their imaginations. But not here in the Commonwealth, not in Mirrabay. A godling did not belong here on these shores.

Utho thrust the ignited ramer at the entity. The fire whip extended from his hand to slash the thing's components into steam and spray. The godling lunged closer.

"Onder!" he shouted. "Help me!"

But the other Brava stood like a statue, hand upraised, ramer sputtering as he stared.

The godling battered Utho with its shifting body and knocked him aside like chaff in a wind. He struck out with his fiery hand, but the hot lash did no mortal damage. The wild entity smashed him again and hurled him to tumble end over end in the air.

Utho's heavy cloak and his finemail armor barely protected him when he crashed down onto a wood-shingled rooftop. Stunned, he slid down the roof, fighting to control his body, to wake up. He felt the pain of countless injuries, rolling, sliding, and just as he dropped off the edge, he managed to grab a gutter.

As he held on and tried to recover his bearings, he saw Onder in the streets below, not far from the furious half-corporeal creature. The younger Brava turned and fled in the opposite direction from where the villagers were rallying.

Utho was astonished by what he was seeing, and his heart tightened with black disappointment.

The godling rammed into another warehouse, flattening the walls, sending long planks flying, uprooting support timbers. Fishing nets strung out on repair racks flailed about like giant spiderwebs and landed in tangles. With a burst of energy, the entity pushed into the town, knocked down walls, smashed windows, ignited rooftops. Fire leaped from home to home as it raged onward.

Repulsed by his cowardly companion but unwilling to surrender for himself, Utho let go of the gutter and dropped to the street, keeping his knees bent as his armored cloak draped around him. Pain flared from broken ribs and bruised skull, yet he drove back his dismay with a ruthless disregard for his own safety. The fight was not over yet. His ramer remained clamped around his wrist, although the magical flame had guttered out when he briefly lost consciousness. Blood still streamed from the ramer's golden teeth, and he clutched the metal band, calling fire from his wreth heritage. His hand burst into purifying flame again.

In the streets, the people of Mirrabay fought Isharan soldiers who surged to shore from their landing boats in the wake of the godling's wrath. Carrying torches, the raiders set more buildings aflame, running from house to house. They clashed with fishermen, dockworkers, boatwrights, and shopkeepers. They killed many, but clubbed and captured others with nets, dragging them back to their landing boats. Utho was sickened by the prospect of what those vile people would do to the poor captives.

His vision clouded with a red haze as he thought of his wife, who had faced a situation much like this. He knew Mareka would have fought back and killed many while trying to save their daughters. At least they had *died*, rather than being dragged away to be raped and enslaved—or worse, sacrificed to the godling.

There was a reason the Bravas had declared a vengewar against the Isharans centuries ago. . . .

The wild deity continued its rampage, toppling the town's bell tower and silencing the call to arms with a roar and a clang. Charging through the streets, the godling leveled Mirrabay's remembrance shrine, which preserved the names of all the past lives from the town—including Mareka and the girls.

Fighting by himself now that his cowardly companion had fled, Utho ran after the creature, flaring his ramer bright. The raiders were dispersed through the town, caught up in their own battles. Isharan soldiers lay dead in the streets, along with many more murdered villagers, and although a lone Brava could have slain dozens of the enemy, he knew the godling was the greater threat.

He fell upon the thing again, slashing ramer fire through its barely tangible body. The godling's expenditure of wrath had already weakened it, and Utho's renewed fury damaged it further. The abomination was smaller now, less concentrated. Once a godling left the shores of its own continent, it had none of the land's native magic to draw on, and he knew the Isharans could not revitalize the entity's power with prayers and sacrifices alone.

Apparently satisfied with the swath of destruction it had caused, the wild entity circled back to the edge of the water, needing to return to the sanctuary of the Isharan warship. Stretching itself, the monstrosity toppled one of the watchtowers, dumping the bonfire beacon into the bay. The thing was fading, as if it knew it did not belong here in the Commonwealth.

The retreating godling slipped away, but Utho needed blood to satisfy his own personal vengewar. Turning his violence toward the remaining enemy soldiers, he pulled a fighting knife from the many weapons at his side and intensified the lash of his ramer. While Mirrabay burned around him, he waded into the fray of battle, ignoring the pain of his injuries. He struck down five Isharan soldiers, but he took no joy in the victory.

Utho made his way to the smoking, splintered piers where destroyed boats drifted in the water around the invaders' ship. Now that the magical wind had died away, the warship's striped sails hung limp. At the bow stood a stocky, bald priestlord in a midnight-blue caftan, watching the turmoil from a safe distance.

The priestlord struck a gong, calling the Isharans back aboard. The metallic crash rang out even louder than the screams of the wounded, the clash of swords. The last of the invaders dove into their landing boats and rowed to the warship, taking at least ten captives from Mirrabay with them.

The godling responded like a pet being called to dinner. It leaped into the water, roiling toward the Isharan warship. Though still fearsome, the thing was clearly diminished compared to when it had arrived. It flowed through the open hatch covers at the waterline and back into the ship's hold, leaving murky, churned water behind it.

No matter how hard the villagers fought to defend their homes, no matter how many invaders he slew with his ramer, it was not enough. Utho of the Reef extinguished the fire and looked at the devastation. Half the town was smashed and burning, countless bodies strewn through the streets, the wounded dying in pools of their own blood.

He choked back a sob. This was what the town must have looked like decades ago . . . when Utho had not been here to protect his family.

Animals!

W<small>HEN</small> Elliel approached a mining village called Scrabbleton in the Dragonspine Mountains, she paused to consider her options. For her, as a disgraced Brava, it was always a gamble whether to avoid people or seek their company. Would they welcome her or curse her? Even though she no longer wore the traditional black garb of a Brava, her half-breed heritage was plain on her face, in the almond shape of her green eyes. Would the towns-people know or care who she was? *She* didn't even know who she was.

Whenever she saw her reflection, Elliel could see that she was a beautiful woman, although the sight of her own face still surprised her. With her mem-ories gone, she didn't know what to expect. She was tall and well proportioned, with generous curves that drew the attention of men—and toned muscles and fighting reflexes that kept their unwanted attentions away. She had let her burnt-cinnamon hair grow much longer than a typical Brava would, but she was not a typical Brava. Not anymore.

Fortunately, most people would not understand the tattoo on her face.

Since losing her past, Elliel did not have a plan from day to day or place to place. Scrabbleton seemed as good a spot as any other. She straightened her shoulders and maintained a steady pace along the crushed-rock road.

Around her, the rugged peaks were capped with old snow even after the long summer. The mountain range was aptly named, rising like a back-bone across the Commonwealth, its jagged ridges reminiscent of the im-mense dragon Ossus, who was supposedly buried deep beneath the world. Prominent and conical, Mount Vada loomed over Scrabbleton, occasionally exhaling a plume of white smoke—a snort of the restless dragon, according to legend. The town was renowned for rich mines that produced gold, sil-ver, and copper, along with dragonblood rubies and diamonds called mothertears.

Elliel assumed the mines would need diggers or haulers, so she could find work in exchange for food and shelter. She made no decision about how long she might stay. Every day was a new question for her.

Chuckling streams ran down the wooded mountainside, turning the wheel of a mill on the outskirts of town. Sweet blue woodsmoke wafted from the chimneys of cottages along the main street and near mine openings that burrowed into Mount Vada. The town square held now-empty booths that suggested a regular market for crafts and produce. She noted a well-maintained wooden building with carved lintels and open doors, the town's remembrance shrine not far from the inn.

She had spent countless nights on the road, camping in the forest, choosing her own company over the uncertain welcome of strangers. Her dusty clothes were like those of any ordinary traveler: linen trousers, sturdy leather boots, an undyed flaxen shirt, and a rough wool cloak that doubled as a blanket.

The ramer at her side—which she could have clamped around her wrist, if she still had any magic to draw on—often attracted attention, however. The golden cuff was more of a reminder to herself than a threat to anyone else, since she could no longer use it. Scars on her wrist reminded her of failed attempts since she had awakened to her new empty life.

Here at the western border of Osterra, many days' journey inland from the capital city of Convera, people would know and respect Bravas, even though they were rare. Many Bravas were independent paladins, offering their services to villages or entire districts, while others were bonded to particular lords.

Elliel reached up to her cheek, touching the design there, the rune of forgetting. Though the sting of Utho's tattoo needles had long since faded, the knowledge of her crime perpetually weighed on her. She could not remember details, but she knew what she had done, because of the tattered and often-read letter she kept tucked inside her shirt. In spite of its reminder of her shame, she couldn't bear to throw the hated message away. . . .

Elliel drew attention as she walked down the street, partly because she was a woman alone and partly because of her demeanor, the implicit strength she carried. Although the townspeople did not seem unwelcoming, she was the first to offer a smile. "Could you direct me to the mine boss? I'd like to see about work."

A mother sat in front of a cottage, mending an old skirt while her children ran about chasing chickens. She gestured with her chin. "Hallis is in the building by the central mine tunnel." Elliel saw a set of dark openings dug into the rocky cliffside at the far end of town and a wood-and-stone building just outside the largest tunnel.

Hallis, the mine boss, was a short, tough man with knotted forearms, biceps, and neck. Inside the small building, he sat recording figures in his ledger with a lead stylus. Tacked on the wooden wall were maps of the tunnels with indications of the particular metals and gems found in each one.

When Elliel entered, Hallis rested his elbows on the desktop and looked appraisingly at her. Without introducing herself, she said, "I'd like to work in the mines."

He looked at her with interest, as well as surprise. "You look strong enough. Why should I hire you?"

"Because I would do a good job," Elliel said.

He turned to a page in his ledger filled with names. "Good enough. Who are you? Where are you from?"

"My name is Elliel, and that's about all I know." She touched the mark on her cheek. "I have no past, but I'm determined to make a future."

Hallis kept staring, as if he could see right through her. "You're a Brava, then?"

"I was. Now, I'm just Elliel. Other Bravas erased my legacy."

The mine boss regarded her with suspicion. "You must have done something horrible, then."

"I must have. I know what they told me, and I assume the story is true."

Hallis's brow furrowed. "I couldn't hire a dangerous criminal. I need to know what you did."

She steeled herself to give him the answer. "I'll tell you, but only once. And if you still choose to hire me, I promise you won't regret it." She reached into her shirt, touched the paper folded against her heart, and recited from memory what she knew.

Elliel remembered vividly the day she had awakened in nondescript clothes with some money in a pouch at her side and the ramer clipped to her belt. It was more than two years ago, the moment her new life abruptly began. Everything before that was a blank.

She had found herself in the back of an open wagon, cold and wet, pulling a drenched woolen blanket around her. Rain streaked down from the
gray-locked sky as the wagon rattled toward an unknown village. Looking
around, she saw she was huddled among sacks of dirt-encrusted potatoes,
now slick with mud.

In front of her on the buckboard, the driver wore a floppy, wide-brimmed
hat. Rain pattered on the leather and dripped in a fringe down onto his
shoulders. He stared ahead, holding the reins.

She leaned forward in the wagon bed. "Where are we?"

The driver turned to look at her. His whiskers were a mixture of black
and gray on his leathery face. When he gave her an uncertain smile, she saw
that one of his front teeth was missing. "I was told you'd wake up before we
reached town. That's all the farther I'm supposed to bring you." When he
nodded, more rain slid off the brim of his hat. "The Brava man said you
were on your own."

Refusing to answer more of her questions, he stopped his weary old horse
at the outskirts of town and told her to climb out of the wagon bed. But she
didn't know who she was, only her name: Elliel. She felt stinging pain on
her cheek. "What is this?"

"It's not very attractive, I can tell you that," said the driver. "Some sort of
spell rune, but I don't know about such things." He drove off into town with
his load of potatoes.

Ducking out of the rain, Elliel went into an inn, where the people stared
at her. She just wanted to sit out of the rain, where she could think. The innkeeper told her to go find a barn and stay dry with the animals, but she
found the few coins in her pocket and instead paid for a mug of broth so
she could sit by herself near the fire.

That was when she discovered the letter, in which Utho described what
she had done, and that he had found her guilty.

According to the letter, as a wandering Brava, Elliel had served farming
towns in the northern rural counties of Osterra. One day, maddened by a
high fever, she had gone into a bloody rage, ignited her ramer, and charged
into a school, where she used her fiery hand to massacre everyone—sixteen
boys and girls, along with their teacher.

When she came back to herself after the fever rage, Elliel fell into such
despair that she tried to take her own life, but the great Brava Utho arrived

in time. He seized her, disarmed her, and pronounced the sentence himself. Accepting his judgment, Elliel had let him tattoo the rune of forgetting on her face, wiping her legacy clean.

That rainy day, as she had sat by the warm fire in the inn, she read the devastating account again and again, absorbing Utho's damning words, trying to remember a single moment of it. She wanted to crumple the letter and throw it into the flames, but she didn't dare. This document was all she had of her past. She had to keep it. . . .

Now as she faced the mine boss across his desk, Elliel said, "For the past two years, I made my own life. I wandered across the Commonwealth, and I've been in the Dragonspine for a while now. Just surviving."

She had found work in towns, sometimes only for a day or two, other times for a month or more. She occasionally offered her services as a fighter or bodyguard because she was a former Brava, but she avoided that sort of work if she could, for fear she might fly into a rage again. What if she lost control? Who could defend themselves against her if she went on another rampage?

Sixteen little boys and girls and their teacher, all dead . . .

"I am strong and I will work hard, sir," she said.

"Let me read the note for myself," Hallis said. "You must still have it."

She gave him the paper, and he squinted at the words, his bushy eyebrows drawing close as his frown deepened. His face was filled with questions and doubts as he handed the letter back.

"I don't remember any of what I did," she insisted. She had neither the strength nor the desire to lie.

"Bravas are always honorable," he said. "You must still have some spark of that within you. And you are well now?"

"Since the day I woke up in that wagon, I have never been . . . ill again."

He leaned heavily on his small desk, and the wood creaked. "If you give me any reason whatsoever, any hint of instability, I'll cut you loose. Down in the mines everyone depends on each other."

"And they can depend on me, just as I'll depend on them."

He nodded again and wrote her name in his book.

5

STANDING before the wreths that had emerged from the dust storm, Adan faced these alien strangers with a straight back and square shoulders. *I am King Adan Starfall.* His people needed him to be strong.

Wreths. Legendary creators of the human race. And warriors who nearly tore the world apart in their endless thirst to destroy each other and kill the mythic dragon. *How can this be? They vanished thousands of years ago.*

Their return could not bode well.

As the silence drew out at the gate of the walled city, the reptile mounts shifted, flicking black tongues out of their wide mouths. The regal woman on the largest auga regarded him with eyes the color of cracked amber. Her long golden hair was flecked with a metallic sheen. With her right arm, she held a triangular green shield that looked like a single scale of some tremendous reptilian beast.

The eerie wreths wore brown leather armor with a coating of scales, and they carried an assortment of sharp weapons: long spears with shafts twisted into a tight spiral, white blades fashioned from crystallized bone or daggers that looked like shards of oily black obsidian. Other wreths, clearly a different caste, were unarmed, their heads shaven, their faces craggy; these strange men wore heavy robes of brown leather stamped with looping spell patterns.

Penda and her father stood close behind Adan at the city gate, flanked by nervous guards. Her ska croaked in alarm, peering cautiously over her head.

Adan took one step closer to the visitors and spoke in a voice that was both neutral and firm. "I am the king of Suderra." The golden woman seemed to be waiting for something more from him. Long ago, wreths had expected their humans to be subservient and bow. Could that be what she wanted? If so, she would be disappointed. "And I know my history. You are wreths?" Adan faced her as an equal, which seemed to put the woman off balance.

She responded. "We did not think we were forgotten. I am Queen Voo of the sandwreths, and we have come from the deep desert." Her evocative voice held a hint of amusement. "We would see what you have done with the land in our absence, as we might have need of you again."

Despite the warm sunshine, a chill ran down Adan's back. Standing his ground, he said, "What have we done? We survived. We helped the land recover after the wreths almost destroyed the world."

Voo sounded wistful. "And yet the world endures." She swung her long, bare leg over the back of the lizard creature and dropped to the dusty road. "I am glad we found you. We have much to discuss, your race and mine." She gestured toward Bannriya's thick sandstone walls, crowded buildings, and high towers. Colorful banners had already been restrung after the storm. "You rule this place? You built it?"

"My ancestors built it long ago, after the wars. This is how our race survived the most difficult times."

"Interesting." Her amber eyes sparkled. "Escort us into your city so we can discuss a matter of grave importance. Your world is about to change again, and we wish to make you an offer. An important offer."

Two riders beside her also dismounted, a tall, cocky wreth man who might have been Voo's brother, and a bald older man with a deeply incised face and an embossed leather robe. Behind them, five more sandwreths slid from their augas.

Penda took Adan's hand, and he felt her strength flowing into him. In a clear voice, she said, "We welcome the wreths for an open discussion, but not your entire army." She gestured to the hundred armed, lizard-mounted warriors. "They must stay outside our walls."

"Our entire army?" Voo gave an offhand glance to the numerous sandwreths on their burly augas. "But this is just the smallest honor guard! Once, our armies swarmed like locusts across the landscape, clashing with the frostwreths." She sniffed in disappointment. "If you are truly worried about such a minimal party, then you may not be able to help us after all."

Help them? Adan's thoughts spun. He had not offered any help, and if history was any guide, humanity owed the wreths no favors. As king, though, it was his duty to receive the delegation, if only to learn what they were about. "We would consider it a gesture of good faith if you left your honor guard outside, however small you think it is. We will speak with your representatives in the castle."

Standing in front of her auga, Voo appeared unperturbed. "I will bring my brother Quo and five wreth mages. The rest will remain here." She glanced up at the sandstone walls and added in a dismissive tone, "It is not as if your defenses could stop them if they wished to enter."

On Penda's shoulder, the ska made what sounded like a rude noise, but the wreths ignored it.

Realizing the folly of insisting on an even smaller group, Adan led the queen and her party through the high gates and into the city, with Penda and Hale Orr at either side of him. Though clearly unaccustomed to following rather than leading, the wreths nevertheless walked behind the king and queen in a procession, all the while looking around curiously, as if judging Bannriya.

Adan explained, "The dust storm blanketed our streets and buildings. We've just begun to clean up."

"Like everything else in the world, dust is a resource," said the wreth queen. She nodded to the wreth mages, who in turn moved their bronzed hands to create breezes that scoured the dust from the street, blasting grit from the buildings and doorways ahead of them, doing the work of days in only an instant.

Penda acknowledged the mages. "Thank you, although we could have finished the sweeping ourselves, in time."

"Of course you could." Voo's tone had an oblivious lilt. "Humans have always been good at menial labor."

An indignant hiss from Xar covered the sound of Adan's sharply indrawn breath. Penda shushed the ska, and the king forced himself to ignore the insult, for now. These strange wreths were obviously powerful, but not necessarily enemies—at the moment. He could not afford to take offense too easily. He sensed there was a great deal at stake here.

People watched the procession from doorways and windows. A troop of armed Banner guards followed in close formation, weapons ready, though Adan doubted the sandwreths were afraid of his soldiers.

Many millennia ago, the elder race had been created and blessed by their own god Kur, who was one among the many gods who made countless worlds. This was the first world created by Kur and he was fond of it, though because it was his first, it had many flaws. He gave the wreths the task of purging the world of all evil, which was manifested in the great dragon Ossus. If they succeeded, he promised to return, take his chosen wreths, and remake the world into its perfect form. That was their legend and their sincere belief.

But the wreths broke into two great factions that warred over which ones would be Kur's chosen. Using their own magic, trying to set themselves up as gods, the wreth race then created humans to be workers, breeding servants, and foot soldiers in their perpetual wars. Thousands of years of conflict followed before the tattered remnants of the wreth factions retreated into obscurity, leaving their humans to survive in the magic-depleted wasteland that remained.

Every human knew about their race's origin and the downfall of the wreths. Ruins of once-great wreth cities were scattered across the landscape. But so much time had passed, while human civilization thrived across the Commonwealth in the meantime, that no one gave much thought to the lost race or their long-departed god. Adan could not imagine why the sandwreths would reemerge from obscurity, unless they meant to cause great trouble.

Your world is about to change again, Voo had said. A threat? A promise?

Adan wrestled with his duty as king. He would do anything to defend his people, to keep them safe and prosperous, though he was not a bloodthirsty man. He didn't dare declare war on their own creators.

We wish to make you an offer. An important offer.

King Adan Starfall would listen and then decide.

The procession arrived at the castle in the center of the city. As they stood at the front stone archway, the brother of the sandwreth queen looked down at the toppled ancient statue at the gate with an oddly curious smile. "Look, Sister. They still have reminders of us."

Voo frowned at the weathered sculpture. "That one was not worth remembering. I am surprised they would keep it."

"The statue was brought here from the ruins many generations ago, by one of my predecessors. No one remembers its significance," Adan said, hurrying them forward into Bannriya Castle.

Inside, he took them to the parley hall, rather than his throne room. He had no idea whether Queen Voo might take insult if he sat looking down on her from a raised throne dais. He wouldn't put the question to the test just to see her reaction.

The queen, her warrior brother Quo, and the five wreth mages gathered around the table, as if they found it quaint. Penda's dark eyes flashed with concern, as if she and her ska sensed something portentous, and Adan longed to hear what she thought. They took adjoining high-backed seats, and Voo chose the chair on the other side of Adan as if it were her due.

Several vassal lords, out-of-place ministers, worried-looking advisers, and half a dozen functionaries joined the other courtiers, filling the room. They were still in the castle only because of the storm, but they were too fascinated by the strange visitors to leave.

Fixing her amber eyes on the king, Voo spoke in a voice full of laughter and razors. "Adan Starfall . . . *King* Adan, we are impressed by what you humans managed to accomplish while we were gone. We expected to find only a few squalid remnants, if any of you survived at all. I never knew that humans had such ambition or independence! Your race seems surprisingly strong. Now that we have awakened from our long spellsleep, we want to know how you've thrived, how many cities you built, how large your population has grown. We feel . . . responsible."

"Why?" Penda asked, without tact.

The wreth queen took no offense. Her answer startled them like the sharp drop of an executioner's ax. "Because the final war to wake the dragon is coming, and we want you to be our allies against the vile frostwreths."

One of the servants dropped a tray of biscuits and jam in her shock.

Adan answered slowly but firmly, sharpening his words. He could feel the agitation of all the observers in the chamber and knew they would have countless questions, but he was the king. "Your wars caused untold damage thousands of years ago, to the world and to us. The land recovered under *our* stewardship, and the Commonwealth is at peace under my father, the konag. We have no interest in your reasons for fighting each other, and we will certainly not assist you in waging war."

"But the *real* war is not over, and it never will be until we defeat the descendants of Suth," Voo said. "The frostwreths will come down from the north, and when they do, your lands will be like a strip of metal between a hammer and an anvil."

Though his face burned, Adan kept his voice level. "If you came here to bring threats, then you and your people are not welcome in Bannriya."

The warrior Quo snorted. "Oh, there *will* be war, whether or not you welcome us. At least my sister brings you hope."

Voo nodded. "I offer you a chance, King Adan Starfall. Join with us. You humans have no gods watching over you, as we do. Nevertheless, you may prove useful as allies against our enemies. Join us and have our protection." She smiled again. "It is in your best interests to accept."

T HE autumn skies were blue, and the changing aspens turned the hills honey-gold around the northern city of Fellstaff. Though Kollanan, king of Norterra, knew that winter was just around the corner, warm weather had lulled him into postponing repairs to the roof on the castle's main keep. Still, he and the carpenters had to get the work done before the cold set in, and this was the perfect day to do so.

Shirtless, wearing only leather boots and breeches, the king perched high on the sloped roof. He looked at least a decade younger than his fifty years, with broad shoulders, strong muscles, and a flat stomach. Relishing the sun on his bare back, he raised his hammer and pounded long nails through tarred shingles, anchoring them to the roof boards.

He enjoyed the staccato patter of hammers, hearing a certain music in it, and he took satisfaction in the work. He would never command his people to do something he wasn't willing to do himself, and he hated leaky ceilings. Now the keep would stay warm and dry throughout the cold winter and into the rainy spring.

High above the crowded city, his view of Fellstaff's winding streets and open marketplaces gave him a sense of peace and satisfaction. Koll felt comfortably at home. He was the king of all he could see, from the snowy mountains and expansive lakes in the north to the forested hills down toward Suderra, to the eastern farmlands and the scattered wreth ruins across the plains.

Humming to himself, he brushed a hand over his thick beard, which was sprinkled with more gray than he liked to admit. Despite the cool air, he could feel the prickle of sweat in his hair—good sweat that came from work instead of from killing. He was no longer in the Commonwealth army, and the war with Ishara was over decades ago. This was his life now, and this was the kind of king he wanted to be, a paternal manager rather than a battle commander. He plucked a nail from between his lips, positioned it on a shingle, and pounded it into place—a carpenter's hammer, not a war hammer.

During the war in decades past, people had called him Kollanan the Hammer, because of his weapon of choice when he and his brother Conndur went to fight the Isharans. Now, he found the Hammer epithet fitting because he liked to build things. His war hammer hung on a wall in his private study, where it would stay.

Thirty years ago, he had returned to the Commonwealth with a new bride acquired as a spoil of war, but he had never bragged about his fighting in Ishara. He had left the war on the shores of that other continent, and when they came home he made certain the tales focused on his brother, who would become konag of the whole Commonwealth. Koll had been glad to retire to rule the distant northern kingdom with his queen, Tafira.

He and Conndur were great friends. When they were young, they had been starry-eyed with imagined glory and eager for victory. Neither of them had bothered to consider the consequences of war, and now it was Conn's duty as konag to consider the fate of the three kingdoms. Koll didn't envy him the responsibility. As king of Norterra, he had more than enough to worry about: his people, his vassal lords, the crops, the mines, the roads . . . his wife, and his daughter and their two grandsons living in a village to the north . . . A good life. Not easy, but satisfying.

The roof's trapdoor hatch opened and an elegant figure emerged. With black hair and shapely curves, Tafira was like a manifestation from the gods—if wreth gods had ever paid attention to humans. "Early dinner is ready, Husband. Your presence is required, because I do not wish to dine alone." His wife had a rich smoky voice that still held the hint of an Isharan accent, even thirty years after she'd come home with him.

The other workers on the rooftop chuckled. Koll clipped his hammer to his belt, nimbly keeping his balance on the shingled slope. "Men, you've heard the ruler of the kingdom issue her commands. I am the Hammer, but I must bow to the nail." He spread his hands. "Or face the consequences."

The rungs creaked under his boots as he climbed down through the hatch after Tafira. Alone with her in the shadows, he smelled the lingering spices that clung to her. "You cooked something very flavorful."

He leaned close to kiss her, and she swatted him. "Put on a shirt. You sweat like a horse!"

"There are no horses on rooftops." He pulled her close. "You never minded before."

"I mind when I choose to." She pulled away with a smile, and he admired her, shaking his head at how lucky he was. Tafira could outmatch the beauty of any woman half her age. Truly, she was the most precious spoil of that awful war.

The household crew prepared to serve the early dinner, one of the few Isharan traditions his wife kept from her past life. Though Fellstaff Castle had skilled cooks, Tafira supervised them in the kitchens because she knew the right combinations of expensive imported spices. Her Isharan dishes were distinct from the venison, mutton, fish, and root vegetables common in Norterra, but her recipes were the only things she still cherished from her childhood home, along with one small figurine that represented the minor godling from her home village. Tafira held no fondness for those days, which was not surprising, since her own people had tried to kill her.

During that war, he and the Commonwealth army had spent more than a year living off the land from village to village, conquering Isharan territory even though their roving army didn't have sufficient numbers to hold it. For months, Koll's troops struck and retreated, then struck somewhere else, keeping the Isharans in a state of fear.

Because the people in the Commonwealth had no gods to please, their greatest personal goal was to lead a long life and leave a great legacy. Their deeds were all that endured after they were gone. The soldiers had sailed off to invade Ishara with heroic hearts, but constant pillaging, hatred, and distance from home changed the men. Even Koll the Hammer had become jaded.

Some of his soldiers went mad with bloodlust, their hearts full of poison instead of compassion. He saw brave men and good friends become monsters. Once, when riding back from patrol, he came upon his troops ransacking an Isharan village called Sarcen. Seeing easy prey, his soldiers set homes on fire, rode down and trampled children, hacked old women with their swords. In their shock, the people of Sarcen couldn't even awaken their weak local godling from its slumber. But Kollanan charged in among them, twirling his battle hammer over his head and commanding his own men to stop. He was forced to kill two of his out-of-control line commanders to stop the massacre. That was when he had also saved Tafira.

Three decades later, she still looked as compelling as the day he swept her up, placed her on the back of his horse, and rode away from the smoking aftermath of Sarcen.

Now, after washing up, Kollanan pulled on a fine cotton shirt, strolled into the castle's withdrawing room, and poured himself a glass of a dry Suderran wine as he waited for dinner to be set out.

A muscular blond man entered the room, quiet as a cat. The Brava's face was square and weathered, with flat features, high cheekbones, and the familiar almond eyes. He wore his traditional black leather breeches, boots, and jerkin, the finemail draped like silk over his chest, an assortment of weapons at his belt, as well as the golden ramer band. Comfortable in the castle, Lasis had left off his finemail-lined cloak, though he would never let down his guard.

Businesslike, the loyal Brava held out a sheaf of papers. "I have monthly reports from all eight counties, Sire, including harvest projections from the farmlands, a report of cotton growers disputing a boundary with Suderra, and also a proposed demarcation of forestland for the woodcutters so they can enlarge our winter stockpiles of firewood."

Koll picked up the reports, scanned numbers from the vassal lords. "Didn't we discover a rich vein of coal in the western counties? Can't the villages use coal to heat their homes?"

"Most prefer fresh wood, Sire—as do I." Lasis sniffed. "The smell of coal is not to my liking."

Five years after the end of the Isharan war, when Kollanan had retired to his kingdom to live in peace, the young Brava had come to Fellstaff to offer his services. Lasis said he liked the idea of a king who walked away from conflict to devote his life to farming instead of war. "I don't like conflict either."

Koll remembered that day and recalled his skepticism. "That seems a dubious qualification for a Brava. Are you afraid to fight?"

Lasis had not been insulted. "I am no coward, but you will need my strength if you want true peace in Norterra. The only way you can have peace is with a man like me bonded to your service. I will ensure that it happens."

Lasis stayed in Fellstaff Castle for much of the time, but he also roamed the eight counties as a paladin, helping where he was needed, saving people where he could, or meting out justice if he couldn't arrive in time to save them.

Because the Brava did his work so well, and because King Kollanan ruled so effectively, Lasis soon found that his services as a guard were not needed as much. With the king's permission, he would ride off on sojourns of his own. He stopped an assassination attempt down in Suderra during the first year of young King Adan's rule, when one of the deposed regents sought to return to power. Lasis refused to tell Kollanan the details of what he had done there in the southern kingdom. "The results are all that matter, Sire." And Koll had accepted that.

Now, sitting in his chair, Koll scanned the documents and nodded his approval just as Tafira called them to dinner. "Let Konag Conndur worry about politics, taxes, and history. My kingdom is doing well enough."

He sat next to Tafira at the head of the grand table. She served braised venison cut into bite-sized pieces mixed with noodles, a brown sauce, and pepper flakes that sizzled like fire on the tongue. As they ate, she glanced at several empty seats at the table. "I wish Jhaqi and her husband would visit. It's been too long since we've heard from them."

Koll turned to his wife with a knowing smile. "You just want to see our grandsons." He took a gulp of wine to wash down the spices. "But now that you mention it, there should be more traffic from the north. It has been nearly two weeks since we've had word from Lake Bakal."

"Shall we send a messenger? Next week is Tomko's birthday. We should send gifts."

"He'll be five years old, won't he?"

"Four. Birch is five. You lose track of time, Husband."

"Only because I'm so happy to be with you, beloved." She accepted the compliment as her due. He made up his mind. "I'm due for a nice ride. I'll head up there myself tomorrow, while the weather holds. I carved some new toys for the two boys, and I can deliver them in person."

Lasis finished his meal. "I will accompany you, Sire, for your protection."

"I don't need protection in my own kingdom." Koll huffed, though he knew the Brava was merely doing his duty. "It's only three days—I've made the ride many times."

He didn't want to cause his wife any concern, but as he considered, he found the long silence from their daughter, and the entire village of Lake Bakal, to be worrisome. Koll intended to get to the bottom of it.

7

WITH the weakened godling huddled in the cargo hold as the warship departed, Priestlord Klovus watched black smoke rise from the devastated village. His heart swelled with triumph as the sails billowed with magical wind that drove the ship eastward, back home to the continent of Ishara.

Wasting no time, Klovus summoned the bound prisoners taken from Mirrabay. They would serve their purpose now, because the godling needed rejuvenation. Some of the Commonwealth men and women struggled and spat, while others seemed too defeated to resist as he hauled them in front of the golden chute. Their blood was weak, but so was the godling after its exertions. Far from the magic-infused shores of Ishara, the deity dwindled, even though the faith of the sailors remained strong. Klovus had to be careful not to let them see any weakness.

As soldiers held one prisoner after another, the priestlord slashed their throats and drained their blood into the chute that poured into the hold. Once used up, their bodies were tossed overboard.

"Hear us, save us!" the crew chanted as each victim serviced the godling.

Their blood fed the deity, but its energy remained at a manageable level, still within the priestlord's control. Klovus knew this godling personally, had tended it when he had just been an ur-priest at the harbor temple, before his promotion to the main temple in Serepol as key priestlord of all Ishara.

When the captives were all used up, Klovus sensed that the godling was stabilized. He examined the sleeve of his caftan and noticed a blood spot on the fabric. He scratched it with a fingernail, but the stain ran deep. He would have to burn the garment later, since it was contaminated with the blood of the godless.

With the magic strengthened again, their voyage home would be safe and swift, but the priestlord would face his next battle when he saw the empra. She did not agree with his plans, had not sanctioned this raid. In fact, she preferred peace to power. . . .

During the quiet voyage, the Isharan soldiers nursed their wounds on the open deck. Three surgeons sewed up the worst injuries suffered at Mirrabay, many of which had been inflicted by the Brava man. Twenty-four raiders had died in the attack, but the coastal village had lost hundreds, thanks to the godling, in addition to the ten sacrifices they had just made here.

Meanwhile, the entity rested down in the hold. Through his sandals, Klovus felt energy pulsing through the deck boards from below. Taking advantage of the respite, the captain ordered his men to check the hatch covers on the hull ports to make certain the godling was secure. The captain was a religious man, but also sensible, and they all knew what the thing could do if it broke free. Klovus would keep it weak enough, yet content.

As priestlord, though, he wasn't overly worried about the godling. He had bought its loyalty and knew he could control it, even if none of the sailors did. He used his symbiotic connection, drawing upon the deity's innate strength, calming and feeding it in return. Klovus had always felt the great bond, the strength of the many godlings. He was their true speaker, their true representative.

The entity had expended its rage in an appropriate fashion and could now lie dormant until it was needed again. When the warship returned to Serepol, Klovus would restore the godling to its home temple at the harbor's edge, sealing it behind its spelldoor. This one wasn't even Serepol's greatest godling—Klovus would never have taken all protection from the capital city, no matter his disagreements with the empra.

As the ship sailed on, the captain approached him. His sleeveless hemp shirt opened on a hairy chest, and he had tied a white head scarf in place. "Are you satisfied with the raid, Priestlord?"

"The godling demonstrated its power, and the people of Mirrabay will never forget us. Stories will travel across the three kingdoms. Everyone will fear what we can do." *Perhaps even the empra . . .*

Frowning, the captain leaned closer. "Aren't you worried that Konag Conndur will strike back? He'll want revenge against Ishara for what we did."

"If he tries, he will be devastated." Klovus hoped, in fact, that the Commonwealth would respond, and then Empra Iluris would have to take her role seriously. "They have no gods. Therefore, they have no chance against us."

The captain glanced toward the deck hatch. "I think the godling is still hungry, even after the sacrifices. It used so much energy when it attacked the village that the sailors are concerned. We should have taken more prisoners for sacrifice."

Klovus hid his expression of disgust. "The godling doesn't thrive on the tainted blood of such people." He also didn't want the entity to grow too unruly before he could seal it back into its temple. "Have no fear, the godling will grant us a safe voyage. We'll be home soon."

The captain remained uneasy. "But what if we are beset by storms? Tomorrow we sail past Fulcor Island—what if the Commonwealth garrison there sends warships to attack us?" He lowered his voice so the other sailors couldn't hear. "In its current state, is the godling strong enough to protect us?"

Without the anchor of its home temple, Klovus feared the entity might decide it liked freedom better, but he could maintain the balance. "Our sailors can offer more blood if they wish. Let them sustain the godling during our voyage. Have no fear."

"Hear us, save us." The captain nodded with a relieved smile. "I have no fear, because I know its strength." Adjusting his scarf, he went looking for volunteers among his able-bodied crew.

In Ishara, each of the thirteen districts had its own primary godling in a temple managed by a ruling priestlord, but other villages and localities had lesser godlings that were created, strengthened, and maintained by the nurturing believers. The inherent magic in the new world distilled their beliefs into a tangible entity, a local godling endowed with the very powers the people believed in. Seeing the physical manifestation of those beliefs served to strengthen the people's faith, which in turn strengthened the godling. The cycle fed itself. Most Isharans did not understand or question the nuances, but the godlings reflected the mood as well as the nature of the district and the people.

Ishara was a pristine continent, settled by ambitious pilgrims who had left the devastated old world well over a thousand years ago. The wreth wars had wrung out the old continent like a frayed washcloth, and the land held very little magic anymore. The people of the Commonwealth were too weak to create godlings of their own.

But the faith of the Isharan settlers, amplified by the magic in their land, had manifested something marvelous. With this raid, Klovus had demonstrated the power of a relatively minor godling, even far from home. With that evidence in hand, he would have the leverage to insist that the empra resume construction on the Magnifica temple in Serepol. When finished, the Magnifica would be the most wondrous structure ever built by humans, housing the most powerful godling ever manifested . . . but only if the stubborn empra would let it be completed.

Upon taking the throne three decades ago, young Iluris had halted construction, much to the dismay of the priestlords. She first used the war against the Commonwealth as an excuse, and had concocted other reasons every year since. She simply didn't want the godlings or the priestlords to have too much power. She had always been difficult. . . .

On the third day of the voyage home, the waters turned choppy with a gathering storm, and Klovus conceded that it would be wise to strengthen the godling. Sailor volunteers stood in line near the golden chute, passing a knife from one to the next. The crew members slashed their forearms and spilled blood into the chute, collecting enough to satisfy the deity.

Klovus led them in their prayers. "Hear us, save us."

"Hear us, save us."

On the far side of the deck, he saw the surgeons speaking in low voices, concerned as they tended a severely injured soldier who lay coughing and convulsing. They knelt over him, their garments stained with his blood. They had wrapped strips of linen around a deep sword cut in his side, but the bandages were soaked with red. Klovus knew the man was breathing his last.

The priestlord stepped away from the collection chute, took the knife from the line of sailors cutting their arms. "I need this." Holding the blade, he stepped over to the dying man. In his blue caftan, he loomed over the bleeding soldier, who reached up with a clutching hand. Klovus quietly asked the surgeons, "Is there no chance?"

They shook their heads.

The wounded man raised his head. Though he could barely see, his eyes locked on the priestlord's, and he choked out the words, "Give me to the godling. Please."

It was exactly as Klovus had hoped. Even if the man hadn't offered, the priestlord would have taken matters into his own hands. To the dying soldier, he said, "You are a brave man, and it is a worthy sacrifice." He called two of the sailors. "Help me carry him to the sacrificial chute. Quickly! If we don't do this before he dies, the strongest power will be wasted."

The injured man groaned as they lifted him from where he lay. "Careful," one of the sailors whispered. "Gently."

"We don't have time to be gentle," Klovus said. "The blood of a dead man is a far inferior sacrifice. Hurry."

Choosing speed over delicacy, the sailors carried the man to the opening above the hold, leaving a pile of blood-soaked bandages behind. The priestlord grasped the dying man by the shoulders, while the sailors maneuvered into position.

The soldier gurgled and twitched over the golden chute. Klovus grasped his matted hair, yanked his head back, and with a quick jerk of the sacrificial knife, slit his throat. The sailors held the man by his feet while he bled the last of his bubbling red life down into the hold.

"Hear us, save us."

The godling absorbed the blood, the magic, and the strength. The ship itself seemed to thrum with the entity's delight at this unexpected feast. Klovus looked at his sticky fingers as the dead man sagged. The sailors lowered the body and rested his gaping throat on the chute, so as not to waste a drop, until the soldier had nothing left to give.

When the blood was drained, Klovus said, "He offered all he had. The godling appreciates the sacrifice."

Feeling tangible strength return to their ship, emanated by the deity below, the soldiers celebrated. As the warship continued across the open sea toward Ishara, the priestlord inhaled deeply, smelling salt air and victory instead of the lingering stench of blood.

From the pinnacle tower in her palace, Empra Iluris stared out at the busy harbor of Serepol, the capital city of Ishara. Numerous fishing boats, trading ships, and armed patrol vessels plied the waters, but she still saw no sign of the warship that Priestlord Klovus had commandeered.

The damned fool is trying to start a war!

She had instructed her hawk guards to inform her the moment the rogue ship returned to Isharan waters. She wanted to tear the key priestlord limb from limb for what he had done, but politics would prevent her from doing so. Considering the flames he had already fanned among the people, Klovus might even be welcomed home as a hero. Though her reign had been marked by decades of peace, some Isharans truly wanted war rather than the prosperity she had brought to the land. Klovus's provocations might ruin everything she had worked for.

Iluris was empra of Ishara, all thirteen districts, all the priestlords, all the people, but the priestlords controlled the godlings, which gave them a different sort of power. Publicly, they swore loyalty to the throne, but that didn't stop Klovus from justifying whatever he wished to do. *Damn him!*

Iluris had not sanctioned this provocative raid, but the key priestlord did it anyway, supposedly for the good of Ishara. If he returned victorious, the empra would not be able to punish him, at least not publicly . . . and as leader of Ishara, how could she want the raid to *fail*? She was in an impossible position.

But it was time to put the ambitious man in his place, to diminish his ill-advised victory. It would have to be done carefully, subtly, and for the good of Ishara. She would have to think along unexpected lines.

With hawk guards outside in the corridor keeping her safe, Iluris paced in her tower chambers. She was forty-seven with ash-blond hair, her face still smooth despite decades of rule and three worthless husbands. Seasoned and experienced, she was more than a match for Klovus, who was ten years her junior.

From the opposite high window, she looked inland toward the heart of her city, her gaze drawn to the temple quarter, where a vast foundation and half-constructed walls stretched over an area that would have encompassed an entire neighborhood, the first floor marked out and partially constructed. The priestlords had ambitions to raise it ten times higher, if she ever allowed them to complete it.

The Magnifica had been a dream of the priestlords for nearly half a century. Beginning in the reign of her father, Emprir Daka, work armies had razed street after street, and the temple's foundations were laid down with huge blocks of stone. From across the land, each district had donated materials, money, labor. Even in its initial stages, the temple inspired awe and pride, and the priestlords were giddy with self-importance. The Magnifica would host the primary Serepol godling, the *Isharan* godling, and make that entity the most powerful in the world.

But the main Serepol godling was already immense and intimidating, and she worried what so much concentration of power would do to the entity. Why would the priestlords need the godling to be so strong? Were they even sure they could control it once the temple was finished?

When young Iluris took the throne after her father's death, she had been wise enough to see the danger and the consequences. Citing the war with the Commonwealth as the ostensible reason, she had halted construction on the Magnifica, hobbling the priestlords' ambitions. The broad foundations and the half-constructed walls served as a temporary temple to house the Serepol godling. Enormous piles of construction material remained, enough to build an entire town, waiting for the work to resume.

Klovus had been no more than a boy of seven when the Commonwealth war ended. The Magnifica temple had been stalled for most of his life. He had served as an acolyte, where he discovered he had a real affinity for the godlings, and that helped him rise quickly through the ranks. As a priestlord, he could control some magic, even if he let the godlings do the work for him.

Iluris, though, had no discernible magic of her own, in spite of coming from a long and respected noble lineage. If the priestlords ever decided to battle her outright, maybe even try to assassinate her, she wasn't sure she would survive, so Iluris protected herself in her own way. Her hawk guards, whom she called adopted sons, would give their lives to keep her safe, and she had developed her own deft skills and political maneuvers.

She stared out the high window. Still no sign of the raiding ship's return . . .

As empra, she worried about the future of Ishara. She remained childless despite her three marriages, and she had taken no new husband in years, seeing no value in marrying yet again, not at her age. If she died without an heir, the priestlords would replace her with some starry-eyed puppet who would let them build their Magnifica temple and give extravagant power to their godlings.

She was determined not to fail, because she owed it to herself and to her people. Isharans did not deserve yet another corrupt leader.

Iluris stepped to the edge of the open tower window and looked down to the courtyard, dizzyingly far below. Placing her hands on the sun-warmed sill, Iluris watched the tiny figures down there. Such a long way to fall. This was the very tower, the very window, from which she had pushed her father. That was how she'd become empra at the age of seventeen. . . .

Emprir Daka had been a hard and loveless man who killed two wives—not with a blade or poison, but through persistent emotional abuse. Iluris was the daughter from Daka's second marriage, and after he destroyed his wife, his own daughter became his next target.

The emprir had fathered three daughters, two of whom died in early childhood. Iluris had survived only because she was protected and cared for, watched every day by nannies, servants, and guards—of their own volition, rather than by any command from Emprir Daka. Only later did Iluris piece together the hints and realize that the servants were sheltering her because they knew the other two girls had not died by accident. Although Daka became resigned to having Iluris as his heir, he punished her simply for not being male. Soon enough, though, he took advantage of her for being female.

When her monthly courses started flowing at age thirteen, the court advisors informed the emprir that Iluris had reached full womanhood and could be considered for a marriage alliance. Daka took the news a different way, however. With his wives dead, he began to slip into his daughter's room late at night. He would lock the door and force himself upon her, telling her it was part of her training to be empra.

She fought back, but he was stronger, not just physically, but because he had the power of command. Once, he brought in his personal guards to tie her down, then commanded them to witness as he raped her. She lay sobbing and screaming. And they did nothing.

When she went to the priests and begged them to make her father stop, they chided her for trying to circumvent what the godlings wished. She wondered whose "wish" it really was. Despite her pleas, they gave Emprir Daka permission to continue molesting her. Iluris never forgave the priestlords for that.

One night, when Daka came to her drunk, she was ready. She had hidden a drugged needle beside her bed, and when her father forced her down under his weight and his hot breath, she vowed that it would be the last time. She snatched the needle from the bedside and pricked his shoulder. He was so preoccupied with his passions that he didn't even notice the scratch.

The drug quickly took effect, rendering him dizzy and nauseated. Iluris coaxed him over to the window of the pinnacle tower, just for a breath of air. As he stood there, naked and sweating in the low light of the braziers, still swaying, Iluris pushed him. He toppled out of the high window and fell with only a low moan until he struck the paving stones.

When the guards rushed in, followed by stunned priests, Iluris managed to summon tears without betraying that they were tears of joy. "He came in to give me a good-night kiss, but he must have had too much wine. He went to the window for some air and lost his balance." She drew a breath. "Such a great loss for Ishara."

Thus, she became empra during the war with the Commonwealth, which ended shortly thereafter. Over the years of her reign, Iluris led Ishara to prosperity, despite lingering resentments against the old world. Her concern was for the thirteen districts, the cities, the people, the schools. She wanted to make Ishara a better home for humanity than the damaged old world her people had left behind so long ago.

But now, without asking for her blessing or permission, the fool Klovus had launched a provocative attack that Konag Conndur was sure to answer. The priestlord had managed to sneak away with the godling from the harbor temple and a duped crew. A priest courier had informed her only after the warship was long gone, ensuring that she could not stop Klovus under any circumstances.

Now, Iluris needed to assert herself and put the key priestlord in his place.

Gazing out at the harbor again, she knew it might be days yet before the ship came home, and even once the sails were spotted on the horizon, the ship would take many more hours to reach port, so she had plenty of time to take action.

With her secular power, the most resounding punishment she could impose on Klovus would be to reallocate the stockpiled construction materials and tools from the Magnifica temple square. She smiled. For the past year, the priests had quietly added to the mounds of building supplies, enough to continue the project in earnest, whenever they thought they could get away with it. So many resources.

Iluris decided to commandeer as much of the stockpile as possible in the name of Ishara and use the stone blocks and wood, paid for by the priest-lords, to build schools to teach young Isharans their letters and numbers, to repair roads, to increase trade among the districts.

Yes, that was it. Her land would thrive.

Her dream was to keep Ishara a land of plenty. She would do what was best for her people. No matter what Priestlord Klovus desired, the last thing she needed was an all-out war with the Commonwealth.

9

⚱

Lightning crashed and thunder boomed like a battle in the sky, unleashing a late-night downpour. Jagged white bolts danced among the clouds over Convera Castle, which sat high on a defensible wedge of land above the river confluence.

Rain hissed against the latticed windows in Konag Conndur's library, but a fire of seasoned oak in the hearth kept him warm and comfortable.

Earlier, for dinner, Conndur had hosted a group of ambassadors, lords, and successful businessmen from around Osterra. The konag believed that diplomacy worked better in a relaxed situation, especially with roast herbed lamb. Other than minor boundary disputes and squabbles over tariffs, the three kingdoms of Osterra, Suderra, and Norterra had coexisted peacefully for many centuries. The open-hand symbol of the Commonwealth had been well chosen.

During the dinner, Conn brokered a deal between a man who owned flocks of sheep and a lord who had idle spinners and needed the wool. Lord Cade, from the rugged northernmost county, presented a sack of perfect salt-pearls and described how his brave divers retrieved them only by swimming deep in the dangerous currents.

Prince Mandan, Conn's elder son, had also attended the dinner, because the konag insisted that the prince participate in governance. Adan, Mandan's younger brother, was king of Suderra and well liked by the people—quite a change from his predecessors—but even greater responsibilities awaited Mandan as the future konag of the entire Commonwealth. The prince had been schooled in geography and mathematics, culture and art, but he had no instinct for *people*, alliances, obligations, friendships, and enmities. Mandan was not at all ready, did not seem anxious for the throne, and had never shown the leadership abilities Adan had. At twenty-five, the prince was already older than Conndur had been when he became konag.

After dinner, Mandan bowed out of the conversation as soon as he could, wanting to work on his poetry. The guests bade him good night, and he hurried to his quarters. Only Conn realized that his son was uneasy because of the thunderstorm brewing outside. The young man had always hated storms. . . .

Now that the guests were gone, Konag Conndur relished the quiet time in the hours before midnight while the rain came down. Sitting in his chair by the fire, he perused a volume chronicling the deeds of konags from the past. The inscription read, *Long life and a great legacy.*

That benediction summed up the greatest success any human could hope for, since their entire race was a secondary creation. When making humans to be their servants, wreths had not endowed them with souls, nor given them any place for an afterlife. They had to make their mark in *this* life and leave a legacy to be remembered for as long as possible. Their deeds would be their immortality.

Conn skimmed the stories in the book. All the names were also recorded permanently in the great remembrance shrine in Convera City. The men and women in this chronicle had achieved that goal, and he hoped that when his own chronicle was written, his legacy could exist proudly beside those of his forebears.

A roar of thunder rattled the windows, and the rain streamed down. He was glad he wasn't out on a military campaign trying to sleep in a wet tent with water dripping through the seams. Such experiences were for younger and more foolish people—unlike stargazing. Unfortunately, the rain clouds would prevent him from going out on the rooftop platform tonight to study the stars, a cherished activity he had often shared with Adan. But with Adan on the throne in faraway Suderra for the past few years, those intimate times happened only rarely now.

Conn had tried again and again to teach his other son the constellations, but Prince Mandan never could marvel at the lights of those other worlds created by the ancient wreth gods. Sighing, the konag closed the volume of history and leaned back in his chair. If only Adan had been the firstborn . . .

Conndur himself was a second son who had never expected to become konag. It should have been his brother Bolam, the firstborn. As heir apparent, Bolam had been trained in statecraft, skilled in strategy games and the arts, a well-liked young man with many interests, great intelligence, a calm disposition, and a gift for negotiation. Bolam would have made a great konag.

When war broke out with Ishara, their father Konag Cronin dispatched his two younger sons, Conndur and Kollanan, to lead the expeditionary armies. Conn the Brave and Koll the Hammer led skirmishes across Ishara for more than a year. While his two younger brothers were in the thick of the dangerous war, Prince Bolam remained home in Convera Castle, safe and protected . . . where he caught a fever and died.

Devastated, Konag Cronin lost all heart for the war. With his oldest son's body consumed by the funeral pyre and Convera City decked in black crepe, Cronin gathered every last warship in the Commonwealth, adding coastal passenger ships and swift Utauk trading vessels into a breathtaking fleet. That enormous navy crossed the ocean and converged on Serepol Harbor.

But instead of burning the Isharan capital in rage and revenge, Cronin had sent a message to young Empra Iluris, calling for an end to the war. In his deep grief, he wanted nothing more than to bring his remaining two sons home safely, and the giant fleet sailed back home.

Even though the war was never resolved, the Commonwealth retreated. Koll the Hammer accepted the throne of Norterra, where he settled down with his new Isharan bride and retired from military life. A disheartened Konag Cronin groomed his second son as his successor, and Conndur the Brave was crowned two years later.

A long life and a great legacy.

While Conndur brooded, immersed in the sound of drumming rain, the study door swung open and a tall black-clad man strode into the library. His cloak was sopping wet, and he pulled back his hood, shaking rain from his face. His steel-gray hair was plastered to his head.

Startled, Conn rose from the chair. "Utho! You must have had a terrible journey in this storm."

Without speaking, but full of words to say, Utho removed his gloves and shucked off his finemail-lined cloak, which he hung on a peg by the roaring fire. His face carried the weight of terrible news.

The konag braced himself. "What is it, Utho? Tell me."

"It's Mirrabay, Sire. I . . . I did my best."

"You always do, old friend." Conn ignored the rainwater that dripped from the Brava's dark leathers onto the tile floor. "What happened?"

As if breaking a latch that held his voice, Utho said, "The Isharan animals attacked in an enemy warship and"—the words caught in his mouth again. He made a strange sound. "They brought a *godling*, Sire. They unleashed it on our shores. The abomination killed hundreds of people, set fires, destroyed homes, and Isharan soldiers came ashore to finish the job."

Conn reeled. "But you drove them off? You defeated the godling?"

"We fought hard, but there was so much damage. I managed to weaken the godling. I don't think it could have survived much longer on our shores. When the Isharans returned to their ship, they carried off prisoners." His dark gaze was haunted. "Probably to feed it."

Conn remembered that during the previous war Utho's family had been killed in one of the early attacks. Ah, yes, in *Mirrabay.* "I'll rush troops there to help them rebuild, and we'll increase defenses so the Isharans can't strike them again."

The grim Brava turned away. "That won't be enough, Sire. We have to answer this attack with a counterstrike. Hit Ishara with our navies and make them *hurt*. Bring the ships we already have stationed at Fulcor Island." His wide face showed great determination. "We could do more than punish the Isharans. We could wipe them out once and for all, take over their continent, set up our own colonies. We deserve it! That is where the Brava home should be."

Behind him, the crackling fire popped as a sap-filled knot of wood burst into flame.

Conn tried to calm his thoughts, remembering to be the leader. "But, open war? The Commonwealth learned that lesson thirty years ago, and many other times before that. Ancestors' blood, we can't get carried away! What happened at Mirrabay—was this a real military strike, or just hot-blooded raiders acting on their own? Do we know that Empra Iluris sanctioned this incursion? That does not sound like her."

"Sire, they brought a *godling*," Utho repeated.

Conn paced, deeply disturbed. "The forefathers of the Isharans departed from here a long time ago and made a new home on the other continent, while we stayed here in the ruins. Why do they hate us? And why do we hate them so?" Though he had been given many reasons, he had never completely *understood* the answer.

Utho stood close to the fire, and his wet clothes began to steam. "Because they're animals, Sire. Because they use magic and imagination to create their own gods. And because we have none."

Conndur lowered his voice. "Is that reason enough for war between two continents?"

The Brava stared at him as if the answer were obvious.

Lightning flashed in a blinding, skittering display outside the windows, and thunder boomed with such ferocity that it shook the stone walls. When the roar faded, a disturbing sound came from behind the heavy doors of Mandan's quarters across the hall. The prince let out a terrified scream.

10

❧

UNDER clear skies that showed no hint of the terrible sandstorm, the sandwreths departed from Bannriya, riding their augas back toward the distant desert. They left King Adan with many weighty matters to consider.

He had long depended on Penda and her father as sounding boards, and now he summoned them, along with his vassal lords, advisors, trade representatives, diplomats, and military experts. Word had passed swiftly through the city after the wreths were gone, and his chief councilors present in the city came at his call, though the vassal lords from more distant counties in Suderra would be several days arriving.

As the meeting began, young Hom scribed notes, doing his best to keep up with the stream of suggestions and arguments made by the gathered dignitaries. No one had answers about the wreths, because few had even considered such a question before.

Only a few years ago, their greatest concerns had been possible civil war in Suderra as the boy king Bullton was ousted from the throne, the corrupt regents sent into exile, and Adan Starfall acclaimed as the new king. No one had ever expected, much less wanted, the aloof creator race to return.

Finding his ornate chair uncomfortable, Adan got up and paced the room. "Why would the wreths come back now, after two thousand years? Have they been in hiding all this time? Recovering?"

Though the others offered uninspired theories, Penda looked at him. "They are back because they expect to fight a war that will remake the world."

"*Cra,* they may intend to *cause* the war themselves!" Hale muttered. "You know the legends. They need to wake the buried dragon and kill it, then their god will return, save his chosen ones, and make a new world from scratch."

"I don't see how that benefits humans in any way," Adan said.

"Humanity will lose, no matter which wreth faction wins," said Lady Yl-loh, a plump middle-aged widow who ran her county with extreme efficiency.

"Why would the sandwreths want us as allies?" Adan asked. "What can we offer them? You all saw how they summoned a dust storm."

"And are the frostwreths better or worse?" Hale asked. "Why should we choose sides, when we are doomed either way?"

Penda drew her brows together in a skeptical expression. On the stand, Xar ruffled his wings and leaned forward to peer at each speaker in turn, as if he disagreed with every word spoken. On a stool next to the green ska, Hom glanced up, then returned to his writing, catching up with the conversation.

Hale Orr tapped his good hand on the tabletop. "Maybe the Utauk tribes could venture into the desert and see what the sandwreths have been doing out in the Furnace. We could say we are trying to initiate trade. Yes, why not? We will make it true."

"You're welcome to send an expedition out there, but don't expect your people to return." said Lord Buroni, who ruled one of the larger counties. He had come to Bannriya for a wine festival and delayed his departure because of the dust storm. "No one comes back from the Furnace."

"Unless the sandwreths help us," Adan pointed out, though the words didn't ring true. "Queen Voo made no threat other than to warn us of a disaster that may come."

"Just as a spider makes no threat to a fly hovering near its web," Penda said, drawing a circle around her heart. "Wreths make me uneasy. *Cra*, they're like . . . goose bumps in my mind." She shivered as if from something she sensed, but could not define. Xar squirmed on his post, absorbing Penda's emotions through their heart link.

"We can't go to war with an entire race, especially not the wreths," said Lord Adoc, a war veteran from the hill country. "We don't know how much is legend and how much is truth, but we do know that their last wars wrecked the land. We spent two thousand years healing it, and their ruined cities still litter the countryside." His stony expression became defiant. "This land is ours, Sire, and I'm not keen to hand it back to them. The wreths created us. Do they still consider themselves our masters?"

"What if they do?" asked Adan. It was a disturbing possibility. "What can we do about it?"

❧

The sky was thick with stars when Adan stepped out onto the open gazing deck that night. He had spent countless hours on countless nights looking for patterns in the sky, letting his thoughts wander, but tonight the universe gave him no peace. Until now, he had been satisfied with the world and his place in it, ruling Suderra with the woman he loved, with their first child on the way. As king, he was giving the people a fresh start, and he would do right by them.

While being raised as a prince in Convera Castle, he and his father had often stood on a similar gazing deck, watching for streaks of meteors. *Starfall*. His own name reminded him of those times. Here in the southern kingdom, he made meticulous notes about the stars overhead and wrote letters to his father describing how the constellations were different from those back in Osterra. Now, it was imperative that he write his father a warning letter. The konag needed to know about the return of the wreths.

"You prefer to spend your hours out here alone rather than in a much friendlier place—with me?" Penda stepped out to join him in the darkness, with Xar on her shoulder. Now that the wreths had gone, the ska seemed much calmer. Penda wore comfortable attire for the night, a loose white gown that seemed all the more alluring because of its simplicity. "Come to our chambers, my Starfall."

"Even the stars can't compete with such an offer." He kissed her on the cheek, let his lips linger there as he breathed in the scent of lavender and sage from the soap she used. "Do you think the baby would be scandalized if we made love?"

Penda took his arm. "The baby had better get used to it. We certainly haven't worried about it thus far."

The ska extended his wings to balance on her shoulder and looked accusingly at Adan. The king laughed. "Oh, Xar, I owe you a debt of gratitude. If not for you, Penda and I would never have found each other."

The reptile bird made a rude noise and preened his long green feathers.

"It wasn't entirely up to him," Penda said, stroking under the ska's faceted eyes. "But he did his part."

Adan remembered well how they had met. On a bright, sunny day shortly after taking the throne of Suderra, to wide acclaim, Adan had gone out to reassure the people of Bannriya who had gathered for the celebration. The young king wore a high-collared cape, a brocade vest, and a gold pendant that dangled on a thin chain around his neck. Addressing the people from an elevated dais, he had opened his arms to cheers and applause, and sunlight flashed on the pendant.

Just then a wild green-scaled ska swooped in with startling speed. When the king reeled backward in surprise, Xar snatched the bright object from Adan's neck and flew away with the prize, burbling and clicking in triumph. Momentarily stunned by the reptile bird's audacity, Adan had stared up into the sky. The crowd gasped in horror and many shouted that it was a terrible omen.

The new king, however, let out a loud, genuinely heartfelt chuckle that immediately dissolved the tension. He pointed to the sky. "I may be the ruler of Suderra, but it seems the skas plan to be rebels!"

Taking their cue from him, the people also laughed, the sounds swelling into a chorus of relief and amusement. He continued the day's celebrations without mentioning the incident again.

King Adan was sure he had lost the pendant permanently, but the next day a beautiful young daughter of the Utauk tribes presented herself at the castle doors, begging to speak with him. A green ska rode on a leather pad on her shoulder, his wings tied down with a thong. The reptile bird twitched, seemingly incensed.

But Adan kept his attention on the young woman. She had deep brown hair that flowed below her shoulders, dark eyes that reminded him of the night sky, and full lips set in a serious expression. Adan immediately wondered what they would look like if curved in a smile. Meeting his curious gaze, the young Utauk woman extended her cupped hands, opening them to reveal the gold pendant he had lost the day before.

"My ska took this from you, Sire. He is greedy and hard to control." Adan glanced at the scaled bird, while the young woman contritely averted her dark eyes.

"I've heard that is often the case with skas," Adan said. "What is your name?"

"I am Penda Orr," she said in a soft voice that could not hide her pride, "daughter of Hale Orr of the Utauk tribes. We do not steal." She shot a glare at her ska. "Xar needs to learn that as well."

Intrigued, the king rose from the throne and walked down the marble stairs to accept the pendant from her outstretched hands. He held it up, letting the gold chain dangle, and it caught the ska's faceted gaze. "Thank you for returning it to me, Penda Orr. I didn't expect that at all. Be thankful that under my rule we don't execute thieves." He wanted to know more about this young woman. Pocketing the pendant, he continued in a serious voice. "But they must still be punished. Don't you agree?"

"You are the king, and that is your prerogative, Sire." Penda remained tense, while Adan paced. Xar ruffled his feathers. She added, "I have a heart link with my ska, and I feel the guilt as well. What sort of punishment would you suggest?" She seemed to be beginning a negotiation, which was not unexpected from an Utauk.

Stroking his lip, Adan said, "The pendant has been returned, so in this case, I think imprisonment is sufficient. For a week."

"Imprisonment, Sire?" Penda asked, alarmed. The ska buzzed and clicked.

Remembering that his predecessor King Syrus had kept falcons for hunting, Adan called for a cage to be brought from the castle's storage rooms. "We'll keep your ska here in my throne room, on display as a thief. Perhaps other skas will learn not to cross me." He hoped Penda understood he was teasing.

She gave an uncertain smile. "I'm sure Xar will learn his lesson." She drew a circle around her heart.

Though Xar grumbled and twitched, Penda forced him into the cage and closed the door. She waggled a finger at her pet. "*Cra*, it serves you right for what you've done. Stealing from our new king!"

Adan found Penda Orr intriguing, and he continued with mock seriousness. "There is more to the punishment. Unfortunately, I have no experience in caring for a ska, therefore you have to remain here at the castle to tend to the prisoner until his sentence is over."

His plan worked perfectly, and the beautiful young woman stayed with him for the required week. Since she had to pass the time somehow, Penda ate meals with Adan, and they talked. She taught him Utauk games of chance, which she always won, while he showed her Osterran games he had learned as a prince in Convera. Her company seemed quite natural to him, and it became the favorite part of the day.

Because he required Penda to stay for so many days, her father's caravan had to depart without her. The large convoy of families and goods headed off into the hills, so Penda resigned herself to stay in Bannriya until such time as the tribes circled back to the capital city.

But since he was king, Adan decided to solve that problem for her. When

Xar's formal sentence was over, he mounted an expedition. With Penda and her ska, they rode hard to catch up with the much slower Utauk caravan, and Adan delivered the proud young woman to her father, much to Hale Orr's delight.

Only later did Adan learn that Penda had *trained* her ska to snatch the pendant, just so she would have an opportunity to meet him. A devious plot! But considering how their romance had blossomed, how could he resent it? He could not have planned it better if he had tried.

Now in their chambers with candles burning low and giving off a sweet scent of beeswax, the two engaged in a slow dance of disrobing, paying attention to every touch of fabric, silken hair, warm skin. They kissed deeply, trading warm breath with each other, in no rush.

On a stand near the wall, Xar drowsed, basking in their contented emotions after two tense days.

Adan brushed his lips along Penda's shoulder, kissed her ear, stroked her hair, letting his fingertips linger and absorbing every small whisper of sensation. He pulled off her soft white shift, and she helped him remove his loose shirt, speaking no words. They reclined together on their bed. Penda purred while he kissed above her heart and then reverently touched the smooth swell of her golden belly where the baby was just beginning to show.

He kissed her again and caressed her skin with his palm as they gradually worked themselves closer and closer together. She wrapped herself around him, holding him, building their passion until he carefully, gently entered her.

They embraced and rocked in a perfect duet for a long while until they were warm and spent. For nearly an hour, Adan had managed to forget about wreths and a war that might destroy the world.

Afterward, Penda held him, whispered in his ear, "Starfall, you are truly a good ruler, a good husband, and a wonderful lover." He drifted off to sleep, barely hearing her final sad, whispered words, "And there is so much you don't know."

11

〜

THE next morning, as Kollanan prepared to ride north to see his daughter and grandsons, he adjusted the blanket and cinched the saddle straps on his warhorse, a sturdy gelding named Storm.

An Utauk trader arrived in the courtyard, and his pony's saddlebags were nearly bursting with goods to sell. Koll recognized the balding trader. "Darga! It's about time you came back to Fellstaff. Tafira says our pantries are nearly empty."

Darga's rounded cheeks were flushed in the morning chill as he tied his pony's halter to a post. "I have a full load of spices, Sire. Expensive and rare. I hope the lady offers me a good price for them."

"If she didn't, you wouldn't keep coming back."

The Utauk laughed. "*Cra,* that's true!"

Queen Tafira emerged from the keep wearing an embroidered day-robe lined with rabbit fur. "Did you bring cumin seed? Fire-curry leaves? Black mustard?"

"A bit of everything, my lady." The Utauk opened pouches to display powders and dried roots. Even from several feet away, Koll could smell the mingled scents, some pungent, some bitter, some sweet. The trader held up a packet in his stubby fingers. "Red and yellow pepper, enough to make your eyes water—clears out the tear ducts, so you never need to cry." He continued to rummage. "Mace, crisroot, nutmeg for your bakery, even some blue poppy seeds."

Tafira inspected other pouches and pulled out a tiny paper packet, opened it, took a sniff. "Saffron? Real saffron?"

"Indeed, and cinnamon bark, rolled and dried. All obtained at great effort and expense."

She gave him a knowing look. "Most of these come from Ishara. Did you trade with the spice farmers in the jungles of Janhari District? Did you buy them in a market at Serepol?" She lowered her voice with a cautionary tone. "Or were they confiscated from Isharan ships during raids by the Commonwealth navy?"

Darga drew a circle around his heart. "Utauk traders are neutral and we go where we wish. I couldn't identify the origin of each packet here, my lady."

Tafira frowned. "I want to know if there might be an aftertaste of blood, if they were taken through piracy."

Darga's expression hardened. "You mean the blood of Commonwealth men? Or the blood of Isharans? There's been enough spilled on both sides. Utauks see it all."

Tafira didn't deny that and looked away as she set aside the pouches she wanted. "It ruins the flavor in either case."

Emerging from the keep, Lasis ignored the trader's haggling and went directly to his king. The Brava wore his usual black leather outfit and traveling cape, with the golden ramer band and a fighting knife at his belt. "I'm prepared to ride with you, Sire. Two of us can travel just as swiftly as one."

Koll patted the sword at his side. "The northern road is wide and well traveled, even if we haven't heard from Lake Bakal in a while. Stay with Tafira and help her fight the household battles."

Though not convinced, the Brava relented. "As you wish, Sire. You've made the ride many times, and I have spent years scaring the lawless away. The roads are safe." He flashed a very small smile. "You are perfectly capable of taking care of yourself, as you've shown many times."

Leaning close to him, Koll said, "You serve me well, Lasis, but sometimes it's good for a man just to be alone. Let me get reacquainted with my own thoughts."

The Utauk trader departed smiling, and Tafira had enough fresh spices to supply her kitchen for months. Saying goodbye to his wife, Koll wrapped his muscular arms around her waist and crushed her against him. She chided him, "I'm not a silly romantic girl anymore!"

"That's still how I see you, beloved." He kissed her, then swung up onto the black warhorse. "Don't ever change!"

Koll rode out of the courtyard and Storm pranced along, as if proud to be out on a grand ride. Leaving the castle, the king made his way through the city of Fellstaff. The thick defensive walls were built from a mixture of fieldstone and perfectly cut blocks scavenged from wreth ruins. He waved to the guards as he rode through the northern gate and headed on the main road toward the mountains in the distance. The forests were still lush with golden aspen and red maples, but in another few weeks the leaves would fall, leaving the trees bare.

Enjoying the beauty, Kollanan no longer thought about the old war with Ishara, but rather considered his land and his people. He thought of their daughter Jhaqi, who had grown from a spunky tomboy into a fine young woman who married the town leader of Lake Bakal, a calm and caring man named Gannon who was altogether too proud of his mustache. Their two sons, Tomko and Birch, were delightful and energetic grandchildren; they often had other village children over to play, creating even more chaos for their mother to manage.

Tucked in his pack Koll carried carved wooden animals, a fox, a spotted cat, a bear, and a trout, as gifts for the boys. He liked to carve new ones while the two watched with rapt expressions. He would press a block of soft pine to his ear, saying things like, "Listen, there's an animal inside here! I think it's a pig. I'd better let him out." Then he'd carve with his hunting knife, flicking curls of pale wood onto the floor as he wore down the edges, shaped the curves, and produced a little pig. Because Tomko liked the first one so much, Koll had been forced to carve a second pig so that his other grandson wouldn't feel slighted.

Lake Bakal was a beautiful town on the shores of a mountain lake ringed by sharp crags. The waters were deep and blue, surrounded by rocks with small swatches of beach. Year in and year out, the town's activities were dictated by the seasons. With autumn setting in, the fishermen would haul in large catches to be smoked or salted for the winter months. Hunters would bring down stags in the forests, while woodcutters stockpiled logs for each cottage, as well as an extra load for the town leader's house. The cycle never changed: predictable, comforting, and traditional. The Utauks had a saying, *The beginning is the end is the beginning.*

With the changing season, Koll could imagine that Jhaqi and her family were too busy for social visits, but their silence concerned him. They rarely went more than a week without sending a letter. Surely other travelers or traders had passed through from Lake Bakal? But Fellstaff was a large city, so maybe he hadn't noticed. He'd been busy fixing the roof on the keep and building new shelves for Tafira's winter greenhouse.

After two days of riding, he approached the mountains that rose up to embrace Lake Bakal. The skies turned iron gray and the temperature dropped. He pulled a fur-lined cloak around his shoulders and hunched forward to absorb some of the horse's warmth. Koll could hear the silver pines brushing together in the wind, their needles whispering rumors.

When at last he came over the rise from which he could look down to the lake and the village on the far shore, Kollanan saw an utter disaster.

White flakes danced on the wind, skirling veils of snow that rippled from the lakeshore, while more snow blew in from the craggy highlands beyond. Despite the unseasonably warm autumn down in Fellstaff, the lake was entirely frozen, its surface solid gray ice. The village was covered in white, as if slathered with plaster by an arctic mason. He saw no fishing boats, no movement in the town. Runnels of snow and ice flowed through the streets.

His battlefield instincts awakened, and he jabbed his heels into Storm's sides, urging the horse forward. The closer he got to the village, the colder the temperature became.

Breathing hard, feeling his lungs burn with the cold, Koll rode faster. The big warhorse charged through drifted snow, hooves clattering on unnatural ice that covered the road. He came upon the first outlying cottage at the edge of town, found it drifted over with snow. Inside an open door lay sprawled the frozen body of a woman in an apron, now covered with a glaze of ice. Beside a drooping, ice-encased apple tree in the yard, he saw the snow-crusted shapes of two lifeless children and their dog.

Eyes wide, Koll pushed ahead. He touched the sword at his side, though he had never imagined he might need it on this simple trip. He wanted to shout his daughter's name, but some instinct told him to keep quiet. He rode into the silent town and found more people dead in the streets, struck down in everyday activities, many covered over with snow, others frozen solid like statues.

Spearlike icicles dripped from the gutters and windowsills. The town's bell tower was rimed with frost. Breezes moaned through open windows. These people had been taken by surprise, perhaps on a warm autumn day. Koll's heart felt as frozen as the village. His unsettled horse plodded toward the main square, and Koll's dread grew.

The town leader's dwelling was open. Shapes lay in the yard: two larger ones like a woman and a man, and two smaller ones, all mercifully covered over with a blanket of snow that revealed only patches of skin and icy hair. Koll could not see their petrified expressions, but he did spot one small hand protruding from a clump of snow, its bluish-white fingers wrapped around a wooden toy, an all-too-familiar carving of a pig.

A scream built within him. His vision was blurred by more than the snow.

Storm snorted in fear. Koll tugged the reins and whirled the warhorse around to see tall figures watching him as they emerged from the side of the bell tower. The strangers had long hair the color of dirty snow and almond-shaped, watery blue eyes. Their gray-and-blue armor was adorned with silver scales. They carried spears, knives, and swords, the blades made of obsidian and ice, the long handles twisted in tight spirals.

Koll's glove tightened on the reins, and with his free hand he pushed aside his fur-lined cloak and touched the hilt of his sword. The warhorse snorted, stood his ground.

Koll called out a challenge, "What sort of demons are you?" Seeing the devastation of the village, he had no doubt he would have to fight to the death.

The lead warrior, a male with blowing ivory hair, smiled with pale gray lips, showing sharp, evenly spaced teeth. "Why, we are wreths. We are your makers, your masters."

"I have no master. I'm the king of Norterra."

The wreth warrior seemed witheringly charmed. "Oh, so you have kings now?"

The strangers stepped closer, each one taller than Koll. Their arms were bare, displaying pale skin, but they seemed unaffected by the cold. The metal plates of their armor sparkled with frost. Nearby stood monstrous mounts, shaggy creatures like white-furred horses, but with smoldering eyes and wide paws instead of hooves.

Storm shifted several steps backward, snorting. The lead wreth strode toward them. "I am Rokk, Queen Onn's chief warrior. We came to take what is ours and found this surprisingly quaint village."

Rokk looked at the frozen bodies, at the snow-encrusted forms of Jhaqi and her husband, the shapes that must be Koll's two dear grandsons. "Maybe we should have kept more humans alive. That was a miscalculation, since we will need workers for the times to come. Ah, it has been so long since wreths had human slaves, we forgot what to do with them. And with the land's magic so diminished, we are unable to create more. Our attempts have been"—he sniffed—"unsatisfactory."

Koll ripped the words from his throat. "You murdered them! My daughter, my grandsons—everyone in Lake Bakal."

"They were in the way." Rokk shrugged. "The village was in the way, and we have better things to do with this place. More wreths are coming from the north with building materials and weapons." He skewered Koll with his ice-blue eyes. "We need to construct fortifications to prepare for the coming conflict, the final war against the sandwreths."

The warhorse spooked and skittered sideways. The wreth warriors seemed to find it amusing, but Koll saw his chance. He dug in his heels and yelled. Storm galloped away down a side street, crashing through drifted snow.

Koll knew he had to escape, to race back to Fellstaff and sound the alarm across his kingdom, to summon his armies. The warhorse charged headlong in terror, and Koll hung on, gripping his sword with one hand. His cloak whipped wildly around him.

At any moment he expected the frostwreths to summon a wall of cold that would freeze him solid like the rest of the town. But he got away. Apparently, Rokk and his wreth companions felt no threat from him, nor did they care what he knew about them.

Koll rode like a madman from Lake Bakal and the stranglehold of ice. He could think only of his daughter and her husband, the two boys, the smothered village. *The final war . . .*

As the horse pounded along the frozen road, the eerie cold in the air continued to intensify, turning Koll's tears to icy tracks on his face.

12

❧

WHEN the thunder crashed, Prince Mandan screamed again.
With Brava reflexes, Utho launched himself down the corridor like an arrow loosed from a longbow. He snatched his ramer, ready to clamp the band around his wrist and ignite the magical flame. "My prince!" He cast a glance back to Conndur as he ran. "I'll protect him, Sire."

Conn followed, though with less urgency, having already guessed what the screaming was about. "You can't protect him from a loud noise and a flash of lightning."

Lightning skittered outside, illuminating the rain that streamed down the windows, and another frightened moan came from the prince's room. Two night servants rushed down the halls, alarmed by the screams.

As far as Konag Conndur was concerned, Utho was overreacting, enabling his son's weakness—and in full view of the castle staff, too. He pulled the fur-lined cape around his shoulders so that he looked like a ruler. Appearances mattered, and respect had to be earned. How could the people of the Commonwealth revere a leader who cringed at every crack of thunder? He was relieved that Lord Cade and the other important visitors had not seen the prince like this.

Mandan was a sensitive young man who preoccupied himself with painting and reading, studying maps of the three kingdoms, learning his history, the legendary wreth wars, the building of human civilization. Conn loved his son and heir, but he wished the young man were stronger. *Adan* never would have hidden from a flash of lightning.

Utho reached the door first and stormed inside with the konag behind him. Just as Conn suspected, there were no attackers, no dangers.

A low fire in the hearth illuminated a large bed with dark wooden posts, the mattress covered with quilted blankets. Maps of the three kingdoms hung on the walls, with smaller charts of specific counties and an intricate map of Convera City at the confluence of the two rivers, showing the streets of the lower town, the two riverside districts, and the roads leading up the high bluff to the castle.

The room smelled of turpentine and oil. An easel stood in the main work space, adjacent to a table covered with jars of oil paints, a palette with smears of bright colors, numerous brushes. The prince's painting was nearly finished, a portrait of a lovely young woman—although the depiction showed little of her beauty. Mandan had not been impressed with the latest marriageable daughter offered to him. In sharp contrast, a painting of his mother Maire, with her long red tresses, oval face, full lips, and alabaster skin, hung above the prince's bed, far more beautiful than she had ever been in life.

Mandan hunched on the floor beside his bed, winding the sheets between his fingers like a drowning man grabbing a lifeline. The rush of rain rattled the windows, and wind whistled through a gap in the casing.

Prince Mandan of the Colors had a narrow face, hazel eyes, and carefully cut brown hair, now rumpled with sleep. At the moment his expression showed complete misery. Utho bent over him, dominant, powerful. "You are safe, my prince. I'm here. I will protect you."

Keeping his face set so as not to show his disappointment, Conndur entered the room. This was a father's job, but the Brava was pampering the boy. *Boy?* Conn sighed; he had to stop thinking of his son that way. Twenty-five years old! It was long past the time when Mandan should have taken a wife, had several children, raised his necessary heirs—as Conndur himself had been forced to do. Duty was duty. He glanced at the idealized portrait of Maire over her son's bed.

"An Isharan army with a ferocious godling would be something to fear," he said. "A bit of thunder and lightning are not. You're safe in the castle, Son. Nothing can harm you here."

Mandan blinked as if he didn't recognize his own father. "Something can always happen. Even my mother wasn't safe." He pressed his face against the finemail armor on the Brava's broad chest. Utho held him with a steel-hard arm, offering strength but Conndur saw it as only encouraging weakness.

"That was a long time ago, my prince," Utho said quietly. "This is just a storm." As a concession, he added, "I will stay here if you need me to." He lowered his voice, as if talking to himself. "I couldn't be there when my own family needed me, but I can stay at your side." Utho looked up at the konag with a startlingly intense gaze. "The attack on Mirrabay has made all those wounds fresh again, Sire."

Conn felt an ache in his heart, more for his faithful Brava than for his son. He spoke as if Mandan weren't there. "You have my sympathy, old friend, but please don't coddle the prince. The future konag must learn to be strong. He should face his fears. We need to toughen him."

Utho fixed the konag with his almond eyes, but didn't move away from the prince's side. "I will devote my attention to it, Sire, but not tonight. Nights like this remind him of when he lost his mother."

As a boy, Mandan had been the one who found Lady Maire's cold, still body after she killed herself.

Conn placed his hands behind his back to hide his clenching fingers as he looked at the painting over the prince's bed. "Maire is long gone now. Her name is written in the remembrance shrine, and we won't forget her legacy. That's the best we can do."

"I miss her," Mandan said in a small voice.

"We all do." In Conn's case, it was partly a lie. After his older brother died from a fever and Konag Cronin recalled the Commonwealth troops from the Isharan war, young Conndur the Brave had become the new heir apparent, the next konag. Cronin had strongly encouraged him to marry and have a family as soon as possible. Upon reviewing the candidates, and gathering much advice from counselors who didn't once consider romance or compatibility, Conn chose a tall, milk-skinned woman named Maire, who had wavy red hair and doelike eyes. He liked her well enough.

"Don't waste any time," his father had told him in a private conversation. Since returning from the Isharan war, Conn had seen deep grief in the older man's eyes, as if he still couldn't comprehend that he had lost his brilliant heir to something as stupid and capricious as an illness. "Life is short."

Once they were married, Conndur and Maire set about the business of making heirs, and their lovemaking held a sense of duty. Within a year, Maire gave birth to Mandan, and old Konag Cronin clapped a hand on his son's shoulder in a clear sign of relief.

Two years later, Adan was born, and then the following year a stillborn daughter came into the world with a gush of blood, cramps, and pain. The loss of that daughter *broke* Maire. She insisted on holding the dead baby in her arms for nearly a day before the midwives finally took the rag-wrapped body away for burial.

After that, Maire avoided Conndur's bed and doted on her firstborn son. She spent her days with the young prince to the exclusion of all else, singing to him and teaching him poetry, but Mandan's true aptitude was in sketching and painting. Conndur had tried his best to be a good father, taking the prince out riding and hunting, teaching him archery and the basics of sword fighting. A future konag needed to learn the things that a konag must know.

Though Maire was still young enough to bear more children, Conndur never again shared her embraces. She drove him away with cold bitterness. No matter how much time she spent with her favorite boy, it was clearly not enough. Maire retreated into the refuge of the blue poppy, saying the medicine dulled the pain in her heart and the dark memories in her mind.

One night during a furious thunderstorm, a frightened Mandan sought his mother's comfort, and when she didn't answer his knock, he opened the door. In the flashes of lightning that burst through the windows, he saw her lying on the bed, eyes open and glassy, mouth wide, skin white. He held his mother's body, wailing, shaking her, kissing her.

The konag knew, as did most others in the court, that Maire had taken a deadly amount of poppy milk, but official messengers announced to the people that the queen had died from a "sleeping sickness." That was how Conndur insisted her legacy be written, and Mandan even came to believe it, but the prince had never been entirely right after that night.

Now, on another stormy night, the konag watched Utho holding the young man, calming him. He did not resent the bond between the Brava and Mandan, but Conndur had had enough. "Come, old friend, and finish your report on the Isharan attack on Mirrabay."

At the reminder of the bloody raid, a flash of anger crossed Utho's face. "The news will not change, Sire. I'll meet you in the library after I've made sure the prince is asleep."

Utho remained, and though his strength comforted Mandan, it took a long time for the young man's sobs to fade. "I'll protect you, I swear it."

The prince looked up at him with swollen red eyes. "You're sworn to protect my father. I'm not the konag."

Utho stroked his rumpled hair. "Bravas are sworn to protect this land, whoever the konag is. You'll be konag someday, and then all of my loyalty will belong to you."

13

WHEN the returning warship entered Serepol Harbor, the head of the empra's hawk guards rushed to inform her, but she guessed it was already too late. Key Priestlord Klovus had prepared his ur-priests ahead of time, and they had assembled crowds to greet the crew with great fanfare. Celebrations sprang up near the harbor temple, home of the lesser godling that had served on the raid.

"Thank you, Captani," she told him. "Klovus will claim a great victory over the Commonwealth, and there's nothing we can do but pretend to be supportive."

Captani Vos bowed his head. "I'm sorry, Mother." Her lead guard had deeply tanned skin, and his cheeks were clean-shaven.

She had her own victory of a different kind, and she would relish it. "Have the building materials from the Magnifica temple been redistributed?"

Vos nodded. "Most of them, Mother. The bulk went to two new schools and a road project, and the rest will benefit dozens of homes."

She smiled at him, satisfied. "Then we have done a good thing, too."

Iluris could hear victorious drumbeats echoing throughout the crowded streets and from the tiled rooftops and whitewashed buildings. Ishara's scarlet banners were raised high on watchtower poles, showing a vigilant eye at the center of a symbolic sun, a reminder that godlings watched over the new world. Klovus and his returning raiders were feted as heroes, even as they made the option of open warfare again seem attractive.

Her expression tightened. "Send the key priestlord here without delay." She made up her mind that she would not lose this battle entirely.

Waiting for Klovus in her throne room, Iluris wore a lavish silk dress with gold embroidery and delicate silk slippers with cabochon jewels. The pleats of her dress rustled with each movement, the vibrant magenta, orange, and green cloth draped artfully. She also wore a jeweled collar and headdress. As empra, she looked magnificent.

The key priestlord arrived an hour later with an entourage of robed ur-priests. He wore a dark blue caftan trimmed with crimson, the fabric quilted to make himself look more imposing. His head and round cheeks were freshly shaved, and his skin glistened with scented oils.

As soon as he strode through the doors, she rose from her throne and faced him. The echoing reception hall held decorative sculptures of the primary godlings that protected the thirteen districts. Her displeasure was evident in her voice. "You took your time to arrive, Priestlord. I asked you to come immediately." Her gold-uniformed hawk guards stood on either side of the throne dais, curved helmets in place, scarlet capes hanging at their shoulders. "I see you found the opportunity to bathe and change—while I was waiting for you."

His smug smile faltered. He laced his fingers together over his stomach, and lowered his gaze in an attempt to look respectful. "I bore the stink of the ship and blood from our battles on my clothing, Excellency. It would have been disrespectful to appear before you in such a state."

"I've seen sweat and dirt before, Priestlord." She stepped back to her throne. "I would rather you obey my orders than tend to your personal hygiene."

He bowed even more deeply, but he seemed to be bursting with satisfaction. "My apologies, Excellency. I was so caught up in our exciting news. As you can see, the people are already celebrating!" He gestured behind him as if to encompass not only all of Serepol, but the entire continent of Ishara. "You'll understand the importance of this day. We attacked a village on the godless coast and left many dead and grieving, while our losses were minimal." He grinned.

Her chamberlain Nerev, tall, dour, and silent, stood near a writing table with an inkpot and sheets of paper, in case Iluris might need his services.

"Best of all," Klovus continued, "our godling demonstrated tremendous power—and it was just a minor godling, taken from the harbor temple. Think what we could accomplish with stronger godlings from the primary temples. We could purge the Commonwealth, once and for all."

"And how would my people benefit from that?" The empra held her annoyance in check. "The old world is worn and weak, damaged in the ancient wars, its magic faded to almost nothing. Why would we want it? Why is it worth Isharan blood, when we have so many untapped resources here, so much to do?"

Klovus looked startled, as if the answer were obvious even though he couldn't articulate it.

Iluris continued, "We have our own pristine continent, lush with magic. Under my rule, Ishara has prospered and the citizens are content. The godlings reflect the mood of the people, and they are mostly benevolent and calm. Why would you want to change that?"

His expression pinched. "Contented godlings are weak godlings. When the people grow lax, they think that sacrifices are no longer necessary. But during my raid, the harbor godling proved how necessary they are." A flush came to his rounded cheeks.

"Your entire raid was unnecessary! You create conflict to perpetuate conflict, and we don't need it." She pointed a lacquered nail at him. In the throne room, the hawk guards and Chamberlain Nerev watched in uncomfortable silence. "Klovus, I did not authorize this offensive. You didn't ask permission to take *my* navy and *my* soldiers off to fight."

Several of the ur-priests were alarmed at her open chastisement, while others maintained unwavering beatific expressions. Despite the scolding, the key priestlord acted innocent and jovial. "Ah, but it all turned out for the best. We achieved a singular and unqualified victory for Ishara. The people will celebrate in your name and increase their sacrifices to the godlings. We both benefit. How could anyone quibble?"

Iluris took her seat in the tall ornate chair and regarded him in silence. She did not give him leave to relax. Her hard gaze did not waver.

He fidgeted, looking up at the throne until his expression finally showed a hint of anxiety. "Excellency, the priestlords have always given our devotion to you, as we did to Emprir Daka before you, and all the others in a long line of rulers. Every priestlord, ur-priest, priest, and acolyte is loyal to you. We wish only prosperity for our people and victory over our enemies. With this glorious raid, I wanted to convince you how important the godlings are to our future. They anchor the beliefs of the people and protect them from storms and outside attacks." His words picked up urgency. "But our grand vision has rested quietly for too long. Half a century ago, your father began constructing the Magnifica temple. Ishara's primary godling is strong, but cannot achieve its full potential until the temple is completed. Serepol will be home to the strongest godling ever to manifest in the entire world."

Iluris frowned as she waited for him to catch his breath. "And what purpose would such a tremendous godling serve? Our land is already thriving, and our people are strong. What possible threat does Ishara face that would require such a defender?"

Klovus sputtered. "Why . . . the godless Commonwealth! We have to be strong against them. That is why we need to build the Magnifica temple and let our godling grow, so it can be the powerful protector Ishara needs."

She arched her eyebrows. "Oh? Didn't you just boast that with only one warship and a minor godling, you destroyed an entire town? Isn't that why my city is now celebrating?" Her gold-flecked eyes flashed. Outside the palace, the cheering continued.

"Why, yes . . . but one can never be sure. What if the godless konag and his people rediscover some magic in their tired old land? Their armies invaded Ishara when you were barely seventeen, and we must never let that happen again. The only way to defend ourselves is to make our godling so strong that no one can stand against us." He stepped right up to the edge of the throne dais. "The Magnifica temple must be built. The people are ready!" His eyes were pleading, his voice solicitous, but she could still see the razor within him, the smoldering anger because she wouldn't do as he wished, and thereby she denied him the clout he so craved.

Klovus lowered his voice. "Your people want this, Excellency. We see them at their worship every day, in every district. They are ready to build."

She adjusted her embroidered silk skirts, tapped one bejeweled slipper against the other. "Alas, Ishara has more immediate needs, but I agree the people are ready to build. While you were away on your raid, I redistributed the construction materials stockpiled at the Magnifica site so they could better serve the Isharan people. Since we won't continue work on the temple in the foreseeable future, those tools and supplies will build roads and homes and schools, which the districts need right now." She smiled. "The people are grateful for what you have done for them, and I am sure the godling will be pleased."

Klovus nearly lost control of himself. "But . . . but you had no right!"

"The temples exist for the good of the people, as you have reminded me so many times. We both have the same goal: to keep Ishara strong. But I am the empra, and I decide whether or not we want war." She rose from the throne and glided down the stairs to take his arm. "Now come with me out to the balcony, Priestlord. We'll address the gathered people and tell them of your great victory at Mirrabay, and you will receive credit for your generous donation of the construction materials. But it will end there." She gave him a sharp smile. "We are much stronger together, don't you agree?"

Empra Iluris could tell that Klovus knew his best play was to show solidarity with her. But despite his manufactured smile, she knew that cooperation was the farthest thing from his mind.

14

⤺

DIGGING in the mines of Scrabbleton was hard work, but Elliel found peace in the day's labors. She had her pick and shovel, a bucket for bringing debris to the larger carts that hauled rocks out to the sorting bins. The glow of lantern light and the close warmth in the humid passageways comforted her. Some claimed that the fires deep in Mount Vada were the exhalations of the sleeping dragon Ossus, though that was surely just a myth. Each time she took a breath, she did smell sulfur.

As a Brava, she had deceptive physical strength, but instead of using it in battle, she swung her pick and struck the unyielding wall, chipped away more rock. The Scrabbleton miners had worked the mountain for centuries, worming their way through ore veins like termites boring through rotten wood. In her short time here, Elliel had grown fond of the wholesome and honest townspeople, who had in turn begun to accept her. This place might actually serve as a home for a while.

Elliel worked alone in a section of the tunnels, without having to answer questions about herself. Down here, she could let her thoughts fall into dull silence. After awakening to her new life with her legacy gone, she had accepted Utho's damning letter. Elliel had wandered from place to place ever since, fleeing her past. She had murdered those poor children and their teacher, and she wanted to be far from where she had done it. She could remember two winters, so it had been at least two years since she had committed her crime.

Her first memory of waking in the rain in the back of the wagon had been in one of the counties to the northeast with highland terrain, but the villages looked much the same. She hadn't asked the names of the places, but she knew the first town was in one of the northeastern coastal counties. Some driving force made her keep going farther and farther away.

Somewhere back there, she had left the darkest of tragedies. She had not dared to visit the scene where she had committed such a heinous act, nor did she want to provoke the grieving townspeople, who would never get over the slaughter of their children. They might not consider Utho's punishment sufficient. . . .

In her travels, as she had wandered over the rugged central mountain range, she was always listening for gossip, lest someone tell stories of a murderous Brava woman. So far she had kept ahead of the rumors, and Scrabbleton seemed the right sort of place for her, at least for a time. Elliel devoted herself to the work. Right now, that was all she needed.

She chopped more rock, searched the rubble for glittering veins of quartz, the distinctive greenish brown of copper ore, or the sparkle of gold, but she saw only plain rock. She shoveled the debris into her bucket and raised the iron-tipped pick again.

After each shift, she welcomed the ache of sore muscles. As a Brava, she assumed she had wielded a sword or her fiery ramer, but she took satisfaction from the ache of exertion in the mine, knowing it came from an honest day's labor. And it did not involve killing children.

Throughout the tunnels Elliel could hear the staccato sounds of nearby miners hacking at the rock, searching for valuable gems or ores. As a special prize, they might find rubies so dark and rich that according to legend they were the blood of Ossus hardened into jewels during his long, wounded sleep.

As she worked in the flickering lantern light, Elliel could understand how miners might let their imaginations run away with them. In the inn, where weary workers drank the local ale, played games, and talked, she had heard them tell bone-chilling stories. Shauvon, the innkeeper, would roll his eyes as he bustled about the common room.

Elliel had secured a small room for herself in the inn, and in the evenings she would relax at a table by herself. The miners glanced at her and turned away a little too quickly, talking in low voices, but she was used to it.

When she asked mine boss Hallis not to repeat her tale, she had known the promise would not hold for long. By now the whole town knew her tragic story, her shame, and the meaning of the tattoo on her face. They would accept her eventually, or she would move on, as before. She felt no overt aggression or antipathy from them, though. They seemed to be softening, especially the miners she worked with.

For now, she was not Elliel the disgraced Brava, she was just Elliel the digger. To these Scrabbleton miners, a long life and a great legacy meant having a comfortable home and children to carry on after they were gone. Elliel envied such simple goals, never expecting such a life for herself. . . .

Hallis had spent the first day guiding her through the mines. He knew each tunnel, side shaft, and dead-end pocket even without carrying a map because he explored so often. The mine boss had spent a lot of time leading mine crews in his younger days, but due to stiffening muscles and aching joints, he could no longer do the strenuous work. But he still remembered those days.

As they walked the tunnels, he explained the different types of rock, teaching her how to identify silver, iron, copper, tin, lead, even powdery yellow sulfur, which was useful for treating skin conditions and for making matches to light the lanterns. Mount Vada was a treasure trove.

The mine boss lifted the lantern so he could study her expression. "I see that you're overwhelmed. Don't worry. You can just swing your pick where the other miners tell you. We haul the ore out in carts and sort it later."

"I can do that." She gave him a thin smile. "And dragonblood rubies? How will I find them?"

"Such gems are precious. They'll find you, if you're lucky enough."

During each shift, miners split up in the cramped tunnels, hewing the rock wherever there was room enough to swing a pick. Today Elliel accompanied miners named Klenner and Upwin, neither of whom had any objection to working near a woman, especially after watching her work. They joked, but not at Elliel's expense, and she warmed to the two. She could hear both men in adjacent shafts, hammering away, shoveling the debris into buckets, which they dumped in the cart in the wider shaft.

Elliel did not keep track of the time. The shift would be over when her lantern candle burned three-quarters of the way down, but meanwhile, she lost herself in the work. She felt the pick penetrate the stone, and a fine, sharp spray of debris stung her cheeks and forehead. The crumbling rock yielded with startling ease.

Suddenly, hot red liquid gushed toward her as if from a severed artery, then sealed off. With Brava reflexes, she jerked to one side. The smoking crimson fluid hardened in the air and broke into crystalline droplets. Rubies pattered to the floor, each as large as her thumbnail. In wonder, Elliel bent to pick up the gems. They were still warm in her palm. "Klenner, Upwin! Come see this."

Since she spoke so rarely, the other two miners came running, amazed by the gems she held. "Bless my ancestors!" said Klenner. "That's a rich haul. You'll have a year's bonus from Hallis."

Upwin ran back to the stone wall where Elliel had been digging. He kicked debris aside and held up his lantern, pressing his face to the rugged wall. "Stand back, there might be more."

Gathering the handful of rubies, Elliel let Upwin excavate the same place, widening the gouge, but he encountered only more rock, none of the hot fluid.

"It was liquid when I struck," she said, "like red water."

Klenner clapped her on the back. "That's dragon's blood, all right. You struck it, and now you've been blessed. There'll be celebration in town tonight. This doesn't happen often."

Just then, she felt a vibration in the mine walls and floor. A loud rumble thrummed through the mountain. The two miners recoiled in panic. "Better run! The tremors will get worse."

As the rumbling and shaking increased, the three backed out of the small tunnel and ran along the wide passageway. Rocks pattered down from the ceiling, threatening to bury them alive, but before they had taken a dozen steps, the vibrations faded, and the stone walls became still again. Elliel could hear only her heavy breathing, the pulse pounding in her ears. The other two miners flicked their eyes from side to side, and eventually relaxed.

"It's over," Klenner said.

"Just a little one," said Upwin. He looked at her. "That's what happens when you dig deep into the Dragonspine. One of these days we're going to poke Ossus in the wrong place."

Elliel placed little stock in the stories. "The dragon is just having nightmares of the ancient war that almost killed him."

"You know what'll happen if Ossus awakens." Klenner sounded serious. "The world will end!"

"Then we'd better not wake him." Elliel tucked the handful of fresh rubies into her pocket.

15

Utho of the Reef summoned nine Bravas to a dark and secret meeting place in the Convera City lowtown. Their business was grim and it would mean the loss of one of their own, but after Onder's cowardice at Mirrabay, the Bravas had no choice.

Utho chose a small remembrance shrine on the Crickyeth River side of the lowtown. Unlike the gigantic remembrance shrine in the heart of the city, the wood-walled building was only the size of a shop, but it served as a place for the locals to record the names and brief legacies of their many fallen loved ones.

After the old legacier locked the doors for the night, Utho knew that he and his elite Brava companions could meet there undisturbed. It had been a long time since they were forced to mete out such harsh justice for one of their own. Utho had done this to Elliel more than two years ago for entirely different reasons, but no one could doubt that Onder deserved this punishment.

Two Bravas waited in nearby alley shadows, invisible in their dark garb. They emerged as Utho approached the closed shrine. He gave them a silent acknowledgment as he used the key and swung open the door to let them into the shrine, where they lit just enough candles to see. Their boots made the floorboards creak. Two more Bravas arrived, and the five of them cleared the table where patrons reviewed the names of their ancestors and read notations of the legacies they left behind.

"Can you be sure Onder will come?" asked Klea, a muscular middle-aged woman who had dedicated her services to a lord in a county just south of the Confluence.

Utho slid a bench from the wall over to the table. "He is still a Brava. He still has his code of honor and his heritage." *For now.* The thought made Utho ill. There were few enough Bravas left, true half-breeds with both human and wreth heritage. The wreth bloodline had been diluted greatly over many generations, but Bravas kept their lines strong, their training rigorous. Because of their prowess in battle, Bravas were in great demand. Most signed on to serve a lord or a powerful business leader. One minor lord boasted four bonded Bravas, not because he needed so much protection, but to inflate his own importance.

More than a millennium after the wreth wars, the undiluted half-breed descendants of wreths and humans had sailed across the ocean to establish a colony in the new world, but the fearful Isharans murdered the settlers by unleashing a horrific godling, a kind of creature which at the time no Brava had ever seen. After barely surviving such unprovoked aggression, the re-maining Bravas felt they had to develop a rigid code of honor. It was their safety net, their armor, and now it was their obligation.

"Tell us what happened in Mirrabay," asked Gant, a gruff brute of a Brava who moved another chair to the table in the dark shadows of the remem-brance shrine. "What exactly did Onder do? Why did he run?"

"He will tell the story himself, when he arrives," Utho said. "That is part of his punishment."

The group took their seats and waited. Klea went to a shelf in the back, retrieved another candle, and lit it. Four more Bravas came in a group, but none of them engaged in light conversation. With each new arrival, the Bra-vas rose in greeting, then sat down again.

Finally, Onder arrived, looking paler than usual in his black garb. His short hair was unkempt, and the shadows around his eyes were deeper than could be explained by the dim candlelight. The other Bravas remained seated at the table, refusing to give the young coward any sign of respect.

Klea said, "We're glad you came, Onder."

"Not glad," Utho said, "but we acknowledge the necessity of what we need to do."

Hanging his head, the young Brava closed the wooden door behind him as if he were cutting off all hope. As the others turned to face him, he stood at the foot of the table, arms limp at his sides, like a scarecrow built out of shame.

Utho addressed them. "A Brava is a rare thing, and we cherish every mem-ber of our people. We keep our bloodlines strong. We train in our isolated settlements before we venture out to serve the Commonwealth. But what we cherish even more is our code of honor. Without that core, we are nothing. Onder, you no longer have that moral core. After tonight, you will no longer be a Brava."

The young man trembled where he stood.

"We are here to sever you from our community. Everyone in the Commonwealth will know that you betrayed your people and your honor."

Onder's lip quivered, but he did not speak.

Gant spoke up in a coarse voice. "Tell us about Mirrabay, lad. We need to understand what you did and how you failed."

"So that it may never happen again," Klea said.

Onder began, "I was a paladin, moving freely up and down the coast. I fought bandits, I protected the villages. I rescued a family when a flooded creek washed away their home. I—"

"Did you swear to protect Mirrabay?" asked Klea.

Onder hesitated, then nodded. "Yes, Mirrabay and other towns. I went there to see Utho. He and I came from the same Brava training settlement, we had the same training master." A plaintive undertone in his voice seemed to be searching for sympathy, but Utho had none for him. "I was there when the Isharans came."

"And had Utho himself sworn to protect Mirrabay?" pressed another Brava, a man named Bron. "Was he bonded to the town?"

"No, he was visiting on behalf of the konag, gathering information for a report. When the attack began, we thought we could defend against the Isharans. The two of us ignited our ramers, ready to face them, but. . . ." His voice cracked. "They had a godling, like the one that destroyed our colony of Valaera so long ago." The Bravas muttered around the table and continued to look intently at the pale man. "When the thing attacked, it was so huge and powerful. It—"

Utho interrupted, "He fled in panic, leaving the people undefended. A Brava with a ramer is worth any ten regular fighters. Their homes burned. The villagers of Mirrabay were slaughtered, just as they were thirty years ago."

Onder looked down at his hands, squeezing his fingers together. His face was shadowed in the low candlelight. "But a godling once wiped out a whole Brava colony! What chance did *two* of us have? It would have killed us. I would have died if I faced it."

"You should have died fighting," snapped Bron.

"I fought it," Utho pointed out, "and yet I survived."

"I wish I had fought," Onder groaned. "I wish I had died. But I can't change that now."

"We can." Utho nodded solemnly. "With that one act of cowardice, you erased your legacy, so we are here to complete the task."

Onder swallowed hard. "And I am here to submit to it."

Klea drummed her fingertips on the tabletop. "Are you certain it's necessary, Utho? He's young, and his bloodline is strong. This hasn't been done since Elliel . . ."

"Elliel's crime was so great that I did the purging myself," Utho said. "But here, in Convera, I called all of you together. Is there a single Brava among us who doesn't agree our action is necessary?" He looked around the table, from one face to the next.

Onder waited, his expression hopeful, but no Brava spoke up in his defense. Utho had known they wouldn't. The disgraced man's shoulders sagged.

Utho removed a leather-wrapped packet from his black jerkin and unrolled it on the table to reveal a set of needles and two small vials of ink, black and red. Seeing them, Onder let out a quiet moan of dismay.

"Your legacy is gone, and it shall be forgotten," Utho said. "Those of us here will remember your crime of cowardice, but you will not. Everything that you were up until this point, every memory, every deed, will be erased."

The others stood up with a scraping of chairs. As Utho removed his needles, he said, "Bind his arms. Make him sit before us, alone." Two Bravas took Onder by the elbows, lashed his wrists together, and pressed him down into a sturdy chair at the end of the table. He didn't resist, but his eyes filled with tears.

Utho picked up the needles, opened the vials of ink. "I will place the rune of forgetting on your face for all to see. The spell will reside in your skin and work its way into your mind." He bent close to the younger man's face and used the back of his hand to brush away a tear that trickled down Onder's cheek. When the skin was dry, Utho dipped one of the long needles into the black ink and pricked the other man's skin, stabbing and stabbing as he traced out an intricate pattern for more than an hour.

Over time, his wrists ached from the repetitive motion, and his fingers grew numb. He infused the design into Onder's cheek in such a way that the spell would draw its power from the young man's wreth blood.

The disgraced Brava wept openly. Utho switched to red ink, ignoring the tears as he continued inscribing the tattoo. The witnesses remained solemn and silent while he completed the task.

Klea took a blank sheet of paper and wrote out in painstaking detail the story of Onder's cowardice. When she was done, she folded the paper and tucked it inside the young man's shirt. "At some time later, you will find this. You'll read what you did, so you can know what happened to you, but you won't remember it. That is not a blessing. Your entire legacy is gone."

Onder didn't struggle against the bindings on his arms, but his shoulders shook. He seemed utterly defeated.

"This punishment is used in only the rarest and most unforgivable circumstances." Utho dipped the needle into the red ink again and bent closer. "When I complete this line, the rune of forgetting will take effect. You will no longer be a Brava. Your finemail armor is forfeit. We will replace your cloak with one of plain wool, leaving only your common clothes and your ramer. But you will be an empty vessel, always knowing only a hint of what you lost."

He finished connecting the spell lines in the tattoo, and Onder's pale skin began to glow. The ink smoked as it burned its way into his tissues, and the young man went rigid. His expression fell slack. Utho stepped back to regard his handiwork, then nodded. Just as he had done with Elliel.

The Bravas removed the ramer bands from their belts, and as Onder made inarticulate mumbling sounds, they clamped the golden cuffs in place. Blood welled up, and they drew upon their inner anger to ignite the flames, which swallowed their hands. Together, the nine Brava witnesses stood with blazing fists raised, filling the dim remembrance shrine with light.

In the chair, Onder blinked and sat up, struggling against his bonds. "What happened? Who are you?" He looked from side to side, staring at the ignited ramers and the Bravas. "Who am *I*?"

"You are no one," Utho said. "Not anymore."

In unison, the Bravas extinguished their fire, and Utho set the disgraced man free. Later, when Onder found the note in his shirt, he could read it over and over again. And that was all he could ever know.

16

As he walked the streets of Bannriya, Hale Orr used good cheer as a mask to hide his real thoughts. This was not a normal day. The sandwreths had left a shadow over the city.

He wore a loose maroon tunic that fell below his hips, embroidered with the circle symbol. *The beginning is the end is the beginning.*

In the ancient walled city, people continued to repair windows and roofs after the storm. Farriers groomed horses, wheelwrights fixed carts, blacksmiths hammered a sharp metal rhythm into the air. Grocers haggled with farmers for better prices on the loads of winter squash, carrots, and potatoes they brought to market from the foothills. Hale chatted with merchants, sampled pastries and fried corn dumplings from vendors who had set up stalls around the great bazaar.

In the years since Adan took the throne from the unpopular regents, the mood in the city had brightened, trade increased, and Utauk groups came through more often. Hale wanted to speak with the leader of the caravan that had arrived from the plains today. With ponies and horses tied up near watering troughs, the people set up camp in the streets and the square. Utauks could afford rooms at the finest inns, but they preferred to sleep outside, where they felt free. This group wouldn't stay long within the walls of Bannriya, and Hale wanted to get their news as soon as he could.

The pack animals carried pouches of sweet raisins, bolts of cotton fabric from the south, bushels of nuts from a village aptly named Walnuts, barrels of pressed cider, sacks of roasted squash seeds. In the main bazaar square, the caravan had erected a silk pavilion for the caravan master and his family. Children splashed in the water troughs and fountains.

Hale had led many caravan treks and sailing voyages in his younger years, although now, thanks to Penda's marriage and his impending grandchild, he was content to stay in Bannriya. *Cra,* he was growing soft!

He approached the green pavilion and pushed open the flap to greet Melik, the bearded, slow-voiced leader. Melik was on his second marriage, and very happy with his life. He gestured for his visitor to sit on the cushion next to him, offering strong tea.

Hale situated himself. "So, you've had another successful journey across the land?"

Melik drew a circle around his heart. "Any journey is successful when we arrive with our goods intact."

Hale asked with careful curiosity, "Have you seen anything interesting to share and be shared?" The Utauks had an unparalleled network of information that was not available to outsiders.

"I have." Melik took a deep sip of his tea. "You've seen strange things in Bannriya, too, I hear. Wreths from the past? Is it really true?"

"*Cra,* I saw them myself." Hale added honey to the tea, as if that could temper the bitterness of his words. "A hundred of them riding on the heels of a dust storm. Who knows how many more are out in the Furnace?"

"Too many," Melik grumbled. "We have seen signs in the sky. Our skas have flown wide and far, scanning the landscape, and when we view the images from their mothertear collars, we are troubled. In the southwestern hills, we saw roaming bands that we could not identify. They might be wreth scouts." He finished his tea with a loud slurp and poured himself a second cup.

Hale rested the stump of his wrist on his lap as he played the conversational game. "What else did you see?"

"A great deal more. We have watchers everywhere, collecting records, skas recording images. I'll give you a complete copy of all their documents for Shella din Orr."

Hale set his empty cup on the low table. "Our great gathering will take place soon, and I will give it to her then. I have a report for you as well, to share and be shared."

Hale handed him a code-written document in their secret language, a summary of intelligence gathered from around Bannriya, including information that noble families and wealthy merchants thought was private. In exchange, Melik slipped him a densely written set of charts and notations, records of the places and people his caravan had encountered, opportunities to be considered, warnings about certain untrustworthy individuals, as well as a handful of mothertear diamonds with recorded images of what the skas had seen.

After he left the pavilion, Hale smiled outwardly but felt more troubled than ever. As he walked away from the fraternal chaos, a dark-skinned girl in dirty, oft-mended clothes trotted up to him. "Thinking of going on a caravan again, Father? You've been too long in this stone city." She moved with a graceful catlike stride. "Need to remember Utauk ways!"

Hale let out a loud laugh to see the orphaned girl. "Glik! Do you travel with Melik's caravan now?"

The girl scoffed. "Just the last three days. Caravans are too crowded, noisy, and smelly. I go my own way, you know that. Was by myself for nearly a full month before that."

"We worry about you out there all alone."

She made a rude noise. "I'm both inside and outside the circle. I find my place." Glik closed her eyes and drew a circle around her heart. "The beginning is the end is the beginning. And I am somewhere in the middle."

Beneath her serious expression, Glik's face was streaked with grime, and her raggedly cropped dark hair was a tangle that might have served as a bird's nest. "You look like you could use a good meal," Hale said. "Come back to the castle, and we'll feed you."

Glik followed, weaving back and forth as if she found straight lines too dull. "Only if I don't have to wash beforehand. I am part of the earth."

Hale assessed her disheveled appearance. "You look like you're wearing half of the earth. The cooks will complain about dirt falling in their food. You have to clean up a little."

Glik was twelve or thirteen, as best as he could tell. All the Utauk tribes welcomed the orphan girl, who flitted in and out of the community, always searching for something. More than most Utauks, Glik was sensitive to circles and signs in nature, to meaningful dreams that did not always have a clear explanation.

They walked together down the wide road, past two men fixing the broken wheel on a cart while a mournful-looking donkey stood by. Bright banners flapped in the wind from the rooftop of an ornate remembrance shrine near the heart of the old city.

Recalling the ominous report he had just received from Melik, he asked, "What did you see out there all by yourself? Did the land speak to you?" He brushed a smudge of dry dirt from her cheek.

Glik often struck out on solitary vision quests, returning only when she had something to report, or when she was hungry for human companionship, which wasn't often. She answered Hale with a nod. "Saw plenty." Her expression had a haunted undertone, and her eyes were red rimmed, as if she had slept poorly, or cried a great deal.

Hale became serious. "Tell me."

"Went to the far southern mountains and explored the fringe of the desert. Spent two days out in the red rock canyons before running out of water. Had to come back. Even caught a glimpse of the Furnace."

He thought of the dust storm and the sandwreths. "Better you than me."

"In the forested hills up above the desert, a lot of tall trees are covered with sand. Small settlements, a farmer's house or two, even a tiny village, swallowed up, as if they'd never been." She flashed her dark eyes at Hale. "People *gone*. Just dust and nothing else!"

Hale muttered a curse. "Can you show me the images? Your ska's mothertear would have recorded them." He suddenly realized what was wrong. "Where is Ori? Is he out scouting?"

The girl looked like a flower drooping in a sudden drought. "No, he's . . . gone. Lost him on this last trip. He was getting old, but I thought our heart link was still strong." Grief welled up in Glik and seemed to engulf her. With a trembling hand, she drew another circle around the center of her chest. "Ori left me, flew away and broke our bond." Tears trickled from her reddened eyes. "The beginning is the end is the beginning."

"The beginning is the end is the beginning," Hale repeated, wrapping his arm around her bony shoulders. He held her for a long moment. "Tell me what happened, if you can."

Older skas often left their masters and flew away to die alone. Glik had bonded with Ori after the reptile bird was already full grown, when the girl was only eight, but the two had been extremely close, more than pet and partner.

Glik sucked in a deep breath, drawing courage to tell the story. "Ori flew off into a dust storm. Could see him, just a speck up in the clouds, caught in the winds. Screamed for him to come back. Felt the fear in his mind, but there was something else—I could tell. Couldn't control it. Pulled on the heart link, but I knew . . . knew he had made up his mind to leave me." Her voice broke.

"Wanted to chase after him, but the storm was coming for me, too. Had to run and take shelter in a cluster of rocks, still sending out my thoughts to him. But he didn't respond. Spent hours listening to the hissing wind, and I dreamed of the scouring dust, the howling storm, and *wings* . . . giant black wings." Her eyes had a glazed, distant look. "Survived and dug out, but Ori never came back. Lost his thoughts. Just an empty hole inside me now."

"Sometimes Utauk luck deserts us." Hale lifted his stump as proof.

Though much of the magic in the land had been used up during the devastation of the ancient wars, Utauks could still draw on their enhanced luck, a subtle form of magic. They could increase their odds just a little, give a hard-to-define nudge so a fish might notice a lure in a stream, or help dice roll to the right number, or deflect an enemy's arrow by just enough to miss a vital organ.

But Utauk good fortune was capricious and unreliable. Hale's left hand had gotten cut during a knife fight when he was young. Either Utauk luck had failed him, or his rival had more luck than he did. The cut went deep, and his opponent declared victory as Hale wrapped his bleeding wrist in bandages. In the following days, the wound grew infected and gangrenous, until his grandmother was forced to chop his hand off.

Hale touched Glik's shoulder with the smooth end of his stump. "You'll find another ska, child. Some of the tribes sell them. I could inquire among the caravans."

"Nothing can replace Ori," Glik said, forlorn. "He helped guide my dreams, kept the nightmares from getting so bad."

The two climbed to the outer gates of the castle, which were draped with the banners of Suderra and the Commonwealth. Penda hurried out to welcome them, with the green ska on her shoulder. When she saw the orphan girl, Penda lit up. "Glik, you're back!"

The girl came forward to touch Xar's elongated, scaly snout. "I always come back, Sister." She shook her head and snorted. "You're married and pregnant! Haven't given up on seeing the whole world, have you? Come explore with me."

Xar flapped his wings, clicking and buzzing as if to say *he* wanted to go out and explore. Penda touched her abdomen. "My days of traveling aren't over yet."

Glik stroked the reptile bird's feathers. "Beautiful ska."

Xar fluffed up his plumage at the compliment, but Penda's expression fell. She sensed something wrong. "Ori?"

"Lost in a dust storm," Hale explained for her.

"More than just a storm," Glik said. "Ori broke our link and left me. We always shared our visions. Can't be sure, but I think he wanted to protect me from something."

Penda touched her adopted sister's tousled hair. "I'm so sorry."

Awkwardly, Glik changed the subject, flashing a glance at Hale. "I want to eat. You promised."

"First, you have to get cleaned up," Penda said, making the girl grimace. "And while you eat, I need to speak privately with my father."

Hale wondered if Penda had received another strange premonition. "Of course, dear heart. Let's go to my quarters, where I can sit and have a rest."

She snorted. "Rest? Aren't you the man who once walked for four days straight without sleeping while you were courting my mother?"

"That is how the story goes. Alanna was worth it."

After Glik ran off with servants, Hale guided his daughter to his private quarters behind them. Even inside the castle, he had made his rooms a reflection of his past, covering the stone walls and ceiling with cloth hangings, and dangling incense burners on chains, so he felt as if he were living inside a lavish Utauk tent. He had come to enjoy the warm fireplace, dry blankets, the roof over his head. He didn't miss traveling endlessly in caravans, building encampments in the hills, or standing on the open deck of a trading ship, but he remained very much involved in what the tribes were doing, what they saw and knew. With the ominous portents his people had seen, the information network seemed more important now than ever.

After placing her ska on a stand next to the door, Penda sat on his bed. He knew his daughter well enough to notice the worry lines on her forehead, the concern in her eyes. "Now then, dear heart, what do you need from me?"

"I've thought about this at great length." She reached into a foldpocket in her swirling skirts and withdrew a honey-gold lump of amber wrapped with gold wire. "You gave me this pendant years ago. With all that's happening in the world and the baby growing inside me, it is time for me to spend this."

Hale remembered the day he had given the promise to her, the day she had become a woman. He had explained what might be expected of her, as the daughter of a prominent Utauk chief. He had planted dreams in her, promising her good fortune and a great legacy, but when she held out the amber promissory pendant now, he balked. "Let's not be hasty, dear heart. I am your father, and I will always love you. But this can only be claimed once."

"Once, yes, and the time is now. I vowed to my Starfall."

Hale remained reluctant. The talisman was a promise between father and daughter, a symbol. She could use it to claim any favor from him, at any price. The Utauk tribes did not take such things lightly.

"I'm determined," she said.

"You always were determined." He stroked her brow with his good hand. "So beautiful, surpassing even your mother. Adan Starfall didn't stand a chance when you made up your mind to have him."

"You still think it was just part of a scheme," Penda said with a sniff.

"It was a scheme, whatever else you think. We discussed it in great detail—that you would find him, lure him, seduce him. You did what I asked, dear heart. In fact, you've done more than I asked. I never thought you'd succeed so well."

"You taught me not to do anything I don't want to. It was my *choice* to marry Adan. I love him."

Accepting the amber pendant from his daughter, he sighed and slumped back among the cushions. He cupped it in his palm, rolling it back and forth. "What do you wish to spend this on?"

"It's for me and my husband." She hesitated. "And for all of Suderra."

"That must be quite a wish."

She crossed her arms over her chest. "Just as I am now part of this land, wedded to the king and in the line of Suderran kings, my husband is a part of the Utauk tribes by marrying me." She looked at him defiantly. "Do you deny it?"

"I can't fault your logic."

Penda knelt beside him like the sweet daughter he remembered. She folded his fingers over the amber pendant in his hand, forcing him to hold it tightly. "If the wreths are returning, then there can be no secrets. No secrets at all. We have to do this, Father." Her brown eyes met his, and she pressed the amber pendant harder against his palm. "I want you to tell my Starfall everything."

17

༄

ALTHOUGH Empra Iluris had thwarted further construction on the Magnifica temple for decades, the priestlords continued their work underground, unseen. The temple was already far larger than any outsider suspected. Loyal acolytes had constructed underchambers and vaulted containment areas for Ishara's most powerful godling. They would never let it become weak.

The hidden chambers were also used for other secret activities. At the moment, Priestlord Klovus's gaze was intent on the group of men trying to kill one another. His attention did not waver.

The six fighters were barefoot, stripped to the waist. Sweat and oil slicked their golden-brown skin. They carried no weapons, not for this part of their training. No Black Eel needed more than his body to kill or maim. Each one of the elite assassins was himself a living weapon.

Klovus watched the candidates, assessing them. The underground training chamber echoed with the smack of flesh against flesh, hard blows into knotted muscle, an outburst of breath from exertion, a hiss through clenched teeth. But never a hint of pain. the priestlord's eyes followed the blur of their movement. These duels had already winnowed down the best fifty to thirty, and these new ones were nearly ready for full deployment.

Though he was not easily impressed, Klovus knew the capabilities of these killers and was satisfied by what he saw. *Black Eels.* Nightmares incarnate, quick as shadows and as deadly as rumors. Among the common people, they were known only in whispered stories. No one but high-level priestlords had ever seen Black Eels; even their victims rarely saw them coming.

Once, Empra Iluris had asked Klovus about the mysterious assassins. "Tell me, Key Priestlord, do these Black Eels exist?" The woman could be sweet and cooperative, hinting at just how strong their alliance might be, but he knew she didn't share his vision for an invincible Ishara.

Klovus had responded to her question with an innocent and curious look. "Black Eels, Excellency? How do you even know that name?"

"Because people love to talk." She pressed, "Now, do they exist?"

He waved a hand, flashing his many rings. "The people make up stories to amuse their drab and difficult lives."

"Yes, they do . . . and sometimes they are correct." She offered a sweet, poisonous smile and repeated, "Do the Black Eels exist?"

Recalling a dismissive comment Iluris had once made about the godlings, Klovus finally answered with an obsequious smile, "If you believe in them, Empra, and if the people believe in them, then in some fashion they *must* exist."

Of course, the Black Eels were quite real, and Klovus controlled them.

In the vaults beneath the unfinished Magnifica, the six candidates attacked in a melee of blows with fists, elbows, knees, feet, and shoulders. Each fighter defended himself perfectly. These trainees followed no rules, because in real combat there were no rules—only life or death, skill or failure. Each Black Eel had the goal of defeating all the others. Sometimes they squared off individually; other times they formed fluid alliances, four against two, three against one. They were not allowed to stop fighting until at least one of the six lay defeated or dead, but they were all so equally matched.

For now, none of them would use magic, though Black Eels did have the ability to summon constrained bursts of fire or to harden parts of their skin into iron, making them impervious to a sword strike. Conversely, they could soften their skin like clay and make their features malleable. With intense concentration, they could shift their appearance to take on another person's form. That skill proved useful when stealth, physical strength, and deadly weapons were insufficient.

Black Eels were sworn from childhood to serve the priestlords and the godlings. To serve *him*. If only all the people in Ishara were so devoted . . .

The stone walls of the chamber were adorned with both fearsome and benevolent aspects of the primary Serepol godling. He glanced at the images and could sense the presence and the power concentrated here.

Most Isharans could feel godlings thrumming in their temples, but others had a much closer affinity to the entities. Such people were the ones drawn to serve in the priesthood, where they could commune directly with the god-ling.

Klovus had felt the pull of the entities since he was just an acolyte, and after sacrifices he felt the power strengthen, the beliefs of the people made manifest. He rose in the ranks from acolyte to priest to ur-priest. He had managed the temple of the harbor godling, then rose to become priestlord of Serepol District. Finally, through his ambition and talent, because of his special connection with the main Serepol godling, he became the key priest-lord of all Ishara.

In order for their land and their culture to survive, each person had to make sacrifices. All the people knew it, and Priestlord Klovus became the recipient of their devotions and offerings. He was an energetic man in a very important position, and he had his own needs and appetites.

Women petitioners offered their warm bodies, dedicating themselves to the Serepol godling—through Klovus. He had numerous lovers and more requests than even he could accommodate. He hated to disappoint anyone so eager, because it seemed disrespectful to the godling. Everyone had to give what they could as part of their sacrifice.

Some of those women, particularly the young ones, were nervous and weepy, their bodies trembling beneath him. Some were bitter and resentful, young wives devoted to their sad-eyed husbands, but driven by desperation to make sure their prayers were heard. Klovus reassured the guilt-racked wives that love for a godling was entirely different from love for one's hus-band, even though it might appear to take the same physical act. Klovus ac-tually preferred the reluctant ones, for when those women gave themselves to him, he knew that the price meant something to them. Sacrifices could take many forms, but they had to be *felt as sacrifices* in order to strengthen the godling.

Others behaved like whores, giving themselves with wild enthusiasm, us-ing their hands and mouths in ways that never failed to surprise him. When they had proved their sheer devotion, Klovus would bless them, promising to do what he could to achieve their requests, though the godling often worked in subtle or intangible ways.

He also received young boys as tender offerings. Even though such plea-sures were not to his tastes, he felt it was not fair to deny them. The people offered whatever they could, and some families only had young boys. He re-membered the first time an angry father had presented him with a shivering and dull-eyed boy, no more than nine years old. "Take him and have your way, then give us your blessing." When Klovus had tried to brush them away, fury flared in the father's eyes. "Who are you to question our devotion and our sacrifice to the godling? Are we to be damned because we have no daughter to spread her legs for you?"

Realizing the truth of the statement, Klovus reminded himself that he was the godling's representative, and it wasn't his place to judge or decline a sacrifice. That was what the people believed. What if the godling wanted this?

The father had roughly shoved the boy forward. "I've already broken him in for you. He knows what to do."

And the boy did.

While he reveled in such physical pleasures, Klovus needed other tools to build up the power of Ishara. Such as the Black Eels.

The cadre of assassins trained under his general guidance. These six were among the most competent Black Eels, but new recruits were always being tested beneath the district temples. Children were taken from the streets, pressed into service, and put through a trial by fire. Barely one in ten survived to this point.

As they fought each other, he tried not to fixate on the Black Eels as individuals, because so many died in the process. In this excellent group, though, he did know the one named Zaha, who was perhaps the best of the trainees. Zaha had thick black hair and bushy, dark eyebrows that could easily be altered through his camouflage magic. He fought against the other five, not as their commander, but as simply one other trainee.

The Black Eels broke into three one-on-one fights. Zaha and his opponent were equally matched, meeting blow with blow. Even such remarkable speed and skill, however, took on a certain monotony after half an hour.

Then, Zaha's opponent faltered, missed a block, and Zaha landed a hard fist in the middle of his face, breaking his nose with an audible crunch. In a blur, he pushed his opponent backward into the two adjacent fighters. Interrupted, they turned upon the new enemy, instantly joining forces against the weaker opponent. Vek, Klovus remembered. The injured man's name was Vek.

The three pounced together, driving Vek to the hard stone floor. The man, already gushing blood from his smashed nose, raised his hands in a blur to defend himself. One of the other Black Eels caught Vek's arm and drove it hard against his knee, snapping the arm at the elbow.

Even then, the fallen Black Eel did not let out a grunt of pain. The second fighter began raining hammer blows on Vek's ribs and kidneys. Zaha grabbed the man's ears, lifted his head, and with a sharp crack, snapped his neck.

Exhausted, the three stood, looking down at their work. The dead assassin lay on the floor, his face covered with a wide splash of scarlet blood. The other dueling pair also stopped their fight, and the remaining Black Eels turned to face Klovus.

Vek had been trained for years, and it seemed like a waste, but by his own requirement, the elite group could include only the best of the best. The training was also a winnowing, and that particular Black Eel had failed. With one gone, now the rest of them could move forward.

Zaha glanced at the blood staining his knuckles, and wiped it on the cloth wrapped around his hips. "We are Black Eels," he said, in a deep, dead voice. "If we can be killed, we should be killed."

"You lost one of your number," Klovus said, "but the rest of you have gotten better. Elevate more new trainees from the other groups and harden them as quickly as possible. I don't know how soon I might require your services."

Especially if Empra Iluris continued to be problematic.

He departed from the underlevels of the Magnifica temple and decided he would accept a sacrifice this evening from the pretty female supplicants who came to worship.

18

⁊Ɛ

THE terrified warhorse galloped along the forest paths, racing away from the unnatural, bitter cold. Hunched over Storm's back under the dense silver pines, Kollanan rode as far and as fast as he could, but after a time when he heard no sounds of pursuit from the shaggy white mounts, he realized that the wreths had *let* him escape. They simply didn't consider him a worthwhile threat.

His tears had long since dried, but his heart was consumed with grief and anger. Koll clung to his exhausted horse, staring into the distance of memories that swirled with the now-silenced laughter of Tomko and Birch. He remembered the boys playing with their toys, squabbling as young brothers did, then quickly forgetting the feud. Jhaqi would chastise them, but in a good-natured, patient way, and have them play with other boys their age. Her husband Gannon had been a calm man—too calm, Koll thought, because he didn't get angry even during town council meetings. He wondered what they had thought as the malignant blizzard swept over the town, killing every person at Lake Bakal. Because they were *in the way*.

The warhorse carried him toward home. Koll lost track of time. He was in a hurry, yet he dreaded telling Tafira what he had seen. All those poor, good people . . .

On visits, he would sit with his grandsons out on the wooden dock. Fishermen rowed out into the deep lake for the biggest fish, while Koll and the grandsons dangled their lines to catch the bass and sunfish that flitted under the dock. Tomko and Birch had been more interested in threading fat worms onto the hooks than in actually catching fish. When the lines went taut, he had helped them pull in their catch. Afterward, they would all have a delicious, if scant, dinner of the small fish they had caught.

When he blinked his tears away again, Kollanan was surprised to see that he had reached the city walls and open gates of Fellstaff, the tall buildings, and the fortified citadel on the most defensible hill within the walls. He could make out the patchwork of new winter shingles on the roof of the main keep. Slumped in the saddle, he rode through the northern gates. The guards recognized him and called out a greeting, but Koll could not answer. Seeing his bleak expression, their voices faltered. He rode directly to the main castle. It was late afternoon, but he didn't know of which day.

Finding his way home, Storm trotted into the courtyard, where a stable boy hurried to take the reins. Koll slid out of the saddle and steadied himself on uncertain legs. He had ridden so long he could barely straighten his knees.

Tafira emerged from the kitchens of the keep, her lush black hair tied back with a red ribbon. "I'd welcome you home anytime, Husband." She came close to kiss him, then froze as she read his eyes, his drawn face. "No . . ."

Two of the kitchen staff watched from the doorway, eyes filled with questions, but Kollanan's thoughts were only for his wife. He opened his mouth to explain, but his throat had frozen solid with unspeakable news. Instead, he just gathered her in his arms and held her close. Resting his bearded chin on her shoulder, he sobbed.

Sipping a goblet of mulled wine, Koll needed half an hour to tell Tafira the entire story. The words kept catching in his throat. "All frozen . . . everyone in town. Drifts of snow through the streets, the whole lake . . . solid ice. The people didn't have a chance, didn't even have time to understand what was happening."

Tafira coaxed the details from him, but he wasn't sure he could convey the piercing, unnatural cold, the ominous frostwreths, the heart-wrenching certainty upon seeing the buried boy's frozen hand wrapped around a carved wooden pig.

When Lasis heard the report, he was angry and determined. Standing in his full black leather outfit, his finemail shirt, his black cloak, the Brava looked determined to take on the entire ancient race. "I should have gone with you, Sire. The two of us could have fought those wreths. With my Brava magic, my ramer—"

"We would have been killed." Koll felt the hollow in his heart. "And Jhaqi and her family would still be dead. This way, at least we know."

Lasis remained stolid, ready to do whatever needed to be done. "How will we respond to this? And how many wreths are there? They haven't been seen in thousands of years, that we know of. Do we gather an army, ride north to Lake Bakal?" The Brava's loyalty to Kollanan and Norterra was without question.

"We'll get our revenge, don't doubt that," Koll said. "Right now, I am weary to my bones. . . ."

Silently, the stricken Tafira led him to their bedchamber because neither wanted to be with anyone but each other. In public, Tafira often maintained an emotional distance from the people, building an invisible wall that she only let down for a close few, but now she shuddered against Koll, and he held her tight. He lied to her that it would be all right, because he knew she needed to hear the soothing words.

When Tafira finally fell asleep, he extricated himself from her embrace and stood naked near the fire, staring at the embers of the charred logs. After a while, he pulled on a fur-lined robe and quietly left the chamber.

In his private study, the hearth was dark and cold, and white breath curled out of his mouth and nostrils in the chill air. He lit a candle on his writing desk, found paper and ink, and struggled to chronicle the terrible things he had seen. He gripped the quill and willed sentences to come. Tonight, he had many important letters to write.

The first was to his brother, the konag. If what the destructive frostwreths claimed was true, then some great war was coming to the Commonwealth. As Koll began to write, his fingers were cold and stiff. The ink smeared, and he scratched out several words, started again. The ink blotches looked like black tears on the page, and the words were no better. In a halting and convoluted recounting, he laid down the events, leaving nothing out. Conndur had to know everything, but how could he respond? Would the konag call all the armies of the three kingdoms to prepare for a war unlike anything they had ever seen?

Yes, that was what Koll wanted.

After he sealed the letter to his brother, he took more sheets of paper and wrote brief missives to his vassal lords. Tomorrow, he and Lasis would spend hours discussing strategic alternatives. He hoped the Brava might know something more than mere legends about the ancient wreths.

Koll glanced at the wall above the cold fireplace, where he had mounted his old war hammer, hoping he would never need to use it again. *Koll the*

Hammer . . . If the frostwreth Rokk stood before him now, Koll would swing the heavy weapon and smash that evil face.

He finished letters to be dispatched to the eight counties in Norterra, commanding his vassal lords to prepare to defend the northern kingdom, to reinforce their own strongholds as a precaution. He encouraged them to tear down the varied wreth ruins and use the stones to build up their castles. It was only fitting.

They would all face a new enemy now, one they had never expected to return from the mists of history.

As soon as Kollanan left their bedroom, Tafira sat up in bed. She had not been asleep, but managed to lie still, her breath little more than a feather's touch. She had suppressed her own weeping for her husband's sake, but now that he was gone, she let the tears flow without brushing them away.

In her hometown of Sarcen, the people believed that tears drained the sadness out of a person's body. But Tafira did not feel purged of her sorrow, no matter how much she wept.

On a shelf near her bedside sat a clay figurine no larger than her hand, the local godling in Sarcen. It was a frog with human hands and a shield on its shoulder, its appearance based on the summer frogs that made droning, cheerful music after the rains. The villagers had built a small temple to the frog godling, asking for good crops and happiness.

Many Isharan towns had similar rudimentary temples and local godlings, weaker than the primary entities in each district's main temple. With quiet days and a content existence, the villagers had not maintained their temple very well, and the frog godling became weak as it received few prayers and fewer sacrifices.

Thus, her village had been woefully unprepared when the Commonwealth invaders came into town. The panicked people tried to awaken their lethargic godling and make it strong, but to do so would require a great cost in blood. In desperation, they had seized the young girl Tafira, choosing her as the most expendable sacrifice among them.

Tafira had been scorned by the locals as the bastard daughter of a wealthy farmer, and although the farmer acknowledged his daughter and adopted her as his own when her real mother died in childbirth, his wife resented the girl as a constant reminder of her husband's infidelity. When Tafira's father died, he left her with nothing. When the people of Sarcen needed a sacrificial victim, her stepmother volunteered the girl without a second thought.

Despite her lowly birth, Tafira had been liked in the village, and many opposed the choice, but the ransacking soldiers were approaching. Filled with stories of Commonwealth bloodshed, fire, and rape, the Sarcen villagers agreed to sacrifice Tafira, but the raiders arrived before they could do so, and Sarcen's godling never manifested to defend its people.

In the end, the town's only true defender had been Kollanan himself, who brought his blood-maddened soldiers under control and saved much of the village. Koll had also rescued Tafira from her own people, taking the trembling young woman away with him.

As his exotic, foreign wife, Tafira had been accepted here in Norterra for decades. She had built a new life for herself with him based on love, not superstition and treachery. Their daughter Jhaqi had been a living reminder of that love, and she had found love, too. But now Jhaqi was dead, along with her husband, their two beautiful boys. . . .

Kollanan let Tafira keep reminders of her Isharan heritage, accepting that she still had the frog godling figurine as a token of her past life, even though it also reminded her of how her own village had turned on her. It was not a fond token of her lost home, but a symbol of the terrible things that people could commit.

Tonight, when she looked at the figurine, it was just an impotent decoration. It could not protect her, or her daughter, or her grandchildren. Here in Norterra, the thing was useless against the frostwreths. It would never have defended her, and it could not bring her loved ones back.

Tafira didn't need the reminder; she needed only herself and her husband. And she knew they could be formidable.

Before she could control herself, Tafira hurled the clay figure at the fieldstone wall around the fireplace. The frog statuette shattered into powdery fragments.

19

IN the pristine, snowy waste beyond the boundaries of Norterra, the frost-wreth palace rose like an outburst of crystals from the glacier. The labyrinthine walls were built from blocks of ice solidified so quickly that glimmers of ancient sunlight were trapped inside.

The blizzard wall whipped around the towers, whistling hypnotic music through the holes and crenellations. The palace was a city unto itself, a warren of private chambers and huge gathering halls. Drawing upon the reservoir of ice to reconstruct the glacier as needed, mages continued to reshape, extend, and grow the outer walls. Ice and stone buildings rose around the perimeter as more wreths awakened from their long, periodic hibernation.

Now that most of the noble frostwreths had finally awakened from spellsleep, their race was rejuvenated. The royal caste had the largest chambers in the towers, while mages occupied ornate laboratories deep inside the ice. Wreth warriors practiced and fought out on the snowfields, longing for the day when they would face their mortal enemies again in the final war. They would wipe out the sandwreths and then wake the dragon Ossus. That would bring back the god Kur, who would remake the world, with them as his chosen.

In her shimmering throne hall at the heart of the palace, Queen Onn lounged in her ice-hard chair, tapping long fingers on the translucent throne. One sharp nail carved a gouge in the ice, peeling up a curl of frost that evaporated into the chill air. Her skin was pale, her hair sumptuous and the color of bone; it hung down to her waist, for it had continued to grow, albeit slowly, throughout her centuries of spellsleep and recovery. Her eyes were just a shade darker than pure water. Her smile held little warmth even as she greeted her lover.

Chief Warrior Rokk presented himself to her clad in sparkling armor and boots lined with thick white fur from the enormous bears that frostwreth children killed for sport. A crystal knife hung at his waist, but he had left his long spiraled spear at the arched doorway of the throne room.

Even as he bowed, he kept his ice-blue eyes locked on hers, in flirtation rather than defiance. "It is good to be back, my queen. The clean white cold makes me feel at home after enduring the lands to the south." He rose into a relaxed stance. "I realize that war preparations are necessary, but I would rather stay at your side."

"You have always been lazy, Rokk," she said.

He looked scandalized. "Merely waiting for the appropriate time." He tossed his pale hair behind his shoulders. "My scouting team descended out of the cold to the fringes of the main continent. We established a distant beachhead at Lake Bakal, but there was a human infestation. In the thousands of years since we left them, our slaves managed to eke out some kind of existence without us."

She raised her pale eyebrows. "Some of them survived after the wars? How industrious."

Rokk came closer, though she hadn't invited him to do so. "They built many rudimentary structures, but we easily disposed of them. For now, I left the mage Eres in charge to build our new fortress from ice, wood, and stone."

Onn considered. "Such survivors would be hardy, I suppose. You killed them all? You should have captured and conscripted them because they could serve us again as slaves. We might have put them to work, as in the old days. Humans were much better than the clumsy drones we have now."

Rokk sniffed. "That seemed too troublesome. We simply wiped out the town. The people were frozen before they knew what was coming, but I believe there are plenty more elsewhere, if you decide you need them, my queen. One man did arrive to investigate after we had erased the town. He even had the audacity to call himself a king." He laughed.

"They imitate us," Onn said. "That means they still remember the majesty of the wreth empire, before it was torn apart."

The chief warrior paused and smiled. "But I did capture one human child as a gift for you. A little boy. I brought him with us on the ride back here. I thought you might be curious."

Intrigued, she raised her eyebrows. "What would I do with a weakling child?"

He shrugged. "Throw him out in the snow and watch him freeze, if that is what you wish. He is yours. Once we warmed him up, he said his name was Birch. He was shivering too hard to tell us much else."

She sighed. "Bring him in, and I will have a look." As Rokk shouted into the ice corridors, Onn ran a fingertip across her pale lips.

Two wreth warriors entered with a very small human between them, a boy of no more than five years, hunched under a heavy blanket that had been draped over him. The child had a mop of dark hair, and his eyes were red rimmed. The warriors nudged him across the ice floor.

Onn looked at him curiously, wondering if the boy would know to bow before her. "He looks very weak. I am surprised he survived the journey here."

"Humans are tougher than I expected," Rokk said. "I should have brought an older one, though. This boy can't tell you anything."

Onn mused, "On the other hand, he is a blank slate. Maybe he can learn to be useful." She spoke in a sharp voice. "Boy! Do you know where you are?"

The child sniffled and shook his head.

"What is your name?"

He trembled for a moment before answering. "Birch. It's a tree . . . pretty, with white bark." He pulled the blanket tighter around his shoulders.

"You will see enough white up here." Onn indicated the far corner of her dais. "Go sit there until I decide what to do with you. Hope that I find you interesting enough to keep."

As the child shuffled over to the step, Rokk climbed the dais to stand next to Onn's frozen throne. A sharp spear hung on the wall behind her. The relic from ages past had a barbed tip stained with an ancient varnish of rusty blood from when the queen's great-grandmother Dar had wounded the dragon in a furious battle. Onn intended to use that same spear when Ossus emerged from the mountains again.

Rokk said, "I accomplished what you asked, my queen. Now you may show me your gratitude. It will be an enjoyable experience for both of us." His lips curved in an annoyingly confident smile.

Uninterested in his attentions at the moment, Onn stroked the thin line of a scar across her left cheek, a wound inflicted by her treacherous cousin, Voo. "We have waited thousands of years for the right time. We must take our plans seriously." She flashed a quick glance at the huddled little boy. "Watch this, Birch! Learn your history."

She gestured. A delicious cool tingle flowed through her fingertips, and the mirror-smooth floor of the throne room rippled as she manipulated the ice like soft wax, forming figures from old wreth legends. "Our god Kur left very clear instructions of what we must do before we can be saved."

The boy watched, his tear-swollen eyes going wide in fascination.

The shape of a monstrous reptilian head rose out of the ice floor and opened its fang-jagged jaws. Birch backed up the dais stairs, getting as far away as possible. When he bumped into her cold blocky chair, she let the dragon's head sink back into the rippling floor.

"Once we prove our worth to Kur by killing the dragon, then we—and not the sandwreths—will be his chosen creations and join him in a new, perfect world." Out of the ice, she fashioned the head and shoulders of an exquisite male with handsome features that only a deity could imagine: Kur, the god who had shaped this world and created wreths. She imagined touching him, pleasing him. "We have waited a very long time."

The queen had slept off and on for centuries, placing herself and most of the wreth royalty into spellsleep, which made them functionally immortal. The great warriors and mages had also gone into stasis, though they awakened frequently to keep building their resurrected empire.

Onn herself revived only every century or two to assess how her race was healing and to see how much of the land's strained magic had returned. For two thousand years, she had been disappointed, but now the frostwreths were nearly recovered. As, no doubt, were their rivals from the desert. She eagerly anticipated the war to end all things, so their god would come back.

Birch crouched near the throne, shivering under his blanket, and she found she did not detest having him nearby. In fact, she was beginning to find his non-wrethness interesting. "Watch this, boy, so you understand! Let me start at the beginning." Every wreth knew the story, but the captive boy did not.

"There were many gods and they created many worlds, one for each star in the night sky, but *this* was the first world Kur had ever fashioned, and he was fond of it. Next, he created wreths to populate the land, and he became fiercely attached to what he had made. The other gods scolded him, because they considered their creations to be disposable, but Kur loved us too much."

The warrior lounged against the side of her throne, stroking Onn's hair. She ignored him while she continued to dabble, raising her ice figures out of the floor. Beside the image of Kur, she fashioned a strikingly lovely wreth woman and told the story like a puppet show.

"The part of Kur's creation that he loved most was the woman Suth, my ancestor." Onn smiled wistfully. "How could he not? She was the most perfect woman he had made, and Suth's beauty must have been nearly equal to a god's. Kur took her as his lover, showing her a passion unlike anything the wreths had ever known."

Rokk's eyes sparkled. "She could not have been as lovely as you."

Onn alternated between being pleased with his persistence and being irritated by it. She focused instead on the sculpture of her great ancestor, the ancestor of all frostwreths. She adjusted Suth's nose slightly, made the cheekbones higher, the chin more delicate.

The little boy didn't seem to understand much of what she was saying, nor did she expect him to. Her lips puckered into a frown. "Eventually though, for whatever reason, Kur took another lover, Raan, who was Suth's younger sister." With sharp exaggerated movements, she shaped a second young woman, whose beauty rivaled Suth's. Queen Onn's face twisted in a flicker of anger. "Raan tried to steal the god away from her own sister. The jealousy led to violence."

Onn bent her long fingers, and Raan's frozen face distorted and shattered into fragments that tinkled across the floor. The warrior Rokk laughed in delight, and Birch let out a gasp.

"Kur said that while both women could claim his love, neither could claim him as their own. But in their actions, he saw his error. Kur was a young, idealistic god, and his first world was flawed by dark emotions of hatred, anger, jealousy, violence—a reflection of fundamental flaws in himself. Kur's own weaknesses were manifested, and amplified, in the wreth race he had made.

"So Kur purged those defects from within himself, and out of them he fashioned Ossus, the great dragon that embodied all the flaws of a god, the darkness and poison. Thus purified, Kur knew he could have erased the world and made a better one, but he was too attached to his own creations . . . to Suth." Onn pouted. "And I suppose to Raan as well. So he gave his people a chance at redemption."

Birch blinked up at her. Onn crossed one long leg over the other.

"The world could never be perfect so long as it contained all his anger and violence, as personified in Ossus. If his children, his wreths, could destroy the dragon at the heart of the world, then he would take them away to a new paradise."

Rokk casually came around to the front of her throne and sat at Onn's feet, leaning against her legs as he watched the sculpture show.

"And then Kur vanished. He has not been seen for many thousands of years." The boy continued to stare at the sculptures on the floor. "The wreths split into factions, those following Suth and those following Raan, who became the sandwreths. Their hatred for us was as pernicious as the evil embodied in Ossus himself. The followers of Raan meant to destroy us so they could have Kur to themselves. They did not wish to share paradise."

When Onn huffed, tendrils of cold steam curled out of her mouth. Birch looked up at her, as if she had blown smoke rings for his amusement.

Before she could finish her grand tale, a small figure entered the throne chamber, one of the silent drones that served the wreths. It was gray skinned and humanlike, its features flat and crudely formed. Drones were poor imitations of even the human race, which the wreths had created so long ago when their power was strongest, but because the land's magic had been wrung dry, Onn and her mages could no longer make creatures as sophisticated as humans. Now, in these latter days, such drones were the best the frostwreths could fashion.

Perhaps she could learn something from this human child who sat cold and hungry on her dais.

In meek servitude, the drone walked forward with a tray bearing small bowls of food, which he offered the queen and Chief Warrior Rokk.

"I assume you are hungry," Onn said to Rokk.

"I'm hungry for your love, my queen." He sprang to his feet and gallantly snatched the tray from the drone's hands. "But we can dine first." From one of the plates he plucked fleshy, spiced lichens that grew within the cracks of the glacier.

"Feed the boy," Onn said. "He needs to eat to stay alive. Since you bothered to preserve him, let us see if he can be useful to us."

"*I* should feed him?" the warrior asked in disbelief, then snapped at the drone. "Feed him!"

The drone handed one of the dishes to Birch, and the boy stared at the food for a few seconds, as if it might be some kind of trap, then ravenously devoured it.

The drone quietly turned and walked away across the frozen floor, avoiding the translucent carvings of Suth and Kur that rose from the tiles.

Onn watched the diminutive creature. It served adequately, like all the others, but drones were interchangeable and disposable. When it reached the middle of the floor, she worked her magic, shaped the ice, and the head of the dragon rose silently behind the drone and opened an icicle-fanged mouth.

Birch dropped his plate with a clatter. The drone turned, then looked up in dismay as the Ossus sculpture plunged down and swallowed him before withdrawing down into the ice of the floor, as if it were a deep lake. It disappeared beneath the mirror-smooth surface.

Onn chuckled as she melted all the figures to leave a placid pool that froze solid. She glanced at Birch. "Did you enjoy that, child? Have you learned your first history lesson?" The wide-eyed boy didn't seem to know the answer she wanted. She explained, "Once we eradicate the sandwreths, the daughters of Raan, we must slay Ossus to eradicate evil and violence from the world. Then Kur will return and bring us with him to paradise."

"It may still take a long time," Rokk said.

"Then we should start now." She lowered her voice to a whisper, like the cold wind playing music around the towers of the frozen palace. "Oh, Kur must be a perfect lover. . . ."

Rokk stroked her arm. "In the meantime, you have me, lovely queen."

"A poor substitute."

Birch sniffled again, tugged on his blanket, and hunkered down to wait.

Rokk kissed the side of Onn's face and ran the tip of his tongue along the scar her cousin had inflicted. "I will do my best, lovely queen." He made it clear that he was no longer interested in history or legends, and after a few moments, neither was Onn.

20

Long after dark, Konag Conndur basked in the comforting presence of the stars. It had been two days since the thunderstorm, and only a few puddles remained on the gazing deck of Convera Castle. The stars twinkled like ice chips overhead. Normally he felt refreshed and clear minded up here, but tonight his thoughts were heavy as he tried to look for answers. The stars were bright lights, other worlds—supposed paradises created by the old wreth gods. Conn didn't know if he believed those ancient stories.

He lay back on the padded bench with his arms at his sides, and stared upward. He could imagine falling into the sky. The adjacent bench remained empty. No matter how many times he brought Mandan up here, the prince complained about the cold, the late hour, the waste of time, unlike Adan, who had always shared his fascination with the stars.

One dark night when Adan was fifteen, the two of them had spent hours in companionable silence watching a meteor shower that slashed across the sky. One particularly bright line of flame was accompanied by a shrill whistle and a popping noise before it vanished. Shortly afterward, Prince Adan had declared his choice of epithet—Starfall—and had never changed his mind. After his younger son became king of Suderra and traveled to the far side of the Commonwealth, he and his father exchanged frequent correspondence, full of wonder, speculations, and ideas.

But the letter Conndur had received today brought disturbing and perplexing news. Why, after thousands of years, would the ancient race return from the depths of the desert? *Sandwreths. Queen Voo.* Names and events from those half-forgotten wars seemed like nothing more than children's stories. The wreths had nearly destroyed themselves in their attempt to kill the mythical dragon—and each other. They had wounded Ossus, driven it deep underground, then battled themselves into near extinction. The surviving humans had spent two thousand years rebuilding the land, never imagining the wreths would come back.

Adan would never make up such a tale. He was not prone to undue alarm, did not cringe from thunder and lightning. . . . According to his letter, the sandwreth queen warned that the human race should prepare for a great war, even hinted at an alliance. How great a crisis was this? How many wreths were there?

But how could the konag worry about legends and vague warnings from the far side of the land when Osterra was under direct attack from Isharans and their godlings? The heinous raid on Mirrabay was just the latest in a string of incidents that included skirmishes at sea, warship sightings from the Fulcor Island garrison, innocent Commonwealth trading and fishing vessels gone missing. The real threat to the three kingdoms was obvious.

Conndur could barely control the rage of his own vassal lords, and the people on the coasts were terrified of the raiders. Lord Cade, nearly apoplectic about the danger to his people high on the northern coast, had already used his own saltpearl wealth to equip a private standing army.

But . . . wreths? Conn found his son's report as intriguing as it was unsettling. As konag, he should arrange to meet with sandwreth emissaries, even if he had to travel all the way to Suderra. But first, he had to rebuild Mirrabay and defend against further Isharan attacks.

Wreths! What could it possibly mean?

Convera Castle stood high on a wedge-shaped bluff above the confluence of the two great rivers. The Bluewater poured down from Norterra, wide enough to accommodate barges and cargo boats for great distances. The wilder Crickyeth River flowed out of the Dragonspine Mountains, the rugged boundary between Osterra and the other two kingdoms in the Commonwealth.

With fertile farmlands all around, the city had built up along each river and filled the wedge of land in between. The defensible bluff between the joined rivers rose more than two hundred feet at the point, with sheer cliffs plunging down to the water. The castle had stood above the ever-growing city for more than a thousand years. A warren of passageways, reinforced storerooms, prison cells, and armories ran throughout the bluff beneath the castle proper.

Utho knew of other secret chambers down here, used for darker purposes. Someday perhaps he would show Prince Mandan, if it became necessary, but not today. He had promised Conndur he would teach the prince more about the harsh realities of leadership and warfare.

Utho led the reluctant young man into the winding passageways inside the bluff. The tall Brava carried a crackling torch, ducking to avoid the low ceiling, while Mandan held a small lantern, impatient with the walk, which took him away from his other interests. "Why do we need to look at all the stored weapons? We haven't used them in years, and nothing has changed."

"The political situation continually changes. The Isharans are always out there, always wanting to kill us. Remember Mirrabay. Never assume defenses are as strong as you expect. I've sworn to protect you, and the Commonwealth, but I cannot do it alone. In order to be a good konag, you need to see all this, and learn."

Mandan ducked under an even lower stone ceiling at an intersection of tunnels. "I wanted to finish my new painting today. It's Lady Surri, another girl they want to make me marry." He frowned with disinterest.

Utho nodded solemnly. "I understand, my prince. Sometimes we have love, and sometimes we have duty." He had truly loved Mareka, his human wife, but he also had a responsibility to keep the Brava bloodline strong, and he had other children he would never know. "Flesh, blood, and heart are different things. We do our best to satisfy all three."

Mandan reluctantly accepted what his mentor had to say. "Someday I'll decide." He suddenly smiled as an idea occurred to him. "Maybe it would help if I painted Mirrabay and the godling, so others can see the horrors the Isharans inflict on us. If you describe all the blood and death in detail, I can capture it and make everyone afraid of the Isharans." He sounded eager now, interested. "I've never seen a real battlefield."

"Be thankful you did not see it with your own eyes. Mirrabay was beautiful at one time . . ." Utho remembered when the sun would rise out of the eastern sea, and the light shattered into bright beams and reflected into the town. He held on to the beautiful memory, then put it away, refusing to let the Isharans ruin that image for him. "We have to be ready if those animals come here to the Confluence."

Mandan swallowed, as if he had never imagined the possibility.

Utho stopped at a thick door, removed an iron key from a pocket, and turned it in the lock. "If we are ever attacked, my prince, you need to know what weaponry the Commonwealth has. Someday you might have to lead the armies yourself." Extending his torch, he stepped into an enormous chamber with rough ceilings supported by pillars at regular intervals. "This room alone contains enough steel to equip a marching army." The yellow light reflected off countless metal blades, tarnished with age. "Five hundred swords right at hand, with another thousand in additional chambers throughout the bluff. We also have fortified armories distributed across Convera City."

Interested despite himself, Mandan followed Utho. Holding up his lantern, he paused to look at a rack that held ten upright pikes. "These are all leftover from my father's war, aren't they?"

"Yes, the thousand ships brought these weapons home from Ishara after the death of Bolam, and they probably left as many behind in enemy corpses." Anger tightened his chest, but Utho couldn't deny his satisfaction at the thought of countless dead Isharans. He looked in a barrel filled with assorted armor components and made a mental note that these would have to be cleaned, repaired, sorted. "We have helms and shields, spears, maces, war axes. Other rooms hold thousands of fletched arrows and quarrels, quivers, longbows, and crossbows."

Mandan picked up a heavy weapon. "And a battle hammer, like the one my uncle Kollanan used."

"Each weapon has a precise name, a specific use, a particular method of training. You need to learn them, and I will teach you. Harden you." When Mandan looked overwhelmed, Utho added quietly, "But not all at once. We'll start simply." He led the prince back out of the armory chamber and locked the door behind them. "Come to the overlook. It will give you a greater perspective on how defensible Convera is."

Utho went to the outer walls of the bluff to a large barred window, from which they could look down the cliffs to the rivers below. Mandan rattled the iron bars, fascinated by the long drop. "Are these bars meant to stop invaders? No one could climb all the way up from the river anyway."

The prince was still quite naïve, which was all the more reason for Utho to direct his training. Any Brava could scale these cliffs if necessary, but he did not point that out. "There are thirty more such openings up and down the bluff, guarding both rivers. From up here, defenders could hurl boulders, rain down arrows, and cast fire on any enemy vessels that came up the Joined River from the sea." His nostrils flared as he drew in a long breath.

"The day I see Isharan ships sail up the river, I'll know that we Bravas have failed the Commonwealth." His hand drifted to the gold band clipped at his side, letting a finger stray across the sharp points that could draw blood.

Mandan looked down. "You'd protect us with your ramer. You'd save me."

Utho removed the spell-etched metal band, held it out. "A Brava should use his ramer only when needed." The prince's eyes widened, but he seemed afraid to touch the cuff. "We are alone here, my prince. Let me show you what we can do. A Brava does not draw on the fire lightly."

He fitted the gold band around his wrist and clamped it tight. A bead of dark red blood welled up from the sharp golden teeth, and a fringe of flame ignited around the rim, fed by the fuel of his magic and the anger in his blood.

As Mandan backed away, Utho extended his anger, and the flame grew, wrapping over his hand as he straightened his fingers, forming a far brighter torch than the one he carried into the tunnels.

"Many humans have wreth blood of varying degrees. Our creator race took human lovers, especially in the latter years of the war when they needed to breed more fighters. After countless generations, many people across the land don't even know they have wreth blood."

"But the Bravas know," Mandan said.

"We remain as pure as possible, half-breeds as strong as our first generation. Bravas can use some wreth magic, which we have adapted into something entirely our own. In particular, this."

Utho lifted his hand and watched the bright flame sear the air. "The gods created wreths, and wreths created humans, but wreths never acted as our benevolent creators. We were nothing to them, but they are long gone . . . and we remain. We're on our own, my prince. We live our lives and make our legacies." The ramer brightened, its flame extended. "And unlike the Isharans, we don't create those abomination godlings. Our race already has everything we could need."

The coiled energy was difficult to control, and the blade extended longer. He thrust his blazing hand through the bars, where the ramer fire could snap and thrash outside in the open air.

Concentrating on his hatred for the Isharans, who had killed his family and soiled the history of the world, Utho extended the fire into an incandescent whip. Far below, riverboats drifted down the Bluewater, and he could see tiny figures on the deck, pointing up at him.

Mandan was brave enough to reach out and touch his arm, intrigued by the dangerous weapon. "Why do we need that if the Commonwealth isn't at war?"

Utho came back to himself, drawing his arm back inside, and letting the ramer blade die to a flickering ring around the band. He extinguished the flame and unclipped the ramer from his wrist, where blood still oozed out of the wounds. "We may be at peace, but one can hope that won't always be the case."

21

WHEN Priestlord Klovus requested a meeting with the empra to discuss the future of Ishara itself, Iluris realized that he was expecting a public meeting in the palace's throne room, for show. For his own prominence, he wanted to be surrounded by nobles and courtiers, permanent members of the priesthood, and hundreds of spectators. He thrived on the attention that such situations brought him. Iluris didn't intend to give him the spectacle.

Instead, she responded to the eager priest courier with a benevolent smile. "I will speak with him at once. Tell Klovus to meet me in the courtyard gardens where I'll be enjoying the flowers. The cacti are beginning to bloom. We can talk uninterrupted, just the two of us."

As key priestlord, Klovus was the most powerful man in the thirteen districts, and she had to treat him carefully. His control of the temple godlings made him someone to be reckoned with, a useful ally . . . but only if he chose to be an ally. His two predecessors had known their place and accepted her as the political ruler of Ishara, and Klovus also needed to understand the proper hierarchy. He couldn't be allowed to think the empra was at his beck and call, and she certainly would not let him drag Ishara into war just because he wanted to show off his godlings.

The courier fiddled with the rank amulet that hung on a chain around his neck. "Now, Excellency? Perhaps a more formal appointment might be appropriate?"

Ignoring the courier's discomfort, Iluris rose from her throne. She adjusted her light headdress. "Why be cooped up in a shadowy chamber when it's such a lovely day in the gardens? Send him here quickly. My schedule is quite busy."

As the courier hurried out of the throne room, she made her way outside to the enclosed palace gardens, which were so well tended they looked natural. With a rustle of leather and steel, Captani Vos and two other hawk guards followed her, their red capes flowing behind them. Her adopted sons were a constant, comforting presence, always close, but the guards also understood that sometimes Iluris preferred her space, her time to concentrate.

Throughout the gardens, pedestals held carvings that ranged from terrifying to heartwarming—artists' interpretations of the main godlings from the thirteen districts. She breathed in the tart scent of yellow hibiscus blossoms so bright they were like shouts. Islands of lilies dotted small pools that rippled as goldfish swam in endless circles.

Following the crushed gravel paths, Iluris reached her garden of spiny succulents from the arid areas far to the east, particularly the high deserts of Rassah District. Honeybees explored cactus flowers as large as her cupped hands.

An incongruous water clock rose tall above the sand and rocks, twenty feet high. The device had been built three generations ago and still functioned with precision. Water from a reservoir at the top trickled in a steady flow that filled graduated cylinders, lifting floater disks that dumped the cups to fill lower basins, minute by minute, hour by hour. At precisely midnight, all the basins were emptied, then plugged again so the water clock could measure out another day. She listened to the soothing sound of the trickling water, the reassuring flow of never-changing time.

One of the hawk guards cleared his throat politely, calling her attention to an approaching visitor. Puffing, Klovus rushed along the path in his dark blue caftan. He held out his pudgy hands, showing his rings, as if they would impress her. "Empra! I came immediately at your summons." His smile did not reach his eyes.

"I didn't summon you."

He faltered. "Ah, but I was told to come meet you in the gardens."

She didn't want to argue. "Your courier said you wanted to speak to me about the future of Ishara. That is a serious request, but not very specific."

His slight bow should have made him look humble. "I am thinking of the future, Excellency, as should all Isharans. As I pray in the temple to our powerful godling and monitor the sacrifices that maintain its strength, the future weighs heavily on me."

"No more than it weighs on me," Iluris said.

Klovus looked embarrassed. "You understand what I meant, Excellency."

"I usually do, Priestlord." One of the minute cylinders of the water clock filled, tipped, and spilled into the hour cylinder with a loud splash.

"You have reigned for three decades, and you have led us to prosperity. I congratulate you for that. Our land has been at peace since the end of the war with the godless Commonwealth. In every temple throughout the district, our godlings are content with the faith of the people." His voice lowered. "Although with the Magnifica temple unfinished—"

She cut him off. "If you mean to open that discussion again, you may leave. I haven't changed my mind, nor am I likely to. The godling is already powerful and benevolent in these contented times, but with the completion of the Magnifica, it might become so strong that even you couldn't control it."

"My connection to the godlings has always been great, Excellency. I understand them, and I only want them to achieve their own greatness, because they help us so much. . . ." Klovus fidgeted, cleared his throat. "But temple construction is not what I intend to discuss today. Rather, I want to ask about how we can plan beyond your reign. That is a vital consideration for Ishara."

A female servant arrived, carrying a tray with an ornate silver pot and two glasses stuffed with bright green mint leaves, along with a plate of date biscuits. Iluris sat on the stone bench, adjusting her layered skirts. Klovus sat on the other end of the bench, though there was little room for him. The servant placed the tray between them and poured hot sugar water into each glass.

"Thank you, Excellency," Klovus said without looking at the servant, then remembered to glance up. "And bless you, too, my child. The godling knows your service to us all." After the girl blushed and hurried away, he picked up one of the date biscuits. "Let me be blunt."

"That never seems to be a problem for you."

"You have no heir. Under normal conditions, if you happened to die, your husband would take your place as ruler, but your husbands are all dead, and you are . . . childless."

"No need to be embarrassed. I'm fully aware that I have no children. None of my three husbands ever managed to get me pregnant. They were often so drunk they couldn't perform even the most basic biological functions." She took one of the biscuits herself.

All of her husbands had fathered children from lovers in the city, however, so she couldn't blame their weak seed. Also, since she had never conceived a child during the four years when her father had regularly raped her, Iluris had long since concluded she was probably barren. A fourth husband wouldn't fix the problem, especially now that she was in her late forties and for the most part past childbearing age.

Klovus bowed. "That is why we have to consider other answers. You and I haven't always agreed, but you know my greatest loyalty has always been to Ishara. I want to be your partner. What could be more beneficial than a strong alliance between the empra and the key priestlord? What could be more natural?"

She didn't know what he was getting at. "Aren't we already allies? For Ishara?"

"I meant a more, ah, formal arrangement. I've considered this long and hard, and I believe the best solution for the good of the land would be a marriage, you and I, uniting the power in Ishara." As Iluris blinked in disbelief, he continued in a rush. "That way the leadership would remain stable no matter what happens, and the two of us are certainly aligned in our love of Ishara."

Iluris controlled her expression so as not to ridicule him. "You are ten years my junior, Klovus. Some might accuse me of marrying a mere child." He laughed, but she continued in a barbed voice as she ran her eyes up and down his portly form. "It may be that I'll outlive you, though. You sample from the sacrificial platters too often, and the offerings weigh heavily on your bones."

Despite his scandalized look, he didn't deny it. "I suggest myself as your husband only out of the greatest duty and sacrifice. If I am not to your liking, then choose a successor from among the other priestlords." He forced the words out of his mouth with as much effort as a man struggling to push a feral cat into a small box.

"There are indeed many attractive priestlords," she mused, and a flush came to his cheeks. The flow continued to trickle in the water clock. One of the full cylinders slowly tipped over to spill its contents into the next larger basin down the line. She decided not to torment him further. "It may surprise you, Klovus, but I don't see you as an enemy. My life is devoted to a strong Ishara, a peaceful and prosperous future, for the good of the people. We can aspire to so much. Therefore, I agree with you in principle."

He held a date biscuit halfway to his mouth. "You do?"

"It is well past time for me to choose my successor. All Ishara should know who will be the next empra or emprir after I am gone. We should always be prepared for death. When my dear father fell from the high tower window, it was quite unexpected."

When Klovus grinned, she saw for the first time what a truly sincere smile looked like on his face. "I would be most honored, Excellency, if you chose me to rule at your side."

"Let's not go that far, Klovus." She knew she had to tamp down his ambition. "I have no compunctions about marrying for political purposes, obviously, but I'd rather *choose* the proper replacement based on who would be the best leader for Ishara. It must be someone with the range of knowledge, temperament, and flexibility—not to mention personality—to lead our continent, whether in times of prosperity or crisis. We have had decades of peace, but that may not always hold. Actively selecting my successor from among the best, well-considered candidates seems a far better method than merely accepting whichever dollop of slime happened to get in the right place up between my legs."

Klovus was horrified by her coarse words, but she continued, "Such a choice should be drawn from the widest possible pool of candidates. I'll have Chamberlain Nerev write up descriptions of the qualities we need in a leader and distribute the list across the land." She looked at him across the top of the tea glass. "Then we'll see who we find. Your priestlords are welcome to submit themselves for consideration. I want to be fair to everyone."

Klovus slid off the bench and stood facing her, his face red. "What can you possibly mean? That anyone can suggest themselves for such an honor?"

"Why shouldn't all Isharans have a chance? The candidates can be male or female as long as they can convince me that they deserve to be the next leader, and that they reflect my goals for the future of Ishara. I have no sons or daughters of my own, but I can adopt whomever I choose. That person will be my legitimate heir."

She smiled as possibilities flashed in front of her. "We'll have great tournaments so candidates can demonstrate their prowess in speed and strength, and scholarly pursuits. We may find great orators, or successful city leaders. Some priestlords may be eminently qualified as well, as I said. I won't prejudge them." Klovus was pale now, but she continued, having made up her mind. "The selection process will unify and engage all of Ishara. I'm excited to discover the best our people have to offer."

She finished her date biscuit and gave him a sweet smile. "You see? We can agree. You won't be stuck with me forever."

22

ADAN was up in his writing room, where he liked to work without interruptions, although his squire often troubled him to ask if he needed anything. The king had already met with three councilors, the leader of a merchant company, and military advisors, but he wanted an hour alone to think. When Penda and Hale came to see him, though, he found time for them.

He looked up at his wife and father-in-law. "You two have joined forces against me? I can see it in your expressions."

Penda's smile faltered, despite his light tone. "Not *against* you, my Starfall. It's very important." He felt a chill as he saw her reaction.

Hale Orr stepped forward. He was dressed in a traditional nomadic outfit of crimson and black silks, as if ready to ride out on a caravan. "The return of the sandwreths changes things. My daughter insists that you go with us to the camps in the hills for our large gathering."

"I have something to show you," Penda said in a solemn voice. "It is the secret heart of the Utauks."

Troubled, Adan looked down at the documents, the mundane but necessary business of the kingdom. "Just ride out into the hills? For how many days? I can't leave my duties here." After his people had suffered for so many years under a bad ruler and corrupt regents, Adan had promised never to brush them aside.

"You are also king of the Utauk tribes in Suderra," Hale pointed out. "What we offer you has never been shared with an outsider before."

He knew neither of them would make such a request lightly. He rose from his desk with a nod. "We'll pack up and leave as soon as possible. I can delegate most of my work for the next several days." He looked deeply into Penda's dark eyes, searching for a hint. "Is this some kind of celebration, like our wedding festival? I enjoyed those times among your people."

She stroked the side of his cheek. "No, this is much more important, but in a different way."

Two years ago, the formal preparations for their wedding festival had been overwhelming. The konag had ridden to Bannriya with a large entourage and his uncle Kollanan the Hammer came down from Norterra. While the whole city was bedecked with colors for the formal Commonwealth ceremony, Penda had sneaked Adan away in the thick of the long festivities to where the Utauk tribes had held their own celebration in the hills beyond the city walls.

Caravans from across Suderra had converged in the foothills at an enormous and colorful encampment. Thousands of people. The number stunned Adan. "I didn't think there were so many Utauks in the entire world."

Hale Orr, his future father-in-law, had cocked his eyebrows. "*Cra,* what did you expect? I'm a very important person in the tribes, and so is my daughter." He drew a circle around his heart.

Seeing the huge camp, Adan had been worried that such a great influx of people, along with all the guests from across the Commonwealth, would place a strain on Bannriya's resources, but the tribes took care of themselves and remained outside the walled city.

In the center of the celebration camp, a bright yellow pavilion had been set up, which Hale proudly designated as their wedding tent. Even though the official Commonwealth wedding ceremony would not occur for four more days, the Utauk tribes insisted that Penda Orr be married there first.

After the two were wed under the stars to cheers and drums and whistling music, the Utauk representative drew a circle on each of their foreheads. "The beginning is the end is the beginning." Adan had felt happier than ever before in his life.

When they sneaked back to rejoin the official celebration, Konag Conndur married them formally in a much more sedate ceremony before vassal lords from all fifteen Suderran counties. Neither Adan nor Penda explained their secret smiles. . . .

Now, as he took in the serious expressions on Penda's and Hale's faces, Adan knew the Utauks were not planning a celebration.

The three of them rode out from the castle stables, pointedly without an escort, much to the consternation of the Banner guards. Penda brought her ska, which balanced on her shoulder, enjoying the trip. Occasionally, Xar would take flight, circle high to look at the landscape, then come back. The diamond in his collar, called a mothertear, acted as a lens to record anything the ska saw in his flight.

They rode in among the tall pines which sighed in the gentle breezes and filled the air with a resinous scent. In the distant hills, patches of birch, maple, and oak had begun to change color with autumn. The three riders left the main road and followed narrow game paths, but Adan noticed that even these faint trails were well traveled. Splashes of powder-blue poppies growing in the underbrush seemed to mark the route.

As the horses moved along, Hale used his good hand to open a pouch at his waist, from which he plucked a few black seeds and scattered them on the ground. "This is one of the small details we wanted you to know, Adan Starfall. We leave many secret messages in the world. If you see blue poppies growing, then you know that Utauks have come this way."

Penda added, "To anyone else, they just seem like wildflowers."

Adan spotted more poppies highlighting a faint and wandering trail. "I never noticed before."

"Few do," Hale said.

They camped in a pleasant clearing under towering oaks, then rode hard again all the next day, winding deeper into the hills to places Adan had not bothered to note on his sketchy maps of Suderra. So much of his kingdom was wild, sparsely settled, even unexplored.

On the third day, after following the sporadic blue poppies, Hale led them to an isolated valley. Adan heard the sounds even before he saw the thousands of tents, haphazardly arranged wagons, paddocks for livestock. There were ten times as many people as had come to celebrate his wedding to Penda Orr.

Hale shifted in his saddle. "This is a gathering of our core tribes. It is only called in a time of crisis."

Penda reached across to take his hand. "The world has secrets, Starfall, and it's time for you to know of them. Utauks collect secrets."

Adan drank in what he saw, but it was like trying to swallow an entire river. For all the apparent chaos, he recognized that the camp was in fact well organized. The livestock was kept far from the stream that threaded the valley, so as not to foul the water. Families set up clusters of tents showing distinct clan colors. Cookfires filled the air with a haze of smoke.

Children flew kites made of colored paper on birch-twig frames. As the boys and girls ran among the tents, tugging on the strings, skas flew around, seeing the kites as prey as well as playthings. Several Utauks had reptile birds as companions; some of the creatures rode on shoulders, others perched on crossbars outside tents. Xar spread his green plumage and hissed and clicked in greeting to the other skas.

After tying their horses to a tree, Hale led the way to the middle of the camp, greeting everyone they passed, calling many by name. Few seemed to know Adan, or if they recognized that he was king, the Utauks didn't seem to care. The noise and the laughter, the whirlwind of faces, made him dizzy. Adan wondered what he had gotten into.

Penda held his arm. "Utauks try to look at life through happiness, but you should not misjudge the seriousness of this meeting, my Starfall."

Hale paused. "Normally, when it comes to Utauk business, we would tell you only what you needed to know."

"As king, don't I need to know everything?"

Penda elbowed her father before he could answer. "Yes, you do."

"My daughter called in a favor," Hale said. "Although it was a surprise to me, I now agree with her. All humans need to be concerned about the wreths. I'll take you to the matriarch of our clans. It is high time you met Shella din Orr."

On the way, Penda introduced him to a girl with dirty clothes and unkempt hair, who ran forward. "This is Glik, my foster sister. She takes care of herself, but whenever she needs something, she can ask me."

"Maybe I need your ska," the girl said, waggling a finger in front of the green reptile bird on Penda's shoulder. "I miss my Ori so much."

Indignant, the ska clicked, then flew off to circle above the camp. "Xar is heart-linked to me," Penda said to Glik. "You need to find another ska of your own."

"I will, you'll see. I dreamed about it. I don't want a tame ska from a merchant. I'll get a new ska from an egg in one of the mountain eyries. My heart link will be even stronger that way." Glik traced a circle on her heart and went off, clearly determined.

As the families settled down to eat, Hale took Adan and Penda to the main tent with decorative tassels as large as horse tails. "We will dine with my grandmother. She wants to see you in private."

The spacious tent was lit with candles and lanterns, decorated with silk hangings, plump cushions, and furnished with carved wooden chests and shelves. Orange fires in braziers warmed and lit the tent, sending smoke up through a hole at the apex.

Though he was the king of Suderra, Adan sensed he was in the presence of someone extremely important. On a rug woven with threads of countless colors sat an ancient woman, her body shrunken and twisted with age. Her skin was wrinkled like the bark of an old oak tree, but her eyes were bright sparks full of intelligence. Her withered mouth formed a smile, revealing that even at her age she still had at least three of her teeth.

Hale bowed deeply. "This is Shella din Orr, matriarch of all the tribes."

"And Hale Orr is my grandson," the woman said in a raspy voice. "One of a thousand or so. It's so hard to keep track. My own children have outdone themselves in reproducing."

Penda led him forward by the hand. "This is Adan Starfall, king of Suderra, son of Konag Conndur in Convera." She met the ancient woman's gaze. "And he is my husband, the father of our child to come. Therefore, he is one of us."

Shella nodded. Her gray-white hair was as thin as spiderwebs on her skull. "Yes, one of us." She patted the multicolored rug beneath her. "Sit next to me, young king. And your wife, too. I remember Penda . . . such a sweet girl." Her grin widened to reveal that, yes, there was a fourth tooth embedded in the back of her gums. "She seems to have married well."

"I did," Penda said with a smile.

"And so did I," Adan added. "I am honored to meet you, Shella din Orr." He sat on a cushion and looked at the thread patterns in the rug.

The matriarch ran a long, hard fingernail along the weaving. "Each thread, each color, represents a different Utauk family, all of them interconnected, forming a beautiful pattern that is difficult to discern unless you study it for years. Even though my eyesight has gone dim, I like to look at it and think. The world faces many troubles now, and I do not envy those who will live long enough to face them." Her words had an ominous undertone.

Adan admired the complex pattern in the carpet. "Thank you for welcoming me, Matriarch. Is that what I should call you?"

"Call me Mother. Everyone does."

Adan recalled his own mother, Lady Maire, who had died many years ago from a sleeping sickness. He didn't remember ever seeing her happy. "Your tribes astonish me, Mother . . . all these families." He adjusted his knees on the cushion. "I'll be happy to meet as many Utauks as wish to introduce themselves."

"You are here because your wife demanded that we share our Utauk secrets," said Shella din Orr. "She called in a debt that had to be honored."

"And why did she demand it?"

"Because she wanted you to know what we know, so that as king of your people you can make the proper decisions. We have much to share and be shared."

The old woman clapped her hands and let out a high, shrill whistle. The tent flap opened and three broad-shouldered Utauk men stood there, waiting for instructions. "Go to the library tent and bring the books. It is time to show the king a small part of what we know."

The men soon returned with another ten helpers, all carrying leather-bound volumes and wrapped scrolls, stack after stack. They placed the first ones on the writing table near the braziers, then they piled books on the floor of the tent. The mountain of knowledge grew minute by minute, already twice the size of the library at Bannriya Castle. "You carry these with you as you travel?"

"They are books. They are important," said Shella. "They hold information the Utauks have gathered since the end of the wreth wars. This is our heart camp, and we have several wagons of books, but every Utauk caravan, every clan, every camp has its own library of the world. Our information network is connected with thousands upon thousands of observers, all of whom take notes and share what they see." She casually indicated the volumes. "Choose a book. Any example will do."

Adan picked one from the nearest stack and extended it to the old woman, but she did not take it. "Open it. Any page."

He flipped to the middle, where he discovered charts, ledgers, and drawings. He found lists of towns, names of people, extraordinarily detailed maps of rivers and lakes, rock formations, valleys, roads, unknown mountain passes.

"No one knows more about the three kingdoms than the Utauk tribes," Shella said.

Adan tried to grasp what it all meant. He had maps back in his castle, but nothing in such detail. Neither the libraries in Bannriya or Convera nor any remembrance shrine could match this. He looked up at the ancient woman from the stacks of books. "This information is accurate? And recent?"

"Dear boy, we have collected knowledge for nearly two thousand years." Shella sounded as if she herself had been there since the first page was written. "We keep track of all villages and towns we trade with, customers on farmlands, a family here, a camp there, even isolated Brava training settlements." Her brittle gray eyes became sharper. "Our records are current. And hear me when I tell you that some towns have disappeared. Villages simply aren't there anymore, erased from existence."

One of the stocky nephews interrupted, "Shall we bring in the mothertears too?"

Hale blurted out, "Of course bring the mothertears! *Cra*, that's the most interesting part."

Xar flapped his wings on Penda's shoulder, bobbed his scaly head, and preened to show off the diamond in his own collar.

When the tent flap moved aside again, two burly nephews carried a heavy chest. Wheezing, they set it down on the many-colored rug in front of Shella's knobby legs. The old woman opened the lid to reveal countless diamonds the size of Adan's thumbnail tucked into cloth-lined cubbyholes. Each mothertear was labeled with an amazingly small piece of paper and fine handwriting.

Shella selected and scrutinized one. "These diamonds record the landscape of the kingdoms, every tree, every rock. So much detail, it can be overwhelming." She picked up another gem, squinting at the facets. "It takes quite some time to find what you seek, but it is here."

Adan leaned close. The facets of the mothertears reflected faint rainbows, hinting at the images preserved inside them. "Are these all from the skas? Images recorded by their collars, like Xar's?"

"Yes. For many centuries," Shella said. "If you want to see the village of Broken Wheel from six hundred years ago, we have it." She clucked her tongue against her gums. "Though I don't know why you would want to."

He glanced at the reptile bird on his wife's shoulder. "So you aren't the only spy, Xar? Skas are watching the world all over?"

Xar turned his faceted eyes toward the king, as if proud of what he had done.

Penda said, "Skas see things we cannot, and the Utauks travel where most people don't go. This legacy of our tribes holds the whole world and all its history."

"But times are changing, and we suspected as much long before the sand-wreths rode out of the dust storm," Hale explained. "That's why my dear heart convinced me to bring you in on the Utauk secret. The reports we've received, the vanishing towns and villages, families whisked away from their homes . . ." He sorted through the gems with his one good hand and pulled up one in particular, held it in his palm.

When he activated it, an image shimmered in front of them showing hill towns in the west of Suderra—Adan recognized the terrain. He saw un-tended orchards heavy with fruit, croplands never harvested, sheep and cows wandering loose.

"I don't see any people," Adan said.

"Exactly!" Shella broke in. "After the skas alerted us to this, we sent a trad-ing party to investigate, but they found no sign of the population, only a few abandoned buildings filled with drafts, dust, and mice." She rummaged among the stored gems, removed another one as Hale dissolved the first images and put the diamond back in its place.

The matriarch displayed a new projection, wooden cabins in a deep pine forest, all of them just as empty and silent. "This was the home of Bravas, one of their training settlements. Again, all gone."

Penda was deeply concerned. "I told you my dreams worried me, Star-fall."

He looked around the tent piled with books. He had never known that such a vast trove of knowledge existed. And now that he knew, he was trou-bled by what it showed.

23

PLEASANTLY sore from another day in the mines, Elliel relaxed in the inn's common room, enjoying her second cup of the local ale, although she felt only a slight effect from it. Bravas had a high tolerance for alcohol or drugs; their wreth blood kept them clearheaded and alert, even when they didn't wish to be.

After finding the dragonblood rubies, Elliel had received a significant bonus, but since her needs were modest, she asked Hallis to distribute most of it among the other miners, with an extra silver coin for Upwin and Klenner, who were with her when she'd found the gushing red liquid. Such generosity earned her gratitude and welcome among the townspeople, but Elliel was not trying to buy friendship. Who would want her as a friend, knowing what she had done?

She sat by herself at a small table, absently eating dinner. Shauvon had brought her a spiced venison sausage and a hunk of white cheese on a wooden board, even though she hadn't asked for it. The pleasant innkeeper and his wife went out of their way to look out for her.

The other townspeople gathered for regular fellowship. Upwin laughed with his friends, playing a game with stone dice. Two miners sat with their wives and an assortment of children for a family meal in the inn. The children kept staring at Elliel and whispering as if she were a strange creature, but their mothers shushed them, pulled them back.

Preoccupied, she thought of her last two years of wandering. Since awakening to her new life, she had traveled much across Osterra, generally heading west and south, finding work where she could. Bravas were in great demand, even disgraced ones. For a time, she had bonded herself as personal guard and protector for an ambitious merchant. She wanted to start rewriting her legacy, to do good for a change, but she soon realized that the merchant wanted her to be his enforcer, to twist arms, set fires, and collect debts in any way possible. After a month, Elliel's discomfort and shame reached the point of intolerability.

The merchant had sent her to confront a farmer who owed him a quarter of his harvest because of a past-due loan. He ordered Elliel to take a torch and offer the man a choice—pay, or have his face burned. But when she saw the farmer's terrified expression, saw the helplessness of his wife and their four children, she turned her back and stalked away. That day she severed her bond with the merchant.

He was outraged. "Bravas are required to obey orders from their bonded masters!"

She simply regarded him. "As you've reminded me many times, I am no longer a Brava."

Glad to leave that obligation, she had wandered for months, seeking work that didn't rely on her fighting skills. Here in Scrabbleton, she actually liked being a miner.

Now she looked around the common room at the wooden tables and the fire in the hearth, listening to the hum of voices. These people knew one another and relaxed after their long shifts with an ease of camaraderie. At a table against one of the stone walls, two young lovers shared a potato pie. They leaned close, speaking softly, though their eyes communicated more than words. Their hands touched, lingered, as if to reassure each other of their mutual affection.

Watching them filled Elliel with questions about herself. Had she ever experienced love? She was young and pretty. Had she ever kissed a young man in the shadows, giggling and touching? Had she given her heart to someone? Had she been married, to a human or to another half-breed Brava? Or was she still a virgin? Elliel had no idea.

Alone at her table, she flexed and unflexed her fingers, staring at her palm as if she could find secret answers written in the lines there. The little finger on her right hand was shortened, the top cut off at the upper knuckle, leaving only a smooth scar. Had an animal bitten it? Had she suffered frostbite? Had the finger been severed in a knife fight?

She glanced at three children crawling by their mother's skirts under a table. Did Elliel herself have any children? A chill shot through her like a bolt of icy lightning. What if she had *killed* her own children? What if her sons or daughters had been among the victims in that schoolhouse?

She touched the golden band clipped at her side, the metal worked with ornate spell symbols and sharp metal teeth. Only a Brava carried a ramer, a rare object she no longer had the knowledge to ignite. The inability reminded her of what she had been, what she had done.

She removed the band and placed it on the table. The gold seemed dull to her now. The symbols mocked her. She turned the cuff in the dim light of the inn's common room, musing about the things she must have done. What sort of legacy had she built before Utho had stripped it all from her?

She clipped the ramer back in place and got up to leave the inn. Upwin called after her, "Thanks again for the bonus, Elliel! Let's find more rubies tomorrow." She nodded absently, tossing her long cinnamon hair behind her.

In the quiet night, smoke curled up from a few chimneys, and a faint orange glow shimmered near the summit of Mount Vada, where a crack revealed fires within the mountain. She paused before the town's remembrance shrine, which was built with dark wood and carefully fitted stones. The door was open, welcoming anyone who wanted to remember lives long gone.

Entering, she saw the shelves filled with volumes that listed the names of families from Scrabbleton: mothers and children, husbands, wives, miners who had died in tunnel collapses, young people who had gone off to seek their fortunes. They were all noted here, remembered. The people of Scrabbleton recorded everyone, from stillborn babies to men so ancient they no longer knew what year they'd been born. In the dimness, Elliel traced a finger along the spines. The shrine smelled of leather, old paper, dust.

At least these records existed, while she knew none of her history, except the one horrendous act that had cost her legacy.

Elliel returned to the inn and entered through the back door. Shauvon's wife was in the kitchen, scraping trenchers and soaking mugs in a washbasin. The woman's orange hair had gone mostly gray, and she kept it tucked up in a gray bonnet. "Elliel! Help me clean up?"

Happy to help—to be *invited* to help—she toiled in comfortable silence beside the woman until the pots were scrubbed and the mugs rinsed. When they were done, Elliel went to her room. She closed the door, lit her lantern, and turned down the wick because she didn't need much light. She undressed, removing her belt and setting it aside, peeling off her linen work jerkin and placing it on the chair. She stepped closer to the lantern. The orange light bathed her naked skin, and she ran a hand over her arms, her chest.

Thin scars and thick welts formed tortured patterns across her body.

Beneath her breast, she felt an X-shaped scar that was hard under her fingertip, as if someone had cut it with the tip of a dagger. With a palm she brushed her breasts, closed her eyes, and wondered if a lover had ever done that. Gooseflesh ran down her arms.

She let her fingers trail down slowly to her flat abdomen, pausing at the long nasty welt that curved from her right side to just above her navel, where it stopped abruptly. Such a deep cut should have been fatal, but she had survived. She felt a twinge of pain from the long-forgotten wound.

She tried to imagine herself in battles as a Brava, using a sword or a knife, or igniting her ramer in great struggles. A waxy patch on her upper left arm was obviously a burn. How had that happened? Each of these scars had a story, all of which had been erased from her legacy.

When Elliel tried holding a sword, she instinctively knew what to do. Her muscles felt right, her reflexes well practiced. She must have been a fearsome warrior, expertly trained. The memories might be gone, but fighting techniques came naturally to her.

Elliel's fingers played across her stomach, touched the taut skin, and she stepped closer to the lantern's glow. She searched, but couldn't see any stretch marks to indicate that she might once have carried a baby. But what if she had? Had she given up the child?

Tears filled her green eyes. No matter how much she might want the answers, she would never know them.

She blew out the lantern.

24

❧

THE primary remembrance shrine in Convera towered seven stories tall, built of quarried marble that gleamed like the fresh, bright memory of a loved one. The shrine was the largest such structure in the Commonwealth, but even this monument could not adequately reflect the history of what the human race had accomplished on its own.

At least that was what Shadri thought, and she had thought about it a lot.

Each time the young woman entered the giant building for her daily work, humming and smiling, she paused outside to admire the beautiful statues flanking the open doorway, two ferocious lions of memory. The lion on the left roared to proclaim the glory of the lives preserved within, while the lion on the right looked contemplative, as if mulling over the legacies recorded here.

Shadri greeted the silent lions as she did every day, then hurried inside the enormous structure. The fact that she was allowed to work in the remembrance shrine every day put a spring in her step and a smile on her lips. Her sixteenth gift day had been two months ago, and she had celebrated by spending an extra hour reading.

Her heavy eyebrows often drew together as she thought of questions she wanted to answer. Straight brown hair, parted in the middle, framed her plain face. Her body was solid and a bit stocky, muscle not fat. She came from a family of workers and wore patched red skirts, the dye faded to a rusty brown, but they were clean and comfortable. She didn't bother with embroidery, ribbons, lace, or frippery, because the last thing in the world she wanted was to be noticed. Shadri had a joy of learning and a bullish curiosity that made her happier than the attentions of any flirting boy.

So much to learn, so much to study! The shrine held a wealth of names and history, each floor boasting archive rooms filled with packed wooden shelves. Shadri knew the maze by heart, and every time she turned a corner, another thing caught her interest. She already knew the legaciers and scholars in the remembrance shrine, but many had learned to avoid her persistent queries, especially Chief Legacier Vicolia.

When she was just a young girl, Shadri's father had also grown exasperated with his young daughter's curiosity. "I just run a lumber mill! Why would I need to know answers to all those questions?" Now, at least, she was around kindred spirits in the great shrine. The legaciers, most of whom were women, devoted their lives to preserving stories, legacies, and names of those who lived in Convera.

Entering the cool and imposing shrine, she heard the reverent whispers of patrons, researchers, and family members. They consulted with the staff legaciers, whose job it was to know where to find the name of every distant relative. Shadri delighted in watching the patrons' faces as they found the record of a loved one.

The marble walls had neat rows of chiseled names with birth and death dates. Shadri walked briskly past a father who stood at one wall, holding the hand of a little girl. With a finger, he traced the letters of a woman's name in the marble. His wife's, perhaps? "There she is, for us to remember." His lip trembled, and the wide-eyed girl nodded slowly.

"Long life and a great legacy," Shadri said to them in blessing as she passed. She paused, letting her curiosity get the best of her. "What was she like? Tell me about her. Did she enjoy music? What was her favorite food?"

The man grew misty-eyed as he talked about his first wife, how she made a honey and sunflower seed bread that no one could match, how she made up songs with nonsense rhymes and taught them to their little daughter. When he said this, the girl sang one of the rhymes she remembered.

Shadri walked off, humming the rhyme to herself as she left them to their memories. She climbed the stone stairs and scanned the engraved names, row after row after row. When she reached the next landing, she admired one name boldly carved in letters an armspan tall. The man had paid a vast sum so that his name could be the most prominent in the shrine. MYRIAN BRUNT. Shadri blew a loose strand of brown hair away from her face. Everyone in Convera knew his name despite the passage of centuries, but it was not a *true* legacy, since no one remembered who Myrian Brunt *was* or what he had *done*. Just his name.

Whenever her work duties allowed it, Shadri would pick a volume from the shelves and study the recorded lives, the accomplishments of countless generations. She was pleased with what humans had done after being abandoned by their creator race. She didn't think that wreths had ever paid much attention to science, discovery, or history. Humans, though, kept track of everything . . . well, at least people like Shadri did.

New parents would pay to have their baby's name written in the archives, but the legaciers' greatest business came when families paid to memorialize a lost loved one. Trained chroniclers would write down brief biographies for the vast archive. For a fee, they would chisel a name on one of the stone walls of the shrine, or for a lesser fee, they would write the names in fine calligraphy in the permanent books.

Long life and a great legacy . . . Such a wonderful blessing to give someone! Every person deserved to be remembered, and Shadri did her best to remember them all. Her people had done rather well for themselves, even if no gods watched over them.

Wooden study tables had benches to accommodate many scholars. The day was bright and the windows were open to let in sunlight; candles would be brought out for people who wanted to read into the night. She herself was one of those. The legaciers were used to seeing her at all hours.

In the back of the room, a team of scholars recorded extended family trees that marked the branchings of marriages, children, stepchildren. In red ink, they indicated known wreth bloodlines, descendants of half-breeds, bastard children born when the ancient race had taken human lovers.

Shadri considered the interconnected family lines to be like the roots of trees in a giant forest. She herself was just one tiny twig . . . and her twig would end, unless she ever married and had children. Someday, when she was older, she supposed that was another thing she would have to learn. For now, she scared off most boys when she pestered them with questions about their work, their apprenticeships, their games, their trades or crafts.

On her way to her duties on the upper floor, she picked up some books from the patrons' table and returned them to their proper places. The chief legacier entered the room and skewered Shadri with a disapproving glance. Vicolia, a stern and haughty woman, held a prominent position that gave her a sense of inflated importance. "Why are you wasting time with those books? It's not your job."

Shadri patted the volume's spine to make it even with the others on the shelf. "These were left out on the table by a patron. I returned them where they belonged."

"It isn't your place to do that." The woman huffed. "Now I need to have a real legacier make sure you haven't gotten it disorganized."

"It's not disorganized," Shadri said. "I know what I'm doing."

"How are we to be sure? We don't let unqualified people touch the records." Vicolia kept her voice low so as not to disturb the other patrons. "Shadri, your behavior is growing tiresome. I've indulged you these past months, and I admire your dedication to studying, but I'd rather you spent the time doing your proper work. Up on the top floor you'll find your buckets of water and scrub brushes. You left them there last night, because you didn't finish the job."

"Yes, ma'am." Shadri lowered her eyes and tried to slip past; she had indeed gotten distracted before completing her duties.

"When you finish polishing the windows up there, you can do the next floor down. The shelves of the main archive require dusting, and the underground levels need more sweeping than usual. See to it."

"Yes, ma'am," Shadri said.

"Our last cleaning woman wasn't so distractible," Vicolia muttered. "Now, don't disturb the patrons as you get about your chores."

Shadri continued up the steps, dreading the amount of sweeping, scrubbing, and cleaning that lay ahead of her, but at least she would be among the books, in the company of the names carved in the walls, and surrounded by history.

25

IN the Utauk camp Adan tried to fall asleep under the stars. Penda's arm was loosely draped across his chest as she snuggled close on their soft blankets. Xar roosted on a low shrub nearby. The reptile bird snorted and wheezed in his sleep.

In the crisp air, Adan could smell the smoke of campfires and hear the low music of a stringed instrument being played more for meditation than entertainment. He could still taste the flavors of the spiced meal he had eaten in Shella din Orr's tent.

Wide awake, he absently stroked Penda's long dark hair, enjoying her beauty in the starlight. He pondered the sheer trust she and her father had shown by bringing him into the Utauk secrets. Their people had an unbelievable trove of information and a network of spies and observers that no one else noticed.

Other Utauk travelers had reported mysterious rumors from the north, maybe manifestations of the wreths. A different faction of wreths? Were they the mortal enemies that Queen Voo had warned about? Adan wondered if King Kollanan had seen any cause for alarm up in Norterra. The young man had already written his father about the sandwreths, but his uncle Koll might need to be warned. What if those other wreths had already swept down from the ice-locked vastness to attack Norterra?

Lying there awake, he felt a chill. Taking the danger seriously, he decided to waste no time and just ride north himself to see Kollanan face-to-face. He could reach Fellstaff in five days, if some of the Utauks would show him the shortest way from here. That would be much faster than returning to Bannriya, preparing an expedition, writing letters and sending couriers, and then setting off again. He would just *go*. Somehow, he felt the Utauks would applaud the decision.

By her steady breathing, he could tell that Penda was sound asleep against him, feeling safe in his presence and among her people. Looking up at the stars, Adan saw a yellow streak overhead, the quick whisper of a shooting star, and he thought of those times with his father on the gazing deck of Convera Castle, pondering the many other worlds the wreth gods had created.

For thousands of years humans had settled the war-torn continent, restoring the natural beauty even if the magic had been weakened. But what if sandwreths from the arid wasteland and frostwreths from the north wanted their land back? What if they intended to enslave humanity again, as they had done before? Voo had suggested an alliance, but could he trust her?

Adan had to do more against this mysterious danger. He would talk with Kollanan as soon as possible.

As the sun rose, the Utauk camp revived. Cookfires crackled to life to heat water for morning tea. Shella's nephews made a pot of honey-sweetened porridge, and Hale Orr cradled three bowls, somehow balancing them all as he offered one to Adan and Penda. From the bags under his eyes, Adan could tell the older man hadn't slept much either. Judging by his straight back and firm expression, Hale seemed to have come to a conclusion of his own.

"I need to stop sitting around adding fat to my bones, dear heart," he announced to Penda. "Although I enjoy the comfort of my quarters in Bannriya Castle, I can't just ignore what is happening in the world. This is too important, and I haven't finished building my legacy."

Penda held her bowl of porridge, but didn't take a bite. "What do you mean?"

"I need to take a journey to get some answers. *Cra*, I can do my part! I'm not an old man yet, and I think I have another journey or two left in me." Holding the bowl of porridge against his chest with his left forearm, he used a wooden spoon to scoop up a mouthful. "I'm going to Ishara. I'll find an Utauk trading ship and sign aboard." He mused. "With my family rank, they may even make me merchant captain."

Adan knew Utauks could travel with immunity, even if tensions were high between the Commonwealth and the new world. "Why go to Ishara? What do you expect to find there?"

"I want to see if there are any rumblings about the wreths over there. We need to know."

"Wreths were never part of Ishara," Adan said. "They fought on this continent."

"And they nearly destroyed it," Penda said, then changed her tone as a thought occurred to her. "*Cra*, magic is still strong in the new world! What would stop the wreths from going there?"

"We need to know." Hale Orr scuffed the tip of his boot on the ground, making a divot. "I'll come back and report whatever I learn."

"And you'll report it to Starfall as well, since he's part of us, our family, and our tapestry."

"As we agreed, dear heart."

Adan cupped the bowl of porridge in both hands. The cooked oats and honey smelled delicious. He confessed, "I made a similar decision myself last night. I intend to set off for Norterra to warn King Kollanan. If the frostwreths are as bad as Queen Voo warned, he needs to know."

Penda turned to him in surprise. Xar flapped his wings and burbled, as if telling Adan to leave right away, and good riddance.

Hale cautioned, "I wouldn't trust Queen Voo, either. Remember what the wreths—all wreths—did to us in ancient times. They created us and used us as pawns and playthings. They bred with us, enslaved us, and tried to destroy the world. No Utauk—no *human*—should celebrate their return."

Adan nodded. "I don't disagree with you at all."

A sparkle of mirth shone through the concern in the older man's eyes. "My son-in-law is a wise man."

Penda was still waiting for explanations. "That's a long journey. Did you intend to take me with you, without asking?"

"No, I need you back in Bannriya. Yes, I have advisors, ministers, and delegates, but I want *you* to watch over the people in my absence. You're good at that."

Penda sniffed. "You plan to send me home to manage the kingdom on my own?"

Her father chuckled. "You can do it with one eye closed, dear heart."

"Of course I can, but I did not give Starfall permission to go." She straightened her back and faced Adan. The ska fluttered his wings as if to reassure her that he at least did not intend to leave. Her expression softened, and she lowered her voice. "But I dreamed that you would be far away, so when I woke up I knew you were going. I just didn't know why or where. I will miss you."

His heart ached and he wrapped her in a hug. "I'll be back quickly, I promise. Why would I ever want to leave you?"

"Why indeed? Make sure you're back in time to see our child born." She
glanced at her father. "Both of you."

"That is a promise I intend to keep," Adan said.

"Me, too," Hale said. "The beginning is the end is the beginning."

26

∽

I N his sunlit chambers in Convera Castle, the prince finished a portrait of one of the many potential brides offered to him. Once again, Conndur was disturbed by what he saw, but didn't know how to express his unease. He and his older son had not been able to communicate well since Lady Maire's death.

Mandan seemed satisfied with his work, as unsettling as it was to his father. The young man used a narrow brush and bright white paint to add his signature. *Mandan of the Colors.* When painting, he never used the title of prince. In this, he was an artist, and he was unquestionably skilled. The idealized portrait of his mother that hung over his bed proved that.

He stepped back with a critical smile. "I've captured Lady Surri quite well, don't you think, Father?" He seemed eager for praise, but his voice also held a hint of taunting.

"I recognize Lady Surri, no doubt about that," Conn agreed, trying to keep his voice neutral. He was certain her noble parents would not appreciate the depiction. There was nothing specific about the portrait that anyone could fault, and he couldn't quite put his finger on why the painting disturbed him so much.

Mandan had accurately portrayed Surri's narrow face, blue eyes, pert nose, and wavy brown hair that fell to her shoulders. When her father presented her at court, she had indeed worn those pink ribbons in her hair, as well as a string of saltpearls given to her as a gift by their neighbor Lord Cade. Surri did have a wash of freckles across her cheeks, but in Mandan's painting they looked like flecks of mud on her fair skin. The small mole high on her left cheek appeared far larger and darker in the portrait than it really was. Her lips should have curved in a contented smile, but somehow they looked twisted. Her features were ever so slightly *wrong.*

Conndur had thought Surri was quite pretty when he first met her, but obviously the prince was not impressed. "So you won't reconsider her as a potential wife, then?"

"I'm afraid not, Father." Mandan sighed and set his brush and paints down. "There was no spark, and I found her company tedious. She isn't the right woman for me."

He glanced toward the portrait of Lady Maire, her rich red hair, her pale skin, the protective expression in her sea-green eyes. Conn had seen the beauty in the woman back when he married her, and had felt the sting of her loss after her suicide. But Mandan still saw his mother as an unrealistically perfect woman, which meant that no bride would ever measure up.

Frustrated with his son's pickiness, Conn couldn't help but remember his own arranged marriage with Maire, even though they had never felt any particular spark. He said with a hint of exasperation, "You'll be konag someday, Mandan. You need a queen. Among the ones offered to you, find one you can tolerate."

"You've said that many times, and Utho has told me as well, but I'm not ready to give up on true love yet." Mandan looked at the portrait he had just completed and sighed. "Lady Surri will be disappointed, as will her parents, so I'll give them this lovely portrait as my way of repaying their consideration." He stepped back, locked his hands behind him. "The idea that they would offer their daughter is a sign of great respect. We should be happy with that."

Conn gave a quiet sigh. His son would present the portrait to the girl's parents with great pomp and ceremony, and they would feel obligated to hang it prominently, as a gift from the prince, even though the depiction was a quiet insult. Just like all the others.

Conn had to hope the prince would eventually accept one of the candidates, though he had never seen his son show any interest in romance or physical pleasures, preferring his art and music to carousing. Sooner or later, though, the prince's marriage—and heirs—would become a political necessity.

Conn smiled as he remembered his own youth. He and Koll had certainly taken advantage of the willing young women who wished to spend time with the sons of the konag. While Bolam was groomed to take the throne, Koll and Conn became well known around Convera for their exploits. That was before the war.

Now he tried a different approach. "You've seen how happy your brother is, how suited he is to marriage. Adan and Penda are already expecting their first child. But you're my firstborn, not Adan, and I expect you to give me grandchildren. Suderra is much too far away for me to adequately spoil the new baby once Penda gives birth."

"Yes, marriage suits Adan well," the prince agreed, but his voice was noncommittal.

Knowing he wouldn't get a better answer, Conn turned to the business at hand. "I've dispatched troops and supplies to Mirrabay. The town has much rebuilding to do after the raid. That's one of the things a ruler does."

Mandan nodded solemnly. "A konag should always take care of the people when tragedy strikes." The prince said the proper words, but without emotion, as if reciting a meaningless phrase he had been taught. Suddenly, his voice hardened. "Especially when it's the result of an Isharan attack. They are animals."

Conn blinked in surprise as he realized that the prince must have been talking to Utho; the Brava's hatred of the Isharans bordered on obsession, though with good reason. He continued, "I'm also sending wagonloads of food, since we won't finish rebuilding the town before winter, and the cold storms can be harsh."

Mandan walked over to a map of Osterra on the wall. The prince had always enjoyed maps, more for the art than the geography. He drew his fingernail along the small harbor that marked Mirrabay. "I know where it is. A konag needs to know the entire land he rules. He must also know the history and the culture of his people." When he frowned, the young man's face took on an unexpectedly sincere expression. "I know I'm not like you, Father. You don't approve that I spend more time with art than with military training, but that cultural knowledge makes me stronger and deeper as a man. Isn't that also important for a konag?" He seemed to be trying hard to please him.

Conn considered. "Yes, I recognize that. My brother Bolam was an accomplished musician, and he could play several instruments. Our music library still holds some of his remarkable compositions. I never faulted him for his artistic interests—and I don't fault you. But you cannot neglect statecraft and physical combat. If war comes again, you must be prepared to do more than paint. That's why I asked Utho to train you harder."

The young man paled. "I . . . I understand that. I don't look forward to war, no matter what Utho says."

"One can't always anticipate the reasons for war. Sometimes there's no choice. You remember the story of Queen Kresca."

The devastation after the wreth wars had led to centuries of squalor and violence among the human survivors, the strife and desperation as they survived on scraps, without their creators and without gods. Some tried to kill anyone they saw, while others attempted to rebuild civilization, a *human* civilization. The people wanted a leader to manage and guide them, to bring help where it was needed.

That person was a great queen named Kresca. She had built a kingdom in Osterra and erected the first fortress at the confluence of the two rivers. She had a well-fed and healthy population, which was unusual after so many centuries of austerity. Kresca's farmers irrigated large areas of reclaimed land, so that instead of tending small plots to feed a family or two, they planted vast fields and harvested enough grain to carry an entire city through lean times. She was able to gather a large army of defenders.

Naturally, the rival kings from the north and south wanted what Kresca's people had. They joined together to invade, but Queen Kresca's people fiercely defended what they had built. She announced to the invading rulers that if they conquered her lands and took over the fields, they would have supplies for now, yes, but they would destroy the very reason the supplies existed at all. Did they not understand *why* her people were well fed and strong?

As the three armies prepared for a terrible battle, Kresca went to face the two rival leaders. Standing before them, she asked if they were afraid. They laughed and said that they were not afraid of her. She said, "Not afraid of me—afraid of *the truth*. I want peace, because with peace we can all prosper. We can show you how to reclaim the old battlefields, how to irrigate the land, how to feed your people. Then you won't need what we have, because you will have great kingdoms of your own."

After much powerful advice from their councilors, the kings agreed. Kresca became the very first konag, with the new kingdoms of Norterra and Suderra independent but part of the Commonwealth "so long as our lands shall prosper." As centuries passed, the prosperity continued, and humans reclaimed the world that the ancient race had abandoned.

"Are the reasons for war always valid?" Mandan asked now. "What about the war thirty years ago? No one seems to know exactly why it started."

"I'm sure there were reasons," Conn muttered, though he couldn't name them. "My father considered the reasons sufficient when he sent Koll and me across the sea to fight."

"Prince Bolam was the firstborn, and he didn't go to fight," Mandan pointed out. "If we go to war again, can't I just send Adan and Uncle Kollanan? Why do I need to learn how to fight?"

Conndur frowned. "That wouldn't be the way of a true konag. And sometimes the fight comes to you."

"But Bolam didn't go to war." Mandan kept pressing. "Konag Cronin sent the two of you instead, and you told me Bolam would have made a great leader."

Conn sighed. "Sometimes you ask too many questions, Mandan, and they aren't the right questions." He gave the prince a quick hug, which startled them both. "I'll help you where I can, my son. We will lead, and we will do our best for the Commonwealth. Together."

Surprised, Mandan trembled as he hugged his father back, then they awkwardly broke apart. Conndur left the room quickly as the prince resumed his stance in front of the portrait, nodding slowly to himself.

27

As the konag's bonded Brava, Utho often left Convera to conduct busi-ness with other counties, meet with noble lords, or inspect the secret saltpearl operations in the far northeast. Sometimes, though, he had to make a journey home to fulfill his other duty as a Brava.

Over the centuries, the half-breed race had established unmarked settle-ments, which would be impossible for bloodthirsty Isharans to find if the enemy ever invaded the Commonwealth. The Bravas had vowed that their people would never again reside all in one place, like their hopeful colony of Valaera long ago. That left them far too open for slaughter,.

As Utho rode through the forest on his sorrel horse, he felt the ever-present vengeance swirling inside him, like a fire in an oven, but he damped it, controlled it. He smelled oaks and evergreens, and then woodsmoke as he came upon the first of the dwellings. This Brava settlement had only twenty buildings, comfortable log homes with small vegetable gardens. A wooden aqueduct diverted water from mountain streams to the houses and animal pens. At the center of the settlement, children practiced with blunted swords in an open ring.

An old teacher stood at the edge shouting encouragement and criticism to his wards. Four Brava children, three boys and one girl, fought in a melee that was a combination of deadly serious and play. Their instructor was shirt-less, his cheeks and head clean-shaven, his lean body such a mass of mus-cles that he looked carved from driftwood.

The girl struck one boy in the shoulder with the flat of her blade. "Dead!" she cried.

"Not dead! I can still fight, even with one arm!"

"Yes, you could," said the old teacher. "And you might have to." Hearing the approaching horse, he turned to look at the rider and immediately brightened. "Utho!"

"I heard that these children need a better trainer, Onzu."

The old man scoffed. "I was good enough for you."

Dismounting, Utho tied his horse to a tree. "In the coming days, they may need to be better than me." His expression darkened. "The Isharans raided Mirrabay again. If Konag Conndur listens to reason, we may at last have war with our enemies."

Onzu beamed. "Ah, then you bring good news."

"Nothing about Mirrabay is good news," Utho said, growing grim again. "Not this time, and not last time."

"Pain is the goad that drives us forward, because we Bravas cannot bear to look at the past."

Utho shook his head. "We *have* to remember the past. What the Isharans did to Valaera must never happen again, must never be forgotten."

"It won't be. That is why we keep the Brava bloodline pure so our magic is strong. That is why we remain ready." Letting the children continue their sparring, old Onzu came to clasp Utho's hand. They walked together toward his small log home. "Are you here to visit me? Or have you come to do your duty?"

"I always do my duty," Utho said.

"Cheth will be pleased. She arrived yesterday for the same purpose. She is fertile for the next few days." The old man grinned. "I think she was concerned that *I'd* be the one who had to share her bed."

"You often take on that duty," Utho teased. "Too many Brava children have your eyes and your nose."

Onzu clucked his tongue. "I serve where I am called."

"As do I." Utho followed him. In the old teacher's garden stood the carved wooden figure of a Brava man in ancient clothing: Olan, the optimistic leader of Valaera, the ill-fated colony he had established in Ishara. Utho reached out to stroke the carved face, thinking of the ancient man's dreams. If only Olan had succeeded there, the Brava race would be thriving on a continent of their own. . . .

Onzu saw his interest. "The Isharans still attack us, and we still vow to kill them. Should later generations pay for the crimes of their ancestors?" He shook his head. "There has to be an end to it."

Utho was not convinced. "Maybe after a thousand generations they will have paid enough for what they did to us. But not yet."

Centuries ago, a group of Bravas decided to leave the old world and seek their promised land, where they would establish a colony. Led by the visionary Olan, they constructed a fleet of ships to carry them across the sea to the new continent, far to the east. Explorers had described the shores of Ishara in glowing terms—lush forests, fertile plains, and a handful of settlements built by the first humans who had gone there at the end of the wreth wars. Crowded aboard their ships, a thousand Brava colonists sailed away from the old, bruised land.

Arriving at their new shores, intending never to look back, they dragged their ships high on the beach. Then the pioneers cut down trees, quarried stone, and constructed a perfect colony, which they named Valaera. They planted crops, hunted, and enlarged their settlement.

Before long they were discovered by the Isharan people, who treated them with suspicion, uncomfortable with these strangers, these invaders—especially since the new arrivals looked similar to the terrifying wreths from their past. The optimistic pioneers underestimated the hatred and fear of the Isharans. The Bravas believed they could defend themselves.

But not against a godling.

One night, two years after the founding of the colony, Isharans rode in, surrounded Valaera, and unleashed one of their abominations to destroy the colony. Of the thousand initial Brava pioneers, over seven hundred were slain in that attack. The rest, led by a badly wounded Olan, were driven to the sea, where they salvaged some of the original vessels they had hauled high on the shore.

As they limped back home to the Commonwealth, only hatred kept them alive. By the time they arrived, the Bravas were hardened and they made up their minds to forge themselves into a new kind of fighting force. Olan spread the word about the unprovoked violence of the Isharans, and the returned Bravas swore their loyalty to defend the Commonwealth. Among themselves, the half-breed race kept alive the burning need for an eventual vengewar.

Some Bravas did form families with humans. Utho certainly had. His love came as a surprise to him when he met Mareka, who had only a drop of wreth blood within her, but she was special to him, and so were their daughters. More than thirty years ago, when he was asked to help guard

Fulcor Island against an Isharan incursion, he could not refuse because of his vow to the konag. Utho had said goodbye to his family in Mirrabay and sailed off to the island garrison, leaving his wife and daughters undefended. . . .

History already demanded that the Isharans never be forgiven for slaughtering the Valaera colony. After the Isharans also killed his family at Mirrabay, Utho could never forgive them in his heart either.

While the wreth bloodline dwindled as the mixed-breed descendants had more children, the pure Bravas swore never to grow weaker, never to let their magic fade. To maintain their race, each Brava had the solemn duty to conceive one or more children by another pure Brava so that their children maintained the same amount of wreth blood from generation to generation. For Utho there was no romance in it. He had loved Mareka, and there was no more love left in him. But he could still breed.

Throughout the afternoon, he and Onzu talked inside the old man's home, sharing news and reminiscing. When Utho stepped out the front door, he found a Brava woman waiting with her arms crossed over her chest. Cheth was tall, well proportioned, in her midthirties with a long face and close-cropped ash-brown hair. She regarded him as he paused in the doorway. "You'll do. The next three days will be my best time to conceive."

The Brava children born of such unions were left in the settlements to be raised and trained. The teachers were seasoned warriors, sometimes patient, sometimes ruthless. Onzu was a little of both. Utho had been raised here, trained here, formed bonds with other Brava children here, before setting off to establish his long legacy.

He would spend the next three days with Cheth, and then he would return to Convera and his work for the konag. As the afternoon sun slanted through the trees and the children continued their rigorous training, Utho followed Cheth into the guesthouse and closed the door, so that they could both do their Brava duty.

28

Late at night, Captani Vos came to the empra's tower chambers, a private place for a private and personal ceremony. His eyes twinkled. With his cleft chin and high cheekbones, the leader of her hawk guards looked rugged and dangerous, enhanced by a crooked nose that had been broken in a training exercise in his youth.

Empra Iluris rose from her settee when the captani entered. She had been waiting for his arrival. Unlike many of her frustrating obligations, this part of her duties warmed her heart. Of all the achievements in her reign, creating the hawk guards might be the best thing she had done.

Vos stood in his full formal armor, a gold breastplate, red cape, golden bracers on his arms, sturdy boots, greaves, a sword at his side. Every element of his outfit was neat and polished, presentable for his empra, but Iluris was much less formal when she received people in her own rooms. She had removed her jewels and relaxed in a comfortable robe with a sweet herbal tea and a bowl of tart berries. Her hawk guards understood that she was also a woman, a person, a mother—*their* mother. Her elite troops, her adopted sons, were allowed to see her in ways that no one else did, and they loved her for it. They could know who Iluris really was, and they would give their lives for her.

Captani Vos held out his left hand to display three golden rings cupped in his palm, each one fashioned with the head of a hawk. He wore a similar ring on his own finger. "You will be happy with the three new candidates, Mother. I tested them myself, and I want to install them into service before you begin your pilgrimage to search for a successor. I'm confident they will be among your best."

"You are my best, Vos," she said. "But I love you all equally."

He had been brought to Iluris in the tenth year of her reign, when her hawk guards were just coming into their own. The elite guards were developing their ranks and traditions, understanding their paramount role of defending the empra. She did not trust the insidious politics, the backstabbing and treachery her father had actively encouraged. The young empra had needed her own protection, a special force that was loyal to her above all.

Vos was a young man from a large family that had too many mouths to feed, so his parents had signed him over to the Isharan army. He felt as if his family had discarded him. Six months later, the coughing flu had swept through Serepol and killed his entire family. Only Vos was left, an orphan with no one but the Isharan army. Iluris had adopted him herself. She had no children of her own, and all of the hawk guards became her surrogate children. Each one was special to her.

Now Vos signaled back into the torchlit corridor. Three young men entered her chamber garbed in uniforms similar to the captani's, though their capes were darker maroon, less likely to show blood if the recruits were injured during hard practice fights.

As Iluris stepped up to welcome them, the three nervous young men averted their eyes. She teasingly scolded them. "Look at me! You should not be overwhelmed in my presence or you'll never be able to protect me."

The young man in the middle stepped forward. "We will protect you, Excellency. We promised. It is how we serve."

"That's the correct answer," she said, intentionally casual. Once they became full hawk guards, these young men would spend enough time in rigid formality, backs straight, arms at their sides in her throne room. "Tell me your names."

Captani Vos took a step forward, ready to introduce the candidates, but Iluris cut him off. "They can speak for themselves."

The one in the middle spoke first. "I am Cyril, and I'm honored to be chosen. I will not let you down, Excellency."

The second young man introduced himself as Nedd, and the third was Boro. "They will be fine additions to my family," she said, studying each face. In their eyes, she read pride, eagerness, and anxiety. "You have no families of your own?"

The three young men shook their heads.

"All orphans," Vos affirmed.

"They are no longer orphans," she said with a smile. "They are part of our family now."

She took the three gold rings from Captani Vos and slipped the first one on Cyril's finger. He clasped his fist tight as if to make sure the ring would never fall off. She did the same for Boro and Nedd. All three young men looked up at her with tears welling in their eyes.

"I now have three new sons to ensure the peace and prosperity of Ishara," she said. Iluris had no doubt they would be fierce fighters, would sacrifice themselves for her. They were hers entirely.

She opened her arms wide, waiting. The new hawk guards were hesitant, but Vos nudged them. They came forward, and she enfolded all three into an embrace. "After tonight, you may call me Mother, because you are part of my family."

29

WHILE the godling of Serepol chafed in the incomplete Magnifica temple, Klovus attended worship where he had once been ur-priest. The harbor temple, which housed the lesser godling that had attacked Mirrabay, was also a good place to set up his secret meeting with the other district priestlords later that night.

At sunset, fishermen, dockhands, porters, innkeepers, and brothel workers gathered to give thanks to their godling. "Hear us, save us," they chanted. The temple had a tower as tall as the mast of a ship and lintels carved with hypnotic designs reminiscent of wind and waves. Ceramic tiles prominent with the designs of Serepol covered the façade.

Klovus and a group of his chosen deputies joined the worshippers as the temple rang brass bells, each person bringing sacrifices of things they valued. He had donned his finest caftan, and wore gold chains around his neck, filigreed bracelets on his wrists, and a jeweled shadowglass amulet as wide as his palm. As key priestlord, he was revered almost as much as a godling.

In the expansive temple chamber, a polished granite altar stood in front of the spelldoor that held the godling in place. The new ur-priest of the harbor temple, a former fisherman named Xion, stood by his altar. "Priestlord Klovus, we are honored that you join us again. I'm so proud our godling helped in the fight against the godless. Hear us, save us."

Klovus nodded. "Hear us, save us." Everything seemed to be in order.

The people showed their devotion, bringing their most precious possessions as offerings. Some with bandaged hands carried jars of dark blood, which they would feed to the godling. Others gave practical offerings of food, fresh fish, and baked breads for the priests. Some women looked with shy flirtation at Klovus. Such pleasures would have to wait, though, for he had important business later in the harbor temple's underground chambers. That was the real reason he had called this ritual. It was a perfect diversion.

Ur-priest Xion and his assistants poured the blood offerings into a gold trough behind the altar, and the red liquid spilled into the base of the glowing spelldoor. The rainbow lights of the contented godling flashed brighter, which drew awed gasps from the observers. Their belief always increased when they could see the power of their protector, and as their belief increased, so did the godling's power. The innate magic in the new world created a cycle of faith and proof.

All the godlings of Ishara were connected by the faint network of magic that infused the continent, a web that emanated from this city, where the first human pioneers had settled after the wreth wars. Klovus understood the mysterious source of their power, but most people didn't.

Klovus could feel the energy inside himself, too, the special affinity he had always felt for the entities. They were real, and powerful, even if they were created out of imagination and magic. If only the Magnifica could be finished, then all of Ishara would have a central protective deity of such might—under his stewardship, of course—that no force in the world could hope to stand against. Which was why Empra Iluris had good reason to be concerned. Klovus was sure he could control the godling, no matter how powerful it became. . . .

Xion willingly relinquished his role, and Klovus spoke to the audience in the harbor temple. "Your godling rejoices in your devotion. He caused great harm to our godless enemies across the sea, and now he is home to guard Serepol Harbor—so long as you continue to believe."

Behind the spelldoor, the godling radiated contentment, and Klovus could feel its warm glow.

"Hear us, save us!" the crowd chanted.

After all the sacrifices had been received, Klovus blessed the crowds and sent them away, then he also dismissed the local ur-priest. "I require your temple this evening, ur-priest. You may go. See that we are not disturbed."

Xion looked protective and uneasy, glancing at the spelldoor as if worried that Klovus would take his godling away again, but the key priestlord made an impatient gesture. "No, that is not our business tonight. Your godling will remain undisturbed."

Relieved, Xion bowed. "Thank you, Key Priestlord. Thank you for this honor. My temple is yours. Hear us, save us."

"Yes, yes. Hear us, save us."

When the temple was finally empty and full night had fallen, Klovus issued instructions to his trusted deputies. They opened the hidden doors and prepared the thick-walled lower chambers, which he had often used during the time he had served as ur-priest here. They lit torches and cleared the musty room for the real meeting.

When Klovus had sent his summons across Ishara, the other twelve priestlords could not refuse to attend. He gave them enough time to travel from the other districts, and they arrived in Serepol as discreetly as possible.

After dark, the twelve priestlords came in disguise to the harbor temple, where they were ushered down into the underground chamber. Small braziers burned in the corners, sending curls of sweet-smelling stimsmoke into the room.

Klovus greeted each guest as they removed their drab coverings. A tall priestlord with a high forehead and a deeply seamed face looked out of sorts as he entered. Klovus said, "Priestlord Dovic, thank you for coming. You came a long way from Sistralta."

Dovic drew his brows together. "An incredibly long journey. The roads were miserable—a muddy quagmire through the entire Janhari District. The food was poor, and my body aches." As if suddenly remembering to whom he was speaking, he gave a quick polite nod. "It is always an honor to come to Serepol, Key Priestlord, especially if you summon us."

Klovus hid the twinkle of anticipation in his eye as he spoke with the man. "Someday I'll return the favor and make a pilgrimage to your district. Though Sistralta is far away, I hear your godling is powerful."

"It has to be," said Dovic. "Because of our grass hills and muddy valleys, we face frequent fires and floods, and thus our godling is often called upon to defend us." He glanced meaningfully at the two plump, contented-looking priestlords from Tarizah and Rassah, districts that faced few threats.

The priestlords talked among themselves, and tension pervaded the air as the men and women speculated about why Klovus had called them. Finally, the last priestlord arrived, a stern woman named Neré from Tamburdin

District, which was on the edge of the unexplored territories. "I have greater concerns than meetings or social gatherings," she said, arranging her tight braids on her shoulders. "The barbarian Hethrren have attacked us several times, and our walls can barely hold them back."

Klovus frowned, stating the obvious answer. "You are a priestlord. Use your godling and annihilate them."

The hard woman looked away. "The more angry and desperate my people become, the stronger and more vicious our godling grows. It strains against my control. I'm concerned that if I unleashed it in this state . . ."

Klovus snorted. "Any priestlord who cannot control a godling is not worthy of the title. Learn to guide your people's sacrifices and prayers so that the godling does what *you* want it to." He insisted that she take her seat at the long table, so that he could start the meeting. "I called you all here because we need to consider Empra Iluris and the future of Ishara. I fear she grows more intractable."

The dozen priestlords muttered, nodding and frowning. Adas, priestlord of Ishiki, said, "We heard her ridiculous proclamation about looking for a successor, as if it's a game. She wants to make a mockery of our traditions?"

"Thankfully, we priestlords can keep Ishara stable," said the Janhari priestlord, a brown-skinned old man.

The frail Mormosa priestlord let out a deprecating cackle. "Since she's looking far and wide for her successor, Klovus, I take it that the empra declined your offer of marriage?"

Other priestlords covered their snickers, and his cheeks burned. "It was never a romantic overture, but rather a business proposition. Iluris is stubborn and refuses to see reason. Therefore, we must find an alternate course of action."

Hurried footsteps whisked down the stone stairs through the secret passage from above. A tall man entered, disguised in the unmarked robes of a midlevel priest. He had a high forehead and deep wrinkles etched into his long face. He was out of breath, flustered. "My apologies, Priestlord Klovus. I only just arrived from Sistralta." The other priestlords looked up in surprise, and the newcomer gazed curiously at each of them. "I was delayed in travel. It is a very long trip across muddy roads."

The newcomer stopped abruptly when he saw a man identical to himself seated at his assigned place at the table. "What is this?"

The other priestlords muttered in confusion.

"You see?" Klovus looked from the seated Priestlord Dovic to smile at the standing, newly arrived Dovic. "The first part of our demonstration is a success."

The seated Dovic's shoulders straightened and his face bunched. His skin crawled as if all his facial muscles were spasming at once. His brow sloped and shrank, the color of his hair darkened until it became blue-black. The lines in his long face smoothed over, and his chin retracted.

"Remarkable!" Klovus turned to the surprised priestlords. "Allow me to introduce Zaha, the current champion among my Black Eels. They have been practicing camouflage magic."

The real Dovic stared, aghast. "He looked exactly like me."

Once Zaha reverted to his normal appearance, he rose from the chair. "Priestlord Dovic, you may have your seat."

"The Black Eels can change the color of their hair, the tone of their skin," Klovus explained. "They can adjust their muscles and take on new features using actual manipulation of flesh in conjunction with a hint of a glamour spell. If trained well enough, my Black Eels can look exactly like anyone they wish to be." He smiled. "Which could prove a very useful skill indeed."

Several of the twelve guests were disturbed, but some were clearly excited. "How can we use this?" asked the Prirari priestlord.

"That depends on Empra Iluris. She has been given every opportunity to strengthen the godlings—not just the primary godlings but the smaller local entities as well. Our people must continue to believe, because that is what feeds our power. That is what makes Ishara strong."

"And if the empra's wishes don't align with ours?" asked the Rassah priestlord. "Should we wait for her successor, since she has already begun her search?"

"We *could* wait and hope for the best." Klovus looked at the Black Eel champion, who stood imposing and completely silent. "Or, we could consider more immediate options."

30

THE sandwreths headed back to the Furnace across the stark outer desert. The soft open sand slowed the pace of their augas, but on rocky ground their wide, three-toed feet were quite nimble. With wreth magic, the sturdy reptile mounts had been bred to the desert wastes, the perfect creatures for travel across the desolation.

Queen Voo was intrigued by her encounter with the humans, their quaint king and their walled city. After hearing reports from her scouts, she had been eager to see for herself what they had done. It seemed impossible that the wreths' orphaned creations had built cities and farmlands across what had once been vast battlefields. Not only had those poor creatures survived the apocalypse, but their independence and ambition came as quite a surprise. Voo had not guessed that the lowly humans possessed such determination, but perhaps they only needed incentive, a trial by fire.

She mused aloud as the augas plodded along, "When we created humans, maybe we added more strength than we realized."

The wreth party passed among misshapen pinnacles of rock. Her brother rode beside her, holding the leather reins from his auga's wide muzzle. "Is that why you took so many human lovers before the end of the war?"

Voo's face pinched. "That was for no reason but entertainment, and the entertainment was paltry. Surely I took no more than ten or fifteen of them into my bed. It has been so long, I cannot recall."

"I found their women worthwhile, as something different," Quo admitted. "I do not know if I ever had any children by them. I paid no attention."

"Humans were created for a purpose, and they served it. Now we must start over, and there is very little magic left in the land. We have to rely on the humans that remain." As the augas passed under the shadow of a rock pinnacle, she blinked up at the sun. "They may be useful again."

"What if they do not want to ally with us, my queen?" asked her primary mage Axus, a tall, thin wreth with a grayish complexion, large eyes, and hairless skin. His brown leather robe hung on him like a shed skin.

"Then they are fools. They will be crushed between our army and the frostwreths either way." Her thin lips quirked in a smile. "Choosing to be our partners in the coming war is a much better option for them. We can always force them."

"And we have in the past," Axus said. "We do not need their cooperation, but you are making the process more convoluted than is necessary, as we have already proved."

"I enjoy it, and the end result will be the same." As her auga moved along, Voo imagined shapes in the lumpy hoodoos. "This conflict has lasted since the dawn of our time, since the split between Raan and Suth." Her voice dropped to a husky whisper. "We remember what started it all."

She pulled her auga to a halt and held out her left hand. She pictured an image in her mind, sketched in the air with her pointed nails, and the changes manifested on one of the prominent hoodoos. Rock chips flew away and red dust skittered into the air as she reshaped the pinnacle into the face of a beautiful woman. "Raan, the wronged party . . . the reason for our war, and the reason why Kur abandoned us."

Her brother leaned back and watched critically. "How can you be sure that is what Raan really looked like?"

"It is how she should have looked." Voo sketched in the air again, manipulating a stunted hoodoo until a second female face appeared, nearly as beautiful as Raan, though with a sneer on her stone expression. "No one ever said that Suth was not also lovely. Kur chose the sisters for their beauty, after all, but we know that Suth was twisted and ugly inside. Her black heart was plain in what she did to Raan and the poor child that could have changed the world."

With an offhanded burst of magic, Voo shattered Suth's face. Shards of rock crumbled into dust and debris. She turned to Quo and asked in a surprisingly vulnerable voice, "When Kur comes back, do you think he will find me as beautiful as Raan?"

"I cannot speak to the tastes of a god," said Quo with a frown, "and one should never ask a brother how desirable he finds his sister."

The augas swiftly crossed the outer desert, creating dust devils in their wake. As she rode, Voo thought through what the sandwreths needed to do before Kur would return to save them. They had a world to save, and to destroy.

Ages ago, when Kur manifested himself as a magnificent man among the wreths, he seduced the beautiful Suth, but eventually found her younger sister Raan even more desirable. When Suth became angry and jealous, Kur responded, "Are you not both my creations? I love and care for you all. Do not make a god choose."

Raan became pregnant with Kur's child, even though Suth had been his lover for a longer time. Unable to control her poisonous envy, Suth saw the dragon moving in the night, the personified evil and wickedness, all the inner darkness that Kur had purged from himself. The very presence of Ossus corrupted the evil Suth, twisted her.

In secret, she gave her sister a poison that nearly killed her and did make her lose the baby—who was half wreth, half god. Raan survived the ordeal, and when she discovered that her own sister was responsible, she commanded her warriors to kill Suth in vengeance, and the great battles began.

When Kur heard that his unborn child was dead and the two sisters were trying to kill each other, his rage became uncontrollable. Even though he had tried to make himself perfect, the dragon was too strong here. Kur appeared before Suth and Raan as a towering angry visage. He told them he would remake the world and correct his mistakes, but he commanded the wreths to destroy Ossus first, thus erasing all evil and violence. Only after the dragon was killed would he save any wreths who proved themselves worthy. Then he vanished. . . .

They had succeeded in wounding the dragon and driving him deep underground, as well as devastating the land and nearly destroying their race. Now, Voo vowed to lead her sandwreths, the descendants of Raan's people, to victory over the evil descendants of Suth.

Riding fast, their party entered the outskirts of the Furnace. They passed the shadowed canyons of the ever-growing camps, fenced-in clusters of squalid homes. Most of the arid wasteland was uninhabitable, but with the last tatters of magic, Voo and her wreths could make any place habitable. She would need vast numbers of workers and fighters to sweep across the land that humans had tended for them as stewards. It remained to be seen whether King Adan Starfall would decide to cooperate.

During the long war, wreth armies had an inexhaustible workforce of humans, for they could simply create more of them whenever they chose to. The endless battles had broken and drained the land itself, yet they had only succeeded in wounding the titanic dragon.

Voo's ancestor Rao had fought Ossus, cornering the great beast while a contingent of frostwreths also attacked the dragon. Badly hurt in their bloody battle, Ossus had crawled deep underground to hide and heal, rippling the landscape into the sharp mountain range called the Dragonspine.

But wounding the dragon had not achieved their goal. Ossus needed to be killed, and the frostwreths had to be destroyed, so that Kur would take the sandwreths with him to the new perfect world he would create afterward.

Ahead, Voo saw the giant fortress of sand and stone her wreths had sculpted. Peering into the shimmering heat, she admired its smooth towers, high walls, and spiky crystalline crenellations.

Amused by her thoughts of history and legend, she let her creative magic flow and fused hunks of sand into an image of the dragon that shifted, then faded into crumbling grains. Beside her, Axus also participated, fashioning sand figures of wreth armies, making them clash against each other in slow powdery engagements. Then, with a sweep of his hand, the mage wiped them all out.

Voo gathered sand again, depicting the final face-off between herself and Queen Onn, with sandwreth armies butchering frostwreth armies in the surrounding mountains. Voo and Onn had already dueled among the crags of the Dragonspine, queen against queen. Swinging her sword, Onn had chopped off a length of Voo's golden hair, and Voo had retaliated, slashing the frostwreth queen's face. As the battle intensified, the two women—and their armies—nearly wiped each other out.

Her force decimated, Voo's soldiers had dragged her away from the remaining wounded frostwreths, while her mages raised a powerful barrier so they could fall back and take their queen to safety. Both sides had retreated in tatters, exhausted at the end of the war.

Only a handful of surviving human workers had huddled in hiding places, where Voo had expected them to starve or die of exposure. Retreating to the seared deserts, she and her armies had placed themselves into cycles of spellsleep for centuries, leaving only a few sentinel wreths to keep track of the world.

Now Voo had awakened for the last time. She was ready to fight.

With a sneer, she flung out one arm in a slicing gesture, and all of the sand figures were not only flattened, but turned into a sheet of hot glass in the desert.

"That is what we will do to the rest of the world when we succeed, level it and start over," she said. "Then Kur will finally come back for us."

31

⤫

THE Scrabbleton mines smelled of sulfur, and Elliel sweated as she swung her pick and cleared the rubble. She had burrowed through hundreds of feet of solid rock, following veins of useful ores, precious metals, and unexpected gems. It was honest, hard work, requiring just enough concentration that her mind didn't wander to dangerous thoughts.

A person without a memory had time to create a new legacy. In this mining town, she wasn't likely to accomplish great deeds, but did every person need to be a hero or leave an epic life story? Wasn't it possible just to be a normal, quiet person with a quiet life? Her days were peaceful, if unremarkable. She had a room at the inn, a meal every night, and she knew what the next day would bring. That was enough. She didn't need to be a fearsome Brava warrior—just Elliel.

Because of her accidental find of dragonblood rubies, other miners now wanted to work near her, hoping for more of her luck. Klenner, one of her usual mining partners, was at home recovering after an unexpected rockfall smashed his left hand. In his place, a young man named Jandre had joined her and Upwin in the tunnels.

"I heard a story about Bravas," Jandre said loudly enough to be heard over the sound of picks and shovels. "Two wealthy noblemen each had a bonded Brava, and each one thought his was stronger, so they challenged their men to fight." He swiped perspiration from his forehead. "Do you know this one, Elliel?"

"I don't know many stories about Bravas at all," she said, hoping he wouldn't keep talking.

Undeterred, Jandre continued, "The nobles placed high wagers. In the town square, the two Bravas fought each other, hand-to-hand, for hours. The crowds grew. More wagers were made. The Bravas inflicted terrible damage on each other, but they used their wreth magic to minimize the injuries. Can you work healing magic, Elliel?"

"Never tried. I try to avoid serious injuries in the first place."

"The Bravas fought for a full day, with their nobles growing more and more agitated, wagering larger sums as the day wore on. Finally the opponents stopped, battered and bloody, and held each other up. Instead of fighting, they faced the crowd and spat blood. 'Bravas will fight to defend the Commonwealth,' one said. 'Bravas will give their lives to defend the konag and the people,' said the other. 'But we are done fighting for your amusement.'" Jandre grinned in the lantern light. "Both Bravas broke their bond to the nobles that day, claiming a higher code of honor, and they walked away, supporting each other."

Elliel broke away more rock. "A good story." At one time, the tale might have resonated with her, but now it was just a distant story.

"Do you think it's true, though?" Jandre pressed.

"Who am I to judge what is true or what isn't? I am no longer a Brava." She moved her lantern closer to see the distinctive greenish-brown smear that indicated copper ore. "This is what I know to be true: If we work together we can fill a cartload with this ore and send it back out."

The two miners came to help with the digging, carrying lanterns that spilled bobbing circles of light in the tunnels. Elliel struck the wall with her pick, loosened chunks of ore, and knocked the rubble to the floor. Upwin and Jandre shoveled it into a wheelbarrow.

With her next blow, though, a large section of the wall fell away with surprising ease, revealing an unexpected empty pocket. Grabbing her lantern, she shone it inside, and the light reflected back at her with startling intensity, sparkling from a forest of quartz crystals that lined the curved wall of a small, hidden chamber. What a strange discovery.

Upwin shouldered up close. "You found the unexpected again, Elliel."

Jandre grinned. "That's why I wanted to work with her, though I was hoping for rubies instead."

The men shoveled away the rubble while Elliel widened the gap with her pick. After more of the wall crumbled, she reached inside to pull out a handful of milky-white crystals. "Pretty. Are they valuable?"

"Just quartz."

"Sometimes mothertears are found with quartz," Jandre suggested. The eager young man picked up one of the heavy buckets of rock. "We're all working together. If you strike any spurting red liquid, like when you found the dragonblood, we split the bonus, right?"

"As you wish." Elliel had no objection to sharing. In fact, she had found that, despite her independent nature, the quiet sharing of work or reward brought her a faint feeling of pleasure. Jandre trudged back down the tunnel while Elliel enlarged the opening to the quartz-lined hollow.

She sensed the rumble building in the mountain before she heard it. Her lantern's candle flickered as an errant breeze whispered through the wide crack she had just exposed. Instantly alert, Upwin set down his pick. "Tremors again!"

The shouts of frightened miners and the clatter of dropped tools came from adjacent tunnels. The floor shook, and powder dusted down from the ceiling. Upwin grabbed his lantern and turned to run.

A severe shock split the wall in front of Elliel, and quartz crystals tumbled out like glittering projectiles. Part of the ceiling collapsed, and a boulder crashed down, but she dodged it as her lightning-fast Brava reflexes took over.

The sound inside the mountain grew until it was as loud as the roar of a waking dragon. Steam hissed through new cracks in the walls. What if Ossus was indeed digging himself out from under the mountains?

Elliel braced herself and searched for a way out. They were so deep inside Mount Vada that even at a dead run, she wouldn't be able to make it to the surface fast enough. Upwin bolted up the passageway, and farther along the tunnel, Jandre screamed and his lantern winked out as tons of rock fell, crushing the young miner.

Great slabs of the wall in front of her collapsed inward to reveal a small natural cavern encrusted with crystals, and the room held more than quartz. She now saw metallic ribs—*artificial* ribs—in reinforcing arcs that held up the rock walls and curved ceiling. Hoping for better shelter, Elliel leaned into the small chamber as rocks fell around her. Her lantern's glow ricocheted off the angled facets of quartz.

Inside, she was astonished to see a tall, pale man tucked in among the crystals, as if embedded in the quartz. He stood motionless, either asleep or dead. He had strange features, a wide face and large almond eyes, a mane of dark hair, and gray garments that camouflaged him against the quartz.

The metal support girders bent and groaned. The crystal ceiling cracked, and shards rained down. The stranger began to slump forward, released from whatever bonds had held him in place. A boulder slid down, breaking his femur like a stick of wood, and tumbling quartz crystals tore his skin.

Dropping her lantern, Elliel scrambled toward the mysterious man, instinctively trying to save him. Maybe it was her subconscious Brava instinct. When she extricated the man from the debris, he was bleeding, and he stirred—alive and in pain! He blinked his large eyes, and a low groan came from his lips as she shoved the rock aside to free his broken leg. She *had* to help him. She draped the man's arm over her shoulders and dragged him backward into the main tunnel, although that offered no safety either. The rumbling and crashing continued.

Holding him up in spite of his broken leg, Elliel pulled the stranger along with her, but the exit was impossibly far away. The tremors continued. Rocks pattered from the ceiling, and yawning cracks spread along the tunnels. As she staggered along, the stranger tried to help with his good leg, but his efforts supported little of his weight.

She could see an intersection ahead. Two miners ran up the tunnel yelling, their own lanterns like dancing lights. "Wait!" she shouted. "I need help!"

But they didn't wait. No one would survive if they didn't get out before the tunnels crumbled. Dragging the stranger along and dodging rubble, she came upon Jandre's crushed body. Seeing the dead miner kindled an even greater urgency to get this stranger out—and to save both of their lives.

The wider tunnels were braced with wooden timbers, which meant she was not far from the exit. The rumbling had gone on for minutes now. She pressed on, somehow finding incredible strength.

The dark-haired stranger gasped, clinging to her. He opened his eyes blearily, and couldn't fathom where he was.

With one final aftershock and a loud, grinding groan, the ceiling broke and rocks began to slide down in front of them. Elliel put on a burst of speed, running toward the collapse. Though she knew they would likely be buried in it or trapped behind it, she could see no other way out. Their escape would be entirely blocked.

But as the ceiling fell, the stranger moaned, and she felt a tingle through his skin. The air glowed in front of her eyes, and an invisible force shoved aside the falling rocks, leaving a narrow path clear for them.

Elliel didn't question what had happened. She ran onward, pulling him into the outer tunnels, where panicked miners continued to run for the entrances. Like a miracle, she saw blessed sunlight ahead, though it was hazed by rock dust and steam that gasped out of the shafts. Elliel realized she was crying.

Not giving up, she pulled the man along, and he clung to her. Her throat burned from the effort, from the sulfur fumes, from the dust. She struggled out into the daylight and felt a warm satisfaction to know that she had saved this exotic stranger, whoever or whatever he was.

32

So that King Adan could reach Norterra as swiftly as possible, Shella din Orr offered five well-traveled Utauks to guide him out of the wilderness. The hearty tribesmen found a much shorter, and more private, route than the main road.

When they finally came within view of the walled city of Fellstaff several days later, the Utauks bade him farewell, and Adan rode ahead alone. Sensing an ominous undertone in the air and a brooding gray chill across the sky, he thought of Queen Voo's warning about the frostwreths. He hoped he had arrived in time.

Troubled workers toiled on either side of the main road outside the city, adding barricades even as the dusk darkened. Stonecutters hauled wagons of rocks and scavenged building blocks to fortify the outer walls. Trenchers dug deep to expand the defensive moats. Adan felt a chill. His uncle was obviously making military preparations.

Once past the gate and riding through the streets of Fellstaff, he saw numerous black banners hung from the chiseled stone walls. The remembrance shrine, the bell tower, and the castle itself in the middle of the city seemed to be draped in mourning. Lanterns were lit in the streets as the dusk deepened. He slowed his horse to a walk, pulled the Utauk travel cloak around his shoulders, and inhaled the sharp chill in the air. No one recognized him as the king of Suderra, since he wore common riding clothes.

As he brought his horse up to the castle entry, which was also draped in black, he faced a pair of guards standing in wary welcome. They wore leather chest armor, mail hauberks, and greaves. Each man held an ash spear with a jagged iron tip. Such weapons were mostly considered ceremonial, but they looked deadly now. The two men greeted him with flinty, challenging expressions. "You arrive late in the day, sir. We're about to close the castle gates for the night."

"Then I have arrived just in time. I am King Adan Starfall from Suderra, and I need to see my uncle on urgent business."

The guards were surprised, but not shocked. One of them was obviously relieved. "Aye, I think he'll be glad to see you. We may need Suderra's help."

The other said, "Is the south in danger as well, Sire? Terrible changes around here. Tragedies." He shook his head.

Adan felt a greater urgency and dread. "Take me to Kollanan. Quickly!"

Inside the castle, black window coverings filled the chambers with unnecessary shadows. Torches burned in holders on the walls, and the smells of pitch and smoke were not comforting.

His larger-than-life uncle met him in his private study, where his famous war hammer hung above the mantel. Kollanan rose to greet his visitor. "Adan Starfall, how I wish I were seeing you under other circumstances." His normally neat beard looked unkempt, his gray-streaked hair disheveled, his eyes haunted. He wrapped Adan in a surprising bear hug. "Young nephew, I'm glad you came. How did you know?"

When he squeezed back, Adan could feel the weariness and weight that filled his uncle's bones. His voice came out hoarse. "I come with news of my own, Uncle. I fear neither of us will take much joy in each other's stories."

"No joy," said a woman's slightly accented voice. "And great danger for all of us."

Queen Tafira was seated in a high-backed chair facing the fire. Long gray skirts hung down to her slippered feet, and her hair was tied back in a black ribbon. "Our daughter and her family are dead, our two sweet grandsons murdered. . . ."

"The entire town of Lake Bakal is wiped out," Koll added in a harsh voice. "I can't believe I am saying this, but we are being attacked by an enemy from legends. I've seen them with my own eyes."

"I know." Adan looked deep into his uncle's gray eyes. "The wreths."

Koll looked as if he had been struck with his own hammer. "How do you know about the wreths? They came out of the north, white and deadly. They engulfed an entire town, people we knew. Our poor . . ."

Adan spoke into the sad silence. "Down in Suderra, wreths came from the desert wastelands, but they didn't attack us. Their queen warned me of a great war to come, and she said that the Commonwealth would be caught between a hammer and an anvil. She told us the frostwreths would be coming from the north, and I rode hard to warn you." He looked away. "I'm too late."

"Too late for our daughter," said Kollanan, "but this is just beginning. We're preparing defenses across the kingdom, and I sent a letter to Conndur, asking him to rally the entire Commonwealth army. My eight vassal lords are building fortifications, learning how to get ready for war again after all these centuries."

For the next day, Adan, King Kollanan, and the Brava Lasis discussed strategy and defenses. They decided to head north, swiftly and discreetly. Koll wanted them to see firsthand what the frostwreths had done to Lake Bakal.

The three men rode hard through golden forests of aspens and birches, but within a day the surrounding trees were skeletal and bare. They saw no travelers at all. Villagers, woodcutters, huntsmen, and traders seemed to be avoiding the road, or maybe they had all been killed.

Sitting astride his black warhorse Storm, Koll squinted ahead through naked trees interspersed with thick silver pines. "I wonder how many other settlements have been emptied or destroyed. The frostwreths might have spread widely already."

The air held such a biting chill that the horses snorted steam and Adan hunched under a heavy cloak of bear fur that Kollanan had given him for the ride. He said, "Suderra is always warm and dry. I'm not accustomed to this."

"None of us is," said Kollanan, nudging the horse forward. "It will get worse just up ahead when we see Lake Bakal."

Lasis sat tall in the saddle, his black finemail cloak hanging from his shoulders. His hand touched the ramer at his side. "And when we see the wreths."

Koll gestured with a gloved hand to where the road wound up to a high point. "Tafira and I always looked forward to crossing that ridge when we came to visit our grandsons. From there, Lake Bakal is a glorious sight, deep blue water surrounded by thick silver pines, and the town on the shore, fishing boats on the water."

As the horses topped the rise, Adan took in the expansive view of the lake, above which swirled a gauze of white wind. The deep waters were gray as metal. The boats were gone, crushed and frozen into the ice. The mountains beyond were barely visible due to blowing snow in the distance.

"Ancestors' blood," Koll muttered. "That fortress is entirely new."

On the shore of Lake Bakal rose an enormous structure of stone and ice. Blocky defensive walls, support arches, and unfinished towers loomed high. Work crews moved about like ants, and even from this distance Adan could see that they weren't human. Some of the wreths used magic, cutting ice from the lake, moving huge blocks of stone, dragging fresh pine logs. A large section of the lakeshore had already been denuded of trees.

"That fortress covers much of the old town." Koll glowered, not bothering to hide his anger and disgust. The muscles on the side of his jaw bunched. "The wreths told me that we were in the way. They said they could take whatever they wanted—and now they've done so." He exhaled loudly, and steam curled from his mouth. "I will not let myself be swept aside because they decide I am *in the way*!"

Lasis fixed his gaze on the construction site, as if calculating how many wreths he could slaughter if he ignited his ramer and charged in among them, but he came to his senses. "We will have to gather a vast army to drive them out. We can push them back."

"I wouldn't even begin to know how to fight them," Adan said, "no matter the size of our army."

As they stared at the wreth fortress, Storm snorted. They heard rustling branches, a crunching of snow behind them. The three men whirled to see movement in the underbrush, an elusive figure scuttling for shelter. It was a scrawny human dressed in rags and furs, with matted hair.

Kollanan called out. "We won't hurt you!"

"Unless it's a wreth spy," Lasis said as he lurched after the figure. "What if we've been seen?"

The rustling in the frozen scrub oak stopped. "I'm not a spy, and I hate the wreths!"

Koll turned Storm about. "Come out and show yourself. I'm your king, Kollanan the Hammer. If you're from Norterra, then you know me."

Lasis snatched a gangly young man out of the underbrush. He couldn't have been more than sixteen years old. "I know my king!" the boy squeaked. "You're Lady Jhaqi's father. I did some work for town leader Gannon."

Koll felt heartsick. "You were from Lake Bakal?"

Adan swung down off his mount, took off his heavy bear-fur cloak, and wrapped it around the miserable young man. "He looks freezing—and starving."

"B-both," the young man said. He shivered. "And my face is dirty, too."

"What's your name?" Koll asked.

"Pokle. I was out here when the blizzard wall came. I saw the frostwreths, I saw the lake freeze." He gasped.

Koll said, "Keep your voice down, boy. Tell us what happened." The Brava led the group deeper into the shelter of trees on the ridge.

"I set my rabbit traps all around the lake, but that day I was just . . . just fishing, sitting on the rocks. I had two lines in the water, one pole in my hand, the other propped up between the boulders." He pulled Adan's furs tighter around him. "I thought the gray sky looked like snow, but not like any blizzard I've ever seen. I saw the wave come in, air so cold it shattered the trees. Wind and snow blowing, howling! Then the lake began to freeze, spreading from the opposite shore. It was solid ice!" He turned to Adan with a desperate edge in his voice. "I swear I saw it! Solid ice that spread across the lake, moving as fast as fire on dry grass."

Pokle seemed surprised that nobody questioned his fantastic story. "I scrambled away from the lakeshore just in time, and the ice froze my fishing lines solid. Then the snow came. I ducked into the bushes and felt the cold roaring around me. I huddled for hours, and when I climbed back out, uh—" His voice hitched. "The town was frozen. I never saw magic like that before!"

"And you've been hiding here since then?" Koll asked.

"I couldn't go back home!" Pokle cried. "What was I going to do? I went to my traps and found three rabbits. I had enough to eat, and I used their fur to make hand coverings." He held up his hands, which were wrapped in warm scraps. "It was a nice autumn day when it all started—I wasn't dressed for cold like this."

Lasis regarded him curiously. "Why did you stay? With the town and the lake frozen and everyone gone, why didn't you make your way to the road? Head south to Fellstaff, or at least one of the villages?"

The boy glanced around wildly. "There are frostwreths here! They slip through the forests, and they're always watching! How did I know the wreths hadn't frozen the entire world? I found a hunter's shack where I could keep warm, and I hid there. I was afraid to go out into the open. And then I saw you." He looked from one king to the other, and a glimmer of hope lit his expression. "Did you come to fight the wreths? Are you going to drive them away?"

"I don't know yet, lad," Koll said. "But we'll find a way. This is my kingdom, and I promise I'll keep you safe. Come back with us, where it's warm."

The boy was shuddering. "Yes, please. I think . . . I think I've had enough of this place."

Adan interrupted, "This fight goes beyond just our two kingdoms. The Commonwealth is at stake. I wrote to the konag already—"

"I wrote to my brother, too, but a written message will not convey the danger of the wreths." Koll looked at him. "You and I must go see Conndur in person, Nephew. We have to make him understand how urgent this is."

33

AFTER the Utauk tribal gathering, Hale Orr rode hard toward the coast of Osterra, where he hoped to find a ship. His overland ride was exhilarating and exhausting, but he felt the extra weight he had put on during his quieter—yes, lazier—life since his daughter had married Starfall. He had meant to retire from the nomadic life and watch Penda thrive alongside her husband. Now he had his own adventure.

Dressed in colorful silks and riding a horse with a saddle studded with brass circles, Hale looked like any other trader, but the Utauks in Windyhead, the southernmost Osterran port, recognized him for who he was. The crimson and black and the family symbol on his leathers told others that he was a grandson of Shella din Orr.

Walking out onto Windyhead's longest pier, he waved to the crew of a two-masted trading ship, the *Glissand*. They were busy inventorying their goods: leather hides and fur pelts, packages of dried winterberries wrapped in oilcloth, small chests of dragonblood rubies and saltpearls.

He spoke with the voyagier, a man named Mak Dur, who gave him a bow of respect. "We would be pleased to have you aboard, Hale Orr. If you join us, I'll name you merchant captain."

"*Cra*, it's been a long time since anyone called me that! I accept your offer, Mak Dur." Hale traced a circle in the air, and the voyagier responded in kind. As merchant captain, Hale would not command the *Glissand*, nor manage the crew—that part remained under the purview of the voyagier, who was the real captain—but he did choose their destination. "Put on extra food and water because we have a long voyage. Instead of heading up the coast, we'll turn east to the open sea. Our first stop will be Fulcor Island."

Mak Dur's eyes lit up. "Ah, the watch station is due to be resupplied, and we are always paid well by the konag to support them."

"But we will only pause there briefly." After a moment, Hale continued, "I intend for us to sail the rest of the way to Ishara. I have important questions to ask in Serepol."

The crew muttered in surprise. They were not afraid to trade with the distant continent, but this meant they would be longer away from home.

"Yes, that will be more profitable for us," the voyagier pointed out. "I've had a crate of shadowglass packed in the hold for two months, but no priestlords to sell it to. This is a perfect opportunity."

Shards of the strange black material were harvested from ancient wreth battlefields. Hale himself wore a tiny chip of shadowglass in an ear pendant. Isharan priestlords paid extremely high prices for the substance, which allowed them to view their godlings.

The next day, the *Glissand* sailed off from Windyhead with the villagers waving farewell. Utauk trading vessels were distinctive in design, with a wide-beamed hull, riding low in the water, and two masts with tan sails painted with a large circle.

The open sea and bright sunshine were invigorating, and Hale Orr drew a deep breath of the clean air until he felt his lungs would burst. They headed toward Fulcor Island, a large bastion of rock at a strategic point halfway between the two continents. Fulcor was currently held by the Commonwealth, but over the course of history, control of the stone-walled fortress had shifted again and again like the marker ribbon in a rope-pulling contest.

The Utauk tribes had always been neutral, willing to trade with the three kingdoms and with Ishara, but remained loyal to their own way of life. Other than its strategic importance, Fulcor Island was of little commercial interest, except for the fact that the garrison's isolation made the soldiers eager customers. Commonwealth ships brought basic supplies as needed, while Utauk traders delivered other amenities, reminders of home, and they were always welcome.

Hale faced the wind and let himself be lulled by the deceptive peace while he considered the dangerous reports from the Utauk network, as well as the unsettling arrival of the sandwreths. Isharans had their own magic, with godlings and priestlords. As far as he knew, wreths had never been part of Ishara, so it seemed unlikely they would have seen any sign of the ancient race on their shores, but he had to know what the Isharans were likely to do if an unexpected conflict broke out in distant Suderra. Given the stories of coastal raids, Hale feared that the Isharans might be gearing up for war, too.

They held a historic grudge against the old world and wanted to strike back, which would be nonsensical and destructive to both sides.

For more than a millennium, the wandering Utauk tribes had laid down a safety net of commerce, trading among all villages and towns and fostering the need for imported goods. Barely noticed, the ubiquitous traders knitted the fabric of dependencies together. Utauk ships filed no voyage plan and did not present their logs to any harbormaster on either continent, but they brought goods back and forth. It was the best way to promote peace between Ishara and the Commonwealth.

Hale had no idea how to calculate the cost of a war with the wreths, though.

Two days into their voyage, the lookout spotted the gray outcropping of Fulcor Island ahead. It rose like a mountain from the water, surrounded by churning foam that marked reefs extending like claws around the fortress.

Mak Dur consulted his charts, licked his finger, and thrust it into the air to caress the wind. "Exactly where we want to be." He handed Hale a spyglass tube filled with focusing oil. With his good hand, Hale placed it against his eye and fumbled to adjust the runes. The twisting curls of oil brought the distant island into clear focus.

Fulcor looked stark and uninviting. Other than fresh water, the island had few resources. Its value was primarily strategic because of its location between the two continents. The sheer cliffs merged into the gray stone wall of the squat and forbidding fortress. Even at high tide, waves foamed around the reefs, adding an extra angry line of defense.

The voyagier took back the focusing glass. "We are approaching from the southwest, so we'll have to sail around. There's only one narrow, defensible harbor cove enclosed by high cliffs, which is on the north end. The reefs are more dangerous on this side." Mak Dur frowned. "There have been recent Isharan coastal raids, so most Utauk trading ships stay close to the Commonwealth shores. We haven't been out this far in months."

Still watching the island, Hale gasped and stepped closer to the rail, as if those few feet would make a difference in what he saw. "*Cra*, look—those are people! Over the cliff!"

Extending his good hand, he took the focusing glass back from the voyagier and turned it toward the fortress. Black specks plunged from the high stone walls, flailing figures too large to be swooping seabirds. There were men and women tumbling from the fortress wall, either jumping or being hurled down into the gnashing water around the reefs.

"Three more!" Hale kept staring, adjusting the optic oil. "Why are they jumping?" Four more bodies went over the wall and fell to their deaths. The swirling currents would quickly wash them away, leaving no bodies for anyone to see. No evidence.

The voyagier grew serious and took the lens back. "Do we keep going? Is there a threat to us?"

Hale spoke with confidence that he hoped was justified. "We are Utauks, and we bring much-needed goods. We are always safe." He paused, then added quietly, "*Cra,* we have to go there and learn what we can. Something is happening here." He unconsciously lifted one finger to make the sign of a circle in the air.

While Mak Dur adjusted course, the sailors extended the tan canvas to make sure their Utauk circle was visible, so the *Glissand* wouldn't be attacked by any Fulcor naval vessels. Their course avoided the danger of the reefs and took them away from the bloodstains in the water.

34

As the wagon procession moved down the wide imperial road, jouncing over hard ruts, Empra Iluris rocked with the motion of her carriage. The high wheels seemed to magnify the bumps in the road, despite her plump cushions.

The empra's procession across the districts of Ishara was led by Captani Vos and twenty uniformed hawk guards in polished helmets and red silk capes marked with the coat of arms of her family, *their* family. Her newest adopted guards, Cyril, Boro, and Nedd, had joined the company, and Iluris saw the warm expressions on their faces. She believed that kindness and generosity were the surest way to earn loyalty. Fear also worked, though it was a far less certain method.

The priestlords and their godlings drew strength from the faith of the people, but the people loved and revered their empra as well. As she traveled among them, she realized that as ruler she drew a certain kind of magic from the land as well.

Iluris sat back in the carriage and watched the countryside roll by. Behind her, she could hear the clop of hooves, the rattle of wheels, and the jingle of fine decorative bells that sounded like a delicate rain of metal. Supply wagons and two other passenger carriages rolled farther down the line.

On their way to the town of Olbo in the Dhabban District, Iluris took advantage of the blessed hours of silence to contemplate her own thoughts, rather than listen to Priestlord Klovus. Because she had invited him to join the procession, the key priestlord imagined that he had returned to her good graces, but she hadn't forgotten his unsanctioned raid on Osterra. Klovus still basked in his victory, the fool. He claimed the tensions made the godlings stronger. Any day now, Iluris was sure a violent counterstrike would come from Konag Conndur and the Commonwealth navy, and then Ishara would be forced to respond.

Reaching into a pouch tucked between the cushions, Iluris removed a bitter almond, bit into the furry green nut, and enjoyed the tartness. Upon starting her procession five days ago, her entourage had traveled in a great circle around the outskirts of Serepol. She listened to her people cheer, sent out the call for candidates to be considered as her successor, then rode away to the outlying lands. She would tour all thirteen districts, see the whole land, and be reminded of how her people had thrived in the decades of peace.

She had already crossed the districts of Ishiki and Salimbul, and now the procession rolled across the grasslands of Dhabban, where families wandered the open plains tending herds of sheep and antelope. The achingly green grasses stretched as far as she could see. The dirt road looked like a long, tan ribbon draped across the grasses. Captani Vos had declared they would reach Olbo before sunset, and Cyril rode ahead to prepare the town. There would be feasts, games, and exhibitions, and inevitably some people would make their case as to why they should be Ishara's next leader.

So far, she had heard interesting pitches from wily businessmen or grizzled old battle commanders who had fought in the last war against the Commonwealth. She liked some of them, but none seemed perfect, not yet. She wasn't in a hurry, though. Dhabban was only the fourth district she had visited, and there were so many people, so many *good* people, in Ishara that she had no doubt of finding a worthy successor.

The procession leader shouted for a halt, and voices called up and down the line. Iluris looked out the open carriage window and saw a twisted black tree that had been struck by lightning. It stood like a sentinel in the grasses, the only visible landmark on the plain.

Captani Vos rode up on his dapple-gray horse, his armor, sash, and cape covered with dust from the road. "Mother, we can see the town ahead, and I wanted to give you warning, in case you need to prepare."

"Thank you, Vos." Her legs and buttocks were sore, and she needed to relieve herself. "Set up the privacy pavilion for me, please. I should ride into Olbo refreshed."

Her hawk guards unpacked a bolt of blue silk, which they wrapped around a framework of poles stuck into the soft grasses. The empra entered her privy, while the men simply relieved themselves on the side of the road. Priestlord Klovus scuttled off into the taller grasses.

She finished quickly, and the guards packed up her privy, ready to ride on as soon as she had situated herself. She was plumping up her cushions when Nerev, her lanky chamberlain, tapped politely on the door of her carriage. "May I join you for the ride into town, Excellency? I would like to discuss the list of candidates so far."

Iluris knew her quiet hours were over, and she decided that if she had to have company, her chamberlain was better than a demanding priestlord who would keep trying to convince her to go to war. "Of course, Nerev."

Carrying his tablet, he climbed into the carriage, folded his long legs, and adjusted his red chamberlain's robes. When he swung the enameled door shut, Iluris called through the open window, "Captani, let's be on our way. I want to arrive while there is daylight."

The leader whistled from the front horse and the procession moved along. The carriage bounced and rattled on the well-traveled road. Far behind, Key Priestlord Klovus hurried back from the tall grasses, calling for them to wait. Iluris saw one of the last supply wagons pause so the stout priestlord could swing himself up.

Sitting back in her cushions, she turned to Nerev. The chamberlain stroked his dark, pointed beard as he looked down at the names in deep concentration. He read them off, and Iluris pondered, then asked him to cross out three names. She would see who else they might find before she made up her mind.

Olbo's town square had been cleared to make room for the empra's wagons and carriages. Pavilions had been erected so she could meet with candidates who came to speak with her. At a long wooden table under the largest pavilion, she dined with the town leader, a sleepy-eyed man who was unaccustomed to so much activity. Klovus was seated far down the table so he could speak with the local priest and other important people of Dhabban.

They were joined by the local ranchers with the largest herds and the greatest number of workers. One master shepherd, a man named Gren with a flock of ten thousand sheep, produced wagonloads of wool for the weaving houses in the Ishiki and Tarizah Districts.

Gren sat beside Iluris, explaining his business. "It's a vast enterprise, Excellency." The rancher savored a bite of roasted lamb covered with honey and slivered almonds. "This is one of my sheep. My flock is perfect, down to every scrap of meat and every fiber of wool. Managing such an operation can't be entirely different from the work of being an emprir."

The honeyed lamb melted in her mouth. "If the quality of this meal is a reflection of your ruling skills, then you should be considered for the job," she said, half in jest. "But I warn you that ruling all thirteen Isharan districts, as well as managing a navy and a standing army to face the constant threat from the Commonwealth, all while maintaining peace so that our land can thrive, is different from managing a herd of sheep."

"Likely so, Excellency, but I can always learn."

She told Nerev to write the man's name in his book.

After the meal, an unusual form of entertainment began as the audience sat back and drank sweet mead. Driven by dogs, twelve bleating sheep were turned loose in the square. The empra's hawk guards closed ranks, ready to defend her, but the town leader said, "Just watch, you will enjoy this."

Three strapping young men bounded in among the sheep, carrying loose coils of hemp rope. Each of them tackled a sheep, tied its thrashing legs together, then jumped up to snatch another one. Five were down and tied in less than a minute. The young men rounded up the rest of the sheep, assisted by the barking dogs, and soon all the sheep lay immobile in the square. The Olbo townspeople laughed and applauded.

"A remarkable skill," Iluris said.

"Now, we shear them," said the most muscular of the men, a giant who stood taller than most and had shoulders nearly as broad as a cart. With a razor-edged knife he slashed off a hunk of white wool, which he presented to Iluris with a grave bow. "The finest, purest wool you'll ever see, Excellency."

She accepted the gift, felt the softness in her hands, pressed it against her cheek. The crowd laughed even louder as the giant picked up two of the tied sheep, one in each massive arm, and raised them over his head. "You see, I'm the best shepherd, the best shearer, and the strongest man in Dhabban." He cracked a wide grin. "Maybe I should be the next emprir."

"That is certainly one qualification." Iluris turned to Nerev. "You'd better write down the young man's name."

Grinning, the giant let the sheep down, and the other young men finished shearing them to raucous cheers and rhythmic applause.

꙰

After leaving Dhabban, they arrived next at a border town on a small river in the Tarizah District. Citrus orchards lined the banks, and the people caught catfish from the river.

Iluris was surprised when the townspeople had no candidates to offer for her consideration. Their leader, a square-chinned, no-nonsense woman, bowed, as if to gently deliver bad news. "We are good people here, Excellency, well fed, content, kind to our families. We are pleased you have come to visit us, but no one here is inclined to become the next emprir of the land."

Klovus came up to the town leader, puzzled. "Surely you have a local temple? Your godling protects you and keeps you safe."

"We have a temple on the bank, and our godling lives in the river. He is content, as are we."

"You pray and you sacrifice?" The priestlord sounded challenging. "You keep the godling strong, for such time as you may need him?"

"If we need him, the godling will be there. We sense him. Last year, he protected us from a terrible storm that blew down many trees in the forest, yet none of our homes were damaged. Five years ago, a fire swept through the grass hills and could have wiped us out. We were ready to evacuate in our boats, but the fire worked its way around our town, and the godling snuffed it out. Yes, we know he is there."

Iluris looked at Klovus. "You see, Priestlord, that is exactly how godlings were meant to serve us. I must commend the Tarizah priestlord. He has done excellent work."

Klovus looked troubled. "Yes, he has. But the godlings should be kept as strong as possible, in case we face more dangerous enemies than rainstorms and grass fires."

The town leader placed a finger on her chin, still considering the empra's original question. "We do have one person you should talk to, though. Wayman is a learned old man. Such a wise person might make an excellent leader. You could ask him?"

Some townspeople took Iluris in a boat down the river, accompanied by Captani Vos, two hawk guards, Chamberlain Nerev, and Priestlord Klovus. When they arrived at a hermit's shack on the bank with a small wooden dock extending from the front door, they called out his name. "Wayman!"

The old man had long hair and a thick gray beard, well brushed. As if it were a complicated operation, he worked his way into a well-worn wooden chair at the end of the dock and rested his wrists on his knees as he watched them. "You are Empra Iluris."

"I'm told you are a wise man. I was hoping we could discuss Ishara."

"We can discuss anything you like." When he smiled, his teeth were yellowed, but intact. She couldn't guess his age. "I've read much over the years, and I have had many years to read. My home is filled with books, and loyal travelers bring me more books each week."

"How many books have you read, then?" asked Klovus.

"One thousand, six hundred and thirty-two. I've kept track since I was a young man." He laughed. "I can't say they were all good books, though, and sometimes the information contradicts what is written in other books." He tapped his fingernails on the arms of his chair. "What has the world come to if you can't trust what you read in books? Astonishing! I guess I need to read more books."

"Do you remember what you read?" Iluris asked.

"I remember every word. It's a trick of my memory." He tapped the side of his head. "Sometimes it's a curse, though." He looked up at her. "Think of your own life, Excellency. Are there not some things you wish to forget?"

A flash of her father's drawn face, his set jaw as he held her down and forced himself upon her . . . "Yes, many things. I am crossing all districts, seeing Ishara and meeting people to find a worthy successor."

"I read that in a letter a traveler brought. I am surprised you reached Tarizah so quickly."

"We came to see you, Wayman," said Chamberlain Nerev. "You are extremely wise and well read."

His dry laugh turned into a cough. "Oh, I have no interest in ruling a land. I have my dock, and the river, and the fish." He let out a slow sigh. "And my books. I am already an emprir, but of a much smaller territory."

Iluris was charmed by the old man. "If you have so much knowledge, why don't you want to be considered for the role? I might insist that Nerev write down your name in his book. You could be my advisor, if nothing else."

"He can write down my name if he wishes, but I will not accept the post, should you offer it to me."

Without getting up, Wayman reached down beside his chair for a long stick with a string and a hook tied to the end. "You do need a wise empra or emprir, but unfortunately, I am too wise." He cackled once more. "Wise enough to know that I don't want to be a ruler. And I am too old." He found a second pole on the other side of his chair and offered it to her. "Even as empra, you have much to learn, don't you? Why don't you fish with me awhile?"

"I've never done that," she said.

"A person's life is not complete without fishing at least once. I insist."

Wayman gave Iluris brief instructions, and then they fished in companionable silence. A breeze rippled the surface of the river, which sparkled like thousands of gems in the sunlight. Iluris enjoyed herself for the next two hours, even though she still hadn't found what she was looking for.

35

ADAN and Koll delivered the bedraggled teen to safety in the castle at Fellstaff. Tafira promised to help Pokle recover while the two men traveled to Convera Castle to see the konag. Adan dispatched a message to Bannriya, so Penda would know his new mission and that she had to watch over the kingdom's business for a little while longer.

The riverboat rolled down the Bluewater River out of Norterra. Adan stood on deck, leaning against a crate of pottery from the town of Broken Wheel, where he and his uncle had boarded. Kollanan had paid for their passage, but did not reveal their identities; a barge captain didn't need to know that two kings were aboard his vessel. They wore warm clothes taken from the Fellstaff castle stores, woolen shirts and gray cloaks with no insignia.

Out on the open deck, the young king of Suderra watched the shore roll by with deceptive grace: tall trees, a trio of deer grazing in the reeds, gray outcroppings of rock. Koll stood next to him, his shoulders bunched, as if he hoped to make the boat travel faster through sheer force of will.

Both men were withdrawn and serious. Certainly, the wreths weren't done with the harm they meant to do, especially if they intended to wake the dragon and bring about the end of the world. "We have to convince Conndur to send part of the army to Norterra," Koll said. "With my report and yours, he can't deny the threat. We know the frostwreths are building a fortress at Lake Bakal. How long until they move southward? What if they attack Fellstaff? Lasis is there with Tafira, but how can they defend the entire kingdom? I shouldn't have left them alone."

"And I left Penda back home. What if the sandwreths come back?" Adan squared his shoulders. "I trust her to take care of what needs to be done—just as you trust Tafira and your Brava. But everything may hinge on us convincing the konag to help. We need to look my father in the eye and make him see the danger here."

Adan thought about everything he'd experienced in the last few weeks. He looked at his uncle and said, "A few months ago, I couldn't have been happier. My wife told me that she's carrying our first child. My kingdom is prosperous, the regents are gone, the people are happy with my rule. And now . . ." He felt the burn of tears in his eyes. "What sort of world will my child live in? Penda and I are bringing a son or daughter into what might be a terrible war, maybe the end of everything."

He looked at Koll watching the shadows gather on the river. "My grandsons have already left this world. At least your child has a chance."

The riverboat pulled up to one of the main wharves in Convera, just past the first bridge. City guards monitored the river town, stopping brawls, watching out for petty thieves. As Adan and his uncle disembarked, bidding the barge crew goodbye, Koll waved to the nearest guards, shouting in a voice that had commanded armies. "Sergeant! Send a runner to the castle and tell the konag that King Kollanan and King Adan request an immediate audience."

The crew dropped their crates and stared at their fellow passengers. The captain put a hand on his hip and chuckled. "I thought I recognized you, Koll the Hammer! I saw you at a harvest festival in Fellstaff once. Imagine that, two kings on my boat!"

Adan and Koll set off at a determined pace, ascending the streets toward the high bluff overlooking the Confluence. Guards and curious citizens gathered around them, but the two did not stop for small talk. One sergeant said to the armored guard next to him, "I wager they're here to help with the war against Ishara. We've got to strike back."

Adan was startled. "What war with Ishara?"

"The town of Mirrabay was wiped out a few weeks ago. The Isharans attacked us with a godling, and they'll probably do it again." The soldier chewed on his words and spat them out. "We've got to respond to the cowardly strike. It'll be all-out war with Ishara."

"I've already been to a war over there, and I know what it's like," Koll said in a low growl. "We bring news of a different danger."

"And more urgent to the world," Adan added.

They worked their way past mule carts and children at play, barking dogs, women exchanging gossip, carpenters repairing homes, street workers fixing cobblestones. Adan had grown up here, and he savored the smells, colors, and sounds of home, which were so different from Bannriya. Despite the concern in his heart, he looked wistfully up at the castle. He had left here as a prince, and now he came back as a king—with news that would change the Commonwealth forever.

In their nondescript travel clothes, Koll and Adan marched through the gates. Nobles and courtiers hurried about, rushing to prepare for the arrival of the two visiting kings. Adan briskly led the way to his father's throne room.

Inside, sunlight streamed through tall segmented-glass windows. Konag Conndur, wearing a fur-lined cape and a purple tunic, watched as servants hurried about to bring food and drink. Prince Mandan sat fidgeting at a table next to a stack of documents and ledgers, with the tall, steel-haired Brava next to him.

When they hurried through the entryway, Conndur broke into a grin and stretched his arms wide, rising to his feet. "Starfall! Koll!" He strode toward them, but faltered after only a few steps. The bleak expression on his brother's face and the clear worry on Adan's made him hesitate. "I received your letters with the southern star charts." He frowned. "And that odd story about the wreths."

"We're not here about star charts, Father," Adan said in a serious voice. "Yes, the wreths have returned after leaving us alone for two thousand years."

Kollanan added, "It's worse than that, Conn. The wreths mean to destroy us."

"The wreths mean to destroy *each other,* and we just happen to be caught between them," Adan said. "They mean to wake the dragon Ossus so they can kill him."

Utho stood beside his konag, as solid as an oak but with a deeply skeptical expression. "We read your letters, but your news is difficult to believe. How can the wreths wake a mythical dragon? Does it even exist? That ancient race has been gone for so many centuries. What kind of threat can they pose us now?"

Koll's nostrils flared. "Ask all the people they massacred at Lake Bakal, my daughter and her husband . . . my grandsons."

Adan ignored the Brava, since the konag was the one they needed to convince. "Neither of us is prone to fancy, Father. I've seen the wreths myself, both factions, and I believe they intend to start a war that will rival the ancient battles that nearly destroyed the world. We have to decide our best course of action, without delay."

With a huff of impatience, Prince Mandan rose from his worktable, the last to formally greet them. "We are in a crisis here, too. It's a good thing you came, since we were about to send a summons to Norterra and Suderra. The Commonwealth needs you. There's a very real chance we'll be at war with Ishara again, and that is our immediate priority. The konag calls for you to rouse your people, spread the word to your vassal lords so you can raise a great army across all counties. We need all fighters here in Osterra to defend against Ishara."

Unable to believe what he was hearing, Adan looked at his brother in alarm, then at his father. "You can't mean this! Did you not hear what we just told you? The *wreths* have come back."

Conndur gave Mandan a chiding glance for how he had handled the discussion. "Understand what we've been going through here in Osterra. The Isharans provoked us, attacked us directly. Utho fought the godling himself." He let out a long growling breath. "Of course I've heard the legend of the sleeping dragon, but no one has ever seen it. It's just a myth. But here in Mirrabay, Isharans sent a godling to our shores. A *godling!*"

Kollanan spoke gruffly. "No matter what the Isharans did, Conn, they are still just people. You have to reconsider." He swallowed hard. "The wreths are worse than any harassing raids."

The konag lowered himself heavily into the large carved chair at the head of the document table. "What they've done is much more than harassment, Koll. The Isharans are our mortal enemies. The people are howling for blood— and with good reason. A town is devastated, more than a hundred innocent villagers slaughtered. Over the past year there have been five other skirmishes and countless missing ships. As konag, I can't ignore that! The Isharans are clearly testing our strength and resolve. On the northern coast, Lord Cade reports seeing many suspicious ships in the fog. Watchman Osler has put Fulcor Island on high alert, ready for a sneak attack from the enemy navy."

"And yet," Adan insisted, taking a seat, but remaining on edge as he raised his voice, "*the wreths have come back,* Father! Last time, they laid waste to this entire continent." His voice cracked. "Kollanan and I both saw what they did to Lake Bakal. And down in Bannriya, I lived through the terrible dust storm they brought, and I looked directly at Queen Voo when she explained the threat. I believe this time the wreth factions truly mean to wake the dragon and destroy the world."

Prince Mandan chuckled, as if this were just some old quarrel with his younger brother. "Wake the dragon! Wreths! Such fanciful stories." He glanced at Utho, as if for reassurance. "Humans have the world now. The wreths were broken and defeated. No one has seen them since they disappeared."

"*We* have," Koll said in a gruff voice, then turned away from Mandan as if the prince were beneath his notice. Instead, his gaze burned into the konag's eyes. "I saw it, Conn. *I saw it!* The wreths erased that entire town as if it were nothing, as if the people didn't matter. Because they were in the way! And the wreths will keep coming."

"Of course I believe both of you," Conndur said with an edge of exasperation. "But what do they want?"

After an uncomfortable silence, Adan said, "The sandwreth queen wants us humans to fight beside them against their enemies. We will need the Commonwealth armies just to stand against them."

Utho said, "The wreths created humans, but they abandoned us thousands of years ago. They have not bothered us in all that time. But the Isharans attacked us directly, again and again. They murdered so many innocents." He paused, turning his hard eyes to the others gathered at the table. "And the Isharans are *real*. They are the true enemy."

"How can you say that?" Adan asked. "We've seen wreths, talked to them, and—"

"*Talk.*" Mandan scoffed at his younger brother. "Suderra is far away and doesn't need to fear any Isharan attacks. Of course you don't take the threat seriously. Of course you think your problems are more important." He made a rude noise. "Your kingdom is safe, while Osterra is in danger. Our cities are about to be ravaged, just like Mirrabay."

Conndur touched the prince's forearm, making him fall silent. "Mandan, if I wanted to hear Utho speak, I would have asked him myself."

The prince flushed, sounding indignant. "You asked me to learn more about politics, Father. Well, I am learning! Utho teaches me, and I trust his judgment."

Struggling to contain his impatience, Adan looked at his uncle, trying to figure out what to do, what else they could say. Kollanan's eyes were hooded, his face drawn in a grim frown. "You haven't seen what we've seen, Conn. War is coming, worse than anything you could imagine."

"There *will* be war," Mandan said. "On that much we agree."

36

AFTER Kollanan and Adan had departed for Convera, Fellstaff Castle felt empty, cold, and dangerous, now that Queen Tafira knew what was out there. Though the staff built up the fires in all the main rooms, she felt a clinging chill everywhere. Tafira wrapped herself in a fur-lined cape and slipped her feet into rabbitskin slippers. The northern kingdom was much colder than her native Ishara, and she doubted she would feel warm again until Koll came back home.

Throughout the day, she met with the string of nobles who had followed the king's urgent instructions to take a census of their available fighters, to inventory their weapons and armor, and to build up the defenses in their separate holdings. Lords Teo, Cerus, Alcock, and Bahlen rode in from outlying counties after hearing the news, only to find that the king had already departed for Convera. They were full of questions.

"Wreths? Truly?" asked gaunt and skeptical Cerus. "My county has a dozen wreth ruins with broken walls and collapsing towers. People tend to stay away from them, but the ancient race is as dead as my grandsire. How can they pose a threat now?"

"You are welcome to ride up to Lake Bakal and see for yourself," Tafira said, "but I wouldn't expect you to come back."

Cerus gave a slow, respectful nod. "I am deeply sorry to hear about your daughter and her family, my queen."

Lord Alcock paced the floor in the throne room, his back to the roaring fireplace. "Couldn't some natural disaster have frozen the lake? We have seen terrible winters before and did not blame the wreths."

Tafira's voice was heavy with the ice of anger. "I saw my husband's face, and that is all I need to see. He encountered the frostwreths himself, spoke with them and barely escaped with his life. Later, he rescued a young man

who hid in the woods and witnessed the whole thing. Pokle—the only survivor of Lake Bakal, as far as we know—is here now and still scared of his
own shadow. You can talk with him, if you like. You will see at a glance that
he's been through some terrible ordeal."

Lasis entered the throne room, wearing his black leather armor and boots.
"I myself saw the wreths building a great fortress on the shore where the
town was. It appears to be a beachhead, the first step in a full-scale invasion.
Norterra must be ready for them."

Though Lord Teo seemed willing to debate with Tafira, he didn't dare
contradict the Brava. He gave Lasis a slight bow. "Very well, I believe you."
He offered a sheaf of papers to the queen, who also accepted similar documents from Cerus and Bahlen.

Lord Alcock's brow furrowed. "An Utauk trader came through saying
much the same thing about sandwreths down south. They appeared out of
a dust storm, he said. He might as well have been telling tales of dragons, so
we did not take him seriously. Ancestors' blood, we should have believed
him."

"Yes, you should have," Tafira said. "Now that my husband calls us to
arms, we have to prepare. He hopes to convince the konag to send a significant part of the Commonwealth army to defend Norterra and Suderra. If
we all fight together, we can be strong enough to drive off these wreths."

After the lords left, looking disturbed, the Brava stood at attention in the
queen's presence, as if he needed to tell her something. She smiled at him.
"I am glad to have your assistance, Lasis. My beloved is away, but I rely on
your strength to protect the kingdom."

"You are a strong ruler in your own right, my queen, and the defenses of
Fellstaff are improving every day." He glanced out the arched windows that
allowed pale sunlight into the chamber. "But there seems to be more to this
conflict . . . so much we do not know." He raised his square chin. "With your
permission, I would like to gather information, which we can use to plan
our defenses. You need not worry for your safety while I'm gone. I will have
the vassal lords send additional guards to keep Fellstaff secure."

Though the Brava was bonded to King Kollanan's service, he often went
on journeys of his own as a wandering enforcer, a reminder of peace and
law throughout the kingdom. Tafira had grown used to his absences, but she
had never been concerned about an overarching threat to Norterra before.

She looked at him for a long moment, assessing him. "Shall I send a contingent of soldiers with you?"

"For some missions, a single man—especially a Brava—can be more successful than a small army." He touched the ramer at his side. "I need to learn if the wreth attack against Lake Bakal was directed toward killing humans, or if the village just happened to be in the wrong place."

Tafira sat back in the hand-polished chair. "Our people are still dead. Does the reason matter?"

"It does, my queen. Have the wreths declared war on humans? Will they hunt us down the way Isharans raid our coastal villages because they hate us so? Or do they simply consider us irrelevant to their schemes? If the latter, our safest course may be just to stay out of their way. We need to know the nature of our enemy."

Tafira's eyes held his for a long and silent moment. "I trust you to do what you need to do. You have my leave to go. Come back with vital information that we can use to save ourselves."

Lasis headed out before sundown, still regretting that he had let Kollanan go by himself to Lake Bakal in the first place. Even during peacetime, no king should be without his faithful Brava, not even Koll the Hammer.

He chose Char, a sooty gray stallion from the stables. He planned to continue through the night under the full moon, and he knew the mount was reliable and strong. More importantly, as he raced under the shadowy pine boughs that arched over the road, the horse's coat looked like snowfall on ashes and would provide camouflage when he tried to get close to the frost-wreths.

He headed single-mindedly north, stopping only to give Char his feed bag and to drink at clear cold streams that were dotted with fallen leaves. When the stallion needed rest, Lasis stopped for a few hours and napped as well.

After two days of hard solo travel, Lasis neared the high northern lake and slowed the horse to a guarded walk. They reached the crest of the ridge just after dawn. The rising sun reflected from the frozen expanse of Lake Bakal and washed over the looming ice and stone blocks of the frost-wreth fortress.

In the early-morning silence, sounds of construction carried across the high valley. Ice crackled as blocks were cut free from the solid lake, lifted by magic, then stacked and frostwelded into place. Construction stones scavenged from the town's original buildings reinforced the wall. He saw hundreds of the white wreths.

Lasis narrowed his eyes and drew a breath, feeling heat burn within him, a glimmer of the wreth blood that lay so deep in his ancestry. Bravas accepted and respected their half-breed heritage, which gave them access to the magic that let them wield their ramers and draw upon other spells. But Lasis hated his forebears for what they were. The wreths had treated their creations horribly. Their half-breed children, ancestors of the Bravas, were not the result of passionate romance or warm love. No, human mothers had been taken from the ranks of slaves, raped, and impregnated. Wreth women had forced male human lovers to perform or die.

Lasis found no great honor in his wreth heritage, but he could use his strength and abilities against them now. As a Brava, he had sworn his life to serve and protect the king and the Commonwealth. He had to assess what kind of threat this unexpected enemy posed. The wreths would be sorry they had returned.

In the cover of the skeletal trees, he slid off the back of his gray charger. Lasis pulled a gray cloak over his normal black garb and paced alongside the horse, taking advantage of its white-and-gray camouflage. He carried a long traditional knife at his right hip and the ramer clipped to his left, though he did not plan to fight.

Keeping to the shelter of the silver pines, he descended toward the lake. When they reached the edge of the trees at the rocky shore, but still far from the gigantic fortress, Lasis loosely tied Char's reins to a branch, then touched his forehead to the horse's mane. "This part I must do alone."

He crept off, making little sound. His black boots whispered in the snow as he wove through the trees, following the edge of the frozen lake over rough terrain. When he grew closer, he looked up at the fortress walls that rose precipitously from the shore, anchored on the black rocks. The base covered the area that had been the town square and outlying streets.

Peering out from between two pines, he watched the activity. Strange beings worked on the site, smaller than humans, but not wreths either. Their faces and arms were smooth, as if only partially formed out of softened wax that held little detail. Were they some other kind of servants?

He caught sight of several tall, hairless wreths in gray-and-blue robes:

mages. Additional wreths with body armor and long, wild hair shouted orders. Their obvious leader, a lanky warrior who gripped a white spear with a long spiraled shaft, gestured toward the walls and work teams, directing the activity.

Lasis crept closer, lifting a snow-laden pine bough to crouch under it. Loose snow showered onto his gray cloak, and he brushed himself off, inching along the lakeshore. Ripples ridged the lake's surface, indicating that everything had frozen instantly, so that even the stirrings of wind on the water had been locked in place.

The wreth mages used magic for much of their heavy labor, which explained how the construction could have progressed so rapidly, and on such a vast scale. Work crews used coils of black, braided rope and gangs of drone workers to manually haul blocks of ice into position. Gauging the size of the fortress, he wondered if this would be the final extent of the structure, or if the frostwreths would expand it, maybe all the way around the lake.

The morning sun glinted on an enormous block being hoisted high up the tallest tower. As Lasis moved closer so he could see better, a large shard broke off and fell. Like a giant ax head, it tumbled down among the workers, killing several of them. The black rope slipped, and the huge block began tumbling down the side of the tower.

Responding with a shout, two mages lunged forward and raised their hands as the ice block scraped down the immense wall. Their magic seized the block in the air and held it in place. With a flash of steam, the ice block fused to the tower wall, ruining the otherwise perfect symmetry, but at least it didn't smash to the ground. The wreth mages stood concentrating as they melted the imprisoned block. Water flowed in thick runnels down the tower wall and froze there like flat icicles.

Lasis was daunted by the power he had just witnessed. The warrior crew leader was no longer visible, although the tall wreth man had been near the front of the crowd only a moment ago. Feeling exposed, he folded himself in among the pines again. Behind him, a sudden unnatural chill made the air brittle, and he whirled.

Three wreth warriors stood behind him, moving with a silent grace far superior to his own. "We found a snow rabbit," said the tallest warrior, the one who commanded the work crews.

Lasis backed away, one hand straying to the ramer at his side.

"Queen Onn was right, Rokk," said a second warrior. "We should not have killed all the men in this little town. They could serve as better laborers than the drones. Let us take this one alive."

Rokk narrowed his large, cold eyes. "He is a strong one, and my darling Onn will wish to speak with him."

Lasis unclipped his ramer. "I'll fight you."

Rokk chuckled. "That should be amusing. Let us see how you can try."

Lasis slipped the golden band around his wrist and clamped the halves together. Golden teeth drew blood, activating the spell designs. Heat surged through him, and a corona of fire lit around his wrist, engulfing his hand in a ball of flame. By force of will, he extended it into a hot serpentine coil, then swept his arm to lash out with the flames.

Laughing, Rokk lunged forward with his long crystalline spear and met the Brava's fiery whip. Lasis snatched his arm back, coiling the ramer flame around the shaft of the spear, but the frostwreth warrior yanked hard, unleashing magic of his own. The Brava felt stark cold plunge down into his hand, but the blood-fueled fires grew hotter. He intensified the ramer whip until Rokk's spear smoked and shattered in his hand.

The frostwreth warrior recoiled in surprise, looking at the splinters in his hand. "Now, that is unexpected." He cast the debris aside and called to his companions. "All the more reason to capture him."

The wreth warriors closed in, and Lasis lashed the air, drawing a line of fire in front of them. They hesitated.

Then a frostwreth mage emerged from the trees to confront him. Lasis felt a knot in his stomach. He had come here to see what the wreths were building, and he needed to report to King Kollanan. Perhaps it had been unwise to undertake this mission alone after all. But he did not surrender. If nothing else, he would kill as many as he could to avenge the poor villagers who had been swept up in ice and fear.

He lashed ramer fire at two wreth warriors, but they managed to block it with their spears, driving the flame back. Lasis spread his fingers apart, splitting the ramer fire into multiple tendrils and used them to strike at the wreth mage, knowing this was the most dangerous opponent.

"Eres," Rokk said to the mage, "this one seems to have interesting magic."

The mage seemed intrigued as well. "Wreth magic. He must be descended from the bastard children of our nobles. Apparently some of them still live."

Lasis attacked with multiple tendrils of fire like a handful of blazing whips. The flames skittered across the wreth mage, left smoking lines on his blue-and-gray robes, but the lines quickly disappeared. Eres stepped closer, unhurried, and reached out with an open palm, pushing his hand toward the ramer. Its tendrils retracted, withered, dimmed.

The mage closed his palm and fingers over Lasis's burning hand, and the ramer fire guttered.

With his free hand, Lasis drew the long knife at his waist so he could keep fighting, but the pulse of cold backed into the ramer, down his arm, and through his chest. His blood turned to ice. Though he kept trying to fight, he couldn't wrench himself free.

The other two wreth warriors closed in behind Lasis and clubbed him with the spiral hafts of their long spears. When the fire in his hand died out, so did the light of his consciousness.

37

EVEN as she left the great Convera remembrance shrine, Shadri knew she could have spent a lifetime—a hundred lifetimes—reading through the records of names and legacies, but she had overstayed her welcome with Chief Legacier Vicolia. Still, she had many other interests and many other things to learn, in no particular order.

In only a short time, Shadri had read countless legacies in huge volumes, filling her mind with the stories of their lives. She loved working in the remembrance shrine, even as a cleaning girl, and some of the legaciers had encouraged her interests, but the chief legacier constantly reminded her that she didn't belong.

In another time, another life, Shadri might have become a legacier herself. She could have devoted each day to compiling, organizing, and preserving legacies in the great archive, or she could have managed a local remembrance shrine in a smaller town. She would have been fascinated by the work . . . at least for a time.

But becoming a legacier would have limited her possibilities, and this way Shadri was now free to pursue any interests, wherever they might take her. She could learn about forestry or mining if she liked, could study the political history of the Commonwealth, or she could learn about the mythology of the wreths, their legends and their gods. Maybe she would research the Bravas, with their code of honor, their great skills, and their mixed heritage. First, she had to meet one, though. . . .

Shadri packed up her things and left the remembrance shrine, bidding the legaciers farewell with tear-filled eyes. She took her pay, bought a few travel supplies and a pair of good walking shoes, then set off with a heavy pack on her shoulders. Humming, she followed the southern fork of the Crickyeth River away from Convera toward the Dragonspine Mountains.

Along the way, she would find cities and towns, farmlands and orchards, craft bazaars and caravans, wreth ruins, and sparkling waterfalls. Everything she learned would become a new volume in the expanding library of her mind.

That was why, in the next town, she found the dissected body of the dead man so fascinating.

In a village called Thule's Orchard, Shadri used some of her spare coppers to buy a meal of soup and bread at the inn. After shedding her large pack and leaving it outside the door, she had brushed off the road dust and mud. She wore a patched cloak, a drab blouse, and layers of patched skirts that hid her age and the shape of her body. She didn't want to draw much attention.

Still humming quietly, she sat alone watching people, eavesdropping on their conversations, curious about them. She wrote down her thoughts in one of the journals from her pack; she had already filled several journals, all the way to the margins, but if she didn't write down her ideas, she would forget them, and the very thought of lost ideas seemed a tragedy to her.

When a distinguished-looking older man approached her, she was surprised. "Might I join you for conversation?" he asked. "You look like you've been on the road a long time, and you seem to be keeping a thorough account of your travels." He nodded to the open journal on the table in front of her. The man was older than her father, with thick gray hair, a kindly but worry-seamed face, and a white scar on his chin. His eyes hinted that he had seen many things, and Shadri wondered what those things might be.

"Hmm, I accept your company, but you'll have to buy your own food," she said. "I have only a few coins to last me on a long journey."

The older man smiled back at her. "To be honest, I see so few people with books here in Thule's Orchard. If you tell me about your journey, I'll pay for your meal as well as my own. I like to hear stories of other places."

Shadri warmed to him. "So do I, but people say I ask too many questions."

"Here now! There can never be too many questions!"

She suddenly felt much happier to be there.

The man introduced himself as Severn, the town's physician. She showed him her journal as she pushed aside her steaming cabbage soup. "I'm on a journey to understand as much as I can about the world. Still a lot to see and do. I'm taking notes."

Dr. Severn let out a relieved laugh. "Our journeys have similar paths, young lady, for I am also a man of learning, primarily medical knowledge. I want to draw a complete map of the human body—the organs, musculature, skin, bones—to know how everything *works*." He glanced around the inn's common room as the conversation swirled around them. "The wreths created our race a long time ago, and I want to know how they did it. I can only work with the material I have at hand." He lowered his voice. "I have recently come into possession of the body of a hanged bandit, and I intend to get started straightaway. Some people find such studies disturbing."

"Knowledge can be disturbing," Shadri said, "but it's still knowledge, and it has its own worth. I've often wondered about the human body myself." She held a forefinger in front of her eyes, bent it, straightened it, then studied her fingernail.

He leaned closer to her. "The way we learn is by investigating, and I intend to study the cadaver thoroughly. When the villagers asked what I was doing with an unclaimed body, I told them that the bandit would help me be a better doctor."

Shadri slurped her soup. "How can a dead man make you a better doctor? It seems he wouldn't need a doctor anymore."

Severn's bushy eyebrows rose higher. "If you have a severe cut and I need to sew you up, wouldn't you rather I practiced on dead skin beforehand? If your arm is wrenched out of its socket, or you have a stomach wound, wouldn't you prefer that I learned my craft on a dead criminal, instead of making mistakes on you?" Shadri had to agree with his logic, and Severn smiled. "But nobody here will help me. The villagers are too queasy and reluctant."

"Queasy and reluctant?" Shadri weighed her natural revulsion for corpses against the potential for so much learning on an unexpected topic. Yes, for the knowledge, she could do this. "I'm sure I can hold my own." The prospect sounded more interesting by the minute. "I'll stay a few days and help you. Medical knowledge should come in handy, no matter where I go, especially if I need to patch myself up on my travels."

Even as a little girl, Shadri had been curious about everything, much to her family's exasperation. Her father ran a sawmill at a fast-flowing stream. Watching him cut lumber from logs, she had tried to decipher messages in the wood grain. She had plagued him with so many questions he would bend closer to the whining saw blade just to drown out her words.

Shadri had four brothers and two sisters, all singularly lacking in curiosity. Her parents regularly took her into town for market day and let her run among the stalls, so she could ask *other* people her questions: How did potters fire their clay, how did metalsmiths work their gold and silver, how did glassblowers create their own kind of magic from ash and melted sand?

When she grew into a young woman, finding no boys in the village who could tolerate her curiosity, Shadri left home with her parents' blessing—and a sigh of relief—to see the world and pursue her own interests. It seemed a naïve and innocent thing to do, even dangerous, but she didn't give it a second thought. On the road from village to village, she followed her fascinations like stepping-stones across a clear stream, and never looked back.

After she finished her soup in the inn, she followed the doctor to his small clinic. Shadri and Severn worked on the cold cadaver late at night, so as not to cause too much consternation in the town. For Shadri, the work was a revelation. She had never seen inside a body before.

Under the glow of bright lanterns set around the long clean table, the doctor made a deep, precise cut in the abdomen, then used a metal rod to push aside the knotted muscle fibers until he exposed the body cavity.

"I served as a soldier in the war against Ishara years ago," he explained. "I was young, apprenticed to a battlefield surgeon, and I learned how to patch basic wounds, how to save the people who could be saved, and how to comfort the ones who were going to die. I would sit beside those poor lads and write down their legacies, so I could deliver them to the remembrance shrines in their hometowns. That was why I wanted to become a doctor."

He pried the cadaver's red abdominal muscles farther apart to expose coils of intestines. With a probing hand, he reached in and moved the guts aside. Shadri leaned forward, holding up the lantern to study the mysterious body in front of her. Severn asked her to hold open the incision so he could use a larger knife, and he worked with meticulous care. "Better not nick the intestine, or we'll have a much more unpleasant evening."

The doctor continued to talk as Shadri helped. He seemed happy to have someone to listen. "When the wreths created us, they must have had a plan, but often it doesn't make sense to me. I want to understand how the tiniest parts fit together and function." With a bloodied hand, he pointed toward his chest. "The wreths must have known. If I can figure it out, maybe I can fix problems when our bodies go wrong."

She absorbed everything he said. "Did the wreths look the same as this inside, I wonder? The same organs and muscles? What was different about them?" She looked at the purple-red liver, the frothy pink lungs. "Did they consciously make us inferior to them, or were they just incapable of making beings as sophisticated as themselves?"

Severn looked at her in surprise. "Their god created them, so they must be superior. We are just secondary creations." He looked down at the interconnected organs, the mysterious forest of blood vessels. "Though it is still quite impressive work, I must say."

"But how do you *know* the wreths were superior? Just because the legends say Kur created them?"

"Well, because he gave them souls, for one thing, and in all the bodies I've treated on the battlefield and all the cadavers I have studied, I've never found a human soul."

Shadri still wrestled with the question. "But would you even know where to look? Or how to recognize one? For that matter, how do you know the wreths had souls at all? How would they know?"

She could tell that he was becoming flustered with her questions, as people often did. He said, "You go well beyond the boundaries of my knowledge, I'm afraid. As a doctor, I have to be pragmatic. A child with a broken arm doesn't want to hear ruminations on where the soul might be hiding." Keeping busy, Severn cradled the dead man's stomach in both hands. "If you stay, I can teach you how to patch up an injury, sew shut a wound, apply ointment to a burn. *That* is knowledge I can share."

She nodded, considering. "Those sound like valuable skills. I'll stay and learn what I can. This is very instructive."

She spent a week in Thule's Orchard, as promised, helping the doctor with his patients, asking him a litany of questions about medicinal plants and salves, how to treat a rash, deal with types of diarrhea, bring down a fever, ease a sore throat, treat aching joints, mend a cracked skull. And on and on, to the point where the former battlefield surgeon had run out of answers. She could tell she was overstaying her welcome.

Eventually, Shadri grew restless and wanted to move on again. She apologized to Severn as she packed her supplies, clothes, tools, and notebook into her increasingly heavy pack to head out again. "I'll treasure the information you've given me, but I want to understand more than just the human body. I've studied with alchemists, natural historians, musicians. Do you know there's even a mathematics of music? So much to learn." She talked faster and faster. "I want to understand the puzzle of history. Why did so much magic disappear after the great wars? What did the wreths have in mind for our race? And there's always that question about the soul . . ."

The doctor stood outside his clinic, waving goodbye. "In all that, I'm afraid I can't help you, young lady. You'll have to follow your own curiosity."

She set off, humming to herself.

38

After the tremors in Mount Vada stopped, the Scrabbleton miners cleared the tunnels in a frantic search for survivors. High up the mountain's slopes, a fresh plume of gray smoke poured out of a new fissure above the tree line.

While distraught workers carried out several smashed bodies, Elliel tended to the mysterious stranger she had rescued from the quartz-lined vault. She stretched him out on the ground in the open square, checking him for injuries as he revived. Without speaking, the man propped himself on his elbows and looked around in amazement.

The pale, dark-haired stranger intrigued and frightened Elliel. His gray chest armor was some kind of hide with a fine stippling of reptilian scales. A thick black belt girdled his waist above silver leggings made of fine woven metal. His features were compellingly handsome, his face perfectly formed, as if a god had designed it. His eyes were a deep sparkling blue, as if the irises were made of crushed sapphires. His features were more exotic than her own half-breed appearance, and Elliel took a long moment to understand what that meant.

Surely, he was a *wreth.*

Even more astonishing, the symbol tattooed on his cheek—a circle connected by a web of interlaced lines and loops—was almost identical to the rune of forgetting that she herself bore.

The stranger's gaze communicated questions as well as physical pain, but he made no sound. Gingerly touching his leg, she identified where it was broken. "This needs to be set and splinted," she said, hoping he understood her language. "It will hurt."

Without speaking, he gestured for her to get on with it.

She bent over him, knowing what to do. Apparently, tending the injured was a skill that she had not forgotten, perhaps part of her Brava heritage. She put one hand high on his thigh and the other just above his knee. Grasping firmly, she pulled in opposite directions with a strength she was sure none of the other miners could match. When the broken ends of the femur were far enough apart, she aligned them and fit them back together.

He let out a coughing hiss of pain, then breathed quietly. His crushed-sapphire eyes looked up at her with gratitude.

Elliel splinted his leg, using torn cloth and flat pieces of wood as the miners cared for the many other wounded. Busy, focused on the immediate need, the distracted miners at first assumed she had rescued one of their own, but soon they realized they did not know this man from within the mountain, and that he wasn't exactly human.

Elliel found Upwin and was glad to see that her fellow miner had gotten out alive. "Help me carry that man back to my room? He can recover there."

Upwin looked from her to the dazed stranger on the ground. "Who is he?"

"I don't know, but someone has to take care of him. He was inside that crystal vault I discovered." She draped one of the stranger's arms over her shoulder and Upwin took the other. They lifted the wreth man up and he limped along, trying not to jar his splinted leg. They made their way to the inn and carried him past Shauvon and his wife, who were busy preparing food for the exhausted townspeople.

The innkeeper looked at the stranger in surprise, his eyes full of questions, but when a dusty woman poked her head in the front door and shouted for more hot water, he hurried away.

After she and Upwin got the wreth stranger to her room, they gently laid him on her narrow bed. He stretched out his good leg on the straw mattress, and Elliel lifted the splinted leg up beside it. She found a blanket and tucked it in to make him comfortable.

She thanked Upwin, and he hurried to go. "There's more work to do out there. They haven't found Jandre yet. I should . . ."

Not having the heart to tell him she had seen his partner's crushed body during her escape, Elliel gestured. "Go, I'll take care of this one."

She went into the inn's kitchen and put together scraps of fruit, bread, a lump of cheese, a tankard of ale, and a cup of water, then carried all the items back to her room so her patient could eat. She used a damp cloth to wipe his forehead and chin, swipe dust from the corners of his strange eyes, then wash the tattooed rune on his cheek. She hesitated there. "Who are you? Can you speak?"

His brow furrowed as if he were wrestling with an uncooperative mind. Finally a word bubbled to the surface. "Thon."

"Thon? Is that your name? Why were you sealed in that chamber? Who put you inside the mountain?"

He frowned again. "I don't know."

She fed him a bite of cheese, waited while he chewed. "I barely got you out in time. Do you remember the tremors? Is that what woke you?"

He winced, shook his head. "No. Is . . . is the dragon waking?"

She pulled the wooden chair close to her narrow bed. "I don't know either."

He extended a finger to touch the side of Elliel's face, marveling at the similar tattoo there. She flushed, embarrassed. "I'm a Brava—*was* a Brava. I committed a terrible crime, so they stripped me of my legacy." She stopped herself from confessing the entire massacre. He didn't need to know. Elliel wished that she herself didn't know. "Are you guilty of some crime, so that the wreths wiped your memory and sealed you away in that prison?"

Thon's face went blank, and a sheen of tears glistened in his sapphire eyes. "I don't know."

Elliel ate some of the bread and shared grapes with him. "You should rest and recover." She set the tankard of ale at his bedside, next to the cup of water. "I'll be here." She had grabbed a second blanket from the main room and spread it out on the wooden floor. "I've spent plenty of nights on the ground. I'll be comfortable enough."

After she blew out the lamp and darkness filled the room, she lay with her thoughts spinning, her body aching, the sadness of the disaster competing in her mind with the mystery of this ancient man. A wreth! She could sense him lying motionless on the bed nearby. He didn't stir, even a little. His breathing was slow and even, but somehow Elliel didn't believe he had fallen asleep. . . .

The next morning she woke at dawn and lifted herself from the hard floor. Thon sat up in bed and swung both of his legs over the side. With his long slender fingers, he undid the bindings of his splint, pulled the rags away, and removed the wooden sticks that had kept his leg straight.

Elliel jumped to her feet. "Don't do that! Your bone needs to knit properly."

"It already has." Thon rose to his feet and stood uncertainly, flexing his leg. He rubbed his hand down the fine silver-mesh legging, squeezed the middle of his thigh where the bone had snapped. Then he lifted the leg, stomped his boot down, and nodded. "Yes, that was what I needed. The magic here is weak, but it was sufficient." He took an unsteady step toward the door. "I want to go outside. It has been so long, and there is . . . so much I do not know. Everything, in fact."

Elliel stood beside him. "I will introduce you to Scrabbleton. Here, let me help." She took his arm, placed it around her shoulder.

He insisted that he needed no assistance, but he leaned on her anyway. Taking slow steps, they walked into the inn's common area.

Townspeople had gathered for the morning, still stunned after the disaster from the previous day. Shauvon's wife brought out hot tea and fresh baked bread to serve them all. Mainly, the people had come together for discussion and shared grief. Mine boss Hallis was there, already planning the day's recovery efforts. There were still many injuries, but everyone had been accounted for. In all, nine had been killed in the tunnel collapses, and four of the bodies were irretrievable, including Jandre's. In a hoarse voice, Hallis proclaimed, "They are one with the mountain." He said there would be three days of mourning before he would allow anyone back into the mines.

The gathered people looked up with questions and surprise when Elliel brought Thon in among them.

"Where did he come from?" asked Hallis.

"*What* is he?" asked another miner.

"He's a wreth, I think," Elliel said, "from ages ago. I found him in the mine. He was buried deep inside the mountain."

"No one has ever seen a wreth." Hallis took a closer look.

"My name is Thon. I cannot tell you why I am here . . . only that Elliel rescued me." He looked around the room, then fixed his gaze on the door. "I would like to go outside and breathe fresh air, feel the sunlight. It has been a . . . very long time."

Elliel walked him through the crowded room as people stared after them. The wreth stranger felt solid next to her, his muscles smooth and hard. Oddly, he seemed to be supporting her as much as she supported him.

Once outside, Thon turned his face to the sky, blinking into the clear blue distance. "What a marvelous world."

Elliel looked at his perfect features that were marred only by the tattoo rune. "I wish you could remember."

"Now that I've awakened, I have to discover the rest of my history." He turned to look at her. "You say that I am a wreth? And that the wreths are long gone? Maybe I can find them again."

"Is that wise, after what they did to you?"

"I do not know what they did to me, or whether or not I deserved it."

They heard a distant rumble, and the ground shuddered again, another tremor. Gasps of dismay echoed from inside the inn, but the quake abated quickly.

The wreth man stared at curling gray smoke that rose from the upper slopes of Mount Vada. He said, "I may not have much time."

39

ADAN and his uncle stayed at Convera Castle, repeating their stories about the wreths to the konag's advisors and his council of vassal lords. Adan feared that their conversations were going around in circles.

After so many fruitless discussions, a frustrated Koll had dragged his brother into a private chamber and slammed the door. Even through the heavy wooden barrier, Adan and everyone else in the castle had heard them shouting. Koll had pounded his big fist on a table, like his legendary war hammer. Their argument raged for nearly an hour before Kollanan threw open the door again and stalked off to his guest chambers, where he locked himself in for the night.

The next morning, a more conciliatory konag met with the two of them, while Utho stood at his side, like a stony bodyguard. "I believe your story," Conndur said. "Of course I do. These wreths are a matter of great concern, and I especially acknowledge the deep pain of your loss, Koll. Your poor daughter and her family . . ."

With little sympathy in his voice, Utho said, "Many of us have lost families to brutal enemies. Lake Bakal was a tragedy, as was Mirrabay, and we know the Isharans will attack again."

The konag nodded. "They struck a town not far from this capital. Before that, we had news of numerous missing fishing boats, almost certainly attacked and sunk by the Isharans. I can't send the Commonwealth armies away to Norterra to see what the frostwreths might do, when our own coast is so clearly at risk. I have to be prepared for an all-out war, especially if we are now facing godlings. . . ." He clasped his brother's shoulder. "I cannot squander my army on the other side of the land and leave Osterra vulnerable. I must leave you to build your own defenses, Koll. The Norterran people are strong. I know you can keep them safe." He turned to Adan. "The sandwreths seem more cooperative, at least from Queen Voo's words. If they should return to Bannriya, tell them that I would send an emissary to speak with them. I would even come to Suderra myself at some point, if we manage to keep the Isharans at bay."

"Father, if the Commonwealth is caught in the middle of a war between wreth factions," Adan said in a quiet voice, "the Isharan attacks will look like a courtyard brawl by comparison."

Conn's face sagged. "Ancestors' blood, I hope you are wrong." He and his Brava returned to the council chambers.

Later, standing by himself in the rear courtyard gardens, Adan considered the tall hedge maze, which held so many boyhood memories. He no longer held out hope that he could change his father's mind. The Commonwealth army would not be coming to face the wreths. A long-vanished race freezing an entire town and warning of a war to end the world . . . maybe it didn't sound as real and immediate a threat as the Isharans were.

Grumbling in frustration, he marched into the hedge maze, which rose well above his head. The piney scent of junipers and the twitter of birds carried him back to his childhood days spent here in the castle.

He followed the gravel path to the first branching. The maze had been a place of great mystery when he was a boy, and he had spent countless hours exploring, hiding. Sometimes late at night and in complete darkness, he would wander the maze himself, memorizing every twist and turn.

An unexpected voice interrupted his thoughts. "Careful you don't get lost, Brother. I doubt you still remember your way." Adan was surprised to see Mandan there in a quiet corner of the maze, his brown hair over his ears, the gold circlet resting on his brow. He wore a red jacket with gold stitching, large buttons, and wide cuffs that would have made eating a meal impossible. "You've been gone from Convera a long time."

Utho stepped up behind the prince like a watchdog, his flat face showing no expression. "I'm certain he remembers, my prince. You both spent enough time here."

"Shall we run through the maze together?" Adan asked in a challenging tone. "I used to beat you every time."

"You would occasionally win." Mandan's lips quirked in a thin smile. "But I pelted you enough times with rocks from hiding places."

Adan brushed the green fabric of his jerkin. "Yes, it was very un-kingly behavior." The prince sniffed, but he was clearly amused by what he had done.

Adan thought back to when they would hide in the elaborate maze, trying to reach the apple tree at the middle, like a prize. Mandan had craftily made holes in the hedges so he could spy on him and throw rocks, sometimes hard enough to draw blood. Adan still had a faint white scar on his left temple from one sharp-edged rock.

He learned later that Utho had taught Prince Mandan how to prepare an ambush and to lie in wait. "It was part of his training," the Brava responded when an indignant and bleeding Adan accused him. "Any military man must know strategy, secrecy, and surprise, and Mandan is going to be konag."

Finding it unfair, Adan wanted to run to his father to insist that Mandan be punished, but the young prince realized that wasn't very kingly behavior either. Instead, Adan had approached Utho in private, careful to act businesslike. "I'm a prince, too, and I need to understand the same sort of tactics. Kollanan and Conndur went off to fight together in the last Isharan war. What if the same situation occurs?"

The Brava had nodded solemnly. The normally expressionless man had shown a faint smile as thoughts began to click into place. "I agree, the prince needs to understand both sides of a surprise."

Adan planned his revenge—not meaning to escalate the feud or inflict pain on his brother, but to make an impression, to put them on even footing. Late at night, choosing a primary intersection in the hedge maze, Adan dug a deep hole and filled it with foul-smelling nightsoil collected from the garderobes. When the pit was full, he covered the surface with ashes and sprinkled gravel. It wasn't perfect, but at a quick glance, the path looked unchanged.

The following day, Adan taunted his brother and lured him into the maze. Mandan chased him, running headlong. Adan let the prince come close, and when he reached the proper intersection, Adan jumped over the hidden pit and kept running. Mandan ran after him, hot on the chase. Without suspecting a thing, he stepped in the soft gravel and sank in the stinking muck up to his waist. As Mandan yelped as if he were being murdered, he slid deeper into the hole and splashed shit all over himself.

Recalling the scene now, Adan couldn't stop smiling. "You still smell it a little, don't you?"

Mandan scowled, knowing exactly what his brother meant. "Your trap was in a different part of the maze, not here."

Chuckling, Adan clapped his brother on the shoulder. "All in good fun, just two boys playing, like when you struck me with rocks."

Mandan laughed as well, but his humor seemed forced, and Adan realized that the sting still hadn't gone away. "It's in the past," he said in a serious voice. "We have more important things to worry about. As allies." Adan hoped his brother's expression would soften.

Mandan turned away. "We should be allies. Ishara is attacking us, killing our villagers, seizing our boats. And now you come with a story about wreths, trying to distract us from the real enemy."

"There's no rule that says only one problem will occur at a time." Adan extended his hand. "We are still brothers."

Mandan hesitated, then accepted the grip. "Of course we are."

That night, seeing that the dark sky was free of clouds, Adan made his way up to the gazing deck. He wasn't surprised to find his father already there under the stars. Konag Conndur sat with a ledger open on a small table beside him so he could mark observations. But the new page remained blank.

Adan took his familiar place on the adjacent bench, and the two men gazed at the Sword, the Stag, the Castle, all the patterns so familiar from his childhood days. Adan knew he couldn't beg his father to change his mind, couldn't pressure the konag to send troops to stand against the wreths. Right now they were just together, father and son, sharing the same interest.

He was surprised to see tears sparkling in his father's gray eyes. "Oh, Adan," he said, "what if all the stars fall?"

40

Empra Iluris had ruled for more than thirty years, but over the past few weeks she realized how little she'd actually seen of the real Ishara. Her search for a successor had taken her to nine of the thirteen districts so far, and her mind was filled with a breadth of cultures, stunning landscapes, and fascinating people. Iluris wished she had done this a long time ago. Now the land was in her heart.

By the time they reached the Prirari District, Chamberlain Nerev had already filled a volume with candidate names, meticulous notations of their abilities, and his unbiased impressions. He asked the empra to review his recommendations, but she steadfastly shook her head. "I'll keep my mind open until we are finished." The lanky man stood there forlorn, holding his books, and she tried to reassure him. "Since I'm not imminently dying, we can take time to make our choice."

Reaching the Prirari capital, the empra's entourage were given quarters in buildings around the main temple square, while she herself would occupy the top floor of the governor's four-story administrative mansion. The comfortable quarters would be a sharp contrast to their previous stop in a nomadic antelope-herding town on the edge of Tamburdin District.

Klovus joined her when it was time to meet the Prirari priestlord. He looked ragged from the constant traveling. With the strange variety of foods, the changes in weather, and the relentless pace, he had lost several pounds, and his caftan now hung more loosely on him.

"You're looking fitter than usual, Priestlord," Iluris remarked. "You'll be a slim and muscular man before we return home."

"I may be skeletal by then with this indigestion." Trudging forward, he accompanied the empra toward the whitewashed towers of the temple. "I will introduce you to the Prirari priestlord. Erical is a good man and handsome, with a calm disposition, never married. You will like him, Excellency."

"And for what purpose will I like him? As a potential husband?"

Klovus fiddled with his fingers. "I'm trying to be serious, Excellency. Erical would make a fine ruler, if you'd consider him."

"Does he even want the position?" She already knew what Klovus wanted.

"Every priestlord wants what is best for Ishara, and a strong ruler is what is best for our land."

"A prosperous Ishara is best for all." She decided to give him the benefit of the doubt. "Let's see what this man has to say for himself."

They reached the graceful white temple. Four soaring towers stretched like whitewashed arms toward the sky, enclosing a large tiled dome over the main worship area. At the arched entryway, the quiet priestlord waited for them in a gray caftan trimmed with blue. He had close-cropped brown hair, gentle eyes, and a large frame, although he stooped his shoulders as if to minimize his size.

He bowed. "Our temple awaits you, Excellency. I've whispered to the godling at great length, and I believe she will be pleased to meet you." Almost as an afterthought, Erical acknowledged Klovus as well. "It's far more modest than the home of the great godling in Serepol, but the temple is well cared for and our godling is content."

Iluris extended her hand to accept his polite greeting. She'd seen so much ambition, even desperation from some of the other priestlords that she appreciated the necessary reminder that not all of them were the same.

The large worship chamber echoed with their footsteps and whispers. Filtered sunshine streamed through triangular blue skylights in the dome overhead. Other priestlords had created a spectacle for her visit, with crowds of worshippers and great sacrifices just to impress her. In contrast, the Prirari priestlord kept his temple quiet and private.

When she asked Erical, he said, "I wanted your visit to Prirari to be more introspective, Excellency. We're a quiet people, and we prize the beauty of nature. We have lakes and rivers, and our eastern hills are covered with orchards. I hope you can stay long enough to sample our cheeses and apple wines."

"I look forward to it, Priestlord," she said. "For now, show me your godling."

The expansive worship area under the dome was empty except for flower-filled urns around the perimeter. On the back wall, a shimmering silver smear rippled and stirred, like water reflecting gray clouds. Most major Isharan temples had a spelldoor that contained the godling, holding it in some other void until it was summoned.

When the visitors approached, the glowing spelldoor brightened, as if the powerful presence could sense them. Iluris knew they would only see the godling directly if it were unleashed to defend the city, and that would not happen today. Here, they had a more intimate audience.

"She is calm now, because our district is happy and prosperous," Erical said. Mounted on the stone wall beside the shimmering spelldoor was a rectangular sheet of obsidian no more than a foot on a side. It looked oily and slick, and so much deeper than black that the word had no meaning.

The priestlord's eyes sparkled, and he spoke to Iluris privately, as if her entourage did not exist. "Would you like to look through the shadowglass window? We can watch the godling directly in her own world."

She was curious. "A shadowglass window?"

Klovus stepped forward to interject. "It is a special material harvested from ancient wreth battlefields in the old world. Shadowglass has rare properties that allow us to view godlings in their own place outside of time."

A window for priestlords to view godlings? Standing close to him, Iluris peered through the black glass. She heard Erical's breathing quicken and could smell the heat of his skin. He seemed full of wonder, as if he were seeing his own godling for the first time. As her eyes focused on the gleaming dark surface, she discerned an indescribable knot of colors and energy, ripples whirling like the feathers of a bird struck by lightning, with a singular eye floating in the center. It was as if someone had gathered and folded the auroras that appeared in the night sky and tucked them behind the black glass.

When the strange eye turned to look at her, a chill went down the empra's spine, but she sensed no threat, no anger, just benevolence and immense power generated by the unwavering faith of the Prirari people. Fascinated, she gave Priestlord Erical a smile.

Klovus interrupted their pleasant moment, pushing close. He peered into the shadowglass and nodded. "Quite a lovely godling! I understand she can be roused to anger when necessary? Under dire circumstances?"

"It rarely becomes necessary," said Erical.

Raising his eyebrows, Klovus turned to the empra. "As I mentioned before, perhaps you should consider Erical as a possible successor? He has the temperament for it, and he's quite wise."

Occupied with his own thoughts, Erical concentrated on the shadowglass window, moving his lips as if speaking with the enclosed deity.

"Is that what you wish, Priestlord?" Iluris asked. "Would you like to become the next emprir?"

Erical frowned back at her as if the idea had never occurred to him. "Why, no, Excellency. I could never leave this." He touched the shadowglass.

She wasn't surprised.

Having met so many people and traveled so long, Empra Iluris asked to dine alone that night in her private rooms on the fourth floor of the governor's mansion. There was already a large day festival planned for the following morning. With a gentle smile, she told the disappointed governor, "I want to contemplate all that I've seen in lovely Prirari." Klovus volunteered to take her place at the private evening banquet, and Iluris was happy to allow him the honor. For now she craved solitude.

It was a warm night and she opened the balcony windows. Though she ate alone, the table set out for her could have seated ten people and fed twice as many.

Taking Erical's suggestion, she had requested a selection of Prirari cheeses: yellow ones with a hard rind, pale white cheeses veined with gray-blue mold, soft creamy cheeses mixed with dried berries. Some were smoked, others mild, some so strong they made her eyes water, but she tried them all, knowing the servants would probably report back to the cheesemakers. She sampled two types of Prirari apple wine, a dry and crisp variety that paired well with some cheeses, and a far sweeter vintage that she sipped for dessert.

Servants brought in basins of steaming perfumed water. It was not exactly a bath, for the people of Prirari did not believe in baths or full immersion, but she scrubbed her face, rinsed her arms, and soaked her feet, and felt very refreshed.

Through the open windows, she could hear sounds from the square below: musicians playing on multiple flutes, conversations in the streets, water splashing in a large memorial fountain. The outer walls of the governor's mansion were bedecked with vine trellises, and the sweet smell of the night-blooming lilies wafted in on the breeze.

Iluris was satisfied with the procession so far. She'd seen great examples of her people, and she didn't feel sad or worried. She still had four districts to visit, many people to interview, and she knew her successor was out there.

A sudden shout came from the hawk guards below. Iluris yanked her feet out of the basin of fragrant water and searched for a weapon. Was there an assassination attempt? She had been lulled by the serenity of Priestlord Erical, the marvelous godling, the warm reception in Prirari District. The uproar came from the floor below, and she heard the distinctive voice of Captani Vos.

Iluris hurried to the window, looked down, and was shocked to see a wiry girl climbing the vines from the window just below. She had brown eyes, torn clothes, and ragged dark hair. The guards tried to grab her as she climbed the trellis, but the girl kicked at them with a bare foot. Climbing faster, she grinned roguishly, rather than in terror. One of the new hawk guards, young Nedd, used his sword to hack at the thick vines, breaking one loose. The girl lost her footing and swung, then snagged the adjacent trellis and kept climbing up toward the empra.

Guards pulled down on the severed vine, and the girl snatched a different one, scrambling higher, but the trellis splintered, the vine snapped, and she began to fall toward the street below. Her dark eyes met Iluris's for just an instant and the girl's look of determination changed to disappointment.

Captani Vos caught the girl's foot with a gauntleted hand as she tumbled. She kicked again, but Vos and Nedd pulled together and raised the scamp back to the window and dragged her inside.

The empra hurried to the door of her own suite to find two hawk guards standing alert, their faces tight. "What is happening downstairs?"

"An intruder, Mother, possibly an assassin." Indignant, Cyril refused to let her pass.

"You are safe here," Boro assured her.

"I saw the girl," Iluris said. "She didn't look like an assassin."

Boro looked at her with a solemn expression. "One never knows what an assassin looks like, Mother."

"I want to see her. Take me downstairs, now."

Cyril blinked in alarm. "Is that wise? She could still be dangerous."

"You are my hawk guards. I assume you can protect me from a little girl?"

Iluris pushed past them, and the two young guards followed her to the stairs and down to the next level. Inside the room, torn green vines were dragged across the sill. Vos, Nedd, and two other hawk guards held the girl, who wore a ragged shirt and rough-spun pantaloons with frayed cuffs. She struggled like a street cat. Nedd tried to tie her wrists together, but she kept breaking one hand free and striking him in the face. When she saw the empra, the girl renewed her thrashing.

Iluris stepped forward, and the others in the room fell silent. "You're caught, young lady. Do you really expect to escape my hawk guards?"

"Maybe. They're mostly incompetent."

Annoyed by the insult, Nedd tightened his grip, but she stopped fighting now that she had the empra's attention.

"She probably meant to stab you in your sleep, Mother," said Captani Vos.

"I wasn't asleep," Iluris said. "Did you find a knife on her?"

The captani looked at his other guards. "We haven't searched her yet."

"Then you'd better do so."

They quickly and roughly patted down the girl's patched clothes, but to their consternation, they found no weapon.

"Maybe she meant to scare me to death," Iluris said, crossing her arms over her chest.

"I just wanted to see you," the girl insisted. "And to see if I could do it."

Iluris studied her. She had a pointed chin, high cheekbones, a roughly shorn mop of hair. Her large eyes and thin body gave her an ethereal appearance. "What is your name?"

"Cemi. Don't ask for my family or my lineage. It's not impressive."

"She would have been disruptive, Mother." Vos looked embarrassed. "We are sorry for the disturbance. We will deliver her to the Prirari authorities."

"You should be more sorry that you let me get so close," Cemi interrupted with a snort. "Elite guards! What kind of protectors are you, if you let me climb within a few feet of the empra's private chambers? I've been watching you all day. Hawk guards are supposed to be the best, the most loyal, the empra's adopted sons! Yet, I slipped through the square below and sneaked into the governor's mansion. They thought I was a servant! Then I got to the window and started climbing." She sniffed. "I would have made it, too."

"But you didn't," said Vos. "We stopped you."

"Only at the very end. I did slip past five ranks of guards."

Iluris was both curious and impressed. "And how did you do this?"

Cemi huffed. "Through observation and a quick wit."

"Certainly not with modesty," Nedd grumbled.

Klovus scuttled in, looking flushed. "Excellency, I heard you were in danger."

"She was never in danger," Cemi said, before anyone else could respond. "I made it this far with the blessing of the godling. I made a sacrifice at the temple and prayed for a chance to see the empra."

Klovus looked at the dusty girl and scowled. "What kind of worthy sacrifice could you have made?"

"I caught a rat. It was all I had." She narrowed her brown eyes, challenging him. "Have *you* ever given all you had, Priestlord? Isn't that what the godlings value in a sacrifice?"

Iluris found herself chuckling. "How old are you, girl?"

"Too young," said Klovus.

"Fifteen," said Cemi. "I think. It's not as if anyone celebrated my gift day each year."

"Fifteen . . . Do you know that I was only seventeen when I became empra of all Ishara?" She clucked her tongue. "My poor dear father accidentally fell from a tower window."

"Sounds too clumsy to be a ruler," the girl quipped, to the gasps of the guards, the chamberlain, and Priestlord Klovus.

"Maybe he just deserved it." Iluris liked the girl's scrappiness. She gestured to Captani Vos. "Have her brought upstairs. There's far too much food for me to eat, and we may as well share it, so I can talk with her more."

They looked at her, horrified, but Iluris insisted. "If she made a sacrifice in order to speak to me, we wouldn't want to insult the Prirari godling, now would we?" She left the room and headed down the corridor, calling over her shoulder, "I'll expect the girl in half an hour—cleaned up and in fresh clothes."

Cemi yanked her arms free of the guards. "You heard the empra. Bathing water and new clothes!"

Iluris smiled as she walked to the stairs, with Cyril and Boro hurrying to follow her. Cemi had nearly made it up into the private chambers. With a little help and perhaps more training, she might have succeeded. Something about the girl intrigued her. Iluris decided it was worth investigating further.

41

THE Utauk trading ship entered the well-defended harbor cove on Fulcor Island. A Commonwealth warship was anchored at the mouth of the cove, while another patrolled the waters farther out. Five smaller vessels were tied up to a network of piers attached to the gray cliffs at the waterline.

As Mak Dur expertly guided the *Glissand* through the reefs, the sailors flew flags with the prominent Utauk circle to declare their intentions. The navy patrol ships let them pass, and the vessel tied up to the only remaining slip on the wooden pier inside the harbor cove. Sheer rock faces blocked the only access up to the fortress on top of the cliffs. A wood-and-metal staircase was attached to the exposed rock, leading from the dock up to a cleft in the cliff, which granted access into the walled garrison.

Hale looked at the smaller boats sharing the pier and recognized one Commonwealth vessel, perhaps a mail boat or supply ship. The others, though, were of a different design. He frowned grimly.

Isharan vessels, as he had feared.

The garrison soldiers were glad to see the trading ship, knowing that the Utauks brought amenities beyond their basic military rations. Because of the island's defenses, there was no easy way to unload the *Glissand*'s goods and deliver them to the fortress at the top of the cliffs. The sailors had to carry the supplies up the steep, zigzagging staircase to the cleft high above. The crack opened to stone tunnels that led up inside the walled garrison.

Hale changed into fresh crimson and black silks, tidied his hair with a tortoiseshell comb, and tugged on his shadowglass ear pendant for luck. He looked like a respectable merchant captain.

He climbed the steep, exposed steps behind one man with a keg of ale on his shoulder and another man carrying a sack of dried beans. Because of his rank—and because of his missing left hand—Hale wasn't asked to help carry the heavy cargo.

At the top of the staircase, the traders entered the deep, cool shadows of the cleft. There, a thin man waited for them in an Osterran military uniform that looked wrinkled and threadbare. Hale had not visited Fulcor Island since his trading days a dozen years ago, but he recognized dour Watchman Osler, the garrison commander who had been stationed at this outpost for years. Osler had defended the strategic fortress against several skirmishes with the Isharans.

Hale raised his good hand. "Greetings, Watchman. I am merchant captain of the *Glissand*. We trust our merchandise is welcome."

"Reminders from the outside are always welcome," said the watchman. "For the sake of the Commonwealth, we stand guard against the evil Isharans and hold Fulcor Island at all costs, but some of my soldiers do get homesick. Your delivery will keep them happy for a while."

Osler's face sagged, as if his years on the bleak island had made him bleak as well. His stringy hair was long and gray, and could have used a wash; his cheeks were grizzled with gray whiskers. After such a long assignment here, with little contact from the outside, the watchman didn't tend to his personal appearance as he would have back in the Convera military headquarters.

Hale, though, prided himself on his appearance, knowing that an impression lasted long after a meeting. "On this trading route, how could we not make your lives a little brighter?"

He looked around with an intent gaze, watching the mood of the soldiers, but nothing seemed suspicious even after the horrific sight they had seen as they approached the island. What of all those victims they had seen thrown from the high walls down to the churning reefs . . . ?

"We are delighted," said Osler, without even the hint of a smile on his face. "The amenities you bring will be most appreciated. I'll have the cooks prepare whatever we have left for a feast, if you want to call it that. No need for rationing now that you've resupplied us."

"*Cra*, I'm happy enough with a feast of bean stew, old potatoes, and dried meat." Hale kept his voice light, though his mind was filled with questions. He wanted to ask about the unexpected Isharan vessels tied up in the cove, but an Utauk leader was always careful when gathering information.

Watchman Osler led him through the cleft in the rock, which was lit with flickering lanterns that smelled of fish oil. They climbed a set of wide stone steps and emerged into an open-air courtyard surrounded by the towering fortress walls. Inside, he saw several large barracks, an armory, a dining hall. Against the far wall stood the largest structure, a tall main keep with two wings, the roofs of which rose higher than the surrounding wall.

On the barracks buildings, the soldiers put up swatches of colored fabric to remind them of their homeland. Around the barracks were garden plots, the sandy soil mixed with either guano or human fertilizer. Several buildings had cisterns on their roofs, open to the sky to catch rainwater from the frequent squalls.

Hale nodded in satisfaction. "It looks like you have everything you need here, Watchman."

"We have the necessities, but that's not enough to keep the soldiers happy. I know you brought fine cloth, sweetmeats, fresh fruits, and exotic treats, but when the nights grow cold and the sea wind blows hard, we need firewood and warm blankets. Did you bring those as well?"

Hale bowed. "Since we were coming to Fulcor, we took on exactly those items at the port of Windyhead."

The Utauks spread out blankets and unloaded their items inside the walled courtyard, where the soldiers could haggle over luxury items, food, or mementos from home. The energetic preparations reminded Hale of a small Utauk camp gathering.

The garrison soldiers were not wealthy, but they did have an allowance to spend when they went to Convera on leave. If the Utauks did their job right, those men would spend most of their coins here. Watchman Osler was indulgent with his men, even allowing some of the soldiers on patrol duty to come down so they wouldn't miss out. Three soldiers were engaged in a bidding war for a thick multicolored blanket.

Hale wondered how such men had thrown those victims to their deaths in the sea.

Walking among the blankets, Osler studied the displayed wares. "Is that all of your goods? Your ship seemed larger than this would indicate. Are you holding anything back?"

Hale drew a circle in the air. "We have other stops to make on our route, Watchman, but you have first pick of our goods." In many ports, a trading ship could take on new merchandise to add to their inventory, but alas Fulcor had no goods to offer.

Osler's frown made his weathered face look even more rugged. "And where do you go next? Sailing all the way out to Fulcor Island is quite a diversion. Perhaps back to the northern coast of Osterra?"

Hale responded with a casual smile and a dismissive gesture. "Utauk traders travel wherever we expect to find customers, but we don't report our routes or give away our secrets."

The watchman remained suspicious, and his voice took on a deadly edge. "If you're going to Ishara, you'll be sorry. They're not to be trusted. They'll steal from you, kill you."

"We've never had trouble," Hale said. "Our trading partners know they have to treat us fairly."

Osler's expression grew even more threatening, which sent a chill down Hale's spine. "You could be carrying weapons for Ishara. Maybe I should confiscate your cargo to make certain it doesn't fall into enemy hands."

Hale fixed him with a hard gaze. "You wouldn't want to do that. Utauks are neutral and always have been. The war has been over for decades, and I doubt Konag Conndur would want you to start a new one."

"Maybe the Isharans will start a new one," said Osler. "We suspect that the empra is making plans for a full invasion of the Osterran coast, after Mirrabay. We captured part of their underhanded navy, ships that ventured too close to Fulcor Island, disguised as fishing boats. It was an act of aggression."

"You mean those boats we saw tied up to the piers below?"

"We captured one just yesterday, two others in the past month. The Isharans are growing bolder, much more dangerous."

Hale had seen Isharan warships before and knew full well that these boats were of a different design. "They look more like civilian ships. Fishermen, perhaps."

Osler let out a laugh. "Just a clever ruse. They are spies. Our warships captured them and brought them here. After we interrogated the enemy aboard, they were sentenced and executed." He straightened his shoulders, showing no hint of guilt. "Every one of the men and women refused to provide any information, so we threw them from the cliffs."

Hale forced himself not to shiver visibly. "If you got no information from them, isn't it possible that they were just simple fishermen and their families?"

Osler's eyes stared toward the gray fortress wall, but seemed to see right through it. "Enemies are enemies."

Hale decided it would be unwise to argue and he felt suddenly anxious to leave Fulcor Island.

42

THE beginning is the end is the beginning.

For the time being, Glik had been around enough people, had wrapped herself in the Utauk circle and reminded herself that she was just one thread among many in the great tapestry of her tribes. She was also a special thread, an orphan, possessing a vast Utauk family . . . and none. Since the loss of her ska, her thread had frayed.

Inside the circle, and outside the circle.

Ori had been her family, her partner, the link to her heart and to her world, and now all Glik had were powerful visions, nightmares, and driving forces that she couldn't understand on her own. She needed another ska, her own ska. Through the heart link, they could control and interpret the shadowy dreams together.

To do that, though, she had to go far away, by herself. As she often did.

Shella din Orr had given her blessing, clucking a tongue in her mostly toothless mouth. "A girl your age should be playing with others, learning a trade, flirting with boys, finding romance." The old woman cackled. "But you are a seeker. I've always known you were special." She reached out with a gnarled finger to draw a circle around Glik's heart. "When you explore the world, be sure you bring your information back to me."

"I will, Mother." She had already prepared for her quest, finding a plain old collar with a small, clear mothertear diamond so her new reptile bird could record images. Now Glik just had to find where the wild skas lived, deep in the rugged mountains to the north and west. When she gave Shella a warm farewell embrace, the old woman's body felt bony and frail, like sticks wrapped with yarn.

After the great convocation of tribes was over, the Utauk families saddled their horses, packed up their cooking equipment, rolled their blankets, folded down pavilions, hitched their wagons. They headed into the hills along several routes, dispersing like fluff from a dandelion.

Glik set off on foot, alone. In her dreams she saw beating wings, scales, feathers, a faceted eye calling her, and she heard the long-lost song of the skas in her heart. She would follow the pull, even if she didn't know where she was going. On this journey, Glik would only be able to see with her own eyes.

She ached to have the scarlet reptile bird on her shoulder, longed to stroke the sharp-edged feathers, feel the warm scales, scratch under Ori's elongated chin.

Why did you leave me?

When she had first found Ori, the ska was injured, caught in a tangle of branches. She had extracted the reptile bird, tended him, linked with him. Glik had been just a child then, but she kept Ori for five years, five perfect years.

With a stick, she drew a freehand, perfect circle in the dirt and hiked away into the Suderran hills. Glik didn't carry maps, but she instinctively knew the lay of the landscape. From her dreams she knew the direction she had to go.

Glik crossed a line of hills and paused to stare at the rugged sea of melted ground. In all her explorations, she had been to the Plain of Black Glass only once. The mysterious, scarred valley was the site of one of the most terrible wreth battles at the height of their awful wars. Scorched and blasted by titanic magic, the soil had not recovered even after two thousand years.

According to stories, this place was once a wreth metropolis, but in a final battle, the creator race had unleashed so much magic that the ground itself melted. Since the wreths used their human slaves as foot soldiers and workers, countless thousands of people must have died during that holocaust. Maybe their blood was infused into the puddles of shadowglass, which carried remnants of magic.

As Glik picked her way down the slope, she was surprised to see powder-blue poppies planted in the dry soil. Intrepid Utauks had come out here, knowing they could sell the shadowglass to collectors of rarities and especially to the priestlords in Ishara, who used slabs of shadowglass as windows to observe their godlings.

Even under the hot sun, the ground held a chill, as if it had been drained of all life. The uneven ground was interspersed with chunks of obsidian that shimmered with an oily rainbow of colors. Glik was looking at an incomparable fortune in front of her, but the only thing she wanted was a ska.

Shading her eyes, she saw a flash of color against the melted plain—the blue-and-white fabric of a tent. "Hello!" she called as she ventured out onto the rugged half-melted terrain, careful with each step. If she fell, the razor-edged glass might cut her badly.

She heard no answer, only the breezy silence of the empty plain. She climbed the crystal-sharp blocks, seeing bare patches where more blue poppies claimed a foothold in tiny pockets of soil. "Hello!" she called again.

Glik had often been alone for months, needing no other company than Ori because she was never alone, thanks to their heart link. Still, she enjoyed sharing a meal with someone, exchanging stories and news. Inside the circle, instead of outside. This isolated prospector might want company as well.

The tent was empty, though. When the girl poked her head inside the flap, she found only a bedroll, some cookpots, and a waterskin. The tent cloth was tattered, as if it had been there for some time. Maybe the prospector had departed and left his possessions behind?

Wind whistled across the blasted plain, seeming to blow sheer emptiness along with it. Suddenly lonely, Glik shivered. She sensed the powerful remnants of magic deep beneath this haunted battlefield. So many people had died here, both humans and wreths. Had the melted glass captured their dying screams?

She left the abandoned tent and searched the area, not bothering to call into the eerie silence, sure that no one would respond. Whoever this Utauk prospector was, he or she must have gone away, perhaps with a load of shadowglass.

But why leave the waterskin behind?

With increasing dread, she followed marks where someone had chopped out pieces of shadowglass. She climbed over an obsidian hummock and saw a man below—a human figure in a gray shirt, red scarf, brown pants. He was sprawled facedown among chunks of broken shadowglass.

Startled, Glik began to run toward the man, but she knew it was much too late. She slipped, caught herself on a sharp-edged black boulder, and the shadowglass cut a gash across her fingers. Bleeding, she moved with greater caution, making her way to the body.

The prospector must have also slipped. His tools were scattered around him: a chisel, a rock hammer, a pick. The sharp obsidian had sliced down the inside of the man's arm, opening an artery. He had bled profusely, and dark, sticky patches dried across the vitreous rubble. On the lifeless Plain of Black Glass, scavengers hadn't come to devour the body, although a few persistent flies buzzed around the desiccated skin. The man's dead face wore a look of surprise.

Glik considered burying him, but the ground was much too hard, the shadowglass too sharp. The slabs would be too heavy for her to lift by herself. Instead, she went back to the tent and found scraps of cloth which she tore into strips to wrap around her bleeding fingers, then wrapped more cloth around her hands for protection.

In the warm afternoon, she picked up chunks of the black rock and carried them around the dead man to create a perfectly circular ring. She worked hard, knowing the labor was important, filling in the gaps, surrounding him, keeping him inside the circle. "The beginning is the end is the beginning," she said.

When night fell, she went back to the empty tent, taking advantage of the shelter. Glik would remember the man's legacy, as much as she knew of it. Among his scattered possessions, she found a name written down. *Bhosus.* She discovered paper among the supplies and wrote an account of everything she knew about the prospector. At least that was something to mark that this person had *existed*, since the gods certainly didn't care about humans.

When she slept in the whistling silence, dreams came to Glik with rushing noises, countless voices from the ancient battlefield demanding her attention, insisting that she remember their stories as well. It was overwhelming, deafening, and she wished Ori were there with her to help guide her dreams, her visions.

In her dream, with a mental call, Glik asked for the ska's protection, and inside her mind the sound of countless chittering ska voices drowned out the voices of the ghosts in this battlefield, made them leave her alone. She saw thousands of reptile birds flying, swooping together in an enormous flock, so many wings and feathers and scales they filled the sky . . . and they all flew toward black, jagged mountains.

The next morning, Glik emerged from the tent to see sun shining on the distant line of rugged mountains on the horizon, exactly what she had seen in her dream. She took the prospector's supplies and waterskin and left the Plain of Black Glass.

High overhead, she made out the tiny black specks of skas wheeling on the breezes. Their eyries were in the mountains. That was where Glik needed to go.

THE wind made beautiful music as it whistled outside the crystal windows of the frostwreth palace, accompanied by the hiss and scratch of blowing snow. The weak, gray sunlight that penetrated the blizzard wall illuminated Queen Onn's bedchamber.

She concentrated on the sound of her own breathing, the brush of flesh upon flesh, and the sounds of pleasure from the man beneath her. She found the noises stimulating. The captured Brava lay back on the slick bedcoverings with sweat glittering on his pink skin. She could have made each of those droplets freeze into tiny ice crystals so his body sparkled. She enjoyed it when her lovers sparkled.

Lasis kept his eyes closed, lips drawn back as he fought her, though of course he did not succeed. His features revealed that he had wreth blood somewhere in his lineage. Onn's people had once dabbled with their human creations; some even fooled themselves into calling them lovers. For Onn, there was no love, only curiosity.

So far, this one had not lived up to expectations. She straddled him, shifting her hips, and against his will he moved with her. "That's better." She drew a long finger across his forehead.

Lasis kept his eyes closed as if he were imagining someone else. His lips curved in a frown. She stroked the side of his face, along his nose, releasing more glamour, more of the complex chemicals and scent that worked into the man's animal nature. He shuddered, unable to resist.

Onn had always been able to manipulate males, whether they were wreth or human. With her beauty and primal sexuality, she rarely needed to rely on magic. But Lasis had resisted in every way since Rokk had found him skulking around the Lake Bakal ice fortress. As a half-breed, the captive possessed a trace of magic, and she wondered what he could do with it. The mage Eres had said he fought strangely but well.

In a way, this man was as intriguing as the little boy that Rokk had taken from that primitive human village, but unlike the child, Onn could press Lasis into a different kind of service.

The Brava's ramer was an interesting artifact. She had heard it clatter to the cold floor when she made Lasis cast his clothes aside. The captive had endured, stony and angry, as she walked around his naked body, inspecting him.

"I expected to be more impressed." She had reached out to touch him, releasing the first tendrils of her glamour. She saw him flinch, then relax unwillingly. "But you are adequate, I suppose. Let's see how well you perform."

"I refuse. I swore my loyalty to the Commonwealth. I serve none but King Kollanan the Hammer. I—"

Impatient, Onn released a flood of her magic. He shuddered and threw his shoulders back as he struggled, but finally he sighed and shuddered in an entirely different way. "Oh, I don't think you'll refuse."

Onn had taken him to her bed, coaxing and kissing him. Lasis seemed mechanical, struggling to do exactly the opposite of what she wanted, but she could manipulate him as easily as she could shape ice forms. She played him like a musical instrument, moving him faster and slower, letting him rest—just enough—before driving him to a frenzy again.

From the other side of the room, a whimper distracted her just at the moment of climax. In frustration, she looked over to see the human child sitting in the corner, wrapped in the blanket she had let him keep. He said his name was Birch—who named a child after a tree?—and that he was five years old, but could offer little additional information. He played with a small wooden carving of an animal.

Contemplating how rarely wreth had children of their own, Onn kept him nearby. She herself had given birth to two sons, both of whom were killed in the wars millennia ago, and a daughter, Koru. She had lost track of her daughter, a full-grown, powerful survivor, but Koru had a different spellsleep cycle from Onn's, so they rarely interacted.

A young child was different, though, even a human boy. Dabbling in capricious maternal instinct, Onn had decided to keep little Birch with her, to mold his life, since he was young enough to be malleable. As an unformed human, the boy might prove more useful than a drone. He sat where he was told, and he watched without comprehending when she forced the Brava to be her lover.

Dismissing thoughts of the child, she turned back to Lasis, pressed her palms on his bare chest, trying to command his focus. Again, he struggled, turning his head to one side to avoid looking at her. A jolt ran through him as he gasped, "Birch? Birch! He is still alive."

Onn glanced back at the boy, trying to sense some familiarity in the pale young face. "You know him?" Birch turned away from the attention, clutching the wooden figurine he had brought with him, like a talisman.

"He is a boy," Lasis said through clenched teeth. "Nothing more."

"If you know this child's name, then surely there is more to him." She leaned closer, demanding his attention. She found the Brava's willpower surprisingly strong.

"Nothing. A boy."

Uninvited, one of the smooth-skinned drones entered her chamber with a message. This new interruption annoyed Onn, and she snarled at the stupid thing. "What do you want?"

The small-statured drone didn't have the sense to know fear. "Chief Warrior Rokk will soon return to Lake Bakal. He wishes to seduce you before he leaves."

Onn's face pinched with displeasure. "He always wants to seduce me." She turned a wolfish smile down at Lasis, growing bored with his angry apathy. "Send him in. I might have need of him after all."

The drone stared with cowlike eyes as she arched her back, turning her cold breasts toward it. Drones were such a disappointment. "You like to watch us? Or are you going to deliver the message?" When the drone paused, as if pondering the answer, she shrieked, "Get out!"

Birch tried to hide under his blanket, and Onn had had enough. "Take the child with you. Care for him, or I will be very angry!"

Birch looked at her for a moment in disbelief, then sprang to his feet. "Thank you, Queen Onn!" At least someone had taught the child manners.

As Birch ran to the drone with his blanket, the diminutive creature seemed baffled, then the two scuttled out of the chamber.

She knew it did no good to be furious at the ill-formed drones. It was like shouting at a piece of furniture. Some frostwreths even toyed with the drones as sexual partners. Most of the creatures were neutered and incapable, but some could serve the role, especially the females. The idea made her skin crawl. She had debased herself enough in rutting with this lowly half-breed. Perhaps a more cooperative human would have been a better candidate, though there was a certain thrill in making Lasis dance to her wishes.

He glared up at her, and she leaned close, breathing chill steam into his face. "Tell me you are not enjoying yourself."

He followed her command precisely. "I am not enjoying myself."

During the time of the wars, wreths had followed Kur's example and created humans to serve them. The inferior race looked like wreths, though they were less attractive, weaker, and mostly unable to use the magic that permeated the land. Humans had been a successful and tenacious species, and after awakening from the long spellsleep, Onn was pleased to know that they had survived, even after the holocaust.

When the wreth mages awakened periodically over the centuries, they had attempted to create more humans. Queen Onn encouraged their efforts, knowing that the frostwreths would need servants to do the menial work, and to die as fighters when necessary. But the process had been disappointing, the magic in the land too weak after the wars, and the best species the wreth mages could now produce were simple drones, subservient, but not clever. So insufficient.

Rokk sauntered into her bedchamber wearing a hard black vest, a gray cape, and tight blue leggings. "Ah, I see you are already occupied, my queen. Does that mean you have no time or energy for me?" He tossed his pale hair back.

Onn bent over the Brava and felt a flash of anger toward the reluctant man. "No, I was finished with him. He has given all he can give."

The aloof warrior cocked his chin. "Are you already tired of the human child I brought you? I saw a drone leading him away."

"I have not decided what to do with him. I think I will send him with you to the Lake Bakal fortress."

Rokk's eyes widened. "And what would I do with him there? How would I care for him?"

"Have your drones tend him. That is all I would do with him here."

He still seemed alarmed. "But to what purpose?"

"He might have some use as a hostage." Onn looked down at the reluctant man beneath her. "This Brava hinted that the boy is somewhat important, but would tell me no more."

Rokk scowled at the Brava as if glad to divert the discussion. "The man is indeed troublesome. I could torment him for you."

"No need. This one was just an experiment, a failed one." In an offhand gesture, she slashed her razor-edged silver nail across his exposed throat. Blood sprayed out, and Lasis thrashed, bending his head back to splash crimson across Onn's naked form. The blood smelled potent, wet and metallic.

The Brava tried to grab her in his last moments of life, but she knocked him off the side of the bed, where he rolled onto the floor and stopped moving, stopped gushing blood. Onn sniffed, surprised. He hadn't even bled much except for the original spurt, but now he lay cold and motionless.

She turned back to Rokk as he approached the bed, looking hungrily at her. She ignored the dead Brava on the floor. "We will have drones dump it outside in the cold."

Rokk unfastened his dark vest and let his cape fall to the floor. "My pleasure, Queen Onn."

"Your pleasure will come after you have earned it." She considered the spray of blood on the sheets, then intentionally reclined on the stain.

Rokk poured himself a goblet of silverwine and drank it slowly as he regarded her. "For so many years whenever I awakened, you were still in spellsleep, so I would just stand and admire your body in stasis. It aroused me so much that I would have to find someone else to satisfy me, since you weren't available."

"Whenever I awoke from spellsleep, I had plenty of lovers to choose from, too," she said. "You should have made arrangements for us to wake at the same time."

"Now, we are both awake and will stay awake until we rouse the dragon," said Rokk. "Until the world is ended and remade."

Onn beckoned him to her, and he stretched out on the bed so they could touch their skin, feel the tingle of magic as they each unleashed their glamour spells, building to an ecstasy that they would both experience.

"Do your duty, Chief Warrior Rokk," said the queen. "Satisfy me."

44

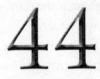

THE people of Scrabbleton had no explanation for the wreth stranger's remarkable healing, other than magic. They already knew that the half-breed Bravas recovered more swiftly than normal humans.

At Elliel's side, Thon walked among the townspeople, fascinating them and frightening them. His broken leg was healed, and he barely limped. The smoke from the summit of Mount Vada seemed angrier and thicker each day, and a gloomy pall hung over the Dragonspine Mountains, as if Ossus were growing restless. Each breath of air tasted of brimstone.

Elliel took Thon to the town's small remembrance shrine, where she showed him the records of human lives, all the people who had been associated with the town for a long time. She read some of the names aloud, because he said he couldn't understand human writing. His face remained blank; the recent history meant nothing to him.

Thinking hard, he asked, "Would you take me back inside the mines? I want to see what remains of the chamber where I was held. Maybe it holds some clues as to why I was sealed inside."

She was concerned. "I don't know if it's safe. Most of the miners haven't gone back inside yet. Some of the shafts have been dug out and reinforced, but we were deep inside the mountains. The tunnel collapsed behind us. I barely got you out before the walls and ceiling caved in."

The wreth man shrugged as if such an obstacle was of no consequence, and his dark blue eyes pleaded with her. "I need to see."

She looked at his strange expression of curiosity and need. She had already decided to stay with Thon and help him solve his own mysteries. Something about him captivated her.

Some miners were shoring up the outer galleries and clearing the main passages of debris, but none had yet ventured into the deep tunnels. Occasional tremors still rumbled through the mountain, so mine boss Hallis had not risked sending in the full work teams.

Carrying a lantern, Elliel led Thon, proceeding with caution. As they picked their way around debris, a warm sulfurous mist hung in the air. When they came upon a wall of fallen boulders that blocked the passage, she shook her head. "We can't climb over or through that."

Thon placed the flat of his hand on a boulder and concentrated. The rock shivered, then crumbled into fine gravel that spilled across the tunnel floor, clearing the way. "It is no longer an obstacle."

Elliel was amazed. "No, it isn't." He waited for her to take the lead.

They worked their way through the rubble, moving down the tunnel until broken slabs formed another impenetrable barrier. Again, the barricade posed no challenge for the wreth man, who simply made the obstruction crumble. When parts of the cracked, unstable walls threatened another collapse, he used the rock debris he had just produced and slathered it onto the rock like plaster to hold it in place, and then it hardened into a solid bond.

Elliel followed the turns, chose the correct intersections as she remembered them, guided Thon farther until they reached the hidden quartz-lined grotto. They stood shoulder-to-shoulder as he peered into what had been his prison.

Glimmers of light shot through the broken crystals, as if his presence activated some inner energy. Without speaking, Thon used his hands and his magic to widen the opening so he would walk through the door without obstruction. Together they searched the small chamber, but found no artifacts, no answers. The reinforcing metal struts in the wall were jarringly incongruous. Thon picked up a quartz shard and turned it in his hand. "No message here. No wreth writings." He was mystified and disturbed. "Someone just . . . sealed me away for eternity without leaving any explanation as to why."

"Do you think you were being punished?" She unconsciously touched the tattoo on her cheek. "Did the wreths strip you of your legacy, too? Or maybe it's something entirely different. You could have been left as a guardian. Or a messenger."

"Maybe I was left here to protect Ossus."

She wasn't sure he was serious. "If Ossus is real."

Thon turned his startlingly handsome face toward her, tilted his head to one side. "Of course the dragon is real. You felt the mountains stir. You saw the collapse in the mines. You see smoke rising from the mountain."

She did not deny the evidence. "I've come to question a lot of things."

Thon sifted handfuls of the crystalline debris through his fingers before letting out a sigh. "We will not find anything here, Elliel. We have to look elsewhere." He moved her out of the chamber, then made intricate motions with his hands. The crystals crumbled from the vault wall, shifted, and drew together to form a jagged sphere that filled the entire chamber, sparkling like a giant snowball. The hidden room was entirely blocked.

Thon backed away farther and collapsed a huge section of the rock wall, to seal the chamber forever. "My answers will be outside."

The next morning, as more of the miners cautiously returned to their regular routine, Thon prepared to leave Scrabbleton. "I must find answers, and they are not here. My path leads north along the Dragonspine, then west. Something is calling me there, drawing me."

"Wreths haven't been seen in thousands of years," Elliel said. "Just half-breeds like me."

"And yet I am here." He gave her a smile that sent an electric tingle through her skin. "Perhaps there are more like me. I need to find them."

"Maybe they aren't friendly if they entombed you for thousands of years." She looked at him for a long moment, then made up her mind. "I'll go with you. As you find answers, I may find answers of my own."

He offered her a sober look. "Our questions are entirely different."

"That doesn't mean we can't help each other."

Elliel had felt content here in Scrabbleton, even at home. The people had welcomed her, and she enjoyed her work as a miner, but she had made no commitment to settle here permanently. Something about this wreth stranger seemed vital. She had to help him, wherever it took her.

Hallis was sad to see her go, because she was such a hard worker. Upwin and the other miners insisted on saying goodbye before she departed, and Shauvon provided ale for everyone as a farewell celebration. Thon joined them in the inn's common room. The townspeople still felt perplexed about him, though not threatened.

Filled with good food and ready for a good night's sleep before setting off the next morning, she and Thon went back to her room, where he had continued to stay. He sprawled on the narrow bed, while she spread her blanket on the hard floor again, but he gestured to her. "Sleep here. You will be more comfortable."

She hesitated, wary of what he might be asking. Even so, her pulse raced when she looked at him. A mysterious magnetism hovered like mist around the strange man. Was she really so resistant to the idea of sleeping with him? She was sure most of the townspeople already assumed they were.

Elliel thought again of her blank past and wondered if she would be a good lover, or if she was entirely inexperienced. As with her reflexes in fighting, maybe some things were instinctive. . . .

Before she could join him on the bed, Thon stretched out, rolled on his side, and faced away from her, leaving half the narrow bed for her to lie upon. Elliel stood for a long moment, looking at the blanket on the hard floor, then surrendered. She crawled onto the bed, facing the opposite direction with her back touching his. Though the bed was more comfortable than the floor, she had a very difficult time getting to sleep.

While Shauvon and his wife were baking the morning bread, Elliel and Thon slipped through the inn's common room, where one man remained, snoring like a growling bear and resting his head on his forearms on a table. Outside, the sky was dark, with only a pale glow of sunrise seeping from behind the mountain range. They set off, wanting no fanfare from the townspeople, and followed the hill roads out toward the western plains.

After two days of walking, they found a very small settlement called Arnasten, with fewer than forty people, and strangers were rare. Elliel bought a hot meal for the two of them, but the villagers stared at them so intently that they left before dark, preferring the less judgmental solitude of the forest.

Four miles down the road they found a sign on a wooden post pointing the way to a hot spring, one of many thermal areas in the Dragonspine Mountains. Elliel didn't know if she had ever been to a hot spring before. After asking her to read the human letters on the sign, Thon smiled. "Let us go there to absorb the energy in the world. It is heat and life."

Following the side path, they found a ten-foot-wide pool surrounded by boulders and drooping, yellowed trees. The water was a milky blue, stirred by tiny bubbles. Steam and fumes rose up, adding a mineral smell to the air that was not entirely unpleasant. They were alone.

"We bathe, and we relax," said Thon. "We talk." Completely unselfconscious, he removed his jerkin, his boots, and his fine leggings to stand naked and muscular beside the pool. His pale skin had a buttery sheen in the last light of day.

Elliel began to remove her loose linen shirt, turning her back to Thon, who stood stretching as if to make sure she looked at him. "Why do you hesitate?" he asked. "Wreths created humans. We know what you look like."

"You don't know what *I* look like," she said, thinking of the scars that disfigured her otherwise fit body. When was the last time a man had looked at it—if ever? She steeled herself and pulled off her shirt, then undid the bindings on her loose trousers.

"You are lovely."

For some reason she believed what he said. With her back to him, she heard the splash as he slid into the steaming pool. She piled her garments on one of the rocks. She turned, intending to get in and submerge herself as quickly as possible, but Thon was looking at her. She found that she couldn't move, though not because of any magic. He ran his appreciative eyes over her breasts, the various scars, the curved loop across her abdomen, the burned patch. He seemed to take in all of it as part of her.

"I was right. You are very beautiful."

When she could move again, Elliel pulled her cinnamon hair back from her face, stepped to the edge of the spring, and lowered herself into the water. The pool was hot and tingling, and the sulfurous fumes made her feel warm and giddy. She let out a long sigh. "This does feel good." The aches in her muscles dissolved like honey in hot tea.

Thon stretched his arms out to either side on the rim of the pool and leaned back. "There is still some magic left in the land. I can feel it here, a heat pulsing into this water."

"Do you know this place? Have you ever been here?"

Thon touched his cheek, tracing the rune marked there. "I do not know."

"I don't know either," she said. Utho's letter was in the pocket of her shirt neatly laid on the dry rock. "The memories of my old life aren't there, but the skills sometimes are."

She sank deeper, all the way up to her chin, and rubbed her skin, running her fingers over the scars. Questions surfaced in her mind. "As a person, I am more than just my past crime, aren't I? My body remembers some of what I was. I'm a talented swordfighter. I tried archery and found I was good at it. I practiced with musical instruments when a minstrel showed me, but I had no aptitude at all."

He seemed amused. "You were trying to find out who you are."

"Yes, and I still don't know."

Daring, she moved through the water and floated just in front of him. El-liel stretched her legs down to where she could just barely touch the soft silt and slimy rocks on the bottom of the deep pool. She reached out to delicately touch his tattoo. "I've looked at my face in the mirror enough times. Your mark is different from mine. There's an extra line here."

"Our tattoos are not the same. Not precisely." He extended his forefinger with the gentlest of touches, no stronger than an infant's breath against her cheek, and traced the markings she couldn't see. "Mine has an extra loop. It is a locking element that prevents my memories from ever being released." Unerringly, he touched the exact spot on the side of his face, even though he couldn't see it. "This cross-mark means my memories are sealed as surely and securely as I was sealed in the vault inside Mount Vada."

"The vault that held you in the mountain wasn't permanent either," she pointed out. "Maybe your memories aren't gone forever."

"Nothing is impossible," he admitted. "But I was placed deep in the mountains, and someone meant for me to forget. Now that I have awakened, it is a mystery I was meant to solve. Am I a weapon? Or a monster? Was I locked in there by the wreths? Or maybe even by Kur himself? I do not know."

She absorbed the soothing heat in the water for a moment. "I feel the same emptiness inside my mind, but at least I'm aware of what happened to me, what I did. I have Utho's letter." The stillness around them deepened as she thought about her lost memories. Thon had said that her tattoo was missing a locking element. Did that mean she could reverse the punishment the Bravas had imposed?

She longed for that, but was also afraid, hesitant. Perhaps it was a blessing that those memories had been purged from her. What would it feel like to know every expression on the faces of the children she had slaughtered? Their screams, their weeping, how their poor teacher had fallen under her ramer.

"Don't you *want* your memories back?" she asked him, but he refused to respond. She continued, "I would like to know why I did what I did." Then she whispered, hardly daring to voice the words at all. "Or *if* I did what they say I did."

DRESSED in black leather armor and finemail-lined cape, Utho was impressive among the fighters in the Commonwealth soldier escort gathered for the departure of Kollanan the Hammer and Adan Starfall. Utho was glad the two men were going back to their respective kingdoms with their unsettling stories about wreths. Given the imminent Isharan threat, the Commonwealth could not afford to be distracted by ancient legends.

Looking sad, Konag Conndur stepped out into the courtyard as his brother and his younger son prepared to leave. They would each have an armed escort of twenty soldiers as they followed separate routes over the Dragonspine to their kingdoms. The soldiers wore iron helmets with swooping cheek guards, swords at their sides, and leather body armor marked with the open-hand symbol of the Commonwealth.

Giving the konag a farewell embrace, Adan said, "Remember what we said, Father. If Queen Voo returns, you must meet with her."

Kollanan said in a gruff voice, "Meanwhile, I'll be gathering my entire army. Don't underestimate the wreths, Conn."

Prince Mandan arrived late, dressed in rich purple silks, as if he were attending a grand function of state. He frowned in surprise to see the armed escort. "Forty troops, Father? What if we need those soldiers here in Osterra? What if the Isharans attack?"

"They will attack," Utho said in a low voice. "Sooner or later."

Conndur said, "We have enough forces to defend ourselves."

Utho warned, "We must have a realistic view of the true danger, Sire. We can't have the common people looking for wreths under every bed, when the Isharans might send godlings and warships to the Confluence at any moment."

As he mounted up, Kollanan shot a sharp glance at the Brava and spoke with bitter sarcasm. "Yes, maybe the frostwreths meant no harm when they destroyed Lake Bakal and killed all those people. With their new fortress, I'm sure they have only the best intentions."

"We'll spread warnings across Suderra and try to be prepared for whatever the wreths do next," said Adan. The two kings turned their horses, impatient to be away from the crowded courtyard. "I know the Utauk tribes are also on the lookout. If anything changes, we will send another warning. The three kingdoms must stand together."

Conndur looked deeply troubled. "Even if our armies stood against the wreths, would they not sweep us aside like insects?"

"Insects can sting," Kollanan said and urged his horse into a trot, leading his escort soldiers out of the gate in a thunder of hooves. Adan's group followed.

That afternoon, Utho continued Prince Mandan's instruction, although it meant interrupting a tutoring session in the arts. As a Brava, he had to make sure the prince knew how to kill.

When Utho stopped at the doorway to the studio chambers, Mandan was attempting to paint a bowl of old fruit, some pieces merely wrinkled, some brown and rotting, or covered with a burst of gray-blue mold. The tutor frowned at the bowl. "Let me get some fresh fruit, my prince. A painter should concentrate on more attractive subjects."

"A painter should depict the world around him," Mandan corrected. "And a konag needs to see the rot as well as the freshness."

The tutor clicked his tongue against his teeth. "You are of course right, my prince."

Mandan's expression lit up when he saw the silent Brava standing at the door. The tutor looked up, sniffed. "We can't be interrupted in the middle of a lesson."

Utho ignored him. "My prince, come with me."

The tutor sputtered, but Mandan set down his paints. "Utho has important training for me, in preparation for becoming konag." The annoyed tutor couldn't gather his paints and palette quickly enough, leaving the bowl of rotten fruit behind.

Utho handed a plain shirt to the prince. "Today we go out to the archery fields so I can train you to handle different types of bows."

"I already know how to shoot a bow," Mandan said.

"In war, you need to shoot without thinking, without flinching." Utho imagined that Mareka and even his little daughters had shot arrows at the Isharans who came to rape and burn and kill, and when they ran out of arrows, he hoped they had used sticks and knives, fighting to the last. . . .

Utho needed to make sure Mandan could fight just as well, if need be, but the prince clearly wasn't interested. "I've gone out on the hunt every month. I felled a stag just last week."

"You *wounded* a stag, my prince. I made the kill shot."

It had been a messy business. The prince's arrow had merely lodged in the deer's ribs, and the beast went crashing and bleeding through the underbrush. Utho brought it down with a single arrow to the heart. He cut the stag's throat so that the deed was done by the time Mandan caught up.

"If the Isharans attack, you won't be able to defeat them with painting," Utho said.

Mandan considered this. "I have you to defeat them, as well as the entire Commonwealth army. If the enemy invaded our shores, all three kingdoms would unite to drive away the enemy."

Utho wasn't so sure, if Adan and Kollanan were off chasing wreths in the hills. "Wouldn't you like to make a kill yourself?"

"I suppose I could shoot an arrow right into the heart of Empra Iluris." His lips formed a strange grimace. "Or maybe I'd shoot her in the ribs, so she would be a longer time dying. Like the stag."

Utho should have chided him for such ignoble sentiments, but considering they were talking about Isharans, the dark glitter in Mandan's eyes seemed appropriate. "Yes, she would deserve that."

They went out into a walled practice yard on the bluff high above the river confluence. Utho brought a regular bow, a longbow, and a crossbow from the armory chambers, along with a basket of arrows and quarrels. Bales of old gray hay stood against the stone wall of the practice yard. To make the target more appealing, Utho had found an old yellow caftan such as the ones worn by Isharan priestlords, plundered from some foreign cargo ship the navy had seized.

Utho hung the caftan on the bales and turned back to Mandan. "Use this as your target. Your aim will be better if you imagine some Isharan animal wearing it."

Mandan smiled. "Oh, I will."

He had the prince use the longbow first. When the young man had difficulty stringing it, Utho bent the flexible wood, pulled its curves down, and slipped the bowstring loop in place. "The longbow's range is tremendous. That is its main advantage. When our archers face an Isharan army on the battlefield, longbowmen can shoot a rain of arrows from a safe distance, enough to decimate the enemy."

"How do you aim so far away?" Mandan plucked the bowstring as if it were a musical instrument.

"If you have enough arrows, it is not so important to aim at an individual target. You just kill them all. Try it."

Mandan took an appropriate arrow from the basket, nocked it, and strained to draw the string back, but the pull was difficult. When he loosed the arrow, it whistled, flew wide, and clattered against the stone wall.

Frowning but patient, Utho said, "Here in the practice yard, however, you *do* have to aim. Let me show you."

Mandan tried three more times, first determined, then flustered. Utho adjusted the young man's finger placement, sighted down his arm, and showed him how to lead with the tip of the arrow. The third arrow struck the bales of hay, at least, which he considered a victory. Utho didn't want to frustrate the prince further, so he gave him the regular bow, the one he used in hunting, and Mandan was far more competent with it. He shot half a dozen arrows, managing to pierce the caftan with two of them.

Mandan looked up at his mentor. "Tell me the story about why you hate the Isharans so much. I want to hear it again."

Utho needed little encouragement. "You know the history, how they slaughtered our peaceful Brava colony of Valaera, used a godling to tear my people apart. Since then we have sworn a vengewar against them."

Mandan sounded impatient. "I know the history, Utho, but your anger always sounds so personal. I know they killed your family during the last war. Why weren't you there to protect them?" The prince shot another arrow, grazing the old caftan again.

Utho handed him the crossbow and four quarrels. "Because I had another assignment. I had to leave them at home in Mirrabay when Konag Cronin stationed me on Fulcor Island."

Mandan looked at the quarrels, holding the crossbow and weighing it. "Is that why you're called Utho of the Reef?"

"That is how I became Utho of the Reef." His voice grew quiet as he told

his story. "Emprir Daka wanted to take back the island, so he dispatched a
trio of the Isharan navy's most powerful warships, which were far superior
to our patrol ships stationed at the island. The Isharan warships anchored
out past the reefs, well beyond the range of even our ballistas or catapults
from the walls. From there, they blockaded the waters, drove away supply
vessels. We couldn't reach the enemy ships, and all they had to do was wait
for us to starve.

"We were trapped for weeks. We drank water from the cisterns, ate the
last of our old stores." He set his jaw. "We were down to nothing, with no
alternative but to surrender, but I knew we had to break the hold, somehow."

Mandan nocked one of the quarrels in his crossbow, wound the string
tight, and set the latch. "What did you do?"

Utho looked out over the wall of the practice field. "I destroyed the warships, all by myself. From the reef."

"Utho of the Reef . . ." The prince smiled. "How did you do it?"

"The Isharan ships were anchored out of range, but when the tide went
out, the rugged, slippery rocks of the reefs were exposed above the water.
For only one hour each day, the reefs became a treacherous walkway.

"On a dark and moonless night, I climbed down the cliff with a longbow—
like the one you were just using—and a basket of pitch arrows. I reached
the waterline and picked my way over the reefs toward the sea. I was nearly
swept away by waves sloshing across the rocks, but I didn't dare fail. In the
dark, I kept walking out across the water until I was far from the island . . .
and within range of the anchored enemy warships.

"They thought they were safely out of reach. The Isharans couldn't see
me, didn't expect me. But I found the perfect position on a large outcropping of coral. I set my basket down, strung the longbow, ignited the first pitch
arrow with a spark of magic. As the tip burst into flame, I drew back the
string and let the arrow fly. My aim was true, and my fire arrow hit the sails
of the nearest Isharan ship.

"I lit and shot all fifteen arrows, one by one, and all fifteen of them struck
home. The flames ignited the enemy sails. Fire rocketed up their masts and
along the decks. Their men cried out in alarm. They had no idea how they
had been attacked, for no one should have been able to approach from that
direction.

"I enjoyed my victory for only a minute, though, since the tide was coming back in. Water already covered part of the reef walkway, so I left the

basket and bow behind and just ran. My feet splashed in tide pools, and waves nearly swept me off the rocks. I lost my balance and tumbled into the sea, but I swam back, pulling myself up onto the coral, and waded along until I made it back to the garrison.

"Behind me, the enemy vessels were burning fast, and I heard the screams of roasting men. All three Isharan siege ships became great funeral pyres." He smiled as he spoke.

"I was exhausted and battered, but we had won. The Isharan navy was defeated, and our warships could break the blockade and attack the other patrolling vessels. It was a great victory, and we celebrated. The garrison was saved." He stared off into the distance. "I took a ship back home to Osterra so I could tell Konag Cronin what I had done, that Fulcor Island was still safe."

Utho paused, feeling sick. He fell silent for so long that Mandan looked at him with eager curiosity. Though a Brava rarely showed emotion, Utho's voice cracked. "But while I was stationed at Fulcor Island, an Isharan raid wiped out the town of Mirrabay, where my family lived. Slaughtered them all—Mareka, our daughters, all dead . . . while I was out on the reef saving the garrison instead of my family."

The prince stared, flushed with anger and disgust.

Utho snapped at him, "Don't just fumble with that crossbow! Shoot! What if we were under attack?"

Startled, Mandan lifted the crossbow, pulled the trigger, and launched his first quarrel. It struck the caftan below the belt, making what would have been a terrible wound in the lower abdomen. He wound the string, loaded, and fired the other three quarrels. Utho's story had sharpened Mandan's intensity, and all of the deadly bolts struck home.

"Good, my prince," said Utho. "Be ready to do the same if ever you see a real Isharan."

46

⤠

WHEN her procession finally rolled back to Serepol, Iluris let out a happy sigh and gazed out the window of her carriage. "One's home city is always the most beautiful place in the world."

"You haven't seen some of the places I've lived." Cemi rode next to her in the carriage, drinking in details. After the scamp had been cleaned up and given fresh clothes, Iluris invited her to accompany the procession to the next district, much to the alarm of the hawk guards, Chamberlain Nerev, and Priestlord Klovus. Cemi had no family, no ties, nothing to keep her in Prirari, and the empra enjoyed her unusual perspective and insights. As they traveled together, the young girl's interest in the world around her never flagged.

At the head of the procession entering Serepol, Captani Vos cleared the way through crowds that gathered to watch the empra return. Cemi peered out the open window on the other side of the carriage, absorbing the capital city. "That giant building! Is that the palace?"

Iluris chuckled. "That's just a warehouse, child. The palace is much larger."

Cemi looked at her skeptically, sure she was being teased. "Truth?"

"The empra would never lie."

"You taught me better than that!" The scamp laughed, then quoted, "Politics, leadership, negotiation, they all involve shades of the truth. Only people who pray to godlings in the temples believe in absolute answers to their questions."

The words warmed Iluris's heart. "Good, you were listening. I'm going to include you among my advisors. Your insights are often sharper than theirs."

The girl leaned back in the rocking carriage. "It's because I've lived a real life, instead of a pampered one."

Instead of her street rags, Cemi now wore a lovely green blouse embroidered with gold and silver, inlaid with cabochon jewels. Scarves wrapped around her neck and covered her short brown hair. She looked beautiful, clean, and completely uncomfortable.

The empra said, "There are many advantages to a pampered life. Your mind has more freedom to think about important things if you aren't worried about catching rats or running from thieves."

"I won't argue with that." Cemi tugged her silk sleeve, plucked at the jewels glued onto the fabric. "But I'd rather spend these gems than wear them. What is the point of showing off and looking so pretty?"

Iluris smiled. "A girl your age has reasons to be pretty."

"They aren't always good reasons."

As the procession traveled across the remaining districts, Iluris had spent hours in the carriage teaching her new ward the history of Ishara, the priestlords and each district's godlings. She described the long-standing conflict with the Commonwealth and the constant depredations of the unruly Hethrren clans in the wild lands south of Tamburdin District.

Everything was a revelation to the scamp, who had survived on the streets without formal schooling, although years ago a kindly old woman had taught her how to read words and sound out names. Iluris assigned Chamberlain Nerev to help Cemi with her reading during parts of the long ride.

Now the girl kept watching everything around her as the carriage rolled past Serepol warehouses, blacksmith shops, lumberyards, large kilns that served potters' street. Stonemasons broke giant blocks of marble into smaller slabs. Farmers drove mule wagons loaded with sacks of grain, baskets of fresh greens, bushels of apples.

One farmer darted in among the hawk guards and reached the side of her carriage. Shouting, the guards drew their swords and closed in around him, but the farmer was no assassin. At the carriage window, he extended a pale green melon. "For you, Excellency. You've never tasted a sweeter one! My best."

She accepted the melon just as Captani Vos seized the man by the arms, pulling him away from the carriage. Seeing the melon, Cemi's eyes lit up. "These are delicious and rare—I stole one once! They're called sunset melons. He meant no offense."

Accepting the girl's assertion, Iluris called out to her dedicated guards, "Release him and give him my thanks. But if this melon is so precious, we have to buy it. Give him a gold coin, Vos."

The captani stepped back, touched his breastplate in surprise. "A gold coin, Mother? For a *melon*?"

"For this melon. It is worth the cost."

The farmer beamed and bowed. As instructed, Vos gave the man a coin, and he danced away with a story to tell his fellows for years to come. Iluris watched him go, recalling her earlier thoughts that she had a sort of strength and protection from the people's faith in her, much as the godlings drew power from sacrifices and faith. She wondered what the key priestlord would think of that.

After the procession regrouped from the disruption, the captani approached the carriage window. "I apologize for letting the man get so close, Mother. He could have harmed you."

Iluris pursed her lips. "Captani, please give me your dagger."

Vos drew his knife. "To defend yourself? We would never let you be in that much danger! We would all die before—"

"I require your knife to cut open this sunset melon. I'm curious to see how it tastes."

As the carriage rolled on, she and the girl spread a cloth over their laps, and Cemi sliced through the hard rind to expose a juicy orange interior with little black seeds. The flesh was musky and sweet, and it melted in Iluris's mouth. Cemi carved out a chunk for herself, ignoring the juice that dripped on her fine clothes.

"This is delicious." Iluris dabbed sweet juice from the corner of her mouth. "See, dear girl, you can teach me things, too."

"Not as much as you've taught me, and I'm very grateful." Cemi clearly meant it.

"When you ask questions, you force me to formulate an answer, and as empra, I'm supposed to have the answers."

"Don't the priestlords claim to have answers?" Cemi wiped her mouth with the sleeve of her dress. "Isn't that why they keep the godlings, to protect us all?"

"Priestlords think they have answers." Iluris's voice grew quieter as the carriage rattled on. "In truth, no one has all the answers."

Finally, the procession passed through the heart of the capital city. The priests came out in their colorful caftans, and Klovus rode in the lead, waving as if he were in charge now. As they rolled past the enormous foundations of the Magnifica temple, Cemi stared. "Is the size of the temple why the Serepol godling will be the strongest godling in the world?"

"The construction won't be finished for a long time yet. Our godling is powerful already, but once that temple is completed, it would become a thousand times stronger. Who knows what it might do with all that power?"

Cemi stared. "With a protector like that, Ishara would be invincible."

"And what if godlings have ambitions of their own? Or the priestlords?" Iluris felt a knot in her stomach.

The rest of the arrival day was a blur of parades and celebrations, receptions, cheering crowds. Iluris endured it all, smiling to her people as the beloved empra. Overwhelmed, Cemi curled up and fell asleep in the carriage before they reached the palace. When the scamp woke up, she stared at the tall towers, fluted rooftops, colorful tiles, stained-glass windows. Cemi poked her head out of the carriage. "Don't tell me that's another warehouse."

Iluris chuckled. "No, this truly is the palace. As I said, nothing is more beautiful than home."

The girl remained silent for a long moment before asking quietly, "And that's going to be my home now?"

"So long as you behave," Iluris teased. "I will keep you around."

That night, Iluris asked the chefs to make a small meal to be served in her quiet tower chambers, and of course they delivered an extravagant feast, much of which would go to waste. After spending time in Cemi's company, she decided to make sure the unwanted food was distributed to beggars from now on.

The girl changed out of traveling clothes into comfortable silks and slippers. She sat on a padded chair at the low table, tucking her feet beneath her legs as she ate.

Iluris had brought Chamberlain Nerev's ledger listing all the names under consideration to be the next leader, with many of the candidates crossed out, no longer in contention. "Let's talk about these."

Cemi had already reviewed the possibilities on the journey, as Iluris suggested, and she kept her eyes open. "Now that you've taught me so much, I see how important it is that we really find the best person to be your successor." She sniffed. "I always thought the empra was just some fancy lady who had banquets and parades but didn't really do anything."

Iluris lifted her chin. "I work harder than that!"

"When my most important concern was to steal an apple to fill my belly, I didn't think about the subtleties of government." Cemi turned a page, scanned the numerous names and brief notations by each one. "I want to help you find the right person."

Iluris was pleased that Cemi's reading skills had improved enough for her to decipher the chamberlain's scrawled writing. Some of his letters were jumpy and jagged because he wrote on his lap as the carriage rattled along the roads.

Fifteen years old, Iluris thought, trying to remember when she herself was so young. Cemi had lived a difficult life, fighting every day, but young Iluris had suffered as well under her abusive father. Even a pampered life wasn't always what it seemed.

"I thought you wanted to be the next empra," Iluris teased. "Isn't that why you tried to break into my rooms in the governor's mansion?"

"Dreams are only good so long as they stay dreams. Reality isn't the same," Cemi admitted. "No one would accept a scamp from the streets with no noble blood, no experience. I'm nothing." She ran her finger down the list of names, tapped on several of them. "But if I can help, I'll help. I don't want the responsibility of what you do."

Iluris pushed aside her half-eaten dinner and bent close so they could both look at the names. The empra said in a conspiratorial voice, "The one who truly wants the power is not the one who should have it. In that respect, you'd be very high on the list of contenders."

Cemi made a rude noise and scrutinized the names again. "I like several of these, and another one here." She flipped the pages, indicated more candidates.

Iluris had an idea. "Then here is your assignment. Consider these and then tell me why each one of them is a better choice than you. What skills do they have that you don't?"

"You aren't serious?"

"I'm very serious. Those names have merit, or Nerev would not have written them down. So, tell me why they have merit. Compare them." She hardened her voice. "And tell me why they are better than you. What do you lack?"

"The list will be long," Cemi said.

"We aren't in a hurry." Iluris began to appreciate the ingenuity of her scheme. Cemi would define the advantages of these other men and women and with respect to the specific skills or knowledge she herself didn't have. With such a list in hand, Iluris could identify exactly how to focus Cemi's education henceforth, to make her the best possible candidate so that she really could become the next empra of Ishara.

47

Six days after leaving Dr. Severn and the town of Thule's Orchard, Shadri spotted the crumbling wreth ruins out in an empty valley. In the low afternoon sun, the ancient abandoned city seemed to beckon her, and Shadri answered that call, already excited about all the mysteries she would find there.

With her big pack on her shoulders, she hiked out of the hills toward the ruins, humming to herself and content with her own company. Her baggy tunic, dusty skirts, and patched cloak hid her stocky frame and showed that she was obviously not a person with any wealth or power.

Shadri knew that few people ventured into the ancient wreth cities. Even after so much time, they considered the places cursed, or at least dangerous. She found them intriguing, however—an opportunity to gain knowledge that few people would seek.

Reaching the gateway to the crumbling ruins, she stopped humming, feeling the weight of silence and history. She saw countless questions, and more questions beyond those questions. When there were no people around to ask, then she asked the questions herself. She hoped this fallen wreth metropolis would answer her.

The ruins were full of shadows and strange curves, doorways that went nowhere, bridges that cut off abruptly in midair. Craning her neck, she faced a graceful stone tower with curved sides that tapered to what would have been a majestic point, but the apex had fallen into rubble. Shards of colored crystal from windows lay scattered on the ground.

Though the fine detail had been erased by time and weather, the tower wall was covered with stone faces sculpted by wreth artisans. Each face bore the distinctive almond eyes, angular cheekbones, and pointed chin of the wreth; expressions varied from contented to heroic to horrified. The realistic depiction of the long-lost race was unsettling, yet fascinating.

The moss-covered remnants of high walls were cracked from centuries of rain and frost. Fluted, corkscrewing pillars held up nothing but birds' nests. She nudged the rubble with her boot, imagining this great metropolis in its glory. So much to see! It seemed a cruel joke to arrive here so late in the day.

An ornamental frieze wall rose in front of her, carved with dozens of detailed figures, two wreth armies engaged in battle. The wreth warriors wore extravagant armor and carried fierce-looking spears with twisted hafts, spiraling clubs with hooked spikes, triangular embossed shields. This stone mural likely memorialized some historic event in which the descendants of Suth had fought the descendants of Raan, since the two factions had warred constantly for the right to wake the dragon and destroy the world. Although the wreths used their human slaves as shock troops, Shadri saw no humans in the mural, only wreths with fury on their faces.

One army sat astride thick-legged reptiles, while the others rode shaggy horses with clawed paws instead of hooves. The opposing captains held their weapons high. The carved scene was pregnant with violence.

When Shadri moved forward for a closer look, she stepped onto a raised flagstone and felt a click. A humming glow throbbed through her body. The mural sculptures shifted, the stone figures rumbling as they slowly came alive, like a puppet show. The battle groups surged together. Reptile mounts careened into the wolf horses. Wreth soldiers slashed with their swords, plunged spears into their stone opponents.

The animated violence grew worse as she watched, the battle more horrific. Stone blood spilled from stone figures. A wreth battle commander skewered his opponent with a jagged spear, then moved forward to chop off his enemy's head. Victorious, he held up his grim trophy and turned toward Shadri. His gray, petrified eyes looked directly at her.

With a gasp, she stumbled back off the flagstone, and all movement in the mural ceased. The figures did not reset to their original positions, but remained frozen in the bloody aftermath of the ancient battle.

She stared at the silent tableau and chuckled. "Interesting. I did not know any of that." She would have to write down the details in her journal as soon as she settled down by a campfire.

As dusk deepened, Shadri hummed to herself again and began to look for a place to spend the night, so that she could continue exploring the next morning. Most sensible people would have fled the haunted ruins before darkness fell, but her questions were stronger than her fears.

"Superstition is the enemy of knowledge," she reminded herself. Spending so much time alone, Shadri often spoke aloud to keep herself company, although she avoided the practice when she was in a town, so that people wouldn't think her addled.

In an overgrown plaza Shadri found a raised rectangular platform, like a stage that had been silent for millennia, and decided it would make a good place to bed down. She shrugged off her unwieldy pack, glad to be relieved of the burden. She rolled her shoulders to loosen them, then gathered branches, fallen twigs, and dry leaves, with which she built a crackling campfire against the darkness. She decided to gather a bit more wood to make sure she had enough to keep the flames going throughout the night.

When she uprooted a dead bush from the flagstones, it came loose with a musical tinkle of crystal. The branches had wrapped around a fallen relic, like a tree made of silver and iron. Blue crystal shards lay around the fallen object.

Only one of the flat, triangular crystals was still intact, the smooth surface covered with wreth markings. After she scrubbed away the caked dirt with her palm, she found a second layer of writing on the opposite side. Holding the fascinating crystal up to the flicker of the campfire, she tried to read it, but the symbols were indecipherable. Shadri wanted to learn the wreth language someday.

She spread out her cloak, propped her pack behind her so she could lean against it, and sat cross-legged near the cheery fire. She puzzled over the triangular crystal, tilting it back and forth in the firelight, but the elusive questions tantalized her.

Her campfire was the only light in the ancient city. If she let her imagination wander, she might have envisioned watchers in the shadows, echoes of the lost race that resented her for trespassing there. But if some wreth were to lurch out of a tomb and stand before her, Shadri would stand up and defiantly demand answers. How she longed for that!

Ready to sleep, she lay with her head against her pack and stared up at the stars—all those other perfect worlds created by the wreth gods—and she imagined the ancient race. What had the wreth been thinking when they created humans? When she and Dr. Severn dissected the corpse together, they had marveled at the intricacies of organs, muscles, blood vessels, looking for where the missing soul might be hiding. How complex humans were! She could feel her heart beating, the blood flowing, the air moving in and out of her lungs, the thoughts spinning through her mind.

Yet humans were only a secondary race created to serve as slaves or tools. Neither Kur nor any of the other gods around the myriad other stars paid attention to humans. Their race was on its own.

She placed her palm against her breastbone and felt her heartbeat. She was alive; she could think; she could dream. What more did she need? Shadri wondered what it would feel like to have a soul. . . .

The idea incensed her. Why were the wreths superior? If Kur had abandoned them, how did the ancient race even know they were so special? "What made you feel different from how I feel?" she demanded aloud, in case any wreth ghosts happened to be listening. "How do you know Kur pays no attention to humans, just because you created us rather than him?" Her forehead wrinkled, drawing her dark brows together, and she lowered her voice to a whisper because the question was so ominous. "How do you even know Kur is there at all?"

She had heard that magic was much stronger in Ishara, where people created their own godlings. If so, why couldn't citizens of the Commonwealth create beings as well? Was magic too weak here? Surely their beliefs could be just as strong! Should people in the Commonwealth be ashamed of this failing? Or was "creation" something they could figure out how to do if they just tried hard enough?

Or was it the other way around? Had the Isharans done something monstrous and terrible when they generated their godlings?

Shadri's questions multiplied, as always, and each mystery spawned another mystery. That was what made life fascinating and worthwhile, but each question mark denoted an empty spot in her knowledge, and Shadri was determined to spend her life filling that emptiness.

Humming to herself again, she curled up in her cloak and pressed the triangular crystal against her heart. Maybe as she slept the answers would come to her in dreams, but she didn't expect it. Answers were usually harder to obtain than that.

The ruins loomed around her, mysterious and protective. She would stay here and find her own answers, poking and prodding until she figured it out.

48

ROCK pinnacles rose out of the ocean of sand deep in the Furnace wastes. The stone monoliths looked like a gateway at the end of the striated gray mountains that pierced the desert.

Queen Voo and her sandwreths were thriving here. The stark heat reminded her of the blasted battlefields from the wars, after she had slashed her rival Onn's face, after her people dragged her away from the boiling landscape under a shield of defensive lightning. The world's magic had been so strong then . . .

The wreth factions had almost destroyed each other in the centuries of warfare, but that war was not finished yet.

Voo hoped that Kur was watching so that he could see her anger, how she and her sandwreth comrades were trying to do exactly as he commanded, in spite of how poorly his lover Raan had been used. The evil Suth had poisoned her own sister and nearly torn the world apart with her jealousy. As the descendant of Raan, Queen Voo would continue that generations-long war of vengeance against the frostwreths.

She shifted the triangular green shield on her arm. No matter what her rivals were doing far to the north, the sandwreths were stronger, and they would wake the dragon—as Kur demanded. It would take time, and first they needed to test their magic, but the sandwreths would be Kur's chosen people.

Ten of her loyal companions rode augas under the shimmering heat, including her brother Quo and the mage Axus. They had left their sand-and-stone fortresses behind in the deep desert, heading toward the mountains. The reptiles thundered along, leaving deep three-toed imprints in the sand. Voo looked behind her at the swirling sand they had crossed, seeing the line of their tracks.

Wearing brown leather and golden scales, they followed the fault line, seeking the resonance point at the far southern end of the mountains. No humans had ever been this deep into the Furnace, because humans could not survive in such a harsh environment. That was why, as a benevolent queen, Voo protected and sheltered her special human servants, kept them alive so they could continue to work and build. That way, only a few of them died, rather than all of them.

Her brother rode up to her and squinted his amber eyes into the heat ripples that blurred the jagged mountain range. "We will use our magic here, Sister? Unleash all of it?"

Her auga lurched along. "I want to see what we can achieve. Let us hit these mountains, prod the dragon. It is only the first step, but I believe we can make him stir."

Quo's smile showed perfectly even teeth. His long hair hung like a mane behind him. "We could level these mountains and break the desert if we wanted to."

Voo shook her head, jingling the gold bangles woven into her hair. "We will not break the desert, but we will shake the mountains. Our magic will run deep."

As the queen slowed her auga, the other wreth mages and nobles joined her, squinting their sparkling eyes across the empty sands. The party rode to the first line of black slabs that rose out of the sand and built upon one another into a ridge that extended to the distant Dragonspine Mountains.

All the remaining magic in the land was connected, all the lines of power that had fed wreth armies for centuries as they systematically destroyed the continent. This mountain range extended into the Furnace like a raw nerve. Voo and her companions would pulse it and jar the entire land.

Having reached her destination, she gracefully slid off the hardened leather saddle. The large-eyed beast flicked out a black, forked tongue. The rest of the wreths dismounted and stood with their queen to study the imposing mountains. The dry dust smelled clean to her, full of potential. She set aside her dragon-scale shield and knelt with her bare knees in the hot sand. She pressed her palms against an angled slab of volcanic rock. The heat burned her skin, but she washed it away with a thought, then pushed her magic into the rock.

"I can feel it. This rock goes deep to touch the mountain, and that mountain goes deep to touch the heart of the world, where the dragon sleeps."

Flashing a grin, she looked at Quo and the wreth mages and nobles. "To-gether we can thrust our magic like a knife into that heart, and twist."

Voo felt the clinging leather of her garment, which still held tendrils of life and magic. Her boots and shoulder patches were made from finely scaled auga hides, but the rest of the leather was cured human skin, which was soft and comfortable.

The queen leaned against the slab, extending her arms to cover as much stone with her skin as possible. She drank in the throbbing heat, the energy, the magic. Her brother did the same, tearing off his leather jerkin and press-ing his bare chest against another slab of stone, embracing it like a lover.

The wreth mages and nobles peeled off their clothes, and every member of her party touched the rock at the root of the black mountains. Queen Voo laid her cheek against the rough stone and whispered to the mages, "Sum-mon it now. Call the magic. Send a wave of force deep into the world, touch the raw nerve, and jar the sleeping dragon."

The mages intoned deep-throated spells, called up frayed remnants of magic, mere scraps that remained in the ground, and intensified them.

Energy surged into Voo's spine, tingled in her solar plexus, sparkled in her heart. It warmed her empty womb and drew upon her source of life, increasing it. Nearby, her brother laughed, and the mages and nobles ex-hibited the same exhilaration as they summoned more power.

They formed a combined hammer and hurled it deep into the rock, pro-ducing a tremor that penetrated the earth. It resonated and rippled along the entire range. The sharp cracks of the mountains shook huge boulders loose from unstable positions. An avalanche slid down the cliffsides into washes and arroyos.

Queen Voo and her companions struck again, throwing a hammer of magic in among the dunes. The sand erupted in towering geysers, and dust swirled like a whirlwind. The shock went deeper.

"We will be ready! We will be strong." Voo poured her concentrated force into the mountain. "Our combined power will wake the dragon."

A final wave struck hard, jolting the nerve at the root of the mountains. The shock rippled all along the range, traveling for uncounted miles into the heart of the Commonwealth.

Spent but exhilarated, Voo slid down the slab of rock and landed in the soft sand. The stone felt cold now. Her naked body was bursting with sweat.

The wreth mages had collapsed. Her brother crawled closer, walking on hands and knees to reach her. "Shall we do it again?"

"We will." Voo hugged him. "But not yet. We must eradicate the vile frost-wreths first. We need to save some fun for when the real war starts."

49

AFTER Rokk departed again for the new fortress at Lake Bakal, Queen Onn guided a group of wreths northward. She had work to do in the snowy mountains.

Wrapped in a cape lined with white bear fur, Onn lounged in the curved seat of her sled. Four small, muscular drones, clad in tattered furs and harnessed to chains, plodded through the snow. Their spiked boots found enough purchase to drag her sled north. Alongside her, two more sleds carrying frostwreth mages crossed the landscape toward the dominant black mountain that rose out of the wasteland.

The mountain, which Onn had not bothered to name, was weighed down by tons of ice and snow, but it was a resonance point. Its bones went deep to the root of this range that extended into the lower continent to join with the Dragonspine Mountains, beneath which Ossus lay. The dragon slumbered, hidden for millennia . . . but it was no longer safe, now that the wreths were strong and ready to awaken it.

She was glad she had not brought the little boy Birch along, since the human child would never have survived the rigors of this journey. She wasn't even certain the fragile thing would last back at Lake Bakal, where Rokk had taken him for the time being, nor did she have confidence the drones would know how to care for him. She sniffed, making up her mind to devote more attention to the boy. Maybe she would summon him back, but later. Her work here at the black-walled mountain was far more important.

The white landscape was interjected with stark rocks. This was the realm Onn ruled, a cold expanse with additional wreth fortresses, walled settlements, and redoubts where her people had gone to ground as they rebuilt their race. For centuries of alternating spellsleep and years of wakefulness, she had fostered her race, helped build their defenses and their weapons. Onn was hungry for a war to destroy the hated sandwreths so they would not be redeemed by Kur when he returned. She touched the scar on her cheek, remembering how she had almost killed Queen Voo long ago. She would be victorious this time.

Onn felt the cold sting her bare face as the drones hauled the sled faster. Ice crystals sparkled on the white bear fur. She could never forget the most important command Kur had given his children before he disappeared, that they must destroy the dragon, the embodiment of all that was evil, hateful, and violent. Such darkness poisoned not only the wreths, but the world itself. Onn was not yet convinced they were strong enough to wake the dragon, but her people grew stronger each day.

The wreth mages in the adjacent sleds were wrapped in thick blue robes; their heads bare and bald, their sunken eyes ice-blue and determined. The humorless mages were poor company, but she needed them for their power. If they could hammer magic into the black-walled mountain, the resonance might be enough to shake the world.

The drones stumbled to a halt on the uneven snow, which made the whispering runners of her sled grind into silence. The pale, slow-witted creatures stared at a wide crevasse that yawned before them. Unable to cross the deep blue-walled canyon, they turned to her with blank and incurious faces.

Impatient, Onn swung herself out of the sled and walked across the snow. The mages also emerged to stand at the edge of the deep crevasse. When they made no move, she snapped, "Do I have to do this myself?"

"No, my queen," said one of the mages. The four of them stood at the edge of the drop-off, their blue robes flapping in the wind, animated by the power they evoked. The snow trembled beneath Onn's feet, and the crevasse began to close, its edges grinding together like a door slowly shutting.

"We don't need to reshape the entire landscape—we just need to cross over," she scolded the mages. Onn raised her hands, called upon her own magic, and manipulated the ice. Its component water melted and re-formed the walls of the crevasse like putty. She filled in the gap, formed an ice bridge solid enough to bear the weight of the sleds, and climbed back into her seat. When she was nestled among her furs, she told the drones to start moving again.

The hissing of the sled runners changed to a loud scrape across the hard, clean ice she had formed. The mages' sleds followed as the drones staggered across the windy plain, their bowed heads shrouded in furs.

Queen Onn shaded her eyes and gazed at the looming black mountain ahead. The pristine covering of ice and snow inspired her, making her imagine what the world would be like after Kur remade it in a perfect form. But Onn could not have her final victory if the dragon still slept beneath the world, and she knew that rousing Ossus would require a titanic effort. She and her mages needed to practice, after so much time of lethargy.

When all three sleds stopped and the drones stood exhausted before the black buttresses, Onn faced the mountain as if it were an arrogant barrier that defied her. Her ivory hair blew about like a wild thing, but she summoned heat from inside herself, calling the magic in her blood. She smiled at the wreth mages beside her. "This will take all of us. Together we can shake the world."

The mages crackled with cold, their blue robes swirling. Onn shrugged out of the bear pelt and stood in only a thin, silken gown that was little more than woven wind. "We have to touch the power ourselves. Let there be nothing between us." She stripped off her gown, tossed it aside. The breezes caught it, and somehow the garment drifted back into the sled. The drones watched without emotion. Queen Onn stood bare-skinned in the frigid air and threw back her head. Her breasts were high, her hands spread as she reveled in the cold.

Likewise, the wreth mages shrugged out of their blue robes and stood facing the glaciers. Without their garments they didn't look less powerful, but rather more majestic.

"This is how Kur created us," Onn said. "This is how we must show him that we will do as he commanded us."

The mages raised their arms over their heads, squeezing doubled fists. Onn took her place in the middle and raised her hands. When she clasped them into fists, she felt the magic crackle.

Beneath her, the thick glacier shivered, as if afraid. They called the deep magic, united as the spell built and swirled around them, and then in unison, they swung their fists down as if to smash the ground with an imaginary hammer.

The magical impact sent concentrated force into the ice, pummeling the black mountain with seismic blows. The ground shook and roared. Onn braced herself. The glaciers covering the mountain shifted, broke apart, and fell away. Great bastions of blue and white slid down the rock wall in deafening rumbles, relieving the mountain of its burden.

Without flinching, the drones stared vacuously at the immense power that had just been unleashed into the world.

When the mountain was nearly as naked as Onn and her mages, they raised their hands, clasped their fists, and summoned the walls of force once more.

"Again—and deeper!" Onn said. "Until all the mountains feel it."

They brought their hands down in a second furious blow that resonated deep, deep into the earth.

Onn watched the ripples shudder across the arctic landscape, and the shock waves continued to build all the way to the horizon, as if she had thrown a stone into a pond. Glacial debris tumbled from the side of the mountain with a sound as loud as the roar of a dragon.

Onn smiled.

50

Together, Elliel and Thon traveled the mountain roads, passing supply trains, ox-drawn ore carts, and pack mules following a familiar route from town to town along the Dragonspine Mountains.

Thon followed the road, trending generally toward Norterra, but he wasn't sure where he needed to go. Elliel watched him gaze off into the distance with a lost but curious expression in his crushed-sapphire eyes. The enigma surrounded him like an aura, and she sensed that this stranger had a deep importance. They also had a unique connection because of their similar situations, both of them with a lost past. What if he did have an important destiny? What if, by being at Thon's side and helping him accomplish his own quest, she built a legacy of her own that was strong enough to wipe out the dark stain in her past? Though it wasn't a formal arrangement, as it had been with others she had served, she considered herself bonded to the wreth man, doing what she had been bred to do. Elliel began to feel like a Brava again.

They followed the mountains for two days after the hot springs. Because of the shape of the rugged peaks, she could imagine early settlers telling stories about the huge world dragon buried there. With its persistent plume of smoke, Mount Vada was the largest peak in the range, and its conical silhouette was prominent behind them each morning when Elliel looked back the way they had come.

She led the way, studying Thon, watching his reactions. Because her companion was a wreth, his expressions were often opaque to her, not normal human reactions, but she tried to interpret them as she learned his personality. Though she felt an undeniable attraction to him, he had made no attempt to seduce her, though he had ample opportunities. When Thon gazed into her green eyes, did he find her pretty, or was he just studying her tattoo?

She was just as fascinated with the rune on his face, especially the loop that formed the locking element. Someone or something had purged him of his memories, sealed him in a quartz-lined grotto deep in the mountain, and he didn't even have a damning letter to give him explanations, like the one Utho had written for her. He was a complete cipher.

She couldn't believe him guilty of some horrific crime like her own, but preserving Thon in a crystal cave seemed far too extravagant a process for mere punishment. Why had they not just executed him, or exiled him, rather than sealing him inside a mountain for eternity? What possible crime could have warranted that? Or was it a crime at all? Maybe it wasn't a punishment. What if Thon had been sealed away there for his own protection, to keep him safe? What if he was being hidden for some purpose? There had to be something more to him, and she was determined to discover what it was.

Observing his soft voice, his kind curiosity, and his calm demeanor, she was convinced that for all his strangeness, Thon must be an honorable man, someone she could respect. In her heart, Elliel considered herself a good person, too . . . yet she had murdered those children and their teacher. Thanks to the rune of forgetting, she would never know exactly why she had flown into an unbridled, murderous rage. She had read Utho's letter so many times, she'd memorized every word, but it sounded like it was written about a stranger, not her. It had to be!

She touched her cheek and walked purposefully along the stony pathway. Next to her, Thon said, "I am glad for your company. We have a long way to go."

Elliel climbed the steep path without losing her breath. "We don't even know where we're going."

He kept up with her, showing no sign of a limp even though his leg had been broken only a few days earlier. "Yes, but I know it is far away. I can sense the call, where I am supposed to be. This way." He gestured toward the top of the ridge. "Maybe by the end of our quest, you and I will both know who we are." Smiling, he reached out to touch her. Elliel felt a chill, as if he were using magic, a glamour that trickled into her skin from his fingers.

Suddenly, he recoiled and his mouth dropped open. "Can you feel it?" He clutched his chest. "It goes deep."

"Thon!" She grabbed him, held him steady. "What is it? I don't feel—"

The ground thrummed beneath her feet, a vibration that bubbled up from the core of the mountain range. She heard a louder sound as the peaks shook, and another sharp shock knocked her to her knees. Thon dropped to the ground beside her, paralyzed.

Up and down the ridge, the tall silver pines swayed as if stirred by a storm underground. Several trees toppled and slid down the slopes along with rocks and displaced dirt. This was immeasurably worse than any of the quakes she had felt inside the mines. It went on and on.

She held Thon, offering comfort and needing his touch in return. He clutched her, his face twisted in a rictus of pain. "The world is tearing itself apart!"

Rocks sloughed down the shelf that held the narrow road, and part of the mountainside came down behind them. Another pine crashed next to them as the tremors increased. Seeing that the top of the ridge ahead was clear of trees, Elliel grabbed Thon's arm. "Quick, up there! It's safer."

They ran, panting and stumbling to keep their balance as the earth rocked like a wild horse. They staggered to the ridge top, where they were above the trees and falling rocks. Shuddering, Elliel and Thon turned back to look at Mount Vada.

The huge mountain had exploded, its symmetrical cone blasted away, leaving a raw wound from which boiled a fountain of ash and smoke that rose in an anvil shape higher than even the winds could reach.

"The mountain . . ." she said.

For many days she had watched the curl of listless smoke far above Scrabbleton, thinking little of it. Now, a river of orange fire dripped like candle wax down the nearer slope, and Elliel feared the lava would engulf the town. Like an angry, violent cough, another expanding ball of ash and smoke vomited out from Mount Vada.

"All the miners!" she cried. "My friends. If they were in the tunnels . . ."

Thon's pale skin had grown even whiter as he stared at the continuing eruption. "Ossus is awakening."

Elliel grabbed his hand. "We have to go back, see if we can help. I know that's what a Brava would do. We can't just run away."

"Yes," he said, in a bleak voice. "If the dragon is stirring, we must go there."

51

VIEWED from the bluff high above the river confluence, the sky seemed to be on fire. At sunset, copper and crimson clouds rose above the distant Dragonspine, and the air stank with a lingering pall of smoke. From the castle walls, Conndur watched the colors grow more violent, and he sensed that something wasn't right. A spreading gray pillar of smoke rose like a thunderhead above the mountain range.

Prince Mandan stood beside him, looking to his father for answers. "Remember ten years ago when the grass hills burned? The smoke made the sunsets look like that. Is it a forest fire?"

Conn swallowed hard, tasting ashes. "If that is a forest fire, then half of Osterra must be burning. Something enormous has happened."

At first, he had viewed the smoke as a curiosity, then a worry, and now the sunset intensified his feeling of dread. Within the next day or two, travelers or eyewitnesses would come from the distant mountains and report. In light of the unbelievable warnings from Adan and Koll, though, what if this strange phenomenon had something to do with the wreths and their terrible magic? If true, that would be worse than any Isharan coastal raid. . . .

Wearing black, Utho climbed the wooden stairs up the stone wall to join the konag and the prince on their high vantage. He stared westward, grim. "It's a grave portent, Sire."

The Brava looked down and saw a pale gray fleck land on his black sleeve, standing out like a snowflake. He brushed it away, but three more drifted down on him. Curious, he picked one up between his fingers and rubbed the tips together.

"Is it snowing?" Mandan asked. "It isn't even cold."

"Not snow, my prince. It is ash."

❧

By the next morning, the sky over Convera was choked with clouds that were not clouds. A blizzard of ash drifted down to cover the streets, and gray-white flecks caught on the walls, the roofs, and the banners of Osterra. Uneasy merchants shook out their awnings; families swept and reswept their doorways. People tied scarves over their mouths and noses.

Conndur and the prince joined Utho in the stable yard as he saddled his mount. He had packed blankets and supplies. The konag thought of devastated wreth battlefields, firestorms of magic unleashed as the factions of the ancient race tried to destroy each other. What if Adan and Koll were right about the wreths? About the dragon?

The konag said, "I can offer a military escort."

"I'll ride faster alone, Sire. Light and fast." Utho's black cloak was dusted with smears of pale gray. By now the air smelled of sulfur and burning, and the ashfall came down even more thickly.

One of the city guards, flushed and breathing hard, found them in the stable courtyard. "Sire, the Crickyeth River has changed. I just came running from the lowtown. It's a disaster!"

With Utho and Mandan following, Conn hurried to the castle wall and looked down to the river far below. The Crickyeth normally ran swift and clear out of the Dragonspine Mountains, but the nature of the current had dramatically changed overnight. The usual swift flow had become sluggish, clotted. The water was gray and brown, as if uncounted tons of silt had poured into the headwaters. Broken pine trunks floated down the river like splintered sticks, so many at once that they tangled, crashed, and scraped against the banks like battering rams.

Along the river, flatboat pilots and fishermen frantically tied their boats to the docks, then scrambled back onto the bank as broken branches and tree trunks plowed through. A huge tumbling silver pine, its boughs still thick with dark needles, swept along like a brush, scouring anything in its way, crashing into the narrow bridges that spanned the river, knocking out small docks.

Warning bells clanged from the lower city's watchtowers. On the other side of the wedge of land, people on the calmer Bluewater bank stayed close to their homes. At the point of the Confluence, the clogged waters of the Crickyeth rolled into the Joined River, spilling a stain of mud, silt, and ash.

As Utho mounted his horse, ready to ride out immediately, a second group of riders galloped into the stable yard. On their saddles in front of them they carried bedraggled refugees: a mother and father, two children dressed in rags. Their feet were bleeding and their faces were even grayer than the ash. The guard captain's red rank sash was also streaked with gray powder. "Sire, these people come from the foothills east of Mount Vada."

The refugee father slid off the saddle and barely kept his balance as he bowed before the konag. "Sire, we had one horse for the whole family! When the mountain exploded, we all climbed on and rode away so fast that it killed the horse. Then we kept running on foot. We made it to the city at dawn." The man coughed until he could speak no more. His two children were sniffling and crying.

Conn came closer. "The mountain exploded? Tell me what you saw. What happened?"

The mother wiped the back of her hand over her crusted lips. "Mount Vada shook and then broke open with a great raging fire. The whole eastern side of the mountain is gone. It . . . bled fire."

"Smoke everywhere," the father said.

The young boy looked astonished, shaking his head. "It was the dragon! Ossus is trying to break out of the mountains."

"Dragons breathe fire," said the little girl. "We saw it."

Utho turned to Conndur, clearly off balance. "This is not possible, Sire."

"Aye, but it happened," insisted the man. "The ground shook, the forests fell."

"Everything devastated," his wife echoed. "Everything."

"This is exactly what Adan and Koll warned us about," Conn said. "This is what the wreths intended to do."

The Brava set his jaw and turned to his horse. "I'll ride out now and see the truth of this with my own eyes. I will bring back my report of what really happened as soon as I can."

The konag felt a knot of fear in his stomach, seeing the torn expression on Utho's face as he struggled with his beliefs and convictions. Conn was not so sure. "I know your doubts, old friend. You say it can't be true, but you also know the legends, and you heard what my son and my brother said. If the wreths have indeed returned, they vowed to wake the dragon beneath those mountains. What if it is true, after all?" He knew the answer to his own question. They might be facing the end of all things.

Conn gestured to the guard captain and the refugees. "See that these poor people are taken care of. Give them food, shelter and clothing." He knew what he had to do. "Stay your horse, Utho. I need more than just a scout. Gather troops, tents, horses, and supplies so we can mount a full expedition."

He placed a hand on the ash-caked cape that covered his son's shoulders. "Mandan, you're the prince. Bring your maps. Let us see what's happened to our land." The ash and smoke in the air made him cough. He caught his breath. "As konag, I have to respond to this in person, see if there is any evidence of the great dragon after all. We were warned, and I didn't listen."

52

⚮

WHEN the Utauk trading ship pulled into Serepol Harbor, the Isharans sent out a pilot boat to guide them to a segregated dock. The proud voyagier directed his sailors to pull on rigging ropes, trim the sails, and tend the rudder so they smoothly reached their designated berth at the far end of the bay.

Resplendent in crimson and black, Hale Orr stood at the *Glissand*'s bow, proudly lifting his chin, but he felt uneasy. After their tense last stop at Fulcor Island, he didn't know what to expect here. The simple Utauk circle on the mainsail identified them as a neutral party, and the Isharans would know that they carried desirable cargo. Most Isharans wouldn't admit that they wanted anything from the Commonwealth, but they bought the items nevertheless.

Mak Dur looked at the foreign harbor with grim satisfaction as the wind blew his purple silks and his long dark hair. When the ship approached the dock, sailors threw down hawsers to burly Isharan workers who wrapped them around stanchions, then heaved the hull firmly against the pier. The Utauks waved at the crowd on the dock already gathering to pore over the goods for sale.

"Bring your merchants and your customers!" Hale shouted. "We have treasures, but not enough for everyone in Serepol. Some will go without! Who will be the lucky ones?" He remembered serving aboard a trading ship in his younger years. Being a grandson of Shella din Orr made him an important man among the tribes, the old woman had so many grandsons that Hale was never all that special, so he had to earn his prominent position by accomplishing great things. That was the way any person should make himself special, no matter what his bloodline might be.

He waited for the first crates of foodstuffs, bales of fabric, and baskets of wrapped trinkets to be brought down the gangway and placed on display. The Utauks strung ribbons and spread out blankets, setting up their market right there rather than venturing into the city. The buyers came to them.

Hale hopped onto the pier, welcoming the Isharan customers, but also keeping his ears open, because he was here to ask questions and gather information as well. The first time he had come to Ishara, he was only twenty years old, cocky and full of curiosity, sure he would make his fortune in a single voyage. Instead, he had lost most of his profits in a gambling game with local dockworkers. He had been naïvely confident in his Utauk luck, not realizing that even luck could be trumped by clever cheating, and the dockworkers cheated. His real good fortune was that they hadn't beaten or killed him, but had been satisfied just to take his money.

This time, Hale was on a mission. *The beginning is the end is the beginning.* He needed to learn if anyone in Ishara had also heard of the wreths returning, even in their far-flung districts. Since no humans had even been to Ishara during the ancient wars, no one knew if the wreths had touched this land. If they were returning in Suderra, maybe they were here as well.

He pondered who might be the best person to ask, someone who had information more reliable than rumors, although even rumors might be worth investigating. Serepol was a bustling harbor with sea captains and wealthy merchants, as well as duty-bound sailors, armored soldiers, and illiterate carters. If any strange incidents had occurred, surely someone would be willing to tell tales.

Merchants pushed their way to the front of the curious customers gathered out on the pier, hoping to buy large quantities. The entire crowd parted, though, as six armored men marched forward in a military file, wearing golden capes and stony expressions. Some people scattered, while others were preoccupied with bidding on the items spread out for sale. The soldiers paid little attention to the displayed Utauk goods, but suspiciously regarded the ship itself.

Looking from Hale to Mak Dur, the guard commander called out, "You come from the Commonwealth. Who is your merchant captain? Empra Iluris wishes to speak to him. She has questions."

Hale drew a circle around his heart and forced himself to maintain a broad smile. "As do I." This was better than he expected. The empra would certainly know if wreths had caused trouble in Ishara. "I expect it'll be a mutually beneficial conversation."

Leaving Mak Dur and the crew with their goods for sale, he willingly joined the gold-uniformed soldiers. They folded around him and marched him along the pier into the city toward the palace. Maybe this was a sign of good luck after all.

He bowed deeply before Empra Iluris under the arched ceilings of the palace's reception hall. "Utauks have always been welcome in Ishara, Excellency. Your people are eager to buy our wares."

"I did not say you weren't welcome. Perhaps you have something I wish to buy," Iluris said. She was thin and small-framed. Her face was pretty, a bit washed out with age and stress, her ash-blond hair mostly covered by the wrapped folds of her headdress. If she had worn normal clothes on the street, she would have drawn no notice, but here, on her gilded throne, she was magnificent. Her hands and throat sparkled with jewelry. "Utauks have been good sources of information for us."

"We sell a variety of items," he answered cautiously.

"Tell me about the Commonwealth's plans for war."

The empra's guards, stationed at the wall in the throne room, had made no move since he arrived. He could sense them watching him, as if he might pose a threat.

The question surprised him. "Nobody wants war, I assure you, Excellency. It is bad for business, on all sides. Trade is better when the customers aren't killing one another."

"I could make you the same reassurances, Merchant Captain. War is wasteful and certainly not my intention after so many years of peace." Iluris drew her lips tighter. "But not every person in this land believes the same. What about honor? What about revenge? What about all the blood that's been shed, recently and in the mists of history?"

"Blood is a costly thing, often more expensive than gold."

A teenaged girl with short dark hair entered the throne room and unceremoniously took a seat beside the empra. She was dressed in colorful finery similar to what Iluris wore, but she seemed awkward in her garments, as if they were a costume. Hale gave a polite nod. "Is this your heir, Excellency?"

Iluris responded with a quick smile while the girl flushed. "That remains to be seen. For now, Cemi is here to learn, and my discussions with you are part of that learning."

The presence of the unexpected girl changed the tone of this meeting. Taking a gamble, he chose to fix his attention on Cemi. "And how may I help? What would be most useful? I have seen a great deal in my travels. I listen and observe everywhere I go."

Iluris spoke up. "Private Isharan vessels and fishing boats have disappeared beyond our coast. We suspect that Commonwealth navy ships from Fulcor Island sank them."

"Or maybe captured them," Cemi added. "Less wasteful, isn't it?"

A fleshy man hurried through the doors, surrounded by imagined importance. He wore a dark blue caftan and a gold medallion around his neck. "Apologies, Excellency. I came as soon as I heard of our visitor." He glanced at Hale. "Is he a spy?"

"We are about to commence negotiations for his services, Key Priestlord Klovus. He's given me no reason to think we're not friends." She turned back to Hale. "Now, tell us what you know about our missing ships, Merchant Captain."

Negotiations for his services? Cautiously, Hale pointed out, "I hear that there is outrage in the court of Konag Conndur over a recent Isharan raid that destroyed a peaceful coastal town. It seems that a godling was involved. Some might say that such raids are not the best way of ensuring peace between the two continents."

A scowl crossed Iluris's face, but Hale didn't think the displeasure was directed at him. "Peace and war tug us back and forth, and we hold on as tightly as we can," she said. "I can assure you that the raid was a lawless act not sanctioned by my throne. One can impose laws, but laws mean nothing to the lawless." Her pointed words seemed to be directed at . . . Klovus?

The priestlord huffed. "But the depredations from Fulcor Island can't be excused! We've let that wound fester for decades, and maybe it's time for us to take back the island. It is, after all, part of the ancestral land of Ishara. Our first ships stopped there on their voyage to this continent."

Hale straightened, looking to the priestlord. "Konag Conndur would argue that the island rightfully belongs to the Commonwealth."

Iluris leaned heavily on the arm of her chair. "The sad fact is, Fulcor is a bleak and windswept rock that no one should covet, much less shed blood over." She turned her hard gaze to him. "I am more interested in purchasing a wider range of information, Merchant Captain. As neutral Utauk traders, you are accepted everywhere. You travel widely and freely. That makes you very valuable. I want to buy your eyes, as an observer. Whenever you come back to Ishara, simply tell me what you've seen in the Commonwealth."

Tempted, he smiled and moved on to the next step in the dance. "I'm glad you asked so bluntly, Excellency. That brings me to the real reason I wanted to come to Serepol. I have indeed seen something interesting, maybe dangerous. This can be the start of our interchange. Share and be shared. My information comes at no charge, except that you must answer a question in return."

She was intrigued. "Oh? And what is that?"

He again drew the circle over his heart. "Wreths. The ancient race. A group of them has reappeared from the wastelands."

"Wreths? Still alive?" Klovus scoffed. "That's not possible."

The priestlord's unfiltered reaction told Hale most of what he needed to know. Still, he looked hard at the empra's stony face. "Has there been any sign of wreths in Ishara, Excellency? This continent has stronger magic than what remains in the old world. The ancient race may come here to take advantage of such a resource."

Klovus started to answer, but Iluris silenced him. "I can assure you I've heard nothing of it, Merchant Captain, and I just completed a procession across all of my districts. No one speaks of wreths here. They are creatures of the old world and the distant past. They have no relevance to Ishara."

Her answer gave him great relief. "There, Excellency. Our relationship is off to a good start."

The empra leaned forward again. "I am not concerned about wreths. I had in mind hiring you for more conventional spying, about more conventional things."

He was more comfortable with a familiar conversation. "I'll take your gold, Excellency, and I will be happy to provide you with information, so long as you don't object if I also sell my information about Ishara to the konag? Utauks must remain neutral. If those are acceptable terms, I am happy to share my observations with you."

Klovus turned red. He opened his mouth, closed it, and then made a rude noise. "Impossible and ridiculous."

Iluris just smiled. "What if you agreed to give Konag Conndur only the facts about us that *I* tell you to give him?"

"So long as what I say is the truth."

Cemi blurted out, "And who decides the truth?"

"In this instance, I do," Hale said, giving her a respectful nod. "No one else."

Iluris pondered for a long moment. The key priestlord shifted from one foot to the other as if bursting to ask questions, but a cold glare from the empra kept him silent. Finally, she rose from her gilded throne. "Thank you for your conversation, Merchant Captain. That's not the sort of bargain I want to make at present."

53

⁊⁊

AFTER the long journey home over the mountains from Convera, embracing his wife was Adan's first order of business.

Penda greeted him at the Bannriya city gates as he rode in with the twenty soldier escorts. Adan focused only on the beautiful Utauk princess he had married. She wore maroon silk skirts embroidered with leaf designs. Penda stretched up to greet him, tilting her head back, and he leaned down to kiss her, running his fingers through her rich, dark hair. The escort soldiers watched, smiling.

When he gave her a chance to draw a breath, Penda said, "I send Xar out to look for you every day, so I knew you were coming. *Cra*, I've been waiting for hours since he spotted you! You should have ridden faster." Adan dismounted and swept her into his arms.

Her ska circled overhead, then landed gracefully on her shoulder with a flounce of green plumage, seemingly unimpressed that Adan was back.

"Suderra was lonely without its king," she said, "just as I've been lonely without my husband."

He touched her stomach, feeling the gentle swell of their baby. "You have a part of me with you at all times."

"I don't want part of you. I want all of you." With her fingertip, she drew a circle around his heart.

"And so you have me." He took her arm, and they walked into the city, with the horses following. Seenan, resplendent in his Banner guard uniform, led the escort soldiers to the Bannriya garrison, where they would be given temporary quarters.

Back inside the castle, Adan told Penda everything he had done in his long journey to Fellstaff, Lake Bakal, then downriver to Convera Castle, and finally back home. The squire Hom was happy to tend his master again, though still disappointed that the king hadn't taken him along in the first place. Remembering the terrible frostwreth incursion at Lake Bakal, however, Adan shook his head. "You would not have wanted to see what I saw."

The boy brought a private meal for the king and queen in their suite, and nearly dropped the tray as Xar flew in and deftly snatched a silver spoon from beside a plate. The ska flew off, hissing and clicking. "You bring that back!" Hom yelled, not knowing whether to pursue or keep the rest of the meal intact.

Xar proudly dropped the spoon in front of Penda, but she frowned at the reptile bird. "That is not how you please me, Xar." Feeling Penda's disappointment through the heart link, the ska drooped his head in forlorn apology.

As they ate, it was her turn to tell Adan of the great tension across the counties as the Suderran people reacted to the news about the sandwreths. His vassal lords had all reported in, and armed local militias were scouting some of the more isolated towns, which had fallen suspiciously silent.

"But Queen Voo sent no further word?" Adan asked. Recalling the disaster the frostwreths had caused, maybe he would have to agree to an alliance for Suderra's very survival.

Penda shook her head. "They vanished back into the desert, as if they were only myths after all."

In midafternoon, the two went up to the gazing deck to look out over Bannriya and the surrounding terrain of the kingdom. Accompanying them, Xar landed on one of the crenellations, bobbing his head.

Penda took Adan's hand as they looked out at the countless tile rooftops. "While you were gone, I came up here to watch for you every day, but this afternoon . . . I sense something wrong again." Her dark eyes met his. Adan felt a chill, knowing not to discount his wife's instincts. "Perhaps another harbinger."

Xar flapped his wings, turned his mothlike gaze back on Penda, and let out a strange sound unlike anything Adan had heard before. His wife shuddered and paled, and he caught her in his arms as she collapsed. "What is it? What's wrong?"

She shook her head as if trying to clear it. "Bright noise, deep shadow! Inside the circle, outside the circle . . ." The ska whistled again, and Penda put a hand to her head, breathing rapidly.

Adan smelled an odd taint in the air, a hint of spoiled meat and sulfur. "Maybe the wreths are doing something."

With a piercing shriek, Xar took wing, pulling into the sky above the towers of Bannriya Castle. Penda let out a gasp, and her eyes rolled up so he could see the whites of her eyes, as if she could see through Xar's eyes. She winced and bent over, clearly feeling a psychic blow through her heart link. Penda's eyes squeezed shut and her breathing came fast and shallow. Though her eyes remained closed, she moaned, "This isn't right, Starfall."

As he held her, Adan felt a tension in the air as if the world itself had shuddered. "Is it the baby?" he asked, cradling her. "Is something wrong?"

"Not the baby," she said, then shivered violently.

Adan supported her, tried to move her to one of the stone benches, but she took his arm and held him still. "I need to see, Starfall! *You* need to see." Strands of dark hair blew about her face. Her eyes remained closed. "There's an anger, an uneasiness in the sky, the world."

Xar let out another strange cry. Penda opened her eyes and pointed urgently toward the east. "Look, over there! The sky is . . ."

He turned, and the sight snatched the words from his throat. "I rode over those mountains with the escort party just days ago."

A monstrous gray blur dominated the eastern horizon, where the Dragonspine crossed the land. A background mutter of dismay came from people standing at windows, all staring to the east. Xar swooped back, landed on Penda's shoulder, and buried his scaled snout in her hair.

Moments later, Adan heard a buzzing in the air, like countless raucous noises overlapped in a distant cacophony. The sounds of the city grew hushed with an ominous premonition.

Rising from beyond the forested foothills on the western horizon, the opposite direction from the great gray cloud rising from the mountains, an amorphous black shape swooped through the air, soaring just above the treetops. The shadow held its integrity for a few moments, then expanded, growing darker, larger. Its outline had great angular extensions, like huge wings, a gigantic body, a long neck, and then the entire mass blurred, breaking apart and scattering, then coalescing once more. His skin crawled from the sight.

Penda moaned from where she held on to him for balance. Xar let out another unfathomable sound. Adan's eyes could not focus on the terrifying shape that filled the sky and swelled larger as it approached Bannriya. But the dark shape disintegrated as it rose above the city, and Adan saw that it wasn't actually a dragon, but a strange storm of living creatures.

Penda pressed her hands to her temples. "Can't you hear it? They're screaming! They're coming here."

Within minutes, the black cloud differentiated itself, shattering into countless flying things, an incredible mass of winged creatures, thousands and thousands of them.

The wild skas arrived, flushed from their secret hiding places in the mountains. The huge flock of reptile birds descended upon Bannriya like a cloud of locusts, filling the air with flapping wings, clicking, buzzing. In terror, Xar clutched Penda's shoulder.

In the city streets, people ran for shelter. Mothers screamed, innkeepers bellowed. Everyone fled inside, slamming doors, closing shutters, yanking down awnings as the noise grew louder. The skas kept coming, flapping their wings, screeching in a whirlwind of sound like a mass migration.

Adan could barely stand it, and he knew his wife heard it much louder in her head. Penda raised her hands and shouted, "The wreths have shaken the world! Starfall, they are trying to wake the dragon! All the skas are driven out!"

He held her tighter. Months ago he would have laughed at the suggestion of the mythical dragon comprised of the worst parts of a god's soul. But now seeing the angry cloud of smoke and ash erupting from the Dragonspine Mountains, as well as this ominous swarm of countless wild skas, he didn't think that any legend was impossible.

He tried to drag Penda inside, but she resisted, pulling away from him. "Wait! They're not attacking." The skas swirled and circled in the air, intimidating in their very strangeness. Xar clung to her, nuzzled her ear, sought comfort. She nodded to herself. "The skas are not what we should fear." The clamor in her mind continued, but remained at a steady pitch.

As the colorful reptile birds squawked and buzzed, swooping closer to the castle on the high point inside the walled city, Adan saw that she was right. The frantic skas extended their wings, flashed their plumage, and they began to alight on the city buildings, covering the roofs and walls like an avian blizzard.

Closing her eyes, Penda stroked Xar's plumage, calming her pet. "I won't let you go! Stay with my heart link."

୭୨

For the rest of the afternoon, then sunset, and throughout the night, the uneasy blanket of skas covered Bannriya like the aftermath of a sandstorm, exhausted in their panic. The people hid inside, shuttered their windows, barred their doors.

But the next morning, as the sun rose, the enormous flock spontaneously took wing again, flying back to where they had come from. Rather than departing in a single great cloud, this dispersal was slower, more uneven, as if the skas were still confused but no longer terrified. Soon enough, only stragglers remained on rooftops and under eaves.

"I've never felt such dread inside me before, Starfall," Penda said. "Never heard anything like it in all of our Utauk lore. Skas do not act like this." She remained pale. "I wish my father had been here to see it."

"Something stirred them up," Adan said as the last few reptile birds fluttered off, heading back to their mountain homes.

The eastern sky remained dominated by the enormous gray pall of smoke and ash, and dust from the deep western deserts added a haze that hinted at some angry turmoil deep in the Furnace, where the sandwreths lived.

54

෫෨

IN the subterranean chambers beneath the Magnifica temple, the Black Eels met their next challenge, an opponent far more brutal and powerful than any they had faced before.

A godling.

Priestlord Klovus wasn't certain the barricade would be enough to protect him against the fury of the entity once the Black Eels provoked it, but surely his confidence and his domination was. He had always controlled the godlings before, but his assassins had to be powerful enough to stand against it, should the worst happen.

The priestlord from Tamburdin District had again reported violent incursions from the Hethrren, and she wanted to unleash her godling against the barbarians, but its need for violence was growing stronger. By courier, Neré had asked for the key priestlord's help in controlling the entity, since she had no doubt of his powers.

Klovus needed to have no doubt as well, and he had to prove he could fight a godling should one become intractable. He had his direct connection to the godlings and his magic to keep them in thrall, and he had no better fighters than the Black Eels. Klovus had never considered fighting *against* a godling before.

Turning the rings on his fingers, he watched the specially trained assassins. No one was more familiar with their deadly skills than Klovus was. His palms were sweaty with nervous excitement. These were the best ten drawn from the best teams. Although some would surely lie broken after the battle, he hoped most would survive. The test would strengthen the surviving ones, the spilled blood would empower the Serepol godling, and Klovus could gauge how well he controlled the fearsome thing. It was a good contest from all sides.

The Serepol godling had existed since the very first Isharans had imagined it into being, and it was the strongest deity in the thirteen districts. The people fed it over the centuries with their increasing faith. Its power had waxed and waned throughout history, depending on how much Ishara needed its supernatural protection, and the captive deity shifted from benevolence to vengeance, as required.

Klovus had sensed it all his life, and with his special abilities he had communicated with the deity, calmed it, channeled it, but also imparted his own anger and frustration, which was reflected back to him. The godling knew its place, knew whom it served.

This was a far greater challenge than the Tamburdin godling would ever be, and after he and the Black Eels reaffirmed their abilities here, Klovus would depart for the distant district, where he could help guide the other godling as it destroyed the barbarians. That was what godlings were *for*!

The underground chamber's stone walls were thick enough that no one would hear any roars or screams once the duel began. The thick exit door was closed and bolted. Klovus had fastened two iron padlocks on the inside and tucked the keys inside his dark caftan. No one would get out of here easily. They—both the Black Eels and the godling—would have to go through him, and Key Priestlord Klovus did not intend to set anyone free. Not until this was over.

The ten assassins stood shirtless in loose training pants and studded leather gloves, as if their fists might be effective against the furious power of the wild entity. Four of them wore tightly laced sandals, while the other six chose to remain barefoot, since the calluses and their sharp, hard nails were deadly weapons. They all carried traditional knives, clubs, curved swords.

Against the far stone wall, the shimmering spelldoor hovered like a hazy irregular blot, leading to the strange realm where the godling lived. Adjacent to the spelldoor, an irregular sheet of shadowglass allowed him to glimpse the godling. He could see its shape congeal into an omnipotent humanlike face composed of features it had gleaned from countless worshippers. As the godling's suggestion of a face changed, Klovus often saw his own visage there. The entity sensed and responded to the key priestlord, and that pleased him very much.

Even though the temple construction had been stalled for decades, the people of the city still sacrificed to the godling. At dawn the crowds would swell for daily devotions, and their prayers and offerings replenished the entity. That was why Klovus had intentionally chosen the dead of night for this combat test, when the godling would be weakest.

Still, the Serepol godling was never weak, but neither were the Black Eels. They would fight the entity with every grain of their strength, using their anger, their fists, their weapons, and anything else they could summon. If they did not succeed, then Klovus would have to drive the godling back himself. He would learn much, regardless.

"Are you ready?" He stood behind a sturdy barricade of wooden beams, crossbars, and stacked crates, as if he intended to protect himself against street rabble. He had reinforced the barricade with his own magic, but *he* was the barrier the godling should fear, if it got out of control.

As a team, the ten Black Eels faced the shimmering spelldoor, looking for shadows lurking behind the magic. Only Zaha responded. "We are always ready, Priestlord."

Klovus smiled. "As is the godling."

He concentrated on the thread of power within him and muttered the words that helped him release the magic. The glowing shape faded around the edges, split through the middle, then unfolded, inward, outward, and sideways. It opened, and the godling emerged into the chamber from whatever void it lived in.

Even stunted by the empra's unwillingness to construct its great temple, the godling was still awesome, a ravening powerful being. It came through the spelldoor, a thunderstorm of faces and smoke, a shapeless blob that extended lightning and blasted like wind wrapped into a cudgel.

Klovus ducked behind his spell-enhanced barricade, but could not tear his eyes away as the Black Eels faced the angry deity. Two of them dove toward the core of the magical storm, flinging their bodies directly into the source. Zaha slashed with his hands, then kicked with a hard, bare foot, but it was like trying to grapple with a tornado. The godling hurled one of the assassins out of its raging nexus and smashed him against the stone wall. The Black Eel used magic to harden his skin just in time, but the blow was still hard enough to stun him. He slid to the ground, shook his head, then lunged forward again.

Another assassin stood motionless, eyes closed, expression calm. He slashed with his curved sword, severing one of the smoky tentacles that extruded from the godling. It dissipated into steam and sparkles.

Diminished, the godling recoiled and retaliated. The Black Eel could not maintain his meditative calm, could not even summon the skin-hardening spell in time before the godling smashed him to a pulp, leaving a ruin of blood and battered flesh.

Seeing the modicum of success, Zaha changed tactics. He had thrown himself into the entity and been rebuffed, but now he also focused his mind. His expression became blank. He reached out and picked up the sword of his fallen comrade, holding one blade in each hand, and glided forward with deadly intent. Two of his companions followed his example and did the same.

The godling was a howling beast, impatient with its captivity. Klovus could feel its energy in his heart, surging through his own veins. This entity was far more powerful than the harbor temple's godling, which he had taken to Mirrabay. This was *Serepol's* godling. This was *his* godling, more than the harbor temple's godling had ever been.

Another assassin used fury and violence against the roiling entity and was smashed against the stone wall, which split his skull with a splash of red.

Zaha and three others maintained their meditative concentration, raised their swords, and walked into the whirlwind. With no more emotion than if they were harvesting wheat, they began to slash, twirling their swords to stab the godling, slice off its roiling tendrils, diminishing the deity bit by bit.

The godling roared with a sound so deep and loud that the thick stone walls vibrated, as did the floor, the air. Klovus could hear the cry, a scream that resonated through the fabric of reality itself.

Methodical, Zaha struck with his blade, spilling out a gush of black thunder. The godling re-formed, shifted its angry tendrils so that screaming and shouting faces boiled up like bubbles in a cauldron. Klovus saw his own face surge to the front, surrounded by an angry halo of storm.

One of the meditating Black Eels opened his eyes and recognized the key priestlord's face. He flinched just for a second—and the godling struck. A blast of shimmering magic slime struck the assassin in the face, driving him backward.

Two other Black Eels lost their concentration, and the godling exploded in wild fury, knocking them all aside, swelling larger as it regained its strength. The cloud of hands and faces, misty tentacles and insubstantial fists swarmed forward, smashed a third Black Eel, crushed his chest. The godling was in a reckless rampage now, intent on annihilating the attackers.

Zaha faced it. The other Black Eels rallied, but the godling was huge and strong. They were all about to be obliterated. Klovus could see that.

He knew it was time to exert his power and influence. This was his test. The priestlord lurched out from behind his barricade, held up his hands, and shouted in his most implacable tone. "Stop! Godling, I command you!" His wall of magic crackled. The connection in his mind surged, and he held the godling in mental chains. "You serve me. I am your priestlord."

The deity crouched and squirmed, throbbed as numerous spectral heads bubbled up and turned to face him, their eyes glowing yellow, flashing with power that demanded to be released. Klovus stepped closer. "Stop, I said!" He walked through a smear of blood on the floor. "I command you."

He glowered at the godling, feeling its immensity, but he knew his own immensity as well. The godling had never questioned its place, and Klovus allowed no doubt in his mind, because the creature would surely sense it. "I feed you, I bring the worshippers. I am your master." He lowered his voice. "I will see that your temple is completed, I promise. Someday. But only if you obey me."

The godling hovered in the air, electrical bolts skittering through its core. The battered Black Eels picked themselves up and stood, ignoring their injuries, not counting their fallen. They faced the entity, accepting whatever the key priestlord decreed.

"This is a test for all of us," Klovus said. "The Black Eels are my most powerful fighters, and I can't have them all killed." In his mind, he struggled to control the deity, sweating profusely as the godling swelled and resisted. "I cannot let you go out of control. Not yet."

The thing eventually pulsed in silence, its storm fading back into calmness. Klovus took another step forward, and the entity retreated toward the far wall. The key priestlord imposed his will, confident again. Yes, he could do this.

With a gesture, he opened the spelldoor. The shimmering white rectangle appeared like a patch of morning fog and seemed to call the godling. In its last moments of freedom, the entity flared up, thrumming its inhuman roar through the air as if insisting that it wanted to remain loose.

Klovus shoved it with his mind, forcing his command, and the godling tumbled back into the void. He sealed the spelldoor, and silence filled the arena chamber.

Looking around at the dead and wounded men, Klovus assessed the damage. The chamber itself was intact, although several of the thick stone blocks showed cracks, broken by the sheer force of impact. Three Black Eels lay dead, one other severely injured with a broken skull. Klovus found it disappointing. Those were greater losses than he had expected, but a godling was no normal opponent.

Zaha brushed himself off. "I apologize for our poor performance, Key Priestlord."

Klovus nodded slowly. "You were never meant to win. You fought a godling face-to-face with no special weapons but yourselves. It was impossible to win."

Zaha's brows drew together, perplexed.

Klovus reached inside his caftan and removed the two keys to open the iron padlocks. "But now I've given you a taste of the impossible. I tested you, I tested the godling, and I tested myself."

Now he was ready to help Priestlord Neré in Tamburdin. The godlings truly were the greatest weapons imaginable, but they were no match for Klovus.

55

WITHIN hours, the konag's expedition departed from Convera, heading west toward the disaster in the Dragonspine Mountains. Conndur dreaded what he would find there, but he had to see for himself, if Ossus was really awakening deep beneath the ground. To the west, the sky was a knotted mass of gray, choked with smoke and drifting flecks.

"Are we really going to go there?" Mandan's face was as pale as the ash in the sky. "Shouldn't we stay in the castle where it's safe?"

"If the dragon is real, then no place is safe," Conn said. "It's our responsibility to help the people." His voice carried weary disapproval. "You'll be the next konag, Mandan. It's your responsibility, too."

"He is right, my prince," Utho said. "We need to see if this is true."

The prince dredged up inner courage and nodded. He mounted his horse and waited beside his father, ready to go. The Brava remained silent and deeply disturbed.

Mandan had packed comfortable clothes that were much too fine for the rigors of outdoor life, but Conndur chose not to criticize his son, not now. When he and Koll had gone to war as young men, neither of them understood how few comforts a person truly needed. Mandan also brought a small book of maps and a sketchpad to draw what he observed, perhaps even evidence of Ossus.

The royal party rode out through the castle gates and down to the lower city. The ashfall covered the streets and showed no sign of ending. More refugees flowed into the city, terrified and lost. The first ones came from the foothills, having felt the extreme tremors in the ground, seen the pillar of fire and ash erupting from Mount Vada like the roar of an awakening dragon.

The expedition rode double file along the river road, and the slosh of clogged water and the groan of drifting trees drowned out the jingle of the tack and armor. Standard-bearers trotted ahead, holding up pennants, one showing the open hand of the Commonwealth, one showing the rising sun of Osterra. The pack wagons came behind, rattling over the wide dirt road. Normally, the Crickyeth River would have been dotted with cargo boats, flat barges, and fishermen, but the debris-filled current was too treacherous.

At sunset, the outriding scouts found a large meadow where the large party could make camp. In an efficient operation, the soldiers removed tents from the supply wagons, while others built campfires and set about cooking beans mixed with onions and sausages in large cauldrons. The gray ash in the air continued its eerie fall, but the clouds overhead took on a different character. Conn sniffed, and he could smell rain even through the burnt odor. A good downpour would knock some of the ash out of the air, but it would also create a terrible mess.

Near one of the campfires, Mandan sat on a fabric chair that had been set up for him, while Conndur contented himself with a wooden stump for a seat. They ate their simple camp meal, the same food as the soldiers had, while the prince brushed at biting insects, tugged at his chafing clothes. Utho was stoic as he faced the road that led toward the Dragonspine.

As the soldiers finished setting up the tents, a small group of refugees came down the road, surprised to see the royal banners. They all looked frightened and desperate, with hurriedly gathered belongings lashed on their backs. They led two goats, a spindly cow, and a barking dog. Covered with ash, the man looked like a ghost. "Thousands of trees flattened, Sire. A tree fell on our horse and killed her. Closer to Mount Vada, some people stayed to pick up the pieces, but we can't live there anymore."

"Has anyone seen the dragon?" Mandan asked. "Did Ossus really come out of the mountain?"

The refugees looked at one another, sharing fears. "We heard the rumbling, saw the fire and smoke . . . but not the dragon himself."

"A lot more refugees are on the road behind us," said the man's wife. "We're heading to Convera, where it might be safe. Do you think we'll find shelter there?"

If so many refugees poured in from the mountains, Conndur wondered how his city could possibly help them all. "Ancestors' blood," he muttered. He made sure the people had some bean stew before they continued down the road as the first sprinkles of rain began to patter down. The prince looked uneasy, especially when low thunder rumbled through the clouds overhead, and he went to huddle in his own small tent.

Weary in his mind and heart, Conn took his blanket and tried to sleep. The downpour soaked the tent fabric and leaked through the stitched seams all through the night. The soldiers tried to keep dry in their tents. Some attempted to keep the campfires burning, but it was no use.

As he lay back with his eyes open, Conn recalled the nights he had spent sleeping on the battlefield in a strange land. He and Koll had led skirmishes even when they were wet and miserable, and many of his soldiers had developed skin sores from soggy clothes or cracked boots. None of it had felt very glorious, despite the legacies they were each trying to build. . . .

The next morning, Mandan looked bedraggled as he emerged from the tent into the cold misty dawn. Utho found dry blankets at the bottom of the supply wagons and wrapped the prince to keep him warm while they waited for breakfast. The camp cooks managed to light the wet wood and boil water for morning tea.

Conn gave his son credit for not complaining. Mandan brought out a cloth-wrapped volume from his tent. "Last night, I traced our path in my books so I could see how far we'd come on the first day, but then water got on the pages and damaged the maps."

Conn took a seat on the wet stump next to him. "I'm afraid the world is damaged, too, my son."

The procession rode out, passing more refugees. As they approached the mountains, ash continued to fall. At night when Conndur stretched out to sleep in his tent, he could feel a deep rumbling beneath the ground, like Ossus growling. Conn thought of the great dragon buried in the mountains, and the warnings Adan and Koll had brought about the wreths. What if the legends were true after all? It had been so easy to assume the Isharans were the greater threat, the more obvious threat.

As the expedition reached the mining region, they came upon an empty town, its buildings burned and collapsed, the streets choked with debris. Dead oxen were sprawled in the town square, mouths open, tongues caked with gray powder. Chickens ran loose, but nothing else moved in the town.

Forest fires burned along the rugged ridges to the north. The road became less passable, because countless trees had been knocked flat by a tremendous blast. Streams were dammed up in bubbling, stinking pools with yellow sulfur scum on top of the water. Thermal vents hissed between boulders.

Conn could not dispute what he saw with his own eyes. The stirring dragon had shaken the world. Even Utho was struck dumb at the unexpected sight.

The procession moved ahead, covered with an ominous gloom. The scouts worked their way forward through the avalanche debris and fallen trees. The standard-bearers no longer bothered to carry their flags, which had drooped, stiff with ash. The troops simply rode with their heads down, trying to keep moving.

The rain had settled out some of the ash, clearing the sky so they could see glimpses of the mountain peaks. Mount Vada rose ahead of them, but it looked as if its entire summit and part of the side had been ripped away by a malicious hand, leaving a raw wound that spewed smoke and ash. Red rivers of fire ran like blood down the steep slopes.

Sitting in his saddle, Mandan peered all around him, frightened. He had taken out his book of maps and opened the water-stained pages to where he diligently marked the progress of the expedition. Now he just stared at the drawn lines, then studied the terrain, unable to reconcile what was marked on the maps with what he observed. Conndur could see the prince struggling for words.

Mandan closed the book, shuddered, and then hurled it to the side of the road among the debris. "I know the maps by heart. I knew the roads, the towns, the mountains. I studied them, because that's what the tutors told me to do!" His voice was choked with all the ash he had inhaled. His lips were chapped, his eyes shadowed. "But all those dots and words—those were real people, real places, and real lives!"

"Yes, my son. They all are," Conndur said. "And as konag, they are all yours. You have to save them, keep them safe."

"But how?" Mandan cried.

"Any way we can, my prince," Utho said. "That is the question every konag must ask."

Riding ahead, they finally came to what was left of a mining settlement called Scrabbleton.

56

◈

COMING home at last made Kollanan's heart glad. The world might be in danger and the future full of dark questions, but Fellstaff would welcome him. Tafira was there, his people were there, and that counted for more than could be measured. His trip to Convera had left him angry and discouraged.

The konag's escort rode fast at Koll's insistence. Once across the boundary into Norterra, they picked up five additional soldiers provided by his vassal lord Alcock, who also accompanied the king, eager to discuss the defenses his people had made to his own stronghold and the larger towns in his holding.

"I have three wreth ruins in my county, Sire," he said as they approached the great stone walls surrounding Fellstaff. "We've scavenged a little from them over the centuries, taking the cut stone to build our homes and boundary fences, but most of the ruins are untouched." He gave a wry frown. "They certainly aren't easy to take apart."

"Good thing we can use something from the wreths, after all they did to us in their wars," Koll grumbled. From the saddle of his borrowed horse, he looked up at the city walls that had stood for centuries.

As the horses approached the gate, Alcock spoke in a quiet voice. "What if they want their old cities back, too? What if they want the whole land back?"

"They can't have it." Koll's defiance had been building for days. He lowered his voice and repeated, "They can't have it!"

The vassal lord had brought a ledger with his report of weapons and armor, how many soldiers he could raise, with a special notation for fighters who actually had experience in war. Since the Commonwealth had been at peace for decades, there weren't many veterans, only a few old soldiers who had served with Koll in the Isharan war. A long time ago, they had followed him all the way to Norterra because they wanted a quiet life where they could forget the bloody battles. As king, Koll had succeeded in giving them that for years. But now . . .

Wall sentries announced Kollanan's return, and as the party rode through the high wooden gates, people came to cheer. Koll forced a confident expression and raised a hand in greeting, heading with determination toward the blocky castle in the center of the city. Home . . . and Tafira.

Riding through the streets, Koll watched his people at their shops, their forges, their homes. Daily lives, normal concerns. Women sat on overturned buckets in front of their houses, mending clothes. Metalsmiths scolded their apprentices in workshops, leatherworkers made boots and saddles, tanners scraped hides and dunked them in large dye basins. Fur traders displayed skins stretched on willow racks.

The castle was still hung with black mourning banners, and a dark pennant flew from the highest tower. Reaching the stable courtyard, Kollanan dismounted and surrendered his horse to a stable boy, while staff guards came to meet the military escort from Convera. Servants arranged temporary quarters in the castle for Lord Alcock.

Koll left them all behind. He flung open the nearest entrance, dusty in his riding clothes. He drew a deep breath of his castle, smelling the lingering spices from Tafira's cooking, the smoke from fires in the hearths, which was so much better than the smoke he had smelled in the air for days.

Tafira hurried to greet him, and their eyes met in an embrace even before they reached each other. Then she was in his arms, and he held her, squeezing tight. Kollanan didn't speak; he didn't need to. He felt her strong stance, her soft body pressed against him. He inhaled deeply of her hair, smelled the honeysuckles she used in making soap. He drew energy just from touching her.

"Did you talk with your brother about the wreths?" she asked. "Is he sending help? Did you and Adan warn him?"

"We did, but I don't know how he will order the Commonwealth to respond."

She pulled away to look into his face. "Why would he doubt you?"

"He has other crises that he thinks are more serious. There's talk of war with Ishara again. There have been bloody raids on the coast, and the people want revenge. Conndur's Brava has even called for an outright attack."

Tafira frowned. "You know all Bravas hate Isharans. A war with Ishara would go on for a long time, as it did before, and in the end nothing would change." The lines on her face deepened as she frowned. "I hated that war. . . ."

He held her tighter. "Yes, and the wreths mean to bring about the end of the whole world. For the time being at least, we may be on our own here in Norterra. We make our own decisions. We fight our own battles."

The kitchens were in a scramble to make the evening meal. The crowded room was already quite warm, thanks to the ovens baking bread, but young Pokle came in, carrying a full load of wood in his arms. He wore warm clothes, a woolen sweater, and extra socks, as if he never wanted to be cold again. "Got to keep the fires burning. Can't let the ovens grow cold." Through the stacked split logs in his arms, he saw Koll. "King Kollanan, you're back!"

"Glad to see you looking warm and healthy," Koll said.

The boy spluttered numerous questions, but Koll was focused on Tafira, and she was engrossed in having her husband back. The queen left the staff with instructions as she led him to their chambers so he could change and wash, and so they could talk in private.

As he tossed his dusty cloak onto a cedar chest in the corner, she poured water from a ewer into a porcelain basin, drenched a rag, wrung it out, and began to wipe the dust and sweat from his face, stroking his beard. He tugged open the lacings of his shirt and pulled the dirty garment over his head. She helped him, then tossed it to the side.

She was reticent, reluctant, and before he could ask, she delivered her news. "I am worried. Lasis departed two weeks ago, riding north. He was going to do reconnaissance at Lake Bakal, gather vital information we would need about the wreths." She rinsed the rag, squeezed dirty water into the basin, and began to bathe his chest. "I've heard nothing from him, and I'm afraid something terrible happened."

"He went to Lake Bakal by himself?" Kollanan filled in the details with his imagination. "Sometimes he is impetuous, but he often rides off alone. He is probably studying their movements, their defenses, gathering intelligence. He could have quite a report for us when he comes back."

"*Two weeks,* beloved! What if the wreths saw him? What could he have done against an army of them?" Tafira asked. She sounded shaken.

Koll could not hide his concern. "Bravas have powerful magic, but their pride sometimes blinds them. Maybe Lasis was too brash. He could have been captured or killed."

He sat back on the bed, and Tafira helped him pull off his dusty boots. He let out a troubled sigh as he washed his feet and put on doeskin slippers. "We'll need an army of our own, because I intend to fight." His shoulders slumped with the weight of his concerns, but he squared them again, straightened his back. "It is the best we can do, and it's the only thing we can do, even without the rest of the Commonwealth army. Norterra is strong. And we'll find out what happened to Lasis."

Tafira stroked the side of his face. "We have to defend our homes."

Shifting the cloak, he opened his cedar chest and withdrew a light woolen undershirt. He added a pale blue jerkin embroidered with the mountain symbol of Norterra. "If we are *defending* our homes, then it's too late. We have to save our kingdom, maybe all of the Commonwealth if Conndur is too blind to see the real danger. Our army needs to be strong enough."

Having traveled over the mountains and across his kingdom, he had seen the rich forests, the crops and the orchards, the flocks of sheep, the small herds of cattle. The sight made him consider how well humans had survived in the aftermath of the wreths. They had salvaged the land from devastation, made their own history, their own legacy.

"This land is ours," he said, in a firm voice. "The wreths ruined it last time, drained the magic—and we spent two thousand years healing it. Will we simply be brushed aside because we're in the way of some other war?" He felt hot tears in his eyes. "Like they did at Lake Bakal? *Humans* are the inheritors of this continent, and we will not be ignored."

He felt a dark twisting in his heart as the grief slowly penetrated. Lasis, his ever-loyal Brava and friend, was quite likely dead, along with his daughter and her husband, his grandsons . . .

"Will we be strong enough for that?" Tafira asked him.

"We have to be."

57

E VERY night on her journey, Glik dreamed of skas.

With the point of her knife, she carved a circle in the bark of a stunted pine just below the tree line on the slopes, and she pushed on into the far western mountains. As she walked, Glik looked up into the blue emptiness of the sky and felt a longing in her heart. In the past when she traveled, her dear Ori had flown high to scout the best route, and then returned to land on her shoulder. Now she was alone. A month without Ori had felt like a gray emptiness.

She was determined to find her own new ska out here. The domesticated skas that were hatched and raised in captivity weren't right for her. She had to find a new egg, not some already-trained pet for sale, because the very strongest heart links were established at a ska's birth.

Glik had never experienced true love with a boy, but she understood what it meant to have her heart broken. Why had Ori left her? In their last few months together, she had sensed the aging ska drawing more distant from her. When the sandstorm came, maybe Ori had been looking for an excuse to go, though Glik couldn't understand why he would do that. If her beloved ska knew he was dying, she would have wanted to be there, to hold and comfort him until the end.

But Ori had chosen otherwise, abandoning her. It had torn her apart inside.

Several days ago on her trek, she had been startled by an uproar of skas, converging in a cloud of wings and scales high overhead. They seemed to come from everywhere. Despite the distance, Glik heard their fearful clamor in her head, like the presence of Ori, but echoing and overlapping by the thousands. This wasn't a vision; it was real.

Drowning in the tide of sounds and thoughts, Glik let herself imagine she was floating through the sky with them. After the wave of skas passed, she found herself on the ground among the dry grasses. For a time, her mind had been carried along with the countless skas flying south, and then she realized she was lying on her back looking up, shuddering and sweating.

Something terrible had disturbed them, but the skas would return. She traced a circle around her heart. After what she had seen, Glik knew exactly where they went to roost. . . .

Now she saw the dark silhouette of a ska high in the sky. Two other specks joined it, circling and playing in the air, dancing on the winds. They were calling her, guiding her. Though these wild skas were not heart-linked to her, as Ori had been, she still felt them. The way ahead became as sharp and clear as a diamond in her mind.

She scrambled to her feet and climbed higher, thrashing through low scrub oak and spiky grasses, and the flying figures swooped lower. Laughing, she waved to them. "Over here! Come see me."

The skas continued to glide on thermals, swooping around in a perfect circle. A sign! As they played and tumbled, she caught flashes of blue plumage, white plumage, and a larger red one. They seemed to be taunting her. "I'm the best companion you could ever find!" Glik promised them. Were they testing her? "Show me where to find your eggs!"

The skas flew toward the sharp mountain peaks over the next ridge, where patches of snow lingered on gray granite. The cliffs were sheer, the climb seemingly impossible, but Glik couldn't stop grinning. *That* was where she would find her egg. She felt the call in her heart.

It took her three more days to cover the distance, and each night she heard the raucous calls of skas in her dreams and the warm music of the link in her heart. She saw Ori in a vision, perched on a bent branch and flapping his scarlet wings, like an old mentor trying to guide her.

In order to reach the peaks where the skas nested, she had to climb rough rocks. Glik sheltered in a deep crack for part of an afternoon as a rainstorm made the wet granite impossible to climb. She shivered and waited, not regretting her decision. Soon she would have a new ska. The perfect one for her. When sunlight dried the rocks enough, she kept climbing.

As she approached the highest crags, she saw the reptile birds flying overhead again, guiding her. She kept working her way up the cliff faces. Her hands ached and bled, but she couldn't let go. She never let herself look down at the sheer fall. Glik's foot slipped, but she caught herself on a knob of rock, holding on with one hand. She just hung there shuddering, then she found a toehold and a handhold, then another and another until she ascended to a narrow ledge, where she rested. Air whistled through her lungs, and sweat trickled down her forehead.

An image of Ori flashed through her mind, and she thought of the new ska she would have. Her vision blurred, and the call grew even stronger.

The reptile birds flew close now, and she located the cracks and cave holes where they built their nests. Glik knew she could make it. Her dreams had brought her here. The wheeling skas watched her, but did not seem disturbed by her presence. Maybe Ori had told them she would be a good master.

The ska nests were right there, inside the fissures. As she made her way into a widening crack in the granite, she could smell the distinctive musk of many skas. Their scales and feathers exuded an oil that reminded her of Ori. How she longed for that again!

The beginning is the end is the beginning.

She wormed her way deeper into the crack in the mountain. Sunlight penetrated through a gap overhead, providing just enough illumination. Ska nests were here in pockets of the rock, cluttered tangles of dry twigs and branches, uprooted vines and loose feathers in a mad motley of colors. Dozens of nests held mottled-brown eggs, any one of which would fit perfectly in her cupped hands. She went from nest to nest, poking among the feathers and the debris, ignoring the broken shells of recently hatched skas and the bones of the rodents they fed to their young.

She closed her eyes, concentrated, drew the circle around and around her heart in a mantra to focus her mind. She could sense ska thoughts all around, but only one of the eggs whispered to her. The splotched and swirled pattern on the shell was hypnotic, beautiful. When Glik touched the warm, fist-sized egg, it vibrated faintly in welcome, and she gave a small gasp. Suddenly, she *knew* the ska inside. It was nearly ready to hatch, anxious for the world . . . anxious for *her.* If she took the egg now, Glik could be out of the eyrie and maybe even out of the peaks by the time it hatched.

Knowing this was the one, she held the egg, stroked the shell, and the throbbing mental voices of other skas fell silent. She didn't need the visions or guidance from the rest of the reptile birds anymore. She had what she needed. This was the one.

Glik wrapped the egg securely in a soft cloth, tucked it into her leather pouch, then tied the pouch inside her shirt, where it would be protected. She would need both of her hands free for the climb back out, and she couldn't risk damaging the egg.

She could care for the little reptile bird, bring it back to the Utauk tribes, and she would be inside the circle again. Glik would no longer be hollow, no longer an orphan twice over. Besides, she would have a grand story to tell. She had climbed into the highest, most inaccessible eyrie.

With her prize secure, Glik prepared to depart, but she felt something more, the dark and insistent throbbing of a vision, a foreboding. The crevice in the cliff widened ahead of her, and she heard a rumbling sound deeper in the mountain. Unable to resist, as if caught in a waking nightmare, Glik squeezed through the crevice and climbed down.

Lit by glimmers of sky from the crack high above, the passage ended at a sheltered grotto infused with a strange glow. The air was warm, stifling, with a hint of brimstone, very unlike the musk of the gathered skas. She realized she was sweating.

Drawn by curiosity and dread, Glik inspected the strange barrier wall. It was not stone, but some kind of resinous substance, like sheets of sheer fibers slathered in layers. It reminded her of the cocoons spun by silkworms grown in farms in southern Suderra. This curved shell was larger than a house, so how could it be a cocoon? The translucent wall contained something faintly luminescent.

Glik touched the blurry wall and felt a vibration that was entirely different from the one she had felt from the warm ska egg. Behind the resinous shell, something stirred, something huge. A lurching vision flooded her mind, like a black cape folding aside to reveal fangs and scales and evil. The unbidden image pounded inside her skull like a thousand thunderclaps. She drew a sharp breath and nearly collapsed.

Ska voices swooped into her thoughts again, this time protecting her, diverting the other dangerous vision, keeping her safe.

Glik backed away from the barrier. Her heart pounded, but she couldn't tear her eyes from it. With an alarming flicker of liquid motion, she saw a shift behind the shell, a glint of something that might have been an enormous faceted eye. It opened briefly, then closed.

Stumbling, Glik retreated, making her way back up to the main rookery. She didn't dare disturb the slumber of that thing behind its cocoon wall.

Cradling the ska egg against her chest, Glik made her way out of the eyrie and into the open air again. She still faced the long and treacherous climb back out of the mountains. She suddenly longed for the safety and comfort of being surrounded by the Utauk tribes. *Inside the circle again.* She wanted to be among her people, to go home.

With her new ska.

58

Days after the flock of agitated skas scattered from Bannriya, Adan still felt tension hanging over his city. He didn't need the incomprehensible behavior of the wild reptile birds to warn him that something was amiss in the world. The bruised and smoky sky over the Dragonspine Mountains remained a mystery.

While waiting, Adan and Penda rode through their city to be seen by the people, to reassure them. They dressed in bright colors and wore gold jewelry adorned with dragonblood rubies. He released wheat from his granary stockpiles and asked the castle's kitchens to bake hundreds of loaves of bread, which he and his staff distributed in the streets. Adan wanted his people to break bread together and remember that they were all one Commonwealth and one race of humans, who had survived and reclaimed the world.

An Utauk caravan had settled in the main square the night before, erecting tents and setting out their goods. This tribe was only distantly related to the Orr family, but Penda welcomed them like long-lost cousins. Utauks followed the king and queen through the streets, playing flutes and stringed instruments, which lightened the ominous mood in the city.

"Suderra might eventually get back to normal, Starfall," Penda said. On her shoulder, Xar bobbed his head, as if the celebration were all about him. The ska scanned the sky with his faceted eyes, as if ready to defend his territory from other reptile birds.

Adan lowered his voice. "I don't think anything will ever be normal again, my love. It all changed on the day the sandwreths arrived." He forced a smile on his face. "But we can at least pretend, and sometimes pretending hard enough makes it real."

Penda touched her stomach. "We have a little more than four months to make the world right. I don't want our child to be born into war."

In the main city square, a giant obelisk towered high, so old and weathered that the engraved markings were no more than shadows and suggestions. The obelisk marked the place where the very first banners had been raised when human survivors claimed the world after the wreths vanished. Inset on two of the obelisk's sides were squares of shadowglass harvested from an ancient battlefield. The tall, intentionally toppled statue of some ancient wreth hero lay faceup in the square, like the one near the front gates of Bannriya Castle.

In an archive room, one of the ancient original flags had been preserved, sandwiched between two transparent sheets of crystal. The red fabric had faded to only a breath of pink, and the cloth fibers were little more than cobwebs. The object didn't hold as much importance as what it symbolized. Humans had dared to build a city here in the wreckage of the world, and they had succeeded.

As king of Suderra, Adan felt the weight of that responsibility, and he saw it in the hope and faith in his people, their confidence that he, King Adan Starfall, would keep them safe.

Even from the wreths.

That thought terrified him. Adan hadn't imagined such a situation when he accepted the throne in the place of the fifteen-year-old child who had been the nominal king for ten years. In the previous generation, dour old King Syrus had ruled as a stern, lackluster man, who did little to earn the devotion of his people. Few minstrels could think of anything to sing about when they told the story of his reign. Syrus seemed to have no interest, no humor, no love.

He died, leaving his young son, Bull—short for Bullton—as his heir. According to Suderran law, the child was managed by a group of seven regents, who in this case were self-serving and greedy. Using money from the treasury, they built monuments to themselves, wrote great chronicles in the city's remembrance shrine, carved their names on stone walls, although they hadn't actually done much worth remembering.

As the boy grew older, he had few wits about him. When Bull reached the age of eight and tutors couldn't even teach him his letters or the most basic mathematics, the regents realized that he was simpleminded and would never be prepared to rule. Bullton didn't like the regents any more than the people did, and several Suderran vassal lords posted complaints to the konag in Convera. Some lords refused to pay taxes; one county even declared itself independent.

As the unrest increased and Konag Conndur grew impatient with the regents, he invoked an ancient law that had been laid down from the earliest days of Queen Kresca, when the Commonwealth founded their alliance. The question was posed to all the vassal lords of Suderra's fifteen counties, and the people were allowed to speak.

None of them liked the prospect of an idiot king, or corrupt regents, and when Conndur suggested replacing the king with his son Adan Starfall, whom everyone liked, the response had been overwhelming. The people acclaimed him, the Commonwealth accepted him, and he took the throne with pride.

The regents were exiled in disgrace to outlying counties, and though people still grumbled about them, Adan did not intend to hunt them down out of vengeance, nor did he hold any ill will toward the former boy king. Bullton—fifteen when he was ousted—was perfectly happy being raised in a hunting lodge in the hills.

In his time here, Adan believed he had ruled well. Suderra was strong. Bannriya prospered. The people had been content . . . until the wreths came, and no one knew anything about the future anymore.

As he and Penda rode through the streets while fresh bread was distributed, Adan could see that the people had faith in him, but how long would that optimism last if Queen Voo and her sandwreths placed a terrible obligation upon them, or if another wreth war laid waste to the entire land?

At last the smoke and distant dust storms cleared enough to show the stars at night again. Seeking peace and contemplation, Adan went to his gazing deck to be alone with the universe. He had spent many nights teaching Penda the constellations, while she had shown him entirely different patterns the Utauk tribes saw. Now, tired from the procession, she let Adan go outside by himself.

He stood alone after midnight, hands clasped behind his back. The ominous changes in the world had dampened his enthusiasm for drawing his own atlas of the heavens. Now it seemed like a frivolous hobby, when there was a real chance the wreth factions would bring about an apocalyptic end to the world.

Now that the moon had set, he saw a faint green glow off to the south, shimmering from the desert emptiness. Dissipated curtains of light danced like a mirage on heat ripples. Auroras were rare, and Adan had no idea what the eerie wash of color meant. Some kind of omen? Another harbinger, as Penda had seen before?

Though Bannriya had quieted for the night, he still heard the simmer of noises in the streets, whispers of conversation, the rattle of a cart heading home up the cobblestones, a family singing and clapping as they played a game. He saw a bonfire and a small crowd celebrating a wedding.

For these people, every day was another day in their legacy. They did not ask too many questions, but Adan looked at the stars. He was the king here, and he silently demanded explanations from the universe, but no one answered him. No one listened. Kur, the main wreth god, was long gone—not that he would have cared about a race he didn't create.

As Adan stared at the starscape, a great silhouette flickered across the sky, blotting out the stars. Could it be another swarming of skas? No, this was different. It flew like an enormous angular kite, swooping across the pastel of the auroras.

With a gasp, he squinted to make out more details. It was a huge winged form, reptilian, larger than any living creature he had ever seen . . . Then it was gone. He could no longer find it against the starry backdrop. It swept across the night, far away.

59

Climbing around fallen trees and rockslides, rushing as fast as they could, Elliel and Thon made their way back to Scrabbleton, fearing what they would find there.

On the way, one of the smaller towns they passed had been entirely buried in boulders and mud. Elliel stared at the collapsed dwellings and smothered bodies and saw nothing to salvage, no one to save. Her heart grew heavier and her fear increased as they closed in on the village she had called home, the kind people she had known.

Fires continued to burn through the forested hillsides, and ash covered the landscape in a somber gray shroud. Smoke clogged the air, and every breath scraped like claws in Elliel's throat. Thon's lean form was streaked with gray, his long hair clumped, his deep blue eyes swollen and red. Several times each day the ground rumbled, and they would scramble for shelter, holding on to great slabs of stone or thick tree trunks, until calm returned.

"Something made the dragon stir beneath the mountains," Thon said. "Is it a coincidence? Or did my awakening have some part in it?"

"I don't know the legends well enough," she said. "I never believed them, but I do know that if I hadn't saved you from inside Mount Vada, you'd be dead now." She negotiated a path over fallen trees that blocked the road. "Who can answer questions about the fate of the world? We'll help the people closer at hand . . . if anybody's left in Scrabbleton."

They faced an impossible barricade of deadfall, huge trees that had tumbled down the slope to pile up across the path, mixed with dirt and rocks. Elliel looked at it in dismay, knowing it would take an hour for them to work their way down and around it to a safer path. "If I could ignite my ramer, I'd carve a path through that."

"Perhaps I have a way," Thon said, looking perplexed and curious. He extended his hand, palm out. "Much like I cleared the rockfall in the mines." He frowned, and his brow furrowed as he summoned magic. The fallen trees shifted, then splintered down the middle to create a pathway through the mound strewn with wood chips. "Move quickly," he suggested as the remaining trees trembled, settling and shifting. "It does not seem to be very stable."

Impressed with his unmeasured powers, Elliel hurried through the deadfall and was relieved when she reached the other side. Thon followed, seeming intrigued by what he had done. They hurried onward.

After two days, they finally reached Scrabbleton again. By now, she and Thon were white spectral figures, like ghosts. Elliel groaned as she saw the rubble of the mining village. Scrabbleton was silent and somber. She heard the sound of rocks shifting, the clink of metal tools as desperate diggers worked rescue operations. A handful of exhausted people wielded picks. Their clothes were torn, their hands and knees bloody as they dug through the rubble that filled the tunnel openings.

Elliel passed the wreckage of the remembrance shrine, where the people kept records of their families and friends. The shrine was now just a heap of charred planks and support beams. A couple of older women in gray skirts squatted in the wreckage, sifting through the remains to find scorched scraps of paper on which names were written. One held up a half-burned sheet. "Eleven names . . . but what about all the others? Their legacy is lost. No one can remember them now. They're . . . gone."

They barely recognized the Brava woman and her wreth companion covered in ash. They got to their feet, brushed soot from their skirts. "You came back."

One of the women flashed a glance at Thon. "Is the wreth man here to save us, or finish the destruction?"

Thon spread his hands. "I don't know."

A gigantic mound of debris had buried the office shack of mine boss Hallis. The streams that had flowed down the mountainside were clogged with debris, leaving only puddles of undrinkable water, covered with a scum of sulfur. Vents of steam gasped out of broken slopes.

Ahead, townspeople clustered around Shauvon's inn, which miraculously remained standing. Part of the roof had been smashed by a boulder dropping out of the sky, but the rest of the building seemed solid.

The innkeeper looked harried and haunted as he gave the survivors important work to do. "Two homes up in the box canyon were buried when a slope came down, and we haven't had time to excavate. Upwin just came back from inspecting them, but it's worth a second look. Someone might still be alive in there."

Even through the layers of dirt and ash, Elliel recognized the miner. Upwin rubbed his raw eyes, smeared powder across his face. "Both houses were buried. We haven't heard a sound from the people inside. They're probably dead." He shrugged. "But we can hope. If anyone has the strength and the fortitude to try to dig them out, we have tools."

"Give us shovels and picks," Elliel said.

"I will help," Thon said.

They went into what had been a quiet, tree-lined side canyon with two isolated homes. The larger dwelling had been destroyed in the avalanche, collapsing the roof. The second home, a small cottage, had been inundated by the rockslide.

Elliel hurried to the cottage, calling out, "Is anyone inside? Can you hear me?" Though she heard no answer, she began digging.

Scrabbleton workers joined them, using shovels to expose one wall, while more miners concentrated on the larger house. The sounds echoed in the narrow box canyon, but the buried homes seemed silent and dead inside.

Elliel coughed, barely able to breathe from the stink of sulfur and ash in the air. Using all her strength, she rolled away a boulder, which opened a hole into the cottage. "Anyone there?" she called as she wormed her way in.

"Two brothers lived in that house," Upwin said, handing Elliel a small lantern. "They weren't in the mines during the eruption, so we think they were at home."

Elliel crawled in to the dark interior of the cottage. One of the walls had fallen, and she saw that great rocks had crushed both of the young men. "They were home." Their chests were buried, their arms outstretched over the splintered remains of a table and a scattering of gambling cards.

She clawed her way back out through the hole, squirming up through the loose dirt, and two miners helped her.

Thon stood before the more difficult challenge of the larger home. As workers dug with picks to clear the main wall, he remained still, staring, his hands outstretched.

"Help us, wreth man," demanded one of the miners. "Don't you have magic?"

"First let me understand the earth and stone . . ." Thon gestured, and the fallen dirt and rocks trembled.

Yelping in surprise, the miners scurried away, as if the vibrations were another quake. Thon pushed with his magic, shoving aside mounds of rubble until he exposed a broken window frame in the front wall. The effort seemed to drain him, but he turned his ash-streaked face toward Elliel. "That was easier than digging. Now look inside."

Elliel's heart leaped when she heard a faint moan through the exposed window. "Someone's in there! Thon, support the walls." Without waiting, she climbed through the broken opening with the small lantern, and worked her way inside the collapsed house, around and under fallen ceiling timbers, shoving aside piles of dirt and stones. She found herself in a dark common room with a downpour of dust trickling from the ceiling, illuminated by a thin shaft of daylight. She heard the moan again and then another one. Small voices . . . children. She froze, suddenly overwhelmed by thoughts of the children she had slaughtered in her blood rage. She needed to save them!

In an eating area, a large wooden table had collapsed halfway, one of the legs broken, and ceiling debris covered the table with stone slabs and piles of dirt. But the children had taken shelter under the table, which had miraculously shielded them. As she dug, Elliel called for help.

Upwin wormed through to join her and gestured with his chin. "The father's over there." She glanced where he indicated and saw an arm protruding from a mound of fallen stone.

"But the children are alive." That was all she could think about.

They both dug faster and cleared the side of the table, where they found a dirt-streaked boy and girl wedged under the back corner.

"We couldn't get out," said the boy.

"Now you can," Elliel said. With great strength she cleared more rocks and stretched her hand beneath the table. The little girl took it, and Elliel pulled her free, dragging the child through the dirt and handing her to Upwin. The miner wrapped his arms around the girl and pulled her back toward the only exit. Elliel ducked under the table and retrieved the boy. She and Upwin emerged to the cheering of miners. It was good news for a change.

"I'm glad we came back," Elliel said to Thon.

Having demonstrated his wreth magic, Thon assisted the villagers, using his powers to shore up crumbling walls, to clear debris from houses, though he looked frayed and drained from the effort. Somehow finding strength and determination, he worked for hours at the collapsed mountainside, pushing boulders away to clear the mouth of the main tunnel. Desperate miners entered, holding their lanterns and shouting for their comrades, but even though they searched long into the night, they heard no answer.

The following day, Konag Conndur and his expedition arrived.

60

THE destruction around Mount Vada shook Conn to the core. The Dragonspine Mountains were a disaster, and tremors and spreading fires resonated throughout the range.

He looked to his Brava. "This is far worse than any attack we have ever seen from the Isharans, Utho. I can't ignore the evidence I see with my own eyes. It changes my entire conception of the world and our place in it. How can we deny that Ossus is stirring?"

Utho was dusted with ash, his black uniform and riding cloak now almost entirely white. He also sounded shaken. "Are you sure of what the evidence means, Sire?"

The konag raised his hands. "Look around you, old friend. How can this not be the dragon? It can't be a coincidence this happened right after Adan and Koll warned us. What else could shake a mountain range like this? The fire and smoke!"

As they rode into Scrabbleton, the Brava remained troubled. "I admit I don't understand it, Sire. It does seem to fit with the legend."

"What if the mountain explodes again? And we're right here!" Prince Mandan looked back and forth. "The people say that boulders rained down from the sky like shooting stars. If we were back in the castle, we'd at least be safe."

"None of these people are safe here," Conn said. "We can't just leave. I am the konag! We have to help them."

The village survivors were covered in dust and tears. One man came forward to speak for the townspeople, surprised that they would come here. "The mayor is dead and so are many others, including the mine boss, but I'm left, Sire." The townspeople muttered in constant fear. "I'm the innkeeper, but I can't offer much in the way of hospitality. We might find some fresh water for your men and your horses. We filter it through rags to make it palatable. But there's nothing more."

The expedition's horses had been unable to drink from the steaming streams or pools of contaminated water for some time. Conndur summoned his guards. "My men will help. We came here to assist."

A tall young woman came forward to meet them. Her dark cinnamon hair was streaked and clumped, her beautiful face marred by a strange tattoo, but she had an imposing presence about her. Conn realized that she was a Brava, though she didn't wear their traditional garb.

His main astonishment, though, was directed toward the strikingly handsome man next to her. The tall stranger had long dark hair, a wide face, and large almond eyes that were a penetrating deep blue. His face bore a tattoo similar to the woman's, but he didn't look quite human. He seemed more lithe, more intrinsically powerful . . . more alien. Conn had never seen anyone like him before.

Recalling what Koll and Adan had said, he realized what this man must be. "You're a wreth!" he blurted out, his voice dry. "A real wreth."

At the same time, Utho froze seeing the Brava woman, and his expression became even stonier than usual. He pointedly looked away from her as if she didn't exist.

The konag slid off his horse and warily approached the strange man, filled with curiosity as well as fear. "There are wreths in the Dragonspine?"

Prince Mandan looked at him with wide eyes. "So the wreths aren't just stories after all? Does that mean the dragon is real, too?"

"They were never just stories, my prince," said Utho, pointedly ignoring the forlorn Brava woman. "But we face so many more immediate threats."

Conn faced the strange man. "Are you wreths here to destroy us all?"

The stranger met his gaze. "I do not know. I can speak for no one but myself." Conn tentatively extended a hand, and the wreth accepted it, first in a firm grip, then more curious, as if the touch of skin were a mystery to him. "My name is Thon."

"My brother and my son reported about wreths in Suderra and Norterra." Conn hardened his voice. "They killed many people in the north. How can we be certain you aren't here to harm us?"

"I am alone. My legacy has been erased. I cannot be certain of anything."

Thon touched the tattoo on his cheek. "All my memories were wiped before I was sealed inside the mountain, but now I am awake and trying to discover my path. She rescued me." He indicated the Brava woman beside him.

Utho interrupted, looking at Thon warily. "You have a rune of forgetting. I know what that means." He hesitated for the barest instant. "Like the one on Elliel's face."

The Brava woman stared at him in surprise and stepped closer. "You know what it is?" She suddenly caught her breath. "You know *my name*?"

"I know you," he said. "I gave you that tattoo myself."

She recoiled. "Utho . . ." She touched her pocket and removed a paper she kept tucked inside her tunic. "You left me this letter. That's all I know about who I am, what I did . . . my whole life."

"It is all you need to know," Utho said, his voice sharp and dismissive. "I did what had to be done, and you would be wise not to ask questions. Make a new legacy and hope that enough time and distance can erase the reasons for your punishment." He lowered his voice. "I'm glad to see that you survived, though. You were so young. I hope you've changed since that terrible time."

Elliel sounded deeply guilty and ashamed. "I am trying. I worked to make amends, tried to fit in. We helped the people here in Scrabbleton—they were very good to me, but I don't know if the town can be made safe. So much destruction . . ."

"Especially if the dragon is stirring," the innkeeper groaned. The konag's escort soldiers held their restless horses, as if expecting Ossus to burst out of the mountain any moment.

Conndur's disbelief had turned into tatters around him. When Adan and Koll told him about the wreths, he had been more concerned about the Isharan attacks on the coast, their destructive godling. But now his skepticism faded. *Ancestors' blood, this cannot be possible!*

Paying little attention to the konag, Elliel approached Utho, who remained in his saddle and made no move to welcome her. She gave him a pleading look. "Tell me more? Please? You were there. What was I like before . . . I did what I did? Who were those poor children I killed? Why? Was it just the fever? That doesn't make sense to me. Was I truly a terrible person?" Her hand strayed to the ramer at her side. "I can no longer use this, but it feels stained with blood. Please, tell me what I need to know!"

Utho's brows drew together. "I can't tell you any more than I wrote in my letter. That part of your legacy has been wiped away. It no longer exists." His voice was stern.

She touched her tattooed cheek. "Thon says this design doesn't include a locking element, that the memories aren't permanently gone. If I can atone, find a way to get them back . . ."

Utho's implacable face grew stormy. "No more questions. Live with who you are, Elliel. That is your only chance for redemption, your only chance for a new legacy. Do not question the past. It is gone."

Elliel retreated, hanging her head. It seemed to take everything she had not to flee.

Conndur kept his gaze focused on Thon. "We know that sandwreths came out of the deserts, and a frostwreth army wiped out a human town in the north. The legends say they want to wake the dragon." He gestured toward the smoking summit of Mount Vada. "Look what happened here. They may succeed!"

Concerned, Thon shook his head. "That is what I fear most. If the wreths have restored their power, they will stop at nothing to complete the tasks Kur gave them. Their efforts to wake the dragon likely caused . . . this." He stared at the damaged village, the smoke in the sky. "Their armies will sweep across the land—your land—and crush each other. They will lay waste to the world, with no regard to humans."

Conndur's thoughts raced. His son and his brother had pleaded with him to send Commonwealth armies to defend against the encroaching wreths, to parley with Queen Voo about a possible alliance. "What do we do?"

Thon seemed mystified. "I am trying to discover the answers myself. They are locked and bound inside me." He turned to the Brava woman. "Elliel and I had set out for Norterra in search of answers for our own questions. We have a long journey ahead of us."

"But we came back and helped Scrabbleton." Elliel still looked pleadingly at Utho as if he might forgive her, but he gave her only a cold response.

Utho said, "A Brava is given the rune of forgetting only under the most extreme circumstances. Only recently, we had to do the same to another who proved himself a coward when he should have helped defend Mirrabay against the Isharan animals." He looked at Conndur with anger flushing his face. "We are still under attack, Sire, and the Isharan navy could raid our coast any day now. We know they are coming. Don't let yourself be distracted by a myth—"

Conn snapped at him, unable to believe what he was saying. "You call this a *distraction*? We'll stay here and help these people, and I'll send messengers to Bannriya and Fellstaff, to tell Adan and Koll that I believe them. We have to concentrate on the wreth threat." He looked quickly at Thon. "Would you like an escort? I can have my soldiers take you directly to the king of Norterra, if that is where you need to go."

"Thank you, but no." When Elliel looked at Thon, surprised he would turn down the offer, the wreth man added, "There is more I must discover. I don't actually know where we're supposed to be."

Disappointed but determined to stay with Thon, Elliel offered a sad farewell to the townspeople, and then the two of them set off, leaving the town in the hands of the konag's expedition.

As the soldiers distributed supplies and established work teams, Conn put together a plan, remembering how he would set up large military camps during the old war. "First, dig trenches and try to find clear water. Filter what we need in the meantime. Set teams to dig through the broken homes and find whatever food we can salvage so the townspeople have enough to eat."

One of his soldiers said, "We could hunt in the forest, but there'll be few animals left."

"There's not much of the forest left," Mandan said. "The trees are flattened or burning."

"We'll do what we can." Reaching the inescapable conclusion, Conn addressed the bedraggled townspeople. "You can't survive here for long. This town won't sustain you."

"This is our home," said the innkeeper. The people muttered in resignation.

"And if the dragon emerges from beneath the mountains, you won't want to be here," Conndur said.

The innkeeper remained stubborn. "If Ossus returns, Convera won't be safe either."

Conn sighed. "No, I suppose it won't."

Utho said, "What if the Isharan navy chooses to attack now? What if they bring another godling up the river to strike the capital? Think of the destruction they could cause—"

Conn cut him off with a raised hand and said in a hard and dangerous voice, "I am not concerned with Isharans right now, old friend. We've seen evidence of the dragon, and we have to focus on the greater threat. In fact, it would be wise to make peace with the Isharans so we don't have to worry about their attacks. A more terrifying enemy has raised its head."

Utho stared at him in disbelief, but the konag grew more determined as he studied the devastation. "These may be the last days of the world . . . and we can't face it alone. A war like this affects Ishara as well as the Commonwealth." He knew it was the right thing to do. "In fact, the Isharans might be the most important allies we have. We may need them against the common enemy. I should talk with them about the very survival of the human race. Surely they will understand."

61

∽

With an escort of four ur-priests and ten Isharan soldiers, Priestlord Klovus rode south to the distant district of Tamburdin. He could save these people from the barbarians by inspiring and controlling their godling. He would show Neré how it was done.

The Tamburdin District was a wild place with thick forests, rolling hills, and rushing mountain streams that glittered with yellow dust. The frontier district provided much of Ishara's gold.

Tamburdin also suffered frequent attacks by the unruly, violent Hethrren who came from beyond the borders. Six months earlier, Empra Iluris had dispatched an Isharan army unit to deal with the raiders, but half of those soldiers had been killed by the barbarians. The best solution was to unleash the power of the increasingly violent local godling, but Priestlord Neré needed Klovus's assistance.

In Serepol, he had asked the empra for a small, swift vanguard to take him to Tamburdin. Iluris was skeptical of his motives, as she always was. "You would place yourself in danger, Priestlord? What can you do down there that my soldiers can't?"

"The responsibility falls to me, as key priestlord of Ishara. With the Tamburdin godling, I will show how it's done." Though he felt a nervous fluttering in his gut, he showed no outward fear. He and Priestlord Neré should be able to defeat the Hethrren easily. He knew the Tamburdin godling was powerful and bestial, a reflection of their wild and rugged district. And hard to control.

Klovus was weary and sore as the riders led him down the stony road to Tamburdin's main city. It was surrounded by a fifteen-foot-high stockade wall of pine trunks lashed together. The tops of the trunks were carved to sharp points, and the walls themselves bristled with outthrust defensive

stakes. At strategic positions around the wall, sentries directed their attention to the wooded hills, watching for the barbarians.

In the town's highest tower, a support cradle held a bronze bell, which
could toll loudly if Hethrren raiders were spotted, calling farmers and shepherds from the surrounding lands into the protection of the stockade. Now
sentries in the watchtowers raised a new set of red banners to signal the approaching procession.

The main gates were open, but well guarded. Tamburdin city guards came
forward to greet them, along with the local priestlord. Neré was thin like a
spindly birch tree, her dark hair hanging in two long braids. Her brown eyes
were like dark knots in pinewood, and her brown caftan had Tamburdin
geometric designs. Her collar and cuffs were lined with fox fur.

Seeing Klovus at the lead of the soldier escort, Neré bowed. "Key Priestlord, I am proud and humbled that you have come. Hear us, save us."

"Hear us, save us," he repeated automatically. "Now, let us get down to
business."

The party rode through the gate into the enclosed town. The head of the
Tamburdin city guard stood at his post, clearly disappointed by the size
of the entourage. "*Ten* soldiers and some priests? That is all the empra both-
ered to send? All together, you may be able to fight four of the Hethrren!"
He had a bushy black beard and a conical iron helmet lined with fox fur.
His leather vest was reinforced with dozens of small metal plates.

Klovus sniffed. "*I* am here, and I will do what the army cannot."

"You can fight Magda herself," Neré snorted to the guard. "We will handle
the rest of the Hethrren."

"Magda?" Klovus asked. "The barbarians are led by a woman?"

"She's huge and muscular. Some say she married a bear because no man
could survive her embraces."

"I fear for the bear," said the bearded guard captain.

Neré gestured for Klovus and his four priests to follow her. He said loudly,
"We must pray and sacrifice to the godling. It exists for the purpose of protecting Tamburdin. That's all we need."

The townspeople muttered, "Hear us, save us."

The wooden buildings were covered with shake shingles harvested from
the nearby forests. A sweet, biting smell of woodsmoke hung in the air. As
Neré led them through the narrow streets, a persistent barking dog harassed
one of his ur-priests. The priest tried to frighten it away, waving his hands

and shouting, but the dog backed into an alley before rushing around the next narrow street, yapping and growling at him again.

"Can we just get one of the guards to kill it?" Klovus grumbled. "Let them practice with their bows."

Neré drew her brows together. "Dogs are useful. We turn them loose in the hills, and their barking alerts us to the Hethrren."

Klovus frowned. "Right now, the barking has only alerted everyone to my priests."

The temple in the center of the city was an ornate structure with wooden walls, the boards sanded and stained dark, the pointed roof covered with wooden shingles like large scales. Eight prominent gables flanked the central spire. The main timbers were carved into imposing symbols of the forest, fierce wooden bears, stags, and wolves. Carved eagles protruded from the prominent gables.

The worshipping hall was built from twisted logs to form uneven, hostile-looking walls. Neré said, "Those logs are from trees that were struck and killed by lightning, so now they hold the power of lightning. The godling can draw on that, along with the sacrifices we share."

"It's a wild and powerful godling," Klovus said.

Neré nodded. "We made it that way, and it has grown even more so lately. Now it is restless and barely contained, which is why I may need your help. The Tamburdin District has the usual dangers of a forested land. The rivers run angry with the spring melt. Wolves, bears, and tree leopards prey upon our hunters."

Klovus said, "Ishara was a virgin land full of magic when our ancestors arrived. We tamed much of it, but humans are still newcomers here. Out on the boundaries, there will always be dangers."

"The natural dangers are not what concern us most," Neré said. "The Hethrren are fiercer than golden bears or starving wolves."

Klovus crossed his arms over his chest and slid his hands into the opposite sleeves of his blue caftan. "What do the barbarians want? Do they wish to take over the city? Does Magda mean to overthrow the district leader and rule for herself?"

"No, the Hethrren want to take what we have and ride back to their own lands. We are sport to them."

Klovus blinked. "That makes no sense. Why would they do that?"

"The barbarians would never live in our cities. They just want to raid and attack, kill some people, steal food and gold—even though they could collect the gold out of the streams themselves if they bothered to make the effort." Neré made a disgusted sound. "No one knows where the Hethrren came from, or why they even exist."

"So, this Magda doesn't want to be a queen so much as she wants to be feared?" Klovus thought he understood.

"When she leads her followers against us, she keeps their violent nature otherwise occupied, then they don't think about overthrowing her." Neré scowled. "And we're the ones who pay the price."

Klovus drew his gaze across the lightning-blackened trunks. A wooden carving of a stag with sharp antlers stood at one wall looking toward the shimmering spelldoor. On the other side of the worship chamber towered a fierce wooden bear twice as tall as a man with massive paws and claws as long as knives. Klovus could feel a tingle of magic in his blood and sensed the godling behind its shimmering spelldoor, restless and protective.

"Call a full worship ritual and sacrifice, with as many people as possible," Klovus announced. "Tonight we will feed the godling and make it more powerful, part of all of us." He stood next to tall, thin Neré. "You and I will be partners, and together we'll give Magda something to fear."

62

THE heat shimmered in the vast desert, sending thermal mirages through the air. Queen Voo could still feel angry vibrations through the ground from when she and her wreths had demonstrated their power. The shock had indeed disturbed Ossus deep beneath the mountains, and she was reassured by her own magic. Voo felt a warm glow in her heart, certain now that her people would ultimately triumph.

The mage Axus and her brother Quo looked at the black mountains that sliced across the Furnace. The mage nodded slowly. "I am impressed, my queen. We cracked the world like a lizard's egg."

Her eyes gleamed with pride. "Yes, we did this. We can still wring magic out of the land."

Quo seemed aloof and cocky. "Then let us do it again and break the rest of the mountains."

"We will, dear brother, but not now. We made the dragon stir, but we are not quite ready to fight him."

Axus squinted at the line of damaged peaks in front of them. "Ossus has a long memory. For now, we will give him terrible nightmares."

Voo led her party to a dry lake bed at the base of the mountains, a white expanse of bitter, salty powder. As crosswinds swirled the dust, a pale haze drifted across the barren lake. The augas had been set loose to romp in the desert, and now they milled about in the powder, crunching through the hard crust and finding pools of scummy water to drink.

In the days when they still had the power to shape living things, sandwreths had created augas to survive in the most desolate environments. That was when the land itself had magic to spare, and wreths could manipulate it as they liked. Her people had been so ambitious back then.

Similarly, they had created the human race from dust, just as Kur had created wreths when he made the world. Since even their own god had not made his children perfect, the wreths could not be expected to make *humans* perfect. And yet, Voo found the subordinate race satisfactory. Recently, she had been impressed by what she saw in Bannriya, the tall buildings, the walls, the persistent civilization. Human progress was much more significant than the small settlements her wreth scouts had first encountered when they began to explore beyond the desert after awakening. When taken in large enough numbers, these people might actually be as strong as she hoped.

Voo had brought a party of twenty wreths with her, including hardy workers from the lower castes. Now they clambered over the fractured cliffs, exploring the slopes on her orders. Some ventured into the main fissure that was like a raw wound in the rock. With the mountains split apart, the interior would be pristine, maybe containing a potent residue of magic undamaged by the old wars.

Maybe something she could use.

Human laborers would not be sufficiently skilled or strong to do work like this, so she turned her wreths to the task. They wormed their way into cracks, calling to one another, lowering themselves with ropes into the mysterious depths.

The next time she presented herself to King Adan, she had even grander ideas of what to propose. If she manipulated them properly, or wielded a powerful enough fist, the three human kingdoms would become her allies against the frostwreths. If she swelled her fighting force with humans, they could conquer whatever armies her rival Onn scraped up from the frozen wastes.

Watching the augas slurp polluted water from the lake crust, she asked her brother, "Would this place be appropriate for another camp, if we brought more human laborers? We should plan ahead, be ambitious."

Axus brushed white powder from his face. "It is probably not worth the effort out here. They are very fragile. The heat would kill them, the water would poison them, and then we would need to bring more and more humans just to replace them."

Quo gave her a petulant frown. "I have enough trouble tending the ones you already gave me."

"Very well, I certainly wouldn't want to inconvenience you," she said, annoyed.

Absently, she swirled salt from the lake bed and fashioned figures of majestic wreth heroes and less-impressive humans. As a game, Voo knocked down the human shapes while Quo crushed them back into powder, then built them up again.

Mage Axus watched them, his seamed face pulled down in disapproval. "If you want the humans to be effective and loyal, you should treat them with greater care. They damage easily, and broken humans are of no use to us."

Voo was indignant that he would speak so boldly to her. "I am not accustomed to having a mere mage question my decisions."

"The reason you have mages, my queen, is to serve as your advisors, and I advise you that we should spend our humans where we benefit most from the cost in blood. They are a resource."

She pouted. "True, but even the lowest-caste wreth is superior to a human." She gestured to her people who were exploring the fissure in the mountain.

"Their chief advantage is that humans breed so quickly." Quo looked down at the crumbled salt figure he had sculpted. "Remember the old days when they replaced themselves as quickly as we could diminish them? Even our people bred with humans."

"If you consider them inferior, then why go to so much trouble?" Axus asked her pointedly.

Voo was distracted by the augas frolicking in the alkaline powder. They snorted and rolled, crusting their scaled hides with salt crystals. She glanced at her brother and said in a disappointed voice, "Axus does make sense. The humans won't be useful at all if they do not survive the alliance."

Quo bridled. "Are you criticizing my management?"

"I am suggesting you give them a few more amenities, maybe an extra ration of water and food. If they are going to die, I would rather they died fighting the frostwreths for us."

He didn't sound pleased. "They are quite resilient. We did not expect to find any of them still alive when we woke from our spellsleep. No matter what we do, some of them will manage to scurry out of the way and survive."

Their discussion was interrupted by shouts from the peak. A muscular sandwreth worker scrambled out of the fissure, waving his hands. "A grotto! It was once sealed, but the walls are broken!"

That didn't sound terribly interesting. She called back, "Are there any artifacts? Things of great power?"

Quo was already starting up the slope, climbing the slabs of fallen rock.

Voo followed, but at a more delicate pace. The muscular worker stood at the top of the fissure, hands on his hips. "We did find something, but I am not sure what it means, my queen. Perhaps one of you can enlighten us."

Three workers struggled to lift a heavy object from below. It was a smooth, curved section of murky translucent material, like a piece of a gigantic eggshell, or a fibrous cocoon. The broken section was as large as one of the doors to her bedchamber in the sand palace.

"We found several fragments in the grotto." The workers rested the large piece on the rocks above the fissure. It seemed to be made of dark milk, solidified. Voo tapped the hard substance with her fingernail, and to her surprise felt warmth lingering there, a vibration of old magic.

Huffing with exertion, the mage Axus joined them. He studied the object. "That is not ancient, my queen. Only recently hatched."

"I suspected as much," she said.

After all their efforts, the wreth workers seemed crestfallen. "You do not find it valuable, my queen?"

"Oh, we will take it back to the sand palace, where it can serve as a curiosity." She pondered where she could display the thing. "We may find a use for it. The thing has intrinsic interest."

Suddenly, a thrum rippled through her heart and mind, and shuddered into the cracked mountains. The wreth workers scrambled away from the edge of the fissure as boulders shifted and loose rock pattered down into the depths.

Queen Voo turned her gaze to the sky rather than down into the fissure. She felt the strongest magic, a pull and pang—high overhead. Her brother followed her gaze, and his mouth opened in amazement. He let out a laugh, pointing eagerly upward. Even Axus brightened.

High overhead they saw an angular reptilian form beating its great wings, raising its serpentine neck as it scanned the desert. Its shadow played across the dry lake bed, and the augas darted about in panic like rodents sensing a predator circling above. The dragon was enormous, its wings triangular, its arrow-shaped head sharp and fierce, its barbed tail like a thick whip. The creature shattered the desert air with a single piercing shriek.

Still staring, Quo said to his sister, "Is that really Ossus? Did we awaken him after all?"

Voo snorted. "No, that is just a small dragon, one of the children of Ossus, but killing it will be good for practice. We need to prepare ourselves."

She watched the monster fly across the sky, following the line of mountains. Its lair would be somewhere in the desert range, and Voo could use
her senses to find it again, wherever it might try to hide. The mages could
summon it, but only when she was ready. Her pulse raced. She hadn't been
this excited in some time.

Voo smiled at her brother. "When we get back to the sand palace, I will
call a dragon hunt. What better way to ready our wreth warriors?" Her smile
broadened as another idea came to her. "Ah, I will even invite King Adan
Starfall to join us. I am sure he would enjoy it."

63

His skin was blue with cold, nearly frozen solid. The blood had paused in his veins. The wind blew hard pellets of snow with a scouring, whispering sound across his bare chest, dotting the frozen varnish of splashed blood.

Lasis opened his eyes.

His naked body lay discarded with the garbage outside the frostwreth palace along with broken crates, glassware, chipped ceramics . . . other bodies. Sluggishly, thoughts carved new pathways through his brain.

After his eyes opened, he heaved a breath. The frozen air sliced like razors in his empty lungs. When he attempted to sit, the sheet of blood on his chest cracked. More red liquid bubbled from the gash in his throat, then stopped as the threads of healing tissue caught and held. He bent his arm, reached up with numb fingers to touch his throat. He pushed the wet, torn flesh together and summoned just a little more of the magic that had saved his life.

As full-blooded wreth royalty, Queen Onn was far more powerful than he could ever be, but as a Brava, Lasis had unusually powerful skills of his own. Wreths knew how to send themselves into spellsleep, shutting down their breathing, their blood flow, their need to eat for centuries at a time. Rather than bleeding to death when Onn slashed his throat, Lasis had instinctively plunged into the deep trance, pulling the magic around him like a blanket and making himself effectively dead. Then Onn's servants had discarded him outside, naked and frozen.

Now that he was awake again, though, he could well die here in the frozen wastes. Blocking any sensation of cold for now, he reached to his side, but he already knew that his ramer was gone. He bent his stiff joints and straightened against the wind, surrounded by unrelenting frozen whiteness.

Behind him, the palace rose high among other frostwreth structures the ancient race had built as they resurrected their civilization. No matter how much Lasis needed food or shelter, he could not go back into the palace. The frostwreths would capture him again, torture him, kill him.

Ahead, away from the fine buildings, he saw low rounded structures, hovels scattered outside the great fortress. They were patched together from scraps of metal, tree branches from a faraway forest, even bones, all cemented with ice and snow. He would try to go there, even though they seemed infinitely far away.

He saw small-statured creatures moving around the huts. A line of them streamed into the frostwreth city, while others worked around their clustered huts to assemble new structures or patch their old ones.

These were drones the frostwreths had created in a clumsy attempt to forge a new servile race. From what he had seen, the drones were ill treated, but he didn't trust them. In order to serve their masters, they might well sacrifice him to Queen Onn. Or maybe they would help. The drones were his best chance to survive and escape, perhaps his only chance. He really had no choice.

Lasis moved with a shuffling gait, barely able to bend, not feeling his feet or his exposed skin. He felt weak, swiftly losing energy, but he was a Brava, bonded to King Kollanan, and he was relentless. He needed to make it back to Fellstaff, to report what he had seen, tell the king and queen what the frostwreths were doing.

And to tell them that their grandson Birch was still alive.

The thought gave him new strength inside. Yes, he must survive at all costs. He lurched forward, trying to focus through frozen eyes. He tripped and fell to his knees, then crawled in a straight line toward the nearest drone hovel.

He didn't make it. Lasis collapsed and sprawled face-first in the gritty snow. He found he could no longer block the sensation of cold. Ice crystals bit into his damaged skin. He inhaled a mouthful of snow, but didn't even have the energy to cough.

Hands grasped him, fingers wrapped around his cold skin. He heard humming words, chittering voices. More small hands dragged him along, leaving a trough in the snow. They were taking him somewhere, but before he learned the answer, Lasis dropped into a sleep that was again close to death.

He awoke to a miracle of warmth, though he heard wind whistling through chinks in the walls. A low fire of oily-smelling crystals burned in a small pit in the ground, adding light and heat to the stuffy room. The skin of some animal with mangy fur had been draped over his naked body like a blanket.

He smelled something rotten burbling in the heat and saw one of the drones pull a small ceramic pot from the glowing heat crystals, perhaps a pot salvaged from a home in Lake Bakal.

Lasis worked to sit up. He was inside one of the drone huts, and they were keeping him here, hiding him. He didn't know whether the creatures had independent thought, if this was a sign of their rebellion against the frostwreths. Why else would the drones save him? Was it just instinctive?

The drone looked at him but said nothing, merely blinked its flat eyes and extended the pot. It opened a toothless mouth, pointed a finger to it as if Lasis didn't understand how to eat. Weakly, the Brava man took the pot and a flattened stick, which he used to serve himself.

The smell of the concoction nauseated him. What sort of flesh had been cooked in it? But he needed to survive, so he forced himself to eat several mouthfuls, knowing it was nourishment of some sort. He chewed slowly, so his body wouldn't reject the food.

"Water," he said, and his voice was a rasping croak. He mimicked the gesture of drinking.

The drone stared at him, showing no comprehension, no excitement, no welcome, but it turned and retrieved a bowl of water, probably from melted snow. Lasis drank a few cautious sips and set the bowl aside with trembling hands.

He fell asleep again, letting his body absorb that small amount of food and water. When he awoke, he felt a thousand times stronger, though his fingers and feet were numb. Now at least he had some confidence that he would live.

More drones came into the hovel, gathering around to stare at him. They muttered among themselves in their own language, but they didn't try to speak to him. As he watched them more closely, he did see a flicker of intelligence in their eyes. They weren't as mindless and mechanical as they let on.

He recalled that the frostwreth queen had instructed the drones to care for Birch. The words drifted back to him, splintered and indistinct. He remembered the exchange between Onn and Chief Warrior Rokk, that she was sending the captive boy back to the new fortress at Lake Bakal. Lasis scrambled through his memories. Had she done so? Yes, that was what he had heard. Birch might be there, if he was still alive, if the drones had tended him as they were tending him now.

He again vowed that he would survive so he could tell the king what he knew, but he could not cross the frozen wastes without the help of these creatures. So he gambled.

"I fought the frostwreths. I tried to kill them," he said. "They are my enemy. You saw what Queen Onn did to me." He touched the wound on his throat. From his pallet, he tried to interpret the light in their eyes, the expressions on their crudely formed faces. He knew they understood his words, because they followed commands the frostwreths gave them. "If you hate the wreths too, then help me."

The drones chittered, and some looked away, clearly agitated.

"Help me," Lasis said. "All I need are food and garments. I will leave at night. The wreths won't know what you did." The drones seemed fearful and uncertain. He pressed, "You've already taken the risk. You saved me. You're hiding me. Now if you let me go, you can be safe again."

After mumbling in some kind of secret consultation, they came forward to surround his crude bed. The drones reached out with their small hands and touched him gently, as if to reassure themselves that he was real.

Clad in a motley of skins, furs, and scraps of cloth, and with a tattered blanket to wrap around himself, Lasis left. The auroras shone bright in the black sky, adding eerie light to the snowfields in front of him.

Before letting him go, the reverent drones had fussed over him, cobbling together the clothes, giving him food. They had also presented him with an object they seemed to revere, a small disk sawed from an antler with little holes drilled through the middle for thread. A button from a human garment. It was a simple object, oddly normal in this extraordinary place, and he guessed they must have taken it from the body of some human victim, perhaps at Lake Bakal. The drones seemed to consider it a symbol, a talisman, and he accepted it, thanking them and tucking it carefully among his furs. They huddled at the doorways of their low hovels, and watched him set off into the night.

Across the rocky, ice-glazed terrain, he saw a road the wreths had made leading south, presumably to their fortress at Lake Bakal. From there, Lasis would be able to find his way back to Norterra and King Kollanan.

At the swiftest pace he could manage, still drawing on his reserves of energy despite days of recovery, Lasis headed home.

64

⤫

THE Dragonspine Mountains fell behind Elliel and Thon as they moved on. Each sunrise was suffused with blood, the sky reddened from the ash and smoke. After Scrabbleton, they were both heartsick but more determined than ever to find answers for the strange wreth man. Did the eruption of Mount Vada mean that Ossus was actually awakening, or just stirring in his restless sleep?

Together, they left the foothills of the Dragonspine range, and traveled the caravan roads across a windy and empty landscape, heading north and west. Each night on the trail they bedded down with their blankets set close together on the hard ground—not close enough to share warmth, but enough to share companionship.

Though Thon remained silent and introspective, Elliel talked about her new life, her real life since the break point. She couldn't create another legacy with a clean slate, because the slate could never be completely clean, no matter how many good things she had done in the two years since awakening. Still, she was young enough that maybe it was best to focus on her new legacy and never read that damning letter again. Utho had certainly been cold to her in Scrabbleton, offering no hope for forgiveness.

She could not erase her past, but she could create her future. She could move forward and help Thon solve his mystery.

As if sensing her thoughts, he reached out tentatively, touched her shoulder. "Thank you." He touched her cheek, lightly ran his fingers over her cinnamon hair.

Thon's presence was a lodestone tugging at the needle of her heart. In ancient history, wreths had often taken humans as lovers, dominating them with their magic, seducing them against their will. But those wreths were not as kind and sensitive as Thon was. Had he always been like this? Since his memory had been erased, she knew only Thon's new heart, not his past. What terrible thing had he done that left him sealed in a quartz-lined prison deep within a mountain? It just didn't seem to be in his character.

But Elliel didn't believe herself capable of the crime she herself had committed, either. Weren't they different people now? Elliel understood full well the curse of empty memories.

Two days later, as they walked through the late afternoon, Thon spotted the ruins of a wreth city in the distance, crumbling towers and ethereal arches, vertical walls made of curves instead of angles. He stared, intrigued. "Where are we? Do you know the name of that place?"

Elliel looked into the slanted orange light of the setting sun. "Wreth ruins. Humans generally avoid them."

His long, dark hair blew in the breeze. "I want to go there."

She forced a smile. "Of course you do, and I will protect you." They left the path and made their way across the tall grasses toward the ruins as the sun set.

By the time they reached the city, a coppery full moon had risen out of the twilight, its usually pale light tainted by the ash in the air. The two of them walked among the soaring towers that stood sentinel over the emptiness. He let out a quiet hum as he tried to call upon lost memories and flickers of residual magic. Moving with childlike wonder, he went to the curved wall of a tower and wrapped his arms around it. He pressed his marked cheek against the stone.

"What happened here?" he asked aloud, as if expecting the buildings to answer. "Who were your people? What was your history?"

The skeletal tower was empty in the ruddy moonlight, and the other collapsed buildings held dust-filled chambers overgrown with weeds. Thon turned back to Elliel, his sapphire eyes sparkling. "I recall vague details about cities like this. I remember the towers, the people, the palaces. Wreths were a magnificent race with a legacy that should have lasted until the end of the world."

"They tried to *cause* the end of the world," Elliel pointed out.

"*I* didn't . . . at least not that I recall." He closed his eyes and rubbed his temples. "I know some of the details, but it is just information, not experiences, not real memories."

Elliel sighed. "I know what you mean."

Under the stars, she found an inviting courtyard with soft grasses and weathered statues, sculptures of male and female wreths that had been smoothed by time. With a childlike fascination, Thon touched one of the disfigured statues, ran his long fingers over the pockmarked stone, closed his eyes. "These two were engaged in some kind of sport that involved a ball, levitation magic, and fire." He seemed surprised by his own memories. "Human athletes participated with the wreths, but they had no magic . . . and they were often injured or incinerated."

Troubled, Elliel took his arm. "Were the wreths just being capricious? Did they enjoy torturing humans?"

"Like most games," Thon explained, "it served as combat training. If they couldn't survive a game, they would not be good foot soldiers on the battle-field."

They spread their blankets on the soft grass among the statues. Elliel opened her pack, removing an apple for each of them and some dried meat that Konag Conndur's soldiers had given them before they left Scrabbleton.

Thon sat close to her as they ate the meager meal. He seemed curious, troubled. Beside them lay the fallen statue of a bare-chested wreth man whose face had been weathered to an absolute blank. Thon touched the sculpted stone as if he could absorb the truth through his fingertips.

"Admit it, you're fascinated," Elliel said.

"I am, but I cannot restore my memories. If I could defy whatever put the locking element in place, then I might know, but what if doing so breaks the spell and causes some other damaging consequence? There must have been a reason. What if I negate my own existence? I was meant to learn in a different way."

Her heart ached for him as well as for herself. "We're both hollow inside, filled with mysteries instead of memories."

She leaned closer, and he reached out to touch the mark on her cheek. His fingers were warm and tingling. "This does not mean we are empty." His fingers trailed down her cheek, cupped her chin. "It means we have room to make more memories."

She pressed her hand to his, held it against her skin. Her pulse began rac-ing and warmth spread through her.

"You are very beautiful, Elliel. You must have had many admirers."

"I . . . I don't remember."

He smiled. "Then let me tell you again. You are beautiful."

He kissed her, and she responded, reaching out to lace her fingers through his dark hair, pulling him close. Their kiss went deeper, and they reclined in the soft grass, where she had spread their blankets.

He seemed so calm and gentle, even as his need increased. She breathed faster, inhaling his own breath, and her lips traced his skin, kissing the tattoo on his cheek as he kissed hers. They began discovering each other with far greater care and fascination than they had explored the wreth city.

Elliel felt uncertain, but she didn't want to stop. "I can't even tell you whether this is my first time or not, or whether I know what to do, or if I can please you."

He silenced her with another kiss and pressed closer, letting her feel the burning softness of his skin. "I trust your instincts."

Whether through memory or intuition, Elliel did indeed know what to do. They held each other, sharing warmth, sharing themselves, stroking passion and contentment on the unwritten story of their bodies like a legacier creating a masterpiece.

Being with Thon restored a lost memory in her—the memory of being happy. Elliel fell asleep with her hair spread out across his chest. He wrapped his arms around her, pressing his cheek to the top of her head.

When they awoke the next morning, Elliel built a fire against the morning chill. They had kept each other warm, wrapped in their blankets, but now in the cool dawn, she wanted to make hot tea. They sat together, smiling and silent, basking in each other's presence.

Elliel finally broke the silence. "We have much more to see in the city. Maybe you'll learn something."

"Oh, I can show you the most important parts," said a young woman's voice, bright and friendly.

They both leaped to their feet.

"That's my specialty. I've been exploring for days. Still, lots of questions, though. So many mysteries." A plain-looking, slightly plump teenaged girl stepped into the statue yard, wrapped in layers of clothes and skirts and carrying an outrageously large pack high on her shoulders. She had a round face, and straight brown hair parted in the middle. "I thought I saw the smoke of a campfire. I was on the far side of the ruins. So much to see here!" She looked from Elliel to Thon. "I'm Shadri, by the way."

Elliel stood wary, but Thon was more open. "What brings you to this old city?"

"I came to learn, of course," Shadri said, as if the answer were obvious.

"Nobody knows much about wreth history and culture—I certainly don't! But what better place to see for myself? I've taken so many notes that I'll need a new journal soon."

The girl walked over to their campsite, distracted by the weathered statues on the grass. When she looked up, she stopped and stared at Thon. "You . . . you're not human, but you're not a Brava either! You look like the statues here . . ."

"I am a wreth," he said. "I was sleeping inside Mount Vada."

Shadri's eyes sparkled at him. "Then you're the best discovery in this entire city! I found some artifacts, explored inside the buildings, saw a lot of writing, though I can't interpret it. There's the most amazing stone mural of a great battle, and it comes alive if you step in the right place. I'll show you. In fact, I'll take you around, unless you already know this place?" Her brows drew together. "Now, if you're a real wreth, I have a thousand questions for you—and that's just to start."

She shrugged out of her large pack, dropped it on the ground, and rummaged among its contents until she pulled out a tattered notebook. "I'll have to sort through my notes to find my most important questions. You can help me a lot. Nobody knows as much about wreths as a real wreth, right?"

Thon looked at her with a sad calmness. "My legacy is a blank book."

Shadri frowned for a moment, then her chatty nature reasserted herself. "A blank book? Hmmm, intriguing. Obviously, I'll want to talk with you about *that*." She gestured to the crumbling wreth city around them. "We can figure it out together."

65

CONN and his soldiers stayed in Scrabbleton for two days assisting the survivors, but they could only accomplish so much. The main problem was water. When his workers found a diverted stream that sluiced over rocks into a pool, they scooped the water out in pots, poured it through rags to filter out most of the ash, then let it settle enough to drink. But the town could never sustain itself that way. At least for now, Scrabbleton was dead.

Though heartbroken, the people agreed to abandon their homes. They wept as they left the ruins of their lives, and followed the weary Commonwealth soldiers on a slow procession toward Convera, where the konag promised them help and shelter.

Distraught and self-absorbed, Prince Mandan said little during the ride back home. The disaster had made a profound impression on him, and his aloof, flippant attitude had changed. Conn hoped his son would remember the plight of these people when he eventually became leader of the Commonwealth.

Torn with many responsibilities, Conndur turned to Utho, who rode beside him. "I know this, old friend. The dragon is not a myth. After Mount Vada, I am convinced the creature is stirring. This is a threat to the whole world, the entire human race."

The Brava turned to him with alarm. "We can't be certain of that, Sire."

"*I'm* certain of it. We saw the fires and the destruction, we felt the tremors, and we also saw a wreth man with our own eyes. We would be willful fools if we don't accept the fundamental change to our reality." He cut off the Brava's words and leaned forward on his horse. "I am not interested in arguing. I need to be back at the castle where I can start preparing the Commonwealth for this unexpected threat. Ride with me to Convera, you and Mandan, with all possible speed."

As the rest of the soldiers led the refugees at their own pace, the three rode off at a full gallop. The skies were a gray soup of clouds, and a constant rain turned the road into a slurry that sucked at the horses' hooves. Reaching the lower city the following day, Conndur saw that one of the bridges crossing the Crickyeth River had been washed out, but intrepid ferrymen were taking people back and forth to the main city on the wedge of land between the two rivers. Shacks and lean-tos that had been erected alongside the road were crowded with refugees. Bleak people stared at the riders as they passed, and Conndur's heart ached for them.

After the Mount Vada disaster, his castle administrators had set up accounting stations where families could ask for assistance. Riders went through the city searching for anyone who might have spare beds to shelter unfortunate survivors. The busy Convera markets had been picked over, since much of the regular trade over the mountains had been cut off after the eruption.

Conndur kept wrestling with possibilities. The Commonwealth army was a mighty force, but how could even the three kingdoms stand against the power that lurked beneath Mount Vada? Or the frostwreths in Norterra that had engulfed a lake and an entire town in a wave of ice? The sandwreths claimed they wanted to be allies, and he considered riding to Suderra so he could meet with Queen Voo, but even if they fought side by side, the wreths would not have the best interests of mankind at heart.

The Commonwealth could never win this war themselves, especially if his armies were also fighting against Ishara. It would take the entire human race to stand against the ancient enemy—their own creators, who were intent on destroying and remaking the world. Conn had an idea to solve both problems at once.

As the three approached the gates of Convera Castle, Mandan grinned at the prospect of being home again, apparently no longer thinking of the plight of the refugees. "I will have a warm bath and a nap in my own bed! I am also eager to paint what I have seen, so others can see the devastation as I have."

Four advisors rushed to report to the konag as soon as he slid out of his saddle and stamped his feet, shaking off the caked ash that plastered his riding clothes. He raised his voice. "Call the council into the main chamber. I will propose an important mission that might mean our very survival. What is happening in the Dragonspine is far more dangerous than an Isharan raid."

Conn insisted that the prince join him for the urgent discussion, right away, which made Mandan sulk at the disruption of his plans for relaxation. For himself, Conn took only enough time to rinse his face and hair from a basin before he stalked into the council chamber. He had his mind made up.

His advisors, vassal lords, and ministers arrived swiftly, and he sat beside the prince at the long wooden table, facing the influential men and women. As they took their seats, the visitors shouted over one another, clamoring to deliver their reports about the damage across the counties of Osterra.

When their voices petered out, Conn said sharply, "The world just changed. For centuries there have been tremors in the Dragonspine, and we thought they were old wives' tales about Ossus shifting in his slumbers. I doubt anyone truly believed those stories. I certainly didn't." He rested his dusty elbows on the table and let out a long sigh. "Now, I fear it's all true. We know from reports delivered by King Adan and King Kollanan that the wreths have returned and they intend to wake the dragon. Perhaps Ossus really is buried beneath those mountains. After I saw the devastation, the fire and smoke, how could I think otherwise?"

The lords mumbled, but Conn's eyes burned with angry tears. "My son and brother tried to warn us, but we were more afraid of the Isharans than the wreths, more than the end of the world! That's like worrying about a pebble in your boot, when an avalanche is crashing toward you." He slammed his fist down on the table. "Ancestors' blood, this cannot be! We've had our disagreements with Ishara over the centuries. They are foreigners with strange ways, and they have godlings, which we don't understand." He swept his glare across all of them. "Yet one thing is certain—they are *humans*, like us, created and enslaved by the wreths, and then abandoned long ago."

Lord Cade said in a sarcastic voice, "Isharans may be humans, strictly speaking, but I've seen enough of them to know that they are quite inferior."

Utho's face darkened. "The Isharans have brought us tremendous harm, Sire. Don't make light of their threat. They mean to destroy us. We cannot let down our defenses."

The konag spoke in a scolding tone. "The Isharans have done us *recent* harm, certainly, and we have caused them harm as well." He scowled. "Don't tell me we haven't raided their fishing boats, captured their people, and killed innocent Isharans."

Lord Cade muttered under his breath, "There's no such thing as innocent Isharans!"

"I fought them too, you know." Conn struggled with his impatience. "I killed more Isharans than I could count, and they killed plenty of our soldiers." His own fighters had felt the bloodlust, had committed atrocities, and the Isharans would not forgo their revenge. "If Konag Cronin hadn't withdrawn us from Ishara out of grief when Bolam died, would that war still be going on?" He swallowed, but the sour taste in his mouth did not go away.

"We cannot be distracted by old quarrels, like squabbling siblings. As konag of the Commonwealth, I must rally all people—all of humanity—to stand against the wreths. We cannot waste our energy and resources fighting Ishara. This threat is greater than either of us."

One of the lords sucked in a quick breath. "You mean fight *alongside* Isharans?"

"Against the wreths—yes." Conndur looked at all of the gathered advisors. "The wreths want to remake the world and eradicate all things. If that happens, what do our arguments with the Isharans matter? We'll all be dead. We need them as allies."

His suggestion caused an uproar. Two ministers rose to their feet, and Utho's face turned a ruddy color. "They will betray us, Sire. If we let down our guard, they'll kill us more swiftly than the wreths would. We can't trust them."

"We have to take the chance," Conn insisted quietly. "You heard what Koll said. What happened at Lake Bakal is just the first step toward much wider devastation. You also saw the mountains shake and the cracks of dragon's fire escaping. We can't blind ourselves." The konag squared his shoulders, issued his decision. "I will write a letter to Empra Iluris and propose that we meet on neutral ground. I can convince her of the crisis that threatens us all. From there, we can discuss possible solutions."

"What neutral ground, Sire?" asked one of the nobles.

He had already decided. "Fulcor Island."

Utho rose to his feet. "You cannot do this, Sire. Fulcor is our hard-fought territory, gained at great cost. You know the Isharans are animals!"

"Some animals can be tamed," Conndur said.

"Why would the empra bother to come? Why would she believe us?" asked another noble—Lady Eudalya, from the county just south of the Joined River.

Conn laced his fingers together. He had to offer them something significant enough to make them agree. "Because if they agree to our alliance, if they throw their might into our mutual defense against the wreths . . . then I'll offer to return Fulcor Island to them. That should get Iluris interested."

The uproar was deafening, but Conndur didn't stay to listen. Ignoring their protestations, he rose and left the table. He was exhausted in his heart as well as in his body, and he'd had enough discussion.

The following day, an Utauk trading ship, the *Glissand,* sailed up the Joined River from the sea and docked on the Bluewater side of the city. The merchant captain, a prominent man named Hale Orr, had just returned from Ishara and he came with news for the konag. Conndur knew the man as the father of Adan's wife, Penda. They had met two years ago in Bannriya at the wedding.

Conndur received the trader, recognizing the hearty man with a neat beard and a gold tooth. Hale had only one hand, but no lack of self-confidence. Dressed in crimson and black silks, he paced back and forth in the receiving room, relaxed and tense at the same time. After brief niceties, Hale spoke quickly with his news. "After our ship traded with the garrison at Fulcor Island, we continued to Ishara, as we do on occasion. I met with the empra herself." He lowered his voice. "She tried to hire me as a spy to report on your movements and your armies, in case of war. I reassured her you were not about to launch an attack on her shores. Which is true . . . I hope?"

Conn raised his eyebrows. "I'm surprised you would tell me this."

"So was Empra Iluris, but Utauks are neutral. I said I would only agree if I could share all my observations with either side. She didn't want to accept those terms."

"They are trying to provoke us. Isharan raiders recently attacked our coast and obliterated a town," Conn said. "It was an act of war, and my people are pressuring me to retaliate. I did not ask for war. In fact, it is imperative that I stop it. I want to make peace between our lands."

Hale Orr's expression darkened. "You may say that, Sire, but the fault does not lie entirely with Ishara. Your ships have been attacking Isharan fishing boats. I saw the proof myself at Fulcor Island, and we witnessed Watchman Osler executing the civilian crews by throwing the prisoners off the cliffs. I assure you, they were only fishermen. The provocation comes from both sides."

Conndur felt angry and sickened to hear this, especially now. "This has to stop! There is too much at stake. Both sides need to change. Desperate times demand it."

He explained about the eruption of Mount Vada, the reports from Kollanan and Adan. Hale gave a solemn nod. "I can vouch that part of it is true. I was in Bannriya with my daughter and son-in-law. I saw Queen Voo and the sandwreths arrive after the dust storm, and I heard what she had to say. It is deeply disturbing."

Conn realized the opportunity that had fallen in his lap. If this man had seen the wreths himself, and he was a neutral Utauk, what better messenger could he send? "I've written a letter to the empra, from one ruler to another, but I didn't know how to deliver it. How would a Commonwealth ship get to Ishara? But an Utauk ship . . ."

"The *Glissand* is not my ship, Sire. I'm merely the merchant captain." Hale paused. "But for an appropriate fee, the voyagier and crew could be convinced to sail back to Serepol. I'll deliver your letter into the empra's hands myself and I'll make her understand how important it is."

66

A TAMBURDIN hunter stumbled out of the forest, bleeding from wounds in his shoulder and shouting about a horde of Hethrren, hundreds of the barbarians on the move toward the city, only a day or so behind him. "They killed both of my brothers. I barely got away."

The hunter's wounds needed tending, but Klovus insisted that some of his blood first be offered in the temple. "We need the godling strong!" he said. "We need it *angry*!" Klovus could barely contain his eagerness. He had carefully planned with Priestlord Neré for the arrival of the barbarians.

The outlying farmers and shepherds retreated into the protection of the stockade walls, and the city prepared for the attack. Anxiety hung over the streets like a cold, low-lying fog.

The next day, the Hethrren swarmed out of the hills in a concerted charge.

Klovus had been happily asleep, making sure he would be well rested for the impending raid, when the town's bronze bell clanged to wake the defenders. He donned his caftan and rushed out to join his ur-priests as the people roused and rushed about. City guards ran to the watch platforms on top of the stockade, stringing their bows and getting ready to launch a rain of arrows on the invaders. Other soldiers gathered at the gates, swords drawn, standing shoulder to shoulder.

Hethrren raiders thundered out of the hills, riding between the trees in scattered formations. They rode huge black mountain horses, using leather blankets rather than saddles. The barbarians had stocky bodies and massive arms, all solid muscle. They howled as they charged forward, using their voices to invoke terror. The men had thick beards and long black hair, and the women rode beside them wielding identical weapons. Their fur-lined leather helmets were studded with polished stones.

Leading them was a woman with a square face and fierce eyes. A wolf pelt on her shoulders flapped behind her as she rode hard, leaning forward on her black horse. She carried a knotted club, its rounded end twisted like the head of a deformed child and varnished with stains of old blood. Her horse snorted as if it felt a bloodlust of its own.

Some Hethrren rode with smoking baskets filled with pitch and kindling. The wicker baskets burst into flame as the raiders swung the containers while galloping toward the stockade. The flaming baskets smashed against the wall, splattering pitch and spreading fire. The Hethrren howled and laughed.

Klovus and his priests hurried to the temple. Neré was there in her brown caftan, her hair pulled tightly back in oiled braids. It was time for them to do their work. Inside, the spelldoor shimmered against the lightning-twisted trees as the impatient godling swelled with the need of its people, stronger than ever and demanding to be unleashed. Klovus could feel its energy rising to a boiling point, and he understood Neré's fears of letting it get out of control. But the two of them joined their magic, which swirled out to connect with the godling. From behind the spelldoor, it sensed them, listened to them. Obeyed them.

Klovus concentrated, felt his connection strengthen, and he turned to the closest ur-priest. "Tell the guards to open the stockade gate—open it wide!"

The priest blinked, startled. "They will refuse, Priestlord. The city is under attack!"

"Unless they want the godling to blast its way through the walls, they had better give it a way out."

The priest ran off.

Panicked townspeople ran toward the temple, chanting, "Hear us, save us!" Klovus feared that the godling would mow them down and scatter them on its escape. If so, he supposed the entity would simply take them as additional offerings to increase its strength, and use that strength to wipe out even more of the barbarian invaders.

Primitive shouts and howls continued outside the city. The bronze bell tolled monotonously. With each assault on the Tamburdin walls, with every scream outside the city, the protective godling grew angrier, more anxious to defend its people, its worshippers . . . its creators.

Klovus could feel the contact with the roiling entity. Neré might indeed have been too weak by herself. His remaining ur-priests backed toward the safety of the wooden temple walls. One man stood beside the huge carving of the golden bear, as if the fierce animal offered protection.

"Now!" Klovus said.

"Now," Neré agreed and raised her voice to the spelldoor. "Hear us, save us. Protect Tamburdin! You are our godling. Save your people."

The gateway shimmered, glowed. "Come forth and do what you were created to do," Klovus said.

They triggered the spelldoor and set the godling free. The entity emerged from its unreal world, the invisible space between here and there. Guided by the two powerful priestlords, it lunged out, released to do only one thing.

Each godling took on characteristics that reflected its area and its people. The Tamburdin deity was from a wild and primal place, worshipped by people who lived and died by the forest. Thus it was a mass of bestial fury, manifesting characteristics of the most terrible forest predators, a storm of curved claws and yellowed fangs, fur and spines knotted together as it swelled and shifted. The godling glowed with dozens of slitted yellow eyes like a pack of wolves seen just beyond the firelight. It thundered forward with the sharp hooves of a rampaging stag, the great paws of a huge bear. It lashed with lightning and the roar of a winter wind that could knock down trees.

It surged toward the temple door. Klovus and Neré used all their powers to guide the godling and keep it focused.

Out in the streets, people scattered. Some were trampled by the charge of the entity, torn apart by its primal explosion of chaos, then it swooped through Tamburdin city and launched itself through the wide-open gates. Guards and soldiers leaped out of its way.

Klovus rushed after the godling, yelling for Neré to hurry. Following the swath of carnage, they reached the walls where they could watch the godling do its work.

Outside the stockade, Hethrren riders stormed back and forth, throwing their flaming pitch baskets to set the walls on fire. Brave Isharan soldiers had emerged from the gate to face the enemy. The leader of the city guards placed himself in front of the barbarian woman and slashed at her horse, making the beast skitter sideways. With a furious glare, Magda swung her twisted wooden club and split his head like a melon.

Then she turned to face the outraged mass of the godling as it emerged from the city walls. The tumble of claws, fur, and horns blurred, shaping and reshaping itself as it swelled on the battleground. The Hethrren horses whinnied in terror at seeing the thing, but the barbarians whipped them forward. They hurled spears at the godling, but the weapons did no harm against the shifting, crackling mass.

Two Hethrren riders charged in to throw burning pitch buckets into the deity, but the fire and smoke only added to its strength, and the godling lashed out with clawed arms, razor-sharp wings, and a panther's tail. The unformed mass of energy tore apart three barbarian warriors and their horses, spraying a fan of blood, gobbets of meat, and intestines. Other riders closed around Magda as she charged forward, swinging her twisted club. With her other hand, she grabbed a spear and threw it at the godling, still galloping straight toward it.

Watching from the scout platform on top of the stockade wall, Klovus laughed. His eyes were shining. Neré was impressed with what her godling could do and also relieved to turn its destruction outward.

The circling barbarians closed in from all sides, as if a united attack could harm the entity. The first rider struck, and the godling killed him, hurling the horse high into the air. More riders closed in, fighting, yelling . . . dying.

When Magda struck the godling, it smashed her backward, knocking her from the horse. Somehow, she released the reins and tumbled free, rolling to her feet on the grass. The entity moved forward, rampaging toward other Hethrren.

Klovus counted at least thirty raiders slaughtered in the first few minutes. Planting her thick legs in a warrior stance on the open ground, Magda let out a howl that was some kind of summons. She brandished her wooden club. As another rider galloped past her, she grabbed his gloved hand and swung herself up behind him on his horse. She whistled and let out a defiant shriek.

The Hethrren kept fighting, but Klovus knew these barbarians couldn't possibly stand against the godling. Magda let out another howl, and the riders closed around her, galloping off in retreat.

From the walls, the Tamburdin defenders laughed and jeered. They launched volleys of arrows after the Hethrren as they rushed back to the forested hills. Three more raiders died with arrows in their backs.

The godling paused, hovering over the smashed remains of horses and Hethrren, then it swelled further. The thing made a buzzing, terrifying sound, like a thousand angry hornets, before it surged off to pursue the riders toward the hills.

Klovus sensed his control slipping and felt suddenly anxious. "If the godling gets far enough away to break free, it might never return. We can't let it loose!"

Neré nodded. "We have to call it back. I need your help."

She had not been wrong to summon him. Klovus seized Neré's hand. "We better be quick. Use all our power."

They concentrated and tugged on the invisible leash, pulling at the wild godling. It struggled in frustration, a ball of fangs, claws, and spines, not wanting to be controlled, not wanting to be tamed, but Klovus ordered it, as did Neré.

"We join our commands," he said, gritting his teeth, and *pushed* out to the godling. "You will obey!"

The priestlords kept concentrating until finally the entity—much diminished now after expending so much power—swirled, tumbled back, and withdrew to the open stockade gates. By now the people in the streets had backed away, clearing a path for it to return to its home temple. The creature growled, buzzed, and purred as it returned to its anchor . . . but it was not meek, not cowed. It was, however, satisfied. The godling's hunger was sated, and it seemed pleased with itself, just as Klovus, Neré, and the people of Tamburdin were pleased with their protector.

Klovus didn't relax, though, until he and Neré had sealed the godling behind the spelldoor.

His heart swelled with the victory, but soon anger seized him, the result of frustration that had been building for years. "Another example of our worth to Ishara," he muttered, "and Empra Iluris wants to weaken the godlings! She refuses to let the priestlords build greater temples. She fears our strength. But that very strength is what safeguards Ishara."

"The godlings are our protectors," Neré agreed.

Klovus contemplated how he would make his report, how he would coax Iluris, how he would argue, maybe even beg. "There might come a time when we need all the strength of our godlings to defeat any enemy. In the end it may fall to us, and only us."

67

The mysterious wreth ruins delighted Shadri. Every day was like a gift day where she unwrapped special prizes, greeting each answer as a treasure to cherish for the rest of her life. Each answer brought a hundred more questions, though. Exactly the way she liked it.

But finding the wreth man—a real wreth who had lived in ancient times!—offered the potential for wonderful discoveries, and the mysterious Brava woman was also intriguing.

After rummaging in her pack and shifting supplies, Shadri removed another notebook, one that still had a few more blank pages. "So many things to know, and you both can help me." Shadri sat on the grass near the two, leaned against her large pack, and cracked her knuckles. That was how her father had always got ready before he guided heavy logs into the winding blade of the sawmill. Her work now would be asking questions and digging out answers.

After marking a note in the journal, Shadri raised her heavy eyebrows to Elliel. "I expect you've had lots of adventures. Bravas are very interesting. Do you know many of them?" Without letting Elliel answer, she rattled on, "I heard the story of a paladin who rescued a trapper's family during a forest fire, drove them out in time to safety, then ran back into the burning woods to rescue another family. The Brava got them out, but nobody saw him escape the raging fire. Later, in the tavern when the grieving people were toasting his memory, the Brava entered, covered in soot but very much alive."

"Bravas have a habit of emerging alive from difficult situations," Elliel said.

"I think he used his ramer to cut his way through burning trees." Shadri glanced at the golden band clipped to the Brava's waist. "Can you show me your ramer? I've never seen one in use." She chuckled. "Well, I've never seen one at all, even when it wasn't in use. How does it work?"

"It doesn't." Elliel frowned. "But it's my part that doesn't work."

She unclipped the band and reluctantly handed it to Shadri, who inspected the intricate craftsmanship and copied some of the spell designs in her margins. "What is your story? Did you rescue people from a forest fire, or something even more dramatic?"

Elliel's expression fell. "My story is not one that I like to tell."

Thon interrupted, "Neither of us remembers our past." He touched the mark on his cheek. "But finding the answers might be important for the future of the world. We need to know about the wreths. We need to know who I am."

Shadri flipped pages in her notebook, looked at the words she had written so tightly to save space. "I'm trying to piece together the greater legacy of history. One story leads to another, then another." Traveling alone and often muttering to herself, Shadri was afraid she would jabber constantly now that she had listeners. "I piece together what I can, but I'm not satisfied with the little pieces."

When the water was boiling over the campfire, they all shared tea. The next question spilled out of Shadri's mouth as soon as it formed in her mind. "Why is it so important now? The wreths have been gone for two thousand years. Do you think that's how long you were buried? Why did you wake up now? What changed?"

Thon was intense. "There must be a reason. I believe I have some role to play in whatever is about to happen. We know the wreths are returning and planning war."

Elliel interjected, "We've seen clear signs that Ossus is stirring beneath the Dragonspine Mountains."

"Ah! I know the story. If the wreths kill the dragon, then their god will return, take them to salvation, and remake the world." Shadri slurped her tea. "Not a good situation for humans, though." She drew her knees up to her chest, adjusting the patchwork skirts, brushing away a grass stain. "That's a good reason to want more answers. I can show you some very mysterious places I've found here in the city. Maybe you'll know some answers, because I can't figure them out. It's all so interesting. Let's go look."

They left their belongings behind, and Shadri took them through the long-abandoned streets with a brisk step, as if she owned the city now. Her commentary was punctuated with frequent offhand questions, but she often didn't wait for answers.

She showed them immense obelisks that had fallen. Towers reached to the sky, the bricks laid in an ascending spiral, wearily straining after so many centuries. Shadri had made notes of the odd curves, corkscrews, and organic shapes. One of the bent walls rippled and twisted, as if a serpent squirmed beneath the blocks. "Did the curves mean something?" she asked Thon. "I've seen other wreth ruins where the walls were straight, but the character here seems different."

He absorbed details as if trying to catch a fluttering thought from a distant corner of his mind. "It is possible that during the battles, the city itself fought back, lashed out against the enemy. Some wreths can control stone. Maybe they turned their own buildings into weapons?" He listened to the breezes that whistled through holes in open parapets. "Or perhaps the city writhed in agony as it was defeated." He shook his head. "I do not know."

Hurrying along, Shadri took them to the mural display wall with stone figures of opposing wreth warriors. She stepped on the activation platform and showed them the moving tableau, the symbolic slaughter of the great armies. She looked at Thon. "You don't remember anything about the wars? How they ended, what drove the wreth factions into near extinction?"

He blinked at her. "No, none of that. I was inside the mountain long before the wars reached that point, I am sure."

One section of streets had collapsed, flagstones and building walls sliding down into a pit like a sinkhole inexorably swallowing the city. A deep hole plunged underground, and old vines crawled out from the depths. Trees had sprouted in the cracks of the flagstones, growing tall.

Shadri went right up to the edge of the dangerous hole. "I wish I knew what caused this. There must be interesting things down there, untouched, but I don't think I could climb safely."

"It was a well," Thon answered. "A central well in the city. The wreths dug deep, tapped into water for their needs as the city grew. It also served as a magical wellspring." He knelt on the edge of the sudden slope, placing his palms on the unsettled flagstones. "They reached a concentrated reservoir of magic, but as the wars worsened, the wreths used up the magic and had to burrow deeper and deeper."

Shadri scanned the streets, saw the thoroughfares bent as if caught in a spasm, buildings frozen in midcollapse, sinking down into a voracious well. Now that Thon was here, the sights seemed more tantalizing.

She looked at trees nearby, gauged the steepness of the slope. "With ropes, we might be able to lower ourselves down there, have a look." The Brava woman looked muscular enough to fight a dragon with her bare hands. She could certainly hold a rope.

"That would not be a good idea," Thon said.

Shadri conceded. "Not today but someday we should come back and investigate it." As they retreated, she continued to pepper the man with questions. "Do you remember Kur? That he created and blessed the wreths, but doesn't pay any attention to humans? Are we really godless, without souls?" She touched her heart. "I don't feel anything missing there. What does it feel like to have a soul?"

Thon looked at her with his gem-blue eyes. "How do you know I have one?"

"I don't, and I don't know how you would prove it. Does Kur even know that humans exist? Did the wreths create us after Kur left the world? Does he ever come back and have a look? Does he know the wreths are coming back?"

Thon said, "I know Kur's name and I know stories. Are you asking me to explain the actions of a long-departed god?"

"I don't know much about gods, except that they created the many stars in the sky and many worlds around them. This was Kur's first creation. Is he benevolent or aloof?" Shadri asked. "Maybe he's proud of what his creations did? How do you know Kur is even there at all, and watching?"

Thon's expression fell into a frown. "He left long ago, or so the stories say."

"Stories," Shadri said with an impatient sigh. "Too many stories and not enough facts."

They made their way back to the camp at nightfall, weary and hungry. As they sat by the fire eating a makeshift meal, Shadri produced the triangular blue crystal she had found on the metal tree. "Do you know what this is, Thon? The letters are preserved, but I can't read them."

He took the crystal, turning it over in his hands. "Wreth mages used such crystals to record history."

Unexpectedly, he dug the sharp point into his forearm, cutting his skin. Dark blood welled up like black oil in the firelight. He dipped his fingertips into the blood and smeared a streak across the front of the engraved crystal.

When he held it up to the firelight, the dancing flames sparkled, and the light penetrated the blood, which activated the layers of letters pressed between the crystals. Glowing symbols appeared on the ground, projected through the magic, the firelight, and Thon's blood.

Shadri laughed in delight. "I wish I knew how to do that."

"Someone wrote an extensive chronicle and stored it here. It tells how the city thrived for many centuries, populated by wreths descended from Suth . . . who was Kur's first lover." He looked up, let out a slow sigh. "That was one of the great factions at war. The dwellers here lived a pleasurable life, their city protected by guardian walls until enemy wreth armies came, the descendants of Raan, Kur's other lover."

He traced out the glowing letters that spilled across the ground. "The siege lasted for two centuries, and the city withered and died. In a final fight, the people unleashed magic from the well, the reservoir at the heart of the city."

"What happened?" Elliel asked.

"The city died. This chronicle was written by one of the last survivors, after most others had died and the rest had fled. Some went into spellsleep in the mountains. This must have been near the end of the wars."

Shadri wished she had thought to take out her notebook and write down his words as he read them. Maybe someday she would have time to translate the entire chronicle, with Thon's help. She would ask him to teach her the wreth language. So much to do and learn!

He returned the crystal to her, and Elliel wiped the blood from his forearm, though the wound had already nearly healed itself. The Brava spoke softly, close to his pale face. "Were you part of that history yourself?"

Thon shook his head. "No, these events happened long, long after I was buried beneath the mountains with the dragon."

"So why did someone put you there?" Shadri pressed. "Was it a prison, or were you a secret weapon? A last resort?"

"A secret weapon?" The thought seemed to surprise him. "That is an excellent question."

68

O N the descent out of the rugged mountains, Glik cradled the egg wrapped in padded folds against her chest. She picked her way down the sheer rocks, finding handholds, ledges, and finally a narrow goat trail that headed to the bottom of the gorge. All along, other skas had circled overhead, watching, approving.

Glik nearly fell many times, but her Utauk luck did not fail her, nor did her visions. She knew instinctively where to go. Finally, with the egg still safe, she reached the river at the bottom of the gorge, where she camped. She removed the rescued egg and marveled at it, relieved to see it intact, alive, full of potential.

As she dozed by her fire, she felt a sudden surge of excitement, like sparks swirling in the air and in her mind. As if pleased to have a stable spot at last, the splotched leathery shell cracked. Glik crouched, moving the egg closer to the campfire's warmth, and placed pebbles around it in a perfect circle. She watched the delicate black fissures streak through the shell until the blue snout of a baby ska emerged.

With cautious awe, she reached forward to touch the hatchling's head— and knew the ska's name instantly, instinctively. *Ari!* Her name was Ari.

Seeing the efforts to break free of the curved prison, she tried to help the newborn ska, but she felt a scolding bolt in her mind. Ari didn't want her help; the ska needed to do this herself, and so Glik let her, watching the beautiful reptile bird's struggles, pushing the shell apart until finally, the fragile and oh-so-perfect creature emerged.

Glik felt her head spinning, and she saw a vivid vision before her: old Ori resplendent in his scarlet plumage on a dead tree near her campfire, bobbing his head in approval. The older ska spread his red wings and sprang into the air, just as when he had flown away into the sandstorm for the last time. The apparition shimmered, then broke into thousands of sparkling fragments. Glik's heart felt happy to see her old companion again, but also heavy with the understanding that she would never see the scarlet ska again.

The girl's whole world was filled with little Ari emerging from the egg. Sensing that the small blue reptile bird would allow her touch, Glik picked up the tiny ska and cradled her in cupped hands, letting the wet plumage dry near the fire's warmth. The sapphire ska extended her tiny wings and shook out the pale blue feathers. From the first moment that Ari stretched, Glik felt the aches and pains vanish in her own battered muscles. She held the newborn ska, looked into the faceted eyes, just as Ari looked into hers. The heart link was like a chain made of flower petals and iron, soft, beautiful, and incredibly strong.

Far overhead in the night sky, Glik heard the shrill cries of other skas. They had followed in order to watch, but once she and Ari were linked, the adult birds circled among the stars and flew back to their crags, satisfied.

Glik drew a circle around her heart, encompassing herself and Ari.

Ari was the most beautiful ska ever, although all Utauks felt that way about their companions. Her scales shimmered like sapphires in the sunlight, and her plumage was long and delicate, as soft as a mother's kiss and the color of a clean sky. From the moment she first held the hatchling, Glik thought of her as a living jewel. . . .

For the next several days, the hatchling rode on her shoulder as she followed the river out of the mountains into more hospitable hills. Ari kept extending her wings, fluttering them, trying to get up the nerve to fly for the first time. Finally, without warning, the tiny ska took wing, flapped above Glik's head, then came back down to settle on her opposite shoulder.

Ari seemed inordinately pleased with herself after the brief flight and preened her plumage, but rode on the girl's shoulder for a while longer, letting her companion do all the work. An hour later Ari flew again, circling higher this time.

Glik laughed and applauded. "Fly, Ari, fly!" The ska fluttered down, as if intending to alight on her shoulder, but Glik felt Ari change her mind at the last moment. The creature executed a midair roll, stroked with hard beats of her wings, and climbed into the air again.

The ska flew, instinctively understanding a thousand aerial maneuvers.

Glik reached out her hands, stretching as if she could join her companion. Ari buzzed past the girl's face, taunting her and teasing her, then swu g up into the sky again, a sparkle of blue. Glik let out a sigh that vibrateu with her own pleasure and contentment.

Yes, Glik remembered this exhilaration from her time with Ori, but it felt different, already stronger. She had linked with Ori when he was already mature, but this beautiful blue ska was young, fresh, and filled with the energy of love and closeness. When she was ready, Glik called her new companion, stroked her back and the sides of her neck, and then reverently attached the collar she had carried with her since the Utauk camp. The ribbon was thin, the mothertear gleaming, seemingly too large for the tiny reptile bird, but Ari preened, delighted to have it. She took wing again.

Ari flew far overhead, and Glik used the heart link to fly along with her, soaring on the winds, exuberant in the freedom of the open air. The sky was an entire kingdom, and the young reptile bird wanted to explore all of it through her link with Glik, a link partly of the heart and partly of magic.

Whole again, the girl reveled in her sense of wonder about the landscape, the hills, plains and rivers, the clear lakes, even the old battle scars from the wreth wars. *The beginning is the end is the beginning.*

Having left the mountains behind, Glik stood on a grassy plain, hands at her sides, face turned upward, just staring at the little speck that was Ari. Her new precious companion soared in the open vastness and feared nothing, but the ska never went out of sight. Glik knew that Ari wouldn't leave her. The tether of friendship could stretch long and thin, but she remained connected to her human partner and would always come back.

Glik could feel Ari's joy secondhand as she gulped a feast of flying beetles. Below her, the girl laughed and ran through the rushing grasses and tall thistles. She couldn't see directly through the reptile bird's faceted eyes, but when Ari came back to land lightly on her shoulder Glik could review the images in the mothertear collar. At the moment, though, she just had to imagine what her partner was seeing.

For the next several days, Glik followed the trails of blue poppies and made her way back into the Suderran foothills. The flowers were only a dash of color to outside observers, but a secret map to any Utauk. She found signs of recent hoofprints, wheel ruts, horse droppings, campfire rings. Her young ska circled overhead, making shrill music as if to communicate with other reptile birds nearby.

Glik came upon a large Utauk caravan camp, although nothing like the recent great convocation that had filled the river valley. Seeing the wagons and the colorful fabrics, Glik realized this was the heart camp that traveled with Shella din Orr herself.

The orphan girl entered the camp to a chorus of happy greetings. Children flew kites in the afternoon winds, and three fully grown skas circled in the air, chasing them. Ari flitted in among the bigger reptile birds, who welcomed her, flying in loops. The little blue ska tried to keep up with them and clicked in frustration when they swirled out of her reach on more powerful wings. As if in a huff, Ari came down and landed on Glik's shoulder, just as the old matriarch's two bearded nephews opened the flaps of the tent to welcome her inside. She moved with a spring in her step.

The crone sat upright on her blanket made with the threads of hundreds of families. "You've returned, dear girl! *Cra,* I hope you brought stories? My nephews only talk business and complain, but you've always been a delight to me."

Glik sat cross-legged on the rug, drawing a circle around her heart. "A mutual delight, Grandmother. Come along on my travels. It would make you feel young again."

Shella cackled. "It would indeed."

Even though Utauks kept a vast amount of ancestral information in their records, Shella din Orr herself remained an enigma. Rumors said that the old woman had five husbands and twenty children over the course of her long life. Shella's bloodline extended in all directions, like the woven threads in the tapestry mat.

Her eyes fixed on Ari, who bobbed on Glik's shoulder as if impatient to be introduced. "I'm glad that you've found a new ska. You were so lonely."

"I was," Glik admitted, feeling a lump in her throat. "Not anymore. Isn't Ari magnificent?"

The reptile bird spread her wings, waiting for the matriarch to affirm the compliment.

"Indeed, a truly beautiful ska and an excellent companion," Shella said. "I can sense the power of your heart link from here. Although my eyes are old and dim, Ari's beauty brings a sparkle to them."

The ska buzzed happily.

Shella ordered her nephews to bring the evening's potage of spiced venison and rabbit with vegetables. Glik tucked her legs beneath her and told of her adventures, from the Plain of Black Glass and finding the dead prospector, to climbing the mountains and retrieving the ska egg. As she scraped the last gravy from the bowl, she looked up at the old woman, troubled. "Found something very strange in the grotto, Grandmother. Like a huge shell or a cocoon wall. Something stirring inside." Her skin crawled as she remembered the shifting shadows, the flicker of an enormous faceted eye. "Had a vision, too, sudden and dark, powerful, dangerous—like great thunder inside my head."

"You found this among the ska eyries?" Shella's frown turned the skin of her face into a wilderness of wrinkles. "I think it was a dragon."

Surprised, Glik looked up. "Never seen a dragon. Dreamed of them lots of times."

"Your dreams have always been strong, child. That's why you're special." Shella sighed wistfully. "I saw a real dragon once, when I was just a girl. *Cra*, they're frightening things, and very rare. Children of Ossus, if you can believe the legends. If you ever see one, it'll change your life, but you better hope it doesn't see you. Or your ska."

Ari squirmed and rustled.

The crone shifted her position on the blanket. "Now then, take that old collar off her. It's too plain, and the mothertear is small." She turned to an ornate wooden chest behind her. With gnarled but surprisingly nimble fingers, Shella worked a catch, twisted a knob, and pulled one of the small drawers open.

"I had a ska of my own when I was a little girl. His name was Uga, and he was with me when we saw the dragon." Shella reached into the drawer and pulled out a strip of blue ribbon. In the middle was a perfect diamond, larger than the one in Ari's old collar. "He was a sapphire bird, just like yours. He flew off long, long ago when he was old." Shella cackled. "What did *he* know about being old! I always meant to get another ska, so I had this collar made, but . . . I would like you to have it, for your Ari."

As Glik took it, tears welled in her eyes. "Thank you, Grandmother." She turned her head sideways, close to the reptile bird. "Like it?"

The ska buzzed and clicked, then hopped down to sit on the rug in front of Glik's crossed legs. Removing the threadbare collar from the young bird, the girl wrapped the new one around Ari's thin neck. "Beautiful." The reptile bird fluttered her wings.

"Now you both will see many fine things," said Shella. "Just remember to come back and tell me everything."

Ari hopped back onto Glik's shoulder, eager to go out and explore the world. Together.

69

I THINK you like the wealth and fame of being a merchant captain, Hale Orr," said the voyagier as the two men waited on the deck of the *Glissand*. They had sailed out to sea again, carrying Konag Conndur's urgent message for the empra. "Why else would you enlist my ship again so soon?"

Hale snorted. "*Cra,* I've been searching for wealth and fame all my life. I can't seem to find it on any of our charts." He grew serious. "How can I enjoy wealth when I am worried about the fate of the world? I fear for my dear daughter and my unborn grandchild."

Normally, upon arriving in Rivermouth or all the way up to Convera, the crew would rest in port for a week, unloading and loading, but when Hale Orr shared the bonus the konag had offered for them to make this special voyage, they were more than happy to change their plans.

Mak Dur tacked north to catch a swifter current that would let them bypass Fulcor Island by a significant distance. Unlike his last trip, Hale could not relax and enjoy the open sea. For centuries, Utauk traders had walked a fine line between the old world and the new, using their neutrality as a buffer between the simmering anger between the two lands. As a younger man, Hale had seen hostilities flare up in Konag Cronin's war, but now with the prospect of a common enemy and an open-minded konag, the two continents had a chance to set aside their differences and become allies. Or at least stop fighting.

That thought was a small glimmer of hope in an otherwise terrifying situation. When he saw Empra Iluris again, he would serve as an ambassador instead of a spy, and he would do his best to convince her. Maybe there was a chance.

Unless the wreths destroyed it all.

He drew a circle around his heart. *The beginning is the end is the begin-*

ning. Seeing him, the voyagier gave a puzzled smile and drew a circle in response.

When the ship approached Serepol Harbor, they prominently displayed the Utauk circle on the *Glissand*'s sail so the Isharan navy would know who they were. While Mak Dur barked orders and the navigator set the rudder, Hale went to the bow as the city came into view. From here he could see the towers of the empra's palace, the various temples with spires and ornate walls, the docks, the harbor buildings. Serepol was a beautiful city, the heart of a great empire.

When they entered the harbor, though, his heart sank and the bright flame of hope died. Two ships were on fire in the water—Commonwealth vessels. As if to prevent escape, Isharan warships drifted on either side of the burning wrecks, far enough away that cinders would not catch on their red-striped sails.

Mak Dur looked disturbed. "Why are those ships burning? Is the harbor under attack?"

Hale answered in a husky voice. "The ships are burning because the Isharans set them on fire." In this situation, how could he expect the empra to accept Conndur's unexpected offer of détente? Would she listen at all?

The voyagier shaded his eyes, and his expression changed as he understood what Hale was saying. "Those aren't warships. They're Commonwealth fishing trawlers."

Hale shook his head. "My guess is that the Isharans called them spies. Another provocation, likely in response to some previous provocation from the Commonwealth." He couldn't forget what the garrison had done to Isharan captives at Fulcor Island.

"Are they holding prisoners for ransom?" the voyagier asked. "Do you think they'll send demands back with us to Osterra?"

"It's possible," Hale lied. He knew there were no survivors. The people would have been executed as soon as the navy captured the vessels, or maybe the poor men and women were being burned alive even now, sealed in the holds of their own ships.

His hopes of delivering a friendly invitation were dashed. Even if Empra Iluris had been open to such discussions in the name of peace, her people would not allow it. The situation had become much uglier.

With his good hand Hale touched the leather pouch that held the konag's formal letter asking Iluris to trust him. Hale's eyes stung as the *Glissand* sailed past the smoking hulks. At the water's edge, he saw crowds of Isharans gathered to watch the enemy ships burn, to cheer the violence.

Hale muttered, "This is not a good sign for delivering a message of peace."

"Not a good sign at all," Mak Dur agreed.

70

FARMERS brought their late-season harvest to sell in the open markets in Fellstaff. Every day, mule-drawn wagons came in piled high with potatoes, hard squash, onions, carrots. Orchard keepers delivered apples and pears, along with barrels of fresh-pressed cider.

Because of the spreading rumors of war, people began to stockpile the harvest in root cellars and granaries. King Kollanan had a standing order to purchase any surplus to be stored in the cool, dry vaults beneath Fellstaff Castle.

Queen Tafira made different plans. She had Pokle accompany her to one of the market squares, where she purchased three pumpkins so enormous she could barely encircle them with her arms. They were soft on one side, beginning to rot. The farmer had hoped to sell them for a few coppers as pig food, or to someone who wanted to roast the plentiful seeds.

Tafira paid a silver coin for all three without even haggling, which the farmer considered an astonishing sum. Pokle was amazed. "But, ma'am, there are better pumpkins. I could help you pick."

The farmer shushed him. "The queen's made her decision, boy. Don't argue with the lady of the castle."

He stammered. "B-but I was just suggesting—"

"The others aren't as big, Pokle. These will do just fine," Tafira said, without explaining why. She had him help the farmer load the pumpkins into his cart so he could transport them to the castle. "Take them to the courtyard near the stables. That's where I'll need them."

Koll sat in his study with the window open. A deep, bitter cold would soon creep downward from the north, with or without the frostwreths, so he wanted the fresh air while it lasted.

At his desk, wishing that he had Lasis to help him with the work, he up-
dated the ledgers with reports from his eight counties. He had no proof that
his bonded Brava had been killed, but in his heart, he was sure Lasis had
gone to confront the frostwreths, and had failed. . . .

Koll had also dispatched other scouts to report what they could about
what was happening at Lake Bakal. The wreths had continued building their
great structure, but had made no other movement. Yet.

Now, he turned back to the paperwork. The mines in the mountains had
orders to produce as much pig iron as possible, and the king had instructed
all blacksmiths to dedicate their efforts to fashioning swords, shields, breast-
plates, helmets. Hunters and trappers redoubled their efforts to bring in
warm furs for the army. Shepherds sheared their sheep and delivered great
bales of wool to make thick blankets and garments. Remembering Lake
Bakal, though, he doubted any blade, shield, or blanket would have protected
the villagers against the unnatural freezing wave. Koll closed his eyes, still
feeling the tears burn when he thought of the child's small hand in the snow,
white fingers curled around the wooden carving of a pig. . . .

Tafira appeared at the doorway wearing long, colorful skirts with just a
few bangles and ribbon flourishes that reminded her of Ishara. She held two
long knives in her hands. "Come with me to the courtyard. There's something I want to show you." Her smoky voice was intense, her accent more
prominent now as it often got when she was determined about something.
She held the knives with a casual ease, and her dark eyes sparkled. She was
being intentionally mysterious.

He had seen this mood before. "You're far more interesting company than
these ledgers anyway, beloved."

Her expression fell, and her eyes darted away. "Please don't call me that
anymore." *Beloved* was the word in her old village dialect for which their
daughter Jhaqi was named.

Kollanan shook his head, insistent. "I'll still call you 'beloved' because
you *are* my beloved, and because I won't forget our daughter even if it hurts
to think of her."

After a moment of silence, Tafira responded with a wan smile. "I accept
your reasoning." She turned to the door. "Bring your war hammer. You
might need it."

He looked at his old weapon hanging above the fireplace. He had not
touched it in a long time. With its long handle, massive head, and sharp maul,

the weapon had earned him a terrifying reputation during the Isharan war. *Koll the Hammer.*

Another king might have placed such a weapon in the great hall so that all visitors could be reminded of his legacy as a war hero, but Koll had never relied on his past, never embellished his stories, never tried to make his people fear him. The hammer was a part of his legacy, yes, and he could not ignore it, but he didn't feel the need to show it off.

Tafira repeated, "Bring your hammer. Trust me."

Trusting her, he went to the wall and lifted the weapon from its mounting hooks. The hammer felt heavy in his hand, both frightening and comforting. "I hoped never to use this again."

"I hoped many things myself," Tafira said. "You made my hopes real a long time ago, but the wreths may try to take them away. We'd better stop them from doing that." She stepped into the hall. "Come with me. Pokle should have the pumpkins set up by now."

Out in the courtyard, the boy had propped the three huge pumpkins against the outer wall of the stable. The farmer's cart had already departed. "Is this good, ma'am?" Pokle asked. "Or did you want them by the far wall?" The teen could not wrestle the big pumpkins very far by himself. Each one probably weighed more than he did.

"That'll do just fine," Tafira said, "but you might want to get out of the way."

Seeing the two long knives in her hands and the battle hammer in Koll's, he scuttled to a distance from which he could watch.

"I always thought Lasis would keep us both safe," Tafira said to Koll, and her expression darkened. "Now you only have me to save you—and I assure you, I can do it."

Koll's heart felt warm. "I thought I was supposed to save you."

"You did that already, a long time ago back in my village. I intend to repay the favor."

"How—?"

Tafira took the long knife in her right hand, balanced the hilt, then threw it in a flash. The long blade spun twice in the air and embedded itself to the crossguard in the soft orange flesh of a pumpkin. "Like that." She threw the knife in her left hand. It whistled through the air and struck with such force that not only did the blade sink deep, but the hilt cracked the rind. "And that."

"Impressive," he said with a laugh, and he meant it. "We'll soon be ready for a war against the pumpkins."

Her skirts flounced as she strode over to yank out her knives. "I can use them to gut an enemy as well."

"Where did you learn that? Have you been practicing?"

"I've been practicing since we moved to Norterra. Not a week goes by in the kitchens when I don't have to throw a cooking knife to skewer a rat in a corner, where he didn't think I could see him." Her lips curved upward. "The entire kitchen staff is terrified of me."

"I love you," he said, "and I'll be glad to have your protection. I hope the wreths are terrified of you as well."

While thinking about what had happened at Lake Bakal, and now knowing that Lasis was missing, if not dead, Koll hardened his anger and made his plans. Lasis had occasionally talked about the hatred all Bravas held toward the Isharans because of their ancient massacred colony. Long ago Bravas had declared a "vengewar," which passed from one generation to the next.

At the time, Kollanan had thought that holding on to such blind hatred for centuries was unproductive, but considering what the frostwreths had done to Lake Bakal in such an offhanded manner, and knowing the wreths were planning to destroy the world because the previous holocaust hadn't been enough for them . . . yes, now Koll understood that hatred. He would declare his own sort of vengewar. There was no logic to it, just emotions fed by blood, fire, and ice.

Tafira stepped back, faced the second pumpkin, and in a blindingly swift gesture, flung both knives at the same time. They impacted less than an inch apart, and Pokle let out a little squeak of surprise from where he watched.

"We can defend ourselves, beloved," Koll said. "But simply waiting here to become victims, hoping we can protect our homes and our people when an attack comes—that's not enough. I never should have believed it would be enough."

Tafira retrieved her knives and was about to wipe the orange smears of pumpkin on her skirts, but instead she threw the knives in a more leisurely fashion, one and then the second. She never missed. "Across the kingdom, our people are making weapons, building defenses. The vassal lords are erecting high walls. The veterans are training a new group of soldiers."

"According to the scouts, the frostwreths are still building their fortress," Koll said. "They don't seem worried about humans at all."

Looking pale and angry, Pokle blurted out, "Attack them and kill them for what they did at Lake Bakal! We have to find a way."

"I'd like nothing more, boy." Koll swung his hammer casually, felt its deadly weight tugging on his arm and remembered the many times he had charged into battle holding the weapon high. He had hunched down over his horse as he swung the hammer to crack the helmeted heads of Isharan warriors.

Making up his mind, Koll turned to his wife and said in a hard voice, "We have to act. The frostwreths don't care that we exist. They don't consider us to be living, thinking beings." He ground his teeth together. "But I will not be ignored by them, and I won't just wait for them to destroy the world. We aren't their meek servants anymore. We control our own destiny, and we must push back, make them hesitate before they attack humans again."

"You mean, fight them directly?" Tafira yanked the knives back out of the pumpkin. "Take a battle to the wreths? They would likely wipe us out."

Koll smacked the end of his hammer against his palm. "We have to stand up for ourselves, even if we fail, because if humans sit back and do nothing, if we cower and whimper and beg, we will be overrun. They are coming, no matter what we do, even if the war has nothing to do with us. They will sweep over us regardless." He smiled. "Better to give them something to think about."

Pokle looked frightened, but Tafira's expression grew more determined. "Yes, and giving up would be worse." She threw the knives one more time and slew the enemy pumpkins. "Still, is it wise to provoke the wreths? Shouldn't we leave them be, for as long as we can?"

"They will never leave us be." Koll had the idea firmly in his head now. "They trampled the village at Lake Bakal because it was in their way. They'll do the same across all three kingdoms in their war against the sandwreths. They won't even pay attention as they destroy our world and crush us." He strode toward the wall of the stable. "They need to respect us, beloved. We have to be like a fierce dog growling in the yard to keep bandits at bay. I doubt we'll defeat them, but maybe at least they'll think twice."

Gripping his war hammer with both hands, he raised it overhead and swung down with all his might. The pumpkin burst in an explosion of orange rind and spraying seeds, all too much like bloody gore.

71

When he saw the Utauk trader sail into Serepol Harbor, Key Priest-lord Klovus knew that something was amiss. He recognized the mystifying circle symbol on the *Glissand*'s sails and remembered the one-handed merchant captain who had so flippantly debated with Empra Iluris. "Why would the same ship return so soon? There has barely been enough time to get to Osterra and back." Maybe the merchant captain had changed his mind about spying for Ishara.

He hurried along the waterfront as the foreign ship approached the available pier. On the way, he commanded five city guardsmen to follow. "We have to interrogate the crew of that ship and find out what they are up to."

The head guard's brow furrowed at Klovus's imperious tone. "They're Utauks, Priestlord. They'll bring items for sale, as they've always done. Maybe they have more to sell after their last successful trip."

"Not after less than two weeks," Klovus snapped. "I want to know why he's back."

The Utauk sailors lashed the *Glissand* to the pier before preparing to unload. This time, they moved only a dozen crates of merchandise onto the docks, a meager haul of goods, which reaffirmed Klovus's suspicions that they were here for reasons other than trade. They hadn't even bothered to restock their cargo.

Hale Orr stood at the rail of the ship, his gold front tooth glinting as he smiled. With surprising agility, he swung over the side onto the dock.

Klovus approached him. "Did you forget something here? Leave behind a sock, perhaps?"

The city guards chuckled. Hale Orr said, "My daughter made these socks many years ago, and they've been mended repeatedly. They are soft and comfortable. Even so, if I forgot them I wouldn't think they warranted a return voyage." He propped the stump of his hand on his left hip, got down to business. "I'm glad you came, Key Priestlord. Now I won't have to bother finding an appropriate escort. Please take me to the empra. I have important business."

Klovus felt sweat prickle on his bald scalp. "She asked you to spy on Osterra, to gather information about the enemy navy and their movements. Have you done so? You may report to me what you found."

"I'm afraid that isn't the information I have. This time I come in a diplomatic capacity." The shadowglass pendant in his ear dangled as he moved. "A disaster has happened in the Dragonspine Mountains, and I need to present a report to her. It has grave implications for the human race."

"What do we care about your mountains?" Klovus asked.

"Because it might mean the end of the world."

The key priestlord considered. "The end of your world, perhaps, but we live in Ishara. Why should we worry about a land that is already dead?"

"Konag Conndur believes your empra will feel differently. My letter comes directly from him." He pressed a leather satchel at his hip.

Klovus stepped forward. "Show me this letter."

The merchant captain's expression darkened, and his thick brows drew together. "Our ship has only been gone a short time, Priestlord. Have you become emprir since we left?"

"I'm key priestlord of Serepol," Klovus said with a sniff. "You don't understand the political power in this land."

"But I do understand my instructions from the konag. I'm to deliver a letter to Empra Iluris. Personally."

"And I gave you instructions, as well. I want to see this letter so I can determine whether it is worth the empra's while." He gestured and spoke in firm command to the head guard. "Bring me the letter."

Hale stiffened, stepped back. The head guard frowned, since priests did not normally command soldiers, but he moved forward and took the leather pouch from the trader's hip. Though clearly angry, Hale didn't resist.

The guard handed the leather pouch to Klovus, who undid the laces and pulled out a folded letter. He frowned at the open-hand symbol stamped into red sealing wax, broke the seal, and read Konag Conndur's astonishing invitation for a parley meeting. His eyes widened, and he read it a second time before the laughter came. "This is absurd." He looked at the Utauk merchant captain, then at the city guards. "He wants the empra to sail to Fulcor Island for a secret rendezvous."

"Apparently not secret anymore," Hale muttered.

Klovus glanced down at the letter again. "She will never agree to this."

Hale shrugged. "Still, the empra needs to read it for herself. Or do you make decisions for her now?"

The city guards muttered, and their leader stepped forward. "We will escort him to the palace now. This is the empra's business." He reached out to take the letter back from the priestlord. "Come with us, Merchant Captain."

Klovus pulled the letter away, quickly making up his mind. "Yes, we'll go now. I'll present this to the empra myself. Bring the Utauk and follow me."

Klovus walked at a brisk pace as one of the city guards ran ahead to inform Iluris of their arrival. They passed statues of Isharan heroes, ornate bubbling fountains, and a water-clock tower in front of the palace. He led them through the arched entrance and down the wide corridor to the throne room where the empra awaited them.

Klovus grimaced with distaste when he saw Cemi at a side table piled with open books. The girl studied columns of mathematical symbols, using an abacus to flick beads back and forth. Chamberlain Nerev sat close to her, watching the girl do her mathematics exercises. A third chair, now empty, had been slid back from the study table.

Empra Iluris sat on her throne on the dais, waiting to receive them. As they entered, her gaze slid past Klovus, and she brightened upon seeing Hale Orr. "You came back, Merchant Captain. Have you changed your mind about the mission I offered you?"

Hale bowed. "I am observant, Excellency, and I do have urgent news to report, whether or not you wish to call me a spy. I brought a sealed message from Konag Conndur that was meant for your eyes only." He flicked a glare at Klovus. "Unfortunately, your key priestlord feels that his eyes are more important than yours."

The empra's expression darkened. "What does he mean, Klovus?"

The priestlord stepped forward, extending the opened letter. "I had to protect you, Excellency. I wanted to inspect this mysterious letter before you—"

"Protect me? You were afraid that if I unfolded the paper, daggers might fly out and stab me in the heart? You've certainly made Konag Conndur into a most terrible enemy."

At her table, Cemi snickered.

Klovus felt a burn of embarrassment in his cheeks. "Words can be dangerous as well." He opened the letter, held it up for her to see the writing. "The konag says that the ancient wreths have returned to wake the dragon and launch devastating wars. He wants us to join their preposterous war and fight at the side of the Commonwealth." He chuckled.

"At the side of the human race," Hale Orr said.

Iluris leaned forward on the throne, speaking to the merchant captain. "Is the konag playing some sort of joke? Does he think I'm a fool?"

"Wait," Hale interjected. "You should read the letter for yourself, Excellency. Konag Conndur asked me as a neutral party to carry this message." He lowered his voice. "As we just witnessed out in the harbor, Osterran fishing boats don't fare well in your waters, so it's good that this was brought to you on an Utauk ship."

The people in the court began to mutter angrily, while the gold-armored hawk guards against the walls remained as silent as statues. Iluris said, "If he is worried about how we treat trespassing enemy ships, maybe he should stop his navy from sinking ours. Konag Conndur has given us no reason to trust his intentions. We also hear he has a brutal camp where he holds Isharan slaves to do dangerous work."

Hale frowned. "An enslavement camp? I honestly know nothing of that, and the Utauks have an extensive information network." He got back to his main point. "I can, however, speak about the wreths from personal experience, as I mentioned during my last visit here. What the konag says is true. I was present when the sandwreths returned to Suderra. I heard their queen speak of a great, new war they intended to fight against their rival frostwreths. We both know the human race barely survived the last war."

"But we did survive," Iluris said. "And our people came to this new world where we are now strong and stable. I want nothing to do with a devastating war—not with the Commonwealth or with wreths."

Hale spoke in an ominous voice. "What happens if the wreths destroy the dragon, and their god does return to remake the entire world? Do you think Ishara will remain unscathed? We will all be erased."

"If these silly stories are true, our godlings will protect us," Klovus said.

Iluris ignored his outburst and said to the merchant captain, "What does Konag Conndur want from me?"

Klovus held up the letter and said, "He claims that the entire human race should put aside their differences, that we should become allies for this greatest battle." He snorted, then continued in a mocking tone. "He suggests that we become *friends* and asks that you meet with him in a neutral place: Fulcor Island."

Hale added, "He's quite serious, Excellency. To show you his sincerity, the konag has offered to return Fulcor to you if Ishara does agree to fight alongside the Commonwealth. That's how much peace means to him."

The empra's brows drew together, and she frowned at Klovus. "Why would he do this if it's just a joke, Priestlord?"

Klovus blurted out, "Because it is likely a trap."

With an impatient frown, she reached out for the letter, forcing the priestlord to climb the steps so he could give it to her. She read the paper carefully. Cemi left her abacus and papers and joined the empra, bending close to read over her shoulder.

After pondering for a moment, Iluris turned to Hale Orr. "We will consider this seriously."

72

⁐

In the dead of night, a vicious pounding struck Bannriya's closed western gate.

Seenan rode hard for the castle and roused the king immediately. "Sire, the wreth man, the one called Quo, is demanding to see you!" The Banner guard waited outside the royal chambers, shifting from one boot to the other. "Shall I open the gates and let him in?"

Adan felt instantly wary. "No. I will go there to hear what he has to say. Don't let him into the city unless I allow it." He sent a bleary-eyed Hom to run and ready horses in the stables. He and Penda dressed in a rush. Before they left the royal chambers, Xar hopped off his perch and settled on her shoulder, as if he was ready to handle whatever the situation required.

Within minutes, they were mounted, and the green ska flew ahead of them, as if to scout. They followed Seenan to the thick sandstone wall, where the pounding on the gate sounded like slow, repetitive thunder. "I think he's losing patience," Seenan said. "We told him we were bringing you with all possible speed."

Adan pulled his horse to a halt at the base of the walls. The heavy pounding was uneven and ponderous, like an attack.

"Ancestors' blood, what is causing it?"

Seenan was pale-faced, sweating. "It's a monster trying to break down the gates, Sire."

Another loud blow rang against the wooden barrier, and Penda flinched. "He will shatter the wood if we don't let him in." Her ska circled in the air, whistling and clicking, demanding attention, but she ignored him.

"Such threats don't make me feel more hospitable toward him," Adan said, dismounting quickly and handing the reins to Seenan. "Let's go have a look from above the gate. We can call down to him."

Another relentless thud slammed the gate every twenty heartbeats or so—a loud, wet blow, as if a giant were hammering with a bloodied fist. At the apex of the stone steps that led to the top of the wall, two guards met the king and queen holding torches.

"It's one of those wreth lizards, ramming and ramming," a guard said, managing to look both apologetic and nauseated. "It'll kill itself."

Adan felt a chill at what Quo was doing to get attention. He went to where he could look over the sandstone wall at the dark landscape. He saw a flickering, shadowy movement outside, and then another loud blow struck.

The king shouted down into the darkness. "I am here, Quo!" He fought to control his anger and barked to the guards in the turret, "Throw torches down there so I can see!"

The guards removed torches from racks and tossed them to the ground. Scattered pools of firelight illuminated the sealed gate and the road that led west into the foothills.

Adan shouted to the unseen visitor, "You should have waited. I came—"

A reptilian beast with a large head and two massive legs lumbered forward, picking up speed, and mindlessly rammed itself into the wooden door. By now the auga had battered itself bloody and senseless. With a wet, bone-crunching impact, it smashed the gate, then reeled backward, a living battering ram. Several wooden beams had already splintered and cracked. The creature staggered back, barely able to keep its balance. Its head was pulped, its mouth broken and bloody. One eye was little more than dripping jelly. After only a moment to regain its energy, the auga charged forward again and collided with the gate.

Sickened, Adan yelled, "Stop, Quo! Why are you doing this?"

A lean figure stepped out of the shadows below, a tall golden-skinned man with long yellow hair adorned with glittering bangles. Quo picked up a fallen torch and held it in one hand like a curiosity. In his other hand he held a deadly-looking spear. "King Adan Starfall! You finally answered my summons," he said brightly. "It takes humans a great deal of time to respond to a knock on the door."

The auga raced forward and crashed against the barricade one more time, leaking blood, helplessly scrabbling against the barred gate.

Bile rose in Adan's throat. "Stop! I'm here. What do you want?"

"Why, to speak with you, Starfall." Quo grinned up at the top of the wall.

"Will you let me in so I can deliver a message from my sister? Or should I let my auga finish breaking down the gate? Either way, I will come inside."

Knowing the barricade would shatter soon, Adan answered with brittle formality, "Even though the hour is late, we will hear what Queen Voo's representative has to say. I am coming down to you. Just wait—please wait. This is not how an ally requests a visit."

"Yes, your culture is strange," said Quo. "Hurry, I bring wonderful news. I have had a long journey, and I am anxious to get back to the deserts. This cold, wet climate does not suit me." His shiver might have been an act.

Adan couldn't tell if the wreth man was malicious or merely oblivious. "If you are in a hurry to go home, then you should not have killed your mount."

Drawn and pale, Penda squeezed his hand. As they hurried down the stairs to the base of the gate, she said, "The news he brings can't be good."

"No, but if he insists on speaking with me, we can't stop him. I expect he will do something even worse if we defy him. This is horrible enough."

Using a pulley and rope, the sentries lifted the huge crossbar, then cranked wheels to withdraw secondary bolts. The battered gates swung open to reveal the tossed torches that continued to burn on the ground.

Just outside, the dying auga swayed on its feet, its head smashed, teeth broken loose, blood spilling from countless wounds. The creature looked at the open barrier and, its mission finally ended, collapsed into a heap in the road.

Quo sauntered forward, tossing aside the torch he had retrieved from the ground. He used his vicious-looking spear as a walking stick. "My sister sends you an invitation, king of the humans in Suderra."

Rather than inviting the wreth man inside his city, Adan stepped through the open gate to face him outside. Penda followed, taking her place beside him. He spoke cautiously. "I am here. Tell us Queen Voo's message."

Quo laughed. "My sister will speak her own words. I brought them with me." He extended his fingers toward the wide, well-traveled road. Magic rippled up and out, and the flat paving split apart to expose the sandy base dirt beneath. Soil churned and swirled, building a mass that rose and took shape. Delighting in his work, Quo moved his hands to make designs in the air.

The sandy soil formed Voo's striking visage with her wide-set, almond eyes, pointed nose, and narrow chin. The dirt sculpture turned and actually looked at Adan and Penda as if seeing them with eyes made of dust.

In a grinding, windy voice, Voo's image said, "King Adan Starfall and Queen Penda Orr, my human friends, I offer you a remarkable opportunity. We have found a dragon out in the deserts, and my wreths will hunt and kill it. As our new allies you must join us to see the power of our magic, as well as our fighting prowess. No human has ever gone on a dragon hunt with wreths. I do you a great honor. You must accept." When Voo laughed, dust and sand swirled around her sculpted face.

"I will send an escort party for you in five days, and they will lead you to me. Quo will give you what other information you need." Her message delivered, her sculpted face sloughed back into a pile of sand and dirt on the broken paving stones.

Adan tried to absorb the words. "A dragon hunt? Ossus has really awakened?"

Quo stepped around the dead auga as if he didn't even see it. "No. It is only a small dragon, but it will still be a challenge to hunt." He tapped the butt of his spiral spear on the ground. "Has it not been ages since humans even saw a dragon? They are unspeakably rare, and we hope to kill them all. This will be an event to remember." His voice hardened, losing all its aloof humor. "We do not extend this invitation lightly."

Adan realized that he couldn't refuse the offer any more than he could have denied the pounding on the gate. The sandwreths would do whatever they liked. He had also seen the power of the frostwreths up at Lake Bakal, and he didn't want either faction as his enemy. He feared the narrow and convoluted path of survival might be to cooperate with Queen Voo, the lesser of two evils.

"I will go," he said.

"*We* will go," Penda added.

"What a wonderful story for you to tell your child," Quo said with a glance at Penda.

She drew a circle in the center of her chest. "We already have many tales to tell our child." On her shoulder, Xar extended his wings and cocked his head at Quo as if to insist that he could fight a dragon as well.

Quo gave the ska a wry glance, then stepped away from the city gate, showing no interest in entering the city after all. "I must be on my way. A sandwreth escort party will come for you in five days. Be ready."

Penda looked at the dead auga sprawled in front of the gate. Slime and gore dripped down the sturdy wood of the door. "You've killed your mount. How will you get home?"

Quo was dismissive. "I have other means of transportation." Dust swirled around him, appearing out of the air like dry mist. As the wreth man retreated beyond the scattered pools of torchlight, he began to trot, and the blowing dust hid him in the night.

73

Now that they had become lovers, Elliel reveled in Thon's presence. The wreth man was compassionate and caring, and he seemed to draw as much strength from her company as she did from his. But they still had no idea who he was.

The closer she grew to Thon, the stronger she herself felt in spite of the dark, empty holes in her past. The damning letter Elliel always carried with her reminded her of the collapsing well in the wreth ruins, a slippery slope that could suck her down into a void. But when she was with Thon, she felt able to stand safely on the edge, look down into the treacherous depths, and not fall.

After exploring the ruins but finding no further key answers, Elliel and Thon decided to move on toward Norterra, where the wreth man felt a strong calling. Shadri continued to find fascinating relics to study in the ancient city, but when the two informed her they were leaving, she ran to retrieve her large pack. "I'm coming, too. If I stay here longer, I might be tempted to stay for the rest of my life, and I can't ignore the rest of the world. Too much to see. I've never been to Norterra."

Traveling together, they moved at a brisk walk all day, although Shadri kept stopping to look at plants, an odd rock, or a bright green grasshopper that landed on her arm. At night, though they ate together in camp, Shadri made a small fire of her own and slept curled against her pack, while the two lovers found a place to themselves.

In the forest shadows Elliel still looked at Thon in wonder. She felt a tingle of warmth as she kissed him, drew his breath into her lungs, felt his skin against hers. He genuinely treasured her, stroking her face with his long, slender fingers. When they lay naked together, he drew his hands over her flat stomach, curious about the lumpy scar from what must have been an awful wound.

"Who could have done this to you?" he asked. "It should have killed you."

She touched the scar, then touched his finger. "As a Brava, I must have been in numerous battles." She touched the other pale lines of her scars, cut marks, the waxy burn, the missing tip of her finger, then back to the big scar on her abdomen. "This one is the worst, though."

"I wish I knew your legacy," he said. "What drove you to that awful crime? It is not like you at all." Even in the darkness, his gaze was intense, piercing. "I can see your heart, and I know what's there."

"Those questions will probably remain unanswered." Elliel touched the scar again, but decided she would rather explore his body instead. She leaned closer and kissed him again. "I want to know *your* story, why you were placed in that mountain chamber. That's much more important. Are you certain we can't find a way to unlock the rune, cancel that seal? At least you'd know what to do, why you're here."

He looked at her with sparkling sapphire eyes. "I wrestle with that decision every day. I do not know if that is even possible. My mark is much more powerful than yours, and I can't remove the locking element. Either I committed a horrible crime and I don't want to remember it, or I have been set as a trap, as a weapon. Or something else entirely?"

He touched the tattoo on her cheek, and she felt a burn, as if he had somehow reawakened the ink in the spell that Utho had imposed. "For you it is different, though. You have your letter, so you know why you cannot remember, why the Bravas imposed such a sentence on you." He held her, stared into her face, and she saw something dark and intense come alive behind his eyes. "There is no danger to the world if you get your memories back. They didn't add the locking element to your design."

Elliel let out a sigh. "But that still doesn't help return my memories."

Thon stared intently at her. His eyes seemed deep and full of stars. "If that is what you want, I need only to add a triggering element."

Elliel sat up quickly on their blankets. "What do you mean? A triggering element? How can you add it?" Her throat went dry.

"I add it the same way any tattoo is made. It would negate the rest of the design, and it's built into the structure of the design. If the half-breed Bravas have enough magic to make the rune work in the first place, then I certainly possess the necessary power to add a new line. I can connect the elements and unravel your erasing." He looked at her with a gaze as sharp as an arrow. "If that is truly what you want."

"Of course it's what I want!" She didn't dare to believe it, and found herself suddenly fearful. "But my memories are gone. Utho said so."

"Nothing is ever gone. The resonances and whispers still live in your mind. The rune of forgetting merely covered them like a blanket of snow. The question is, do you want your memory back? Are you prepared to face the truth?"

She didn't hesitate. "Yes." She had wrestled with her questions for so long, had imagined what she would do if she found the truth, but she had not dared to hope. "Yes," she said in a quieter voice. "I want to know why I did it."

Thon gathered his clothing. "I will ask you again afterward. You might not thank me once you remember."

"But at least I will know."

Though it was late, they found Shadri sitting cross-legged on her blanket, writing in her journal by the firelight. Her enormous pack was propped against a moss-covered oak. Thon lowered himself to a crouch beside her. "I need a needle and some ink, the same ink you use to write your notes."

The girl closed her journal, pulled her pack closer and dug around inside. "That's intriguing. Why do you need a needle and ink under the trees in the middle of the night?"

"To complete my tattoo and break the spell." Elliel's voice was trembling, her throat thick. "You told us you want to learn everything there is to know? Well, this is something *I* need to know. Thon has a way to bring my memories back to me."

Shadri hummed quietly to herself as she pulled out packets, leaves, shiny stones, and finally a small roll of leather, which she opened. "That's certainly worth a needle and a little ink. Will you tell us what you learn? I want to hear the real story." From the leather roll, she plucked a silver needle wrapped in threads. She already had a tiny bottle of ink from writing in her journal. "Can I watch you do it? I've never seen a spell broken before."

Thon looked at Elliel for permission, and she said, "I don't mind. If this works, we'll all learn the answers, no matter how terrible they might be. I don't intend to keep any more secrets."

Taking the needle and ink, Thon sat in front of Elliel beside Shadri's small fire. He leaned close, focused on her face, and dipped the bright, sharp needle into the ink. Without warning, without ceremony, he pricked her skin, then repeated in a blur of tiny sharp pains. Elliel winced, but she forced her eyes open to stare at him. She watched him as he leaned in, working with nimble fingers. The needle stung far less than the returning memories would.

Adding the trigger rune was a complex process, and Thon worked with great care. Shadri observed them, curious and absorbed in the activity.

Elliel felt the burn growing from the constant sting of the sharp needle. Thon paused and looked up from his work to meet her eyes. "Almost finished. Are you certain?"

Elliel didn't nod for fear the movement might disrupt the new lines of ink. Instead, she let out a whisper, "Very sure."

He dipped the needle into the ink, pricked her again and again, and sat back as if in benediction. He touched her sore cheek. "There, it is done."

The lines on her face burned, and she felt a crackle through her jaw, thrumming into her skull. Her thoughts knotted, tangled . . . then unraveled like a tapestry with a snipped thread.

Again, she imagined herself on the edge of that slippery sinkhole into a dark void. Suddenly her safe place crumbled, and Elliel fell—but the bottomless pit was no longer dark. Instead, it was filled with memories, filled with her past . . . filled with the truth.

She braced herself to face the screams of the children she had slaughtered in her feverish rage, the massacre of innocents with her ramer—

But that was not what she remembered.

The flood of returning memories held no murder, no children, no teacher, no fever. No crime at all. Except for one. She had been betrayed.

The story was false. The letter Utho had written was complete fiction. Elliel had never committed the crime she was accused of, and because her memory had been wiped clean, she had never known.

Now, a different guilt filled all the dark and empty corners of her mind—and she remembered everything.

Once she completed her training as a Brava, young Elliel had worked for several hard and dangerous years, serving any need she found. She had been a paladin, wandering in the northern counties of Osterra, enjoying the rugged highlands with cloudy skies and cold mists. She had been self-sufficient and deadly since the age of fifteen, and she spent years hardening herself, laying the foundation for her legacy, the great legacy of a Brava.

At nineteen, beautiful and fierce, she came to the attention of Lord Cade, a powerful noble who ruled a wealthy county best known for producing salt-pearls. The coveted pearls were harvested at great risk by divers who pulled shellfish out of alcoves in the cold churning waters off the coast.

Cade convinced Elliel to enter service as his personal Brava. He was very charismatic, offered her good pay and an important position. The prestige was exactly what a Brava wished for. By bonding herself to him at such a young age, she would already write her legacy large.

She was caught up in the possibilities. Cade himself was politically power-ful back in Convera, and his county was among the strongest, with its own well-equipped standing army. Elliel would be his Brava, ready to protect him and his holdings, to increase his power.

His wife, Lady Almeda, was intense and wealthy, with many connections to merchants in Convera, and marriage to her had brought the real power to his county, although Cade was the one named lord. Almeda was too aloof to be a ruler, uninterested in things that didn't involve her personal comfort, clothing, or baubles. The two were under each other's thumbs, both of them influential, both stubborn, both self-absorbed.

Accepting the bond, Elliel signed the paper, adding her thumbprint in blood, pledging her strength, her mind, and her ramer to Cade's service. This was far more significant than any of the smaller contracts and agreements she had taken as a younger paladin.

Cade swore her to secrecy as his bonded Brava, and demanded that she pledge her absolute loyalty to him and his holdings, on her honor. That was when she learned that Lord Cade's wealth and power came at a dark price.

Although some of his saltpearl divers were swimmers raised in the local villages, most were Isharan slaves, captured during illicit raids, often in collusion with Watchman Osler on Fulcor Island. Isharan boats were seized, their crews taken prisoner and delivered to the rugged northern coastline, where Lord Cade forced them to dive for the pearls. Many died in the risky operation, and some Isharan captives simply drowned themselves to be free from the terrible enslavement.

Elliel was placed in charge of the Isharan prisoners, who were held in ut-terly secret camps. Although she disliked what Cade was doing, she knew the story of Valaera, the Brava colony wiped out by the treacherous Isharans. She had already sworn her allegiance to the lord, and no Brava would break such a vow. She did as he commanded her to do, and because his windswept county was far from the capital, few people knew or cared what he did on the high coast. They did not ask questions, and his own standing army kept prying eyes away.

Every few months, Utho came to the northern coast on an inspection visit. Even though the konag himself knew nothing about the Isharan slaves, Utho knew the truth behind the saltpearl operations, and he grimly approved of how the enemy captives were treated. He and Elliel were Bravas, bound by the same code of honor, and Utho did not interfere with her work.

Soon after she bonded with Cade, though, the nobleman stopped treating her as a partner and loyal defender; rather, he seemed to consider her to be his property. She had her duty and was expected to do it.

Eventually, whenever he looked at her his eyes began to carry an intense, predatory gleam that she had never seen before. Elliel was a confident, beautiful woman. She knew that men found her attractive, but Lord Cade unsettled her. She could tell that he wanted her, and she rebuffed his advances, coolly and professionally, thinking there would be nothing more to it. What lord, however powerful, would dare try to force himself on a Brava?

That was before he drugged her.

Cade brought her to his private chambers to discuss the deaths of several prisoners in the secret saltpearl operations and how to replace them. Unsuspecting, she had tasted a bitter undertone in her wine and thought that the vintage was a little off. Soon she found her arms and legs tingling, her words slurring. Bravas were rarely affected by wine or spirits, but this drug was powerful. Her body couldn't fight it off. As she began to lose control, slumping down, a leering Cade had dragged her limp and weakly resisting form over to his bed.

She could barely struggle while he worked at untying the knots on her black garments. When that proved too slow he took a sharp letter opener from his writing desk, slashed the fabric, and peeled off her clothes so that she lay naked on his sheets, her cinnamon hair splayed out on the pillow. Elliel felt as if she were floating, detached, observing her own actions like a voyeur. Cade stroked her cheek and fondled her breasts as if inspecting property. Then he forced himself upon her.

In the numb fuzziness of her mind, Elliel thought he was ravishing someone else, and that she—a Brava—would come and rescue the poor maiden. But it was *her*, and she could do nothing to drive him off.

When he was finished, he simply left her there in her ruined Brava garments. "You are *my* Brava, remember that. You swore an oath." He kept one of the candles burning for her when he sauntered off.

After she fought off the effects of the drug, Elliel gathered the tatters of her garments but could not find the remnants of her dignity. Impotent to do anything about it, she slipped away from his holding house, keeping to shadows. Shame, confusion, and failure lodged themselves deep within her. Her bonded lord had raped her, and even as a Brava she had been unable to fend him off. She had never experienced such crippling uncertainty in her life, such astonishing helplessness.

But because she was bonded to Cade—*bonded* to him!—Elliel could not simply leave, nor could she kill him to avenge what he had done. Brava honor demanded her service, even as loathing and resentment nearly paralyzed her. Cade was a powerful lord, who could bring disgrace upon her and all Bravas. His saltpearl operations and the secret of the Isharan slaves must not be exposed.

Caught in a labyrinthine quandary, Elliel avoided Cade, seeking answers. She didn't dare let anyone know what had happened, what had changed. She longed for someone to give her advice, like her mentor back at the old settlement where she had learned what it meant to be a Brava. What did all her training *mean* anymore?

She avoided Cade for days, refused to see or speak with him. She remembered him on top of her, while she was rendered totally helpless by the drug. It wasn't her fault, but it *was* her failure. A Brava should have been alert to all dangers! Even now, she felt bound and gagged, but with bonds that only he could see. When Cade glanced at her, his look of provocative satisfaction thrust into her like a knife.

One day she saw him whispering to his men-at-arms, who gave her a similar lascivious look, laughing with one another. Elliel heard men whisper in the village, saw their looks when she went to the tavern to collect a tax payment, as she had always done. Her life and duties were different now. Cade had ruined everything. He had damaged her in multiple ways, and he was an enemy she could not fight against.

Worse, she did not realize that rumors had reached the bitter, jealous Lady Almeda. Elliel was walking through the dark corridors of the holding house, having just delivered a full saltpearl report to the chamberlain late at night, so she wouldn't have to see Lord Cade in person. Her situation was untenable. Elliel might be tempted to kill Cade if she had to face him.

She faulted herself for being unprepared that night. It was her only unforgivable mistake.

Almeda sprang out of the shadows, shrieking at her. She plunged a long knife into Elliel's stomach and slashed sideways to open her gut. By reflex—before she realized how badly she had been wounded—Elliel struck back, punching Almeda in the face, smashing her nose and cracking her head against the stone wall. The sobbing woman slid down the wall and crawled away, leaving Elliel to bleed and bleed on the floor.

Only Elliel's wreth heritage, an instinctive magic that she barely understood, kept her alive by slowing her metabolism. She fell into a deep, slow unconsciousness.

An hour later, Cade had found Elliel gasping and dying in the corridor. He frowned down at her for an interminable moment before he shouted for the healers, and they saved her life by the barest of margins. They stitched her up and set guards at the chamber so Lady Almeda wouldn't try to kill her again. Cade watched over Elliel as she drifted in and out of consciousness for days. She didn't know whether the husband or the wife frightened her more.

During her long recovery, Lord Cade had time to summon Utho to help cover up the scandal. What to do with the wounded Brava woman who had a secret to hold over the nobleman and—because of the secret but vital Isharan slaves—over the entire Commonwealth?

Lady Almeda was outraged, insulted, and inflamed with revenge. With Utho as witness, Almeda vowed to destroy her husband by exposing the saltpearl operations, which might even provoke a new war with Ishara when the empra learned of it. Irrational in her rage, Almeda didn't care what the revelation would do to their noble family, their wealth, or their holdings.

Utho didn't dare let the news get out. He knew how the sometimes-soft Konag Conndur would react to news about the Isharan slaves. One solution would have been to kill Lady Almeda. The other solution would require a great sacrifice from Elliel, at the cost of her memories, her legacy. They decided that a young Brava woman was expendable.

At one point, Elliel slipped into a fever of infection, but overheard what Cade and Utho planned to do to her. She thrashed about so violently that she had to be tied down, and in her delirium she knew little of what was happening to her. While Elliel was bound and feverish, Lady Almeda demanded satisfaction, insisting that the woman who had "tempted" her husband must pay a terrible price.

And Utho complied. It was the best way to end the crisis with the least amount of collateral damage, all told.

Elliel didn't have a choice when Utho's justice was forced on her. The tall, grim Brava got out his needles and his ink. He crouched before her and applied the rune of forgetting to her face while she was still fighting the fever. The explanation would be perfect.

An indignant and vindictive Almeda insisted on watching.

In order to protect their future, they concocted the lie for Elliel, something so horrific as to be utterly believable, for the good of the Commonwealth. The awful letter that Utho had written, the terrible fiction of how she had lost control and murdered helpless children . . . that was just cruel. From the moment Elliel read the note, she had believed it all.

Now she knew the truth.

Reeling, Elliel came back to herself. In the light of the smoky campfire, she looked at the plump scholar girl and Thon, both of whom stared back at her.

She crumpled to the ground, heaving deep breaths, trying to sort the new knowledge, the restored memories. She coughed out her words. "Innocent. I am innocent! I didn't do . . . that."

Furious, she lurched to her feet. Her face felt hot, but it had nothing to do with the new tattoo. She grabbed the golden ramer band at her waist.

Thon and Shadri stared at her, backing away.

Elliel clipped the band around her wrist, squeezing it tight so that the sharp golden fangs bit into her veins, activating the magic with spilled scarlet fluid. The band glowed, and a ring of fire circled the top of it.

Elliel pulled on the magic, added to the blood that fed the ramer's power. The flames grew bright to engulf her hand, rising into a curling sword of flames. She held it high, crackling and bright in the dark forest.

With her other hand she pulled out the rumpled letter that described her false crimes, used the ramer to ignite it, and burned it to ash in an instant.

"I'm a Brava again." She caught her breath and looked at her two companions. "And I have a story to tell you."

74

WHEN Hale Orr returned to Convera Castle with the empra's response, his smile sent a chill down Utho's spine. He dreaded what the Utauk merchant captain would say.

Rushing up to the castle as soon as his ship tied up to the docks at the Confluence, Hale still smelled of salt and sweat. His crimson and black silks swirled around him and his cape was askew as he strode into the konag's parley chamber. Conndur silenced the muttering of the other lords and ministers and rose to his feet, eager to hear the answer.

Utho braced himself.

Hale drew a circle in the air and announced, "I presented your offer, Sire, and told Empra Iluris what I know. She remains skeptical about stories of the wreths, and her key priestlord is sure it's some kind of trick, but I think I convinced her that the danger is not imaginary and that the offer is sincere. Your willingness to relinquish Fulcor Island should she meet certain conditions was truly enough to catch her interest."

Conndur rested his hands on the table in front of him, as if to brace himself. "Did she agree to meet at the appointed time?"

Hale Orr gave his report only to the konag, paying no attention at all to the other gathered nobles. He did not see Utho bristle. "Yes, despite clear skepticism in the Isharan court, she eventually accepted the invitation. She will travel to Fulcor Island with a formal escort at the arranged time." He looked uncomfortable, rubbed his cheek with his stump. "There is one other thing, Sire. When the *Glissand* sailed into Serepol Harbor, we saw the Isharans burning a pair of Commonwealth ships—fishing boats, I believe. Certainly not warships."

With a glance at the other vassal lords in the room, Lord Cade thumped a fist on the table. "How dare they take civilian ships! I'll wager they tortured or enslaved those poor innocent Osterrans."

Utho was amazed the lord could say such a thing without even a trace of irony. For his visit to Convera Castle, the northern nobleman was attended by his new bonded Brava, a blocky man with pockmarks on his face and a nose like some smashed fruit; Gant had served Lord Cade for the past year, secretly helping to manage the enslaved Isharan pearl divers. The choice of the ugly man was a concession to his bitter wife, who insisted that no female Brava ever be allowed in her husband's service again, for obvious reasons.

Hale gave Cade a withering glance and exclaimed, "*Cra!* Are you so unaware of what your own people are doing? The Commonwealth is not innocent in this! The Fulcor garrison is also capturing Isharan vessels and executing the prisoners. Such actions only fan the flames between your two lands." He fumed. "Both sides must stop if there is to be hope of peace. All the people in the three kingdoms, including all the Utauk tribes, will suffer if we can't stand together."

Utho could barely contain his anger, but he remained like a silent statue, for now.

Amid the indignant voices that rose, Conndur added in a stern tone, agreeing with the merchant captain. "Yes, I am aware that our ships have preyed upon them as well, though I never ordered it." He flashed a sidelong glance at Cade, who muttered and turned away.

Utho was surprised by the konag's subtle reaction. Did Conndur actually know about the enslaved pearl divers? He and Cade had worked so hard to keep the secret.

Hale's loud voice broke into the hubbub. He seemed skilled at cutting through an unruly argument. "Hear me! My sense is that Empra Iluris is also frustrated with raids like the one at Mirrabay, which she claims was entirely unauthorized. I detected clear friction in the court, and I am inclined to believe her. She has ruled for thirty years, and her consistent actions suggest that she prefers peace and prosperity."

"As do I," Conndur said. "We both have the same goals, and we both have to endure intractable followers." He glowered at his vassal lords. "It stops now! A complete cessation of hostilities, nothing they can use against us. I command that there will be no more aggression against the Isharans while they have agreed to talk with us. Remember Mount Vada! We may need them, whatever our differences. Ancestors' blood, there is too much at stake."

Utho's heart sank as he saw the deluded determination on the konag's face. This was as bad as he had feared. He had tried to dissuade Conndur from his reckless scheme. He was risking so much to suggest an alliance with the Isharans because of an as-yet-unproven and mostly unseen enemy. As if they could be trusted in anything! After seeing the devastation in the Dragonspine, Conndur was convinced that the end of the world was at hand.

Prince Mandan sat beside his father, wearing a red cape lined with snow cat fur. At least the prince understood the true stakes, even if his father had his heart set on a naïve tea party with their mortal enemies. . . .

"What if the Isharans attack again with their godlings?" asked Goran, another vassal lord. Lord Goran's bonded Brava, a hardened older woman named Klea, stood by his side. "Should we just roll over and die? Flee in terror without fighting back?"

The konag frowned at him. "We need not worry about godlings if I can negotiate peace. Empra Iluris has agreed to meet. They will stop their harassments on our coast for the time being, and that is all I ask."

Utho was so appalled he couldn't restrain his outburst. The slow anger inside him finally reached the boiling point. "Harassments? Those animals just unleashed a godling and burned Mirrabay! More than a hundred innocents killed." He thought of Mareka's brown eyes, her soft and beautiful face. "And all those who died there before."

Conndur sounded sad. "I know you have great pain within you, old friend, but I have to try to convince them, because if I don't try, then I am a failure as konag. The wreths, the dragon . . ." He nodded, as if affirming his own decision. "We'll go out to Fulcor Island and prepare for the empra and her entourage to arrive. After that, we will see."

"Who will accompany you, Sire?" asked Lord Vinay, whose county in the southern foothills of the Dragonspine Mountains had suffered severe damage in the recent upheavals.

"I'll take an escort, and we also have the troops stationed at the garrison." Conndur looked at the uneasy prince. "Mandan, I need you with me. If we can convince the Isharans to be our allies, they need to know that you represent me and speak for me." He nodded toward Utho, who stood frozen with buried frustration. "Utho, you will be at my side of course, and I hope these other lords will let me borrow their bonded Bravas. I could have no better protectors."

"I will go," Klea said without asking her master. Goran seemed surprised at her declaration, but did not argue.

"Lord Cade will grant his permission for me as well," said ugly Gant, although his master did not look happy.

The prince was sweating heavily, obviously terrified. Utho placed a firm hand on Mandan's shoulder. "All will be well, my prince. I will be with you." That seemed to be all he needed to hear, and he visibly relaxed.

Conndur rose, dismissing the council. "Make preparations. I want to be at Fulcor Island a full two days before the empra's party arrives."

Before departing, Utho called an urgent secret meeting of the local Bravas. Late at night, they gathered at the empty remembrance shrine in the lower town. "We must salvage what we can from this debacle. The Isharans are sure to betray us, just as they did at Valaera. They might try to kill Konag Conndur and seize Fulcor Island for themselves."

Gant muttered, rubbing his mashed nose. "Some might say the konag himself betrays us by proposing an alliance with the enemy. We should use the opportunity to kill the entire Isharan party, assassinate their empra, their priestlords, and anyone else they bring along."

Klea paced the small, dark room, troubled by the suggestion. "Then we would be as dishonorable as they are."

Utho remained contemplative. "Honor does not apply where the Isharans are concerned. This is a vengewar."

The gathered Bravas agreed to remain alert and ready to fight, but they would watch how the parley discussions unfolded on the island. Utho had no doubt they would do whatever needed to be done . . . but he did not know what that might be. He dreaded the possibilities.

The following day, the Commonwealth expedition departed in transport boats from the Confluence down the Joined River to the sea. Prince Mandan stood out on the deck, obviously uneasy. "Is it dangerous out on the ocean? What if a storm comes? Thunder and lightning?" His voice cracked. "What if there's a sea battle against the Isharans? What if they unleash a godling against us?"

"I would never underestimate their treachery, but in this circumstance, I doubt they'd be so bold. The empra will hear what your father has to say, if only because she is curious. But then we have to be ready to make our move."

The flotilla of transport ships flowed down the thirty-mile stretch of Joined River to the widening mouth of the sea, where the port of Rivermouth bristled with countless docks. Two warships waited there, provisioned and ready to depart, flags flying with the open-hand banner of the Commonwealth and the rising sun of Osterra.

Mandan stared toward the flat horizon, intimidated by the vastness. "The water just rolls off the edge of the world. It goes as far as I can see."

"Yes, my prince. And somewhere beyond lies the coast of Ishara."

"I hope I never see it," Mandan said.

Utho squeezed the prince's shoulder again. "I hope you never have to."

75

KOLL the Hammer vowed to show the frostwreths that they couldn't simply take back the land they had destroyed. He would fight for his kingdom, even without help from the Commonwealth army. He would sting like a wasp.

At times like this, he missed Lasis more than ever. His bonded Brava was a powerful fighting companion with a solid understanding of legendary things, not to mention his deadly ramer and a measure of magic. But something had happened to him on his mission to Lake Bakal.

On the grounds of Fellstaff Castle, Koll watched new recruits practice with swords and spears, slowly becoming an army. Men and women trained as archers, though it was a challenge for them just to hit their targets. Pokle joined them, determined to learn how to use a bow and arrow. He had hunted rabbits around Lake Bakal, but mainly with snares. Eventually, his aim matched his earnestness.

Queen Tafira also rose to the occasion. She brought out her throwing knives and trained others, including the kitchen staff. "But we aren't soldiers, my lady," complained one of the baker women whose particular skill was in making pies.

"If wreths overrun the castle to rape and kill us all, wouldn't you like to cut a few throats before you go?" Tafira asked. The pie woman chewed on that thought, then applied herself to the training with a grim determination.

Explaining to Koll, the queen said, "We can only justify a pampered life during quiet times. These are no longer quiet times, and I won't be a quiet companion."

"No, beloved, you are not complacent or quiet. I wouldn't have it any other way."

One morning, a scout rode to Fellstaff Castle with a troubling report of

three unusual travelers making their way to the city. "One of them is a female Brava traveling with a teenaged girl, and . . ." He scratched his head.
"And a stranger."

"What kind of stranger?" Koll asked.

"I think . . . Sire—I think it's a *wreth*."

Koll had the scout turn around. "Take me there. I'll saddle up Storm so we
can go meet them on the road." He turned to Tafira. "If someone captured a
wreth, then I am determined to gain as much information as possible."

Several miles down the road, they came upon the three travelers, who were
by now escorted by more wary scouts. A plain teenaged girl with limp brown
hair hiked along carrying a pack half as large as she was. The Brava woman
was tall and attractive, dressed in loose traveling clothes, rather than the traditional black leathers and finemail of a Brava. Her deep red hair was gathered behind her shoulders in a single band. A strange tattoo marked her face.

The third companion drew all of Koll's focus, though. He was lean and
handsome, but alien looking. His eyes were long and narrow, his chin
pointed, his teeth unnaturally even. His mane of black hair was wild like a
thunderstorm. He wore silvery leggings, chest armor with prominent shoulder pads, and a tattoo on his face similar to the Brava woman's. The stranger
had haunting similarities to the frostwreth warriors Koll had faced at Lake
Bakal, yet there was something different about him, too.

Reining up, Koll sat high on his warhorse. "You look like a wreth."

"I believe I am," the man said with no hint of sarcasm. "And you look
like a king. I am honored to meet you."

Koll growled. "I don't know if there's any honor in meeting a wreth. Your
people destroyed an entire town and killed the people who lived there, including my daughter and her family."

The wreth's deep blue eyes met him squarely. "For that, I am sincerely
sorry, but I do not belong with them. My name is Thon."

Disturbed, Koll turned toward the woman. "What is your name, Brava?"

"I'm Elliel." Her expression was guarded, and her green eyes showed an
edge of pain.

"She was accused of a terrible crime and her memories were erased," the
plump girl said, adjusting her pack. "But she remembers everything now.
She was betrayed. She didn't really commit those crimes."

"Doesn't every criminal say the same?" Koll asked.

"Do you expect a Brava to lie?" Elliel asked.

He considered. "In my experience, Bravas are honorable. My own was the most loyal man I've ever met." He lowered his voice. "We think the frost-wreths captured or killed him." He turned Storm around. "Come with me back to Fellstaff. I want Queen Tafira to hear your tales as well. She often has more insights than I do."

Inside the castle, Tafira joined them in the banquet hall for a detailed conversation. Pokle brought in wood for the fireplace and helped carry food trays. He flinched from the wreth man, fearful, but seemed even more nervous around the talkative scholar girl, who was about his age. Shadri ate with great enthusiasm, asking Pokle questions about the food he served, how it was prepared, what spices were used. The gawky young man promised to take her to the kitchens to show her everything.

As if strengthening her resolve, Elliel formally addressed the king and queen. "When I got my memories back, I became a Brava again." She held up her ramer, then turned her wrist to show the half-healed scabs there. "Now I can call the fire and wield my flame, just as I did before. I will offer my skills here, if you can use them, Sire. I am not bonded."

Shadri said quickly, "You would do well to have her in your service, King Kollanan."

Koll nodded slowly. "I know the value of a Brava, but your service will not be a simple task, and you'll need to do more than just frighten off the occasional bandit. I fear the frostwreths intend to run roughshod over our lands." He glanced accusingly at the stranger. Anger and questions had built up inside him for too long. "What do you wreths want from us? Why did you come back?"

Thon looked deeply troubled. "I wish I could tell you, but I have no memory of wreths since the beginning of their great war long ago. I know only that I am awake now, the dragon is stirring, and fire is bursting out of the mountains. It is only part of many great upheavals in the end days of the world."

"You don't inspire me with confidence, wreth man," Koll muttered.

Thon insisted that he was neither part of Queen Onn's army to the north nor Queen Voo's army in the deserts beyond Suderra. He claimed never to have heard of either of them.

Elliel spoke up on his behalf. "Thon does want to help, Sire. He's no part of this new war, and he is not allied with either faction of the wreths."

"How can you be sure of this?" Tafira asked.

"Because I believe him. And I'm a Brava, for what it's worth."

The queen wasn't convinced by the argument. "A Brava, perhaps, but you said you were disgraced, your legacy wiped. And now you say you never committed such a crime?"

"No, I did not."

Koll said, "You had better tell us the entire story." In harsh detail, Elliel explained about Lord Cade and the rape, the poisonously jealous Lady Almeda, the threat of exposure and how Utho had made her a scapegoat to cover it. She said in disgust, "It was politics. And now I am adrift. I can offer you my services and do my best to defend your kingdom in these troubled times."

Koll's expression darkened. "Cade's county is far away, but my brother should know what his vassal lord is doing." After what he had already told Conndur, though, and how he had been rebuffed, he doubted the konag would welcome more disruptive news. "I'll deal with the politics in its own time."

Elliel seemed to be wrestling her past into submission. "And what about Utho? The konag's own Brava is not to be trusted. Doesn't he need to know that?" Her voice caught. "What Utho did to me—"

Koll's expression was as hard as an iron mask. "Utho is no friend of mine either. He was one of the strongest voices against Konag Conndur providing help to Norterra against the wreths." He felt the heat in his cheeks. "I will write my brother. He needs to know about Utho and about Lord Cade. But right now, we are on our own here. We are facing the possible destruction of Norterra, maybe a war that will tear the world apart."

He lowered his voice, looked appraisingly at Elliel. "Yet kings do depend on their Bravas. Since Lasis is gone and possibly dead, I do need a Brava here with me. Whatever your past, I know your abilities. When a man buys an old sword, he only worries about the sturdiness of the blade, the sharpness of the edge and point. He doesn't care how many other people the sword has killed in the past." He studied Elliel in silence for a long moment. "If you swear your service to me, you'll be a weapon in my hand."

"I will accept a bond to you—but only if you swear to be honorable to me." Her answer shocked Koll, and Tafira gasped, but Elliel crossed her arms. "I will accept nothing less than such an oath from you, to me."

After the moment of tension, Koll chuckled. "After you told me your story, I see that as a perfectly reasonable request." He saw a haunted hurt deep behind her eyes. "I have no qualms whatsoever in swearing to uphold my honor to you—or to anyone else in Norterra."

Elliel nodded and visibly relaxed. "Then I accept."

With greater suspicion, though, Koll turned to Thon. The dark-haired wreth was an enigma and certainly dangerous. "You, however . . . how can I accept the cooperation of a *wreth,* when I know what the wreths did at Lake Bakal? Jhaqi and Gannon, poor Tomko and Birch, all of them frozen to death on a whim and a winterspell!" His voice rose as his temper did.

Thon said seriously, "I do not know my part in what is to come, but I believe I can help in ways that no one else in your kingdom could imagine. Let me use my wreth magic in your service."

Queen Tafira studied the wreth man intently, then turned to her husband. "When you brought me back to the Commonwealth, Husband, your people were shocked, suspicious. They saw me as an Isharan, an enemy, not to be trusted. Even so, you took me as your wife, you believed in me. You loved me, and I've never given you reason to regret it."

Tears stung his eyes. "No, beloved, I never regretted it for a moment."

"If you'd listened to the fears and suspicions of others, you might have let the villagers sacrifice me in Sarcen. You might have abandoned me back there and taken a fine Norterran bride instead."

"But I didn't. I loved you."

"This wreth man deserves a chance as well, if he says he can help us. Are you so confident in your ability to fight the enemy alone?"

Kollanan couldn't disagree with her. "Ancestors' blood, we'll see what this wreth can do." With that, he opened the shutters in his mind just a crack and let himself consider possibilities.

76

WHEN the ships arrived at Fulcor Island, Konag Conndur disembarked onto the sturdy pier in the harbor cove. He had never personally visited the isolated garrison, although Fulcor had been an important strategic asset for many years. Knowing he was initiating a portentous event, he felt the weight of his legacy, yet he also felt hopeful.

Seabirds swooped overhead, scolding the visitors. Sharp breezes whipped into the cove and up the sheer cliffs. Farther out to sea, waves hissed and boomed over the reefs.

Conndur stood on the dock as Watchman Osler came to greet the party in his military uniform and a rust-colored old cape that might once have been bright red. The sword at his side looked ornamental, but could well be used for battle. "Our brave garrison soldiers are pleased you'd come on such an important mission, Sire." Osler's expression became troubled. "Though we wonder why you'd invite Isharans here . . ."

Conn clasped the man's extended hand. "Because the future of the human race may depend on stopping these hostilities and allying against an even greater enemy. Therefore, I must try."

Osler gave a dubious bow. "As you command, Sire."

Conndur looked up the winding staircase mounted on the outer cliffs, then even higher to see more than a hundred soldiers peering down from the high walls of the fortress above. The prince and Utho followed him off the ship, and more of the party disembarked. Half of the crew would be stationed inside the garrison as the konag's personal retinue, while the others would remain aboard the ship, always ready.

Watchman Osler led them up the cliffside steps until they reached the cleft in the rock, which led them to the interior of the fortress. Osler spoke over his shoulder as they followed. "The garrison is on high alert, Sire. We spent days working on the main hall, the courtyard, the fortifications. We doubled up the men in the barracks to clear rooms in two separate wings of the main hall. Your party will stay in one wing, and the . . . others will have quarters in the second wing. We have to keep you separate from the Isharans, for safety."

Conn read grim tension on the old veteran's face. "Thank you, Watchman. There may be great changes ahead." He didn't reveal the possibility that they might even relinquish the island garrison if the Isharans agreed to fight beside them against the wreths. Osler and these dedicated soldiers wouldn't approve of that, not at all. He didn't much like it himself either, but he knew how necessary this was. Having witnessed the quakes and fires in the Dragonspine, having heard the pleas from Adan and Kollanan, he had to do what was right.

As they passed through the narrow cleft in the cliffs and up to the open air above, Conndur regarded the soldiers lined up in ranks in the courtyard. He touched his chest to acknowledge them, which sparked loud applause, cheers for the konag.

Then Watchman Osler called out. "And also show a special welcome to Utho of the Reef, one of the greatest heroes of Fulcor Island."

The Brava revealed neither pride nor embarrassment, but accepted the wave of cheers that rolled over him. Prince Mandan looked at him with deep admiration.

More Commonwealth troops came up the stairs from the dock, carrying supplies and filing into the open courtyard. Conndur watched the activity, satisfied. "The empra arrives in three days. Make sure she feels welcome."

After the traveling chests, diplomatic supplies, and ceremonial weapons were unloaded and the Commonwealth retinue had chosen quarters in the main wing, Utho found Mandan in his stone-walled quarters down the hall from the konag's larger chamber. The prince's room had a narrow, open window through which breezes whistled, and Utho knew how cold it would be at night. Fortunately, he saw blankets placed on Mandan's traveling chest, and a fireplace in the corner with a stack of wood. He doubted the prince would realize the sacrifice that private fire entailed to the other soldiers, with wood so scarce on the island.

Mandan had changed into a silk tunic, fine trousers, and brown leather boots, as if he were going to a formal ball. He was already bored. "Why did we have to come three days early? I wish I had brought my paints."

Utho said in a firm, paternal tone, "You are here at Fulcor Island for a very important meeting. Learn from it. You will see our enemies face-to-face, so plan to study their mannerisms, their habits, their weaknesses—and then remember everything. This is an opportunity you won't have again."

"Why would I want it?" Mandan asked.

"Answer that for yourself, and if you're a wise leader, you will find an acceptable reason. Learn everything, observe everything." He took the prince outside the main hall and up to the top of the fortress wall that encircled the crown of the island. "From up here you can watch the ocean in all directions."

Mandan peered into the distance. "So we're able to see the enemy coming?"

"You always want to see them coming. Otherwise they may attack before you know it."

They followed the walkway on top of the wall, gazing back toward the Osterran coast. "Isharans have captured Fulcor Island many times throughout history, and each time our brave fighters seized it back." Tendons stood out on Utho's neck as he struggled with his anger. "For decades, we have held this garrison at great cost in blood, and now the konag intends to hand it back, just to foster an unnecessary alliance. He knows how many Osterran lives they've already taken."

Mandan pointed westward, back toward home. "Look, you can still see some smoke in the sky from Mount Vada all the way out here." His brow furrowed. "What is really happening, Utho? What if my father's right? What if Ossus is awakening, and the wreths want to destroy the world? Shouldn't we all try to fight together? Maybe it is the only way."

Utho frowned. "There are things we can imagine, my prince, and there are things we *know*. We *know* that the Isharans are monsters. Do we ignore everything we know because an ancient story *might* come true?"

Uncomfortable, the young man went to the edge of the wall and stared down to where the reefs extended like protective claws around the island. He asked in a quiet, awed voice, "Is that where it happened? Where you walked out to sea at low tide, so you could launch fire arrows at the Isharan ships?"

Utho gestured down and to the left. "Over there. When the tide is out, the reef is exposed and a nimble man can jump from place to place, but it has to be timed perfectly."

Mandan's eyes shone with admiration, drew a deep breath, and spoke in a loud, confident voice that sounded almost like a leader's. "Utho of the Reef has returned to Fulcor Island. Let the Isharans beware."

77

ADAN and Penda spent the next days preparing for their uncertain trip into the desert with the wreths. Hom bustled about gathering their necessary items, sick with worry.

Adan's council was in an uproar over the idea that their king and queen would participate in a dangerous dragon hunt. The Banner guards demanded to go along as an armed escort, and although he couldn't deny the knot in his stomach, Adan tried to sound convincing. "We have to accept Queen Voo's guarantees of safety. The sandwreths are a great and terrible force, and we will show that we trust them."

Penda raised her eyebrows. "Do we trust them?"

Adan considered, and chose a pragmatic reply. "I think we'll be safe. If the sandwreths are trying to woo us into an alliance, it would be bad form for them to let us be killed, wouldn't it?"

As she packed for hard travel, choosing sturdy Utauk garments rather than frilly regal ones, Penda gave him a quirk of a smile. "*Cra*, it is interesting to be your wife, Starfall." She got out her leather pants, sturdy boots, and crimson and black silks. Seamstresses loosened them to accommodate her growing pregnancy.

After five days, Quo and the sandwreth escort arrived just after noon—golden-skinned warriors with hair the color of honey and bone, intertwined with bangles of beaten metal. Apart from one dour mage, the wreths carried short obsidian-tipped spears with slender spiraling shafts, and they rode sturdy augas. Two of the creatures had empty saddles, ready for their guests.

The wreth party remained outside the gate, which still bore the dark stain where the mindless beast had bashed itself to death. Adan and Penda were ready with their packs and traveling clothes. Xar rode on Penda's leather shoulder pad, as if looking for a way to cause trouble.

From his mount, Quo grinned down at the king. "Adan Starfall, I am glad you heeded my invitation."

"I thought it was Queen Voo's invitation," Adan said.

"My sister lets me speak for her." He pouted, then brightened. "You will both enjoy our dragon hunt."

Adan nodded. "It will be good to see, just in case Bannriya is one day plagued by dragons."

Quo turned to the wreth mage and the other warriors, chuckling. "I like this human king!"

The people of Bannriya crowded at the walls and gate to watch the departure, but their cheers sounded subdued. Adan turned back to wave reassuringly at them. "We're off on a fine adventure with our new friends. Penda and I are building our legacies. We will have great stories to tell when we return."

"Undoubtedly," Quo said and gestured to the two augas with empty saddles. "Let us be on our way."

Adan studied the strange low-slung saddle. He turned to help Penda, but she sprang onto the mount with an ease and grace that he would never be able to match. She sat astride her auga, ready to ride and waiting for him. Holding on to her shoulder, Xar flapped his wings and gave a buzz of approval.

Stepping up to the second auga, Adan managed to climb into the saddle without making a complete fool of himself. He took the reins, feeling the powerful creature shift its weight beneath him.

The wreth escort turned their augas around, and the beasts trotted off down the road, heading to the hills and the deserts beyond. Adan glanced back at Bannriya, then faced forward, trying to prepare for anything.

As they moved along, the augas raised a great deal of dust, and Adan soon realized that the brown haze was a sort of camouflage summoned by the wreths. Quo called out, "My sister is anxious, and that dragon will not wait for us." He cocked a thin smile. "Hold on. You should find this invigorating."

With a lurch, the augas sprinted off on their massive legs. Black tongues spilled out of their mouths, licking the air. Adan clutched the horn of the hard saddle and glanced over at Penda. A bright smile flashed across her face as her dark hair whipped behind her. Despite the tension, she seemed to revel in the freedom. Xar sprang into the air with a flash of green plumage and cruised overhead, following the mounted party over countless miles.

The wreths made little conversation, even with one another. The ominous mage in his leather robe spoke not a single word, though he did send frequent skeptical glances at the two human companions.

Quo gave the mage a dismissive frown and spoke to Adan loudly but conspiratorially. "I make no excuses for Axus. He is a sour sort."

"What have we done to make him resent us?" Penda asked.

"You were not born wreths. Many of our people are surprised that my dear sister places so much stock in humans. Axus considers it a bad precedent for our queen to honor you with this escort as if you were equals, since we created your race long ago."

The wreth mage rode grim-faced, staring ahead without replying.

Adan said, "He resents the escort? But Queen Voo asked us to join your dragon hunt. If you didn't provide a guide, how else would we get there?"

Quo sniffed. "She could have demanded that you come by any possible means."

The terrain grew more rugged as they left the foothills, crossed the mountains, and entered sheer canyons with strange rock formations at the edge of the expansive desert. Adan knew that some of the greatest battles in the ancient wars had taken place out here, and the signs were clear. Although humans had reclaimed much fertile land in the Commonwealth, parts of the world were still uninhabitable, especially down toward the Furnace. Over the years, some intrepid Suderrans had ventured out into the wasteland to mine crystals and agate, but they had not penetrated far. The sandwreths, however, had found a way to tame the worst of the desert for their own purposes.

The augas raced onward for three days. At night, the wreth camps were simply for rest, not for jovial gatherings as in the Utauk settlements. Adan and Penda kept each other company, trying to maintain a normal conversation though they were sore, tense, and tired. They would remove Xar's collar and view the stored images in the mothertear. From the ska's high perspective, the canyonlands were beautiful and harsh, a tangle of impassable arroyos, rocky washes, and misshapen boulders that had tumbled down from the mountains.

Xar ranged farther afield as they traveled, but when they entered the deeper desert, Quo glanced upward and chided, "There are dangerous thermals and flying predators here. You would do well to keep your pet close at hand."

Penda heeded the warning.

As they rode on into the fourth day, Adan was concerned with the harsher terrain ahead, but Quo dismissed his worries. "Be patient just a bit longer, Adan Starfall. Our destination is up in that widening canyon."

The augas expertly found their way along a wash that led into an expansive elbow of a canyon, where they found that Queen Voo had built an entire city as her camp. Nearly a hundred sandwreths and their augas had crowded into the area surrounded by red rock walls. The temporary settlement was fashioned out of the rocks and sand, which the wreths shaped like pliable clay into curved shelters.

As the augas strode into camp, more sandwreths came to meet them, nobles in fine clothes, wreth mages in leather robes, and contingents of wreth warriors in scaled armor. Queen Voo stepped forward to receive the guests, her long hair flowing, her scant leather armor revealing much of her golden skin. She wore coppery gossamer fabrics that swirled unnaturally, like heat shimmers in the air. Turning her hands up to the king and queen, she said, "I trust your trip was pleasant enough."

Penda swung herself out of the auga's saddle and dropped to the ground. "As pleasant as possible, considering the terrain."

Adan's legs were so stiff he had to steady himself against the sturdy creature to keep his feet after he dismounted.

"We built this fine encampment to welcome you, because we know humans are fragile," Voo said. "Our warriors are eager for the hunt. A great many years have passed since last they killed a dragon."

The queen led them into the heart of the bustling camp. Adan saw no fires, merely flat dark rocks that exuded heat for cooking. A flow of water gushed from the side of the cliff, an unnatural spring created by sandwreth mages who had summoned water from deep underground.

Voo said, "Accept and enjoy our accommodations."

"Will we stay here long?" Adan asked. "Before the hunt?"

She laughed. "Of course not! This is merely temporary, to welcome you. Once the dragon is sighted, we will range far and wide across the Furnace."

"So you've seen the dragon already?" Penda asked.

"Oh, yes. We have only to find it again . . . hunt it, and kill it."

Her brother grinned. "It will be excellent practice for the truly great battle that lies ahead."

78

AFTER returning to civilization with her new ska, Glik stayed in Shella din Orr's camp for several more days, reconnecting with her extended Utauk family. She gave herself some time to remember that she was part of these people, inside the circle, but before long she was anxious to be off again. She and her new ska were excited to learn more about each other on their own, to strengthen their intertwined lives and their heart link.

Glik followed a small caravan for a while through the Suderran hills, then grew impatient and set off at a faster pace on her own. Ari took wing, flying high and free, and in her heart Glik soared with the reptile bird, experienced the wind simultaneously through her hair and her feathers. With her new partner filling the hole in her heart, she felt whole again.

Nothing could replace her first ska, but nothing was like Ari either. The blue reptile bird put on a burst of speed, chasing after a panicked sparrow. Ari could have caught it, snapped the bird in her jaws, but for now she was just playing in the sky.

That night Glik made a solo camp in a birch grove by a chuckling stream. The young ska landed on a swaying twig nearby, watching her while preening and showing off her fine new collar from Shella din Orr. Ever since seeing that ominous shape lurking in a resinous cocoon in the mountain eyrie, Glik had been troubled with dire dreams that threatened to wake her in terror, yet trapped her in sleep.

After many years on her own, the girl knew how to deal with restless visions and demanding dreams. Her heart link with the ska could help, just as old Ori had both guided her visions and shielded her from them. The young blue ska hopped down from the unstable twig and took a comfortable position on Glik's shoulder as she sat cross-legged close to her small fire. She stared deeply into the hypnotic flames and beyond.

Sometimes, Glik could summon visions for herself, force them to appear behind her eyes. This process was new to Ari, though, and Glik had to teach her young ska and strengthen the heart link. They were partners in the visions. With one finger she traced the circle around her heart and readied herself to enter the trance.

"The beginning is the end is the beginning," she mumbled aloud and traced the circle again, round and round. "The beginning is the end is the beginning is the end is the beginning." She repeated it until it became a chant.

She felt the presence of the eager ska in her mind and heart. Around her through half-closed eyes, Glik saw circles in nature, stones that fell in an unnatural ring, birch leaves on the ground like a yellow crown, circular ripples in the stream's flow. They were all omens.

She went deeper to feel the thrumming call of the world, wispy threads of magic that remained even in the wounded land. Her mind drifted along and took flight again, but this time she and Ari were flying together alone in the sky. Soon they were joined by other reptile birds. The vision became sharper, the images intensifying.

"The beginning is the end is the beginning is the end is the beginning." Glik kept tracing heart circles, falling deeper into her trance. She closed her eyes to see her inner journey and imagined herself high above the ground, streaking along. Her body had long blue feathers and sapphire-scaled skin. She was a ska . . . among many skas, thousands of them. They flew together in the greatest flock she had ever imagined, creating an uproar of chirps and buzzes and clicks in the sky. Their musky odor communicated many subtleties.

The innumerable dream skas swooped and soared above a vast ancient battlefield. Looking down, Glik saw giant armies, countless fighters in exotic armor, pale warriors and bronze warriors, along with human troops that were being slaughtered. *Sandwreths and frostwreths.*

An enormous city loomed in the distance, larger than Bannriya and Fellstaff combined. Mages from both factions unleashed havoc with knots and twists of magic, summoning fiery geysers or sheets of ice that crashed into opposing troops. Ruthless wreth warriors cut one another to pieces until the plain was a carpet of blood. Sandwreth mages hammered the ground with invisible shock waves, but their faction was losing, and the bronze-skinned warriors fell back toward the enormous city.

In her vision, she and the clouds of skas observed from high above, safe from the fray. More and more reptile birds joined the flock, flying in tight formation as if they meant to assemble themselves into a mosaic, and Glik was part of that puzzle.

Inside the great city, sandwreth mages erected a huge framework made of gems and inset with magical lines, a horrendous weapon designed to slay the dragon Ossus. It would eradicate the enemy army as well—if the mages could control the blast.

Glik gasped as she realized where she was in the vision, what she was seeing. The battlefield below would become the Plain of Black Glass.

As soon as the thought came to her, an enormous flash of light roared out from the mages' device like rainbow tornadoes. The wash of uncontrolled magic crashed forward, disintegrating the armies that filled the plain—both wreth factions, and all of the humans.

Then the magic weapon broke loose from the control of the exhausted mages and spun, blasting its magic in vast arcs that engulfed the entire city, smashing it flat and turning the valley into a pool of melted glass.

Glik and the vision-skas flew higher to avoid the shock waves from the annihilation below. Ari's presence helped guide her escape.

But now Glik felt a force even more ominous, something huge and rumbling. The enormous flock streaked at impossible speed across the land and over towering mountains: the Dragonspine range. Beneath them, the world began to crack open. Mountains shifted and split, and great lines of fire rocketed upward as a vast presence stirred below.

Buried deep in her trance, Glik struggled to get away. She didn't want to see this. It could destroy her!

Ari kept pace inside her mind, refusing to let go. All of the skas in the great flock swooped down, picking up speed . . . flying straight toward the upheaval in the mountains—

With a harsh cry, Glik awoke next to the stream, shaking and sweating. On her shoulder, the reptile bird flapped her wings, nuzzled Glik's ear, clicked and burbled, as if in apology. The campfire had died down to dull orange embers.

"What did we see?" Glik asked in a hoarse voice. She pressed her palm against her chest, felt her heart beating, and traced one more circle, fearing that she had seen an end that would have no new beginning to follow.

❧

She made her way to Bannriya, needing to see her foster sister Penda, as well as Hale Orr. Inside the vast walled city, Glik gradually began to shake off the dread from her vision. She always enjoyed exploring the wilderness of streets, the back alleys. Ari fluttered into the air, then came back to rest on her shoulder, not yet used to the close buildings and noisy crowds.

The girl talked with the food vendors, musicians, potters, weavers, washerwomen. She didn't understand how anyone could be content staying in one home, seeing the same people and the same sights every day. She compared city dwellers to trees, with roots planted deep and growing tall, but stuck in the same place. Glik was more like a red fox, going wherever she liked.

Hoping to get a good meal in the castle kitchens, even if the staff made her wash up, Glik went to the lower side door. The thick-waisted head cook remembered her and teased, "Why, it's the dirty little girl!"

Glik followed the woman into the kitchens. "Proud to wear the dust of all the miles I've traveled." She inhaled the delicious smells of the ovens and cauldrons. "Here to visit my sister. Hope you won't make me dress in fancy clothes?"

"Ah, the queen's not here, child, but you can have a fine lunch with me." The cook rummaged around the kitchen, scrounging day-old bread and a bowl of the previous night's soup that still simmered in the bottom of the pot. Glik tore open a hard roll and fed pieces of crust to Ari, who gulped them down.

Taking a stool across from the girl, the head cook adjusted the white bonnet that held her gray-brown hair. Her face bore a troubled expression. "Queen Penda and King Adan left with those terrible creatures." She lowered her voice as if simply uttering the word would summon the ancient race. "The sandwreths!"

Glik's interest was piqued, and she also felt a flash of concern. "Captured? Taken as hostages?" Ari flapped her blue wings, sensing her partner's alarm. "I'll go rescue them!"

"Oh, dear, no, not that. They went with an escort party riding on those lizard things." The cook's eyes went as wide as saucers. "Queen Voo invited them on *a dragon hunt.*"

"Dragon hunt? *Cra!*" Glik almost choked on her bread, remembering her dreams of scales and dark angular wings. "Not possible." She recalled what Shella din Orr had said. "Way too rare."

"The sandwreths think they know where to find one. They wanted our king and queen to witness it. Quite something to put in a legacy, I should say . . . but not for me!" The cook looked very worried.

The reptile bird burbled and buzzed until Glik gave her the rest of the hard bread, which she happily crunched and swallowed.

The girl made up her mind. "Ought to witness it, too, I guess. You know which way and when?"

"They left a few days ago. Who can say how long a dragon hunt is supposed to take? They headed for the outer desert, toward the Furnace."

"Sounds like enough time to catch up with them." Glik wolfed down her soup.

"Xar went with the king and queen, if that's any help," the cook said. "Maybe your ska can follow."

"Maybe. Come on, Ari," Glik said. Through their heart link, she made sure the ska knew Penda and could find her even out in the great open desert.

79

As King Kollanan's new Brava, Elliel devoted herself to protecting not only him, but also his kingdom. She was bonded to a deserving master and his people, so she set about learning the politics of Norterra, their allies, their history. It was all part of her now.

This job was fundamentally different from the oppressive service she had given to Lord Cade, who—secure in his political power—had drugged her, assaulted her, and cost Elliel her very identity as a Brava. He was far away on the other side of the Commonwealth, considering himself safe. For now.

Then there was Utho.

She walled those thoughts away. Elliel had bonded herself to King Kollanan the Hammer, and his kingdom was being threatened by the frostwreths. She had a higher responsibility than personal retribution.

Kollanan had already sent a warning letter by Utauk courier off to Convera Castle, detailing the secret operations Lord Cade kept up in his county and explaining exactly what Utho had done to her. The news would likely cause quite an uproar once the konag learned of it. Elliel would also need to address the matter herself, at some point, but Thon had taught her patience. . . .

For the time being, she struggled to meld the new person she had become with the person she had been in the past. Her brain was packed full of details, like a remembrance shrine with countless volumes waiting to be read, and she hadn't had time to review her own life. She had two different legacies for the same life.

Now that she had returned to formal service, Elliel wanted to look like a true Brava. The king provided her with leather armor, boots, and finemail, as well as traditional weapons to supplement her exotic ramer. When Kollanan looked at her, he gave a nod of appreciation and respect. "Lasis would have approved of you." She considered it a compliment.

When his eight vassal lords arrived for the next urgent meeting, Elliel was beside Kollanan, confident and intimidating. This was the first time the other nobles had seen the king's new Brava, and she did her best to make an impression. He introduced her to each of the lords, and she memorized the names, the faces: Alcock, Teo, Vitor, Bahlen, Cerus, Ogno, Iber, and Oren. Through keen observation, she learned their personalities, assessing which nobles were loyal and cooperative, which were isolated, and which might be resentful of their king's commands. It was so much to drink in.

During the meeting, Elliel stood behind Kollanan's chair, like a guardian. He looked around the table at the eight lords. "I've made my decision. We will strike the frostwreths, make them sting. I hope that will be enough of a warning for them to leave us alone."

"I understand your anger, Sire," Lord Alcock cautioned. Elliel decided that he served as a frequent voice of reason. "I feel the heat of revenge, too. What happened at Lake Bakal could have happened to any of our towns, and I grieve for your daughter, your grandsons, all those people. But we are mere humans with traditional weapons against such a terrible enemy."

Koll pounded his fist on the table. "I refuse to accept that we are *mere* humans. We are survivors! We rebuilt the world after the ancient race wrecked it, and we will not be considered irrelevant. We have to fight. We have to do *something*!"

Lord Teo gestured to Elliel and the three other bonded Bravas who had accompanied their vassal lords. "They have their ramers, but even that magic must be insignificant compared to the wreths. You lost Lasis to them, did you not?"

Kollanan's brows drew together and he looked down at his hands. "That remains to be proven, but I assume so, alas."

Elliel's hand strayed to the band at her side. The wounds on her wrist had healed, but she felt the tingle in her skin, the burning in her blood. She longed to use the weapon again, against an appropriate enemy. This was a pure weapon, a Brava weapon, and she knew now that she had never misused it, never actually killed children. What Utho had said was a lie. . . .

Kollanan squared his shoulders and sighed. "I am not suggesting we launch an outright war against the frostwreths, though it may come to that.

We just need to sting them like a wasp, make them realize there'll be consequences if they don't leave us in peace. We don't want anything to do with their ancient vendetta, or their dragon, whether or not it exists."

"I would happily smash them all," said Lord Ogno, a square-built man with a blocky face and hands as hard as rocks. "But if you do this, they will smash us back. Are you ready for that? Will our armies be enough?"

Queen Tafira sat beside the king, intent on the war council. She drew two long daggers, one in each hand, and slammed them point-first into the table. "My husband has convinced me. If we can't find a way to make the wreths respect us, then we might as well all just surrender ourselves to be their slaves. Is that what you want? If so, then we'll assign more appropriate nobles to run your counties."

Elliel watched their expressions, listened to their muttered words. No one volunteered.

"Even if it brings down retribution on us, we must assert our humanity," Kollanan said in a lower voice. "Or we won't have any left."

Thon quietly entered the chamber. His dark hair flowed down past his shoulders, his silver leggings shone, his chest armor was burnished. Seeing him, the eight lords muttered uneasily, although Elliel was glad of his presence. "Perhaps I can offer suggestions?"

"Or perhaps you're a spy," snapped Lord Teo. "How would we know?"

"There are many things we do not know," Thon said in a level tone. "But rather than be afraid, I am trying to understand, as should you all."

Lord Cerus grumbled and reached for a knife at his side. Lord Bahlen, accompanied by his own bonded Brava, a young man named Urok, gripped the table in front of him. They had all heard about the wreth stranger, but most were seeing Thon for the first time.

King Kollanan said, "I have accepted this man among us. I admit there's a risk, but there is great potential benefit if he can truly use wreth magic. I'm willing to hear all ideas."

"I will share some possibilities." Thon locked his gaze with Elliel's, then with a placid expression scanned the others around the table. "But I may need your help to refine them."

Once welcomed into Fellstaff Castle, Shadri immersed herself in the records in Kollanan's private library and also absorbed the information in the city's remembrance shrine. One of the legaciers even wrote a frustrated note to the king, complaining that the young woman asked too many questions. Kollanan wrote a brusque reply: "No one can ask too many questions. Answer them."

Pokle spent a lot of time with Shadri, though he seemed too shy to speak much. She took it upon herself to educate him, delighted to have an attentive audience, even if it was hard to tell whether the gawky young man was interested in the actual subject matter. She was happy to talk about whatever facts happened to tumble out of her head.

Shadri followed him around in his duties about the castle, enlightening him on a variety of subjects. Pokle rarely made comments, and certainly offered no debate, but he made frequent enough acknowledgments that she knew she had his complete attention.

Once, while she was describing different types of migratory birds and the formations they flew, a distracted Pokle burned his hand by picking up a hot rack from a fireplace. At his yelp of pain, she immediately stopped her monologue and stared at the angry red line across his hand. Blisters were already forming.

Remembering what Dr. Severn had taught her in Thule's Orchard, Shadri grabbed him by his wrist. "Come with me. I know just what to do. I can treat this." Flushed with the pain, Pokle stumbled after her as she marched him down the stairs to the kitchen, where she demanded honey, lard, and specific spices that Tafira kept in the pantry. The kitchen staff stared at the girl, but got out of her way. "I studied with a battlefield surgeon," she explained. "I know how to be a doctor—at least a little."

While pokle soaked his burn in cold water to ease the throbbing, Shadri mixed up a salve that she slathered on his palm, while one of the cooks boiled a strip of rags to be used as a bandage. Pokle looked greatly relieved as the salve eased the burning sensation. He looked at her with wide, appreciative eyes. "You must be a magic healer." Her attentions seemed to be a better pain reliever than the salve itself.

Shadri deftly wrapped the bandage around his hand. "Nothing magic about it. Just knowledge. I spent many hours dissecting the dead body of a hanged thief, so I could learn." She didn't notice how the boy's expression turned squeamish. "Now, I'm applying my knowledge."

∽

Elliel held her long cinnamon hair in one hand, hesitating but knowing what she had to do. She had not cut the rich tresses since she'd awakened without a legacy, without memories, and with a letter full of lies in her pocket. Now she took a sharp knife and slashed the hair short around her head. It was a symbolic gesture, a change, but she felt she needed to do it. Now, when she looked in her reflection, Elliel saw a different woman from the one Cade had raped, and a different one from the woman who had wandered the land without a memory. *This* was who she was.

Her muscles and reflexes had always remembered what she was, and now she began to train again with knives and swords, as well as in hand-to-hand combat. Thon was an excellent fighter, and the two sparred in the castle courtyard. They clashed, counterattacked, and threw each other to the ground in rough, exhilarating moves, until they both gasped with exhaustion.

Elliel gradually recalled times in her past when she'd been called upon to fight. The details came back in clusters. One time in a dark alley—she couldn't remember the name of the town—she had fought three would-be robbers who meant to kill the merchant to whom she was bound. Elliel had only been sixteen but fully skilled, trained throughout her childhood in a Brava settlement. One of the thugs carried a torch, the other two had knives. The whip-fast young woman yelled for the merchant to run for his life, and he scrambled away in panic, bleating like a shoat. Elliel threw herself upon the three attackers. She slashed one man's throat with the first strike, kicked, punched, and stabbed the second thug. But the third man jammed his blazing torch into her arm, smearing some of the pitch on her sleeve. Her jerkin had caught fire, but she killed the third robber before she took the time to extinguish her own burning skin. That was where the waxy burn scar on her arm had come from. Now she remembered.

Later, she returned to their quarters where Thon was waiting for her. These chambers had belonged to Lasis, and Elliel could feel the presence of the lost Brava here. Though Kollanan's first bonded Brava had been at Fellstaff for many years, the chambers were austere. A banner of Norterra on one stone wall was the only decoration. The room had a washbasin, a wardrobe, and a bed big enough for a large man but pleasantly cozy for Elliel and Thon to hold each other.

When she entered the room now, the wreth man smiled at her in wonder. Coming closer, he ran his fingers through her close-cropped hair. "This is a surprise. You still look beautiful, but it is another you. I so loved it when your hair would fall around me like a flood of fire."

"You'll have to put up with me this way. I like it better for fighting."

"I believe I have already adapted." He laughed and kissed her.

She reached around the back of his head with both hands and stroked the long dark locks that felt like unraveled silk threads. "But please don't cut your lovely hair."

"We should enjoy each other as we are." He helped her undress.

Joy and energy filled her as she responded to his touch. A jolt of sickening pain flashed through her mind as she remembered what Lord Cade had done to her, but she shoved the thought away. No, Thon was her first and only lover.

He feathered kisses on her skin. Elliel groaned and ran her hands over him, trying not to remember Cade at all. That was one memory she wished she could erase. Thon touched the curved red welt on her stomach, evidence of the deep wound that had healed, but left its irrevocable scar.

Elliel gasped as that memory surged to the front of her mind—Almeda lunging out of the shadows at her, howling in jealous rage, stabbing and slashing with her long knife . . . willing to murder someone just to keep a man she had never cared about anyway, a man who had drugged and raped Elliel and treated her as his property.

She shuddered, and Thon held her now and loved her. She crushed him against her. They lay in warm silence, and he just watched her with his sapphire eyes. Gradually, Elliel focused not on her disgraced past but on the fact that she was a Brava bonded to King Kollanan. *That* was who she was now, and she was sworn to defend against the terrible wreths. She had to protect a kingdom now.

"Fight for us, Thon," she whispered in his ear. "King Kollanan and the people of Norterra need you for this. I need you."

"You already have me," he said.

"The others don't trust you. They fear the frostwreths, and when they see you, they see only an enemy. But for this attack King Kollanan is determined to launch on Lake Bakal, you have magic more powerful than any weapon they can use."

"You have great faith in me. You saw me use my magic in the mine tunnels and to help Scrabbleton." He smiled, showing his even teeth. "Though I cannot remember my life, I know in my bones that I will fight to do what is right. You helped me to believe it." He held her close again. "Yes, I have something to offer the raid. I can use what I have within me."

When he traced a fingertip over the long, angry scar on her stomach, she no longer felt the burn of past pain.

The next morning a patchwork man dressed in tattered furs and rags arrived at the Fellstaff city gate from the north. Barely more than a walking skeleton, he was so emaciated, scabbed, and encrusted with dirt that no one recognized him. At first the sentries thought he was a beggar, but finally someone noticed by his features that he was a Brava.

Lasis.

King Kollanan rushed down to the lower city, because the Brava was so weak the guards were afraid to move him. Doctors got there first. They gave him water and washed away some of the dried blood and grime, trying to assess his injuries.

When Koll finally arrived, he was both distraught and overjoyed to see his friend. "Lasis! We thought we would never see you again." He knelt beside the Brava. "Can you speak? What happened?" He bent close to listen.

Lasis opened his eyes, reached a hand toward Kollanan, and spoke in a raspy whisper through cracked lips. "The frostwreths . . . Birch, your grandson . . . is alive."

80

Fulcor Island rose from the choppy water like a sharp gray tooth. As the Isharan warships approached, Iluris studied the rugged cliffs and remembered the long, unpleasant history that shrouded this place.

Next to her, Cemi gazed ahead into the brisk, salty breezes, not impressed. "It's ugly. Why would anyone fight over that?"

Iluris had wondered the same thing herself. "Why indeed?"

Per the terms in the konag's invitation letter, three Isharan warships had departed from Serepol Harbor on the appropriate date, their distinctive red-and-white striped sails billowing in the wind. The empra had handpicked fifteen of her adopted hawk guards, led by Captani Vos, along with a full contingent of standard Isharan soldiers.

Iluris had left Chamberlain Nerev behind to continue winnowing his lists of candidates as her successor, but Priestlord Klovus insisted on accompanying the mission. He urged her to let him secretly bring a minor godling in the cargo hold, in case the enemy meant to betray them, but she adamantly refused. "That would be tantamount to declaring war—a war you already provoked when you took a godling to their coast."

Klovus sniffed. "How else will they fear us, Excellency? The godless need to be reminded of the power we represent."

"I will remind them myself, with my own words. But first I agreed to hear what the konag has to say."

As they sailed across the water, Iluris taught Cemi about Fulcor Island, how possession of the rock had changed hands over the centuries. In one instance, the enemy garrison had surrendered quickly in a relatively bloodless transition, which then lulled the reigning emprir into complacency, and the Commonwealth had seized back the island within five years. Another time, the Commonwealth defenders refused to stand down after a long naval siege and were slaughtered to the last person.

"We almost took the island back in the last war," she mused. "Our navy blockaded Fulcor and cut off their supplies to starve them out. Our ships were anchored at a safe distance, but a lone man somehow made his way out on the water and got close enough to set our ships on fire. We lost that siege, and the Commonwealth has held the island ever since."

Cemi looked skeptical. "And you believe Konag Conndur will give it back just because he wants to be friends with us? That sounds like quite a desperate bargain to make." Her lips tightened in a pinched expression. "I wouldn't do it, if it were me."

Iluris had thought of that many times. "He must be serious. He wants our help in fighting the wreth armies. At the very least, he wants to ensure that hostilities cease between our two lands, so he can concentrate on his other war without worrying about an attack from us." She shook her head, and the winds ruffled her loose head scarf. "I need to hear this for myself, to see if he can convince me. Personally, I would not be disappointed for an excuse to end the raids on both sides. I see no advantage to it."

As they approached the island, Priestlord Klovus emerged from his cabin and hurried across the deck, casting a troubled glance at the stark island. "I advise you never to let your guard down, Excellency, even if you think you can trust the konag."

"I didn't say I trusted him, Priestlord. I said I would listen to him."

He still grumbled. "It's an obvious trap."

"It is so obvious, in fact, that I am dubious it will turn out to *be* a trap after all. I want to know what he's really up to."

Cemi spoke up. "What if the konag and the Utauk trader are telling the truth? What if the wreths did return to start their war again? What if they really do intend to wake the dragon?"

Klovus snorted. "Then let the wreths finish the job they started two thousand years ago and wipe out the dying old world. We're perfectly safe in Ishara."

"We are all part of the human race, Priestlord, and we were all created and enslaved by the wreths," Iluris said. "They did do our ancestors great harm, long ago. Is there no circumstance under which we should stand together?"

"The godless are not the same sort of humans as we are. They have no magic, no protectors, but we have our godlings. We are superior."

"Hear us, save us," Iluris said with only a hint of sarcasm. "Then we are honor bound to help those less fortunate than we. Isn't that what the priests say?"

Klovus grumbled. "If we regained control of Fulcor Island, we could at least claim a victory, but I don't expect the konag to release it anytime soon, no matter what he promises."

The third Isharan ship anchored far out at the edge of the reefs, while the other two vessels continued to the island, as agreed. Guided on a careful course by the nervous captain, the flagship approached the sheltered cove that served as Fulcor's defensible harbor. Staring up at the imposing stone cliffs, Iluris felt a chill. The place reeked of threat and danger. Priestlord Klovus had good reason to be suspicious.

A Commonwealth warship was tied up to the main dock inside the narrow harbor, but the Isharan captain decided—with the empra's permission—just to drop anchor outside the cove, where there was no chance they would be trapped. "From here, we will take landing boats up to the dock, Excellency."

Captani Vos rallied the hawk guards to serve as the empra's escort. The Isharans tied their striped sails and dropped anchors, one on each side of the ship.

Iluris waited with Cemi, resting a gentle hand on her ward's shoulder as they watched Commonwealth soldiers gather on the battlements high above. The empra said, "Cemi and I will board the first landing boat, along with Captani Vos and my hawk guards. The second landing boat will carry Key Priestlord Klovus and a contingent of Isharan soldiers."

"Yes, Mother," said Vos.

Trying to dispel her uneasiness, the empra went to the landing boats. As they were lowered into the water, she dared to hope, but remained wary. Waves washed against the rocks, and seabirds shrieked overhead.

Empra Iluris prepared to meet her mortal enemies.

81

AFTER the konag's hopeful mission departed for Fulcor Island, Hale Orr was done with his responsibilities in Convera. He just wanted to head back home to Bannriya to be with his people, with his daughter and her husband, to help defend Suderra. Most importantly, under no circumstances did he intend to miss the birth of his first grandchild, other world-shaking crises be damned!

He'd left the gathering of Utauk tribes more than a month ago, crossing the land to Windy Head, sailing to Ishara and back, and now riding back to Bannriya. When Hale was younger, such travel would have been a grand adventure, but now he looked forward to his comfortable quarters in the castle. Not only did he feel old, he also felt *done*. Sensing tension in the air and smelling the smoke from the distant eruption, however, he knew that the dark times were a long way from being over.

He rode inland, alone, and within three days encountered an Utauk caravan moving in the general direction of Suderra. The caravan leader, a salty heavyset woman named Rondi, recognized his colors and missing hand, and broke into a broad grin. Her bent front tooth gave her a rakish appearance. "*Cra,* I know you, Hale Orr! Any grandson of Shella din Orr is welcome among us."

"You must have a lot of welcome people, then, since she has many grandsons." Hale swung down from his horse and gave Rondi a formal embrace, lowering his voice to a conspiratorial whisper. "But I'm one of her favorites."

"That's what hundreds of them say!"

The caravan consisted of ten pack horses, three ponies, and a mule, along with forty people: Rondi's grown children, her brothers, and their children. He rode along with them, and they traveled throughout the day. That night the caravan stopped on an open prairie, and the people set up camp with a handful of tents and three main cookfires. The animals were tied where they could graze.

Rondi invited Hale inside the main tent for a bowl of barley-and-vegetable stew. She was joined by two older men, both of whom needed a shave, one with a potbelly, the other with an eye patch. Rondi introduced the potbellied man as her husband and the one-eyed man as her lover. Hale was surprised that the husband took no offense when Rondi flaunted her infidelity. Seeing his dubious expression, the man said in teasing tone, "*Cra*, no one man can stand her for very long. We need to take turns to give each other a rest."

Rondi made a rude noise. "No one man can satisfy a woman like me."

The lover said, "It's a little of both. At least I can send her back to her husband if I get bored and want to find a lustier young woman."

She snorted again. "Have I bored you yet?"

The man with the eye patch lounged on the ground, cradling the bowl of stew on his stomach. "It's only been seven years. As long as you still have a few tricks, I'll stay."

The husband rolled his eyes.

Hale was unnerved by the enticing look Rondi gave him, but he remained polite, recalling the last time he'd been with his own wife, Alanna. It seemed so very long ago—Penda had been only eleven. Even then, Hale had grand plans for his beautiful daughter, although Alanna wanted him to be more realistic, expecting that Penda would marry an influential tribe member, maybe even run off with some boy she fell in love with.

Hale's wife was particularly good with their pack animals, tending them, training them, rounding them up each night as the tribe made camp. When one of their pregnant mares had a difficult time birthing, Alanna spent the night under a tarp tending the animal as a cold downpour splashed all around her. At long last, she helped the horse bring forth a spindly-legged foal . . . but afterward, Alanna caught a fever that raged for days. She coughed until it sounded as if her lungs would fly out of her mouth. Alanna died with Hale holding her shoulders and young Penda kneeling beside the camp bed.

Since then, it had been just him and his daughter. He had taken no women after Alanna, despite having many subtle—and some blatant—offers. Although his self-image was still of a young and dashing adventurer, Hale knew that he shouldn't be so picky. During normal peaceful times, he might have changed his mind, but these were not normal times. And so he slept alone.

Hale remained with the caravan for three days as they traveled the main road south and west across Osterra. When they reached the dwindling southern end of the Dragonspine range, they encountered the periphery of devastation from the eruption. Smoke still hung in the air from forest fires that burned in the ridges to the north, and settling gray ash dusted the pines like snow.

The caravan camped outside a village near an area of sulfurous steam vents. The town had been descriptively, and accurately, named Foul Stench, because of the active exhalations. The bubbling hot springs were even more active since the restlessness beneath Mount Vada, but despite the dangerous changes, the townspeople stayed. If Ossus did crack through the mountains and emerge into the world, they would all die in their homes.

As Hale tried to sleep in camp, he felt the ground tremble. He spread his palm against the dirt and sensed some *presence* far below, stirring. . . .

Next morning, he got up at dawn and drank his morning tea, but the water from Foul Stench had a bitter, soapy taste. Hoping he could find clear streams farther on, he bade the caravan leader farewell, ready to head off at a faster pace on his own.

Rondi smiled with her crooked-toothed grin. "If you stayed with us, I'd make you feel more welcome."

But Hale mounted his horse and took the reins. "Another time, maybe. See that my information gets spread among the Utauks. We need our network now more than ever. So much happening in the world." After drawing a circle in the air, he galloped off.

He pushed the horse hard, covering many miles, until he realized that he would never get home if he wore out his mount. At a slower, steady pace, he traveled for days across the fertile counties of Suderra, always with an eye toward Bannriya.

When at last he reached the open eastern gate in the sandstone walls, he rode in like any other traveler, drawing no attention to himself. This city had been his home for two years, and he'd been well familiar with it even before his daughter married Adan Starfall. He had visited Bannriya during the reign of King Syrus and the later uncomfortable time under the regents. Those had not been good years for trade or travel. Times had improved much under young King Adan, but now all that might change again.

One of the Banner guards recognized him, and Hale gave a tired wave.

"*Cra,* I'm back from my long journeys. I'll ride directly up to the castle. I have a lot to discuss with my daughter and the king."

"I'm afraid they're not here, sir. They've been gone these past several days."

"Gone? Where would they go?" Hale wondered if the Utauk tribes had summoned them again, if Shella din Orr had some new information to impart.

"The sandwreths came, sir. Took King Adan and Queen Penda into the desert on a dragon hunt."

"A dragon hunt? Ancestors' blood! A dragon has been seen?" Hale urged the weary horse to greater speed toward the castle, where he received the same report from two ministers and the household staff.

After such a long journey, Hale had looked forward to relaxing in his quarters. Since Adan and Penda were already gone, he took his time, bathed and rested, ate a large hot meal, which was quite different from the camp dinners he had made for himself. But that night as he slept under quilted blankets and slick sheets, in the room that he had decorated to look like a tent, he realized that the amenities in a big castle did not comfort him after all. No, he was an Utauk down to his bones.

After staying only one day in the city, Hale headed off again into the hills. He hoped to find an encampment where he could spend long hours talking with other Utauks, exchanging news. To share and be shared.

The world never ceased to surprise him. A dragon hunt! And Adan and Penda had gone willingly with the sandwreths, though he doubted they'd had any choice.

Hale followed the blue poppies, which would eventually take him to one of the large camps. The future depended not only on the Utauk information network, but on the konag's bold offer of an alliance with the Isharans. Humans would have to stand together against the wreths.

But if Ossus awoke, he knew that the Utauk luck would finally run out.

82

ON Fulcor Island, Priestlord Klovus was among the godless in a place as bleak as their beliefs. The tired old Commonwealth had too little magic left in their land, and the people had too little faith in their hearts. They were incapable of creating godlings to protect them. They were flawed, inferior.

In Ishara, though, Klovus always experienced the warm strength and benevolent power of the entities that watched over them. He understood the temples, knew that the people unwittingly used the land's intrinsic magic to manifest their guardians.

Now that he was far from Ishara, though, inside the austere stone walls of the Fulcor garrison, he felt naked and alone. Unsafe. Adrift and abandoned. Was this how the godless felt all the time?

Under his breath, he cursed Empra Iluris for refusing to let them bring even a minor godling. Now they had only swords and armor to protect against Konag Conndur's schemes. Klovus knew he would be safe, personally, since he had hidden four Black Eels among the common Isharan soldiers. But what of Ishara itself? Treachery would be bad enough, but an honest overture of peace and complacency might be even worse for the people and the godlings. In comfortable, prosperous times, the Isharans no longer felt so dependent on their deities. Therefore, people had little reason to sacrifice to them, or even *believe* in them, which would only weaken the entities.

As key priestlord, he feared that gullible Empra Iluris might pose a danger as great as the Commonwealth. Even before she agreed to meet with the konag about his absurd proposal, she had done much to weaken the godlings back home, touting her reign of peace while stalling further construction on the Magnifica temple. Why did she fear the benevolent deities? Or was she more afraid of the priestlords having too much power? Would she sell out her land and people just to put him in his place?

When Iluris and her hawk guards had stepped from their landing boats onto the dock, Klovus expected a flash of swords and a spray of blood. The godless soldiers could easily overwhelm that first group. Iluris was so naïve, so trusting.

And yet, the Commonwealth guards treated the empra with respect and led her entourage up the steep cliffside stairs to enter the looming garrison above.

When the second landing boat docked, Klovus disembarked, stared up at the cliffs, then set off at a brisk pace to catch up with the empra's party. By the time he was halfway up the exposed steps, he was red-faced with the effort.

Passing through the cleft in the cliff, which could well have hidden a deadly ambush, he climbed into the walled enclosure that encircled the top of the island. Fulcor had stood as a bastion for many centuries, but history was unclear as to who had actually built these ancient, sturdy defenses. Some said the island had been settled as a stopping point when the original Isharan settlers left the old world in search of new shores, without knowing where they were going. Though barren and unwelcoming, Fulcor was the only foothold of dry land in the expansive ocean. After pausing there, those pilgrims had set off again, dreaming eastward into unexplored waters, hoping for green shores, and they had discovered an entire virgin continent. At some point, this island stopping point had become contested territory, and a handful of defenders had turned it into a fortress. Eventually, the Isharan pioneers lost possession of the island to the barbarians from the old world, then the Isharans took it back . . . and lost it again. Over and over.

Now, for some unfathomable reason, Konag Conndur had offered to return Fulcor to the Isharans if they agreed to some incomprehensible alliance. What could the man possibly be up to? "Hear us, save us," Klovus muttered, though he was too far away for any godling to hear him.

The wide walls had evenly spaced lookout posts, from which garrison soldiers could watch the ocean for approaching warships. The enclosed area held a parade ground, two sets of barracks, an armory, a mess and recreation hall. The most imposing building was the main keep, a blocky, two-story structure that rose even higher than the defensive walls. Every roof held a cistern to catch water from the frequent rainstorms. Trees and shrubs added a splash of green, along with small garden patches the soldiers had planted.

Klovus caught up with Empra Iluris and her party just as they were being received by the garrison troops and the konag's party. The priest-lord looked around at the uniformed Isharan guards around them, and even he couldn't tell which of the soldiers were his Black Eels, because their camouflage was so complete. He lifted his chin as he marched forward in his blue caftan, making sure everyone could see that, other than perhaps the empra, no one was more important.

With each additional load of Isharan soldiers that entered the garrison, Klovus felt slightly safer. Dour Watchman Osler met the arriving groups with a flat welcome—insincere words delivered in a grim and brittle voice.

The empra and her important guests were given quarters in the northern wing of the main keep, separated by a great hall from the southern wing, which held Konag Conndur and his entourage. Klovus found his quarters unremarkable, chill and prisonlike, but he doubted he could improve them even if he made complaints.

Under normal circumstances, the diplomatic parties would have rested and settled for a day or more before beginning their business. Fortunately, this was not a social meeting, and Konag Conndur wanted to begin discussions right away. For his own part, Klovus was anxious to have the ordeal over with. He wanted to know what they were up to.

The workmanlike garrison kitchens produced basic food for the soldiers stationed there, but bean soup was not adequate for such esteemed guests. Thus, the Commonwealth ships had brought a fresh side of beef as well as some caged game birds that were killed and roasted for the welcoming dinner.

The banquet table was a long, squared-off horseshoe. Konag Conndur and Empra Iluris had the two most prominent seats at the cross table, while the Isharans sat at one leg and the Commonwealth representatives at the other. The empra's hawk guards stood along the wall, alert and staring at their counterparts across the room.

Three black-garbed Bravas stood at attention, ready for violence. Klovus knew that most of the half-breed Bravas had been wiped out along with their invasive colony on the Isharan shores hundreds of years ago, although he remembered seeing two Bravas fighting the godling with fiery ramers during the Mirrabay raid. Perhaps the half-breeds were more prevalent than he thought. He studied the one called Utho, the konag's personal Brava, sensing that he was a man to be feared. Utho's face was studiously expressionless, but Klovus sensed a smoldering tension about the black-garbed man.

Directly across from Klovus, a troubled-looking Prince Mandan picked at his meal. The future leader of the Commonwealth did not impress the priestlord. Conndur, on the other hand, seemed a formidable rival, determined, strengthened by the weight of many decisions.

With so many uncertainties looming in the air, the brief, innocuous conversation could not last long, and finally Iluris slid aside her plate and turned to the konag. "It serves no purpose to avoid the question foremost in our minds. Why did you bring us here, Konag Conndur? Although your message and your representative explained some things, I cannot fathom what is on your mind."

Conndur nodded slowly and gave her an uncertain smile. "You want to know what could possibly be so important that I would anger my people by asking you here for open talks? Why I would let myself be called a madman by my closest advisors? Why I would offer to give up this strategic island, just to show my sincerity in wanting an alliance?"

"Precisely," Iluris said. "The Utauk merchant captain told preposterous stories about wreth armies and restless dragons. Don't ask us to believe such fancies. Why did you really bring us here?"

Despite a stir of mutters among the Commonwealth representatives, Conndur kept his eyes fixed on her. "That *is* the truth, Empra. I called you here because of the wreths and a dragon."

Klovus rolled his eyes as the konag told of sandwreths emerging from the deserts with news of a coming war. He talked about frostwreths sweeping down from the north swallowing villages whole and building great ice fortresses. Then he described the shaking ground and explosions of fire from the mountain range under which Ossus was supposedly buried.

Iluris sipped her goblet of wine. "Well, peace is always worth considering, whether or not the situation includes dragons or ancient races. Ever since your grieving Konag Cronin withdrew the great fleet and ended the war thirty years ago, our two lands have been at an uneasy standoff."

"But not a complete truce," Conndur said. "We both remember that war, Empra. Younger ones might dream of the glories of battle, but you and I know better, do we not?"

A look of understanding passed between them, which made Klovus uneasy. With calm pride, Iluris said, "Since that time, I've maintained prosperity, and the Isharan people have thrived. Why would you make an overture now? What has changed? Many told me to beware of a trick, but . . . I would be a laughingstock if I ran home sounding an alarm about dragons and wreths."

"I've seen the proof with my own eyes," Conndur said. "That is why I feel such urgency to change our relationship, to cement a peace before it is too late for the world."

"That is exactly what the Utauk trader said." Iluris steepled her fingers. "While some of my people might be skeptical of you, Konag, I can't conceive of a reason why the neutral merchant captain would lie. Or for that matter, why you would make up such a preposterous story when you could have come to us with a far more traditional overture. How would it serve your ends—unless you were telling the truth?" She seemed to be convincing herself to take the risk. Priestlord Klovus wanted to shout at her not to listen as she continued. "Even if your stories are true, however, we live an ocean away in Ishara. Our land is safe. Why should we care about an ancient army ravaging your outlying kingdoms?"

The konag answered clearly, "Because if the wreths devastate the Commonwealth and succeed in waking the dragon, it will rip apart both the old world and the new. The god Kur will return, rescue his chosen wreths, and then erase the rest of his creation. The human race will be beneath his notice. We'll all be dead, Empra."

"*Only if* the legend is true," Utho interjected, his voice sour.

The konag cast a scolding glance at his Brava. "We can't deny that *something* happened in the Dragonspine Mountains. We can't deny that the frostwreths attacked Norterra. We can't deny that the sandwreths came to Suderra with their own dire warnings. It all fits the legend. We would be fools to ignore it."

Klovus bit his tongue. How could an intelligent leader believe such nonsense? He spoke to Iluris, knowing everyone else could hear him. "Excellency, if the konag's own Brava doesn't believe him, this must surely be an imaginary threat."

Utho turned surprising vitriol directly on the priestlord. "Who are *you* to scoff at *imaginary* threats? Don't your people worship their own *imaginary* gods and imbue them with powers? Even imaginary beings can be dangerous." His dark eyes narrowed.

Klovus bridled. Angry mutters rippled along both sides of the table, and the konag and the empra raised their hands at the same time to quell the conversation. Iluris smiled as an idea occurred to her. "Ah, now I think I see! You want to enlist our godlings to help in the fight against this terrible enemy? If the legends are true, that might be your only hope against the wreths and a dragon."

Conndur's plain surprise showed that he meant to suggest no such thing. Next to the konag, Utho growled. "You will not bring your abominations to our shores!"

Conndur cut him off. "Not yet, Empra, but if the situation continues to worsen, we'll have to consider many unorthodox strategies. As a first step, though, I am only proposing a cessation of hostilities between our peoples. We would all benefit. After that, maybe we can form an alliance against the wreths if they launch their war to end all things."

At the far end of the table, Watchman Osler banged his cup down. The grizzled old man had served himself three goblets of wine, and his voice was faintly slurred. "Ha! An alliance would be easy enough if Empra Iluris married Konag Conndur! They're both widowed. If they simply did battle in bed, there'd be far less bloodshed, and many of my soldiers could go home from this bleak rock."

Indignant gasps rolled around the room. It was difficult to tell who was most insulted. Though surprised, Conndur chuckled. "Our marriage wouldn't solve anything. Prince Mandan is my appointed heir."

"I haven't formally selected a successor yet," Iluris said, though her eyes darted toward Cemi.

Appalled by the suggestion, Klovus let out a sneering laugh. "Our empra would never marry a godless king! She's been offered many potential husbands and turned them all down." He didn't mention that he himself had been one of them. "She would never accept someone like you."

Iluris made a dismissive gesture. "Don't be so dramatic, Klovus. These are merely preliminary discussions. Sometimes marriages can solve political impasses, whether or not there are wreths or dragons hiding in the shadows."

The priestlord's stomach tightened into a knot of poison. She was actually serious about seeking a possible peace with their long-standing enemies! And the empra had just belittled him in front of everyone. Klovus would have to do everything possible to prevent this alliance from ever happening.

83

For an unknown time after he stumbled back to Fellstaff, Lasis drifted in a deep recovery slumber, but he could not afford to lie back and rest anymore. He feared that too many days had already passed, that he might be too late.

As consciousness returned, he realized he was in the castle. Though the candle burned low, he thought he recognized the room he was in. Seeing only dim gray light through the narrow window in the stone wall, he pushed away the woolen blankets. He wore a loose gray shift. Bandages and salves covered some of the worst frostbite patches on his skin, but his real injuries and scars were deep inside.

His body had recovered enough to function, and that was sufficient, but even so Lasis felt like no more than a collection of sticks and stringy muscles wrapped in gaunt flesh. He had endured greater suffering than even a Brava should have been able to survive, yet he had vowed to make it back to Fellstaff, and he had succeeded. He was not used up yet.

When he stood from the bed, his joints felt petrified, his muscles an agony of straining fibers. Forcing his legs to function, he took a stumbling step. He had walked countless miles from the frozen wastes; it should be a simple matter to walk down a castle corridor.

As he made his way along, his vision shrank to a narrow circle in front of him with the destination as his obsession. Lasis had spent so many years here that he instinctively knew where to go, and his feet took him. Time blurred, and he didn't know how long he walked, one step at a time. He had to find King Kollanan and tell him what he knew.

When his mind sharpened out of the fog to clarity, Lasis found himself leaning against the heavy wooden door of the king's private study. Pushing the gap wider, he heard voices, saw a crackling fire in the hearth. As he held on to the creaking door, he heard gasps of welcome from inside the chamber.

Koll the Hammer lurched from his desk and ran forward to greet him with open arms, catching him as he began to collapse. Queen Tafira was also there, along with an unfamiliar Brava woman and an exotic dark-haired man. Both of them had tattoos on their faces . . . runes of forgetting?

Dizzy again, Lasis caught himself on Kollanan's shoulders. As others rushed toward him, his knees buckled and he was assailed by a vision of cold wind and the blinding whiteness of snow filling an empty landscape.

Kollanan held him up with a bear hug, careful not to break his fragile frame. "Lasis, tell us everything! You said Birch is still alive?"

"Can it be true?" Tafira was also there, clutching his arm. "How did our grandson survive? Where is he? Did the wreths capture him?"

Lasis took a moment to reorient himself. "Queen Onn has him." His voice was weak but damning. "They held me captive too, tried to kill me." He heaved a deep breath. "They did not succeed."

The Brava woman and the strange man came close, their eyes sharp with interest. *The eyes.* Lasis flinched when he noticed the man was not a Brava, but a wreth. Yet he was different from Onn and Rokk and the frostwreth warriors he had seen.

Recalling the frostwreths, Lasis heard an empty roaring in his ears and felt unsteady again. He still wasn't entirely recovered, despite his wreth healing powers. Lasis focused on the marked faces of the two strangers. "I know what that tattoo means." He looked accusingly at the Brava woman with short cinnamon hair. "I know what you are. Traitor. Criminal. Without honor."

Her green eyes flared. "You do not know who I am, and you don't know how this symbol was abused." Her voice grew angrier. "I am Elliel. I was made into a scapegoat by a powerful vassal lord, then betrayed by Utho himself. He wiped all of my memories to cover the crime of Lord Cade. Politics over honor. Worse, he convinced me that I had committed horrific murders, and I believed it." She glanced at the wreth man beside her. "But thanks to Thon, I know the truth now."

Not quite believing her, Lasis looked at Thon. "And who are you? Frost-wreth or sandwreth?"

"Neither," said Thon.

Holding him up, Kollanan led Lasis into the warm chamber. "Come and sit, my friend. Elliel also serves as my bonded Brava, and I have accepted this man as our ally. We have so many questions for you, but the answers I most want to hear are about my grandson. This changes our plans! Our armed soldiers are already preparing a swift attack against the frostwreth fortress up at Lake Bakal. We don't know if we can retake the area, but we *will* cause damage. We'll hurt them."

Tafira helped him to Koll's chair near the fireplace, and he slumped into the seat. Lasis tried to grasp what the king was saying. "An attack on that fortress? A futile gesture. You can't destroy it."

When Tafira heard this, her expression tightened, and she turned to her husband. "That is what I feared, Koll. I don't want to lose you, too."

"We have to do something," the king growled. "Especially if our grandson is alive! But how does he live?"

"Let me tell you . . . tell you what happened." Lasis touched the thick, fresh scar on his neck where Queen Onn had slashed his throat. Dark walls formed a tunnel around his mind and memories, and he could barely see the people in front of him as he spoke. He explained his capture at Lake Bakal, how he had fought the wreth mages and warriors, before being dragged far up to the frozen wastes. He described seeing Birch, terrified and shivering, treated as a pet by the queen. But *alive*.

"But I saw the boys' bodies under the snow," Koll said, as if afraid to believe what he had heard. "I saw the little wooden pig I had carved, a boy's hand wrapped around it."

Tafira said, "Tomko and Birch often played with other children in the village. You didn't see their faces under the snow." Her voice cracked. "Maybe it was one of their friends. The boys each had one of your carvings, remember?"

"The frostwreths took Birch," Lasis insisted. "The queen used me and discarded me, believing I was dead." He explained how he had barely kept himself alive with his innate wreth magic.

Elliel seemed surprised. She spoke up. "It is instinctive. The same deep healing sleep is what kept me alive when Lady Almeda stabbed me." She touched her stomach, showing an involuntary grimace.

Lasis described how he had recovered with the help of the drones, and then his long and painful journey south through the snowy wilderness. "Your grandson is still with the frostwreths. Before she cut me, I heard Queen Onn tell her warrior to take the child back with him to Lake Bakal. I remember it clearly. I don't know what they intend to do with him, but he may be there . . . a hostage, or a pet. Maybe some kind of bargaining chip."

"We are going to attack Lake Bakal," Koll said. "If my grandson is there, we will rescue him." His gray eyes intensified as he looked at Tafira. "Now this won't just be a pointless, reactive strike to hurt the wreths. There is a purpose. We need to find Birch!"

Elliel said, "We can still mount the strike you were planning, Sire. Hit the frostwreths with a vengeance, but the central assault will only be a diversion, with a different objective. Thon can help us with his magic." She glanced at the wreth man, then nodded toward Lasis. "While all the frostwreth defenses are concentrated on the main attack, a smaller group can infiltrate the fortress and try to find your grandson."

Kollanan squeezed his hand into a fist and pounded on the writing desk. "Ancestors' blood, we will make them reel. We will *sting*!"

"I will be at your side." Lasis felt stronger, more alive. "And I will need a new ramer."

Elliel was King Kollanan's bonded Brava, and it was not her job to measure the difficulty of a task she was given. That was what it meant to be a Brava, to offer her service and her loyalty. The prospect of the raid on Lake Bakal was daunting, but she would make it succeed, because that was what Kollanan needed.

Even though she had never met the king's daughter or her family, she nevertheless hated the frostwreths who had destroyed that town. She thought of Scrabbleton and the hearty miners, good folk just trying to live their lives in peace. Lake Bakal must have been much the same sort of place. All those innocent people . . .

Elliel listened as the king explained the revised plan to his vassal lords, emphasizing what they hoped to accomplish, not just a damaging strike but a search for his grandson—and a rescue. The lords had already been incensed and vengeful, but now their bleak anger was tinged with a flare of hope. They still looked to Thon with a mixture of awe and fear. He had offered to assist, and the lords were relying on the wreth man's unknown magic to make a difference. Somehow.

Before they launched the desperate raid, Elliel had to test his abilities. They both needed to know what he could do.

As she took him out to the courtyard by the stables, Thon was troubled, distracted. His long, dark hair hung loose, and his blue eyes glittered with both uncertainty and curiosity. He smiled at Elliel. "You promised them abilities I am not certain I have. I know what I have done thus far, but it was instinctive. I feel there is even greater magic within me, but I do not know what it can do."

Elliel hardened her gaze. "Then we figure it out! See what magic you have. Even when I lost my memories, I always had my skills, such as fighting. These skills came out when I needed them. Your skills will, too. We just have to put them to the test. You'll find them."

He took it as a challenge. "I suppose I will."

A large rain barrel stood at the corner of the stables, nearly full after the late-autumn storms. The graying wooden staves were weathered, but watertight.

"I know what you want me to do at the lake," Thon said. "King Kollanan is counting on me, and I want to assist with your part in the rescue." He turned his intense gaze toward the water in the barrel. "Do you trust me?" His lips quirked in a brief smile.

"I do, and I *believe* in you. Show me."

The wreth man squeezed his hand into a fist and plunged it into the water up to his elbow. His eyes slid closed, and he calmed himself. His hair drifted about as if charged with static electricity, and he let out a puff of air, exhaling as he concentrated.

The water in the barrel snapped and froze solid like stone around his immersed arm. As it expanded, the ice loudly cracked the staves in the barrel. He glanced up at her, with his arm locked in the ice. "I think you are right, Elliel."

His eyes rolled back and he concentrated again, *pushing* hard with his rediscovered magic. The water melted, filling the barrel and leaking out of the new cracks between the splintered staves. But Thon didn't stop there. He continued to push with his magic. The water frothed with small bubbles, and a moment later, the water in the barrel boiled and clouds of steam rose up, as if from a soup cauldron.

Fascinated, Elliel laughed with delight.

Thon pushed one more time. He let out a cry, and all the boiling water flashed into steam, exploding out of the barrel, shattering the staves into splinters. As the vapor plume billowed out, it sparkled into gold flecks and transformed into dry dust that fell around the stableyard, piling up in little drifts of powder.

Thon appeared both surprised and satisfied. "I believe that is what we needed to know." He brushed himself off, and nodded at her. "Yes, I can do what King Kollanan requires."

84

❧

As she went after Adan and Penda, the desert was stark and fascinating, beautiful in its harshness. When Glik sent her ska to soar high above her, Ari coasted on the thermals like an iridescent blue falcon, snatching bugs from the air, but the reptile bird did not find what she was really seeking.

Through their heart link, Glik impressed the image of Penda upon Ari's mind. She sent a mental image of her foster sister's green ska, since it might be easier to locate Xar. The jewel in Ari's new collar recorded everything she saw, and each time the reptile bird returned from a scouting flight, Glik would hunker down among the red rocks to review images of the unforgiving landscape. She scratched a circle on the rock next to her to indicate that she had been there, though she doubted anyone would ever find it.

The mothertear images helped Glik plan her route, thus avoiding sheer cliff drop-offs, dead-end canyons, and a maze of rock hoodoos. She had enough water for now, and she easily caught lizards sunning themselves, which she roasted over a small fire built from the dry bushes that grew in salty hollows.

But as they continued into the uncharted desert, Glik felt something draw her onward. She continued to have dreams and visions, guided by her connection with the ska. As she half slept, she saw an enormous beast, all scales, claws, and beating wings, but it wasn't the same terrifying vision she had experienced in her first real dream link with Ari. It seemed as if the young reptile bird shielded her from some parts of the raw visions. Protecting her? Or was Ari hiding something?

Knowing she was being guided by something, Glik went deeper into the desert, expecting to discover the reason she was here. Was it more than just to witness a dragon hunt with the sandwreths?

The beginning is the end is the beginning.

With Ari flying happily above, Glik kept her eyes turned to the sky. How small and defenseless the ska was! If there truly was a dragon out in the desert, would it see her pet as a quick meal, like a falcon snatching a songbird? Anxiety twisted Glik's heart, and the ska grew wary as well, but neither of them saw any sign of a real dragon—nor any hint of Penda Orr or a sandwreth hunting party.

Glik drew a circle around her heart. She took a cautious swig of water, called her ska back for now, and set off again into the great empty expanse.

As she walked in the utter silence, hearing only the hiss of blowing dust and the patter of dislodged pebbles, Glik once more pondered the sealed grotto where she had taken Ari's egg, the immense shape inside that mysterious translucent shell, the moving faceted eye.

Maybe, in fact, she had already seen a dragon. . . .

85

O N the first night in the desert camp, Adan and Penda dined with Queen Voo and her brother, five wreth nobles, and their intense mages. The food was strange, some form of reptile meat along with cubes of sweetened cactus, a sliced starchy tuber baked into delicate pastries, and goblets of chilled spring water to accompany small vials of a golden liqueur so potent that a mere sip sent Adan's head spinning. He set it aside, preferring to keep his wits about him among the possibly dangerous strangers. Perched on a nearby rock, Xar observed the activity, but when Penda offered him a morsel of wreth cuisine he turned away.

Afterward, Adan and Penda lay down on soft sand in a gauzy brown tent that let cool breezes pass through. They dozed off while listening to raucous wreth conversations. Adan awoke in the middle of the night and slipped out of their tent to stand on the canyon floor, looking up at the desert sky. He studied the constellations and thought of the konag, wondering what Conndur would do in a situation like this. He missed his father and also missed the peaceful days when he was a young prince, contemplating the gentle path of a future like a slow-moving river current. Adan feared that such times were now gone forever. The wide and languid river of the future had turned into a furious white cascade of uncertainty.

He knew he needed to arrange a meeting between the sandwreth queen and the Commonwealth's konag. As soon as the dragon hunt was over, Adan assumed they would discuss their possible alliance in greater detail, unless the event went disastrously wrong.

He woke into a hazy dawn, the air stirred by breezes that raised a fine powder of dust. The sandwreths broke camp like magic, moving so swiftly and cooperatively that the pavilions seemed to vanish, packed up and stored on the augas. They left the shade of the red rock canyons and rode their reptile mounts out into the arid devastation.

The sandwreth queen was eager to hunt. Voo's hospitality left much to be desired, but Adan was in no position to argue. He made sure that Penda was rested well enough, especially given her pregnancy, although she seemed as tough and prepared for rigorous travel as he was. Utauk women did not let childbearing slow them down until their water broke, and Penda had several months to go yet. . . .

From what Adan could see, Queen Voo considered the expedition an exhilarating party. Heat thrummed around the Furnace wastes like a living thing. Shimmering curls in the air made the empty sky look like molten glass.

Queen Voo rode high on her auga, her gold-flecked hair flying behind her. "The dragon awaits!" she called in a voice like a war song. The sandwreths hooted and cheered. Quo raised his long, bone-tipped spear, jabbing at the sky as if to poke the dragon out of hiding.

The loping augas churned up dust, leaving three-toed footprints in the sand. The heat slammed down upon them by midday, but Penda had come prepared, wrapping a long strip of white cloth around her head and face; she handed another scarf to Adan, who likewise covered himself from the baking sun.

Preoccupied with the hunt, Voo was oblivious to their discomfort. Adan could feel his skin chafe and burn, and he worried about Penda. When he finally asked to stop so they could share water, the queen was surprised to realize their need. "Of course!" The wreths provided waterskins, and after his wife had quenched her thirst, Adan drank deeply of cold and pure water that tasted as if it had just been dipped out of a snowmelt stream.

Voo said, "I apologize, Adan Starfall. It is easy to forget how fragile you are." She scolded one of the mages. "Axus, do not let this happen again. We must keep our human allies comfortable for the dragon hunt."

The craggy-featured mage nodded, and the seams on his face deepened as he concentrated. When he lifted his arms, his brown leather robe flapped in the breeze he had summoned. The air dimmed over their heads, and Adan looked up in surprise as the temperature noticeably dropped around them.

"It is a trivial spell to filter out some of the sun," Axus grumbled. He seemed offended by their weakness. "I diverted the light and heat elsewhere, so you will remain comfortable. The desert does not mind."

Penda took no insult. "Thank you. Now, let us find the dragon." She urged her auga forward, nearly dislodging the ska from her shoulder. Xar flapped his wings and gripped the leather pad.

The red rocks and pinnacles gave way to an open baked pan of cracked dirt, blistered sands, and white powder. They followed a line of stark mountains that looked like mounds of coal and hardened ash. The day's heat increased as the sun burned high overhead, but the mage's atmospheric shield made the heat tolerable. Adan concluded that without the wreths, he and Penda would have perished swiftly here.

In the early afternoon, Voo called a halt, and the augas milled about as the riders conversed. "We will set up camp here at the edge of the mountains, and the mages can make preparations to call the dragon." She stared at the vacant sky. "This is a perfect place for our ambush."

Adan looked around, saw the flat expanse of sand and dust, the rugged black peaks and the open sky that offered no shelter. "Ambush? The dragon will see us."

"We want it to see us." Quo lazily twirled his spear. "It will not know what to expect. No dragon has seen wreths for a very long time."

86

Aᴀ ꜰᴛᴇʀ hearing Iluris and the godless konag speak so openly and *coop-eratively*, Priestlord Klovus was unnerved. He often disagreed with her priorities, especially when she basked too much in peacetime contentment. Even though she caused harm by stifling the godlings in favor of building schools and roads for the people, in his heart Klovus had always believed that both he and the empra wanted the strongest future for Ishara. Now, though, he feared she had gone entirely mad.

An alliance with an enemy who had been abandoned by gods and unable to create their own? Iluris actually believed the konag's ramblings about a restless dragon and a long-vanished race. She had to be stopped by any means possible, for the good of Ishara, and Klovus had to do it before she caused irrevocable damage.

After nightfall, with his thoughts in turmoil, the key priestlord climbed to an isolated section of the wall behind the keep. The empra and her entourage had separate quarters away from the Commonwealth representatives. Her own hawk guards were stationed near her private chambers, while handpicked Isharan soldiers patrolled nearby. Iluris seemed oblivious to her danger.

Outside on the wall, Klovus did not let his guard down in the chill and windy night. His blue caftan did little to keep him warm against the breezes as a storm whipped up over the sea. Thick clouds obscured the stars, and the air smelled heavy and damp. He waited alone on the rampart.

A lone Isharan soldier on patrol walked up to him, as planned. "I am here at your bidding, Key Priestlord."

Klovus looked at the plain-featured man in his Isharan armor, a regular soldier wearing a leather chest plate, a short sword, dark boots, a leather-and-steel helmet. His bland features were easily forgettable, exactly as they were supposed to be. The priestlord nodded. "I've come to a conclusion, Zaha. It's time I gave you an important mission."

The soldier straightened, ready to receive instructions. Four Black Eels had accompanied the expedition, posing as nondescript soldiers. He still hoped to insert one among the empra's hawk guards, but her adopted sons were much too tightly knit for a Black Eel to maintain the disguise for long. Because Iluris considered them part of her own family, she knew each of her guards, understood their personalities, their memories.

"I am ready, Key Priestlord," said Zaha.

Klovus considered the inevitability of what he was about to do. He was a loyal Isharan, but his faith belonged to the land itself, to the magic there and the godlings his people had created. His ultimate loyalty was not to any one woman, especially not Iluris, and she refused to choose a worthy successor. Without Iluris standing in their way, the priestlords would achieve their rightful place, guide the Isharan people, complete the Magnifica temple, and further strengthen the godlings throughout the land.

He had to look at the ultimate good. Empra Iluris would bring them all to ruin.

Klovus kept his voice low as he spoke with his trained assassin. The crash of waves and the wind from the approaching storm snatched away his words before anyone could eavesdrop from the guard posts. "The empra is our leader, but she is naïve and dangerous, maybe even willfully oblivious. Despite many warnings, she has already fallen into the enemy's trap. . . ." He ground his teeth in anger.

In the guise of a typical soldier, Zaha stared back at him with an expressionless face.

Klovus continued, "The key to ruling a land, to binding its people together, is to unify them with a common goal. If their attention isn't fixed on the same point, they will be distracted by other problems. They will see what their own lives lack, and they will grow restless." He looked over the wall to the luminescent white foam curling around the reefs. "The key to holding power and controlling a population is to direct unrest *outward,* at a target of our choosing—an external enemy."

"The Commonwealth," said Zaha.

"The godless," Klovus corrected. "Konag Conndur and how he lured our dear Iluris into a vulnerable position. His treachery is shocking." He clucked his tongue against his teeth. "It is terrible and tragic."

"You uncovered a plot, Priestlord?"

"Uncovered? No . . . but we will create one." He crossed his arms, slipped his hands into the opposite sleeves of his caftan. "Even though we are far from Ishara, you're one of my Black Eels. Your magic is strong. Are you still able to control it, as needed?"

"We bring our magic with us, Priestlord." The soldier held up his hand, turned the palm toward his face. The soft flesh on the back of his hand crackled, turned gray and stony. "I can create my own armor to deflect the blow of any blade, if that's what you need."

"And fire?"

Zaha cupped his palm, extended his arm. Orange fire flickered upward, brightening to an intense heat.

Klovus waved his hands. "Enough! Extinguish that before anyone sees." The Black Eel closed his fingers, snuffed the flame.

Klovus said, "That's not the same as a Brava's ramer, but none of our people have ever seen a ramer. Your fire will burn bright and hot, and that will be enough. Afterward, the evidence will speak for itself." He stepped closer, regarding the man's plain face. "Most importantly, I need your camouflage spell. Shift your skin and bones, your features, change your height, your hair color."

"Easily done. Who would you like me to be?"

"You've seen the bonded Brava who guards Konag Conndur. Utho is his name. Can you become him?"

The unremarkable Isharan soldier removed his helmet and concentrated. He hunched his shoulders, pressed his arms close against his sides as if squeezing the material of his body, stretching his bones. He became taller. His features flattened, his cheeks widened, his eyes grew distinctive to suggest wreth heritage. His hair thickened, turned steel gray, his chin became more square. The soldier's armor fit more tightly now because the body was larger, and Zaha loosened the leather breastplate. He stood ready, a perfect duplicate of Utho. "Is there a way we can obtain the black uniform of a Brava, Priestlord? Witnesses will more readily identify him that way."

"I'm afraid not, but that will be part of our tale. Obviously, the murderous Utho would disguise himself in order to slip into the Isharan wing of the keep. We'll say he stole the uniform of one of our soldiers, probably killed the poor man." Klovus nodded as he made up his tale. "Yes. I'm certain that's what happened. See that a body is provided, the garments removed."

The storm was closing in, the air heavy with the smell of rain. Thunder rumbled far out to sea, and he watched a play of lightning hidden inside the clouds. "Restore your appearance as a common Isharan soldier until you're actually close to the empra's chambers. You need to make certain you can get inside, past her hawk guards. Kill them and let their bodies be found after you're done. The other Black Eels can help, if necessary."

"One of us is already in position." Zaha stared at him through Utho's eyes. "And what am I to say to the empra, Priestlord?"

Klovus sniffed. "Say? There is nothing you can say. I want you to kill her. And when you escape, make sure that others see you. They have to know that Konag Conndur's personal Brava is responsible for the heinous act. Use your fire so that everyone believes she was attacked by a ramer." He smiled. "Then we'll never again have to worry about an Isharan alliance with the godless."

That would solve many problems.

87

FURTHER discussion would not diminish the risks of the strike on Lake Bakal, nor would it make the plan seem any more sensible. But he believed what Lasis had seen. His grandson was still alive, possibly held captive in the wreth fortress, and Kollanan's mind was set. Since the moment he understood what had happened to that poor unsuspecting town, he had wanted to fight back, to punish and warn the frostwreths. No one could argue with his reasons, and he didn't dare wait longer.

Lasis was much recovered and strong again. Elliel and Thon were ready, and the wreth stranger assured Koll he could do the magic he had promised. The chosen soldiers understood what they were about to do.

During the final preparations, the council members had bolstered each other's courage, raising loud shouts in the echoing conference hall, but their cheers had been offered in a safe warm room, where it was easy to make dangerous boasts. But now as the war party looked at the open gates and the reality of the confrontation sank in, the king feared they might slide on a slippery slope of doubt. He was anxious to get moving, to start the inevitable wheels turning.

Dressed in new black leather armor and a finemail-lined cape, Lasis faced forward, a distant expression in his eyes. All his weapons were in place, including a new ramer at his belt, which he had received from one of the Brava training camps in Norterra. Beside him on an ash-gray mare, Elliel wore Brava garb similar to his, while Thon wore his odd silver leggings, heavy shoulder plates, and chest armor. Lord Cerus had also brought along his bonded Brava, Urok.

Standing beside his warhorse Storm, Koll slipped his arms around Tafira's waist and looked into her flecked brown eyes. Her face was achingly beautiful to him, still reminding him of the frightened young girl he had rescued in the burning town of Sarcen. As decades went by, Koll had not noticed the lines or wrinkles on her face, the widening of her hips as she became a mother as well as a queen. Now he kissed her lightly, tenderly, tasting her breath.

"You know I want to go with you," Tafira said. "I can fight as well as these others. I can help save Birch."

He was sorely tempted as he held her, but remained firm in his decision. "Someone needs to rule these people if anything happens to me. You know that. Stay and be their queen. Be their protector. I will find Birch and bring him back, if I can."

"I should have brought my wife along," said gruff Lord Ogno with a forlorn look in his eyes.

When Koll pulled away, Lords Alcock, Cerus, and Ogno sat high in their saddles, impatient to be off. Before their doubts could delay them, the king mounted Storm and urged him through the gate, leading his vassal lords, three Bravas, Thon, and fifty heavily armed soldiers. Tafira shouted after them, "Sting, Husband! Be a wasp and sting them! Then come home to me *with* our grandson."

As they rode off, the fighters lifted their swords high, like bright steel stingers. Lord Alcock called back to her, "And we'll try not to get swatted."

Kollanan carried his war hammer. *That* was how he wanted the wreths to remember him. In the next few days, he intended to add a new part to his legacy: King Kollanan the Hammer fighting for his people.

According to news brought by an Utauk trader, Conndur finally believed the warnings about the wreths—apparently convinced by what he had seen at Mount Vada. The konag was willing to go to unusual lengths, even meeting with Empra Iluris on Fulcor Island, of all places. Though the idea of an Isharan alliance made him uneasy, Koll was glad his brother finally saw the danger, and that made his heart stronger. Now there was a chance the entire Commonwealth army would come to help defend Norterra, and if the forces of Ishara joined the three kingdoms to stand against the wreths, the human race might even win.

But any advantages from those negotiations on Fulcor Island would occur far too late to affect this mission to rescue his grandson. For now, Norterra was on its own, and Koll would sting first.

After their showy departure, the horses galloped hard up the northern road for half an hour, then slowed to a sustainable pace for the long trip. As the war party strung out along the road, Lasis rode in preoccupied silence. The gaunt Brava man had physically recovered from his ordeal, but he clearly was not eager to face the wreths again. Nevertheless, he would not be dissuaded from joining the assault force.

Lord Bahlen dropped back with his personal Brava, who rode alongside him. Bahlen had a thin face and dark goatee that emphasized his high cheekbones, and his arched eyebrows seemed too low on his forehead. The lord cleared road dust out of his mouth and spat before he spoke. "As we head farther north, Sire, should we keep our horses to the trees, stay off the road? There may be wreth spies about."

Koll shook his head. "That would slow us down by at least a day. Our scouts have already given us a report. Although these ancient enemies are mysterious, they are also arrogant. They won't be watching for an attack from us. They're not thinking of us at all. Humans have no relevance to them."

He thought again of the child's frozen fingers clutched around the carved wooden pig, the two small figures covered with snow. Had it been Tomko and some other neighbor boy? He could hardly believe Birch was still alive. Now he regretted not going back for the bodies so that his daughter and her family could have a proper burial. They deserved it! Then he would have realized that Birch was not among the dead. . . . Koll squeezed his eyes shut and let Storm continue trotting along.

Back in Fellstaff, he and Tafira had spent hours in the remembrance shrine, writing down all they remembered about the grandsons, how they would squabble and then become the best of friends again within the space of minutes, how Birch liked to chase chickens, how proud Tomko was of his ability to climb trees, although more than once he had been trapped up in the high branches without the courage to climb back down.

He clung to the golden thread of hope. Oh, if Birch was still alive . . .

Tafira had written down memories about their daughter Jhaqi, the tall girl with an Isharan caste to her features and a big heart that broke so easily. Jhaqi's first love had been the handsome son of a prominent baker; he had made the thirteen-year-old girl giddy with infatuation, then crushed to the deepest despair when his romantic interest wandered elsewhere. But Jhaqi found true love when she was courted by the young town leader of Lake Bakal; then, when she and Gannon had come riding in during a harvest festival, she had told them she was expecting her first child. Birch.

As he rode along, Koll narrowed his eyes as if he could focus those sad memories down to a pinprick.

When they finally reached the forested ridge overlooking Lake Bakal, Koll called the warriors to a halt as the afternoon sun lowered behind them. Still on horseback, he and Lasis looked out over the frozen lake and discussed the next step.

"We must keep to the cover of the trees," Lasis said.

Koll agreed. "Even if the wreths aren't watching for an invasion, they have eyes, and sunlight glinting on our armor might draw their attention. We'll wait until dusk before we move closer."

Together, they observed their distant target across the lake. Lasis described in detail what he knew of the fortress and settlement, although he had not seen all of it before his capture, and it was much larger now. Outside the milky walls of the fortress stood many wooden buildings, storage sheds, stockpiles, and squalid dwellings for their odd drone workers. The fortress walls and towers showed expansive windows of transparent crystal, so the wreth commanders could survey what they intended to conquer.

Koll's mind kept returning to his grandson, who might be held prisoner somewhere over there. Lasis knew only that Birch was alive, but not *where*. Koll could not understand why the wreths had captured him in the first place, but he would do everything he could to save the boy. His grandson might be held among the drones in their hovels, or he might be inside the immense fortress . . . or somewhere else completely. The king held on to hope. Regardless, Kollanan intended to strike these wreths who had already killed so many people.

Not far away, Elliel conversed with Urok, Lord Bahlen's Brava, both of them clad in their traditional black armor-lined cloaks, while Thon stood nearby, distracted and intent. The wreth man touched one of the bare aspen trees and blended into the crosshatched shadows of the naked branches, as if marveling at the simple wonder of the gray bark. He looked up and stared at the fortress, the solid ice-block walls, the rising towers, as if astonished by the sight of that as well.

Lord Ogno clenched his massive hand around the hilt of his broadsword as he approached the small group. Wary of the vassal lord's intention, Koll dismounted and walked closer as Ogno confronted Thon. "Does the sight tempt you, wreth? Does it make you want to join them and betray us?"

Thon turned to him with a curious expression. "No. Observing the handiwork of these wreths clarifies one thing: I don't know who I am or what I am, only that I am not one of *them*."

"Right now, you're our ally," Koll said. "That is what matters tonight."

Thon reached out to take Elliel's hand. "We know what to do, King Kollanan the Hammer. I have my instructions, and Elliel and Lasis have theirs."

Lasis joined them. "She and I will find the boy, if he is there. The rest of you simply need to battle all the other frostwreths."

While waiting for night to fall, the soldiers tended to their horses, screwing studs into holes drilled in the iron horseshoes, which would give the mounts traction for when they had to gallop on ice.

Standing on the shore under the cover of trees, Koll and his lords made their final plans for the attack. When darkness closed in and ice-chip stars twinkled overhead, Elliel kissed Thon goodbye as he set off by himself down the slope to the boulder-strewn shore of Lake Bakal. He had made his promises to the king, and Kollanan counted on him.

As Elliel and Lasis prepared to slip away, Koll bade his two Bravas farewell. "My hopes go with you. Find Birch if he is there. Save him."

On foot, Elliel and Lasis crept around the lakeshore in the shelter of the trees, heading for the outskirts of the fortress and the site of the destroyed town, where they would wait for their opportunity and make their move as soon as the major distraction began. The main assault should provide all the diversion they needed.

For the frontal attack, the king and his strike force—his wasps—rode over the ridge and down along the main road to the shore of Lake Bakal. On horseback, they gathered on a gravelly crescent of beach where children had once gone to swim. The frozen lake was a field of dark ice, likely solid all the way to its bottom. They carried no torches, but relied on starlight to show them the way across the flat expanse of ice to the looming fortress.

As the soldiers assembled on the frozen shore, their horses' iron shoes and studded screws clinking on the rocks, Koll raised his hammer high. "We will make them feel our sting. Draw their attention so that Lasis and Elliel can do what they must."

"The frostwreths might kill us all," grumbled Lord Cerus. He had always been dubious about the plan, yet was one of the first to volunteer. "But they'll try to wipe us out sooner or later. Maybe they won't succeed tonight, though, and we'll never have another chance like this."

Urok mounted up next to Lord Bahlen, and Koll gave the Brava man a nod of appreciation. "Ignite your ramer when we get halfway across the lake. The fire will be our beacon for the charge."

"I'll make sure the frostwreths see it, Sire," Urok said.

The horses were traveling light, with only the tack needed for riding hard and fast. The soldiers wore fur-lined cloaks, leather armor, and carried their weapons of choice. Each archer carried a goodly supply of pitch-wrapped arrows, and a group of soldiers brought Y-shaped aspen stands, each as tall as a man's shoulders, with an elastic leather cord. That afternoon, they had assembled the catapults, which could each fire stones the size of a small melon.

Koll regarded his fighting troops in the starlight and saw that they were as ready as he was. Carefully, he led Storm out onto the ice, testing the grip of the studded horseshoes and the strength of the ice. It was as solid as granite, and the screws gave the warhorse plenty of traction. He set off toward the distant shore across the expanse of ice, and the rest of his attack party followed.

As the wind whistled over the frozen lake, fifty fighters cantered forward, heading toward the frostwreth fortress.

Crouched in the rocks on the shore, Thon scanned across the ice toward the giant structure. Its frozen towers rose above the site of what had been a peaceful village. Though he had never seen the original town, he could imagine that it must have been pleasant like Scrabbleton.

Thon extended his long fingers to sense the thickness of the ice, the depth of the cold. His dark hair hung loose and his sapphire eyes glittered in the starlight.

From out on the lake, he heard battle cries, the ringing of studded iron shoes as horses galloped toward their target. He saw the spray of launched fire arrows, like sparks from a grinding wheel, and a brighter fire as Urok ignited his ramer.

The sight made him think of sweet Elliel. He hoped that she and Lasis would complete their mission. He needed her to return safely to him.

Cold glowing lights intensified inside the fortress as the wreths flared into wakefulness. From where he crouched, he could hear the shouts of Kollanan's fighters, drawing the enemy's attention so Elliel and Lasis could search for the boy.

He got ready to do his part.

88

ONCE Conndur retired to his private suite in the keep on Fulcor Island, Utho knew he had time. Watchman Osler had vacated his own quarters for the konag, moving to the barracks with the other soldiers during the days of the diplomatic meeting. Utho would visit his old friend Conndur later, for he had a terrible thing to do, but first, he devoted his attention to Prince Mandan.

As thunder rumbled over the ocean, the young prince grew noticeably anxious in his room. Mandan shivered, despite the warm blanket over his shoulders and the fire in his hearth. He flinched away from the narrow window, avoiding the black clouds, the lightning. "I don't like stormy nights," he said, with Utho standing beside him. "Bad things happen on stormy nights."

"A bad thing happened to you one time long ago, my prince, and the storm wasn't the cause of it. If your mother had died on a sunny day, would you be afraid of all sunny days?"

"I would still hate the fact that she was dead." Mandan's eyes were haunted.

"Try to sleep. We don't know how many more days we'll be on the island, but I'm sure we'll go home soon . . . whatever happens here." Utho's voice became brittle. Ever since their arrival, the Brava had struggled with his inner turmoil. He couldn't allow the konag to make such a terrible mistake, and he had hoped—a thin fraying thread of hope—that Conndur and Iluris would quarrel and depart with their hatred properly in place.

"I'd be calmer if I had my paints." Mandan winced as the rumbling thunder drowned out the crash of waves outside. "There's nothing to do here."

"Maybe you can sketch Empra Iluris and give it to her as a gift from the Commonwealth," Utho suggested. He knew full well the prince's penchant for adding subtle insults to his portraits.

Mandan scowled at the suggestion. "I can barely look at her, knowing how the Isharans murdered all those Brava pioneers who settled in Valaera. Such a terrible story." He turned from the window to look at Utho. "Although, if your people had remained in Ishara, then we wouldn't have any Bravas left in the Commonwealth. And we need you, now more than ever."

"I wouldn't want to live in a world where I didn't know you, my prince," Utho admitted, "but I wish my people hadn't suffered such great losses. And think also of all those poor victims in Mirrabay, slaughtered by the Isharan animals."

"We all suffer," the young man muttered petulantly, slumping down on his bed. He set aside his lead stylus and the papers he had used for sketching. "I don't have any heart for drawing either. I won't be able to sleep. I'll lie awake and listen to the storm."

"You need to rest. I could go to the garrison's apothecary, find a potion to help you doze off. Maybe a few drops of blue poppy milk?"

Mandan shuddered. "Never that!"

The prince's reaction answered a question that Utho had always wondered about. Although the official story was that Lady Maire had died from a mysterious "sleeping sickness," the truth was that she had consumed too much poppy milk and died in a permanent slumber on a stormy night like this. Finding her body had shattered her sensitive young son. Until now, Utho had thought that Mandan believed the polite fiction, but it seemed that the prince knew all along that his mother had really killed herself.

The Brava had cared for young Mandan of the Colors, knowing the prince was too soft to be a ruthless leader in times of war. That would have to change, and Utho would make it happen. He would teach Mandan the necessary lessons, the hard lessons. Peace was for the weak, and the prince was the best hope for the Commonwealth's future.

That meant, however, that Mandan was going to have another very difficult night.

The prince flinched as more lightning flashed outside. Utho would steady him and guide him, to make sure he made the proper choices. Utho would salvage the situation that Konag Conndur had created.

For now, though, he had to go. "The fire in your hearth has plenty of wood, my prince, and you'll be warm enough through the night. I'll check on you later, but I have to attend your father. I am his Brava."

Though clearly disappointed, Mandan nodded. Utho left the prince's chambers, closed the door most of the way, and walked down the quiet corridor to the main chambers. He knocked on the wooden door, waited for Conndur to acknowledge him, and entered.

The temporary quarters had been made into an acceptable royal residence. Attendants had changed the sheets, added new blankets, and hung his standard, a forest-green banner with the open-hand symbol of the Commonwealth. A plate of dried fruit and smoked fish sat on the writing desk, but Conndur had not touched the food. He had been documenting his thoughts at the writing desk.

The konag brightened upon seeing his Brava enter. He scratched the graying beard around his chin. "This meeting is going well, old friend. Even though I know you had your reservations about an alliance, I think we are going to find acceptable terms, and then the three kingdoms can devote all of our military resources to preparing for war with the wreths. It will be for the best."

Utho closed the heavy door and slid the lock bolt into place, blocking the view with his body.

Conndur continued, "My legacy weighs heavily upon me. What we do here will change the state of our world more than any konag has in centuries. If the wreths mean to wake the dragon and destroy the world, it is time to put aside old hatreds."

"The world has already changed greatly, Sire." Utho remained straight-backed, showing no emotion, although his stomach roiled. His heart hammered. "Konag Cronin declared war on Ishara thirty years ago, and we survived. Those were terrible times, too, and we will survive these—unless we do something foolish."

"My father's war served no purpose," Conndur said impatiently. "This is different."

Utho whispered in disbelief, "Served no purpose . . . ?" He wanted to scream. His wife and family had died in that war while he was away from home, at the konag's orders! *No purpose?*

Mareka and his daughters had been gutted, their throats slit, their bodies burned. They were long buried by the time he returned from saving Fulcor Island, but Utho could not stop thinking of what the animals had done to them. *No purpose?* Conndur didn't even realize what he had said. "It has to be for something, Sire!"

"I'm sorry. So many tragedies, so much senseless killing." The konag looked down at his open ledger, blotted the ink. "The crisis we face now might shake the very world to its core. You saw Mount Vada! Even with the armies of the Commonwealth combined with the fighting force of Ishara, would that be enough against Ossus? Against the wreths? This is far more important than the old war." Conndur inspected the last sentences he had written, blew on the ink to dry it. "You understand what's at stake, and I hope you can support me. If the Isharans do agree to an alliance, I want you to work with them. It'll be a difficult transition for all of us, but they may be our best hope."

"More likely they'll betray us and kill us all," Utho said. "Don't let yourself be duped."

Conndur let out a nervous chuckle. "Blunt and honest, exactly as I need you to be. I value your wisdom and experience, old friend. You're a wise sounding board, but you must also listen to me. Maybe I can change your opinion."

"The facts cannot be changed, Sire." The pounding in Utho's head was louder than the thunder outside. "History can't be changed." He knew what he had to do, and he hated it. With every word he spoke, he felt more anguished, but Conndur was forcing his hand. His words came out sharp and harsh. "You are too naïve, even gullible. You refuse to see how treacherous the Isharans are."

Conndur's expression fell. "You still hold that opinion, even now that you've met Empra Iluris? She seems perfectly reasonable. She wants the best for her people. She wants an end to this senseless conflict between our lands."

"She also brought her despicable priestlord," Utho said. "What if they have a vile godling hidden in one of their anchored warships? They could unleash the monster to tear us limb from limb, just as my Brava ancestors were ripped apart at Valaera, those innocent people who just wanted to make a new home for themselves!"

Conndur's brow furrowed at the other man's vehemence. "That was many centuries ago, and it has no real bearing now. What if Iluris is sincere, and they can help us against the wreths? I know the real danger to my people. As a Brava, you are sworn to protect the Commonwealth. We have to concentrate on the *wreths,* and put aside old differences."

Utho trembled inside as his thoughts raged. He felt ready to explode with as much fire and fury as Mount Vada. With an aching heart, he whispered, "I'm afraid I cannot allow that."

He had roiled through his decisions, not daring to consult even his two fellow Bravas on the island, but he knew Gant and Klea would agree with him. Fulcor was a point of balance, and island halfway between two warring continents, and Utho needed to disrupt that balance. As a Brava, he had sworn his loyalty to protect and defend the land, and by extension to guard the konag with his very life. But sometimes those two duties were irreconcilable, and Utho's dedication had to extend beyond this one misguided man. His duty was to the Commonwealth and to the future.

When he took a step closer, Conndur looked up at him curiously. Utho said, "I have always liked you, Sire. I considered you my friend, but we all have our duties to perform, and you, as konag, have the greatest duty of all. This will be your legacy."

Conndur pushed aside the ledger and the quill, disturbed. "What do you mean, Utho? You're worrying me."

"There can be no peace, Sire." He hardened his voice, tensed his muscles. "Not until all the Isharans are wiped out."

Conndur recoiled. "What are you talking about?"

"You have to die, my konag, and I'll make sure they believe the Isharans did it. The treachery will be plain for all to see." He shot out a hand and grasped Conndur's throat. Although the konag struggled, kicked, tried to pull away, Utho did not release him. His grip was tight enough to cut off Conndur's breath, so his attempts to shout for help came out as nothing more than muffled gurgles.

Utho loomed over him, pressing harder while the konag clawed at his arms, tried to break free of the grasp. Now that he had made his move and the inevitable wheels were in motion, he felt calmer, more determined. He was doing what was necessary for the Commonwealth, as a Brava was sworn to do.

"Because the Isharans are such heinous animals, I'm afraid I can't make this easy for you. I am sorry." His lips trembled; his voice was hoarse, cracking with the strain. He paid no attention to the sounds Conndur made, to his ineffective struggles. He squeezed harder, rendering the man unconscious and pliable as he focused on the awful things the Isharans had done to Mareka and his daughters, and he wept not just for what had happened to them, but for what he had to do to Conndur, the konag . . . his friend.

Tears blinded him, but he did not lose his resolve throughout the entire long hour as he killed Conndur, slowly and painfully.

In his early struggles, the konag knocked over the small pot of ink, spilling a black splash on the writing desk. But soon enough, so much red had been thrown about in the chamber that no one would pay attention to the ink.

89

As wreth workers set up the desert camp, thrusting poles into the sand and stretching awnings for shelter, Queen Voo and her noble companions lounged in the shade. The colorful wreth encampment had sprung up like desert flowers after a rainstorm.

Adan watched Penda absorbing all the details. She caught him looking at her. "*Cra,* never in history have our people witnessed anything like this. I hope we survive to tell about it. I want to report to my people." Xar squawked in agreement and fluffed his green plumage.

"I hope we survive for a lot more reasons than that." He stroked her arm. "Especially our child."

A group of wreth mages marched out to the flat expanse of the dry lake bed, while others headed up into the rough crags and climbed the rocky slopes. As the mages walked across the salt pan, they extended their cupped hands behind them, trailing out a line of magic that melted a glassy trail that curved and turned at abrupt angles as they changed course. Together, the mages scribed their spell design on a gigantic scale.

In the nearby mountains, Axus stood high on a pinnacle of rock. The bald mage raised his hands, directing his counterparts. From that towering vantage, he would have been able to see the lines and marks of the spell drawn on the canvas of salt.

From beneath the shade of the awning, Adan could see only part of the pattern. Penda leaned forward, squinting; her hair and most of her face were still wrapped in the white scarf. "I recognize the type of symbol. We've seen letters like those in the wreth ruins, where Utauks often camp."

As Voo chatted casually with her brother and the wreth nobles, Adan caught her attention. "What are those mages doing? Is this part of the hunt?"

Quo sniffed. "Of course it is part of the hunt. We cannot succeed in our hunt if we have no dragon."

Voo explained more patiently, "The mages are starting the process of summoning the dragon."

The mages finished making their symbol on the flat pan, drawing lines in the sand that spiraled to a focal point in the center, then they stood together. Queen Voo and the wreth nobles emerged from the awnings and walked to the edge of the design. She gestured to Adan and Penda. "Come, you will want to witness all of it. I insist."

As the heat roiled like shouts around them, Adan and Penda adjusted their head coverings. Voo's tan skin glowed under the yellow sunlight, and a haze of dust hung over the basin. The other wreths gathered to watch.

At the focal point of their spell design, the gathered mages raised their hands and brought them down together in an invisible hammer blow. Bright lights shot out from the spell line, and the glassy sand erupted, spraying sheets of gold light up into the air, like the curtains of an aurora.

The wind whipped up, blowing in a circle that followed the lines of the spell drawing. Dust swirled into the air, rising higher and higher. Adan held Penda as she leaned closer to him, anchoring him. The white cloth around their faces flapped, and Xar spread his green wings to keep himself steady.

Then, after a long silence, a shrieking cry shattered the air, a roar of condensed fear, anger, and hate, mixed with acid. The noise was a primal thing, and Adan felt his skin crawl. Instinctively, his hand strayed to the hilt of his sword. Adan was ready to face the fight of his life to protect his wife, and Penda touched her long knife, as if to save him.

Queen Voo cheered, pointing to the sky. "It comes!"

Whooping, the sandwreths drew their spears and crystal-bladed swords. Voo raised the triangular shield that she claimed was a single scale from Ossus.

Out on the expanse, the wreth mages continued to release their magic, shining a beacon of golden light that tangled into a spell design in the sky.

The dragon swooped in, a sharp-edged shape flying so high that Adan couldn't gauge its real size. It angrily flapped its great wings like the sails of a warship. The creature arched its serpentlike head, spread open its jaws, and let out another roar.

The wreth warriors raised their weapons, ran for their augas, and mounted up. Voo and Quo were the most eager among them. As the wreths charged into the desert, the dragon plunged down toward them.

The ska shrieked, and in a flutter of wings abandoned Penda, flying away to hide.

The dragon came down toward them, its head a frill of spikes that writhed and twisted, its green hide mottled with oily black stains, as if the evil shadows of its existence had begun to leak out of its body. Its faceted eyes gleamed with hatred.

The golden light of the spell sputtered out and faded as the wreth mages began their attack. They raised milky walls of rippling air that slammed into the dragon, knocking it aside in the air, but the monster arced up and swooped back, its barbed tail lashing.

Two mages stayed in the center of their spiral design, trying to pull together another spell, while the remaining mages scattered. The plunging dragon snatched one of them in long talons, then flew high again. Not content just to let the wreth drop, the creature hurled him to the ground, smashing the mage into a bloody stain on the dusty flats.

Wreth warriors thundered out onto the sands, riding their augas. Quo cocked back his arm and cast his spear, augmenting the throw somehow with magic so that the weapon flew high and straight, spinning along its spiral shaft.

The dragon backflapped, changed course, and the spear tore through its stretched wing membrane. The creature dove back down like a hawk seizing a pigeon. It nearly slammed into the dust, but it pulled up just before impact, snatched another wreth mage, and smashed him to the ground.

The panicked augas scattered, but Queen Voo threw her spear from her saddle, and it penetrated the dragon's lower haunch, striking a spark from its scales. The monster roared and lashed back, returning to attack.

Realizing how exposed they were, Adan grabbed Penda's arm. "We need to find shelter! Let them fight the thing." Though they had their own blades, neither weapon could do anything against such a monster.

The two ran for the colorful camp of awnings and fabric pavilions, but the dragon got there ahead of them. Flying low, the beast dragged its curved claws, uprooting tents and scattering the clustered augas that remained in a makeshift paddock. It grabbed one of the reptilian mounts and bowled it into the others as if playing a game with gambling sticks.

Adan dove to the ground, pulling Penda down with him. Dust and sand flew around them, and he quickly, desperately scooped some over Penda and himself, hoping to camouflage them. They covered their faces with the white cloths.

The dragon ravaged the sandwreth camp. Wreth workers grabbed their weapons and inflicted a few minor wounds before the monster massacred them. Adan watched at least five wreths torn apart.

He and Penda lay low and he gripped his sword, ready to hack at the claws if the dragon came for them, but the creature didn't seem to care about the two humans when the wreths kept provoking it.

The dragon flew up again, rising close to the black cliffs—and Axus appeared on his high outcropping. The mage summoned boulders from the crags and flung them like giant hailstones. One rock smashed the dragon's wing, breaking its tip. The monster flew much higher, beating its wings to gain altitude.

Axus followed with another volley of rocks, and one smashed the base of its tail. The boulder shattered on impact—as did the dragon's tail. Though it was high in the sky and barely visible, Adan saw a chunk of the barbed tail *dissolve*, breaking into smaller black pieces that seemed to take flight, scattering toward the volcanic cliffs.

As the dragon flew onward, Penda dug herself out of the sand and tugged on Adan's arm. "While we have a chance, we should get to the cliffs and hide in the shadows."

Adan agreed. "Let the wreths finish the fighting. It's their foolish hunt, not ours."

Quo rode up on his auga as Voo ran on foot beside her brother, a fierce grin splitting her face. Around them, the wreth camp lay in ruins. Many of her people had already been killed, but she summoned the mages. She tossed a flippant look toward Adan, then swung herself up behind Quo on the saddle of a new mount. She whistled to rally her companions. "Come, the hunt has just begun!"

The sandwreths gathered their weapons. Without showing the least bit of fear, they ran off in pursuit of the dragon.

90

THE galloping horses charged across the ice. Their studded shoes dug chips out of the frozen lake, and they ran with a sound like thunder and breaking glass. The frostwreths would know the war party was coming. Kollanan urged Storm to greater speed.

He hoped that Lasis and Elliel—as well as Thon—had reached their positions and were ready.

Cold blue light shone from within the towering fortress. Koll wondered how many frostwreths resided inside. With only fifty fighters, he couldn't kill them all, but he could shock them. He could sting them. He could make them think twice.

Urok rode adjacent to the king. As they galloped across the ice, the Brava man snapped the golden band to his wrist and squeezed it tight to ignite a corona of fire. He shouted a primal cry, and the fire surged up to engulf his hand, creating a long spear of fire—a beacon that could not be ignored.

Kollanan's archers lit their pitch-covered arrows, and dozens of bright orange flames spat and crackled from the ends of the arrows. They launched a rain of shooting stars that flew in perfect arcs to land around the shore, the outbuildings and storehouses. The wood began to burn.

Urging his horse ahead of the king, Urok drew more fire into his hand. Recklessly, he raced up to the shore near the towering gates of the fortress. The huge wooden door had been built out of whole silver pines.

Koll's other fighters dismounted on the ice and set up their makeshift catapults, forked aspens anchored to hurl rocks from the elastic bands. The first four projectiles struck the ice-block walls, leaving white starburst impact patterns. The fighters adjusted their aim, pulled the band farther back, and shot the missiles higher. One volley shattered a huge crystal window overlooking the lake.

In front of the fortress, Urok lashed out with his blazing hand and shot a long stream of fire that began as a sword and extended into a deadly whip. The magical fire crashed against the wooden gate and left a smoking black scar. He slashed with his hand again, putting all his might behind the blow. He struck across and down, and finally the ramer shattered the gate. The thick wood splintered into a shower of burning brands.

Around the base of the fortress walls, small figures ran about in confusion among the burning barracks and stockpiles. By now, Lasis and Elliel would be among the drones, hunting for Birch, and if necessary they would venture into the fortress itself. Kollanan did not see the other two ignited ramers, not yet.

Out on the ice, the war party didn't have long to wait for the wreth warriors to respond and come after them.

As broad sheets of shattered crystal crashed down from the large window, fifteen ominous figures appeared at the wreckage of the gate. They were tall and pale, their long hair like windswept snow tangled with mist. Koll instantly recognized the leader of the frostwreths, Chief Warrior Rokk. Clad in a silver and blue breastplate, carrying a long spiraled spear and a shield with razor-sharp edges, Rokk led his companions out of the fortress in an attack.

The wreth warriors rode monstrous shaggy horses covered with white fur. A spiky mane encircled their elongated heads. Their sharp ears were erect, and their eyes smoldered. Their sturdy legs ended in massive feet that were clawed paws instead of hooves.

Koll raised his hammer in the air. "Another volley! Show them our sting."

With an angry howl, his archers launched fire arrows toward the enemy warriors, but all the flames were snuffed out as the frostwreths came forward.

Urok charged toward them, lashing out with his ramer. Crackling like a whip, the fiery blade blasted the group of wreths, but Rokk held up his razor-edged shield and splintered the fiery lash into scattered fire.

Many of the outbuildings around the fortress were burning now, even some of the drone hovels. The aspen catapult launchers hurled more stones, shattering another crystal window in the primary tower.

Rokk roared something in a language Koll did not understand, and the wreth warriors charged on their shaggy wolf horses. Kollanan knew it was time. The provocation was only the first, and easiest, part of the plan. Now they had to escape.

"Turn around!" he yelled. "Back across the lake—fly for your lives!" He had to hope Thon could do as he promised, and that Elliel and Lasis had enough time. Victory could become a massacre in mere moments.

Archers launched the last of their fiery arrows, though few struck useful targets. Koll wheeled Storm about, and his soldiers retreated with a loud clatter on the solid ice. The horses snorted and began to gallop back toward the far shore.

Kollanan and his raiding party raced back across the indefensible expanse of Lake Bakal, pursued by their enemy. From behind, Rokk and his murderous frostwreths came after them on enormous white beasts.

When the attack began and Elliel saw the king's riders charge across the ice, she turned to Lasis. "It's time."

Her companion narrowed his pale eyes as if purified anger had crystallized in his gaze. "I know."

Together, she and Lasis slipped out of the dense silver pines and ran toward the side of the looming frostwreth fortress. Beyond the ice-block walls, clusters of crude huts marked where the drones lived. The Brava man crouched as they hurried toward the hovels, built where the ruined village had been. "In her northern palace, Queen Onn assigned the drones to watch over Birch. If she sent the boy down here with Rokk, the drones may still be caring for him. The chief warrior did not seem overly paternal." He grimaced. "He didn't want the boy with him."

Elliel touched the sharp fighting blades at her side for reassurance. "We'll search the hovels first while the wreths are distracted." She glanced at the lake, where the furious battle had intensified, and saw the bright flare of fire as Urok struck with his ramer. The enemy would not be watching for any furtive approach from this direction.

"If the boy isn't with the drones," Lasis said, "then we will have to get inside the fortress."

The two made their way toward the storehouses and low shacks. Under the rain of fire arrows launched by Kollanan's group, the drones were already stirring in alarm as small blazes caught on the structures and set the roofs on fire. The drones remained eerily silent as they scurried about.

No longer bothering to hide, Lasis strode forward, his black finemail cape hanging heavy on his shoulders. Elliel accompanied him, drawing her fighting knife, rather than the ramer. Spotting them, the creatures froze in astonishment, then swarmed toward the two Bravas, more curious than afraid. The tallest drone barely came up to Elliel's chest.

Lasis stepped in among the strange crowd and spoke to them. "I am the enemy of the frostwreths, as is this woman." The drones seemed unsettled and confused. Lasis swept his pale gaze across them like a weapon, and the creatures stared at him as if hypnotized. Elliel was fascinated by the connection he seemed to have with them. "Others of your kind helped me when Queen Onn left me for dead at her palace far to the north." He reached inside his chest armor and withdrew a pale ivory object, which looked to Elliel like a simple button. Strangely, the drones seemed to revere the object. "See, I have proof. One of your people gave this to me. Now we need your help again."

Chittering, they gathered closer around him, as if fascinated. Loose fires continued to spread among the outbuildings, and the first fringes of the blaze had reached the outer hovels, but the drones made no move to extinguish the flames.

Out on the lake, a troop of frostwreth warriors rode out toward Kollanan's raiders, leaving the fortress behind. Elliel knew that she and Lasis had to make their move, quickly. "We'll never have a better chance to find Birch."

Lasis spoke urgently to the drones. "Queen Onn is holding a human boy prisoner. We are here to save him. Is he with you? In your homes?" The drones chittered, as if confused. "Did Onn ask you to care for him?"

The fires continued to spread, reaching several more hovels. Impatient, Elliel said, "They don't understand you. We have to search ourselves." She ran past them and pushed aside the tattered skin hanging across the door of the nearest hut. The interior reeked of rot, rancid oil, and unidentifiable odors. She called out, "Birch! We're here to rescue you." In the dimness, she saw no human boy, no one else at all. She hurriedly searched the next hovel, also without success.

Lasis rushed from hut to hut, and the drones imitated the Bravas, hurrying about and looking inside their own homes, as if they didn't know what might be inside them.

Before long, Elliel was convinced the child wasn't among the drones and she turned to face the impregnable ice walls. "If the boy isn't here, then we have to search the fortress, while we can." The battle still raged out on the frozen lake.

Lasis nodded. "Rokk may have kept him as a trophy."

Understanding now, three of the drones moved toward a section of ice blocks that was transparent rather than milky blue. But there was no obvious door into the fortress.

Elliel removed the golden band from her belt. "No time to be subtle. We'll cut our way in." She clamped the ramer hard around her wrist, felt the bite of gold fangs drawing blood and magic from within her. Lasis did the same, and together they ignited torches around their hands. Standing shoulder-to-shoulder, they swung their arms as if wielding hatchets of fire. They chopped into the ice, and the ramer blades flashed the frozen barrier into steam.

They hacked a hole all the way through the wall, and Elliel looked inside. With the three eager drones following like squires, the Bravas pushed their way into the wreth fortress.

91

❦

REGARDLESS of his appearance and uniform, Zaha was a killer.
He walked down the drafty torchlit corridors of the keep's northern
wing, hearing thunder, blowing wind, and the patter of rain outside. The
halls smelled of mold and salt, along with smoke from the torches. Fulcor
Island was a miserable place.

The Commonwealth soldiers and staff who normally resided in this wing
were staying in the crowded barracks buildings on the main grounds, no
doubt anxious for their unwelcome visitors to leave. The keep had the best
quarters the garrison could offer, and Empra Iluris herself seemed satisfied.

Zaha had orders from the key priestlord. He looked like a common
Isharan soldier, dressed like the guards who patrolled the halls. Iluris considered herself safe here with her increased guards, giving the konag the
benefit of the doubt, trusting him in their open negotiations.

Failing to understand the repercussions of cooperating with the enemy,
she did not cast her net of suspicion wide enough and look to her own people
as a threat. The empra's foolish actions would weaken the godlings and cause
incalculable damage to Ishara itself. The Black Eels had been created by and
for the priestlords, and the intense, secretive assassins were imbued with a
magic that they drew from the land itself, and they would serve.

Zaha would serve.

He moved toward the empra's suite, just another Isharan soldier on patrol. Black Eels could move with utter silence, using stealth for protection,
but at the moment there was no reason for stealth. Instead, his greatest
weapon would be guile. He walked like a normal man, and his boots echoed
on the stone floor.

The scamp Cemi had taken residence across the hall. As the girl accompanied Iluris, Zaha had noted her avid curiosity, her dangerous diligence.

Black Eels did not like attentive people who might notice things they shouldn't. He would need to be careful around her.

Although it was long past midnight, Cemi often spent late hours with her mentor, discussing ideas or playing games. If so, Zaha was prepared to kill the girl, too. With the empra herself murdered, what did an orphan street child matter?

He encountered no one along the torchlit corridor until he reached the closed doors of the empra's chamber. Two hawk guards stood at attention outside, one on either side of the entrance. Zaha approached slowly, studying their eyes, reaching out with his senses. The elite hawk guards would sacrifice their lives—in vain—to protect the empra's life.

But the Black Eels had planned ahead. One of the two men standing at the door made a furtive hand signal to him, and Zaha relaxed. The guard was a Black Eel, wearing the guise of a hawk guard, while the other remained loyal to the empra, an adopted son. Earlier that evening, the Black Eel had killed the actual guard, altered his face and body to look like his victim, and assumed his identity. The body was likely stuffed in a storage chamber or thrown over the walls to be devoured by the waves. Zaha knew no one would ask too many questions once the shouts and alarms started.

He stepped up to the pair, saw the real hawk guard grow wary, but he could feel the camouflage magic that simmered in the Black Eel's flesh, behind his eyes. The real hawk guard drew his sword to look intimidating, and beside him, the imposter drew his fighting knife.

Zaha walked up to them without hesitation. "I have a message for the empra."

The real guard said, "She asked not to be disturbed. The message will have to wait until morning."

"That is not for you to decide," Zaha said.

Without making a sound, the disguised guard shoved the long knife into his comrade's side, thrusting through the kidney and liver, into the spine. At the same time, Zaha lunged forward to clamp a palm over his mouth to stifle any sound he might make. The dying guard struggled, trying to raise an alarm as he fought and bled, but he lost his battle and sagged with a muffled clatter against the wall. Then Zaha and the other Black Eel eased him quietly to the floor.

"He was beginning to suspect me," the Black Eel said. "He asked me too many questions, and I didn't answer. Apparently, he and the other one were friends."

"A murdered guard is another good detail," Zaha said. "They will find his body just before they find her. When is the changing of the guard?"

"Not for another hour. You will have plenty of time."

Zaha nodded toward the door. "Is she asleep?"

"She remains awake, but quiet. Reviewing papers, I believe."

Zaha removed his helmet, set it on the floor, and checked the curved sword at his hip. He loosened his leather chest armor to give himself room to physically grow. He drew a breath and called upon his shaping magic, stretching his bones, rising taller. Like a sculptor, he adjusted his flesh, widened his cheekbones, elongated his eyes, changed the color of his hair, until he was a different person, easily recognizable as Utho of the Reef.

"Traditional Brava garments would have completed the image," he muttered as he ran a hand over his cheekbones, his mouth, and along his chin to massage the fine details. "But a man intent on murder would wear less recognizable clothing." He studied the Black Eel. "You should go. As part of the plan, I hope to be seen, so there will be witnesses to accuse Utho, but if they see me with you, I will have to kill you as a hawk guard."

The other man understood. "If another corpse is required, I will serve." He looked at the slain hawk guard on the floor.

"Such a waste would be unfortunate. Stay hidden until the alarms are sounded, then come to fight for your mother the empra, as any hawk guard would." The other Black Eel showed no relief, no emotion whatsoever. "There won't be time for questions if we fan the flames properly and create the necessary chaos."

The imposter guard slipped away, making no sound.

Zaha faced the door, grasped the latch, but did not knock. He would give Empra Iluris no warning, although soon enough he would need her to scream. He rattled the latch, but the wooden crossbar was in place; she had locked herself in. He cursed quietly. Obviously she was not as complacent as Klovus had expected.

Her voice came through the thick wood. "What is it? Who disturbs me?"

Zaha considered tricking her to open the door, but chose to be more direct. For the narrative, Utho must be a brutish, violent assassin. He turned his hand to stone, hardening the flesh of his fingers and knuckles, then twisted the latch, splintered the hasp. He shoved it inside, punching a hole through the thick old door. Thrusting his hand into the hole, he reached up to knock the crossbar out of place before the hardening spell faded. He shoved the door inward and burst into the empra's quarters.

Iluris was in her nightclothes, a gown of gray silk, and her long hair was down. She pushed back from a desk lit by a candle in a pewter holder. Her gilded traveling chest sat open against the outer wall near a stone bench under the window. Lightning flashed outside. The sheets on her bed were rumpled as if she had tried to sleep, but had gotten up to do more work.

She lurched to her feet. "Who are you? How dare you intrude?" She took a step backward, looked around for some defense. "Guards! Where are my hawk guards?"

Outside the door, she saw the uniformed man lying in a pool of blood. Zaha answered in a low voice, "I am here to kill you in the name of the Commonwealth."

The words did not trigger the terror he expected. Instead, she seized the pewter candlestick. "You're the konag's Brava, Utho of the Reef. I know you."

"Yes, you do."

She knocked the burning candle loose and it fell onto the desk. The flame guttered out, leaving the room lit only by one other candle by her bedside. The shadows deepened, jumpy and angular. She held the heavy candlestick as a weapon, but Zaha knew it would do her no good.

He called upon magic to ignite fire in his hand, then threw it. The ball of flames struck the side of her bed, setting the pillow and quilt on fire. Iluris ducked, crouching with the candlestick in hand, but he had missed her intentionally. He had to leave convincing evidence. Another blast of flame struck the stone wall, leaving a black scorch mark, just like a ramer would.

"What sort of treachery is this?" Iluris shouted, "Help—guards! I'm being attacked!"

Not confident he would have as much time as he wished, Zaha drew his sword and summoned more fire. He could cut and burn his victim in ways that Utho might have. The fiction would be easy to maintain, especially once others recognized "Utho" as he fled the scene of the murder. With intense fire in his left hand and the sword in his right, he moved forward to kill her.

❧

The candlestick felt heavy in her hands, yet useless against a skilled Brava. But Iluris herself was not useless, and she would not surrender to this man. Could he really be the konag's grim bodyguard? Bravas hated Isharans because of their tragic past history, and festering memories had kept that vengewar going.

But she sensed something strange about this man. She fixed on the almond-shaped eyes that indicated his wreth ancestry. Wheels spun in her mind as she tried to find a reason for this attack. What did Konag Conndur have to gain by killing her now, especially in such a blatant way? Their negotiations had proceeded well so far, and assassinating her would surely trigger all-out war between the lands again. That wasn't what Conndur wanted. This made no sense.

Therefore, the answer lay elsewhere.

And then she knew.

"You're not the Brava. What are you?"

The man with Utho's features hesitated. "You have heard of the Black Eels?"

The blood curdled in her veins. "Black Eels are just rumors. They don't exist."

"Only our victims have ever seen us. They never survive." The man raised his sword in one hand, held magical fire in the other.

Without hesitation, she threw herself at him with a wild scream and swung the candlestick. She startled him, hammering the heavy pewter object down on his left shoulder. The man twisted out of the way and slashed with his sword.

Iluris ducked and narrowly avoided having the top of her head sliced off, more by luck than skill. He hurled another ball of fire, which struck the writing desk, scorched the wood and ignited the papers. The flames ricocheted, burned the side of her gray silk gown, and caught some of her hair on fire. Scrambling away, she slapped at her hair, and extinguished the flames.

"Key Priestlord Klovus sent me." The assassin cocked back his arm, summoned more fire to incinerate her. "I do this for Ishara."

In anger and disbelief, she cried, *"I am Ishara!"*

Just as he flung the flames at her, Iluris felt an outside force ripple past, a shape made of distorted air and wind, a barely controlled presence that boiled around her and smashed into her attacker, driving him back.

Iluris didn't know what had just happened, but she felt the presence ripple, then fade away as it whisked past.

The Black Eel looked at her in amazement, then his false face twisted in anger. His malleable features distorted, flickered, resolved into a different face before he restored the appearance of Utho. Her bed was burning, the chamber filled with smoke.

The man roared toward her, and Iluris tried to retreat, but her long night-dress tangled around her ankle. As she stumbled away, she stepped on the wax candle she had dropped on the floor. Iluris fell backward, dropping the pewter candlestick as she tried to catch herself.

The back of her skull smashed against the stone bench beneath the window. The crack resounded like an explosion in her mind, and she drowned in blackness.

92

THUNDER rolled across the sea, echoing over the angry waves, and light-ning flared closer in Prince Mandan's window. He gave up all hope of sleep in this miserable place, on this miserable night. The coals in the hearth had died down to an orange glow. The garrison towers would be high enough to attract lightning on the bleak, rocky island. Even the guards patrolling the open courtyard were vulnerable to a jagged bolt from the sky. He pulled the blankets over him, shivering.

On a stormy night like this, so many years ago, he had run to his mother for comfort and found her sprawled on her bed, mouth open and eyes half closed as if drowning in sleep. It had been on a night like this . . .

Mandan moaned low in his throat and struggled to stay calm, but this strange, gloomy place magnified his fears. Maybe he should have let Utho give him a small dose of poppy milk after all, so that he could fade into a blissful oblivion. Sleep would shelter him from the storm more surely than these stone walls could.

His mother had sought comfort like that after her stillborn daughter. Even though she had Mandan and Adan to love, the baby's death had left a cold black void in her heart, a void that even her beloved son couldn't fill, no matter how much he tried.

If his father saw Mandan's mood now, he would scold him and remind him that he was the future konag of the Commonwealth, that he was twenty-five and still refused to take a wife. Mandan had studied politics, agriculture, taxes, trade agreements, history, warfare; it was as much as he could hold in his mind. And still there was more.

He had pored over the maps of the three kingdoms, learning the coun-ties and their vassal lords, as well as the mountains, rivers, lakes, cities and towns, mines, forests. He thought he knew the Commonwealth, but he felt distant from the actual land and people. The devastation in the Dragonspine Mountains drove home to him the difference between real people—*his* people—and statistics, tables enumerating supplies in the granaries and warehouses, population figures for settlements, counties, kingdoms.

He had seen such terrible destruction from Mount Vada, yet there would never be a proper accounting of how many had died . . . and Mandan couldn't grasp how many had lived there in the first place. The results of the loose census eight years ago meant little to him. From the walls at Convera Castle, Mandan often looked out across the lower city, the intersecting rivers, the farmlands on either side of the Confluence. He had believed he knew the streets, the rooftops, the markets. He had always thought he could use his abacus, study projections, and make decisions based on what he saw, like a strategy game. But he didn't *understand* anything.

When he was in Scrabbleton, his heart didn't fully grasp the life or personality of the woman trying to get a cupful of gritty water for her child, both of them covered with ash. He had watched her pour the clogged stream water through layers of cloth, filtering it four or five times until the murky liquid was tolerable to drink. While there in the ruined town, Mandan had seen a depth of compassion in his father's face, a determination to save those people, or at least help them, but that sort of deep caring was missing in Mandan. He didn't know if it was something he'd ever be able to learn. He had tried. Truly, he'd tried.

A roar of thunder shook the walls of the keep. Rain sheeted down against his window.

He heard distant shouts and alarms, and a bell rang in the courtyard. He pushed off the woolen blankets, suddenly concerned. Danger? His eyes darted around his chamber, and he wondered if he should throw the crossbar and barricade himself in the room. What if the Isharans were attacking? What if the keep fell! Maybe the Isharans had used his father's overtures as a pretext to capture the fortress.

He wished Utho were here. Barefoot, Mandan crept to the door in his linen nightshirt, opened it a crack, and listened. The keep resounded with distant outcries, but they seemed to be coming from the Isharan wing. He heard the running guards, probably garrison soldiers rallied by Watchman Osler. He glanced up and down the corridor, wondering why he didn't have a private guard of his own. He was the prince, after all! At least Utho should have been there to defend him.

Farther down the corridor, he saw the thick door of the konag's chambers. It was partially open, and bright light streamed out. His father must be awake.

Leaving his quarters, Mandan hurried down the hall, but hesitated when he heard the noise outside rise to a crescendo. The courtyard bell rang and rang. For now, the corridor seemed safe, but he knew he would be safer with the konag. He pushed open the door without knocking. "Father! Something's happening out there."

The stench struck him full in the face. A wave of burnt hair, scorched flesh, the gagging wet-metal smell of blood—so much blood!

Mandan screamed.

Lit by hanging lanterns and two burning candles, the konag's chambers were an abattoir. Conndur the Brave lay sprawled on the bed, horrifically mutilated, the pieces of his body in the wrong places. Mandan couldn't even understand what he was seeing. His father wasn't . . . right.

The blankets were dark and wet, as if someone had poured oil over them— but it was blood, his father's blood, spilled everywhere. Both of Conndur's eyes had been gouged out and sat like small round fruit next to a lantern on the writing table. They stared at whomever might come in and discover the body.

The konag's arms and legs were spread-eagled, but his hands had been cut off and lay beside him on the bed. His hair was burned away, leaving only a black mass scorched onto his head. His chest had been split open, the ribs pried apart to remove his heart, then the red bloody mass stuffed down between his legs as if it belonged in his crotch.

Mandan realized that he was shrieking. His vocal cords burned as he screamed and screamed, but the crashing thunder drowned out his wail. He no longer knew where he was or what had happened. His thoughts, his vision, everything had shut down. A new kind of thunder boomed inside his head. This was infinitely worse than the stormy night when he had found his mother dead. He screamed again.

Before long, he felt someone shaking his shoulders, powerful hands gripping him. He turned away from the bloody horror and saw Utho standing beside him, his face ashen and shocked. The Brava grabbed him. "I have you, my prince. I'll protect you. You are safe."

Mandan clutched the big man's strong form, then lurched away, doubling over as he spewed vomit across the floor to mix with the wild splashes of blood everywhere. Utho held him, steadied him. The Brava's voice came out in a growl. "The Isharans . . . are animals. And now they've shown us all that there can be no peace between us."

93

ꙮ

HOOVES thundered back toward where Thon lay in wait on the shore of Lake Bakal, building his magic, feeling the instinct rise inside him. A clear thrill vibrated through his veins, and he knew he was actually looking forward to this. A clear purpose.

He saw King Kollanan and his fifty light soldiers racing back across the frozen lake, and a pursuing party of wreth warriors came after them wearing heavy armor and riding enormous white beasts. The frostwreths let out an unearthly cry like wolves closing in on a wounded stag.

Kollanan and his fighters put on a burst of speed, racing across the ice . . . coming toward Thon.

In a moment of dizziness, he realized how much faith—the fate of this entire mission—the humans had placed in his magic. Elliel trusted him. She loved him. He wouldn't fail her.

Crouching, Thon leaned over the surface of the lake and spread his hands. He placed his palms firmly on the ice, pressing down. He could feel waves of power trembling from his body, making the air crackle. His hands melted the ice and his arms sank in up to the elbows.

The frostwreth riders came closer. On their shaggy white mounts—huge wolf steeds with wild fur and the paws of a snow bear—they crossed the ice at an unbelievable pace.

Kollanan and his fighters rode hard, hunched over their swift, light horses. Their iron-shod hooves with hard gripping screws clattered and cracked on the ice.

Rokk and his frostwreth warriors closed in. Thon sensed that they relished the chase, the audacity of the human gadflies. Koll the Hammer had chosen to be a stinging wasp, but like evil children, the frostwreths would enjoy pulling the wings off that wasp.

Thon closed his eyes, clamped his jaws together, and *pushed*.

His hands glowed scarlet beneath the murky shield of ice as he forced heat into the lake. A wave of intense energy shot through the water and vaporized the ice, tunneling out until the surface cracked and split. Steam shrieked out, and geysers of hot spray roared through the broken ice.

Even though Kollanan and his riders knew what Thon intended to do, they shouted in alarm. But the surge of heat that flash-melted the ice wasn't directed at them. He controlled it, sent it past the humans. And then upward.

Rokk and his armored companions thundered ahead, voicing battle cries, sweeping their weapons in the air. Their wolf steeds reared as the ice cracked around them like a breaking pane of glass. Steam spewed up in a blinding mist. The frostwreths turned their wolf steeds about, and their shouts echoed across the lake, all but drowned out by the tumult of escaping steam and boiling water and the roar of grinding ice blocks as the center of the lake began to churn.

On his black warhorse Kollanan led the fighters in a blind dash to the shore where Thon waited. The bright flame of Urok's ramer signaled the tail end of the war party, and the frozen lake bucked and heaved behind them.

"Here!" Thon raised his voice, exhilarated. "To me!" He continued to pour energy into the lake, blasting the ice from the bottom up.

One of the horses in Kollanan's party lost its footing and fell. The animal tumbled, and the ice cracked around it. The rider scrambled to his feet, but a fissure opened beneath them and boiling water gushed out. Kollanan turned back, trying to rescue his man, but rider and horse were both gone in an instant.

"Ride!" the king shouted to the rest of the raiders. "Ride!"

The sounds of the frostwreth pursuers had changed from taunting battle cries to screams of anger, then disbelief. Rokk's voice rang out, commanding his riders. "Use your magic! Summon the ice again."

Thon smiled. It would not be enough—not against him.

Steam and mist swirled around the frostwreths in a cold cyclone as they tried to freeze the lake, but on the far shore Thon leaned farther forward. His arms sank up to his shoulders, and he released another burst.

The ice around the frostwreths and their shaggy predatory mounts buckled. Slabs of ice tilted upward, dumping the warriors into the roiling water. With an angry cry, Rokk fell from his mount and plunged into the lake, and the wolf horse sank after him. The trapped frostwreths tried to swim, but steam whistled around them. The water bubbled. Ice chunks surged.

Thon opened his eyes and slid his arms back out of the water. The residual heat in his hands flash-dried them.

The frostwreths scrambled for purchase among the bobbing chunks of ice.

With a thin smile of satisfaction, he clenched his fists and pounded the surface of the lake. A wave of intense cold crackled out, like a storm wind of frost that expanded in a crystalline flood—sealing the melted lake around the bobbing slabs, freezing Lake Bakal completely solid again.

The white shock wave rushed toward Rokk and his scrambling warriors, encasing the frostwreths in the lake ice. The thundering boom kept rolling all the way to the far shore, where it slammed up against the ruined gate of the wreth fortress. This freezing wave must be like the chill that had swept over the town here, killing all of those innocent villagers.

Exhausted, Thon collapsed back onto the shore rocks. He felt surprisingly weak, and wished Elliel were here. She would take care of him.

But he was alone, at least for now. His long hair was damp with sweat, and he shuddered—then realized that his shuddering was *laughter*, overjoyed laughter! Though he couldn't remember who he was, Thon was amazed by what he had done. He held up his hands, spread his fingers, and studied them. He couldn't wait to tell Elliel that he had achieved exactly what she asked of him . . . exactly what King Kollanan needed.

He hoped she would return soon.

Thon gathered his composure as the raiding party closed the remaining distance to shore. By now, Elliel and Lasis should have had a chance to find the boy.

If not, he might have to tear down the entire frostwreth fortress for her. Right now, Thon thought he could do it.

The three drones hurried ahead, leading the Bravas deeper into the ice fortress. With her ramer blazing, Elliel still tried to get some response from the eager creatures as they ran down the passageways. "A human boy? Is he held somewhere in one of these chambers?"

Turning a corner, she and Lasis surprised two tall frostwreths, not warriors or nobles, but a lesser caste. They carried large tomes in their thin arms. Startled by the unexpected Bravas, the wreths dropped their heavy books and grabbed for white knives at their belts.

Elliel and Lasis moved together as if they had choreographed their actions. They struck the wreths with their ramers, cleaving them into smoking halves. As the bodies fell, Elliel didn't pause to think, but pushed the stunned drones faster, not knowing where they were going. "We have to find the boy!"

Past the next intersection, another male wreth emerged from a large, well-lit chamber. He looked like an administrator of some sort and held himself in a pompous manner. He looked from the three drones to the Bravas with their ignited ramers. He roared in indignation, but before he could form words, Elliel slashed across his abdomen, burning all the way to the spine. He collapsed, still trying to articulate his rage.

"We should interrogate the next one," she said. "We'll never find the boy in time."

A wreth mage emerged from the well-lit chamber wearing a garment made of frozen skins and wrapped in an aura of intrinsic power.

Lasis stepped closer to Elliel. "The wreth mage will know where to find Birch." They faced the ominous man.

The mage's expression grew stormy as he recognized Lasis. "You are the Brava we captured before! Do you remember me? I am Eres, and I defeated you easily the first time. I thought Queen Onn had killed you already." His icy eyes gave Elliel a withering look. "And now you have brought me another one. Is she a better fighter than you were?"

Lasis crashed his ramer blade against the wreth mage, but the man deflected it with a shield of shadow. Elliel struck him at the same time, and Eres pushed back her blade with a cold wave. A chill ran through her bones, a weakness in the power that thrummed through her. Her ramer fire flickered.

"We came to free the boy, the hostage Rokk took from Lake Bakal," Lasis said sweating and straining. "Where is he? Tell us where he's being held."

"The boy?" Eres sneered. "Queen Onn still has him in the northern palace. Rokk did not want to be bothered with such a burden."

Elliel groaned in dismay and attacked again with her fire, but the mage deflected it. The three drones seemed paralyzed with fear.

Lasis staggered back. "The queen commanded Rokk to take him back to Lake Bakal! I heard her."

"Rokk was too impatient and Queen Onn feared he was likely to kill the boy as a nuisance. She changed her mind and decided to play with the child, to see if she could shape him." He laughed. "He is not here!"

With a cry of anger, Elliel hammered the mage, but Eres smacked her back, as if this entire battle were a waste of his time. Her flailing ramer cut a deep gouge in the frozen blocks of the wall.

Then, as if by some strange silent communication, the three drones scuttled toward the mage with unexpected speed. They held small ivory knives that looked like bits of sharpened bones. Eres wasn't expecting them, and the drones stabbed him in the calves and thighs, leaving small wounds.

The mage cried out in annoyance and clapped his hands together, summoning magic. A ripple of cold shuddered out, freezing all three drones solid. They shattered into heaps of flesh-colored ice crystals on the floor.

But that moment was enough, and Elliel and Lasis did not waste the drones' sacrifice. In tandem, they lunged in and brought their ramers down together, lopping off the mage's head, leaving only a smoking stump of neck on his shoulders. Eres's face looked appalled as his head dropped to the frozen floor. With a follow-through stroke, Lasis cleaved his chest in two. The dead mage collapsed, and the blood from his wounds turned to smoke.

The two Bravas exchanged a look of weary disappointment. Lasis said, "If Birch is in the northern palace, there's nothing more we can do here."

Elliel looked at the still-frozen debris of the murdered drones. "But at least the boy is still alive. We will need to go north."

"But not tonight," Lasis said. "Now, we must inform King Kollanan."

Keeping their ramers ignited in case they had to fight their way out of the fortress, they rushed back through the corridors and made their way outside to freedom.

94

Driven by the sandwreths, the augas loped across the desert in pursuit of the wounded dragon. Queen Voo rode hard, her topaz eyes gleaming, her face filled with obsession and joy. She commanded Adan and Penda to also mount the reptilian creatures and follow the hunting party. "No place is safe out here. I insist you join us, so that I may protect you."

She didn't seem to give them any choice.

The augas churned up dust and sand as they raced across the desert pan, following the arm of dark mountains. Overhead, the dragon roared, flying high even though the damage to its wing and barbed tail caused it to fly erratically.

Penda said, "The beast is torn between its need to get away and its desire to come kill us all."

Adan said, "The wreths will never let it get away."

"*Cra*, the wreths may not have any say in the matter—unless their magic is greater than I suspect."

The dragon let out an echoing bellow ripped from the acid in its lungs. The wreth mages raised their arms and drew upon the magic in the desert, sending starbursts into the air. The monster tried to dodge the blinding flashes of light.

"Rally!" Voo cried. Her wreth warriors spread out, racing their augas in an arc across the sand.

Adan gripped the saddle as his mount bounded along. He drew his sword, and Penda pulled out her fighting knife. Why had Voo brought the two of them along at all? Was it just to make the humans feel insignificant? How did she expect them to help fight against such a creature? If Voo was trying to judge human fighting ability in the upcoming war, Adan feared she would be very disappointed.

The dragon plunged down, stroking enormous tattered wings and extending its talons. Adan was sure the beast would seize one of the wreth warriors and rip him into the air, but as the dragon descended and opened its jaws, the sandwreths sprang a trap.

With defiant laughter, Quo and Voo leaped from their augas onto the ground and pounded their fists into the heated surface. A pillar of sand and dust rocketed up directly at the dragon, and the blast engulfed and blinded the creature. Two wreth mages did the same, stamping on the desert surface, pulling magic from beneath the world, and launching another sand geyser that pummeled the great beast.

The dragon rebounded in the air, backflapped its wings, and curled its serpentine neck. Shrieking in fury, it headed toward the shelter of the nearby black mountains. The sandwreths were off in pursuit again, racing on their augas.

As the dragon retreated to the shelter of the rugged cliffs, Axus stood out on one of the outcroppings. He sent a thrumming vibration through the mountain itself. Stones flaked and exploded from the cliffside, bombarding the dragon with a barrage of rock splinters. Broken stones pierced its wings and hide, greatly wounding the creature. To Adan, its blood looked like black oil.

Two flying boulders crashed into the support vanes of one wing and broke the hollow bones, which sent the dragon flapping and tumbling. Unable to keep itself aloft, the beast flailed its wings. One fluttered uselessly, and the other drove it in a downward spiral until it crashed into the desert at the edge of the mountains.

Adan shaded his eyes against the heat shimmers and disturbed dust. He thought he saw pieces of the dragon break away and dissipate into flying shadows, dark fragments that darted off like strange birds.

Queen Voo raced at a breakneck pace on her auga toward where the dragon had slammed into the ground. Flopping, struggling, the dragon lifted its serpentine head, snapping huge fanged jaws at unseen enemies.

Adan kept Penda at a safe distance, but the wreths had no caution whatsoever. Two mages approached the broken beast and stopped just out of its reach. When they summoned their magic, shimmering green lines streaked out of the sand, looking like ropes of light that connected and crisscrossed to form a net that trapped the dying dragon.

The creature's broken wing had crumbled, the leathery flaps disintegrating.

Penda urged her auga forward. "We have to witness this, Starfall. Think of what we can tell our child!" She seemed to have been infected by Queen Voo's lack incautious eagerness.

Adan joined her. "I wouldn't miss it."

Voo approached the defeated dragon, holding her obsidian-tipped spear and black sword. She plunged the spear deep into the heaving, scaled chest. The dying beast struggled against the binding energy threads that tied it down. Stepping closer, she raised her black sword.

Quo bounded in to join her, lifting his own blade. "Wait for me, Sister!" Without pausing, he swung the sword down to hack the base of the beast's long, scaly neck. Voo plunged her sword under the dragon's chin, thrusting into its head.

The monster shuddered, twitched, and *collapsed.*

Adan and Penda hurried up on their lumbering mounts, awed to be so close to the magnificent dragon. The reptilian body writhed, then *boiled,* as if it had come alive in a thousand different parts. Adan thought of a corpse swarming with maggots. Pieces of the dead dragon squirmed and flowed away, burrowing into the sand as if the beast were decaying before their eyes, leaving only hollow remains.

By the time Adan and Penda dismounted from their augas, the dragon's carcass was little more than a framework of curved bones and green scales mottled with black stains. The corpse crumbled in on itself, leaving little but a skull and scraps of horns, teeth, and many scales.

The glowing green webwork of bonds faded into a mist of sparkles.

Putting her sharp-nailed hands on her hips, Queen Voo planted a foot on the remnants of the dragon's large skull and crunched down with her heel. The eggshell-thin bone broke easily, and she kicked the skull aside. "Dragons are fragile things, though they think they are fearsome."

Her brother waded into the carcass, yanked out a rib bone, and waved it in the air.

"What happened to it?" Adan asked. "I've never seen anything like that."

Queen Voo's ivory-and-gold hair flew about in the breeze, unmarred by perspiration or dust. "Do you humans remember the legends? Do you understand *what a dragon is*?"

"We thought dragons were myths," Penda said. "Obviously, we were mistaken."

"Dragons are a physical manifestation of evil and hatred. They are the embodiment of the dark, poisonous emotions that Kur purged from himself. A dragon is composed of all those terrible things, made flesh. We can kill the physical manifestation, but its evil remains in the world."

"But you said this isn't Ossus," Adan said.

Quo chuckled. "Of course not. Look at the puny thing."

The carcass disintegrating into the sand was at least fifty feet long, the head alone the size of a wagon.

"This one is just a splinter of Ossus," Voo said. "But it provided great sport, did it not? Now that the real dragon is stirring, there will be more of them. We will enjoy further hunts."

She bent to the gaping mouth of the crushed skull and wrenched free one of the pointed teeth. While cupping it in her palm, she strolled along the dragon's neck to where the thickest, largest scales remained. She yanked loose a triangular scale as large as a man's head.

Voo still carried her own, far larger shield fastened to her left arm. She lifted it to show Adan. "This one is a small scale from Ossus." She rapped knuckles against her shield, then extended the lesser scale to him. "I give this tiny one to you, King Adan Starfall of Suderra, as a trophy to remember your first dragon hunt with us." She presented the tooth to Penda. "And for you, Penda Orr, queen of Suderra—may your mind always be as sharp as a dragon's tooth."

Penda accepted the fang, which filled the palm of her hand. Adan held the scale, feeling how light and hard it was.

"You must come with us on another hunt someday," Quo said. "We will give you proper weapons next time so that you may actually fight beside us."

Uneasy, Adan glanced over at Penda. "We may not be able to go on more dragon hunts. Our child will be born soon."

Quo chuckled and said in a hard voice, "But your child will be born into a world where humans need to know how to fight dragons."

"Then we'll surely train our child to do so," Penda said.

Since the enormous carcass no longer interested her, Queen Voo went back to her auga. Quo jogged beside his sister and sprang into the saddle of his own mount. "I will arrange an escort to return the two of you to Bannriya. This hunt was most instructive. I trust you were entertained."

Adan and Penda thanked her and mounted up, still trying to understand exactly what they had witnessed.

As he rode past them, Quo reached out to clap Adan on the shoulder. "Now we are allies."

95

THE empra's shouts drew a response faster than Zaha expected, and he had to fight for his life, but he had done that many times before.

Iluris had struck her head hard on the stone, cracking her skull. Blood stained her ash-blond hair and pooled on the floor. More blood trickled out of her ears. She breathed, although just barely, but he knew she wasn't likely to survive such a massive impact.

He was more concerned about the strange power that had manifested in the chamber with such a guided intent. Had that force emanated from the empra? Had she summoned some protection spell? No one else had been in the room. Empra Iluris had never shown any aptitude for magic, but it felt to him as if *she* had summoned that invisible blow, a roiling, barely seen *thing* that drove him back. . . . It was like a godling.

He would worry about explanations later. Shouting soldiers were coming down the hall. Zaha spun inside the smoke-filled chamber, prepared to kill everyone, if necessary. He could not allow himself to be captured or killed. If he were revealed as an imposter, it would ruin the key priestlord's plans. That was unacceptable. He needed to be seen wearing the face of Utho, and he had to vanish, even if it meant he had to die . . . so long as no one found his body.

Though the hour was late, Cemi did not sleep deeply. She rarely did. Growing up on the streets of Prirari, she had lived her life on the wary edge. No matter what sheltered hole or garbage-strewn alley she found, someone was always after her—gangs that wanted to hurt her, street thieves who intended to rob her even though she had nothing to steal, lecherous old men who wanted to grab a scrawny street girl.

Cemi never let down her guard, even under Empra Iluris's wing, even with a full belly, clean clothes, and a spacious room of her own. She couldn't quite believe her new situation, nor did she trust that it would last.

Now, Cemi came alert behind her closed chamber door. Would she ever learn how to relax? Probably not. Despite the empra's soldiers and dedicated hawk guards, Cemi had barred her door and made sure she had a knife under her pillow as well as a heavy stone close at hand.

She heard sounds of a fight nearby and a muffled scream. *That* was what must have awakened her. Instantly alert, she grabbed the knife from under her pillow and raced on silent, bare feet to the door, but kept the bar in place as she pressed her ear against the wood. She heard running boots, the sounds of battle, an alarm being raised.

Then another scream—the empra's scream!

Only a month ago, Cemi would have dragged the bed against the door and huddled in a defensible corner with her knife raised. But fearing that Empra Iluris—her mentor, her friend—needed help, Cemi knocked the crossbar out of place, pulled the door open, and ran down the torchlit corridor.

Shouts of alarm reverberated through the keep. Another scream. Booted feet charged across the tile floors. A hawk guard lay dead on the floor outside the empra's chambers, and the door itself had been smashed apart. Cemi smelled smoke.

Inside the room, an attacker fought several guards in a whirlwind of blows and blades, and when he dashed out of the empra's quarters, she saw him—a tall man with strange features, not an Isharan, much less a hawk guard. She recognized the wide face, the almond eyes, the steel-gray hair: Utho, the Brava who attended Konag Conndur, but now he was dressed in the armor of a common Isharan soldier. He held fire in one hand as he clashed with the soldiers who had rushed to the empra's defense.

Cemi knew that Bravas used some sort of wreth flame magic to burn their victims. Utho flicked a glance at her—just long enough for her to lock his features into her mind—and then broke from the soldiers and bounded toward the stairs on the far end of the corridor.

Without a flicker of hesitation, she raised her knife, ready to follow the soldiers charging after him, but the dead hawk guard on the floor stopped her. Her highest priority was to find and protect Iluris. "Empra!"

The smoke was thick inside the chamber, and she found the bed on fire. The writing desk was overturned, and ash from burning papers fluttered in the air.

Then she smelled blood, rich and heavy.

Hawk guards stormed after Zaha, urgent with vengeance. The closest guard slashed at him with his sword, but the Black Eel unleashed another burst of fire from his hand. He was nearly spent, his magic waning because Fulcor Island was so far from Ishara, but the fire scorched the guard nevertheless and drove him backward.

Disoriented by the flame in his face, the man let down his guard, and Zaha thrust his sword through his chest. Yanking the blade back out, he kicked his victim backward into two oncoming soldiers. That bought him a few seconds, but he could not fight here in the confined corridors. More soldiers would come, and if Zaha failed his mission, Key Priestlord Klovus would be displeased, which would also displease the godlings.

He raced up the stone stairs, climbing past two landings, and then burst out onto the flat open rooftop above the perimeter wall. When he rushed into the night, the Black Eel saw Watchman Osler and ten Commonwealth soldiers charging from the opposite side of the joined rooftop.

The alarm bell continued to clamor against the thunder, calling the garrison to arms. From the rooftop Zaha could see more than a hundred Commonwealth soldiers racing across the rain-slashed courtyard, splashing through puddles. Why were *they* responding? Isharan soldiers were also rallying to defend the empra. Everyone on the island had been poised for treachery, but no one was prepared for *him*.

He held up his sword and let the flame spell die. Zaha feared that the real Utho might arrive and ruin his perfect deception. He had to get away. Now.

While Watchman Osler and his garrison soldiers approached from across the keep's roof, hawk guards and regular Isharan soldiers raced up the stairs just behind him. Zaha whirled and hacked at them with a blur of his sword.

"Godless bastard!" A hawk guard threw himself upon Zaha with a surprisingly competent attack. Zaha slashed his sword point across the man's neck, and he collapsed, gushing blood between his fingers.

Watchman Osler, the grizzled veteran who had spent decades on Fulcor

Island, strode forward with armed soldiers close behind him. He stuttered to a halt as he saw Zaha's face. "Utho of the Reef? Ancestors' blood, what are you doing?"

"He killed the empra!" a hawk guard shouted as more Isharan soldiers rushed onto the rooftop.

Osler was wary but curious. "Did the konag order you to do this? Why are you wearing an Isharan uniform?" His lips quirked, showing his crooked teeth. "Did you really kill the bitch empra?"

"It's Utho!" cried the other Commonwealth soldiers, as Isharan guards closed in behind him.

Zaha stood near the edge of the rooftop. It was a ten-foot drop to the wide defensive wall below, and beyond that was the long plunge down the cliffs to the churning reefs.

Flushed and puffing, Priestlord Klovus charged up onto the roof behind the Isharan guards. "The empra's been attacked, her quarters set afire by . . ." Zaha thought his manufactured alarm was quite convincing. "It's the Brava, the konag's henchman! He commanded this attack."

Zaha's eyes met the priestlord's, and Klovus gave a quick nod.

He made the flame reappear in his hand, flaring bright. Watchman Osler raised his sword defensively, his face contorted in strange confusion. "That's not your ramer, and why would Utho . . . ? You're not—"

With a vicious sidestroke, he decapitated Watchman Osler. The grizzled man was still shouting as his head tumbled aside. Zaha let out a flash of fire, throwing it from his hand in hopes of dazzling the people in the pelting rain.

Then he jumped.

The uproar from the attack was precisely what Klovus had hoped for, and enough people had seen the Brava's face. The plan was set, and inevitable. Surely the real Utho would claim to have an alibi, and Conndur would vouch for his man—which wouldn't matter. There were too many witnesses. With so much violence and confusion, no one would ask subtle questions, and details would be lost in the fog. Once a handful of Isharans were convinced, they would spread the tale after leaving Fulcor Island. Long-ingrained hatreds would come into play.

Before the Commonwealth soldiers and the Isharan guards could close in on him, Zaha leaped from the rooftop, dropping ten feet down to the wide perimeter wall. Lightning flashed again, and Klovus saw Zaha land on his feet and brace himself. More garrison soldiers came running along the top of the wall with their swords drawn, boxing him in. Klovus saw the Black Eel's skin turn white and hard just before he sprang sideways over the edge. He plunged down the side of the cliff.

The garrison soldiers ran together, staring into the dark waters below.

On the rooftop of the keep, the infuriated groups let out a groan of dismay. One of the garrison soldiers knelt beside the decapitated body of Watchman Osler, then looked up with hatred at the Isharan soldiers and hawk guards. Howling for blood, the Commonwealth fighters charged toward their natural enemies. The Isharans prepared to defend themselves.

Klovus flinched. This was exactly what he had intended. Now he just had to get off this rooftop alive.

Down in the water, storm waves foamed over the jagged reefs around the base of the island. Another whitecap slammed against the cliff.

Zaha surfaced and swam against the current. He could no longer maintain the stone spell that had briefly turned his soft skin into armor. After surviving the impact, he had dropped his weapons and shed his heavy armor. A wave hurled him against an outcrop of sharp coral, and he felt his now-soft skin tear.

Swimming with powerful strokes at an angle to escape the rip currents and smashing surf, he escaped the roughest waves, and then stroked across the stormy water. He summoned all the energy he might need, because a Black Eel never gave up. He swam toward the distant, anchored Isharan ships.

He had completed his task. Key Priestlord Klovus would be satisfied.

96

〰

A RED dawn rose over Lake Bakal. King Kollanan and his surviving fighters gathered at the rocky shore, exhausted. The riders slid down from their weary horses to stand unsteadily on the snowy banks, heaving great breaths. One man collapsed to his knees and retched.

Lord Ogno let out a roar across the refrozen lake; then, with a gauntleted fist, he slammed the bark of a nearby silver pine in a gesture of victory and release.

Koll dismounted from Storm, standing with one foot on the solid ice of the lake, the other on the shore. Accompanying Ogno, he also shouted aloud, and his wordless yell transformed into loud, uncontrolled laughter. The wasp had stung! They had hurt the frostwreth warriors, and he hoped their attack had given Lasis and Elliel the time they needed to find and rescue Birch.

Lord Bahlen and his Brava were shaken but satisfied as they counted and organized the surviving fighters. Urok made his inflectionless report. "We lost only two raiders, Sire. That's acceptable, considering the damage we did."

Koll watched the rest of his soldiers gather on the rocky, snow-encrusted beach. Red-gold light spilled across the lake, illuminating the frozen surface made choppy by the turbulence that Thon had created. The jumbled ice had cemented in place a macabre sculpture, a frostwreth spear protruding from an uneven block, the shaggy white back of a wolf horse poking through the surface, a glint of wreth armor, a gloved hand reaching into the air. All frozen solid . . . just like the innocent people of Lake Bakal. Koll drew a grim satisfaction from that.

Lord Alcock laughed. "I wish I'd been able to see the frostwreth faces when the lake thawed right beneath them."

"Any closer and you would have fallen into the water with them," Koll pointed out.

Ogno chuffed. "It was enough just to hear them screaming. Did you hear it? The cracking of the ice was so loud, but still . . . they sounded like cats and little girls!"

Some soldiers chuckled, although they were weak and shivering with relief at what they had seen and done.

Koll's heart hardened. Although he felt pleased to see Rokk and the frost-wreth warriors wiped out, none of it was enough to make up for one little boy's frozen hand, clutching a wooden pig. Tomko's? No victory over the wreths would bring back his daughter and her family.

But maybe Birch—

Two black-clad figures emerged from the shadows of the silver pines, coming from around the lake. Their armor and cloaks were scuffed with dirt and dusted with snow.

"Elliel!" Thon hurried forward, his face a sunrise of joy. "I did what I promised. It was marvelous."

For a moment Koll's heart surged, then sank when he realized they were alone. He had hoped to see his grandson with them, bounding ahead, running into his grandfather's arms.

Lasis came forward to face his king, and Elliel joined him, putting aside her reunion with Thon for the moment. Kollanan asked, because he could bear it no longer, "The boy is dead then?"

"Not dead, Sire," Lasis said. "He is still alive, according to a wreth mage we slew."

Elliel broke in, "Queen Onn brought him to another wreth fortress, far to the north. We will have to rescue him some other way."

"And we will," Lasis insisted. "But he *lives*, Sire. That is one victory for tonight."

"One victory," Koll said, his voice quiet as he imagined the ordeal Birch must be going through. He tried to view this as merely a delay, not a defeat.

Thon looked elated. Grinning, he held out his hand to Elliel, flexing his long fingers. "I do not need my full memories to use my full magic. I was able to call it and do exactly as I wanted."

"I knew you could," Elliel said. "I could feel the power inside you."

The wreth man touched his cheek, unconsciously traced the complex lines of the tattooed rune. He turned to Elliel with a curious expression. "Did I just declare war on the wreths, I wonder? Do you think I was supposed to do this?"

"They don't even know who you are," Elliel assured him.

"Nobody does," Thon said.

Koll strode out onto the ice where the view was unobscured by the pines. The wreth fortress sat like an unnatural growth on the other side of the lake. Smears of smoke rose into the clear, cold sky above some of the outbuildings and drone structures that continued to burn.

The fortress was neither empty, nor safe. Though Rokk and his warriors were dead, the frostwreths would surely come after them eventually. Koll had no idea how many lived inside that grim structure, but he had certainly riled them.

Urok said, "Queen Onn will no longer take us for granted, and she won't assume the Norterran armies are insignificant. Our sting hurt her." He paused. "And now she will be angry."

"Good," Kollanan said, then added with grim resignation as he tapped the head of his war hammer in his palm, "We have to be ready for when the wreths try to swat us back."

The other lords grumbled their agreement as they mounted again. The soldiers hurled echoing insults across the uneven ice, taunting the ominous fortress in the distance.

He hated the fact that the wreths treated humans so lightly, stepped on them when they got in the way. Now, though, Koll had shown their queen that the human race was dangerous. Maybe it would be enough to convince the wreths to leave them alone . . . but he knew that wasn't so.

"You certainly got their attention, Sire," Elliel said, adjusting her warm cloak as she settled into her saddle. Beside her, Thon mounted up.

"I still don't have my grandson back," Koll said. "This isn't close to over."

The raiding party retreated from the lakeshore and into the thick trees. The king patted his black warhorse and took one last look at the frozen lake and the looming fortress. No doubt about it, he had just declared war.

97

GLIK pushed on into the desert for days until her supplies and water dwindled. Her sunburned skin was gritty with sand and dust, and she wondered if she would ever find Penda or the wreths and their dragon hunt.

Ari flew high overhead, still searching. Surely, her ska would find some sign of the sandwreths. Glik hoped she hadn't missed the dragon hunt. She had envisioned it as an exceptional tournament with hundreds of warriors against a huge reptilian beast.

She scratched another circle mark on the red rock. "The beginning is the end is the beginning."

Some odd call pulled her onward. Each night, Glik felt the power in her dreams, sensed a destiny out here, but she had underestimated the vastness of the Furnace. This entire desert might be the scarred remnants of an ancient battlefield, like the Plain of Black Glass.

She hiked along, lamenting the state of her footwear. The rocky terrain had been hard on her boots, and the soles were wearing thin. Discouraged, she stopped, sat on a rock, and removed her left boot to shake out an annoying pebble. Before tugging the boot back on again, she felt the blister. Years of walking had toughened her feet, but apparently she still had some tender flesh left. Once she found Penda and the king, maybe they would let her accompany them back to Suderra. Her ska kept searching.

The girl squinted at the veil of dust clouds that had blown up from a dry lake in the distance. Ari soared over the landscape, but by now Glik could sense through their heart link that her pet also yearned to see trees and rivers again. When the ska let out her familiar call, Glik made a similar sound in her throat, breaking the desert silence. Yes, they both wanted to go home.

She stood up again, kicking her heel to seat her foot in the boot, and set off through a high-walled canyon.

Ari alighted on her shoulder, and Glik stroked the blue plumage. "What did you see from up there? *Cra*, we're not completely lost, because you can always find where we're going, but maybe we should start back." The ska buzzed, her faceted eyes catching the sun. In order to get a better sense of where they were, Glik removed the fine collar that Shella din Orr had given them. She activated the magic in the mothertear, releasing the images it had captured.

The unexplored canyonlands were beautiful, but Glik's heart sank. The arid expanse extended as far in front of her as back in the direction she had come. That was not a good sign. She pulled and expanded the images, looking more closely, trying to find some oasis, a settlement, a wreth encampment.

To her surprise and relief, she discovered a large collection of structures and figures down the side branch of a canyon, not far away. Although cliff overhangs obscured details, she saw walls, buildings, fences ... people. Utauk tribes would only make camp in a place that had water, plants, something to eat. What she saw in the image had to be an oasis of sorts in order to support so many people. This was her best chance, and she decided at last that it was best to give up on the idea of finding Penda or the dragon hunt.

When she replaced the collar, Ari flapped her blue wings. Glik trudged off, heartened now. She drank much of her remaining water, hoping she no longer needed to conserve so tightly. She kept to the shadows at the side of the canyon wall, but the high sun left very little shade.

From the mothertear images, she knew where to go. As she hiked deeper into the canyon with towering rock walls on either side, she saw footprints in the trampled dirt and loose stones. Booted feet, bare feet, and large three-toed reptilian footprints.

Instinct made Glik cautious. Instead of boldly approaching the oasis camp, she kept to the edge of the canyon. As soon as she entered the side canyon, she could smell the settlement ahead, smoke from fires, old latrines, and the stink of countless unwashed bodies. She had been in many large Utauk camps. The tribes insisted on proper hygiene, disposing of garbage and human waste. This, though, seemed squalid and sloppy.

She heard activity ahead, shouts, the clink of metal implements on rock, guttural commands. When she came around a curve in the canyon, the view opened up to reveal walls and fences, barricades across the wide floor. She saw low huts made of mud bricks and fused sand, fabric roofs stretched across hardened rock knobs for shade.

And humans—hundreds, maybe thousands of them—were crowded together like cattle fenced in the butcher's quarter in Bannriya.

Glik drew back. The ska on her shoulder fluttered in alarm.

The humans—prisoners? slaves?—labored in gloomy, silent teams. They worked to build fortifications, digging trenches in the canyon. Standing guard, Glik saw tall, copper-skinned sandwreths with ivory hair, scaled leather armor, obsidian and bone spears, pikes, axes. The wreths roared orders, and the captive humans moved about, sullen and weak.

Glik recalled the empty hill villages she sometimes found on the fringes of the desert, abandoned settlements blown over with dust. She had thought—hoped—that all the people had simply left to find a better life. Now, she realized that they must have been kidnapped and thrown into these sprawling ugly camps. Many Utauk caravans had also mysteriously vanished in the hills.

In her shock, she stared a moment too long. Two sandwreth guards spotted her and shouted in loud voices that echoed through the canyon. Glik began to run, sprinting over the rocky sand of the canyon floor. She didn't bother to cry out in alarm; she just fled. Ari sprang into the air with a beat of blue wings.

The sandwreths came after her, leaping over their fences, racing down the side canyon.

Glik ran for all she was worth, but when she turned the corner into the main canyon, she skidded, her boots kicking up small stones. Two more ominous sandwreths bounded toward her on large augas. The lean warriors raised their spears to block her escape. The others closed in on her from behind.

Glik stopped, fists clenched at her sides, and turned back and forth. She could see no way out.

In despair, she watched her ska fly away. At least Ari would remain free. . . .

98

W HEN Cemi ran into the empra's chamber, knife raised to defend herself, she saw Iluris sprawled on the floor near the wall at the base of a thick stone bench. The empra's skin was gray, and a lake of blood spilled out around her head. Her skull had smashed into the sharp edge of the bench—did the assassin do it?—and now the woman lay with her eyes closed, left hand twitching, fingers trembling. A soldier bent over her, looking helpless.

"Is she dead?" Cemi demanded. "Did that bastard kill her?"

"She lives, just barely . . . and maybe not for long. A wound like this . . ."

Cemi barked a sharp command to the soldier: "Get a doctor—and anyone else who can help!" She suddenly realized there might be more than one assassin, that the danger might not be over. "Bring Captani Vos and the hawk guards! We have to protect the empra. Guard this room." She dropped to her knees and touched Iluris's cheeks, pulled up her eyelids. The empra's eyes had rolled back up into her head, showing only the whites. Blood trickled from her ears.

After the soldier bolted out of the chamber, Cemi grabbed the scorched sheets from the bed and tore off a swatch of cloth much too large for what she needed. She wadded it and very gently lifted the empra's head off the stone floor. The back of her skull felt caved in, too soft. More blood oozed out.

"Oh, Iluris!" She pressed the cloth against the matted ash-blond hair. The empra lay deeply unconscious, on the verge of death.

Furious, the captani of the hawk guards barged into the chamber, stepping over the dead body in the hall and bringing two other red-faced hawk guards with him. "Our mother has been attacked, and Nedd is dead out in the hall." He strode forward, unable to tear his eyes from Iluris and all the blood. "We failed in our job. She's dead!"

Cemi looked up, pressing against the red-soaked rag. "She's alive, but wounded badly. I don't know enough to tend her, not with this kind of injury." Though she was young, the girl had seen more than her share of death, beatings, and slow recoveries on the streets. "She may never wake up from a head wound like this."

"I've treated many battlefield injuries," Vos said, kneeling next to Cemi. He looked up at the hawk guards who had accompanied him. "Bring the rest of our men, all of them. I want them at the empra's side—now! Why is she all alone here?"

"Some soldiers ran off to fight the assassin," Cemi said. "It was the Brava, the one who came with Konag Conndur. Utho."

"Then he should be hunted down and killed," Vos said. "And for certain, his orders must have come from the godless konag. We are all in grave danger. We'll have to make a defensible stand here."

From the distant clamor, accompanied by the sound of thunder and rain outside, Cemi guessed the battles were continuing elsewhere, possibly throughout the garrison. An alarm bell clanged in the courtyard. More Commonwealth soldiers raced to the keep.

"It was a trap," Cemi said. "The konag lured us to this island meaning to kill Iluris all along." She looked up at the captani's face, remembering how she had embarrassed him and his men by slipping past their security in Prirari. But that had been a game, and since then she had gotten to know Vos and the other hawk guards, and she understood they were entirely devoted to the empra. She saw them as kindred spirits.

Cemi realized she was speaking with the tone of command she had learned from Empra Iluris in the last few weeks. Bending over the woman's supine form, the captani went through the same motions she had: touching Iluris's temples, peeling her eyes back. "This is bad." He pressed his fingertips to her throat, found the thready pulse. Without looking up, Captani Vos barked to the additional hawk guards standing at the doorway, "Prepare to defend our mother with your lives. This may just be starting. Once the konag learns that she still lives, he will send reinforcements to wipe us all out."

As soon as Cemi had arrived on Fulcor Island, she had studied the garrison and the barracks, watched the Commonwealth soldiers out in the courtyard. She had a good guess as to how many of them were stationed here. Although the Isharans had brought along a significant honor guard, and their warships lay anchored beyond the reefs, Cemi did the math as if she had an abacus in her head.

"They outnumber us significantly in the garrison, Captani. Surely they mean to kill us all. They have us trapped here." The answer was obvious to her. "We have to stabilize the empra and carry her to the landing boats while the fighting continues and under cover of the storm. We've got to get her to the warship anchored just beyond the cove."

Vos was startled. "It would be madness to leave. She'll die if we carry her now."

Cemi swallowed hard. "She's strong. It's just as dangerous to stay. We're bottled up here, and they will kill us off one by one." She looked intently at him. "Should we just surrender and die? Or should we take a chance, as small as it might be? We've got to save her."

The captani paled and stiffened. "And someone must make it back to Serepol to report what happened here, otherwise the godless konag may try to say it was merely an accident." His voice grew more hoarse. "He could sink our ships and let Ishara believe that the empra simply died on her voyage home! He would be able to claim anything he liked!"

"We have to go," Cemi insisted, "whatever happens. Oh, I hope we can save her."

Vos wrapped tight cloth bandages around the empra's head, as if it were a battlefield wound, and wiped his blood-smeared hands on a torn sheet. "I swore my life to protect our mother empra, and if that's the only way . . ." He stood. "Call our soldiers! Hawk guards, to me! Form a wedge. We will carry her to the gates, retreat down the cliff stairs, and get into our landing boats. We must live long enough to get her to safety."

One of the hawk guards groaned. "We should have brought a godling. Priestlord Klovus said we should have brought a godling!"

"We should have brought a thousand more fighting men, too, but we can't win a battle with wishes. Now go, spread the word to all Isharan fighters. Right now, we can take advantage of the chaos. We have to retreat before the trap is entirely sprung."

Two of the hawk guards rigged a makeshift stretcher to carry the empra, and with Cemi helping, they carefully transferred the limp form onto it. Though rushed, they took exquisite care as they lifted her and prepared to evacuate.

Cemi followed close, not leaving Iluris's side as the guards moved her out of the smoke-filled room. Her hands were covered with sticky blood, and the cloth wrapped around Iluris's head was also soaked. The empra idn't stir. Her expression was slack, her skin clammy.

Cemi felt desperate, but she drew a breath and steeled herself, refusing to act like a helpless, shuddery girl. Their only hope was to get to the ship, and they all knew it. "Hurry!" she whispered, and the armored guards moved at a brisk pace through the keep.

They knew they might have to fight their way across the courtyard, and even descending the steep, rain-slick cliff stairs to the docks would be treacherous for all of them. Cemi was sure they would have to leave some Isharan fighters behind to cover them. Captani Vos would resent that, but getting the empra to safety was the highest priority. The hawk guards had to save her.

As they emerged from the great doors of the main keep, rain slashed down. Men were fighting outside, and she heard swords clashing on the roof above. The hawk guards shouted orders, which were passed on to Isharan soldiers who broke away to fight in the courtyard, providing cover so the smaller party could get away with the stretcher. The clash of metal and screams echoed against the thunder.

Cemi clasped the empra's cold, motionless hand, silently begging her to stay alive. She wished they did have some godling to protect them, but Iluris herself had hampered the godlings and the priestlords. Even if she survived to reach Serepol again, would the godlings deign to assist her? Throughout her entire reign, she had curtailed their power. Perhaps the godlings resented Iluris. Cemi wondered where Priestlord Klovus was now.

The darkness was deep and intense in the pouring rain. Loud, desperate fighting was concentrated on the roof of the keep, and shouting soldiers ran along the top of the boundary wall. The Isharans continued to sound the retreat, their soldiers battling Commonwealth fighters at the barracks, in the courtyard.

Captani Vos was focused on only one mission. His hawk guards formed an impenetrable wedge around the wounded empra as they pushed their way across the muddy courtyard. Commonwealth soldiers converged to cut off the remaining Isharan fighters, but once Captani Vos had cleared a way across the courtyard, the fighting became easier. They reached the gate that led to the cleft in the cliff and access to the exposed stairs down to the docks in the harbor cove.

A bruised, disheveled, and frantic-looking Klovus scuttled after them, his caftan drenched, raindrops glistening on his bald head. Two Isharan soldiers followed him like bodyguards. He saw the motionless figure on the stretcher and rushed closer. "You retrieved the empra's body? We must hold a proper funeral for her back in Serepol."

"She's not dead!" Cemi cried. "We're rescuing her."

The priestlord was taken aback. "Hear us, save us! Yes, we must get her to safety, no matter how badly she's injured. If we weren't so far from blessed Ishara, I could summon magic, and I could help us fight. I should have brought a godling, no matter what the empra said, but she wouldn't let me protect her."

"Then help us escape, Priestlord," Vos growled. They worked their way through the rock cleft, two hawk guards carrying the stretcher, then started down the exposed cliffside stairs. Several defenders volunteered to remain behind and hold off any attacks from above.

The landing boats were tied up to the dock, covered in canvas. The cove's high cliffs blocked most of the rain, but spray made the piers and steps treacherous. Three hawk guards raced down the stairs ahead of the empra. They tore off the canvas and untied the ropes for immediate departure.

Cemi clutched Iluris's hand until they reached the dock and carefully loaded the bleeding woman aboard the boat. "Go as soon as she is aboard! Don't wait," Vos cried.

Cemi sprang into the boat, sitting on the gunwale next to the empra. The captani called back, "Priestlord, come with us to the safety of the warship. We don't have much time."

"I have two personal guards. They must come along as well." Klovus indicated the pair of silent soldiers accompanying him. "They will help protect me."

Vos scowled, but didn't have time to argue. "Bring them, but we have to go now!"

Cradling the empra, Cemi heard the increasing shouts and clang of metal behind them. The fight was intensifying up in the cleft with the enemy soldiers coming after them. One of the hawk guards sprang from the landing boat and back onto the dock. "Go, Captani—take our mother. We will stay here and defend your escape."

"As soon as we're gone, take another landing boat," Vos said. "Get to the anchored ship." Without waiting, they threw off the ropes, and soldiers rowed hard out of the cove toward the warship waiting just beyond the reefs.

Once they were out of the narrow harbor, the waters were choppy. Cold rain poured down, and Cemi leaned over to shield the empra. With a flash of lightning in the sky, she saw the unconscious woman's drawn, empty expression. "Stay alive," she whispered, "please." With such a head injury, Cemi knew that sometimes a victim never woke up. Other times, if they did, the person's mind was gone. "Please stay alive. Please be well again."

The guards rowed furiously toward the anchored ship, and alarms kept sounding on Fulcor Island behind them. Ahead, Cemi saw lanterns appear on the Isharan vessel. The crew aboard knew that something terrible had happened.

Sitting in the stern of the landing boat, Klovus drew his knees up to his chest and wrapped his arms around his rain-soaked caftan. He glanced at his two assigned guards and nodded as if communicating something that Cemi didn't understand.

The priestlord muttered, "The empra still lives." The men nodded, and he lowered his voice. "But it is good enough."

99

With the Fulcor keep in total chaos, Utho wrapped his iron-hard arms around Prince Mandan. The young man sobbed, unable to form words. Utho roared in a voice that echoed out of Conndur's blood-soaked chamber. "We've been betrayed! The Isharan animals killed the konag."

Word spread through the garrison like the cold wind that blew against the island. Commonwealth soldiers howled for revenge. Fighting continued in the yard and on the rooftop.

Mandan wailed, and Utho kept holding him in a cagelike grip. "You're safe, my prince. I'll protect you. I would never let that happen to you."

"He—his eyes! The blood, his h-heart!"

"They weren't satisfied just to kill him," Utho said. "The animals had to show us their contempt. See the true nature of the allies your father wanted to make? These are our enemies, not some ancient legend about a buried dragon. You have to see that!"

Mandan smothered his face against the Brava's chest, muffling his sobs.

The two other Bravas on the island bounded to the konag's chamber and stood at the doorway. Swarthy, pock-faced Gant let out a roar. "I'll kill them all myself!"

Klea said in a cold voice, "No, we will kill them all together."

"There's much killing to be done," Utho agreed, "but first we have to get Prince Mandan to safety. What if the Isharans brought a godling? This could be just the first step in a much larger attack. We need to get him off this island and back to Osterra so we can plan our next move."

"I want to leave," the young man groaned. "I want to go home."

Utho peeled the prince away from him. Although Mandan trembled, looking lost and helpless, the Brava forced the young man to look at his father's mutilated body, the blood on the sheets, the walls, even the ceiling.

The prince needed to remember every detail. "This is an awful betrayal, but what if they intend to do even worse? To all of us? Even this storm may be something they conjured with their magic." Utho shook his head, and snapped to the two Bravas, "Get Mandan out of here." He lowered his voice to emphasize his words. "He is konag now."

A deep understanding flashed among the others as they realized the consequences of Conndur's murder, though not even his comrades would guess what Utho himself had done to arrange this. From the beginning, his fellow Bravas had resisted any possible alliance with the Isharans, but he wasn't sure they would accept the lengths to which he had gone to prevent it. It didn't matter anymore. He had drawn back the bow of possibilities and let fly the arrow of destiny. There was no calling it back.

After tonight, the Commonwealth would never accept peace with the Isharans.

As word of the konag's murder spread, vengeful soldiers streamed out of the barracks and flooded across the muddy courtyard. Sword fights echoed through the main hall and in the corridors. Utho expected that most of the Isharans would be massacred in the next hour, but they were wily and desperate. Some might get away.

Right now, he would whisk Mandan back to the flagship, not merely for the young man's safety, but to keep that arrow flying. The prince could not be allowed to stay, or he might ask too many questions.

A pair of Conndur's soldiers charged into the konag's chamber and stopped, pale and panting, the words ripped from their mouths at the sight of such carnage. One of the soldiers turned away and covered his eyes, shuddering.

"Report!" Utho barked.

The soldier swallowed hard. "We've received word from the rooftop, where there was great fighting. It is not clear, sir, whether or not the empra survived."

Though surprised, Utho could not hide his pleasure, knowing that it would be a good thing if she were dead. "What happened? Was she attacked?"

The soldier seemed confused. "But . . . witnesses said that *you* were the one who tried to kill the empra. How did you come to be here?"

Utho was ready to strike the man in his impatience. "Don't talk nonsense. I have been here since the prince discovered his father. How could I have been on the rooftop? Is there still fighting?"

"Watchman Osler and his garrison men battled bravely, but the watchman is dead, as are many of our soldiers. Rather than be captured, the assassin leaped over the wall and down the cliffs. He's dead. But the witnesses . . . we thought it was you, Utho. Even our own people saw—"

Utho ground his teeth together, trying to understand what the soldier was babbling about. "I would have liked to kill Iluris, but I cannot take credit for it." He issued orders before shock could paralyze the soldier. "When you capture Isharans tonight, throw them over the cliff as well. Feed them to the reefs. They must all die."

He turned to the two Bravas who remained wary in the corridor. "Gant, Klea, with me! We will escort Mandan down to the ship immediately, protect him with our very lives. We also . . ." His voice hitched as guilt surged through him, but he drove it back, dammed it up behind a wall of determination. "We also have to take the konag's body. We can't leave him here. He has been mutilated. What else might those animals do to his remains? Conndur, my beloved Conndur, must go home to Osterra."

Gant let out a low growl. "The people of the Commonwealth have to see what those monsters did to him. My lord Cade will lead a call for vengeance across the land."

Utho realized that particular response was vitally important as well. Yes, he could work with Cade.

Accepting the grim mission, the two Bravas gathered the pieces of Konag Conndur, placed them with the main body, and wrapped them together in a long sheet. They lashed the arms and legs into a separate, grisly package.

Mandan stared numbly while they bundled the remains of his slain father, and Utho let him keep watching. Every instant of this experience had to be seared into the prince's memory. He must never forget.

As the fighting continued, Utho realized that a fire had started in the northern wing of the keep. Normally, garrison soldiers would empty the cisterns and draw up buckets of seawater to fight a fire, but no one seemed concerned about the spreading blaze in the downpour. They were more interested in killing one another.

Utho, Mandan, and the two Bravas stepped out into the rain. Commonwealth soldiers howled curses at the Isharans, and the words gave Utho strength. Their anger had been sparked, and now they understood the revulsion and distrust that Bravas felt toward Isharans. The atrocities Utho had inflicted upon his friend were only a fraction of the horrors that had been visited on Mareka and his daughters, or on the original Brava settlers of Valaera.

A vengewar was not a quick thing, but it was necessary for his people. He would eventually have his satisfaction.

Soldiers fought in the courtyard, swords against swords. When he saw one garrison defender thrust his blade deep into the guts of an Isharan soldier, Utho felt the exhilaration as if he had stabbed the enemy himself.

Lightning split the sky, and Mandan stumbled to his knees in the mud, but Utho grabbed him, pulled him to his feet again. "Come, my prince, I've sworn to keep you safe."

The other two Bravas ran alongside, carrying the horrific bloodstained packages that held Conndur's corpse.

"Some Isharans have already escaped, Utho," called one of the garrison officers who had served as Watchman Osler's deputy. "We killed many, but couldn't stop all of them. They took the empra on a stretcher. She seemed grievously injured."

"I hope she dies." As far as Utho knew, Empra Iluris had not named a successor, and without an heir, Ishara would descend into anarchy and civil war. The priestlords would fight among one another, and other claimants might try to take over the Serepol palace. Good. That would weaken them for when the Commonwealth navies swept across the new world.

"My father wanted peace," Mandan said, stumbling along, as if unable to believe where he was.

"And look what they did to him," Utho said. They ducked through the gate and down the treacherous exposed steps. They headed toward the pier where the Commonwealth flagship was tied up, ready to depart. Others had already sounded an alarm, telling the captain to prepare to set sail immediately.

"The Isharans agreed to come to Fulcor Island as neutral ground. They can't be trusted," Utho told Mandan. "They can't be believed."

They made their way to the docks, meeting little resistance because most of the Isharans were already gone, or slain. Utho gave strict orders for the garrison soldiers and most of the Commonwealth fighters to stay and defend the island. "We dare not let this tragedy allow the Isharans to take over our stronghold here. That may have been their scheme all along."

After they loaded the bloody packages aboard the ship, Utho turned to Klea. "Stay here on Fulcor. I want you in charge. We will sail away immediately with a minimal crew, because I want Mandan safely back in Convera Castle, but you—you're my best choice to be the next watchman of the garrison. Keep the fortress strong and well defended. The enemy could attack at any time."

The iron-hard older woman nodded. "I'll make certain that any Isharan who survives the battle tonight goes over the wall to the reefs."

Utho could not ask for more.

Klea clamped the gold band around her wrist, ignited the ramer, and raised a full blazing blade. She turned back to the cliffside stairs. "I have work to do." She ran with long-legged strides up the stairs and disappeared into the walled fortress.

Utho and Gant settled the prince aboard the ship, while the captain shouted for the anchor to be raised. Iron chains rattled.

Mandan was shivering as Utho pulled him down among crates and barrels on the deck for temporary shelter. They wouldn't go below to their cabins just yet. Utho wanted to watch the departure.

"My father was just trying to help the human race," Mandan groaned. "What about the wreths? The dragon? He was sending a warning. We saw Mount Vada!"

"You saw what happened here tonight." Utho crouched next to the prince. "I don't give a damn about wreths, and neither do you."

Mandan shuddered, but Utho shook him hard by the shoulders. "You're konag now. You rule the Commonwealth. Our future is in your hands—and I'll help you any way I can."

The young man blinked his red-rimmed eyes, his mouth open in disbelief.

Utho hammered the words home. "There can never be peace with those animals."

Mandan continued to weep, but he swallowed hard and drew a deep breath. In a small voice, he agreed. "Never peace. We must destroy the Isharans."

The Commonwealth warship sailed away from the stark cliffs and out into the stormy night.

100

꒰ꕤ꒱

IN the blacksmith's yard, Shadri watched Queen Tafira hurl one knife after another at the practice post. She took careful notes about the different types of blades, knowing she might need the knowledge later.

The blacksmith watched the queen, pale with anxiety. "The post is narrow, my lady, used for testing swords up close. Perhaps we should set up a wider target? A loose blade could fly astray."

Tafira picked up a long knife with a sharp tip. She held it by the point, weighed it, switched to hold the hilt in her other hand, then flipped it over and flung it in an abrupt gesture. The knife spun in the air and embedded itself into the soft upright pine log.

The blacksmith had presented the queen with a full selection of knives, and Shadri inspected them all as Tafira taught her about the different blade designs. "While Commonwealth users often sharpen both sides for a double-edged knife, Isharans strengthen the tang, make the edge long and razor sharp." Shadri was delighted to have her numerous questions answered clearly and patiently, for a change.

Under Tafira's guidance, the blacksmith had been experimenting with different styles. The queen inspected them, offered samples to Shadri. "You'll need a good knife of your own, dear girl. Everyone in Norterra should have a blade for protection, especially now."

"But I'm just a scholar." Shadri flushed. "I can learn about knives, but I've had no occasion to fight with them. If I get in a bad situation, I might be better off running as fast as I can."

"Then *learn* how to fight. When I was a young woman about your age, the people of my village were complacent. They thought their godling would always protect them, but they didn't bother to keep it strong, nor did they keep themselves strong. And when the raiding party came through Sarcen, everyone suffered for it."

Shadri had tried throwing knives, but although her fingers were good for writing long accounts, they did not have the dexterity for blade work. But she made an effort to learn, humming and concentrating. Pokle practiced with her, and the gangly young man showed no more skill than she did. He was good at hunting small game, and at first his fighting abilities had not extended beyond splitting wood, but he was getting better every day. They both were.

Shadri always kept her leather-bound notebook with her, its pages covered with thoughts and observations, but she still had room for additional notes in the margins, and King Kollanan had promised her all the blank journals she needed. Shadri had spent a lot of time talking to Tafira, learning about Isharan culture from the queen's childhood. The two women often sat together by the fire, and Tafira told Shadri wistful stories, pieces of her legacy, how she had come here as a frightened young bride from a foreign land, and how she had fallen entirely in love with Koll the Hammer.

When the queen told stories of their daughter, her deep brown eyes would grow misty. She talked about how rambunctious Jhaqi could climb trees faster and higher than anyone else, how she had nearly drowned in a fast mountain stream while trying to catch trout with her bare hands, how the two grandsons took after their adventurous mother more than their serious father. Shadri had filled her book with notes as she listened with all her heart. In her new role in Fellstaff, she liked to think of herself as a legacier, in practice if not in official designation.

Queen Tafira also had an edge to her personality, an iron determination as she accepted responsibility for the kingdom for the time being. With Kollanan gone on his raid to the north, she did not relax. Instead, Tafira moved daily through the city to meet with blacksmiths, swordmakers, armorers, tanners, and fletchers, all working to build up the defenses of Norterra. And she made herself ready, too.

Now, inspecting the blacksmith's knives, the queen picked a small dagger that could easily be tucked into a boot. She flipped it, then threw it at the post. The thin knife slid into a crack in the pinewood.

Distant shouts rang out from the city wall. "Riders are coming!"

Tafira retrieved her knives and gave a brusque nod to the blacksmith. "These will do nicely for us. Now make hundreds of them." She turned to

Shadri, her expression filled with hope and dread. "Let's go greet them and see how many came home."

Wearing rumpled clothes, Pokle ran out to join them, and they all hurried down the winding streets to the northern gates. A large force of riders approached along the road. Shadri tried to count them, but there was too much dust for her to be sure. "It wasn't a massacre at least, my lady," she said. "Looks like most of the war party."

"They fought the wreths!" Pokle laughed in disbelief. He was squirming with excitement. "They fought the wreths, and they came home!"

"Even one casualty is still a high cost," Tafira said, then added in a resigned voice, "but it's a cost we expect to pay." She ordered the gates to be opened wide.

At the front of the party, King Kollanan rode on Storm. Queen Tafira stood with her arms raised, signaling them, struggling to remain dignified, but failing. Shadri could tell she wanted to run out to meet the party. Tears of joy welled in the queen's eyes.

Shadri gasped when she saw Elliel and Thon riding close beside him. Grinning, she waved both her hands in the air, realizing how worried she had been about her two friends.

The party rode forward, exhausted and bedraggled but eager to get back to the city. Lord Bahlen and his Brava came after bearlike Lord Ogno, with the rest of the fighters strung out double file on the road. Halfway down the line, one man proudly raised the banner of Norterra, and another held the flag of the Commonwealth. When the riders reined in, slowing as they passed through the gates, Shadri saw the shock on their faces, the dirt, sweat, torn cloaks, and scuffed armor.

Tafira hurried toward King Koll as he slid out of his saddle. He wrapped his arms around his wife in a silent hug that lasted a full minute. "The battle was a success," he said. "The wreth warriors were not prepared for us. They expected little when they saw us, and we hurt them. Deeply."

Shadri ran to Elliel and Thon, bursting with questions. "We succeeded," Elliel said to no one in particular. "We damaged their fortress, killed an entire party of wreth warriors." She looked impressive in her black Brava uniform, though her close-cropped hair still looked strange to Shadri.

Kollanan glanced over at the dark-haired wreth, nodding in admiration. "Thon unleashed magic beyond even what I had hoped." He turned back to the queen and shook his head. His voice hitched. "But our grandson wasn't there after all—but he still lives, as far as we know. Lasis and Elliel searched while we diverted their defenses with a frontal attack. They killed a wreth mage, but they got the information we needed." His expression hardened with determination rather than dismay. "Birch is still a prisoner of the frost-wreth queen, somewhere far to the north." He held Tafira tighter. "But there's still hope. We can still rescue him."

Tafira's eyes sparkled with tears, and she rested her head against the king's chest. "Yes, we will rescue him."

"I'll want to hear the whole story, every bit of it," Shadri said, loud enough for all to hear. "I can act as a legacier and write it down in great detail. We can send a full chronicle to all of your vassal lords as well as the konag in Convera. Every remembrance shrine will have a copy. They will know what really happened."

"Ancestors' blood, there is much to tell," Koll said. "You'd better write it down quickly, because soon there's going to be much more to the story."

Shadri bowed, feeling her excitement build. "I'm at your disposal, Sire. I'll write the chronicle, and then copy it, again and again, so the story will never be forgotten." She thought of the stern, self-important Chief Legacier Vicolia from the great Convera remembrance shrine, who was unimpressed with the curiosity of a mere cleaning girl. Vicolia would certainly be surprised now.

"You will have all the paper and ink that you need, Legacier," the king said. Hearing the title warmed her heart. "I will tell you my story, and then you can hear more from Elliel, Thon, the lords, and perhaps a soldier or two."

"All of them, Sire—I have to talk to all of them. This is important. This is the legacy for everyone."

Koll walked alongside his black horse. "It might also be our last legacy." Curious people came out to watch the returning party of soldiers, and Shadri knew that by evening many versions of the account would spread throughout the taverns as each soldier embellished his own part of the tale.

Koll put his arm around the queen as he led them back toward the castle. "First, beloved, I have a long letter to write to Conndur. It's time for the two brothers to go together to war again. Koll and Conn, like when we were younger. We have to summon the armies to Norterra and defend our lands against the frostwreths." He lowered his voice. "Conn will know what to do. I only hope we can hold out here long enough for those reinforcements to come."

101

DUSTY and tired, Adan and Penda headed back to Suderra, guided by Quo and a party of warriors. In the wake of the dragon hunt, the sand-wreths were giddy with their victory.

Adan tried to convince himself the wreths were not overtly threatening, just . . . odd. Surprisingly solicitous, Queen Voo reiterated her desire for an alliance with the humans and agreed to meet with Konag Conndur, because he represented the entire Commonwealth. Once he got back to Bannriya, Adan would send messages and arrange a frank discussion between the konag of the three kingdoms and the queen of the sandwreths. He would also inform King Kollanan that there might be help for Norterra. Maybe they could strengthen themselves enough for the coming conflict.

As they rode out of the desert toward home, Penda kept her thoughts to herself, though Adan could tell she was troubled. Her ska—which had returned to them as soon as the dragon hunt was over, as if nothing had happened—rested on her shoulder. Xar crunched contentedly on a large beetle he had caught.

When they finally reached the forested boundaries of Suderra, Quo pulled his auga to a halt. "There is your kingdom, Adan Starfall." He cocked an eyebrow. "I assume you know your way home from here?"

"Bannriya is half a day's journey," Penda said quickly, as if she were anxious for them to be on their own again. "We'll be fine." She drew a circle around her heart.

Done with a tedious duty, Quo turned his reptile mount around, as did the rest of the wreth escort. "We will contact you soon. Be ready for us." He waited for an awkward moment, expecting something. Adan didn't understand, and Quo added an impatient comment: "We did not offer to give you our augas. You can walk from here."

Surprised, Adan said, "But my wife is pregnant."

"Your wife is strong, my Starfall." Penda dismounted. "We can walk."

Seeing her expression, he did not argue. Adan, too, wanted to be away from the wreths. "I'll enjoy the time alone with my wife." Dismounting, he removed his pack and said farewell to Quo. "Thank you for the remarkable experience."

Quo snatched the reins of Adan's auga, while another warrior took Penda's beast. The reptile mounts flicked their black forked tongues. Without looking back, the strange escort party rode away, leaving the king and queen alone in the hills.

Standing with Penda at the edge of the forest, he took her hand, and he suddenly realized how anxious she was. "*Cra*, they frighten me down to the marrow of my bones!"

Adan was also uneasy. "But I saw what the frostwreths did, too. If we are caught between the two forces, Queen Voo may be our most powerful protector."

Leading the way through the hills on foot, Penda spotted a blooming blue poppy and smiled.

The royal couple arrived home to great fanfare. Adan and Penda told stories of the dragon hunt and showed off the scale and the tooth, trophies from the defeated monster. Hale Orr was there to greet them with a hearty laugh and many stories of his own from Convera to Ishara and back again. He had just returned from several days in the hills with other Utauks.

Young Hom attended them, hanging on every tale, and Hale pestered him to snap to his duties. "Bring food from the kitchens, boy! And have servants heat water—King Adan and my daughter sorely need baths! Have you not been trained in your duties?" The squire scuttled away, and Hale sat down.

Penda picked at her food, claiming not to feel well. "I've learned to trust my senses, Father. The sandwreths are so . . . alien."

"We all trust your senses, dear heart." Hale drew a circle with his finger.

Adan relished the meal. He'd eaten pack food for so long, plus whatever strange victuals the wreths had offered. "I'll tell you this, Father Orr—if that dragon had attacked Bannriya, we could not have fought it. The sandwreths wielded impressive magic. They may be strong enough to drive back the frostwreths if they do march down to Suderra. We should consider them seriously."

"That was exactly what Voo meant to show us," Penda said. "A promise but also a threat. She wanted to convince you that we need her for the coming war."

Adan took another sip of wine. "We do have to consider the possibility. These are not normal times."

A courier burst in, a young Utauk woman who had ridden hard all the way from Convera. Her face was encrusted with dust, and she looked about to drop, as if she hadn't eaten in days. Banner guards rushed her into the dining hall.

"Adan Starfall . . ." the courier gasped. "I was told by the konag himself to present this to you—to place it directly in your hands." She fumbled with a leather satchel at her hip, pulled out a folded letter sealed with wax, a mark that showed a stylized "M."

When Adan accepted the document, the courier collapsed into a chair without asking leave. Penda offered the woman her own meal, and she ate ravenously.

Adan recognized his brother's mark on the wax seal, but also saw a significant change. "What is this? Konag . . . Mandan?" He tore open the letter.

When he read the account of what had happened on Fulcor Island, each word felt like a physical blow to his heart. He could only stare for a long moment, finally whispering, "My father is dead, murdered by the Isharans."

Penda and Hale crowded close to read the grisly description of how Conndur had been assassinated by the Isharans, how Mandan and Utho had fought their way out of the garrison and barely escaped back to Osterra.

Hale's expression turned gray. "I can't believe Empra Iluris would do this! I spoke with her myself. This is not what she wanted!"

"My father is dead," Adan said again, as if he could negate the words by repeating them. "They killed him, and now Mandan is konag." With trembling hands and blurred vision, he read the letter again. "My brother rules the Commonwealth. He demands that all the armies of the three kingdoms join the fight against Ishara. He orders me to arm our soldiers and march them to Convera without delay so he can launch a massive attack against the new world. He . . . he calls it a vengewar."

After what he had just witnessed out in the desert—the sandwreths and the dragon, including Queen Voo's call to war against her own mortal enemies—Adan had not expected this. "But we can't . . . it's not possible."

None of this could be possible. He felt dizzy.

"I was there when the warships arrived back at the Confluence, Sire," the courier said. "It's true. I . . . saw the body myself. Horrible!"

Adan's heart cried out in silent grief for all the times he and his father had watched falling stars in the sky. Now the world was falling apart from within.

Adan went alone to the gazing deck, though it was only late afternoon. It would be a long time before full dark, when he could look at the constellations, but for now he just wanted to be here, to gaze across his city, the sandstone walls, the hills all around.

From here, not long ago he had watched the great dust storm roll in from the desert. *A harbinger,* Penda had called it, not realizing the incredible insight she had shown. Right now, the hills looked blurred and washed out—the haze of another storm coming? When he rubbed his eyes, he realized that he was quietly weeping. Tears blurred his vision, not another storm.

Mandan's letter had described in far too much detail how Conndur had been cut into pieces like a bull in a butcher's yard. *My father is dead.*

With silent grace, Penda came up to him, and the warmth of her presence enveloped him like a blanket. She had left Xar inside on his perch. Now she slipped her arms around his chest from behind and held him close without speaking. He squeezed her arms, feeling the swell of her abdomen as she pressed against his back.

A sharp pang sliced through Adan's heart. "My father will never meet his grandchild. He'll never unify the Commonwealth and the Isharans so we can fight the wreths together. What if Queen Voo is the only ally we have left?" His voice cracked as he spoke the words. He tried to sound like a firm leader, the king of Suderra. Politics was important. The future was at hand. Mandan had declared war—a war that should have been unnecessary. But now, how could Adan argue?

My father is dead. They cut out his eyes, his heart . . .

"No matter what happens in the world, we will keep your father's legacy," Penda said.

Looking up, he saw a flash of blue in the sky, sapphire scales and blue feathers as a ska winged its way toward the castle. Penda saw it, too, and pointed. "Look, it's all alone, but I don't think it's a wild ska." She let out a shrill whistle. She shivered as if an odd sensation had run through her, and her expression became troubled. "This is something we should worry about."

The blue ska circled, sensed Penda calling it, then swooped down. As if recognizing her, it landed on her shoulder, full of energy. Penda caught the small reptile bird, stroked its feathers, saw the mothertear collar around its thin neck. "It's a young one. . . ." She frowned. "The Utauks said my sister Glik caught a young ska, a blue one just like this."

The reptile bird bobbed its head, buzzed and clicked, turned faceted eyes toward Penda's face. "Glik? Do you recognize the name?"

The ska ruffled its blue feathers.

"*Cra,* this isn't right."

"Nothing in the universe is right," Adan said. "Not anymore."

Penda unfastened the collar so she could look at the sparkling diamond. "Watch with me, Starfall. Let us see where this ska has been." With her thumb, she unlocked the images. When the wavering shapes and sights poured into the air, they saw the young, dusty girl in ragged clothes. "That's Glik!"

Adan leaned closer to watch. The images showed the girl trudging through the canyons while the ska circled above. "Why was she out in the desert? Was she near us?"

Penda nodded. "The kitchen staff said Glik stopped here for food, asking about us. She seemed interested in the dragon hunt."

"It would be foolish to wander alone in the Furnace," Adan said.

"Glik is often foolish," Penda said.

In the images, the ska ranged farther and reached a sprawling encampment of fences, mud homes, sandwreth guards . . . and thousands of human prisoners. They were skeletal, barely fed, caked with dust as they labored under their masters. Sandwreths tormented them, whipped them.

Penda's hand wavered as she held the collar. The images from the diamond shook in the air as if blown by a strong breeze. The image showed Ari flying higher, looking down at Glik, who ran in terror. Sandwreth guards chased the girl and others came from the other side of the canyon to trap her. They rode augas, raised threatening obsidian spears.

"They look like the warriors with us on the dragon hunt," Adan said.

In the mothertear image, the wreths captured Glik, even though the girl fought and scratched and kicked. The panicked ska flew away, winging across the sky and over the desert until she finally came to Bannriya.

"The sandwreths enslaved all those humans," Adan said, unable to believe it. "The queen doesn't want an alliance." He remembered the stories the Utauks had told about empty villages, missing people, lost caravans. "Everything Queen Voo told us was a lie."

ACKNOWLEDGMENTS

Creating a new world, new characters, new magic, new history takes a lot of work, and I can't do it alone. Some of the people who helped me bring the Wake the Dragon series alive include: my wife and toughest critic and editor, Rebecca Moesta; my first reader, Diane Jones; my sore-armed typist, Karen Haag; my Tor Books editor, Beth Meacham; and my agent, John Silbersack.

I would also like to give special thanks to Marie Whittaker, Josh Bennett, Kitty Krell for her help on the costuming; Bryan G. McWhirter for the wonderful maps; and my thesis advisor, Tony D'Souza, at Lindenwood University.

And finally, my sneak preview gang of readers: David Von Allmen, Eric K. Edstrom, Martin E. Greening, MaryJane Stricklin, Kristin Jackson, Andrew Bulthaupt, Joseph Bigane III, Daniel Clark, Jeff Evans, Daniel Davis, Richard Pulfer, Ray Tayek, John Everett, and Bradley J. Birzer.